CASUALS OF THE SEA

CASUALS OF THE SEA

BY

WILLIAM McFEE

WITH AN INTRODUCTION BY

CHRISTOPHER MORLEY

THE MODERN LIBRARY · NEW YORK

C.21

Random House IS THE PUBLISHER OF

THE MODERN LIBRARY

BENNETT A. CERF · DONALD S. KLOPFER · ROBERT K. HAAS

Manufactured in the United States of America

Printed by Parkway Printing Company   Bound by H. Wolff

DEDICATION

To those who live and toil and lowly die,
  Who pass beyond and leave no lasting trace,
To those from whom our queen Prosperity
  Has turned away her fair and fickle face;
To those frail craft upon the restless Sea
  Of Human Life, who strike the rocks uncharted,
Who loom, sad phantoms, near us, drearily,
  Storm-driven, rudderless, with timbers started;
To those poor Casuals of the way-worn earth,
  The feckless wastage of our cunning schemes,
This book is dedicate, their hidden worth
  And beauty I have seen in vagrant dreams!
The things we touch, the things we dimly see,
  The stiff strange tapestries of human thought,
The silken curtains of our fantasy
  Are with their sombre histories o'erwrought.
And yet we know them not, our skill is vain to find
The mute soul's agony, the visions of the blind.

INTRODUCTION

M'Phee is the most tidy of chief engineers. If the leg of a cock-roach gets into one of his slide-valves the whole ship knows it, and half the ship has to clean up the mess.

—RUDYARD KIPLING.

THE next time the Cunard Company commissions a new liner I wish they would sign on Joseph Conrad as captain, Rudyard Kipling as purser, and William McFee as chief engineer. They might add Don Marquis as deck steward and Hall Caine as chief stewardess. Then I would like to be at Raymond and Whitcomb's and watch the clerks booking passages!

William McFee does not spell his name quite as does the Scotch engineer in Mr. Kipling's *Brugglesmith,* but I feel sure that his attitude toward cockroaches in the slide-valve is the same. Unhappily I do not know Mr. McFee in his capacity as engineer; but I know and respect his feelings as a writer, his love of honourable and honest work, his disdain for blurb and blat. And by an author's attitude toward the purveyors of publicity, you may know him.

One evening about the beginning of December, 1915, I was sitting by the open fire in Hempstead, Long Island, a comparatively inoffensive young man, reading the new edition of Flecker's "The Golden Journey to Samarkand," issued that October by Martin Secker in London. Mr. Secker, like many other wise publishers, inserts in the back of his books the titles of other volumes issued by him. Little did I think, as I turned to look over Mr. Secker's announcements, that a train of events was about to begin which would render me, during the succeeding twelve months, a monomaniac in the eyes of my associates; so much so that when I was blessed with a son and heir just a year later I received a telegram signed by a dozen of them: *"Congratulations. Name him Casuals!"*

It was in that list of Mr. Secker's titles for the winter of 1915-16 that my eyes first rested, with a premonitory lust, upon the not-to-be-forgotten words.

MCFEE, WILLIAM : CASUALS OF THE SEA.

Who could fail to be stirred by so brave a title? At once I wrote for a copy.

My pocket memorandum book for Sunday, January 9, 1916, contains this note:

"Finished reading *Casuals of the Sea,* a good book. H—— still laid up with bad ankle. In the P.M. we sat and read Bible aloud to Celia before the open fire."

My first impressions of *"Casuals of the Sea,* a good book" are interwoven with memories of Celia, a pious Polish serving maid from Pike County, Pennsylvania, who could only be kept in the house by nightly readings of another Good Book. She was horribly homesick (that was her first voyage away from home) and in spite of persistent Bible readings she fled after two weeks, back to her home in Parker's Glen, Pa. She was our first servant, and we had prepared a beautiful room in the attic for her. However, that has nothing to do with Mr. McFee.

Casuals of the Sea is a novel whose sale of ten thousand copies in America is more important as a forecast of literary weather than many a popular distribution of a quarter million. Be it known by these presents that there are at least ten thousand librivora in this country who regard literature not merely as an emulsion. This remarkable novel, the seven years' study of a busy engineer occupied with boiler inspections, indicator cards and other responsibilities of the Lord of Below, was the first really public appearance of a pen that will henceforth be listened to with respect.

Mr. McFee had written two books before *"Casuals"* was published, but at that time it was not easy to find any one who had read them. They were *Letters from an Ocean Tramp* (1908) and *Aliens* (1914); the latter has been rewritten since then and issued in a revised edition. It is a very singular experiment in the art of narrative, and a rich commentary on human folly by a man who has made it his hobby to think things out for himself. And the new version is headlighted by a preface which may well take its place among the most interesting literary confessions of this generation, where Mr. McFee shows himself as that happiest of men, the artist who also has other and more urgent concerns than the whittling of a paragraph:

Of art I never grow weary, but she calls me over the world. I suspect the sedentary art worker. Most of all I suspect the sedentary writer. I divide authors into two classes—genuine artists, and educated men who wish to earn enough to let them live like country gentlemen. With the latter I have no concern. But the artist knows when his time has come. In the same way I turned with irresistible longing to the sea, whereon I had been wont to earn my living. It is a good life and I love it. I love the men and their ships. I find in them a never-ending panorama which illustrates my theme, the problem of human folly.

Mr. McFee, you see, has some excuse for being a good writer because he has never had to write for a living. He had been writing for the fun of it ever since he was an apprentice in a big engineering shop in London twenty years ago. His profession deals with exacting and beautiful machinery, and he could no more do hack writing than hack engineering. And unlike the other English realists of his generation who have cultivated a cheap flippancy, Mc-Fee finds no exhilaration in easy sneers at middle-class morality. He has a dirk up his sleeve for Gentility (how delightfully he flays it in *Aliens*) but he loves the middle classes for just what they are: the great fly-wheel of the world. His attitude toward his creations is that of a "benevolent marbleheart" (his own phrase). He has seen some of the seams of life, and like McAndrew he has hammered his own philosophy. It is a manly, just, and gentle creed, but not a soft one. Since the war began he has been on sea service, first on a beef-ship and transport in the Mediterranean; now as sub-lieutenant in the British Navy. When the war is over, and if he feels the call of the desk, Mr. McFee's brawny shoulder will sit in at the literary feast and a big handful of scribblers will have to drop down the dumb-waiter shaft to make room for him. It is a disconcerting figure in Grub Street, the man who really has something to say.

Publishers are always busy casting horoscopes for their new finds. How the benign planets must have twirled in happy curves when Harold Bell Wright was born, if one may credit his familiar mage, Elsbury W. Reynolds! But the fame that is built merely on publishers' press sheets does not dig very deep in the iron soil of time. We are all only raft-builders, as Lord Dunsany tells us in his little parable; even the raft that Homer made for Helen must break up some day. Who in these States knows the works of Nat Gould? Twelve million of his dashing paddock novels have been sold in England, but he is as unknown here as is Preacher Wright in England. What is so dead as a dead best seller? Sometimes it is the worst sellers that come to life, roll away the stone, and an angel is found sitting laughing in the sepulchre. Let me quote Mr. McFee once more: "I have no taste for blurb, but I cannot refuse facts."

William M. P. McFee was born at sea in 1881. His father, an English skipper, was bringing his vessel toward the English coast after a long voyage. His mother was a native of Nova Scotia. They settled in New Southgate, a northern middle-class suburb of London, and here McFee was educated in the city schools of which the first pages of *Casuals of the Sea* give a pleasant description. Then he went to a well-known grammar school at Bury St. Edmunds in Suffolk—what we would call over here a high school. He was a quiet, sturdy boy, and a first-rate cricketer.

At sixteen he was apprenticed to a big engineering firm in Aldersgate. This is one of the oldest streets in London, near the Charterhouse, Smithfield Market, and the famous "Bart's" Hospital. In fact, the office of the firm was built over one of the old plague pits of 1665. His father had died several years before; and for the boy to become an apprentice in this well-known firm Mrs. McFee had to pay three hundred pounds sterling. McFee has often wondered just what he got for the money. However, the privilege of paying to be better than someone else is an established way of working out one's destiny in England, and at the time the mother and son knew no better than to conform. You will find this problem, and the whole matter of gentility, cuttingly set out in *Aliens*.

After three years as an apprentice, McFee was sent out by the firm on various important engineering jobs, notably a pumping installation at Tring, which he celebrated in a pamphlet of very creditable juvenile verses, for which he borrowed Mr. Kipling's mantle. This was at the time of the Boer War, when everybody in trousers who wrote verses was either imitating Kipling or reacting from him.

His engineering work gave young McFee a powerful interest in the lives and thoughts of the working classes. He was strongly influenced by socialism, and all his spare moments were spent with books. He came to live in Chelsea with an artist friend, but he had already tasted life at first hand, and the rather hazy atmosphere of that literary and artistic utopia made him uneasy. His afternoons were spent at the British Museum reading room, his evenings at the Northampton Institute, where he attended classes, and even did a little lecturing of his own. Competent engineer as he was, that was never sufficient to occupy his mind. As early as 1902 he was writing short stories and trying to sell them.

In 1905 his uncle, a shipmaster, offered him a berth in the engine room of one of his steamers, bound for Trieste.

He jumped at the chance. Since then he has been at sea almost continuously, save for one year (1912-13) when he settled down in Nutley, New Jersey, to write. The reader of *Aliens* will be pretty familiar with Nutley by the time he reaches page 416. "Netley" is but a thin disguise. I suspect a certain liveliness in the ozone of Nutley. Did not Frank Stockton write some of his best tales there? Some day some literary meteorologist will explain how these intellectual anticyclones originate in such places as Nutley (N. J.), Galesburg (Ill.), Port Washington (N. Y.), and Bryn Mawr (Pa.).

The life of a merchantman engineer would not seem to open a fair prospect into literature. The work is gruelling and at the same time monotonous. Constant change of scene and absence of home ties are (I speak subject to correction) demoralizing; after the coveted chief's certificate is won, ambition has little further to look forward to. A small and stuffy cabin in the belly of the ship is not an inviting study. The works of Miss Corelli and Messrs. Haig and Haig are the only diversions of most of the profession. Art, literature, and politics do not interest them. Picture postcards, waterside saloons, and the ladies of the port are the glamour of life that they delight to honour.

I imagine that Mr. Carville's remarkable account (in *Aliens*) of his induction into the profession of marine engineering has no faint colour of reminiscence in Mr. McFee's mind. The filth, the intolerable weariness, the instant necessity of the tasks, stagger the easygoing suburban reader. And only the other day, speaking of his work on a seaplane ship in the British Navy, Mr. McFee said some illuminating things about the life of an engineer:

It is Sunday, and I have been working. Oh, yes, there is plenty of work to do in the world, I find, wherever I go. But I cannot help wondering why Fate so often offers me the dirty end of the stick. Here I am, awaiting my commission as an engineer-officer of the R.N.R., and I am in the thick of it day after day. I don't mean, when I say "work," what you mean by work. I don't mean work such as my friend the Censor does, or my friend the N.E.O. does, nor my friends and shipmates, the navigating officer, the flying men or the officers of the watch. I mean *work*, hard, sweating, nasty toil, coupled with responsibility. I am not alone. Most ships of the naval auxiliary are the same.

I am anxious for you, a landsman, to grasp this particular fragment of the sorry scheme of things entire, that in no other profession have the officers responsible for the carrying out of the work to toil as do the engineers in merchantmen, in transports, in fleet auxiliaries. You do not expect the major to clear the waste pipe of his regimental latrines. You do not expect the surgeon to superintend the purging of his bandages. You do not expect the navigators of a ship to paint her hull. You do not expect an architect to make bricks (sometimes without straw). You do not expect the barrister to go and repair the lock on the law courts door, or oil the fans that ventilate the halls of justice. Yet you do, collectively, tolerate a tradition by which the marine engineer has to assist, overlook, and very often perform work corresponding precisely to the irrelevant chores mentioned above, which are in other professions relegated to the humblest and roughest of mankind. I blame no one. It is tradition, a most terrible windmill at which to tilt; but I conceive it my duty to set down once at least the peculiar nature of an engineer's destiny. I have had some years of it, and I know what I am talking about.

The point to distinguish is that the engineer not only has the responsibility, but he has, in nine cases out of ten, to do it. He, the officer, must befoul his person and derange his hours of rest and recreation that others may enjoy. He must be available twenty-four hours a day, seven days a week at sea or in port. Whether chief or the lowest junior, he must be ready to plunge instantly to the succour of the vilest piece of mechanism on board. When coaling, his lot is easier imagined than described.

The remarkable thing to note is that Mr. McFee imposed upon these laborious years of physical toil a strenuous discipline of intellect as well. He is a born worker: patient, dogged, purposeful. His years at sea have been to him a more fruitful curriculum than that of any university. The patient sarcasm with which he speaks of certain Oxford youths of his acquaintance does not escape me. His sarcasm is just and on the target. He has stood as Senior Wrangler in a far more exacting *viva voce*—the University of the Seven Seas.

If I were a college president, out hunting for a faculty, I would deem that no salary would be too big to pay for the privilege of getting a man like McFee on my staff. He would not come, of course! But how he has worked for his mastery of the art of life and the theory thereof! When his colleagues at sea were dozing in their deck chairs or rattling the bones along the mahogany, he was sweating in his bunk, writing or reading. He has always been deeply interested in painting, and no gallery in any port he visited ever escaped him. These extracts from some of his letters will show whether his avocations were those of most engineers:

As I crossed the swing-bridge of the docks at Garston (Liverpool) the other day, and saw the tapering spars silhouetted against the pale sky, and the zinc-coloured river with its vague Cheshire shores dissolving in mist, it occurred to me that if an indulgent genie were to appear and make me an offer I would cheerfully give up writing for painting. As it is I see things in pictures and I spend more time in the Walker Gallery than in the library next door.

I've got about all I *can* get out of books, and now I don't relish them save as memories. The reason for my wish, I suppose, is that character, not incident, is my *métier*. And you can *draw* character, *paint* character, but you can't very well blat about it, can you?

I am afraid Balzac's job is too big for anybody nowadays. The worst of writing men nowadays is their horrible ignorance of how people live, of ordinary human possibilities.

A—— is always pitching into me for my insane ideas about "cheap stuff." He says I'm on the wrong tack and I'll be a failure if I don't do what the public wants. I said I didn't care a blue curse what the public wanted, nor did I worry much if I never made a big name. All I want is to do some fine and honourable work, to do it as well as I possibly could, and there my responsibility ended. . . . To hell with writing, I want to *feel* and *see*!

I am laying in a gallon of ink and a couple of cwt. of paper, to the amusement of the others, who imagine I am a merchant of some sort who has to transact business at sea because Scotland Yard are after him!

His kit for every voyage, besides the gallon of ink and the hundred-weight of foolscap, always included a score

of books, ranging from Livy or Chaucer to Gorky and
histories of Italian art. Happening to be in New York
at the time of the first exhibition in this country of "fu-
turist" pictures, he entered eagerly into the current discussion in the newspaper correspondence columns. He
wrote for a leading London journal an article on "The
Conditions of Labour at Sea." He finds time to contribute
to the *Atlantic Monthly* pieces of styptic prose that make
zigzags on the sphygmograph of the editor. His letters written weekly to the artist friend he once lived with in Chelsea
show a humorous and ironical mind ranging over all topics
that concern cultivated men. I fancy he could out-argue
many a university professor on Russian fiction, or Mi-
chelangelo, or steam turbines.

When one says that McFee found little intellectually in
common with his engineering colleagues, that is not to say
that he was a prig. He was interested in everything that
they were, but in a great deal more, too. And after obtain-
in his extra chief's certificate from the London Board of
Trade, with a grade of ninety-eight per cent., he was not
inclined to rest on his gauges.

In 1912 he took a walking trip from Glasgow to London,
to gather local colour for a book he had long meditated;
then he took ship for the United States, where he lived
for over a year writing hard. Neither *Aliens* nor *Casuals
of the Sea,* which he had been at work on for years, met
with the favour of New York publishers. He carried his
manuscripts around the town until weary of that amusement; and when the United Fruit Company asked him to
do some engineering work for them he was not loath to get
back into the old harness. And then came the war.

Alas, it is too much to hope that the Cunard Company
will ever officer a vessel as I have suggested at the outset
of these remarks. But I made my proposal not wholly at
random, for in Conrad, Kipling, and McFee, all three,
there is something of the same artistic creed. In those two
magnificent prefaces—to *A Personal Record* and to *The*

Nigger of the Narcissus—Conrad has set down, in words that should be memorable to every trafficker in ink, his conception of the duty of the man of letters. They can never be quoted too often:

"All ambitions are lawful except those which climb upward on the miseries or credulities of mankind. . . . The sight of human affairs deserves admiration and pity. And he is not insensible who pays them the undemonstrative tribute of a sigh which is not a sob, and of a smile which is not a grin."

That is the kind of tribute that Mr. McFee has paid to the Gooderich family in *Casuals of the Sea*. Somewhere in that book he has uttered the immortal remark that "The world belongs to the Enthusiast who keeps cool." I think there is much of himself in that aphorism, and that the cool enthusiast, the benevolent marbleheart, has many fine things in store for us.

And there is one other sentence in *Casuals of the Sea* that lingers with me, and gives a just trace of the author's mind. It is worth remembering, and I leave it with you:

"She considered a trouble was a trouble and to be treated as such, instead of snatching the knotted cord from the hand of God and dealing murderous blows."

CHRISTOPHER MORLEY.

CONTENTS

CONTENTS

BOOK ONE
THE SUBURB

"Bringing up a family is no joke."

I

ABOUT twenty years ago, late in January, snow was falling over North London. It fell for some hours continuously; "without intermission" the *Evening Star* said, whose sub-editor lived in the neighbourhood; and the said sub-editor sent his nephew, who was learning the business, to the British Museum, to look up heavy snowfalls from 1792 downwards. And by teatime the whole of North London, from the Manor House to High Barnet Church, from Hampstead Heath to Enfield Highway, was very white indeed.

At a few minutes past four in the afternoon the triangular open common land, which is now the correct and asphalted park called Trinity Gardens, Wood Green, was deserted. Save where an open trench for pipes bisected it like a black knife-gash, "all spotless lay the untrodden snow." In the Trinity Road Higher Grade Board School, which fronted this blanket of virginal purity, the Sixth, Seventh, and ex-Seventh Standards were receiving their weekly spoonful of "English," after an exhausting week of French, German, Chemistry, Botany, Electricity and Magnetism, Physiography, Euclid, Algebra, Calisthenics and the Tonic-Sol-Fa Method of Voice Production. The English tabloid for the week was "Hohenlinden," and the senior assistant teacher, who cared more for white blood corpuscles and protoplasmic continuity than *belles-lettres,* misunderstood the obvious excitement among the boys massed beneath the big rostrum. Preoccupied with the biological difficulties of the B.Sc. Final, he selected Bert Gooderich to stand up and read the poem through. Now Bert Gooderich was not a suitable person to stand up and read a poem through. He was a brown-haired, black-eyed youth of fourteen (nearly), built compactly, and solidly, like a sack of concrete cement, with the mouth tied up. He was muscular, with a promise of lengthening bone and deepening chest. His voice had broken a month or so

3

before. His round-barrelled calves touched as he stood
with his feet together. Pulling the London School Board
text-book towards him he held a blue and white handkerchief to his face. He wiped his nose, slid the half-dissolved
sugared-almond dexterously from his mouth, replaced the
handkerchief in his pocket, and sniffed.

> *"On—on Linden, W'en the sahn was laow,*
> *Orl spotless lye the—untrodden snaow,*
> *An' dawk an' wintry was—the—flaow*
> *Of—I-ser—raollin' rapidly."*

I do not propose to spell everything Bert says with the
above phonetic accuracy. But that is how he talked.

He seemed a little startled by the peculiar scanning of
the last line. It seemed wrong somehow, left him with a
chestful of breath. He said that last line again, to make
sure. He looked out of the corner of his eye at the grinning
comrades about him and sniffed impassively. He felt under
no obligation to give the affair of Hohenlinden any
further notice.

"Eezer, not Iser," said the teacher sharply. "I heard
Mr. Talbot tell you yesterday that *i* in German is pronounced *ee.*"

Bert Gooderich looked at the word "Iser" again. There
it was—I-s-e-r. If that wasn't Eyser, he had no use for it.
Possibly the German lesson had contained something like
that, but Bert had been preoccupied with a young Japanese
rat in a condensed milk-tin which Flying Machine Brown
had shown him under the desk.

"Begin again, Gooderich," said the teacher, and Gooderich began again. The teacher looked at the clock. All
the boys save Bert did the same. It was twenty-four
minutes past four. The teacher looked at his watch, and
those boys who had watches did the same, surreptitiously.
Six minutes more, and then—

> *"On Linden, when the Sun was low,*
> *All spotless lay the untrodden snow."*

The teacher with sudden intuition realised exactly the
appropriate nature of the poem to the day, and smiled

through the window at the falling flakes. With the maddening servility of schoolboys the class did likewise. Some even ventured to giggle.

The senior assistant teacher frowned the smile and giggles out of existence. He exerted his authority, and the gigglers found themselves standing on the form, a wearisome penance. It was now twenty-six minutes past four. Bert Gooderich had again tackled the last line with dubious enunciation and heaved a sigh of relief. English literature was not his *forte*.

"Who wrote *Hohenlinden,* Brown?" asked the teacher.

Brown, Flying Machine Brown, in his brother's old coat and his father's Shakespear collar, Brown with his alert yet vacuous features, did not know. The senior assistant teacher found it increasingly difficult to find anything that Brown did know. Sometimes, in the evenings, he would debate with the others who shared his room, who would be top of the Sixth Standard. He never debated who would be bottom. It was always Brown.

One or two hands were put up—self-conscious, apologetic hands. The owners of the hands were obviously anxious to avoid being considered erudite. The others thought you cocky if you put up your hand too often.

"Thomas Campbell wrote *Hohenlinden,* Brown," said the teacher sadly. And the hands dropped quickly. Bert Gooderich sat down and resumed the sugared-almond.

"Yes, sir," said Brown brightly, willing to learn and anxious not to be kept in.

"Yes, sir!" mimicked the teacher. "And you'll forget it before you get home, eh?"

Brown hoped so, but smiled diplomatically.

"All right," said the teacher, "that'll do; Alder, collect the books."

Alder, a Noel Park oil-and-colour-merchant's son, received the books from the end boy of each form, all the others scraping their feet and thrusting exercise books into home lesson bags. Behind the huge green curtains which cut the room in two, you could hear the junior standards clattering out by the back door. A great hubbub arose throughout the school. Caps were snatched from the hooks, mufflers tied on, satchels slung over the left shoulder, and the Sixth, Seventh, and ex-Seventh Standards swarmed out into the chapel yard. It should be noticed that the Higher Grade School was part of the premises behind the Wesleyan Chapel, whose buttresses formed small courts convenient for marbles, chevvy chase, and small-boy torture.

Eventually the whole school was trampling the whiteness of the Trinity Road. Many boys had short sticks, others had "blood-knots," pieces of clothes-line with a knot at one end. All looked eagerly across the triangular common towards the citadel of "the Michaels."

The Michaels were the nearest enemies of the "Graders." The Michaels were cut off from democratic and bourgeois sympathy by their religion, which was church. They were choir-boys, many of them; others were worse—they were Roman Catholics. Their school lay on the high road near the high church, between the devils of the Graders and the surging sea of Boarders or common Board School lads from Whitehart Lane.

By one of those subtle collusions which are the despair of psychology the Boarders had made a truce with the Michaels, with the object of crushing the Graders once for all. Bert Gooderich, purchasing comestibles for his mother at a shop on Jolly Butchers Hill, had met, and fought for six minutes, with the acknowledged leader of the hardy Whitehart Lane army. In the small ring immediately formed, several Michaels had cheered the Boarder. Bert, all his Grader blood boiling, and some of it streaming from his nose, had snatched up his net bag of provisions, and flinging a challenge to both schools to fight the Graders and get licked, had darted away before the odds grew too serious. This happened on the previous day. It took but a few hours for every responsible warrior in all three academies to learn of the fray and the gauge flung down by the Trinity Road hero, and the coming of the snow warned the Graders that a battle of Homeric dimensions would be fought before some of them had tea.

Leaving the kids to skirmish and smother each other with amateurish snowballs, Bert Gooderich and his lieutenants leaned against the railings in front of the sacred edifice and discussed the position. It was nothing to Bert that he himself could have gone home to Bounds Green without harm. The lieutenants lived Noel Park way, Hornsey way, some even dwelt in Whitehart Lane. Bert swung his blood-knot and matured his plans. There was no supineness about Bert now, no sniffing lack of interest. Bert was one of those lofty souls who do not read poems about battles, but fight them with a bloody joyousness that causes poets and suburban residents to appeal to the police. He was a great asset to the Graders, whose ranks were weakened by numerous middle-class boys, poor emasculated creatures who wore white collars continually and who went away to the seaside in August. Instinctively they leaned on Bert, whose father was an engine-fitter at a big works in the City, and whose Augusts were spent fishing in Littler's Pond, bird-nesting out at Enfield, or roaming through Hadley Wood. They leaned on him now, as he swung his blood-knot and matured his plan.

"They're comin', Bert!" called out a lieutenant, peering through the snowflakes. Bert saw "them" plainly enough. He thrust his knot and his hands into his pockets, hunched his shoulders and started to cross the common. The whole school moved forward, like an army, or a flock of sheep. (The reader can take his choice of metaphors.) When he arrived at the pipe-trench, Bert paused and spat. It was half choked with snow, its jagged edges and yawning depth were alike concealed and softly rounded in spotless purity.

Bert spat into the trench. The lieutenants looked at the reddish circle of his saliva with respect. They all knew Bert spat blood. It was one of those mystical attributes of greatness among boys. Many of them longed to spit blood like Bert. One boy who had had a tooth out in the dinner-hour, spat crimson and gained high prestige for a while, but such a means of attaining it was considered cheap, like cough mixture, which only made a brown stain. Bert's bronchial apparatus was adrift somewhere, as was proved when he retched phlegm for the edification of a new boy. It was his crowning distinction, his deathless claim to sovereignty over them. He spat blood.

" 'Ere," he said to Winship, a lieutenant who wore trousers and who lived (slept, anyhow) in Whitehart Lane.

" 'Ere, Art, you go 'ome, that's what you'd better do. Up
past the Alms-'ouses."

"W'y?" demanded Winship with suspicion. "See any
green?"

"Go on," said Bert, stooping majestically and forming
the first real snowball of the fight with deftly-pressing
fingers. " 'Ow do we know the Boarders ain't comin' down
Trinity Road, jus' for a change like? I'm goin' acrost to
mop up these Michaels. So 'urry, Arty, my love."

Arty, Bert's love, threw up his head in enlightenment
and strode off up the bank of the dyke towards the
Trinity Road.

"What's up, Bert?" asked a lieutenant in glasses.

"Come on," said Bert, striding the Rubicon and making
for the Michaels. "We got ter keep this side o' the 'ole
—see?—till I tell yer."

The Trinity Graders, happily delivered of a number of
the aforesaid middle-class decadents who had "gone home"
to their tea and home lessons, and who would be virtu-
ously and insufferably learned on the morrow, now
advanced, a cluster of black dots, across the white counter-
pane of snow. Over against the red brick St. Michael's
school-house, the patrons of that saint were to be seen
plainly, craven hearts whom fear of Bert kept from taking a glorious initiative. When Bert had spat into the
trench, they had retired from the east to the west side
of their road. Now they were inside their yard, round
suspicious heads showing over the wall and a covey of
excited, oily-haired little choir-boys fluttering in the dim
porch. The bigger lads were beginning to think that they
had done unwisely in retreating. Choir practice was at
half-past five, and Bert Gooderich cared neither for God
nor man, neither night nor day, snow nor fine. Bert
punched them furiously whenever he found them. Now
they were in the yard their allies seemed far away, choir
practice was near. Bert and his Nonconformist hordes
were nearer still. He might besiege them till eight o'clock.
Old Plantagenet, the organist, would be wild.

The lieutenants were all agog with delight. Already they
were spotting the Michaels' porch with erratic snowballs;
one downy little choir-boy had remained peeping through

the bars of the gate, when a hard and swift ball caught him in the teeth and he ran screaming into the panic-stricken porch. But Bert was not simply a boy out for a lark; he was a general playing a two-to-one game, he was a tactician with a scheme to develop. Bert looked back across the common to see if Winship had gone through like a coward, or was being chased like a rabbit back to the fight. Snow no longer fell thickly; you could see the lamps of the Freemason's Tavern twinkling away up Trinity Road. Somewhere up there the Boarders were mustering. Bert never miscalculated on the puny defence of the Michaels. He knew they had been in communication with the Boarders. A snowball struck him on the shoulder. He ignored it, staring away towards Trinity Road. Where was the trousered Winship?

II

AT THE northern apex of the triangular common, erected, with superb indifference to man's needs, in the very centre of the highway, was a granite obelisk, from whose walls gushed drinking water except when the Berts of this world had plugged the pores with slate pencils. A sarcophagus with water inside it, and a Scripture text relating to thirst outside it, stood near the obelisk. Two horsemen had reined in near this point as Bert passed those anxious moments waiting for news of Winship. Police Inspector Everett was returned from his inspection of the Y Division. Colonel Corinth-Squires, late 73rd Bengal Cavalry, now of H. M. Science and Art Department, was returned from his afternoon ride. They had met on the Bounds Green Road, had cantered towards home through the snow, and now, like old campaigners, allowed their beasts the smallest possible drink of water before going on to oats and chopped hay. The Colonel, moreover, had offered his silver brandy flask to the Inspector, only to be declined, for the latter drank whisky.

"I knew how it would be, when we accepted the lowest tender for those pipes!" said the Colonel, looking across the common. "That trench has been ready for laying over a week now. Scandalous!"

"I heard," said the Inspector, disentangling his spur from his long blue coat—"I heard that Marsh and Lascelles propose to make a park of this patch, with raised shrubberies and asphalt paths and a bandstand."

"Marsh and Lascelles will take jolly good care they don't pay for the shrubberies and paths and bandstand!" snapped the Colonel. "Now I would make it an athletic drill-ground for the two schools, and what's more I'd set the ball rolling. See the force of the thing! A school each side, with a drill shed, parade ground, football field, and, later on, a swimming bath and gymnasium on this corner. Make it a decent building, with a clock. These poor little beggars have to go by train to Hornsey Road, dammit, to get a bath! Scandalous!"

"The place is a battlefield all the time now," said the Inspector. "My men are always taking names and addresses."

"Names and addresses! Look here, my dear Everett, why on earth can't the police leave 'em alone, so long as they do their fighting on the common? Hang it, it's in the air, this confounded *repression*. They complain of poor recruiting, and I'm not surprised. I'm not a damn bit surprised! Yes, we'll go along Trinity Road. The school and the Sunday-school and the keep-off-the-grass notices in the parks, and the police! How can a youngster grow self-reliant and big in the chest if he's under lock and key all the time? You mark my words, Everett, it's a mistaken policy. In the old days, there were wigs on the green. And now, dammit, if a boy shies a stone he's up before me, and I have to fine his parents!"

"You should live in the country, Colonel. Wood Green is a suburb: Y Division, you know!"

"That's a nice thing to say to me, Everett! My grandfather had Chits Hill Place before Dick Ford organised you. I say, Everett, just wait a minute, will you? Do you notice anything about that mob of youngsters on the green?"

The Inspector, with great good humour, reined his steed beside the Colonel and looked abroad.

"I'm much mistaken, Everett, if there isn't a young general in charge of these Higher Grade boys. Look now! There's a squad keeping back those lads of Whitehart Lane, there's another squad taking the front of the attack on St. Michael's School, the main body are retreating in good order, and by gad! they're covering a detachment of sappers in that pipe trench! See the idea, Everett? I wish I had my glasses!"

The Inspector said nothing, but smilingly watched the fight. The two horsemen might have been officers directing the engagement. The Colonel was excited.

"Look now, Everett! The main body's retreated across the trench. The St. Michael's boys are going to rush it. There's always plenty of snow in a ditch. I remember

that. They'll fall into the ambush. It's magnificent! And
look at the left wing. They've swung round to support
the squad in the Trinity Road. Now look! They're in the
trench, and by Jove, they've got it! No, no! The sappers
are at 'em. Well, I'm blessed! It's a regularly-planned
feint. See, the St. Michael's are on the run, fairly on the
run. Down, too, some of 'em. And look at the main
body. They're after 'em like a shot. No need of a left
wing now. Sappers are always hot stuff in a tussle. The
lad that's bossing this fight is an embryo general. See
how they're keeping the Whitehart Lane chaps from coming out into the open. I *wish* I had my glasses. It's as
good as a play!"

"I'm afraid the play's over, Colonel. It's nearly dark."

"Not a bit of it. These young rascals can see like cats.
And their leader won't stop now. He'll smash up the
St. Michael's and then wheel his whole force round and
chase the Whitehart Lane boys to Kingdom Come. I'm
going round Commerce Road and back to the Freemason's
Tavern to see the rout."

Putting their animals to a trot the two grey moustached
men passed up the shop-lined Commerce Road and
emerged upon the High Road, where the trams now run
towards Enfield. As they came up to the Trinity Road
once more, they beheld what the Colonel justly called the
rout. Penned in between the private dwellings and the
high wall of the Almshouses, the Whitehart Lane boys
were struggling with a furious onset from the whole army
of Higher Graders. Sticks, stones, snowballs, weighted
with flints, blood-knots, and fists were flying in all directions. Hoarse cries of derision and victory blent with the
roar of the High Road. In the forefront of the battle,
with bloody face and empurpled eyes, Bert Gooderich was
hammering home the most famous victory of his life. His
blood-knot was gone, his clothes were torn and wet, and
his satchel was empty. But he was fighting like a demon.
Incessantly he stopped and moulded a snowball from the
blackened slush of the roadway, and with deadly aim he
blinded the nearest enemy. Now and again he closed
with some desperate Boarder, and struck again and again
at the boy's chin until the battle separated them.

It was an immemorial custom of the belligerents to regard the publicity of the High Road as the Romans regarded the Danube. The barbarians of Whitehart Lane might retreat across it. By doing so they earned a respite of twenty-four hours and the mockery of a week. On this particular evening, as the Inspector and the Colonel turned away northward again, the Graders reached the last lamp-post of Trinity Road, and a policeman moved slowly across from the Freemason's Arms to quell the disturbance. Before he was halfway across the barbarian ranks were broken and flying southward, and the Graders, flushed with triumph, retreated with back-turned faces and occasional gibes at the copper. Now indeed the battle was ended, overshadowed by darkness and the anger of the law. Wearily Bert Gooderich climbed the plinth of the granite obelisk and drank thirstily from the heavy copper cup. He had lost his exercise book. There would be trouble with old Piper in the morning.

And there was the long, lonely walk home.

Such are the vicissitudes of greatness!

III

THE Gooderich family, of whom a good deal will be written in this book, lived in Maple Road, a thoroughfare more easily imagined than described. The High Road from Wood Green crossed the western end of it, giving the drivers of pantechnicons and drapery-vans a view of a short, broad, level avenue, with a church at one end of the north side, a church in the middle of the south side, six large houses and eight small villas. The eastern end of this road was shadowed by tall oaks, and tailed off into a quiet lane that wound interminably towards Tottenham. Thus it was that the Gooderich family, who rented the last but one of the small villas, and who had no pretensions to gentility, dwelt in a genteel thoroughfare, and their roof, in the morning, was darkened by the shadow of the ancestral oaks of Verulamium.

Both ecclesiastical buildings in Maple Road were dissenting, but the Established Church, a dry, stand-offish edifice, frowned from the other side of the High Road; the sexton lived at number eight (a small house), and the curate, unmarried and genial, at number four (a large house). Nothing ever broke the calm of this rural neighbourhood, save the Italian barrel-organ at seven o'clock on Saturday evening, and the fact that only six miles separated it from the mightiest city in the world, seemed a wild and incredible myth.

The Gooderich family lived, with lapses for meals, in the back of the house, the front room being occupied by furniture. On Sunday mornings, for instance, there was a further lapse. Mrs. Gooderich would stand a little to one side of the front window, one finger cautiously holding the edge of the curtain, and watch, as in a glass darkly, the Baptists going to chapel. This curiosity of Mrs. Gooderich was perfectly innocent. She was thirty-four years of age and she had a great desire to look at other women's clothes. But the mention of church-going and clothes recalls the fact that the internal economy of the Gooderich family will be badly comprehended without an account of the early career of Mrs. Gooderich. She was born in Berkshire, and her father was a farm labourer. Her five sisters, one by one, went out to service, and it would have been little less than a miracle if Mary had escaped the same fate. The miracle did not happen—no miracle had happened in Wantage since the Reformation—and Mary Higgs, with her small figure, small features, small blue eyes, and small wooden box, was put into the London train to go and make her fortune.

Mary's first, and last, mistress was a stockbroker's wife at Hornsey. There were no children, not many visitors, and not much to do, for the stockbroker was only a junior partner at the time, and he was obsessed by a vision of that famous landscape, "A Rainy Day." So Mary dressed herself in a black dress and white cap and apron every day at three o'clock and chattered with the servant next door through the trellis work that separated the gardens. The servant next door was a flaming blonde with four young men, and she liked Mary from the first. The flaming blonde was a Hoxton girl, and considered it her duty bound to start Mary in social life. The first Sunday out saw them in Finsbury Park. To a girl who had lived in Wantage all her life, Finsbury Park, with its vast lake, colossal refreshment pavilion, broad avenues of stately trees, and its hum of Life, was the Elysian Fields. Mary was introduced to a deep-chested young man who took her for a row on the lake. Boating in Finsbury Park is not the naval scrimmage one finds in Battersea Park. You rowed round and round until your sixpenny worth was up; you kept clear of other crafts and then stepped ashore to eat ices and meringues at little tables. You made due allowance for the fact that personal remarks travel a long way over water, and spoke low. It was like Maple Avenue, genteel. Mary enjoyed it for a month or two, and then the flaming blonde, who wore an engagement ring on these Sundays out, went to Finsbury Park alone, and the deep-chested young man took his airing on the lake in solitary state. Mary was indisposed, so her friend said, concealing the whole truth, which was that Mary was in-

disposed to proceed any further with the tedious business
of a humdrum lovemaking. Mary Higgs was not built
that way. The young man who delivered two Coburgs
and a Hovis loaf daily at the stockbroker's back entrance
was infinitely more amusing. He told Mary diverting
stories, he gave her copies of the *Illustrated Standard* and
the *Mirror of Life,* and he formed the habit of leaving
bags of stale pastry, which Mary consumed in the small
room over the scullery where she slept. And on the
Sunday when she was indisposed, as I have stated above,
she waited until the flaming blonde had boarded the old
horse-tram in the High Road, and then hastened away
northwards towards Jolly Butchers Hill. The baker's cart,
divested of its trade-boards, and looking exactly like a
neat gig, was waiting for her at the top of the hill, under
the trees in front of the Fishmongers' Almshouses. This
was much more to Mary's taste. They drove out past
Winchmore Hill and Enfield, and in the deep lanes that
lead away to Waltham and Broxbourne, the baker's young
man made love in a manner manifestly impossible on the
Finsbury Park lake. And then in the summer evening
they drove across country to Potters Bar and halted at a
public-house on the North Road. Here Mary had a glass
of stout brought out to her as she sat in the trap, and her
swain lighted another cigar.

This was a beginning of a new existence for Mary
Higgs. I don't think she was very much in love with the
man. He had a very taking manner with women, and
seemed to be able to take liberties that they would have
resented in another. He earned good money as a journey-
man, being particularly clever at "smalls," and if she
considered the matter at all, I suppose Mary would have
decided that she was doing very well for herself. He
was fascinated by Mary's *petite* figure, her dark hair
and blue eyes, and the faint Berkshire accent of her
speech. They were both slightly romantic. The fascination lasted for three months, and then the stockbroker's
wife changed her baker.

For the first few days Mary bore the absence of her
lover in patience. Of course he could not come every
day now that he had no reason for calling. One evening,

while buying groceries, she walked past the shop where he worked, but the proprietor's wife was serving another servant with pastry and Mary did not care to go in. Sunday came and went, the flaming blonde went forth to walk out with her young man, and Mary was alone. She was quite at a loss until she formed the desire to find him. She scorned the idea of waiting about until he came by. That was not yet. She had no pangs because she had given way to him. She was merely at a loss.

The week was long and tedious. On the Friday evening she had to run out hastily to get some sponge cakes for a late tea. The stockbroker's nephew and nieces had come for a visit from Twickenham. Mary went to the old shop and bought the cakes from a boy in an apron, a smart well-brushed boy.

"How's Mister Royce?" she asked in the course of a light conversation.

"Him? Oh, 'e's gone."

"Oh." Mary took the change—you get fourteen sponge cakes for one and a penny—and counted the five pennies. "Where's he gone to?"

"Gone to the Col'nies. 'Is brother's out there, yer see."

"Really! You do surprise me."

He did. It was not the first time Mr. Royce's movements had provided a young woman with a surprise. Mary went swiftly home and thought the matter out while she made cocoa and lemonade for the nephews and nieces. She did not care, only—well, she didn't care so long as nothing happened.

You can remain a long time in such a state of mind. You can get used to it, even. You can do your work, and read the newspaper, and talk to a flaming blonde about her approaching nuptials in a perfectly sane way.

And when the Saturday dinner is over and done with, and you run upstairs to put yourself straight, you can even look into the glass at a flushed damp face and heaving bosom, and argue that the flush is due to the hot kitchen fire and the short breath to the hasty climb, not at all to the thoughts of the empty to-morrow. But it makes a change for all that. You will see a crease in the corners near your eyes, and your mouth is a little harder.

Mary did not wait for the breaking point, however. After a fortnight of close-lipped suspense, she paid another visit to the smart well-brushed boy, and asked to see his mistress. The baker's wife, wide of features and slow of movement, emerged from the sitting-room at the back.

"Mr. Royce," said Mary, "'e used to be a friend o' mine. Could you tell me where a letter'll find 'im?"

The baker's wife looked at the small figure of Mary as she ran her fingers to and fro on the curved glass of a Fry's chocolate show case.

"Come in 'ere, my dear!" she said, moving towards the back room, and Mary followed her.

Women have great courage. Half an hour afterwards Mary came out smiling, a piece of paper in the palm of her glove. She shook hands with the baker's wife, who was remarking:

"As I say, I doubt if it's any use, but there it is." And Mary smiled and thanked her. She opened the shop door and the resonant "ting" made her jump.

"Let me know, won't you?" said the baker's wife, and again the girl smiled and thanked her.

The next day was Sunday, a hot September day, and Mary lay down for a while before she dressed. Her hands and lips were dry, and twice she interrupted her toilet to wash and to rinse her mouth.

A street off the Caledonian Road was the object of her search. To the dwellers in outer North London, the geography of inner North London is as perplexing as that of Jersey City or Genoa. One passes high over it all in the train: it consists principally, as far as one can see, of backyards and sky signs. Mary took the Seven Sisters Road tram to the Nag's Head. "You can walk from there," the baker's wife had said. So you can, on a cool day, and if you know the way. But it was a blazing day. The bicycles lifted the white dust of the road into the quivering air, and the sunlight reflected from the sidewalk made her eyes ache.

A policeman helped her. "Third, fourth, fifth on the left!" he told her, and she went on again. When she reached the road, Caroline Road, the number she wanted

was a long way down.   No. 261 Caroline Road, N. It
was what they call a nice little 'ouse. In North London,
if you own a row of such, you will receive more local
homage, reverence, and fame, than an author, a cricketer,
and a trick cyclist put together. Literature? Sport? They
pass, evanescent; the houses stand. You have a stake in
the country. You do not talk or act, you are. After you
leave the saloon bar, men who know you by sight claim
the friendship of your inmost soul. "Don't ask *me* 'ow
many 'ouses 'e's got!" they say, in humorous condescen-
sion, to foreigners.

No. 261 was owned by such a person. In fact, Mr. Royce
Senior was the person and he lived at 261. Consequently,
when Mary Higgs was ushered into his presence, he left
his visitor to make the first move. He was sitting in the
front room, a box of cigars and a bottle of whisky on the
table at his side. When Mary said she was a friend of his
son, he let it pass. When she went on to say that she understood his son had gone to the Colonies, he looked hard at
her but let that pass too. But when she cornered him by
asking for his son's address, he spoke.

"Anythin' important?" he said, blowing out smoke.

"I'm three months gone," she answered with rustic
brevity, "and I'd like to know when he's comin' back."

The owner of twelve nice little 'ouses looked at Mary
Higgs in shocked surprise. He had been against the idea
of his youngest son going out to the Colonies. His idea
had been to buy him a nice little business near by and set
him up. His youngest son was inclined to fall in with this,
had in fact delayed his departure to discuss the matter.
Mr. Royce Senior was rather sorry now that the young
man had not gone after all. Not that he had any objection to
his son marrying a girl in service, for Mrs. Royce Senior
had been a housemaid. But Mr. Royce Senior did not believe Mary's story at all. He had lived in London for a
great many years and he had a large experience of the
villainy of human nature. It was one of his axioms that
while men are liars, young women in trouble are greater
liars still, that they will stick at nothing to fasten a claim
upon some quite possibly innocent young man. He did not
preach on this text save very rarely, in private, to his sons,

but avoided such difficult themes, just as he avoided auctions and deaths in his nice little 'ouses. Moreover, Mr. Royce Senior had no opinion of a young woman who was fool enough to let a man have his own way. It stamped her as unfit to be a mistress of a nice little 'ouse. Mr. Royce Senior's devotion to the solidarity of his class was very deep, very sincere, very unconscious. He was as incapable of ratting as a Tory Duke. His eminence as a houseowner and landlord did not shake this loyalty to his humble class, it confirmed it. He was an embodied respectability, as his wife, now some years deceased, was a disembodied respectability, whose funeral (at Abney Park) was as a second *Anno Domini* to many matrons in Caroline Road. And here was this embodied respectability confronted with a young woman who "tried a new game" by stating unmentionable facts directly and without loss of time; thinking to wring his withers by surprise, he imagined. Well, that was an improbable event, because Mr. Royce Senior was a business man, and he was just as much alive to the interests of his pocket and position on Sunday afternoon as he was on Monday morning. So he turned the matter over in his mind, looking at Mary the while.

"I see 'ow it is," he said at length, looking severely at his cigar. "What you'd better do is to let me move in the matter. I'll write to 'im, see? 'E'll listen to me. I'll 'ave to 'ave 'is side o' the thing, too, 'fore I can move in the matter. What's your address?"

He reached out a fat hand to a roll-top desk at his back and took a piece of paper and a pencil.

"Mary Higgs, 'The Glen,' Eldersleigh Road, Hornsey, N.," said Mary, and repeated it in overlapping instalments until Mr. Royce Senior had it all safely down. "Yes, H-I-G-G-S. Higgs. Double G. The Glen—that's the name o' the 'ouse—El-dersleigh—L-E-I-G-H, Hornsey."

"Yes. All right, I'll attend to it. You see 'ow it is, I can't move in the matter—oh, quite so, I'm not saying that at all. Only nowadays, you know, must protect ourselves." He stood up and laid his cigar down. Mary stood up too. She felt unable to do anything else. Mr. Royce Senior followed her out into the narrow "passidge" and held open the front door. He did not offer his hand, but he maintained the friendly prove-your-case-and-I'm-with-you tone in his voice.

"Don't worry. Jus' leave it to me, see?" And he shut the door.

"It's like this," he said sternly to his son about three hours later. "It's like this. Don't you reckon I'm going ter buy off young women for yer, because I ain't. I don't want ter know whether 'er story's true or not, 'cause I don't care. You're twenty-four an' your own master, not mine. If you want to go to the Colonies, you can go and I'll start yer. If you want to stop 'ere, stop, an' marry the girl, and don't look ter me."

This completes the Royce incident. The briskness of Mr. Royce Junior, the masterly inactivity of Mr. Royce Senior, together with the successful prosecution of stock-broking by Mary's employer, render it unnecessary to detail life as it is lived in Caroline Road.

IV

I DO not know that Mary's mistress was a very uncon-ventional person. In fact, she was very like many young women I have met in suburban society. She was not very religious, nor yet very giddy. As her family grew up, she formed the habit of going to church, because of the children; she liked her husband's friends, and they liked her; she dressed nicely, and knew a good deal about her husband's money matters, because she understood office work, having been in the City for a couple of years as a short-hand clerk. Indeed, like the young women above mentioned, she in no way resembled the stock figures of suburban fiction. I am obliged to emphasise this point, or the reader will imagine I am departing from the truth when I record that she "waited up" on that hot Sunday evening when her maid did not return as usual, at nine o'clock. She was reading a book in the drawing-room when she looked up and saw, through the bow-window, the figure of Mary Higgs coming hurriedly up the path to the front door.

"Why, Mary! Wherever have you been?"

"Oh, ma'am, I am sorry—please excuse me this once. I—I had a fit"; and Mary dropped suddenly into the oak hall-chair while her mistress turned up the light.

"A fit! What was the matter, the heat?"

"Yes, ma'am. I felt all giddy like, and—and I fell down."

"There, there! Come into the dining-room."

Mary helped a little, for she was still faint, sank into a deep chair in the dining-room. Mary's mistress stood by the table and looked at her in perplexity. She wanted to call her husband, but hardly knew what to do.

"What is it, Mary? You're strong enough as a rule. Tell me all about it?"

And that is just what Mary did, with rustic brevity. There was a brief silence when she finished.

"I'll pack to-night, ma'am, an' go in the mornin'," she said.

"There's no need to do that, Mary. Go to bed now. I'll tell you when to pack."

That was all. Mary went to bed, much more light-hearted than her mistress, who bolted the front door, and went upstairs to her husband, who was smoking in the dressing-room.

"Has that baggage come home at last, Trix?" he growled, yawning. "What's up? You've been a deuce of a time!"

"Let's go to bed, dear. I'll tell you afterwards."

It is so much easier to tell intimate things in the dark.

It is here that I must strain the reader's indulgence. That order to pack never came to Mary. The silent darkness, the faint ticking of the clock, the cradled Miracle by the side of the big brass bedstead, the success that was hovering over the business in Copthall Avenue, all these things tended to ease the telling of the tale to the husband. What he thought of it no one ever really knew. Perhaps he did not know himself. That miracle of his own was so recent, so barely detached from fairyland, that at least we may conclude that he did not take Mr. Royce Senior's view of the case. And yet he adopted that house-owner's masterly inactivity, leaving the matter to his wife, and going off to get the nine-fifteen next morning without a single reference to Mary.

That young woman communicated, in a disjointed fashion, the details of her collapse on the blistered sidewalk of the Caledonian Road, the sudden giving way of her limbs, the hot dust impregnated with the smell of manure, the coming-to in the arms of a perspiring stranger, the administration of brandy from a near-by hostelry, the rest in a chemist's back room, the policeman all blue and silver, the curious small crowd. In Mary's mind, the ammonia-reek and the flashing buttons on the vast background of the constable's tunic, were the salient recurring features. Over and over again, as she lay on her bed, she felt the choking sensation in her lungs and saw those buttons like corrugated moons in a blue universe confronting her aching eyes. It was missis' orders that she was to lie still. A charwoman was making the best of it in the kitchen. Nor to worry, either, said missis. Later a doctor, if needful. Mary's eyes closed gradually.

Towards evening she tottered downstairs and entered the drawing-room. Her mistress was sewing, rocking a cradle with her feet.

"Please, ma'am, what'll you be doin' wi' me? I can't stay here. I can't indeed, after this."

"Yes, you can, Mary. I told you before that I would help you. What did you think of doing?"

"Goin' 'ome to Wantage, ma'am."

"And be a burden to your mother? That's foolish. You'll be all right to-morrow again."

Mary was standing looking down at the cradle. The child's face and small arms were uncovered, the hazel eyes were gazing up at her, smiling, smiling. It seemed to the sad, soiled servant-girl that the infinite mercy of high heaven was shining in those clear, flawless little eyes. And she dropped on her knees and bent her head over them in a wild abandon of unutterable emotion.

And so Mary stayed on for another five months. The Spring was in the blue sky, and the tall lilac bush blazed when her mistress said one day:

"Get ready to go home, Mary. There's a train at Paddington at ten-thirty to-morrow."

It had all been explained before, and Mary understood that she was to go to her mother's for her lying-in. Mrs. Higgs had paid a short visit to "The Glen" and received certain instructions. These things are regarded in a very human light by country folk. A trouble is a trouble, and the general idea, in the country, is to treat it as such, rather than to snatch the knotted cords from the hand of God and deal out murderous blows. Mary was the youngest child, and Mrs. Higgs took children as you take your breakfast, as a matter of course. There are quite a number of folk who look at it this way.

I think Mary worshipped her mistress when, seeing the girl's dark blue eyes strained towards the slumbering miracle, she nodded assent. Just one light touch of the lips on the child's forehead, and Mary went out, pale, downcast, and silent, and drove away in a rusty four-wheeler, a diminutive blob of blue cloak, black hat and veil in the corner of the vehicle, surmounted by a brown corded box. And then there was the journey by rail, and a silent old mother on the platform, concealing her emotion under a fictitious care of the corded box. And the walk, the progress up the long tiled path to the cottage set back from the road, into the old home. They had carried the corded box between them from the station, and that was the last thing Mary did for herself for some time.

V

It was the easiest thing in the world for a subdued and considerably changed Mary to stay on helping her mother and tending the baby, instead of standing outside the Old Home in the snow (true, it was summer-time) and peering through the blinds at a tragic couple bathed in firelight and melodramatic grief, which you may find, from theatre posters, is the correct thing for girls in trouble. Her baby showed no signs of violent evil as yet, no scarlet letter blazed on Mary's bosom, and the Church embodied in an Oxford man who feared God much more than he feared hard work, sent old magazines to read and left things for Time to put right. Very gratefully Mary wrote a scrawly ungrammatical letter to the stockbroker's wife, telling her she was well and going on nicely, that the baby was a love, and that she would be very glad and thankful to come back again, if she might, when she could leave the baby. And God bless her for her many kindnesses and no more at present.

It was in July, I think, that Fate, having been occupied with an earthquake in Siam, an insurrection in Lima, and a war in the Balkans, turned his attention once more to Mary Higgs. Mrs. Higgs had a friend living near by whose eldest son, as we have seen, was a fitter in a London shop.

This son, having had his right arm broken and having acquired numerous contusions about the head, had been laid up for some time. More for lack of the opportunity, perhaps, than anything else, the invalided mechanic had never married. A self-contained, *reliable* sort of man, stiff of beard, incalculable of eye, he would stand at the green gate three gardens away, and smoke. Grotesque too, the pipe emerging from the bandages that covered the contusions, while the left hand, white and nerveless, with the black dirt under the finger-nails showing like paint against the blanched flesh, peeped from the end of the square

26

wooden box that enclosed his arm. The inevitable black scarf, changed to white on Sundays, supported this arrangement in a horizontal position. Mary watched him every day for a week when she picked lettuce in the long, narrow garden, or nursed her baby in the porch. And then, on the day she wrote the letter to her mistress, she passed him to reach the pillar-box that was built into the brickwork of the last cottage in the row.

"Mornin', Mary Higgs," he said, nodding.

Mary stopped, startled, looked to see if he were serious in his geniality, and then replied, quietly:

"Good mornin', Mister 'Erbert." Then she went on, dropping her letter into the box, and returned.

" 'Ope your arm's better, Mister 'Erbert."

"Oh, slow an' sure, slow an' sure, Mary. 'Ow's yourself?"

"Nicely thanks; mustn't grumble."

That was the gist of it for some weeks. Mister Herbert developed a latent genius for tact. This is easier in the country, where words mean something, and everybody knows what you mean. For instance, on Sunday morning:

"You ought to go, just t' show you're not unthankful!"

The church bell clanked in the distance, and Mary's face lighted up.

"Oh, I'm not that, Mister 'Erbert! 'E's been that kind you couldn't believe."

"That's 'im. Never seems to see nothink. Same wi' me. Knows I 'ate to 'ave people jaw about me arm. 'E's what I call a Christian."

"So do I."

"Don't matter what it is, a broken arm or—or a broken 'art, eh? All the same to 'im. Good steel all through. No Yankee malleable in him." Mary nodded, and he went on, "That's why I say—you ought to go. I been twice."

"I will then," said Mary.

German science has doubtless full and sufficient theories to account for the novel ideas in Mr. Herbert Gooderich's head. Perhaps his tactful and philosophical nerve centres lay in his right brain, and the enforced use of his left hand and arm developed them. Perhaps that is why so many right-handed folk are difficult to get on with while they have their health. Perhaps it is only nonsense, and the real reason was

that a rather lonely, idle, middle-aged invalid found something attractive, something ineffably romantic, in Mary's
plight.

Mary, too, was in an unusual mood since her first word
with Mr. Gooderich. She had begun to realise the worldly
side of her position. Very gradually it formed itself in
her mind. Towards the baker's young man in the Colonies
she felt nothing save a vague dislike. She was quite useless,
from the weekly newspaper's "betrayed-girl's-desperate-
act" point of view. A certain refinement of soul made her
feel that if she was unfit to be any man's wife, he was unfit
to be any girl's husband, especially hers. His dominion over
her vanished with himself. He was too brisk, he had too
much surface and too little depth to hold her as long as
that refinement streaked her nature. So she waited, wondering, watching the girl-baby.

Congratulations upon the abandonment of the square box
from his arm marked a period in their acquaintance. The
black silk scarf was still in use, but, with care, the arm was
got into the coat-sleeve—when he wore a coat. It was much
pleasanter in shirt-sleeves, reading the rapturous and schol-
arly racing critiques in the *Morning Leader,* and smoking
a colouring clay.

"Back to the bench soon," he assured her.

"You'll be glad to, I expect," she answered.

"Well, p'raps so, p'raps so. 'Ow's the young woman?"

To such a stage had they attained when Mary received
another letter from her mistress. The stockbroker had done
well, solidly well, for two years, and when people in North
London do well, they move a little further North. You go
up, you see, and moving is a small matter. To pantechnicon
yourself across to Putney or Croydon is like going to
Samoa or Venezuela, and the cost is terrifying. So the stockbroker's new address was North Finchley, where dear gas
was set off by low rates. And Mary was asked if she wished
to come back. There would be a cook as well, now, she
learned. She was to let them know soon.

"I 'spect I'll be off out of this, too, soon," she said meditatively, and Mr. Gooderich leaned interestedly over his
gate.

"That so? Old shop?" he asked.

"If I like. Dunno whether to—or not," she mused, moving a pebble with the toe of her boot.

"Leave the young woman 'ere, I s'pose?"

"Oh, 'course I'd 'ave to do *that*. 'What I don't like about the business."

"Awkward, certingly. I been wonderin' you never thought of gettin' married."

Mary Higgs deserted the pebble and looked Mr. Gooderich in the eye.

"It's not my place to think of anythin' o' the sort, Mister 'Erbert, and you know it."

" 'Ow's that? I'm speakin' for meself, o' course. What's to hinder?"

"I'll thank you not to mention it, if you don't mind." And Mary walked away towards her parents' house. But Mr. Gooderich opened the gate with his left hand and came after her through the dusk.

"Jus' listen to what I've got to say, and then we'll know where we are, Mary. Here's me, sick o' lodgin's and wantin' a place o' me own, an' here's you, as you are. I don't see nothing unreasonable 'bout it. I'm old enough to know what's good for me, eh? or p'raps that's it, *too* old. If it is, say so; I'll think none the worse of you."

As Mary stood by her gate, swinging it to and fro and listening to Mr. Gooderich's remarks, a faint wail smote her ears.

"There's baby!" she said, turning to him, but Mr. Gooderich's left hand held her arm.

"There's baby, as you say. I ain't forgettin' 'er, my girl, I ain't forgettin' 'er. Understand?"

The faint wail rose and fell, clucked and died, rose again.

Mary stood, listening to the sound, looking at the serious, bearded, shirt-sleeved man who still held her arm. Then he let her go without a word, his newly-found genius for tact reaching its consummation in the act.

VI

SUCH were the pre-marital days of the small, rather untidy woman getting tea in the kitchen sitting-room of No. 12 Maple Avenue, as Bert Gooderich returned from the great fight. The kitchen was the most important room in the house. You went round by the back way—that is, you did not enter by Maple Avenue at all, but you rounded the acute angled garden of No. 14 at the bottom of the road, ascended its other side and, lifting the latch in a door further up, entered the bottom of your own back garden. And Bert following this route, his shoulders hunched, his coat collar turned up, and his hands deep in his pockets, scuffled through the deep snow of the garden, kicked his boots against the iron dust-bin and then entered the kitchen, letting in, moreover, a gust of wind and snow.

"Oh, so you *are* back then, my lad," said his mother.

"Can't yer see me?"

"Been kept in, I s'pose?"

Bert responded with an incoherent growl about a bit of a lark and subsided into a slow picking of boot-lace knots by the fire. On the other side of the fire-place sat his elder sister Minnie, with his younger brother Hannibal. Minnie was a quiet girl of fourteen now, still without any evil bent, as far as her mother could see, but the manner in which she regarded her elder brother was peculiar. It was not malevolent, nor was it amiable. As her mother said once, Minnie "sized you up." She seemed to be forever sizing-up. It was a cool, balanced, calculating gaze. It made Bert furious at times. As far as it lay with children to do so, they detested each other. Minnie seemed to be saying, "And what may *your* superiority consist of?" She had it then even as she had it, more consciously and challengingly of course, in later years. I remember it as the most penetrating thing in the world, that look, when I think of her, her baby brother resting between her knees as she sat in a low, old cane chair close to the coal cupboard, her forefinger chafing at the corner of that huge *Grimm's Fairy Tales,* and her eyes beneath the level brows bent towards the two clumpish boots on the steel fender, where the balled snow was melting from the heels all over the bright metal. To be quite frank, that demeanour of Minnie's was a source of occasional discomfort to her mother. She was too quiet, Mrs. Gooderich thought. There was no "mother dear" about Minnie. Later on she adopted the phrase, but even then only in a sort of bantering sarcastic way, as when Mrs. Gooderich at Barnet Fair, hearing another girl urge Minnie to come and dance, said, "I didn't know you could dance, Miss," and Minnie, moving away with her friend, twittered, "Lots o' things *you* don't know, mother dear!" over her shoulder, leaving that Hannibal-hampered woman with an uneasy mind.

House work, too, was another trial between Minnie and her mother. Clever enough, even as a child, nothing *perplexed* her level brows, but the will was lacking. Beds cannot be half made. One must not deal flippantly with beds, nor should the slow absorption of *At the Mercy of Tiberius,* interfere with the turning-out of rooms. The American woman who lived next door but one listened with patience to Mrs. Gooderich on this point. "If she was my child, I'd turn her over my knee and give her a good spanking," she replied incisively, but even the un-English vulgarity of the suggestion failed to conceal from the artisan's wife the wild impracticableness of it. You might as well talk of spanking the Empress of Russia, as Minnie Gooderich. She was like that. if you understand me?

At the Higher Grade Girls' School, where Minnie acquired the complicated erudition supplied by the London School Board and the Science and Art Department, there was never any trouble. She slid from standard to standard without noise or clamour, writing unexceptional essays in a beautiful variation of the vertical angular calligraphy prescribed for her by those authorities, making exquisite little coloured drawings of chemical experiments, doing simple equations in a manner quite void of offence. Miss Shelly, her teacher, had moments of rare exultation when she thought of Minnie Gooderich, mistaking that young person for one of her own simple equations, for Miss Shelly was dominated by the Good, the Beautiful, and the True,

and had a glorious belief in human nature. Indeed, you cannot censure Miss Shelly, if you can picture to yourself the
self-possessed Minnie at her desk, with the embryonic Hannibal at her side, her hair in one thick dark brown plait with
an Oxford blue bow, the cream-coloured brows bent to her
tasks, her blotless immaculate tasks. She never impressed
you that she was "not like other girls." She had nothing
in common with Elinor Challis, the chemist's daughter, who
fainted in July, won a scholarship in September, and died
of cardiac syncope in the following April. Nor did she re-
mind you of Muriel Paston, whose father sold linoleum,
curtains, and bankrupt stock in the High Road (old Paston, who would go to prison rather than vaccinate his children). But Minnie's mother, at the time of which I am now
writing, had come to the conclusion that she was, all the
same, very unlike other girls. She had in her something im-
ponderable and elusive, her quiet orderly advance through
suburban childhood had in it something inexorably logical
about it. Her devotion to little Hannibal was not devotion
at all. Little Hannibal remained, in her charge, in a sort
of soporific catalepsy, he was "a remarkably quiet child"
with Minnie. To the gradually opening receptivity of little Hannibal, the figure of his sister was woven into the
wood-cut kaleidoscope of Grimm's illustrations. She was a
sort of fairy stepmother, who froze his soul with a look and
taught him to say strange things. He had two other fairy
stepmothers, Minnie's two friends, strong-limbed, freckled,
plumpish hoydens, who screamed with laughter when little
Hanny repeated those strange things.

Bert Gooderich did not regard her as a fairy at all. He
knew, as he tugged off his sodden boots, that Minnie's
homework was "done," done with that exasperating efficiency that you cannot struggle against. He knew also that
his own would never be done. The smudged and crinkled
copybook in which the work was set out, was lying quite
probably in the slush of the trench on Trinity Green. The
inevitable row with old Piper assumed appalling dimensions
in his mind. He had always heretofore presented some sort
of unintelligible riot of ink and paper in lieu of correct
answers. No work at all necessitated explanations, and explanations invariably preceded hard caning and incarcera-

tion. Old Piper's heart was tender and he loathed corporal
punishment; but Bert's sullenly protesting taciturnity (the
correlative of Minnie's self-possession) roused the primor-
dial devil in old Piper, and he laid on, short sharp blows
raining down passionately upon the hunched burly shoulders. . . .

And then old Piper, sweating a little about the temples,
would try to resume the nineteenth century and the lesson.

Such households as the Gooderichs drag along in a
mysterious fashion. It is useless to calculate two pounds a
week as a hundred a year. When you pay your rent in
shillings per week, when you get your coal at one and
threepence a hundredweight, and you buy your provisions
on Saturday night, you must adopt a quite different arithmetic. You must pay expensively for everything. Week
after week the furniture people, the sewing-machine people,
the wringer people, the insurance people, the piano people,
each take a little nibble from the thirty shillings left after
the rent is paid.

You buy "young Herbert" iron-shod boots to make them
wear, and the oilcloth and stair-carpet are worn out before
you have paid for them. You live on in North London because the rents are low and it is expensive to move, and you
pay double for gas. You change back to oil lamps and start
another little so-much-a-week to the hardware stores. You
try to make a little by keeping a few chickens and the neighbours complain to the landlord, who gives you notice. You
let the front bedroom to a commission-agent, who disap-
pears with three months' rent in arrears. And all the time
it is work, work, work. You get into the way of nagging,
too.

It must not be supposed that Mrs. Gooderich was insensible of her good fortune. Quite unconscious of any irony,
she was grateful that she should be permitted to slave in the
ranks of respectable women instead of living a life of joyous venture among the unclassed. "What would have become of Minnie?" she would think, not deeming it worth
while to ask further, "What's become of Minnie anyway?"

For Mrs. Gooderich, like many driven mothers, imagined
that, barring that incalculable element that made her child

strange, she knew all about her. She ignored the long evenings when Minnie was out with her friends, she forgot
the unchaperoned afternoons in Hadley Woods. The news
that Minnie could dance is a sample of the awakening.

And Miss Shelly was at a loss, and had an awakening. It
was one day in the dinner-hour, when many girls would
bring a packet of sandwiches and a cake in their satchel and
eat it near the stove. In those days you had to come long
distances to school in Wood Green, for the outer ramparts
of London Education were then precariously upheld by
small and desultory "academies" with fees and French,
principals who took select boarders, and assistants who
took their departure without settling their laundry bills.
And Miss Shelly, who had lodgings at Stoke Newington,
lunched at a confectioner's in the High Road and afterwards sat by the stove reading. She was a fluffy-haired
little person, very neat about the wrists and ankles, and a
relentless self-educator. And she sat there, her neat shoes
up on the stove-rail, reading Mary Wollstonecraft's *Vindi-
cation of the Rights of Women,* while Minnie and her
two friends sat near by on one of the forms, giggling over
the open eyes and mouth of little Hannibal. At least the
other girls giggled. Minnie, ever alert as to Miss Shelly's
proximity, bent over the child and whispered, then the two
girls would bend nearer and Hannibal would be obliterated
by three heads of hair. And then a throttled squeal, a giggle,
a scuffle of feet, perhaps a choke, with use of a handkerchief, and Miss Shelly would look at the stove introspec-
tively for a moment.   What *were* those girls romping
about? But it was little Hannibal himself who created
drama out of their idle giggling.

"Go," remarked little Hannibal with agonising distinctness—"Go to—'*Ell!*" and Miss Shelly leapt to her feet as
though she had been shot. One of the girls gave a convul-
sive whoop, choked, and there was a frightful silence.

"Minnie Gooderich," said Miss Shelly, icily, sitting down.
'Come here to me."

It would have given Bert considerable satisfaction to
have seen his sister for the next twenty minutes, for if
ever Minnie felt uncomfortable, it was then. She really re-

spected Miss Shelly, and the knowledge that Miss Shelly no longer believed in her was humiliating.

No brazening could stand against the young teacher's rigid indignation, her awful horror of a girl who could deliberately teach her little brother to *swear*. (To argue that little Hannibal would swear anyway, in a few years' time, would have been futile.) It was the sudden realising of the miry depths in Minnie Gooderich, hitherto unsuspected, that appalled Miss Shelly. She was very pale and preoccupied during afternoon school, and sat for some time before a letter beginning:

> *Dear Mrs. Gooderich,*
> *It is my painful duty to inform you . . .*

But she got no further. She knew enough of children to realise that Minnie would care but little for her mother's remarks. And eventually she tore the letter up. But the Good, the Beautiful, and the True had received a shattering blow. If only Minnie had seemed to care at all! She had been merely apologetic, the cool cream of her rather sallow face had coloured slightly, and her chin had gone out and up instead of sinking on her breast when she said she was "very sorry."

As spring advanced the Science and Art Department advanced too, and prostrated the unfortunate teachers in London Board Schools with a Botany Syllabus. Where possible, Seventh Standard girls were to attend on certain afternoons at the Boys' School, for Elementary Botany. Bert Gooderich received the information impassively because he had never heard of the thing before, but he did sit up in a species of astonished bashfulness when he beheld about a dozen big girls, with Minnie among them, file into the room one afternoon in April and take their seats, with much arranging of skirts and adjustment of elbows, on some vacant forms. And little Hannibal was with them, the most astonished of them all.

"The 'ole bloomin' family!" said Bert to his neighbour. "If my mother comes . . . lummy!"

VII

Little Hannibal was growing, but I think this Botany Class was one of the most vivid pictures of his early childhood, the picture that detached itself most completely from the dull-grey haze of domestic memories. I want you to imagine that rather diminutive child of seven, buried away among those strong-limbed, hoydenish girls, peering out sideways at the boys over the gangway, and staring at the old man who made curious drawings on the blackboard with coloured chalks. His impressions of the boys were shadowy. There were so many of them, all in rows along the desks, each with a shorthand notebook, taking notes of what the man said. He watched Minnie's operations with interest for a time, when he discovered the walls of the schoolroom. They were wonderful walls to Hannibal. There were vast shining charts of fierce lions and tigers, coiling serpents, and amorphous creatures with satirical names like ornithorhynchus and armadillo. There was a full-length figure of a dusky person with a spear, a turban on his head, and (apparently) another turban round his waist. A mild-looking steam-engine, in blue and yellow, occupied another chart, but Hannibal hardly noticed it. He gazed with a peculiar delight upon the Tonic-Sol-Fa chart. He could find endless satisfaction in *outline*. Even his mother's stunted intelligence had observed this trait in little Hanny. He loved the *feel* of a smooth square card-board box, and the stark black letters of the vocal scale attracted him in the same way. How fat and black they were! And you could read them any way; up or down, to and fro, it was all the same. The fettering sequence of C-A-T and D-O-G became fatiguing, Hannibal found. And then he twisted his head a little more and looked over the boys' heads, and saw the largest and newest and shiniest chart of all.

It was a diagram, in all the splendour of Oriental colouring, of the Ideal Plant. There was a wonderful grey root straying symmetrically into the most permeable brown earth, with a straight tapering stem soaring to a heaven of varnished roller at the top. Arranged in a rigid helical progression were branches of broad green leaves, branches of narrow brown leaves, branches of oddly-shaped leaves, until at the very top of the stem was a most miraculous flower, with a complete green calyx, a complete red corona and exemplary pistil and stamens of gorgeous yellow. It was an amazing production, that Ideal Plant. It made you feel keenly what a botched, un-science-and-art-like job the Creator had made of his Flora anyway, with nobody to show him how. But it did not make Hannibal feel that way, because he knew very little about either God or Botany. He revelled in the clean hard outlines, the flawless symmetry, of that Ideal Plant, and rejoiced very frankly in the black lettering. For each part of this plant was stabbed to the heart with a black arrow, and each arrow was labelled with the name of that particular part.

He listened at times to the old bearded man with the shiny forehead. In later years Hannibal always associated shiny varnished surfaces with Botany. As the old man raised his arm to draw on the board, his coat sleeve fell back and the light glistened on his shiny cuff. And the desks where the girls sat were of richly marked pitch-pine, heavily varnished. And Minnie's new text-book shone, glazed and tooled till the eyes ached as they rested on it. Elementary Botany. What garlands and chains of letters there were in this great room!

It was a rich and splendid spring day, and the amber-coloured blinds were drawn over the tall windows as the sun swung round and looked in. And spring was busy in the schoolroom: seeds fell into the soft rich soil of boy and girl hearts, and small ideal plants were beginning to grow here and there, while the old bearded man with the polished forehead talked, and drew on the board.

Bert Gooderich sat next to Flying Machine Brown in the back row, unutterably bored by this new onslaught of South Kensington. At the back of his mind lay a vague hatred of that invisible but relentless tormentor. In some cases the perpetual disturbance of the curriculum was beneficial. It aroused the teachers, maddened them to heroic efforts of brain-culture, drove some of them into journal-

ism and private schools, some of them to marriage and emi-
gration. Often, too, it awakened long dormant intelligences
among the boys and girls. Lads who had droned through
Euclid and Scale-drawing blazed into activity when old
Piper began German; others astonished him by an un-
dreamt-of cleverness at Electricity and Magnetism. It was
curious to watch the amazement dawning in the mind of a
boy who had outstripped the others in Shorthand, as he
watched some stenographic failure leaping into fame in
model-drawing or chemistry. But Bert Gooderich and
Flying Machine Brown sat at the back of it all, blank deterrent failures, drags on the wheel, without hope or ambition. Even old Piper, with his marvellous intuition of the
child-soul, flogged them and broke up the silly little bits of
mechanism that poor Brown secreted in his desk. Brown
would sit silent for the rest of the day, and then slip off
home and become another being altogether. As long as he
could see he would file and tinker and drill, making some
other purposeless ill-finished contrivance, hampered by
lack of tools and material and, most of all, knowledge. And
on Saturdays he and Bert would walk far away to the
Seven Sisters Road, where there was a model-engine shop,
and Brown would sigh as he stared at the beautiful little
engines, all gleaming brass and copper, for they were so
expensive. And then he would get "an idea," "a patent" they
called it, and for a week he would dream and tinker, tinker
and dream, and old Piper would lay on with that thin angry
cane of his. But it was never any use. Nothing could convince Brown that Botany and model drawing and German were more important to a lad who was to become an
oil-shop errand-boy than tinkering and dreaming of flying
machines and Jules Verne submarines. And afterwards,
when I saw him trudging patiently along Mayes Road or
Maple Avenue with a basket of soap and candles, and a
can of paraffin, his blue apron smeared with oil and powdered with drysaltery, I used to think that Flying Machine
Brown was right.

Gradually, as the quiet hum of the school and the amber
light lulled his senses, little Hannibal leaned his head against
Ethel James's shoulder and fell asleep.

VIII

BERT GOODERICH's great day came when he least expected it, came when he had resigned himself to his inevitable black ignominy on examination days. Colonel Corinth-Squires, with his fierce grey moustache and gold-rimmed glasses, was examining the school. I am at a loss to explain why a retired military gentleman should be deputed to pronounce upon a school-teacher's efficiency; but there he was, and there, for all I know, he may be still. Even Flying Machine Brown came away with fugitive honours in spelling. He was the only one who made anything out of "misled" that was not palpably wrong, and stimulated by such unimagined erudition, he put up his hand when Alder, the clever boy in the front desk who collected the books and was considered a rank favourite, failed with "ecstasy." The Senior Assistant Teacher was frankly amazed that Brown, alone of all his class, should be able to spell "ecstasy." Brown himself was a little dazed by his own luck. But perhaps Flying Machine Brown knew more about ecstasy than the Senior Assistant Teacher. He had more of it in his life, anyhow.

But Bert Gooderich looked on at his friend's triumphant progress in consternation. Brown was playing him false. Brown had never shown any learning in class before. He was making up his mind to "have it out" with Brown afterwards, when he heard the Colonel asking each boy what he would like to be. Now this was a question Bert could answer with a rapidity and conviction unusual even in clever boys. No one had ever asked him this question before, and he sat tense and tingling all over as he listened to the answers. Alas! the boys in the clever phalanx were not satisfactory in their ideas. Most of them did not know what they wanted to be. One of them, in despair, decided that the question was not fair, they had never been taught any answer to it. Now and again came a definite call. Macpherson, who had been under an operation early in life, wanted to be a doctor; Harvey, whose parents kept a sweet-shop

39

in the Finsbury Road, was going to be a barrister; and
Hillier, who could draw, voted for architecture. But these
were only the few sparks of ambition flying up from a general smoky mass of uncertainty. Flying Machine Brown
brought an almost unbearable amount of notice upon himself, for every one turned round and looked at him as
though they had never seen him before, when he said,
"Ingineer, sir," and the Senior Assistant Teacher smiled
cruelly and grimly. And then it was Bert's turn, and everybody, having turned round to look at Brown, remained so,
looking at Bert. But Bert saw only the Colonel, and when
the keen eyes behind the gold-rimmed glasses fixed on him,
something inside him made Bert stand up stiffly, his chin
up and his shoulders pressed down and back. *"Soldier, sir,"*
said Bert Gooderich, and waited, trembling, for the end of
the world.

But there was no roar of derision. The Senior Assistant
Teacher looked curiously at the little tableau, the fierce old
martinet looking straight into the soul of the unkempt lout
at the back of the class. He felt as if this was not his business. It suddenly occurred to him that the Colonel was a
soldier. He had never realised it before.

"And by heavens you shall be!" shouted the old Colonel,
staring at Bert's rigid figure and obstinate face. And to
hide his emotion he turned to the papers on the teacher's
desk.

The examination was over, and Bert Gooderich went
home in a trance.

IX

THE usual sudden emergence into young womanhood happened when Minnie was seventeen, and almost immediately afterwards she had a young man. "Boys" ceased to curvette on cycles about the end of the Maple Avenue, and Minnie herself no longer held court at the back entrance in Wood Lane. The lengthening of the dresses to within nine inches of her shoes, the acquisition of a Japanese silk blouse, and the abandonment of a plait for a Langtry coiffure made Minnie impossible to "boys." For two years she had been working as a "retoucher" in the big photo factory up the hill by the "Cimitry" and had learned all there was to know about the positive side of life. Her plain-spoken comments paralysed her mother, who occasionally weighed her daughter's soul against the twelve shillings a week paid for retouching. But the latter won as a rule. Minnie was quite able to take care of herself. Her temperament was "difficult," and the casual philanderers who worked at the factory could make nothing of her. One young man who followed her home after dark appeared next day with a piece of plaster on his cheek, and proved very reticent about the adventure. This was Minnie's own fault, for she chose her girl-friends among those whose reputations were continually under discussion at the chloride troughs, and who were never seen at the corrugated mission near the railway. The philanderers felt the baulk keenly because they were fastidiously careful to leave respectable girls in peace. Many of them were married men, with girls like Minnie of their own.

But the advent of the young man put an end to all this, and Mrs. Gooderich sang a *Nunc Dimittis* in her heart. After all her anxiety—for she had been anxious about her love-child all her life—Minnie was going to be a nice, respectable, refined young woman. The young man was stooping, Mrs. Gooderich thought, for he was a coal agent's clerk, and dwelt daily in a small office near the station, an office with a mahogany truck full of best household in the window. He was a fattish, serious looking young man, careful, neat, church-going, insured. Minnie was lucky. So many girls, etc.

Minnie was calm as ever at this time. The favour of the young man's acquaintance was won tritely enough. For a short time he had been an inmate of that spare bedroom, and Minnie sometimes made his tea. It was not good tea, and I take it as a sign of infatuation that the tea, as made by Minnie, did not drive him to the world again. But when he had taken her for several walks, and had returned from one of those walks with an understanding, the innate delicacy of the coal agent's clerk prompted him to seek lodgings elsewhere. It would look better, it was agreed. The stigma attached to "lodgers" in the suburbs was intolerable to a serious young man. And then came the ring.

Minnie was pleased with the ring. She had a number of spurious ornaments, the usual trash that young girls carry on their wrists and neck and fingers, but this was a thing of price, four pounds ten. He had kissed her when he had slipped it on, on the teak seat that used to snuggle against the old red wall opposite the Cherry Tree Inn, and Minnie submitted. I do not know if it will explain anything of Minnie's character to the reader, but to me it is significant that kissing was abhorrent to her. And since serious young men with small bank accounts think kissing is indispensable and proper and delightful, this diffidence on Minnie's part was a source of microscopic estrangements, though nothing else could have held him so effectually in her toils. "Your breath does smell!" she had remarked once, with terrible calmness, and he had been stricken to a red, angry silence. He was not an imaginative man, and he was quite incompetent to deal with a girl like Minnie. He did not realise that a fancy waistcoat and a well-groomed head of hair are almost negligible factors in the great game, that a young woman is a human being with all five senses cruelly alive.

Another rock on which everything was almost wrecked was his dislike of her employment. He wanted her to chuck the photo factory, "since she was engaged," and Minnie's eyes opened wide with astonishment. "Why, if you please?"

she asked with icy politeness. And he had mumbled something about "the fellers up there." Mrs. Gooderich, too, incautiously seconded this motion, and Minnie explained that her intention was to remain in the photo factory as long as she pleased; if they didn't like it, they could lump it, so there! And the scheme fell through.

Sometimes the young man wondered, in his new lodgings, if he were not brewing trouble for himself, Minnie was so temperamentally different, and he would think, "Never mind, when we're married, she'll settle down and be a good little wifie."

Bert Gooderich, earning his living at the local furniture emporium, lived his life very much apart from his sister. He was surprised enough when she got a young man, it is true, but his mind was taken up with other matters. He was going into the Army very soon, and you cannot expect a young man to take much interest in his sister's affairs. Apart from a detached, sarcastic attitude, assumed only at home towards the young coal-agent's clerk, they entered not at all into Bert's cosmos. Bert offered him "a fag" once, when he came to supper, but the young man did not smoke, which was another trait that Minnie made into a painful deficiency of manhood.

"Don't smoke!" echoed Bert, from the middle of a dense cloud of Wild Woodbine. "Why, you ain't born yet, then. You don't know you're alive, mate."

"You be quiet, Bert," said Minnie; "you'd be better with less of it."

"Oh! What about you, young Min, eh?"

The young man looked at Bert with a sudden suspicion.

"Mind your own business," said Minnie.

"Ditto, ditto, ol' sport," replied her brother, and dismissed the matter from his mind.

But the young man could not so dismiss it. He had that horror of girls smoking that goes with his environment. He was like that. The only women he had ever known to smoke were the *décolletée* adventuresses in novels. The suspicion that Minnie might smoke in secret was torture to him. And he mused wretchedly, as he walked homeward, what might she not do? What did he know of her whose waist he held nightly on the seats distributed about the lanes of Southgate, whose demure eyes looked him over and sized him up with such relentless composure?

"You're not treatin' me fairly, darling," he fretted the next evening. "Why don't you be straight about it?"

"Oh well!" she squirmed, and moved a little away from him. They were standing on a wooded footbridge that crossed a wide shallow stream. A brougham came down the lane, the two brown horses lifting their feet delicately, and throwing fantastic shadows on the high bank at the side. Within they saw a man and a woman, beautifully dressed, bound for the big house behind the pond up the hill. As the carriage rolled slowly through the water the woman leaned towards the open window and saw them standing side by side, and smiled. And Minnie grew angry, and watched the carriage glide up the lane, glide out of sight, leaving them alone again.

"I think it's my right," the young man insisted.

"Is it?"

"To be straight, yes. Of course, if you're sick of it——"

"I didn't say I was. Only, if you will nag so——"

"Who's naggin'? I'm straight with you, aren't I? Nobody can say I'm not patient and all that."

Minnie was thinking of the brougham and the girl who leaned out and smiled. Why could not she have luck like that? To be poor, and slave, like her mother, to be for ever darning and cleaning and living close! She had not smoked a cigarette for years. Even when she had done so, it had only been the schoolgirl's dare-devil desire to see what it was like. If the wretched young man would only leave her alone, she would possibly never have touched them again.

"Well, it's no use goin' on like this," he said in a low voice as they stood at the gate in Maple Avenue. A clear, full moon flooded the road and threw sharp black shadows of the trees on the roadway. Across the way, in the big house at the corner, they could see the family at supper behind the great plate-glass windows. They could see the beautiful room hung with engravings, the soft pink shades of the candles on the table illuminated the scene, the heads bent over the food, the swift skilful servants moving round, the tall clock in the corner with its slow-moving pendulum of gold. The gate of No. 12 creaked a little as Minnie moved it to and fro.

"I must have an understanding," he added firmly.

"Must you?" she said sharply, turning to him so that he quailed. "Well, let's go indoors and you shall have it."

"Minnie!" he said appealingly, but she walked up the little tiled path ignoring him, and he followed.

Her mother sat at the table in the front room, sewing by the light of a smelling oil-lamp. Mary Gooderich had changed greatly in the course of eighteen years.

"Sit down, dear. I'll get supper in a minute." She looked up and saw Minnie's face.

"What's the matter?" she asked.

Bert lounged in from the kitchen, smoking, and sank down on the sofa.

"The matter is I'm not goin' to be nagged at all my life, mother, and so I tell you."

"I've not nagged, Mrs. Gooderich. I've only asked her a plain question and she won't answer it. Nobody belongin' to me is goin' to smoke, that's all I can say."

The young man paused for breath. His rather plump features were drawn with conflicting emotions, his satin tie was rucking up over his collar, and his hands fumbled with the edge of the worn red baize tablecloth.

"What's up—lovers' tiffs?" queried the recumbent Bert in amusement. Minnie blazed at him.

"You be quiet! And nobody's goin' to nag, nag, nag for ever and ever at me, that's all *I* can say," she snarled at her lover. "You get somebody as likes it. I don't." And taking off her ring, she tossed it to the middle of the table.

The young man held to the edge of the table and watched the ring circle about and fall to rest, the tiny stones glinting in the lamp-light. Bert's cigarette stuck to his upper lip as he opened his mouth in his astonishment.

"What d'you mean?" said the young man in a cold, life-less voice.

"There's your ring, that's what I mean."

"I've not deserved this," he answered dully.

"There's your ring, and don't have so much to say, next time."

There was a brief silence that seemed centuries long. And

then the young man slowly picked up the ring, and went slowly out of the house. As the door closed behind him, Bert struck a match, a crackling tearing sound that finished with a hiss and a spurt of flame.

"You've done it now, young Min," he observed critically.

"Done what?" she turned on him hotly.

"Why, *strangled* yourself." He drew at the cigarette for a moment. "I'd 'a' thought you'd 'a' had more sense. Fellers ain't so easy got." And he lounged away, leaving mother and daughter alone.

X

THAT act of very deliberate and unnecessary cruelty by which Minnie Gooderich freed herself from the trammels of betrothal would have been impossible but for her economic independence. Minnie was a girl with a hyper-sensitive brain and atrophied affections. As a schoolgirl she had had her chums like Ethel Turner, but now Ethel Turner couldn't bear her. Minnie bore this with fortitude, again because of her economic independence. If you are earning twelve shillings a week in a station of life where you can live on ten, your attitude towards the world of Ethel Turners will be mildly superior. It is extraordinary how many emotional storms one may weather in safety if one is ballasted with ever so little gold. Mrs. Gooderich, who knew well enough why her daughter's chin was held so high during supper that Friday night, spoke her mind.

"You wouldn't be so free with that tongue of yours, miss, if you had to keep yourself away from home."

"I'd like to be on my own. I'd manage some'ow," she muttered.

"Would you? You're welcome to try. You'd soon find a man's arm useful."

"Oh, mother, don't! Can't you let me alone? I don't want a man's arm. I want peace."

Mrs. Gooderich was silent until Bert took himself off, yawning, to bed. Then she went round to her daughter's side and put her arm round her. She did not speak, only leaned forward and strove to search the girl's eyes. Ineffable maternal solicitude! Her arm tightened round the small waist. Minnie looked up from her plate.

"What, mother?" she asked uneasily.

"Child, I'm not goin' to blame you, as you ought to be blamed for hurtin' a man as loves you true. I'll leave that to your own thoughts. What I do say to you is, don't think as your mother don't know 'ow you feel. Look at me, Minnie.

47

No, you're not your mother over again. I know that well
enough. I used to wonder, when you were a little thing, what
you'd be like when you grew up. I 'ardly dared think, sometimes. I've seen how restless you've been, and I hoped bein'
engaged 'ud settle your mind. You 'urt him, my child. I'll
tell you 'ow I know, because you 'urt *me* often. Minnie,
I've wondered sometimes, if you only knew 'ow near I've
been to wishin' I'd never give you birth, or if you'd ever
understand 'ow near to screamin' I've been for you to put
your arms round my neck an' tell me—tell me jus' little
secrets."

The mother paused, looking intently into her daughter's
face. At length she whispered:

"Child, I'm afeared for you. You 'ave no weakness!"

With unerring precision the mother's instinct had found
the trouble and voiced it with blundering poignancy. But
the child's face was like iron.

"Minnie, didn't you, don't you love that man?"

"I don't think I did, mother. It was all a mistake."

"I can't believe it of you. And yet, I dunno. There, go
to bed, child. We'll be sittin' here all night."

It was about an hour later that she went upstairs with
the small lamp that hung in the passage, and shading the
flame with her hand, threw a monstrous shadow on the wall
of her daughter's room. Then, standing by the bedside, she
let the light fall on the girl's face.

"Yes, mother?"

Minnie lay on her back, one hand behind her head, the
fingers entwined in the dark hair spread over the pillow.
Her breast rose and fell gently like a ship at anchor in some
quiet harbour. And her dark eyes, darker than ever in the
sudden light, were wide open and fixed on her mother.

Mrs. Gooderich set the lamp down on the chest of
drawers and sighed.

"Child," she said, "haven't you anything to tell your
mother?"

Minnie was silent, looking at the ceiling.

"You can't think," her mother went on in a whisper,
"what it means to me to have not a soul to say a word to.
Don't you ever think, Minnie, what you are to your
mother?"

"I don't see what that has to do with it," said Minnie, shifting uneasily.

"With what? With what you did to-night? It's the same thing, my child. You 'urt 'im same as you 'urt me, 'cause you're that 'ard."

"It's no use talkin', mother. I can't help what you say, I didn't mean to hurt you. I didn't know I did hurt you, just because I'm—peculiar, I suppose you'd call it; only it don't seem very peculiar to me not to be silly. That's all."

When Minnie had been small and little Hannibal just born, there had grown up in the vague hinterland of their mother's mind a picture of herself in later years, surrounded by her children as by a wall, protecting her in her decay. That picture had slowly faded. The last flickering outline disappeared as she stood with locked fingers looking down at her daughter. The time generally comes when a mother can see a dim but true outline of the future. But she gains the power to see this at the expense of the power to alter it. Mary Gooderich, looking down at her daughter, felt bitterly the futility of her life.

Slowly she took up the lamp and went to her own bedroom. "'Ard," she muttered, "as iron. She'll go wrong. I can't stop 'er now. She's too quiet. If she'd only cry! Dear, dear! I can't remember when she *did* cry."

For some little while after her mother left her, Minnie lay awake in the dark, watching the square of moonlight degenerating into a more and more slip-shod rhomboid on the wall. At times she could feel the bed quiver slightly as a heavy night goods train thundered over the Great Northern Railway a mile away. She had always felt that infinitesimal flutter of the earth beneath her body as she lay in her bed. At length she slept, smiling a little. The curtain moved gently to and fro between the bed-head and the window like a ghostly wing.

The next morning was Saturday, and Minnie joined another girl on the way to the photo factory. The other girl was in the office. She was trembling with a piece of "news."

"Do you know," she said, as Minnie swung into line with her. "The shop's sold!"

"Gracious! Sold up, Ivy?"

"No, to an American firm. They've got a patent process. Do you know what they mean by Tetratint work?"

"I've heard of it, seen advertisements of it, that is. They roll them off, you see, instead of givin' them to us to run over. I thought it was a machine, though."

"So it is. That's why I asked. They've got advice notes that they've been consigned. The Tetratint Corporation of New York, Boston, Philadelphia, etc. They seem a very big concern. They may give us all a rise," she tittered.

"I don't think," said Minnie sardonically. "More likely give us retouchers the sack."

There was no more said at the time, and they parted at the door of the works, Minnie to her easel, the other girl to her desk. A man in grey striped flannels, a pot-bellied man with a red clean-shaven face and red hair, was in evidence at intervals. Before the morning was half through it was distinctly understood that this man was not asking questions but giving orders. He would stand, hands in pockets, paunch protuberant, an enigmatic figure in the doorway. Girls seemed as though mesmerised by him. He simply stared at them absently until they turned to look. This was to pick out "rubber-necks." It is a modification of the third degree. Some girls blushed, some bridled, some blundered, some rose and fiddled with articles in their jacket pockets on the hooks. For some twenty minutes he stood there chewing a pencil or tapping it against his teeth, until fourteen girls out of the fifteen were in a state of nervous collapse. They had gradually grown to regard themselves as art specialists. They stood for "taste" in a barracks of flying machine-belts and printing frames. They had cultivated the artistic temperament, by which I mean they drank too much tea. You could have seen, had you climbed up the drain-pipe outside the high clear windows, their lips working convulsively and their eyelids twitching. You cannot, if you are still in the teens and highly strung, you really cannot endure the silent scrutiny of a stranger for twenty minutes, especially if you have had two cups of over-steeped tea for breakfast. If any one *had* been able to scale the drain-pipe and peep in suddenly, these fourteen girls would have shrieked themselves into hysteria. One or two jumped and bit their lips when he moved slowly across the floor behind them. He paused, hands in pockets, by Minnie's easel and examined her work. Minnie proceeded. She was nervous, but not having the artistic temperament, her nervousness was visualised as aggressiveness. She could hear the man's watch ticking. She looked up sharply.

"What is it?" she asked, and the sound of her voice slackened the frightful tension in the atmosphere. She could hear the other girls using handkerchiefs and shuffling their feet, but she kept her eyes on the man.

"Just you go on," he said in a low drawl, nodding his head gently. "Don't you mind me a bit. I'm just havin' a look raound."

"I can't work with somebody watchin' me," she retorted, shifting the mirror that threw the light on the underside of her negative.

The screw needed adjustment and she moved a little to get at it.

"Can't you? Well, if that don't beat all!" he remarked, rubbing his chin, his head on one side. For another moment he paused to look her over, and then walked thoughtfully from the room.

A titter, impossible to localise, began in the room. It gathered in volume, broke into a splutter here and there, sharpened to a squeal in a young thing with a plait, and died away to sharp hissing whispers.

"Miss Gooderich, how could you?" came from the next girl but one, throwing her head back and then forward to gain a view of Minnie's face.

"If he'd spoken to me I should have screamed!" announced another girl.

Minnie made no comment. Perhaps her self-possession could be partly accounted for by her preoccupation with the larger problems. One cannot always permit the juggernaut personality of an employer to roll over one's mind. There had been a vibrant quality, a passion, in her mother's voice the night before, that had impressed Minnie in several ways. She had received a short but vivid glimpse into her mother's soul, and she had realised suddenly how impossible it would be to confide. Each

member of the family seemed a stranger to the others.
Bert's lumpish jocularity and candour was but a plant of
forced growth. So she pondered as she worked. Indeed,
when the red-faced man had paused behind her, Minnie
had been asking herself the classic question, "Why not?"
Why not get away from her sordid surroundings, the
strained relations, the coal-agent's clerk? She was thinking
especially of the last when she looked up sharply and
spoke.

At a quarter to one, as she rolled up her black alpaca
apron and set her gear straight, Minnie was still turning
her affairs over in her mind. In the lavatory there was
much whispering and larkish laughter concerning tennis,
for the girls had a court in the neighbouring recreation
ground. Minnie did not belong to the club. The subscrip-
tion was five shillings, one had to buy a racket and shoes,
and Minnie, though a quick worker, a vigorous walker
when *bound* anywhere, loathed violent exercise. Her ideal
was something quite different. Before this book is ended,
you will have a clear notion of what that ideal was.

XI

AT ONE o'clock Minnie was standing in the secretary's private office. Some of the girls had already entered and emerged before her turn came. They emerged holding a business letter instead of the usual small cash envelope. Now as she stood by the table the secretary pushed an envelope from the pile by the cash-box towards her. The red-faced man in the striped flannel suit stood at the desk turning over a file, wetting his thumbs at times. On the envelope was written "W. Gooderich. 12s." The secretary, who came down from the London studios every Saturday, wore a preoccupied air.

He noted the name and amount in his book, and said, "There you are, miss. Kindly read the notice enclosed, and send Miss Milligan in. Good morning."

A presentiment of disaster seized Minnie as she made her way out with the envelope in her hand. As a general rule she walked home through the recreation ground, and along the ballasted line path that brought her out upon the railway bridge. But to-day she took the road by the cemetery, and when she had walked round the bend she opened the envelope. A half-sovereign and a florin lay at the bottom, and taking out the coins she put them in her purse. Then she drew out the letter, slowly unfolded it and read it.

THE BRITISH TETRATINT COMPANY,
402, SOUTH BERNERS STREET,
Dear Madam: W.

In view of the extensive alterations in the company's process work, I am instructed to inform you that your services will be no longer required.

Your engagement will therefore terminate on the Saturday following receipt of this notice.

Yours faithfully,
Joseph Myers, Secretary.

Miss W. Gooderich.

It was a habit of Minnie's to talk to herself when she was walking alone.

"So that's it, is it?" she mused. "Wouldn't he be glad if he knew! He'd come tryin' to make it up. And mother 'ud back him up. And I really believe mother will be glad too. She'll think it's a judgment on me for bein' saucy. I don't care! I daresay I can get a situation at a distance. Oh, Lord, how I hate this place! 'Dear Madam!'" she mimicked. "I think I'm a pretty cheap madam at twelve shillings a week and find yourself. Miss W. Gooderich is no longer for sale at that figure, my dears, and don't you forget it. She's goin' out to have a look round."

And tearing the letter into very small pieces she dropped them through the cemetery railings. There was a species of ritual about this deliberate rending of paper. Minnie was unconsciously celebrating the new momentous cleavage in her life.

From a worldly point of view, there seemed little to engender joy in the young woman's heart. Yet indubitably did she mount the hill with a swing of body and poise of head that had been absent in the morning. At the cross-roads at the top she paused, considering. The sudden appearance of the American woman interrupted her.

"Well, Minnie, finished, I suppose? Where are you going?"

"Well, Mrs. Gaynor, I *was* going to the station."

"This afternoon, I mean."

"Oh, nothing particular."

"Then come with me. I'm going marketing."

"Are you? I'll only be in the way."

"Stuff! Come and talk to me."

"All right, Mrs. Gaynor."

They walked down Wood Lane, and separated at Mrs. Gaynor's back entrance. Minnie went up the garden into the kitchen. Mrs. Gooderich was drying a saucepan of potatoes, holding it carefully upside down over a pan and shaking vigorously.

"Well, child?"

"Mother, you might as well know it at once. I've got the push."

"Got the——" Mrs. Gooderich put the saucepan carefully on the stove and turned to her daughter.

"The push, mother. They're putting down machinery for some new process, and out we go. I do at any rate. There's a new governor. It's a week's notice."

"Whatever shall we do!"

"Do? I'm going to look for a job. I've had enough of it anyhow."

"But you wouldn't give it up before?"

"S'pose I wouldn't. It was different then. I can't help myself now. At least, I mean I *can* help myself. I'm goin' to have a try anyhow. Hannibal Gooderich!"

Little Hannibal, his coat and waistcoat thrown aside, was playing ball against the house-wall. He was counting softly to himself, for the idea is to make a record number of catches from the rebound.

"What you want?" he called swiftly between two counts.

"Come here." Unwillingly Hannibal came, bouncing the ball up and down. Minnie gave him a sixpence.

"Go to the station and get a *Daily News,* a *Daily Chronicle,* a *Daily Mail,* and a *Daily Telegraph.* And bring back the change."

"Can't I 'ave a penny?"

Minnie regarded him from beneath her level brows. He was not a particularly desirable-looking child, with his snub nose, his freckles, his torn knees and carelessly-tied boots. His hands were filthy, the nails packed with black dirt, the knuckles studded with warts which had been split and nibbled. He was a suburban child, sheath upon sheath of grossness encasing the glowing soul within. His mind, too, was sheathed with material "wants." He wanted a penny, he wanted sweets, he wanted papers with pictures, he wanted a fishing rod and sharp knives, he wanted a bicycle. All these wants covered the divine want within, which no one ever suspected. At long intervals, as he grew, the child had glimpses of himself. Now it would be the slow majestic flight of the rooks as they sailed back to their nests in the woods at eventide. Once it was the mysterious chime of the bells at Old Southgate Church coming muffled and thrilling through the frozen air of a winter night. Or at times the thunder of the heavy night-mail beating up the Northern Heights in flame and glowing cinders, roused the innermost soul of him, so that he would climb the railings by the line path, his chin pressed against the pointed stakes, and hold on, screaming for joy. But these were mere temporary obsessions. The world saw but a dirty child, given to truancy, bell-ringing, and petty nuisances. He stood there with the sixpence in his palm, craving a penny.

"Get out of the way, do!" said the mother on the road to the scullery. "What d'you want papers for, Minnie?"

"Advertisements, of course," the girl answered impatiently. "Go on, Hanny. You can have a penny." The boy leapt away, tearing at top speed down the garden and out into Wood Lane. The next moment he was back.

"The Daily whats?" he asked. Minnie repeated the names of the journals which were to show her the way to fortune, and Hannibal vanished.

"That boy runs wild," said his mother, from the scullery. "But I can't keep him in. These long 'olidays! Six weeks! And clean an' cook, cook an' clean day in day out. You'll go to the factory next week, Minnie?"

"Not if a job comes along before. I'll take the first thing that offers. It'll be a start. Mrs. Gaynor asked me to go with her this afternoon. Marketing she calls it."

"She goes to Finsbury Park. You might get 'alf a pound o' Gilray's butter for me. It's better'n anything here at a shillin'."

"All right. But I'm going to look at the papers after dinner. It's funny her askin' me though."

"I can't make 'er out," said Mrs. Gooderich. "She's always talkin' over my head. It's all very well 'er tellin' me this, that an' the other about management, but I can't do it. The other day she says to me, 'What d'you want lace curtains for? I don't 'ave curtains.' And look at 'er front room. There's nothing in it."

"There's room to move in it," remarked Minnie, nursing her knee. Mrs. Gooderich, wiping her hands on a roller towel, regarded her daughter suspiciously.

"That's your idea! Why have anything in the house at

all? As for curtains, everybody can see straight in when you're sittin' in Mrs. Gaynor's front room. Not that she minds!"

"You can see straight into the room at the Lodge," said Minnie. The Lodge was the big house opposite.

"That's pride. They want people to see their nice things. I wish you'd lay the table."

"Mrs. Gaynor, she has her meals in the kitchen," said Minnie maliciously.

"That's a nice way o' livin'! You'd like that, I s'pose?"

"Saves trouble, anyhow. This front-room business is all fiddle-faddle, tryin' to live like people with millions."

Minnie rose and went to lay the table in the front room, taking off her hat as she went. That front room, with its horsehair furniture, often offended her. The table was too big for the room, the bamboo table in the window slewed to one side on its shaky legs, while the mantel-piece was piled high with ornaments and things that are known as "knick-knacks." Sometimes Minnie wanted to sweep that wondrous edifice of knick-knacks to the floor with one mighty crash. This was not the artistic tempera-ment surging out in righteous wrath against Victorian tendencies, it was an ebullition of hatred. Those vases and bowls signified, in their dreary useless emptiness, the dreariness and uselessness and emptiness of the Maple Road spiritual atmosphere. Those fly-specked cards and photographs were blatant with the false ideals of Maple Road. A New Year's card from their cousins Amelia, Florence, Thomas, and John, children of their father's sister at Camberwell, was propped against the paternal shag-box. Often Minnie's lip had curled as she read the turgid doggerel, "dear" rhyming with "Year," "lour" with "hour," and "thine" with "syne."

This attitude of Minnie's towards the gentle hypocrisy of our lives must be remembered later on, for it helps to explain why she seemed so pitilessly brave, so naturally unconventional.

While she laid the table Hannibal came in with the papers. He looked longingly at the change.

"Here you are," said Minnie, giving him a penny. "Now

run away. I want to read." She sat down on the sofa by the window, shook out the vast sails of the *Daily Telegraph,* holding them at arms' length and knitting her brows. Here was the tug of war.

Out of the innumerable legends on that mighty banner she was to select one that would bring to her salvation. What a wonderful panorama it was, all those flats, hotels, bungalows, and "upper parts" to let, all those agencies going begging, those Broadwood pianos going for twenty pounds, those columns of situations vacant! Minnie let her eyes wander over the sheet for a few moments before she settled down to the business of noting addresses. She read down the money-lenders' column with a perplexed look on her face. What could they mean? Was it possible that, by going to one of these angels of mercy, one could get any sum, from twenty-five to twenty thousand pounds, in three hours? Though varied in phraseology, the essence of all was identical. By dropping a card, by 'phoning a message, by pressing a button, one might say, you had any sum you liked to name, "without Fees, Fuss, or Farce," "simply on note of hand," "in a few hours!" Some were more modest than others. From them you could only get five thousand, but it was "with strict privacy."

If you were of good family, a retired major, and public-school man, would protect your sensitive spirit from the coarse world outside. Minnie wondered what it all meant. Why did people remain poor? "Why go bankrupt?" asked one advertiser indignantly. Why indeed?

She turned to the "Situations Vacant." There is something very relaxing to the mind in reading advertisements of situations when the reader is one of the unemployed. The interest is so continually tightened and loosened, the future looks rosy and black with such monotonous alternation, that the mind becomes flaccid and incapable of judgment. So it was with Minnie. She read them all, from the Accountant wanted in Cairo, who got seven hundred a year and had to know French, German, Greek, Arabic, and some Italian, down to the Young Lady Companion wanted by an Irish lady residing in Yokohama, who got no salary and a Christian "Home." Between these two extremes of prosperity and competence lay a welter of travellers, bodice-hands, porters, drapers' assistants, errand-boys, and window-cleaners. Minnie saw them all, hustling as in one big stairway, climbing, stumbling, pushing, getting on each other's backs, tripping unwary juniors and slightly-bald seniors, each for himself. Minnie was in no way foolishly ignorant of these things, she had seen the struggle for existence go on up at the factory. Indeed, it was the vivid contrast, in her mind, between the real strife and the pretended good-will in men that roused the sardonic in her. She had known brisk young men circulate tales about seniors so that their chances of advancement might be bettered. She remembered the very brisk youth who had borrowed money from So-and-so and had then spread a rumour that So-and-so lived as a blood-sucking usurer. She knew of happenings more scandalous still among the young women who had shared her labours up the road.

Only one item seemed at all possible, Minnie thought, after a few minutes of elation and depression. A Young Lady was wanted to nurse a delicate child. Duties light, and most probably the salary was equally airy. But there was nothing for a young woman skilled in the enrichment of photographic negatives. No one wanted a retoucher to proceed at once to Bolivia, at a large salary, to fake portraits. She put the *Telegraph* down and took up another paper. And then her mother came in with the dinner and the three of them sat down to the table.

"Hadn't you better write to your Uncle George about it?" suggested Mrs. Gooderich. Uncle George was the father of cousins Amelia, Florence, Thomas, and John. Minnie sniffed.

"Uncle George wouldn't thank me to do anything of the kind, mother. He's not over in love with any of us."

"He might know of something," vaguely answered her mother.

"I'll try myself, next week."

Mrs. Gooderich was silent. She would have mentioned domestic service, but she knew that Minnie would "bite her head off" at the first words. And like most mothers, she did not believe that her daughter knew anything about keeping house. Little Hannibal, absorbed in the possibilities of a Saturday afternoon with a whole penny to squander, was too busy eating and pondering to ask questions.

"Well, don't forget the butter," said Mrs. Gooderich as Minnie put on her hat.

"All right. Anything else?" she answered absently. She was deep in thought as she walked slowly up to Mrs. Gaynor's door.

Mrs. Gaynor lived with her one child in a mysterious way. She never did anything "for a living," she never seemed in want, and yet she never spent any more than her neighbours. Her domestic economy was extensive and peculiar, and had puzzled others besides Mrs. Gooderich. She talked often in a religious way, yet she never went to chapel. The curate lifted his hat to her, and the Wesleyan minister made an obeisance when he met her, and yet they could not claim her as a communicant. It was whispered that she owned her house, that she was a miser, yet richer than the folk at Maple Lodge. She could not afford lace curtains, apparently, yet it was rumoured that she had plenty upstairs in drawers. After a while the continued discussion of her peculiarities became stale. She remained while the neighbours vanished, some by day, others by night. Her boy, whom no one had ever seen in a linen collar, frolicked joyously in a red jersey and corduroy breeches, a suburban anomaly. People ceased to make remarks. Mrs. Gaynor was an institution. She never asked for credit, and proclaimed herself no lady by bringing her purchases home herself, and so preventing tradesmen from sending inferior articles. The coal-agent's clerk had once revealed a professional secret by remarking that Mrs. Gaynor always ordered her coal, and paid for it, at summer prices, instead of buying it by the hundred-weight. Such was the lady with whom Minnie Gooderich was to spend the afternoon.

XII

"IT's funny you askin' me to go out to-day, Mrs. Gaynor," said Minnie, as they stood waiting for the train. "Because I got a week's notice this morning."

"You did? What have you been up to?"

"Nothing. They've sold the company to an American firm, the Tetratint Company."

"You're not worrying?"

Mrs. Gaynor was a simply-dressed woman of slender frame, grey-green eyes, and very thin but expressive lips. She looked seriously at Minnie, and the girl laughed.

"That's a funny question to ask, Mrs. Gaynor."

"It's essential. Most people miss essential questions. If you tell me you're not worrying, I know at once how to answer you."

"Yes, I am worrying. Who wouldn't, when I don't know when I'll get another job?"

"Worry won't get you a job, child! What do you want to do?"

"Anything."

The train came in, and they took their seats. Mrs. Gaynor waited until they had passed through the Wood Green tunnel before she spoke.

"I don't mean by that, 'what do you want to do for a living?' I mean what do you want to do with your life?"

"I want to live, Mrs. Gaynor, not simply exist! I'm tired of sticking round here, year after year, just muddling along. Mother——" She stopped and bit her lip.

"Go on. What of mother? Mothers are poor things anyway, I know."

"You're laughing at me now. I don't know why I can talk to you better than to mother, but I can. My engagement's broken off, Mrs. Gaynor."

"Who did that?"

"I did, and I'm not sorry, either," defiantly.

"Girls of your age aren't sorry for anything except

themselves. I know that. Did you break it off because you want to live, instead of existing?"

Minnie pondered a moment and then nodded.

"Very well, then, get on with living. Can you pick and choose?"

"Of course not. I'd have to take anything that offered."

"Why not go to a registry office. There's always plenty of places for housemaids. English women are so shiftless that they must have them, and they don't know how to keep them when they get them."

"Housemaid! I don't like menial work," said Minnie.

"Menial! Where I was born, child, there wasn't such a word. You'll have much more chance of living in a woman's kitchen than in her husband's factory. I don't suggest it as something to last for ever. You're too good to make a life-long drudge of. But you want to educate yourself, and find out what life is. Then you can live it, as you say. I know a good deal more about life than you, Minnie, and I'm suggesting something that's more remunerative than what you've been doing."

"Housemaids only get twelve pounds a year."

"Do they? They get twenty in places, and all found. Can you save twenty pounds a year at photograph work? There's an old friend of mine keeps an office in Kensington, and if you like to go there, she'll give you some advice."

"What's a servant want to educate herself for?" said Minnie, poking the opposite seat with the umbrella.

"You don't know what may happen. You don't know what is the matter with you, but I do. We've had girls like you in America for years. You want to spread out, you want all sorts of freedom, and you don't know how to get it. Instead most of you break your mothers' hearts and do ridiculous things. And all the time you miss what you're after—life."

"Have *you* got what you're after, Mrs. Gaynor?"

"Surely, child! I live my life and am happy. What more can one have?"

"I want more than just bein' happy," said Minnie intensely. "I want money, lots of it, and I want to go about. All round, you know. I'd like to go to Paris!"

"That's natural," said Mrs. Gaynor placidly, her hands folded in her lap, and her grey-green eyes watching the enamelled hoardings that flew past the window. "Perhaps you will some day. Many a beggar would ride if he only wished hard enough. Most beggars I know are beggars because they couldn't wish, didn't know how. I'm telling you how you can learn to wish."

"That sounds funny."

"Not funny, strange. Here's Finsbury Park."

"Strange, then. Would you put your own daughter to it, if you had one?" said Minnie, as they alighted.

"Depends on the daughter. She might be very different from you. You've got a real strong mind. No one knows what you may do, some day."

"Do you mean murder?"

"My gracious, child! Why *do* you say such things? Murder! Well now! You say that? I didn't expect it."

"What *do* you mean then?"

"I don't know. I can't see. This engagement of yours— I can't see what's to replace it. . . . No. . . ."

Minnie Gooderich, walking beside Mrs. Gaynor up the Seven Sisters Road, was perplexed at this conversation, though it was Mrs. Gaynor's accustomed tone. Mrs. Gaynor herself looked perplexed too, but her face cleared again.

"Well, child," she said, her thin lips smiling. "Do you worry now?"

"No," said the girl. "I'd forgotten to. One gets talking, and there you are."

"Not altogether. Perhaps somebody else is wishing you not to. That helps, you know, helps wonderful."

Minnie felt her scalp tingling intolerably. She set it down to walking in the sun.

"Here's Risk's Sale on," she said. "Let's go in, Mrs. Gaynor." That lady shook her head. Like most mystics she was very practical.

"Why, don't you believe in sales?"

"Sales are like everything else in this country," said Mrs. Gaynor. "They're splendid things for those who are well off. If you were a rich young woman and wanted two or three party-gowns, you could get them shop-soiled and cheap and yet good. That's a bargain. So with white goods. But if you go in there to get odds and ends cheap, you'll only be buying trash."

In spite of this wisdom of the world, Minnie paused to look. Messrs. Risk's windows were choked with the merchandise of a Summer Sale. In a few weeks they would be choked with that of an Autumn Sale. Mr. Risk himself, having sold the business to a company by guaranteeing a dividend for a stated period, now bred shorthorns and Irish terriers in Hertfordshire seclusion, while the company strove to build up more business by selling their goods at half the cost price. This system demoralises buyer and seller alike, and Mrs. Gaynor would have none of it.

It was drawing towards evening when they reached Finsbury Park again, and sat down on one of the seats beneath the rustling trees of the drive.

"I've been wondering what you really meant, Mrs. Gaynor, when you said I had a strong mind. Does a strong mind, and brains, and all that, bring in any money?"

"Not always. It's a great help though, because you can see where money is. I was thinking you'd probably get views as you grow older, and begin to spread them."

"Me!"

"Sure, you. Wait till you've been out in the world."

"I don't know much about views, but I know I'd like plenty of money, and I like people with brains in their heads."

"Well, just you stick to facts a while. I'll send you to Mrs. Worrall, and she'll have something for you."

"Very likely I'll have plenty o' views when I've been housemaiding a bit," observed Minnie.

"You might get something else."

"What?"

"Companion. Rich Englishwomen are pretty queer. I'll write to Mrs. Worrall about you. Just you call in on Monday morning and see her."

The word "companion" gave Minnie food for rich and splendid dreams during the week-end.

XIII

At three o'clock on Monday afternoon Minnie Gooderich, clad in a neat black skirt, print blouse, black jacket
and straw hat, entered a fancy-shop in the neighbourhood
of South Kensington Station. It was a large fancy-shop.
You could purchase anything from a paper-weight to a
Gladstone bag, from a bottle of ink to a fire-screen.
Within its large glass door you could feel an atmosphere
of rich refinement. Unconsciously you trod softly; you
modulated your voice to the well-bred drone of the west.
A counter piled high with stationery ablaze with the
insignia of the wealthy occupied the left side. To the
right extended cases of expensive leather goods, paper-
knives of onyx and ivory, fountain-pens of wrought and
jewelled metal, prayer-books that retired empresses might
finger. Beyond this banked and terraced merchandise stood
a telephone-box. Through the glazed panel Minnie saw
a lady communicating with the beyond, her lips moving
rapidly yet without a sound. Beyond again, was a ground
glass door labelled "Office," a discreet, genteel-looking
door, a door that had immense possibilities. A young
woman with thin classical features was busy behind the
counter, her head just visible above a cabinet of brass
wherein reposed sample armorial bearings of many colours
and intricate design. As Minnie stood within this genteel
emporium of useless articles, the young woman leaned
over the heraldic cabinet and examined her. One glance
was sufficient. The young woman returned to her occupation.

"Is Mrs. Worrall in?" asked Minnie briskly. The young
woman raised her eyebrows.

"She is engaged."

"Give her this letter, will you?" And Minnie passed
over a square white envelope. The young woman took it
by one corner and read the address.

"Is there any answer?"

"Yes, there is, and I'll wait for it," answered Minnie sharply. The young woman went into the office.

"Come this way, please," she said when she returned, and Minnie stepped forward. The young woman closed the door, and Minnie found herself confronting a stout, richly-dressed lady who was seated at a roll-top desk covered with papers.

"Take a seat. What can I do for you?"

Minnie sat down and told her.

"So I see by Mrs. Gaynor's letter. Have you had any experience of housework?" Minnie shook her head.

"Or of secretarial duties?" Another shake.

"But, my good girl—but let me read the letter through. Hm—hm."

Minnie watched the woman's face as she turned the letter over, and her eyes moved slowly down the page.

"H'm—I see, I see." For a few moments Mrs. Worrall remained in deep thought. Then she took a sheet of paper and a pen and wrote rapidly a few lines. This she folded and put in an envelope, sealing it with green wax.

"I can do nothing for you here," she said. "My connection is entirely among ladies who expect their maids to have testimonials from the aristocracy. As for a post as companion, my clients expect applicants to be *of* the aristocracy, I think. But if you take this letter to this address"—here she wrote the address—"you may be suited. That is all I can do."

"Is this a situation?" asked Minnie, rising and taking the letter.

"Possibly. I wish you success, as you are a friend of Mrs. Gaynor's. It refers to a post I could not offer in the usual way, for certain reasons. It would damage my business. You understand?"

"Can't say I do, ma'am." The lady smiled.

"Mrs. Gaynor remarks in her letter that you have much to learn. If you will deliver that letter—take a 'bus to Chancery Lane—you will begin to learn. Good day."

And Mrs. Worrall resumed her labours at the roll-top desk.

As the 'bus lumbered eastward, Minnie pondered over the mysterious quest upon which the quiet American woman next-door-but-one had started her. What might not happen? In any case, was not this infinitely preferable to the humdrum monotony of working at the factory and walking out? How glorious the world was! All this press of people, the green of the parks, the roar of traffic! Why had she never broken away before? There was a snap of mischief in her eyes as she glanced around her. A youth sitting behind her on the 'bus imagined her to be making eyes at him. He coughed to attract her attention. Minnie turned again and froze him with a look.

The address on the letter was to Mrs. Olga B. Wilfley, 29B, Clifford's Inn, Strand. Minnie was in a complete and very natural darkness as to the nature of an Inn. She did not suppose it to be a public-house. Perhaps it was a hotel. The mystery which surrounded the whole business seemed summed up in this address. 29B was a novel in itself. In a short time it would be explained. In the meanwhile she lived in a simmering ecstasy on the top of the lumbering 'bus. Knightsbridge, Hyde Park, Piccadilly, all passed in brilliant sunshine before her. This indeed was the world. She noted with quick eyes the girls leaning back in victorias which waited at the curb by Swan and Edgar's and Peter Robinson's. They were rich, of course. The sunlight flashed on the silver of the harness and the silk of the coachmen's hats. The 'bus halted, passed on down Haymarket, and she had a glimpse of St. James' Park, with the Government buildings overtopped by Big Ben. And then Trafalgar Square, Charing Cross, and the Strand, all for threepence. Minnie leaned over and addressed the driver.

"Clifford's Inn? You git down at Chancery Lane, miss, that's what you do, for Clifford's Inn."

Minnie enquired what sort of place it was. The driver told her it was "chambers," which was none too illuminating to a suburban girl. He had a brother-in-law, he averred, who had a hawker's licence, and hawked studs and bootlaces and other small haberdashery, and he kept his stock at the porter's in Clifford's Inn. It was handy too, for a hawker, when rain came on, 'cause there was an archway-like. Thrippence a week he paid for keeping his stock there o' nights. Funny old place, with grass an' trees too, right bung in the Strand. The driver rambled on with his monologue, just as his horses rambled along the Strand. Was Miss up from the country? Minnie, with that sudden asperity of hers, replied, "Yes, from Green Lanes!" and the driver resumed his lifelong study of horses' ears. At Chancery Lane, Minnie got down.

Somewhat numb from her ride, she discovered the passage which leads to the Inn. Her simmering ecstasy had faded, she was less confident of success. Mrs. Gaynor, now—what led her to expect so much of Mrs. Gaynor's influence? She marched into the courtyard and stared. She caught sight of a railed-in lawn with trees, and walked through another archway, keenly interested. Was it possible people lived in such queer old places still? Yes, there were people sitting on the seats beneath the trees. Several of them were asleep; one, a woman, was sitting motionless, reading a book. Nothing stirred. The roar of the traffic had fallen to a faint hum. You might almost imagine a magician's spell over this quiet nook, everything suddenly fixed in its place for unnumbered years. It was like, it was like,—Minnie struggled with her stock of imagery for a moment—like a convent, it was so calm, so still on that warm afternoon. What quiet people they must be who dwelt in these black old houses! A tall young man in a black coat and silk hat, and carrying an attaché case of yellow leather, came through from the Chancery Lane entrance and walked past her.

"Which is 29B, please?" said Minnie, suddenly. He paused at once, and looked at her keenly. He had a keen face, his nose was sharp, his eyes were sharp, and his voice, when he spoke, had a sharp metallic way with consonants that reminded one of a machine.

"I am bound there," he replied. "May I have the pleasure?"

Minnie Gooderich did not resemble a maidservant as she stood regarding him from beneath her straw hat. Those were the days when straw hats were in vogue in all walks of life. Moreover, those were the days when the Inn harboured folk of all descriptions. You never knew, Anthony Gilfillan was wont to say, whom you might know, in Clifford's Inn, in those days. He himself, with his yellow attaché case, was eager, anxious, burning to know everybody. Without ado he led the way round the quadrangle, and made a gesture for Minnie to enter the porch.

"A lovely day," he observed, glancing keenly at the girl reading on the seat. "Quite a monastic place this, for the centre of London. But perhaps you do not know the Inn?"

"No," said she, clearing her throat. "I've come to see a Mrs."—she referred to the letter—"a Mrs. Olga Wilfley."

"Oh, really? My hostess. Her flat is at the top. You know she has an 'At Home' to-day? Do you know her? Well, excuse me asking all these questions. Mind these stairs, they *are* rather steep, aren't they? They had peculiar ideas of comfort in the eighteenth century, don't you think?"

The eighteenth-century's ideas of comfort were not more peculiar than Minnie's ideas of the eighteenth century. When they had ascended two floors, she paused for breath.

"Excuse me! I forgot how fast we were walking. Shall I go up and get a chair? Take my arm."

"Oh, no, thank you. I—look here." Minnie, in spite of her protest, touched his arm. "Look here, you're making a mistake. I've come to see Mrs. Wilfley about a situation. There!"

She expected him to draw away, apologise, and quit her. But Mr. Anthony Gilfillan did nothing of the kind. He regarded her face keenly, her ungloved left hand resting on his sleeve, her slim straight figure resting against the broad sill of the landing-window. A type-writer clicked behind a heavy door near them.

"Indeed! I wish you success. Can I be of any service? If you will tell me your name, I shall be delighted to introduce you to Mrs. Wilfley. That is," he smiled, "if you do not object. My name is Gilfillan, Anthony Gilfillan."

"Mine's Wilhelmina Gooderich," said Minnie.

"And you are come about a situation?" Mr. Gilfillan set his attaché case on the sill and showed no desire to rush to Mrs. Wilfley's "At Home." "I take it you are, then, of Mrs. Wilfley's persuasion?"

"I don't know what you mean," she answered shortly. "I've an introduction to her, but I shouldn't know her if I fell over her, I'm sure."

"I see."

"She's not—touched, off her head, is she?" asked Minnie, with a sudden suspicion, born of Mrs. Worrall's guarded manner, shooting through her mind. Mr. Gilfillan laughed and checked himself. He reflected that he had always considered that to be his own private joke against Olga Wilfley.

"By no means; Mrs. Wilfley is a very shrewd woman of the world. Shall we go up?"

As they turned the last corner of that interminable staircase, a low insistent murmur of conversation and a tinkling of teacups reached their ears. The door of the flat was open to either side of the landing, and a messenger-boy, his hair oiled and brushed, stood at the stair head. Another messenger-boy, whose head was even more oiled and brushed, strutted across their field of vision with a tray of bread and butter. A man and a woman followed, the woman listening with head on one side as the man explained something with pats of fingers on palm. The woman lifted her head and saw Mr. Gilfillan.

"Oh, Mr. Gilfillan!" she sailed right at him, hand held high, face all smiles, effervescing a sort of welcome. Mrs. Olga Wilfley's welcome was always more like a glass of soda water than a glass of wine. It sparkled and fizzed, but there was no heat in it. Her hand dropped listlessly from yours, which is the true test.

A few words of polite enquiry, as the oiled and brushed boy relieved him of his hat and case, and Mr. Gilfillan turned to the girl at his side, now really nervous and therefore, being Minnie, trembling to be on the aggressive.

"Pardon me. Let me introduce Miss Gooderich—Mrs. Wilfley."

"So good of Mr. Gilfillan to bring you along," she purred. "Do go in and have some tea. There will be music presently. . . . Who is she, Tony?" she whispered, as Minnie walked with extreme agitation through the nearest doorway.

"Lord knows," he replied, blowing his nose unneces-

sarily. "I found her trying to find your place—says she
wants a situation—so I fetched her up."

"A situation?"

"Yes, she's a letter for you, from somewhere."

"But she may be a servant!"

"Quite likely. I didn't know you took any exception to
servants. Beneath the innumerable sheaths of the Self
there is but one universal individual soul, eh?"

"Tony, you scoffer! Go and look after her, and see she
doesn't steal the sugar-tongs."

Minnie's conjecture, dim enough, that the people in
these old houses would in some way resemble them did
not live long after she entered Mrs. Wilfley's flat. She
found herself standing near the door of a large room with
a gabled roof of dark rafters, from which hung rusty
lanterns fitted with electric globes. The walls were of
brown paper, apparently: the furniture, as far as could
be seen from the people sitting on it, was "frightfully
old," just as the people themselves were frightfully
modern. A grand piano sprawled in one corner. Brass
candlesticks, snuffers, pistols, china-pugs, Japanese prints,
pen-and-ink "sketches," old china, Bartolozzi prints in
circular frames, and all the other rubbish of refinement
were nailed to the brown-paper walls or lay on the
antique bookcases, making it difficult to find a place for a
really modern cup and saucer or a plate of fairly recent
meringues.

The people themselves may be described in the aggre-
gate as journalists. One or two of them had written books,
but I think they were really journalists. One or two had
money of their own, and they wanted to be, really,
journalists. They were all dressed passably well—the
women in short-sleeved summer blouses with low necks,
the men in black frock or morning coats with white slips
in the opening,—and they all had a certain ease of manner,
a certain facility of expression that was hard to distinguish, at times, from real knowledge and culture. But
this facility was rarely felicity. Their tropes and metaphors, for example, were not so true and biting as
Minnie's, though she felt too strange just then to know
that.

Mr. Anthony Gilfillan entered the room briskly, and
shook hands with several people. He then sat down beside
Minnie and began to chat with her. A messenger-boy
brought two cups of tea and another offered a plate of
cucumber sandwiches. It was a characteristic of Mrs. Olga
Wilfley to use messenger-boys for purposes other than
sending messages. Her great ambition was to have a
private orchestra of commissionaires. She habitually used
the piano for a reading desk, and in her bedroom you
might have seen roses in beer-mugs. The bedroom itself
was for the occasion turned into a cloak-room tended by
her charwoman and a red-haired messenger-boy. Fixing
electric lights inside rusty old lanterns gave her real joy,
for her joy was quaintness. It was, as we have seen, very
quaint indeed for Minnie to come "about a situation." It
was deliciously quaint for Tony Gilfillan, the bad boy, to
drag the girl upstairs as a guest. The whole thing, in fact,
was so irresistibly quaint that the hostess stood in the doorway, not ineffective in her silver-grey against the green
portière, and observed the bad boy talking to his
protégée, and so cold-shouldering the lady who did the
phrenological departments of *Stoney Cuts* and the
Rambler. This, roughly, was the conversation of Mr.
Gilfillan and the rapidly-calming Minnie.

"Won't you have some tea, just to revive you after the
stairs?"

"Thank you." Boy presents cups.

"And some cucumber sandwiches? You remember that
bit about cucumber sandwiches in the first act of 'The
Importance of Being Earnest'?"

"Thanks." Boy presents sandwiches. "No, I don't go to
theatres much. I live so far out, you see."

"Oh, you do not live in town?"

"No. That is, I live in North London."

"You mean the suburbs?"

"Yes," with sudden asperity, "but you needn't rub it
in!"

"No, because that's where I live myself."

"What, in——?"

"Stamford Hill."

"I know *that*. I thought you lived——" Minnie paused.

"In this sort of place? No, I'd rather be shot."

"There's some places in the suburbs I'd rather be shot than live in."

"Have you been coming to London to business?"

"No. I've been working at a photo-finishing works. They've sold the place to an American firm and I've had an Irish rise. That reminds me, I've a letter for Mrs. Wilfley. You make me forget what I came for," she laughed.

"Well, that's just what I was out to do," he confessed. "Let me hold your cup. It's empty, will you have some more?"

"Yes, please, I'm thirsty." He rose to find a boy with tea. Mrs. Wilfley came forward and sank like a grey cloud on his chair.

"I'm so glad you came, you know, Miss—Miss—" her voice trailed off dreamily as she caught some one's eye across the room and smiled. "Mr. Gilfillan tells me you wanted to see me."

"Here's a letter from Mrs. Worrall," said Minnie, turning round for her sandwich plate. Mrs. Wilfley took the letter, perfectly conscious that every woman in the room was observant of her movement.

"Thank you so much. Will you excuse me a tiny moment? We are going to have some music before the lecture. A friend of mine is going to sing one of the quaintest Spanish songs. D'you mind?"

"No, I'll wait till you come back." And Minnie munched her sandwiches.

"Awfully pretty rooms, these of Mrs. Wilfley's," said a deep contralto voice on Minnie's left, and she jumped. She was unaware that introductions were superfluous for light conversations at Mrs. Wilfley's "At Homes." The phrenological lady of Stoney Cuts and the Rambler leaned toward Minnie and regarded her with favour mingled with criticism. Minnie, waiting until her mouth was empty, replied that such was the fact.

"Excuse me," boomed the voice again, "but are you a journalist?"

"Me! Good gracious, no!" ejaculated the girl.

"Ah!" The lady again regarded Minnie's phrenological

development. "I thought you were, you know. Awfully clever woman, Mrs. Wilfley. You've read her, of course?"

"No, I haven't, ma'am. I'm afraid I don't know her very well." The lady's glance became a stare.

"Sorry. I did not catch your name?"

"Didn't you?" The sudden asperity was just rising to the occasion with some swift suburban *argot,* when the gallant Mr. Gilfillan returned with her replenished cup.

"Ah, Miss Rathstein, how are you? Are you supplied? Very warm, isn't it? I've been opening a window or two at the back. Yes, it is sugared, Miss Gooderich. Miss Rathstein—Miss Gooderich." He sat down between them and crossed his legs. "Have you seen Bowman lately? Is he safe for an article after all?"

"Yes," said Miss Rathstein, suddenly recalling that she also was safe for five guineas if Bowman put in that article.

"Miss Rathstein is a very old friend of mine," said Mr. Gilfillan to Minnie.

Some one struck chords on the piano in the other room across the landing. Mrs. Wilfley appeared at the door smiling quaintly. There was a general rustle and movement towards the other room.

"Let us stop here," whispered Mr. Gilfillan, laying his hand on Minnie's arm. Nothing loth, she sat down again. She was outwardly calm, intellectually excited, socially adrift on an unknown sea. Mr. Gilfillan was a new species to her, in particular. His attention was vigilant, yet the feminine instinct in her could lay hold of nothing. His whisper had nothing in it beyond the bare literal meaning. He gave her the impression that she was the one person in the world he wished to speak to, yet he made no call to her sex. His keen eyes were animated, yet she detected no flash of desire.

The quaint Spanish song was soon in full swing. The lady who sang it had spent a month in Grand Canary, and had been fascinated by the native airs. In Clifford's Inn, a month at the Santa Catalina Hotel qualifies you forever as an authority on Spanish music. She sang it rapidly in a high tinkling voice. She did not understand the mean-

ing of the words. If she had I doubt if she would have
sung it. That, at any rate, was the opinion hazarded by
Mr. Gilfillan to Minnie, and I often used to find myself
in accordance with his opinions. He had a very fair
familiarity with decorative Spanish acquired while working in a power station at Antofogasta.

"Don't you like music?" Minnie asked.

"It is an agreeable noise," he smiled. "But do you know
what that lady is singing?"

"Mrs. Wilfley said it was to be Spanish, I think."

"Would you like to know what it is about?"

"Is it—saucy?"

"Sauce, yes. Rather hot to the palate."

"Oh, well, I'd like to know then," she dared, looking at
him at last as she was accustomed to look at people.

Mr. Gilfillan was somewhat taken aback. He plumed
himself on his capacity, his proved capacity for reading
character. He maintained it was half the battle in his business, which was company promoting. But to find himself
so very correct in his diagnosis of a casual acquaintance
staggered him.

"You won't blame me afterwards?"

"As if you cared!"

"I do. I care about the opinion every one has of me. If
a man, or a woman, thinks wrongly of me, I would spend
a great deal of time and money to put them right."

"What on earth for?"

"It all counts, in business."

"Does it? Are you in business?"

"I am an engineer."

"Are you? My dad's an engineer."

"Oh, really. Where is his office? I don't know the name."
Minnie indulged a titter.

"His office! He works at McMuirland's, in the City."

"Manager?"

Minnie flushed slowly. "No," she replied. "When I said
work, I meant he's a workman."

"Then he is a mechanic. The word engineer is wrongly
applied to many branches of industry. Your father, for
instance, is engaged in carrying out work designed by

engineers—I know one of the McMuirland's—just as a bricklayer, plasterer, or stone-cutter is engaged in carrying out work designed by architects. An engineer is one engaged in controlling and applying the forces of nature to industrial purposes. He is engaged in the advancement of mechanical science, as our charter of George the Fourth explicitly states. It is important that every one should understand that."

The quiet voice finished with a click. It was natural for Anthony Gilfillan to take the trouble to explain this to a young girl. He would have explained it with equal lucidity and enthusiasm to an old woman. . . . He gave every one the credit for having as good a brain as himself. He himself was interested in all the details of another man's life and work. He was not shocked to find himself talking to an artisan's daughter. He himself was a bootmaker's son.

The quaint Spanish song rattled to a quaint conclusion of abysmal double-meanings and the lady pulled down her veil, took her gloves, and made her adieux. Several others expressed themselves desolated to miss the lecture, and Mrs. Wilfley smiled on the landing.

"How are you two getting on?" she asked roguishly, coming towards them. "Oh, Miss Gooderich, I'm so glad you came. If you can only wait until after the lecture?"

"Certainly," returned Minnie, watching Mrs. Wilfley with some curiosity as that lady accepted a cigarette from Mr. Gilfillan's case. "I'll wait until you are at liberty."

"Thanks so much. It wants talking about, you see."

Minnie supposed it did, though she was still mystified. Mrs. Wilfley sailed away.

"Do you indulge?" The cigarette-case lay on Mr. Gilfillan's palm, open and tempting. Minnie's eyes wandered round the room for a single brief instant in a scared way, and then her hand reached out and took a cigarette.

"Thank you," she said, and he struck a match.

"I prefer a woman to smoke," he observed, "but she must do it because she likes it. Now, so many only light them and incur a headache."

Minnie wondered what the young man in the coal-agent's office would have said now. As a matter of fact, tobacco *did* soothe her nerves. She plunged into conversation.

"What is the lecture about?" she began.

Mr. Gilfillan fixed her with his deeply-set eyes. His face had the tenseness of an ascetic, the deep eyes of a visionary, the alertness of a man of business.

"Do you—but of course you don't—know anything about Oriental religions?" Minnie shook her head, bored in anticipation.

"You have heard of missionaries?" She nodded.

"Going from London to India?" Another nod.

"Well, you will now see a missionary come from India to London, to convert us to her own religion. Come, let us go in and get a seat. You don't mind if I sit next you?"

"Not at all, Mr. Gilfillan. I should be very glad, since I don't know anybody."

"I have a reason for asking that," he returned in his crisp clicking voice, as they moved towards the door. Minnie wondered what that reason might be; but she was arrested in her reply by surprise at the change in the appearance of the other room. Orange-coloured curtains were being drawn over the windows by the messenger-boys, mellowing the light. At a table stood a tawny-skinned woman in a dress of yellow silk, looking straight before her, with large prominent eyes. She looked rather effective in the dim orange-light, her wide nostrils flaring now and again as she exhaled. Other people in the room were grouping themselves about the lounges and chairs against the windows. Mrs. Wilfley was whispering here and smiling there, directing messenger-boys as they removed the plates and cups. She beamed upon Mr. Gilfillan and beckoned with her eyes.

Minnie sat down near a small bronze devil from the East and gave herself up to confused thought. The whole business seemed so astonishingly unreal that she might have expected, had she been imaginative, to wake up in Maple Avenue, N., and find Clifford's Inn a dream. What would the coal-agent's clerk say? What *would* he say? She was not imaginative, and therefore she was unable to tell herself what he would say. She heard Mr. Gilfillan saying something. No imagination was needed to secure

Mr. Gilfillan's opinions. You had them clicked into your ear in excellent English, French, German, or Spanish, according to your nationality. If you were a mother he talked bicycles, babies, and bassinettes, urging the superior resiliency of inflated rubber as a tyre for your infant's vehicle. If you were an astronomer, he presented you with a novel and soul-searching variation of the pyknotic theory, a variation that impressed you even though it might have made Vogt turn in his grave. If you were a teacher, his views on teaching a plurality of languages would confound your more practical brain, and he would admit, with a smile, that though he was a visionary on these matters, his daughter had been educated on his own principles and with much success. If you were by any chance artistic, he would produce a drawing cut out of *Jugend* or the *Figaro,* and it would pay you to listen to his opinion of D. Y. Cameron, of whom he had an early example. And so, since Minnie was an inexperienced young woman at an advanced theosophical séance, he provided her with information concerning that science, information as well-ordered as an algebraic formula, as luminous as one of his own highly-patented electric lamps.

It is true that she did not comprehend a great deal of Mr. Gilfillan's definitions. Those who live, even in a small way, in the world of ideas, gradually adapt common speech, to their own ends. Mr. Gilfillan, who lived in a very extensive mansion in the world of ideas, though his house at Stamford Hill was only rated at thirty pounds, did not, acute as he was, realise that, when he used the word "sympathy," Minnie was not thinking of a general emotion but of black-edged handkerchiefs at a funeral. So, too, when he said "association of ideas," Minnie's mind thought of co-operative associations and political clubs. The saying "Death is, to them, only a recurring incident in an endless life," recalled recurring decimals to her mind. "Goodwill" was to her simply the goodwill of a business, which is the only form of goodwill ever heard of in suburban life. Minnie certainly had heard the phrase "Glory to God, good-will to man," but that was poetry,—it did not count. Altogether, Mr. Gilfillan's whispered preliminary did not assist Minnie very much

as she sat eyeing the bronze devil near by. And then the
tawny woman at the table began to speak, and Minnie
began to understand.

There was no preamble, no introduction, no firstly. The
tawny woman proceeded, in a low penetrating voice, to
outline the latest discoveries of her sect concerning the
mystery of existence. "If," said she, "we dissect a common
flower"—and Minnie's attention was riveted. She *had* dissected a common flower.

"If we dissect a common flower, we find sheath after
sheath, and in the centre the ovule. Within the ovule
which is but another sheath, we find the nucleus, within
the nucleus we find the nucleolus. This is the embryo of
the future plant. This holds good throughout all nature
and super-nature. The ovule, the egg, lying quiescent,
patient, waiting for the male influence to begin its fertilis-
ing work. Without conjunction all will be in vain. So it
is with the world of yesterday and to-day. The world is
composed of sheath upon sheath of protective needs and
interests, within we find masses of nutritious knowledge
surrounding the nucleus and nucleolus of passionate desire,
waiting palpitatingly for the coming of the Sons of Mind.
So it was when Sakya-muni came, so it was when Jesus
came, so it is now!"

It may be doubted if the speaker of these and many
other similar sentences really understood what she was
saying. She certainly had no knowledge of the ranging
impressions which she made upon the different persons in
her audience. Minnie remembered the lectures on the dif-
ferentiation of sex in flowers, though she had not expected
so peculiar an application of botanical facts. Mrs. Wilfley
sat smiling, intently absorbing it all for purposes of
adaptation, for she was an expert pilferer of ideas. She
saw that a dextrous combination of the Sons of Mind
and the Son of Man would "rope in" many more into
her "public," for she had a public. The ideas and terminology of the lecturer were at that time only just emerging
from the brains at Benares, and Mrs. Wilfley saw their
possibilities for quasi-religious literature. Mr. Gilfillan was
also smiling a little, but he was not absorbing. Probably
because he was a Son of Mind. He seemed too penetrating

to absorb anything. A journalistic barrister and a dramatic-critic near him looked firmly at their boots, for they were believers. When you believe in a religion that forbids intolerance and frowns on proselytism, you must look at your boots or perish.

"We must not be led away by illusions as to our own greatness. We must do the petty duties of the home ere we gird up our loins to accomplish the mighty deeds of a Mahâtmâ. We must feel ere we can conquer. We must endure agony and sweat ere we rise in triumph. We must advance, stage by stage, death by death and life by life, till of outward wrapping the Arhat is ultimately free, and we can enter into Nirvana, the place of Peace and Rest."

It was a short lecture, as lectures go, yet they felt as though they had sat for a long time. Minnie felt a certain relief as people rose to pass into the other room, and Mr. Gilfillan's voice clicked in her ear. The tawny woman passed through curtains over a door at the back, and messenger-boys invaded the rooms with coffee and comestibles. A hum of conversation rose, the deep growl of the journalistic barrister mingled with the cultured modulation of a lady in black silk. Mr. Gilfillan pointed out to Minnie a picture representing Mr. Richard le Gallienne carrying a lady's petticoat over his arm. She saw no humour in it. He called her attention to a photograph of Mrs. Wilfley, dressed in a loose robe, one hand on a marble pedestal, her profile showing effectively against a dark background, her eyes raised in the manner now immortalised in "The Soul's Awakening." To emphasise this, a copy of that picture hung near by in an inconspicuous corner, for Mrs. Wilfley had a great deal of that cleverness which consists in knowing just how much people will stand. She knew that artistic, Bohemian people disliked "The Soul's Awakening," but she also knew that they unconsciously made an exception of Olga Berenice Wilfley, author of *The Licencees of Love*. She was aware, also, that a new influence was in the air, and she meant to work that new influence for all it was worth. Yes, the hard rationalism of Huxley and his followers was done for. Religion was going to have another turn. The soul was awakening and Mrs. Wilfley was right there with the goods.

XIV

MINNIE's ideas of the poetry and sensuousness of life
had been formed to a great extent from the works of
Augusta Wilson. *At the Mercy of Tiberius* had stirred her
depths when she had read it, some years before, and,
though by now the impression had dimmed, it was still
there. *St. Elmo* and *Infelice* (pronounced English style)
were fine, but *Tiberius* was terrible. If her somewhat cool
temperament had ever permitted her to soar and dream
a silly girl's dreams, she had imagined herself in the future
as a Beryl Brentano against the world. Perhaps her
occupation having sometimes to do with Christmas Cards
and being at any rate artistic, assisted her, for did not
the stately Beryl, in the intervals of melodrama and to
stave off the romantic poverty of New York City, design
Christmas Cards? Truly the Brentano devoted herself to
her handsome brother, and the beauty of sacrificing anything to either Bert or Hannibal had not been revealed
to Minnie, who generally skipped the affectionate parts
of stories and of life. But Tiberius himself, handsome,
stern, blue-eyed, impossible either to gods or men, seemed
to her a good working ideal; and now Mr. Anthony Gilfillan, quite unconscious of the honour done him, for he
was a widower with a young daughter, was raised to the
shadowy throne and invested with the awful attributes of
a Lenox Dunbar.

One by one, two by two, and in one case in a party of
four, the guests rose, shook hands in a way so distracting
to Minnie that she was hypnotised by it again and again,
and departed with messenger-boys in attendance.

"I find," said Mr. Gilfillan, "that Miss Gooderich lives
in my part of London, so I'll return, if I may, and show
her the quickest route to King's Cross." And he looked
keenly at his watch, calculated with thumb and finger on
chin for a moment, smiled, turned suddenly on the waiting

messenger-boy, accepted his hat and attaché case, and prepared to depart.

"There's no need to trouble," said Minnie, gratified.

"No trouble at all. I have a call to pay in the Charing
Cross Road, I have ten minutes to get there. I shall be
back in an hour exactly. Till then. . . ." And he was
gone.

Mrs. Wilfley looked at Miss Gooderich narrowly.

Miss Gooderich regarded Mrs. Wilfley respectfully,
realising once more that she had come "about a situation."

Mrs. Wilfley rose and stood by the grand piano, arranging and re-arranging some flowers in a Chinese vase.

"I mentioned to Mrs. Worrall some time ago," she
observed with a new inflexion in her voice, "that my work
and my health would force me to secure the services of an
assistant. Certain circumstances"—here she paused effectively—"made it impossible for me to advertise through
Mrs. Worrall in the ordinary way. An alien influence at
work, lack of sympathy in my assistants, would prove to
be a deterrent to my own efforts. I scarcely"—Mrs. Wilfley smiled—"I scarcely expected to hear from my friend
so soon."

"Your friend must have made a mistake," Minnie said
quickly. "I couldn't be your assistant. I've no experience.
I've been in a photo factory."

"Ah, not immediately. My idea was, to train some one
in my own methods. The remuneration would be small
for a time, and then it would depend on yourself. You
could begin learning shorthand and the typewriter, you
know. I should prefer to dictate. The drudgery of writing
is so exhausting, and my health is very precarious."

"What will the wages be, to start?" asked Minnie.
Mrs. Wilfley looked pained at such directness.

"Had we not better, perhaps, leave that for a week
or two. Shall we say, a probationary month?"

"I'd like to know what to expect," the girl persisted.
"I'd know where I was then."

Mrs. Wilfley's pain increased. She coughed into her
handkerchief.

"You see, you have, as you say, no experience. Perhaps
an honorarium of eight shillings a week——"

"I've been getting twelve."

Mrs. Wilfley was sharp enough to realise a bargain. She saw that this cool competent young woman might be the very person she was looking for. She saw, moreover, that the young woman might shy off if the salary were too low.

"Well, shall we say twelve, after a probationary month?"

"I'm sorry I can't live on air even for a month, Mrs. Wilfley. I knew shorthand at school, and I daresay I can soon pick it up again. And I don't suppose the typewriter is very difficult. If you'll give me twelve shillings a week I'll start to-morrow. I shall have fares to pay too, a season ticket and all. It'll be a tight fit for me, even on twelve shillings."

"Very good, then that is settled," knowing she could not get a qualified woman to assist her for less than a couple of pounds a week. "I do hope," she said, going over to Minnie and taking her hands, "I do hope we shall be friends."

"Yes, I hope so," said Minnie, shrivelling a little at the gush. "Will you tell me what I have to do?"

"To-morrow, to-morrow. I was intending to have some one who could live here with me, or at any rate, in the Inn. When I am in the mood, you know, I go on till I drop, and then perhaps I cannot touch a pen for several days. It is the artistic temperament."

"Oh!" remarked Minnie. She was singularly helpless against the mild gush usually affected by women like Mrs. Wilfley.

"You like Mr. Gilfillan?"

"Yes, he is very nice," returned Minnie frankly. "He talked to me all the time."

"I shall be jealous!" with unendurable roguishness. "Quite like some of those quaint romances one used to rave over. The stranger-maiden fascinates the heroine's great friend. You mustn't spoil our palship, Miss Goode-rich. But you must know his little girl, such a jolly little kid."

"Is he married?" Mr. Gilfillan's attitude was now partially explained.

"His wife died some years ago, poor thing. His sister keeps house for him. So different from him. He is awfully clever. Did you like Miss Rathstein? I saw you talking to her. She's very clever. She writes."

During this monologue, Mrs. Wilfley was moving about, taking up books, laying down books, shifting ornaments, finally seating herself at the table and drawing a sheaf of papers from a locked drawer. Minnie watched her dispassionately, thinking of Mr. Gilfillan's little girl. So he was a widower. Mrs. Wilfley went on talking, as she wrote on the margin of a sheet of MS.

"Did you like the lecture? But of course you found it rather deep. Miss Angaralî is so very advanced."

Minnie had a premonition that this sort of thing would prove tiresome. She was unable to understand people like the lady before her, who, without any ulterior motive and quite unconscious, I believe, of the inanity of their conduct, judge heaven and earth, past, present, and future, animate and inanimate, phenomena and noumena, merely as all these things affect themselves. There is no sequence in their excogitations. Their brains work like an exercise in Ahn's First Course.

"Dante saw a vision of Heaven and Hell," you say.

"How quaint! Do you like Dante?" they query.

"I John, saw these things," thunders the prisoner of Patmos.

"I don't care for Revelation, do you? Too mystical for *my* taste."

Minnie, possibly because of her plebeian origin, had a mind of denser texture. Her opinion of Miss Rathstein, for example, had nothing in it of like or dislike. You might as well have asked her if she liked the grass in Clifford's Inn. Similarly with the lecture. If Mrs. Wilfley had said, "Did you *understand* the lecture?" she would have replied promptly, "Some of it." But Minnie had no conception of the rack upon which the Olga Wilfleys torture themselves, the rack of culture which forces them to fake matured opinions and fixed preferences concerning all things that were ever seen in dreams or written down in books.

As a matter of fact, this Board School girl had a clearer conception of the processes used as illustrations by the theosophist than the journalist whose knowledge of flowers was limited to colour, smell, and the extraordinary names in nursery catalogues. Even at that moment, in a corner of the house in Maple Avenue, were hidden those neat note-books, with their little sketches in coloured inks, which "Old Piper" had marked "V.G." and "Ex." with such keen pleasure. Nevertheless, she sat quiescent, waiting for the return of Mr. Gilfillan. The coarser mesh of her intellect allowed things like theosophy and phrenology to drop through out of sight.

At length he came, within a minute or two of the hour he had proposed to take. He was not flushed with haste : he seemed, on the contrary, cooler than ever. Mr. Gilfillan was that sort of man. He did not appear to be in the thick of one of the most exciting events in his career, namely, the flotation of an international syndicate. He had discovered, early in life, that the world belongs to the enthusiast who keeps cool. Like the mediæval saints, he was consumed with a passion for converting the world to his own way of thinking. Like them, also, he sat, so to speak, up to the middle in snow.

Minnie rose, tingling, looking round the walls of the room, after the fashion of one about to depart. Mrs. Wilfley shook hands with Mr. Gilfillan in the manner already dear to Minnie—hands held level with the chin.

"When shall I see you again, Tony?" said Mrs. Wilfley, pushing her manuscript out of the way and rising.

Mr. Gilfillan, drawing his chin back into his collar, and stroking the creases this formed, named a date.

"And there's next Sunday, you know. We're going out to Richmond to lunch at the 'Greyhound.'"

Mr. Gilfillan protested he had forgotten, in the press of business, the affair at the "Greyhound" at Richmond.

"But you don't mean to say you've forgotten and made another appointment?" she cried. He thrust his chin sharply forward, took it firmly in his fingers, and nodded, looking pensive.

"I have done just that," he returned. "For once will you excuse me? I have been somewhat preoccupied . . ."

He did not tell Mrs. Wilfley that he had, since the previous morning, dictated a hundred and forty-two letters, held twenty-one consultations with his board, spoken to thirty people on the telephone, written fourteen telegrams and six cablegrams, and paid several calls to solicitors, patent agents, and underwriters' offices. It would be no use telling Mrs. Wilfley all this. She would only simper and ask what the letters were about. He did not tell her that he had come to her flat that afternoon because he hoped to see Miss Rathstein's employer as well as Miss Rathstein herself. He was not such a fool as to go to a City Editor in his office. The man selling papers at the corner of the street was probably in the pay of the rags which throve on damning speculative businesses. He did not tell her that he had gone to the Charing Cross Road because he might meet the City Editor in the brand new vegetarian restaurant—that restaurant which failed so brilliantly a year later—for the City Editor was a vegetarian as well as a Theosophist. All this was going on and Mrs. Wilfley, who prided herself on managing Tony, did not know anything about it. He had no appointment, as yet, to clash with the "Greyhound" lunch, but in the rush of the past few days Mrs. Wilfley and her outlook on life had grown distasteful. It was only a transitory indifference, of course, for he knew to the full the aptitude of the lady in that art which he himself cultivated so strenuously, the Art of Publicity. He knew how useful to him she could be later on, when he hoped to have the leisure to elaborate the details of his masterpiece, "Gilfillan Filaments Limited." How these two people of diverse yet indisputable cleverness pursued their way up the secret paths to fame and fortune, how they ultimately placed the girl who now stood between them in a position that, to her own astonishment (and their own as well perhaps), developed her powers in a most unexpected way, will be told in its proper place. For the present it will suffice to indicate lightly the limitations of their intimacy.

The worldly relations of men and women often form an equation that cancels out without warning when some insignificant factor has been added to either side. In the case of Anthony Gilfillan and Mrs. Wilfley, Minnie was such a factor. Her unwitting interposition had dissolved the kinetic forces at play between them and left them in a condition of static apathy. Even Mrs. Wilfley, though she had a certain slovenliness of mind that rendered her inattentive to the niceties of psychological analysis, was conscious of a change in the air as Mr. Gilfillan and Minnie took their departure. For a brief moment a faint suspicion, like the clouding of a mirror by a human breath, crossed her mind, a faint suspicion that Tony was not unaware of her wiles, and knew just how strong or how weak they were, just how easily snapped. For a moment this mood was reflected in her face. And then the absurdity of it made her smile. That chit! Ridiculous! Why, she was vulgar and suburban. Good material doubtless, but Tony would fly higher than that. . . . A woman must have intellect to capture Tony, eh? . . .

And the breath of suspicion vanished, like any other breath.

While Mrs. Wilfley was indulging in these pensive reflections, Mademoiselle Minnie and Anthony Gilfillan have got themselves out of Clifford's Inn and are walking down Fleet Street. Unless you remember that the gentleman was rather tall, wore a silk hat, and carried a leather attaché case, you might not be able to pick them out of the human tide that surged eastward down that narrow gorge and swirled into a seething vortex at Ludgate Circus. There they were, however, their shadows lengthening on the flags before them, and at Cook's corner they turned into the shadow and comparative quiet of Farringdon Street. Not before the gentleman had bought papers, however, a pink paper, a green paper, and a white paper, which he folded small and put away in the attaché case.

The conversation, it appears, was of season tickets and the Expense of Life.

"It's robbery and imposition, I know, but they have you in their power. That's why I don't live on that line. My line has competitors, you see, and they are kept straight. People wonder why Home Rails are moribund. No competition. In business a man should love his competitor like a brother. Of course you get the ten bob back when you give up the ticket."

"All these things make it very expensive to be in the City."

"True, but where else can you be? The suburbs are merely vast dormitories, where a man may sleep in comparatively pure air, while his office is being washed, in fact. People complain of their train services. I maintain that we who work in the City should need but two trains a day—the first train and the last train."

"That 'ud be a long day," commented Minnie.

"With a siesta—a rest during midday," he added, with a far-away look in his eyes. "But I am a visionary in these matters. You were saying——?"

"I wasn't saying anything, but I was *thinking* that there'd be a riot if some of your ideas got about."

"Possibly, possibly. You dislike ideas?"

"Me? No, I like people to have some ideas in their heads. Precious few about in *my* part of the world though. And what there are don't do people much good."

"How is that?"

"Well, look at this Tetratint idea. It's a good idea, and I *know* it makes better prints than we can do, and so it ought to be used. And it gives me the push," she added, without ill feeling.

"Perhaps a push is what you needed to make you get on. I owe my success to being pushed out of jobs too small for me. An idea is really a brain-push. Sometimes it pushes a man to success, sometimes to despair."

"There was a minister in our district, a very nice man, who was a bit cranky in his ideas," contributed Minnie. "People didn't know what he was, he preached such queer sermons. Then he got the idea everybody went to heaven at last, and that did it. He got the bag, too."

"A Universalist," laughed Mr. Gilfillan. "Fancy! That must have been a long while ago."

"I was a little girl and heard them talking about him," said Minnie. "His ideas didn't do *him* much good."

"No. Mind the cart. Have you settled with Mrs. Wilfley?" he asked as they passed into Farringdon Street Station.

"Well, I really don't know what to make of Mrs. Wilfley, and that's a fact," she replied. "She had the nerve to ask me to take eight shillings a week, when I've been lifting twelve. That put my back up, I can tell you. And then she wanted me for nothing for a month, if you please. And then she said she wanted me to live in. And after a lot of jabber about her own queer ways I don't even know what I've got to do for her."

They were descending the stairs to the platform, and Mr. Gilfillan stopped, put his hand on the girl's shoulder, and turned her round to him. People passing them were amused.

"I think you will suit Mrs. Wilfley," he said, with a curious grin on his face. "You will be like two cats sometimes, but she will find you useful."

"But what is it I'm to do? Take down what she says in shorthand?"

"At times, but women are seldom in the habit of dictating. You may have to make suggestions, run errands, cash postal orders, and entertain people."

"Me!"

"Why not?"

"Me?"

"Precisely. Mrs. Wilfley will no doubt be glad to use any ideas you have." He nodded to the barmaid who was looking out over a counter on the platform.

When they were in the train, he told her that he would be delighted to see her over at Stamford Hill some evening to meet his sister and daughter. Minnie was interested in that daughter, but she was afraid it would be bad manners to ask questions. So she said she'd be very pleased if it wasn't any inconvenience to them, and, after shaking hands with him, watched him descend at Finsbury Park and vanish among a dense crowd of people bound homeward to High Barnet, New Barnet, Finchley, Enfield, and beyond.

She proceeded to adjust her thoughts to the return to Maple Avenue.

XV

WHILE his sister Minnie was standing in the Kensington Stationery Emporium and High-Class Servants' Registry Office, little Hannibal Gooderich was sitting at a pitch-pine reversible desk in the Trinity Road Higher Grade Board School, engaged in the study of Art. Twenty-three other little boys were in the same business. They constituted the Fourth Standard, and the subject was Freehand Drawing. On an easel beside the teacher's desk hung a book of outline figures, open at Number Six, which was a Greek amphora. The Board School method of drawing an amphora was simply explained on a blackboard near the easel. You drew a centre line very lightly by repeated strokes of the pencil. Then you looked at your neighbour's efforts and compared notes in whispers. If you escaped detection, you proceeded to draw cross-lines indicating the top, the middle, and the narrow waist of the base, holding your rubber in the left hand and so making it unfit for use when most needed. Then you began to build upon this rectilinear scaffolding an approximation of the copy on the easel. It is best to do one side first and then bring the other as near as you can to that. If you had looked over Hannibal's shoulder you would have seen a shaky framework supporting a vague blob of rubbed-out pencil marks, several finger smudges, and a moist patch in the middle showing where Hannibal had been breathing hard. The handles had not yet been attempted. Hannibal never did attempt the handles of the copies. The teacher always gave the word "Line in!" before he had disposed of the body to any one's satisfaction. When the order "Line in," came, you rubbed out all you could of the scaffolding and the erratic tags of the figure, and wetting the blacklead with your tongue, bore down hard and hoped it would look all right.

Having done one side, Hannibal blew out his cheeks,

peeped over his neighbour's shoulder, looked at the clock, the copy, and the teacher, and partook of a pear-drop.

"You said you 'adn't got any more," remarked his left-hand neighbour with some bitterness.

"I ain't. Foun' it in me 'ank'chief," mumbled the artist, squinting horribly with his head close to the paper.

"Gahn'. I can *see* 'em," was the retort, and Artist Number Two twisted round to pick up his india-rubber and incidentally take a view of Hannibal's coat pocket. The clever boy at drawing in the Fourth Standard sat at the end of the form, three boys away, and he now looked severely over the bent backs and whispered with a virtuous indignation intended for the teacher's ears, "Don't shake!"

I often wonder if those clever boys have ever got enough love from women to balance the black hatred that was handed out to them in their adolescence.

Instantly the teacher pounced upon the inverted artist, hunting, like some Congo native, for rubber.

"What's the matter here? What 'yo' doing? Eh? Rubber? Get on with yo' work. There's nothing to rub out yet. Who's eating sweets? Gooderich, stand on the form. Eh? Stand on the *form*, I say!"

Nothing loath, Hannibal relinquished the amphora, and having swallowed the remains of the pear-drop as he raised his eyes in wondering innocence to the teacher's face, climbed upon the form. You can see him now, a thin-legged stocky lad of eleven, his rather uninteresting features set in a mask of anger and contempt towards the industrious clever creature who had complained of some one shaking. It was the clever boy's custom to finish first, and then put up his hand ostentatiously.

"Please, sir, can I line in?"

This was to inform the class that once more he had outstripped them in Art. The class had no objection to this. The whole shoot of them would have seen the clever boy burnt at the stake in a bonfire of his own drawings with loud hurrahs, but the reason would not have been his cleverness, but his insufferable airs of superior friendliness with teacher.

"Please, sir, can I line in?" Then the teacher would

come round and lean over him fondly and a whispered discussion would ensue, and boys farthest away would use the precious interlude to cram comestibles into their mouths and reduce them to invisible proportions before the teacher resumed his glare in front.

This time the monumental figure on the form caught the teacher's eye as he turned to give the order.

"Sit down and get on with yo' work, Gooderich. Line in now."

And with much scuffling of india-rubber, much hitching into new positions, much rapping of pencils against teeth as they gazed, open-mouthed, at the snug perfection of the copy and their own ghastly travesties of it, twenty-four little boys began to "line in."

Hannibal had yet another misfortune before the lesson finished. The teacher was passing behind him with that peculiarly obnoxious way teachers have, shuffling along side-ways to avoid collision with the artists who drew with their books at an angle. Hannibal was perspiring with his lining-in efforts. A partly-dissolved pear-drop lay on his tongue. The teacher leaned over benignantly to see what strange forms Hannibal had been evolving, and even con-descended to flick a crumb of rubber from one corner. Several other crumbs lay about, and Hannibal, anxious to assist the teacher in the good work, tried to blow them away. The elusive pear-drop only too readily slipped from its moorings, shot out upon the paper, and bounded into space.

Tableau!

"Give them to me."

With agony in his heart Hannibal produced a sticky bag of pear-drops. The teacher looked at them with a grimace and pointed to his desk.

"Put them on there and go and stand in the corner."

Strange to state, Hannibal Gooderich had no objection to standing in the corner. It provided him with a quiet spot in which he could take out his hatred of clever boys who could draw, and unfolding it, so to speak, examine it at leisure, adding fresh touches to the vision, devising new humiliations for the intellectuals of Trinity Road. He had no animus against the teacher. He, poor man, was

paid to be a tyrant and a bully, and at half-past four
his dominion ended for the day. Never having heard of a
life without school, save in the frankly impossible careers
of Frank Read's heroes, Hannibal supposed the teacher
to be an unavoidable adjunct to terrestrial existence. But
clever boys had no such justification. They were excres-
cences, freaks, abominations. Board School boys are less
tolerant than any of "exceptional ability." Many of those
who possess it are not slow to disparage it. One boy who
had won a scholarship of twenty pounds a year for three
years, had worked for it under the impression that a mu-
nificent County Council was to hand him each year twenty
pounds in cash to spend as he liked. His horror, when he
realised that it meant more education, was only equalled
by that of his parents, who immediately removed him from
the clutches of the school authorities and placed him in
Everard's Livery and Bait Stables, in Whitehart Lane.
Hannibal used to hear of him, and see him too sometimes,
astride of one horse and leading another, wearing breeches
inconceivably tight at the knees and roomy at the hips,
soft gaiters, and little black-and-white striped collars of
india-rubber. What happiness! Hannibal and many others
immured in the Trinity Road dungeons used to think of
that radiant being as one already in paradise, and modelled
their own dreams of future bliss upon his legendary ex-
ploits.

Hannibal had not long stood meditating in the corner
when a hum of excitement communicated itself to the
class. The Third Standard was on the move, the Fifth was
to be heard tramping overhead, the Sixth, Seventh, and
ex-Seventh were forming up against the great curtains
that divided the room, and the head master came hurrying
in with a bâton in his hand (a "pointer" Hannibal called
it), and conversed rapidly and intensely with the Fourth
Standard master.

A rehearsal of the operetta was impending.

Lest the authorities should, however improbably, in-
sert into the curriculum of the school some familiar and
useful study, the teachers of the school, incited by a new
head master who was extraordinarily keen on music, had
formed the project of producing at the Assembly Hall an

entirely new and original two-act operetta entitled *A Life on the Ocean Blue*. By curtailing the arithmetic and abolishing (temporarily) the reading classes, sufficient time was obtained to make a daily rehearsal practicable. This took place in a large room upstairs at the end of the day, and the romantic pseudo-Italian music effectually erased from the minds of the singers any ideas they may have intercepted during the day.

Hannibal being bidden to return to his place and put his things away, the whole class stood to attention, left-turned, marked-time, right-wheeled, forwarded, left-right, left-right, up stairs, colliding with the Third Standard in the act of deploying to their accustomed seats by the windows, and finally subsided into the forms by the geological specimen case. The upper standards followed, occupying the centre, headed by, the four illustrious creatures who had been selected, after heart-breaking failures, to support the solo parts. Boy after boy had been haled to the piano and given a test-sheet of Tonic Sol-fa hieroglyphics to interpret. Even Hannibal had been tried, and had excited considerable local interest by being unable to utter a single sound.

"Sing *Doh*," said the teacher, and struck the lower C. Hannibal opened his mouth, but without result.

"Do you hear me? Sing *D O H!*"

No sound, Hannibal standing strained and fish-like, with his mouth open. The teacher gave him a shove, the head master called the next victim, and Hannibal retired, disgraced and terribly relieved, to his place. That was a month ago, and the daily practice had hammered something like harmony into the choruses, but the teachers were doubtless correct in giving themselves another three months in which to make the production perfect.

Music is an art so generally diffused, so catholic in intention, that even Board School boys regard musical folk without much misgiving. The four illustrious creatures who sustained the parts of the Captain, the Mate, and the two passengers *en route* to a desert island, were not, so it happened, clever-dicks. They sang naturally well, and the solicitude of the teachers drove them to still higher accomplishments. But the great thing in their favour was that, willy-nilly, their performances gave pleasure. The clever boy who triumphed in German or Euclid, the egregious genius who had whispered "Don't shake" that afternoon, or the intellectual freak who swept the board at essay writing,—what did all their cleverness amount to? Less than nothing. But the singers gave pleasure. They had a right to be superior if they wanted to. To a certain extent the rank and file wouldn't have minded if they could sing too. And when the day came, the great day at the Assembly Hall, they all mustered and joined in the cheering and felt very proud of the performers indeed.

Hannibal piped away all right in unison with a hundred and fifty other voices, and amused himself by singing what was known as "alto." Hannibal's trouble with treble was that every now and then the notes soared out of range. If he descended an octave the lower notes bumped against his diaphragm. The "alto" which he patronised was an ingenious method of balancing the harmony, and giving body to the volume of sound. Where the treble note was high Hannibal sang low, where the treble descended in the scale, up went Hannibal to *lah* and *tee,* and it was a rigid rule that if you sang "alto" you had to finish on a rather flat *fah* or *lah,* while the trebles were pinned quivering on their final *doh.* The effect was very pleasing to the singer. Strangely enough to Hannibal, the head master and the teacher who played the piano made periodical raids on boys whom they suspected of this apparently harmless practice. Indeed, four had once been "smelled out" and placed in front of a blackboard with a song written on it, and they had been compelled to plough right through it again and again. Which made Hannibal very circumspect. He had in fact perfected a habit of moving his lips, and emitting a minimum of sound, for woe betide you if they caught you not singing.

This afternoon Hannibal was fortunate in having an end seat close to the bevelled plate-glass doors of a geological specimen case. Away on his left across the room the sun blazed through yellow blinds, and Hannibal, leaning back in his seat against the desk behind (two of the illustrious ones were singing a duet), moved his head to and fro and up and down in a curious way. This is one of the points where Hannibal slipped off the smooth and shining platform of commonplace accountability. He was imagining a vain thing, but a very comical one in his opinion. By moving his head in various odd ways, he made the distorted image of the head master beating time take on a multiplicity of shapes each more horrid than the last. There he was in that narrow bevel of the glass, waving, leaping, swelling, thinning, vanishing, looming, now all nose, now no nose at all, now a supercilious, long-faced saint, now a squat clawing Quasimodo, now a pallid angel in a prismatic fire-rimmed heaven, now a devil in a bright blue hell. It was an absorbing game. . . .

> *In the solemn hours of duty*
> *Out alone upon the deep,*

sang the Mate with considerable feeling, seeing he was only thirteen years old, and

> *When the stars show forth their beauty,*
> *And the mighty world's asleep!*

added the Skipper, which is just what a skipper *would* sing to his mate on a fine tropical night. And, just to show how insignificant shipowners and underwriters really are, the two gallant young officers carolled together:

> *Then our thoughts fly swift to England*
> *O'er the wide blue realms of space,*
> *In some corner of the Homeland*
> *Find a welcome resting-place.*

And the ship apparently was left to her own devices, which accounts for the collision with a desert island and the ensuing second Act.

Hannibal, engaged in the quest of the absolute in the bevelled edge of the glass, took but little interest in the duet. Like the others, he had no tradition of the sea in his family to induce any interest in nautical things. Like them and all other Board School boys, he knew no English history, and very little geography.

He had never seen the sea.

But he had seen, in a vague and desultory way, that illimitable ocean of unconscious Being in which he and all things else swam with half-blind staring eyes. In this ocean were neither teachers nor boys, neither mother nor father nor brother nor sister, only Shapes, while he himself moved silently among them a strained, thinking Eye. His voyages in this mysterious medium had to be conducted with considerable circumspection, for the people in the Real World, the active and articulate prototypes of those same Shapes, were "dead against it." His father would chuck his chin sharply if he found him sitting in a study, and the pain of a bitten tongue, Hannibal found, was agonising. The teachers, arch enemies of the Ideal, thwacked him with unresilient pointers, banged him with fact-choked books, and Hannibal would awake, sore and chagrined, stranded on the stony beach of the Actual.

But since the rehearsal of the operetta, he had discovered that by the aid of music could he most easily slant away into that alluring condition which I have tried to describe. Probably the identity of matter and form in music served as a sort of pier from which he could slip without effort into the subconscious world. I don't know. The psychology of reflective children is more complicated, I believe, than it appears.

As the music went on, as the duet was rehearsed again and again, and the throats of the illustrious tenor Mate and alto Skipper grew drier and drier, Hannibal's interest in the gyrating image of the head master became more tenuous, and his mind sank deeper and deeper into its trance. He found himself observing with a detached and cynical complacency the movements of those intimate shapes, his Family. They swam in and out of his visual range, his mother—what an extraordinary creature his mother was down here!—his father and Bert and Minnie. Even in this mysterious region of silent Shapes, Minnie was sedate and terrifying. She was rising all the time: each time Hannibal winked she still seemed to rise, a pink shadow. Bert moved also, but his movements were spasmodic, like a wasp on the wing. His father moved from time to time, turning over and over in a curiously helpless way, yet managing to avoid his wife, who was continually

floating towards him. This happened so often that Hannibal grew interested. Why was his father moving like
that? And his mother? It was like trying to clutch something that floated immersed in water, that movement of
his mother. As you clutch, the thing swims away with
the motion of your hand. So moved his father, clumsily
and without poise, a volitionless film.

The crash of the final chorus failed to arouse Hannibal
fully. The entire school rose to its feet with the inevitable
scuffles and kicks. The piano thundered the prelude, and
then.

> *The sea, the sea, the stately sea*
> *The sailor's joy will ever bee—ee!*
> *The sailor's joy will ever bee—ee!*

Yet the boy sat, his back hard against the desk behind,
entranced. He watched the Shape of his mother clutching,
he watched the elusive thing he called his father evade and
yet again evade that frantic embrace, and then—vanish.

With three quick strides the head master was at his side
and raining down blows on his back, and he sprang up
amazed. The chorus swept on—only a few boys could see
what all the trouble was about. The head master pointed
to the open space by the piano, and Hannibal took up his
position there.

> *The sea, the sea . . . the stately sea!*
> *The sailor's joy will ev—er bee—ee!*

While the school was marching out squad by squad, the
head master conferred, with some indignation, with the
teacher who had been playing the piano and who therefore had missed the incident.

"Disgusting, 'pon my word!—Actually!—Asleep!—
Public Spirit—wretched little shuffler!" And so on.

Hannibal, with downcast eyes, remarked that he was
not asleep.

"Oh, indeed, and what *were* you doing then?"

"Thinkin', sir," he replied, and the collected teachers
guffawed, looking into their straw hats before putting
them on. It was a joke.

"Go on, get out of it, you shuffler!" And Hannibal was kicked gently out of the way. He ran down the stairs, snatched his cap and satchel and made across the common to the Obelisk.

It must not be supposed that Hannibal, ignorant of history and geography, had no knowledge of phenomena at all. On the contrary, his observation lessons had included birth, death, and corruption, the saving of life and the planting of a tree. Yet so chaotic was the social fabric in which he was immeshed that no one of his teachers or parents considered these things as in any way important. *"Half-sharp"* the cockatoo voiced Lancashire teacher called him, *"balmy little kid"* according to Bert. But I myself am of a different opinion. That day when Hannibal stood rapt by the Obelisk cattle trough and watched Ike McGillies, the black-haired Irish boy, drown a starling, counting the bubbles of air as they rose; the day when a dozen or so of them, coming through the fields by Palace Gates Station, saw a mare in the throes of premature delivery; the ghastly discovery, in a ditch by Littler's Pond, of a maggoty dog, and subsequently the skeleton; the gallant theft of a wee black kitten from a brutal vendor of crockery; the transporting of a horse-chestnut just bursting into life from a dung-hill to the back garden:—all these things seem to me of importance in the growth of a human soul. Life and death, the warm fur of the kitten against his cheek and the clammy horror of the dead terrier, these things little Hannibal had known even then, and they seemed to him to have some relation to that strange mood where swam the dim shapes of people and things. . . .

And yet he was regarded as a shuffler, a witless incubus, an undesirable, a cypher.

Clear of houses, he took his way along the road to which Queen Bess and her Stile gave a distinctive name in the days when Verulamium was still a noble patrimony. Here on the left the boy paused by an old farmhouse, a decrepit building half-hidden by untidy trees, and flanked by ruined sheds. A vestige of the rural past, it stood there among its burning heaps of manure, backed by a great railway, fronted by a macadamed road, squeezed in between a brick-field and sewage farm. Hannibal paused on his homeward way to peer among the branches,—the house always seemed dead, save for noises in the yard, and a rusty harrow by the gate made it mournful. Who lived there? Hannibal had been born and brought up within a half-mile of it, yet he knew nothing of that lonely farmer. Such was the spirit of the place, for at the bottom of the little hill where ran a brook, the brick houses began, and with brick houses the instinct of Locality becomes atrophied. In self-defence one is not too curious who lives next door. Hannibal had more than once been surprised to find the house next or next but one suddenly empty in the morning, the children he had played with vanished, and his mother's door besieged by bilked tradesmen with, sometimes, a non-committal policeman. Only Mrs. Gaynor was always there, observant at the window, smiling.

The sight of a policeman holding the Inspector's horse outside the red-brick station induced a fresh line of thought in Hannibal's mind. Why did they wear blue? Soldiers wore red in those days. Red, white, and blue, eh? Who ought to wear white? Angels, perhaps?

Balmy little kid!

XVI

OF Mr. Gooderich himself, a word or two here will in no wise be amiss. He was a tradesman, which to the initiated means a man who has served an apprenticeship to a trade. His skill in that trade was very moderate. He had a slow methodical manner, he was careful and conscientious, and thereby gained a surer reputation than was enjoyed by men of greater skill and energy. This manner was the outcome of his view of life. He was a conservative workingman. He was a faithful and reliable member of the "Mals," which is the Amalgamated Society of Engineers, and he set his face like flint against the slightest broadening of its basis or the most trifling extension of its powers. He was interested in racing and, as football grew into the national life, he, like many Conservatives, bought the *Morning Leader* (only they called it differently) for that journal's excellent reports of the game. But I doubt if he ever read the political articles. His conservatism was not of that sort. It was fixed, steadfast, founded on a rock, the rock of obstinacy. He saw things happening, yet he lacked intelligence to infer the inevitable results. Like the pike in the aquarium, he struck his head again and again against the invisible sheet of glass, yet never connected the glass and the blow in thought. No, his conservatism needed more than a leading article to pierce it. "Radical Fudge" was his placid comment on views more porous and ductile than his own. I think "the Empire" made him feel at times, because he once talked of "goin' out" to the Colonies. But the thought of "Ol' Inglan'" which is the obverse of the Imperial medal, held him to his vice at McMuirland's and the book-maker at the corner of Red-cross Street.

He was temperate, kindly in a fatuous way to his children, just to his wife while in employ, truthful in an unintelligent fashion, yet with all this he gave me an impression of despair. He could not move with the times. He presented a spectacle, even in his early married days, of inarticulate protest against a world that was moving, in spite of him, from vestries to municipalities, from private firms to syndicates, from thousands to millions, from muddlers to men. He attributed all the failures of the "Mals" to their lack of trust in the masters. He loved dogs, and he had much of the faithful dog's nature. He would lick the hand that smote him. He was an improver when the men "went out" in the Ferry Road, and he made the one passionate exhibition of his life when he rose amid cheers and jeers to denounce the calling out of the apprentices who had taken the men's places in the yard, and so had defeated the very end for which he fought. It was brutal and cruel, he shouted, to spoil those lads' career in a grown-man's quarrel. And you couldn't make him see his folly. He was Pym, Hampden, Haselrig, Hollis, and Strode all rolled into one that freezing, frenzied afternoon. And when he had carried the day, he went back to his obscurity and never again emerged. A rather cantankerous man, if you were a person with growing pains in your head.

He remained year after year at the bench, while younger men raced past him, perfectly content in the sphere in which it had pleased God to put him. He believed in God just as he had his superstitions about the ace, number seventeen, and the power of Tottenham Hotspurs to lift the Cup. He was one of those men who would have made admirable conservative licenced victuallers, if the God they respect so highly had bestowed a small capital upon them. I can see him, comforably established at Weymouth, or Somewhere-on-Sea, owning one or two blocks of slum property off Jubilee Street (the tenants hailing from Lithuania, Courland, and Esthonia), reading the *Daily Telegraph,* temperately zealous in charitable affairs, yet fearful of "pauperising," which he understood to be the meaning of *"panem et circenses,"* an increasingly portly patriot, recommending young men to join the army or "go out" to South Africa, a prosperous and valuable burgess. Now and again, I imagine, he himself had had a glimpse of this Arcady, this tavern by the sea (forty minutes from London, frequent trains), and had made furtive efforts to acquire a certain capital. He certainly lost a considerable sum on the favourite, that terrible year when Jeddah won the Derby. He was at his bench, as usual, when old Hack, who had been using his privilege as messenger to converse with the paper-man at the corner of Goswell Road, sidled past him and murmured "Sufferin' Moses! A renk ahtsider, Jack. Jedder—never 'eard o' the 'orse afore!" Gooderich hung his head over his job. And his wife was pinched for some weeks for money.

At another time, heated to a dull glow by stories circulating in the shops concerning the possibilities of building societies, and the phenomenal success of a former shopmate, he had formed a resolution to save. Even his wife had grown a little excited about it, 'Erbert being about to save; and had been damped by the American woman's remark, "Before you can save, you must have something to save." They found that remark true enough, and 'Erbert resumed losing half a dollar on a horse every Saturday, and applauding the 'Spurs when they pushed a football through the thorax of every other team in the Southern League. And then a penny-weekly offered five hundred a year and a freehold cottage to the person who could win a word-competition, and the first instalment seemed so easy that the sky was rosy with hope and the 'Spurs retreated to the background for a while. But they were soon back again, and the prize went to some one in Van Diemen's Land. . . .

And in the meantime, while he was busy with these fiddling things, the world moved on. Little by little the work on which he had spent his time was transferred to automatic machines made in Germany and America, great technological institutions arose in the Metropolis from whose doors poured every year swarms of young men pale from night-study, qualified to deal with the newer methods and later mechanism. Everywhere was being preached the gospel of Efficiency. New managers erected glass observation boxes in the very shop where he worked, handed him explanatory literature anent new systems of working, whereby he might earn more money. But Gooderich never earned more money, rather less, for the new system expected quicker work, quicker calculations of time taken and fractions of pence. He resented the new fangled time-keeping. He resented everything new. Everywhere now were young men. "Too old at forty" began to reverberate in the Press. Gooderich was startled, looked at himself in the glass. Something must be done. He must make a definite effort to get out of the rut. Things could not go on like this. For awhile there was another dull glow.

The next day he had purchased a bottle of hair-dye.

Mr. Gooderich was at home when his daughter entered and hung up her hat and jacket. He stood in his shirt-sleeves by the mantelpiece of the front room filling his pouch from the shag-box. His head was turned over his right shoulder in the direction of his wife. They had been discussing her, apparently. Mr. Gooderich was saying dogmatically:

"Give 'er 'er 'ead and she'll soon get winded." Minnie set her face in a mask and entered the room, eyes downcast, one hand patting her hair as though she had been away but a few moments.

"'Ullo!" said her father, screwing his head a little farther round. "Got the bag, I 'ear?"

"Yes, and got another job," she replied quietly, taking a needle and thread from a cigar-box on the sidetable. Her mother looked up quickly and watched her repairing a small rent in her skirt.

"Really?"

"Really, all right."

"What sort o' job?" asked her father suspiciously.

It is one of the characteristics of these people to doubt every word you say.

"Shorthand."

"In the City?"

"Yes."

"Didn't know you could write it."

"I shouldn't like to make a list of all the things you don't know about me, father," she answered, bending all her attention to the repair of the rent. Mr. Gooderich regarded the top of his daughter's head. Mrs. Gooderich lifted her hand in alarm.

"Oh," he remarked at length. "And whose fault is that?"

"Yours, I should think. You never ask."

"If that's the way you talk to your boss, I don't wonder you got the bag. Course, I'm only your father, so I s'pose it don't matter. So long's you keep yourself, you can please yourself." He turned to get his coat.

"*That's* all right," said Minnie, though whether she referred to the rent or her father's words nobody ever knew. She put the needle and thread away and went out of the room. She heard her father in the hall, the striking of the match, the sound of her mother's voice, too low to distinguish. And then her father.

"Not me! *You* brought 'er up, didn't you? Well, then, bring her down. She flies too 'igh for me. She's yours."

And he went out and shut the door behind him. Minnie heard her mother mounting the stairs.

"You mustn't mind your father, child, he's worried to death," began Mrs. Gooderich. "He don't mean 'alf he says."

"He means very little then," commented Minnie. "What's he worried about?"

"His job. He's had several short weeks, and there's no new engines layin' down, he says, and thinks they may pay him off."

"Well, there's other shops."

"Jobs aren't so easy got, after you're fifty," replied her mother. "What's this job *you've* got?"

"A lady author wants an assistant, or something like that. Don't ask *me* whether it'll be any good. I'm not sure myself yet. I'll try it and see."

"Well, that's a nice way to talk. What's the wages?"

"Twelve, same as before. I beat her up to that anyway. Trust me, mother. Your own little girlie can look after herself."

Mrs. Gooderich looked distressed.

"Where're you goin'?" she asked, for Minnie was arranging her hair after a wash.

"Mrs. Gaynor's. She put me on to this job, so I must run in and tell her about it. Shan't be long."

Going downstairs in the dark Minnie almost fell over some obstacle on the bottom step.

"What's that? What'you doing there, Hanny?"

"Nothin'."

Minnie fetched some matches and lit the hall lamp. Hannibal, seated on the stair, was tying a piece of twine round the neck of a jam-pot; a piece of bamboo lay beside him.

"Fishin'?" Minnie was in a good humour.

"Um," responded the boy.

"A lot *you* catch!" observed his sister, and went out into the dusk. Hannibal made a face.

The string adjusted, he scrambled to his feet, grabbed his rod and followed her through the door. His mother, close behind, watched him scuttling away down the road into the obscurity of Walker's Woods. Mrs. Gooderich sighed. Do her duty as she might, she seemed unable to hold either the fear or the affection of her children. They just took no notice. There was Minnie now, away chatting with a neighbour instead of confiding in her own mother.

Mrs. Gooderich stood at the gate for a few minutes in deep thought, and then decided to "run in" herself to Mrs. Gaynor's and assist in the discussion! Closing the door gently until it was almost latched, she went along to the next house but one, and immediately beheld her daughter and Mrs. Gaynor sitting in the uncurtained room, their faces illumined by a gas-jet with an opal globe. Gas-stoves had come in then, but the incandescent mantle lay in the future. And this clear and distinct scene, visible to all who went along Maple Avenue, disturbed Mrs. Gooderich very much. She had an instinctive horror of this sort of publicity. No matter how torrid the weather, Mrs. Gooderich would not drink even a cup of tea in her back garden,—the neighbours might see. As for taking a chair and sitting in the front room with no curtains and a blazing light, it was "strange," and she had spent a good part of her intellectual existence and energy in avoiding anything strange.

So she hurried up Mrs. Gaynor's tiled path as quickly as she could and tapped at the door. And immediately Mrs. Gaynor, aproned and hospitable, stood before her.

"Well, now, if that isn't just what I was wishing! Come right in, Mrs. Gooderich. We're having a nice quiet discussion." She stooped and straightened a corner of the cocoanut matting in the "hall-way," "so bare you wouldn't believe," Mrs. Gooderich was wont to comment of it. They went in, and to her mother's surprise, Minnie did not scowl at the sight of her. Mrs. Gaynor seemed to have the faculty of erasing scowls from people's faces.

The room, certainly in a suburban view, was scantily furnished. The "mantel," as its owner called it, carried nothing but a plain black marble clock, the walls were hung with two or three inconspicuous engravings. There was a sideboard, or in Mrs. Gooderich's terminology, a chiffonier with the accent on the last syllable, a small table supported a small case of books, a table and four rush-bottomed chairs, on one of which Minnie was seated. Mrs. Gaynor herself had been sitting in a deep rocking-chair, almost a curiosity in England in those days. She offered this to Mrs. Gooderich, but it was too strange for her, she preferred something with four legs. As she sat down and folded her hands, she caught sight of little Hiram Gaynor seated on a "hassock" by the window reading a book. The boy looked up and smiled, and Mrs. Gooderich regarded him with renewed perplexity. He was wearing a blue jersey which came up close round his neck, and his round, healthy little face was crowned with a shock of tangled hair that seemed never to be combed. His knicker-bockers were open at the knee, a style old-fashioned even then, for straps and box-cloth finishings were in high favour for boys' clothes. But Mrs. Gaynor did not believe in putting a child into plate-armour, and made Hiram's knickerbockers herself out of navy serge.

Mrs. Gooderich returned his smile, and asked him what he was reading. He said it was a book.

"I'm sure I wish my Hanny 'ud sit down with a book in the evening. He just runs wild. Gone fishin' now." Hiram's book closed, and he favoured Mrs. Gooderich with a gaze of intense interest.

"Is that so?" he asked. "Ma, can I go fishin'?"

"Oh, I s'pose you can, child. I don't reckon you'll do the fish much damage, anyway."

"Where's he gone, Mrs. Gooderich? Littler's?"

"I expect so. Down the Bowes Road, anyhow. But I

wonder you allow it, Mrs. Gaynor. They only spoil their clothes."

"He's none to spoil," smiled that lady, reseating herself in the rocking-chair.

It seemed strange to Mrs. Gooderich, allowing a child to do what he wanted. She didn't approve of such laxity.

"Be in by eleven, child."

"Sure, Ma." And the model child vanished.

"Well, what d'you think of this young woman now, Mrs. Gooderich?" asked Mrs. Gaynor. "She's got a position quick enough."

"I can't think how you're goin' to keep yourself and dress yourself and pay rail-fare, all on twelve shillings a week?" Mrs. Gooderich replied, looking at her daughter.

"To start," said Minnie. "I was just tellin', Mrs. Gaynor thought, that Mrs. Wilfley wants me to live in, and she recommends it."

"Live in," said her mother blankly. Living in was associated in her mind with drapery emporiums, celibacy, and ultimate disaster.

"Mrs. Wilfley doesn't keep a dry goods store," Mrs. Gaynor volunteered. "What she wants is a companion, I s'pose you'd call it, some one to live with her and do little chores in connection with her profession."

"Chores?" This again was an unfortunate word, a strange word, a vague alarming word.

"An assistant, mother," added Minnie impatiently. "What I want is a chance. If I don't get on with Mrs. Wilfley, I'll get out, but anyhow I'll have a chance to look round and p'raps see some other job with better pay. And I can't expect a big screw until I've learned the business, can I?"

"No, I s'pose not. I do hope it'll be all right."

"It will be all right," asserted the lady in the rocking-chair. "Mrs. Worrall is very successful in satisfying her clients."

"Why, from what she said, I thought she'd have a job too, sometimes," remarked Minnie.

"What was that?"

"She said her clients wanted their servants to come

from the aristocracy, and as for companions, she said they had to belong *to* the aristocracy. I suppose she meant poor relations."

"She was talking sarcastic. If she recommends a young woman, even if she hasn't any experience, Mrs. Worrall can place her in good positions. But she would not recommend you, because I told her something of your character in my letter."

"Why, did you tell her——?" began Mrs. Gooderich in dismay. A recital of Minnie's recent behaviour was tantamount, in her mother's opinion, to a bad character.

"The truth," said Mrs. Gaynor simply. "But in a general way. No details. I didn't know them."

"Did you tell her I was strong-minded?" asked the girl maliciously.

"Surely. That was most important. If you like you can read the letter. I always copy my letters."

Singular spectacle! A widow with business habits!

Mrs. Gaynor rose and went to a drawer in the side-table and took out a thick letter book. Placing a sheet of white paper under the last letter but one she handed it to Mrs. Gooderich.

Minnie leaned over.

This was the letter.

> 10, Maple Avenue,
> New Southgate, N.

Dear Olivia Worrall,

> *The young woman who bears this letter to you is a character. She has, I do believe, missed her vocation. She works in a factory. She ought to have gone to college and entered a profession, but in this benighted country a woman doesn't even know what a college education means.*

> *Where could she get instruction?*

> *She has a mighty lot to learn, I'm aware, and learn it she will, if she gets a chance. But we mustn't expect gratitude for helping her. She's a cast-iron image as far as other folks are concerned, though influenced easily enough in the right way. Most girls think they know twice as much as their mother: this young woman thinks she knows twenty times as much.*

Sometimes you'd almost believe she did!

Her young man worried her to death because he thought she smoked. She just chased him out of the district so he'll never come back. Her employers gave her notice last week, and here she is planning another scheme for raising money.

She's a problem, isn't she, now?

It wouldn't do any real harm to recommend her for a rich woman's companion, though it might ruin your business. The rich woman and the young one would be the better for it. But I don't suppose you're so rich you want to offend anybody yet, so you'll just have to use your judgment.

Perhaps you'll rouse up and tell me how you're getting on. I had a newspaper from Alvard the other day—he's still in St. Louis—and there is a paragraph in it saying Adelaide is in charge of the City Hospital for Children.

That girl's a real credit to her country.

Your old friend,
Ann Butterick Gaynor.

Mrs. Gooderich looked at Minnie, and Minnie looked at Mrs. Gooderich. And then they both looked at Mrs. Gaynor, who was looking out into the summer night.

"Well," she said, without changing her position. "Don't you like that letter?"

"It's a funny character you've given me, Mrs. Gaynor," said Minnie.

"Mrs. Worrall's a very smart woman. I guess she took a pretty complete inventory of you while she was talking to you."

"It's a wonder she didn't send you packin'," said Mrs. Gooderich, putting the letter book on the table. "I only hope it'll turn out all right."

"Oh, it *will*, sure."

Mother and daughter rose.

"She'll want some clothes," said Mrs. Gooderich.

"Let her earn them," said Mrs. Gaynor, going over to a cupboard in the corner and taking a spirit-lamp from a shelf. "Sit right down now and I'll make some beef-tea."

By beef-tea Mrs. Gaynor meant beef-extract as made

by Liebig. In a few minutes a copper kettle was on the boil, three large cups received their modicum of the dark, sickly-smelling compound and the needful boiling water.

"I like this," said Minnie, taking her cup. Mrs. Gooderich liked it too, but she did not say so. Her breakfast had been liver and bacon and tea, her dinner stewed kidneys, her tea bread and butter and cheap jam made of turnips and animal jelly, and so, according to Mrs. Gaynor's peculiar view, the poor woman had had nothing to eat all day. Both mother and daughter were the better for the concentrated nourishment in the extract, and the dry biscuit, to their astonishment, was delicious.

They began to talk afresh, discussing the situation in all its bearings. Then they went on to Bert's prospects, Bert who was scarcely ever at home, who was walking out with a girl now, but who was more set than ever on joining the Army. Who was the girl? Mrs. Gaynor enquired, and Mrs. Gooderich had to confess that Bert was inclined to be "light." It had been Ethel Turner, big, hoyendish Ethel Turner, of whom Mrs. Gooderich did not approve. But occasionally other flames illuminated the dark and taciturn soul of her elder son. Mrs. Gooderich was not hopeful about him. She didn't want him to go for a soldier, but he had small prospects at the furniture shop. He was going on sixteen now and he ought to be settled to something. But he would talk of nothing but the Army, and his father "encouraged" him. As if a boy had any prospects in the Army! Mention of her husband led Mrs. Gooderich to talk of his despondent mood caused by so many short weeks. Money got very tight when a man drew so little. Trade was slack, very. There had been rumours of a big job from the Government, but a North-East Coast firm had got it. Mr. Gooderich had dropped the idea of emigrating, but he seemed to fancy work was more plentiful up Tyneside way. She didn't want to go away. She had got used to London. But what was the use?—they couldn't live on air.

Mrs. Gaynor just let her talk, and the woman's mind was eased of its load. That Mrs. Gaynor had any troubles of her own never entered either of her visitors' heads. Why, she owned her house, freehold; people said she had "property," mortgages, shares, and such-like mysterious tokens. How could she have any troubles? Even Mary Gooderich, simple and warped of mind as she was, felt that the "bareness" of Mrs. Gaynor's *ménage* was due to her peculiar American ideas and not to poverty. And Minnie, whose intellect was fifty times keener than her mother's, knew that this quiet lady was *right,* and their own way of existence was disastrously wrong. How to change it? Well, thought the girl, there was Mrs. Wilfley for a start. Her mother had no such ray of hope. She looked down at the green rugs on the linoleum wood-block flooring, which was bees-waxed until it shone, and felt nothing beyond the relief of having a soul to speak to who seemed to understand her troubles. So she talked, and Minnie interpolated now and then, and Mrs. Gaynor listened with nods of comprehension, and they felt their excitement calmed and the future less vague

These two spirits, so temperamentally different, the one puzzled and wayworn, the other aggressively and indomitably young, became permeated by the mysterious quality of silent human sympathy, as, slowly but surely, it exercised its sublime yet invisible functions.

"Good gracious me! Mrs. Gaynor, it's nearly eleven o'clock. Come on, Minnie."

"Well, I'm very glad you came in, Mrs. Gooderich. It does me good to talk about one's troubles. I know that."

"Yes, I s'pose you've *had* troubles like the rest of us. Who's that comin' in the gate? I believe it's your little boy. He *is* a good child. Back before eleven."

They filed out into the hall, where a single gas jet burned low, by the "hall stand." The door was open, and Hiram sprang across the mat and caught hold of his mother as she was turning out the light.

"Sakes, child, what is it now?"

"Oh, Ma!" the boy ejaculated, and looked at Mrs. Gooderich as though numbed.

"What—anything happened to Hanny?" wailed Mrs. Gooderich, and Minnie looked sternly at the little jerseyed figure with the tumbled hair.

"Eh?" asked his mother.

"No, Hanny—he's all right 'nuff. He's down—down there now. He's cryin', he is."

"What ails you, Hiram? What's he cryin' for?"

"There's—there's a man in the brook," stuttered the boy, looking earnestly at his mother. "I—I reckon he's dead, I do."

"Oh!" said Minnie, and Mrs. Gooderich moaned.

"Are you sure, Hiram?" asked Mrs. Gaynor.

"Ask Hanny. He's there now—in the dark—cryin'."

"Mrs. Gooderich," said Mrs. Gaynor, "let Minnie go to the police office with Hiram and we'll go on down the road. I thought you were going to Littler's," she added, to Hiram.

"So we did. We were comin' back by Old Southgate to hear the bells. We caught three fish, we did."

"There, go on now, and we'll put on our bonnets."

"Come on, Hiram," said Minnie, in a low, cold voice; "take my hand." They went out and across the road where a row of lime-trees bordered the half side-walk, and made it dark as a tunnel. The moon had risen, and the road was a broad highway of silver.

"Couldn't you see who it was, Hiram?" asked Minnie, in the same low voice. "Couldn't you see?"

"Yes," choked Hiram, nearly strangled by excitement, running, and possibly fear.

"Who was it, then?"

"Your pa," replied Hiram.

At the time of this narrative, the Apple-tree Inn, situated on the northern side of Southgate Green, was an almost unique example of the old-style tavern: unique, that is, in Middlesex. For even then the craze for rebuilding had seized the breweries, even then comfortable old bar-parlours were being swept away and horrid new high-ceilinged edifices were taking their place. But the "Apple," being off the great highways out of London, and situated some two miles from a railway station, stood immune, and, as one crossed the green, the deep ruby red of the parlour curtains, the tall sign swinging on a pole across the road, the big roomy stables and old wooden horse trough, made up a picture comforting to man and beast, and was amply corroborated by the hospitality dispensed within. Certainly a sane and kindly hand had been laid upon the house: witness the snug billiard-room at the back and the domestic jug-cubicle next the stables. But the very heart and soul of an inn, the fountain of its permanence and prosperity, the parlour, remained in sedate security, a haven of rest and refreshment for the traveller and habitué alike.

You entered this delectable chamber through a small porch in the lane running north-easterly to Chase Side, the inner door opening inwards like any door at home. An oblong room it was, with red plush seats round the outer sides, a fireplace where a real fire crackled and flamed o' winter nights, and a small bar communicating with the general dispensary beyond but screened from vulgar gaze. Here perhaps some fifteen people might sit in quiet seclusion, passing one another the glass water-jug, for soda was not in vogue as it is now. One or two couples (engaged) would be found there, he drinking gin, she port wine. Ladies, married or engaged, generally unbent, so far as to remove a glove, raise the veil above the eyes, and perhaps even adjust a garter, so select and quiet was this room. Young sparks rarely frequented it; perhaps on Saturday night (a bad night for the select) the bar would fill with frivolity, and regular patrons would sit, glass on knee and cigar raised upwards, somewhat jostled, but equable of temper, waiting until the unwelcome tide had ebbed away homeward.

The walls were panelled and so heavily varnished that the original graining was lost in the general duskiness of the glaze, and furnished a perfect background for the pictures, a set of black-framed engravings, Hogarth's own, of *Mariage à la Mode*. They were an admirable comment, these cruelly clever drawings, upon the actual contrasted with the visible life led by the select and serious couples and parties who sat drinking, little finger stuck genteelly outwards, beneath them. One could have wished that sardonic genius to have stepped in some evening, that he might have got the one glimpse necessary for him to project another series, brought up to date.

Who knows? The "Apple Tree" was there before him.

The present scribe would die happy if he could but know that he *had* been forestalled.

Let him not forget one incontrovertible proof of the respectability of the patrons. Every one knew the pictures were worth "a pot o' money." Yet they remained unmolested on their hooks, and there, I hope, they remain to this day.

In order to reach the "Apple" from his home, Mr. Gooderich, an intermittent habitué, took the road which descends with dangerous steepness into the valley dividing the two parishes, crosses the stream at the bottom and mounts with even greater precipitousness the eastern hill, passing between the grey spired church and the Chapel Fields, and debouching upon the Green. It would be difficult to discover in any of the villages environing London a lane more secluded by foliage and high walls or one terminating in a more rural and charming vista. To-night, as Mr. Gooderich passed the permanently muddy bottom and began the stiff climb to the church, the trees overarched it so completely that the moon might have been not yet risen, so dense and palpable was the gloom. On either side between the walls that form the distinctive feature of rural London stretched thickets and woodlands amidst which you might find a number of mansions whose policies, for some mysterious reason, are traversed by numerous public footpaths.

Mr. Gooderich was no longer a young man, and the climb winded him, so that he paused a moment by the church, looked up at the gold face of the clock, adjusted his Ingersoll, and permitting for one brief instant the tiny grain of poetry in his soul to diffuse and emerge, waited for the striking of the hour. The Chapel Fields were bathed in a blinding bath of moonlight; but he stood in the deep shade of the yew hedge in front of the church. The chime of this church was justly celebrated for its penetrating sweetness. Little Hannibal had discovered this, all by himself, one wintry evening. And here was his father protracting his arrival at the "Apple Tree" by waiting to hear the chime.

Mr. Gooderich's mind was sanguine with hope, and it was characteristic of him to be short and surly with his wife at such a time. These people—but why should I mount a pedestal, since right up through all the grades of our social fabric, men act thus detestably to their women. Nor should I blame the man at all since, in this particular case, the unusual and piquant cause of his hope has been barred to women for generations.

The fact was that Mr. Gooderich was attacked at intervals by fits of optimism, as when he resolved to save, when he hoped to win that five pounds a week and a house, when he dyed his hair and worked for a foreman's berth. These fits had burned up, flared, flickered, and gone out. He believed that pre-eminence in life was a matter of luck. Look at Jeddah, that rank outsider! But this time he believed he was about to tread a way of fortunate security. Why hadn't he thought of it before? Well, you see, he hadn't been in the way of it much, and moreover he hadn't got acquainted with Mr. Julius Fife. Mr. Fife it was who, seated side by side with Mr. Gooderich in the "Apple Tree" parlour, had discussed the hardness of times, the decay of old England, and the transcendent advantages of being "in" something. Why had he, Mr. Gooderich, never been "in" anything? He was in his trade union, he retorted, but Mr. Fife had waved that way away with a single flick of his fingers. *That* was all well enough in its place, a very low place, according to Mr. Julius Fife. Had he never thought of joining himself with his fellow-men in one great universal brotherhood? Mr. Gooderich never had, and it may be stated baldly that he never would. Though he was now on his way, sanguine with hope, to discuss with Mr. Fife the possibility and manner of his initiation into Mr. Fife's Lodge, the notion of joining any fraternity for the pious purpose of helping others never entered his head. He had every intention, if luck favoured him, of jumping on others and stamping their faces into the ground, if he could improve his position thereby. Mr. Julius Fife's aspirations were pure and undefiled, no doubt. I do not know him very well, and he is welcome to the benefit of the doubt. But I knew Mr. Gooderich like the back of my hand, and I can assert that he was entirely innocent of philanthropic sentiments. The Great Architect of the

Universe would have been nonplussed to find him a suitable job in the Temple. His talents lay in other directions.

The deep mellow *boom* of the great bell thrilled through the shining night as he stood in the shadow of the yew hedge, and the heart of the man was uplifted. And then the chime—*Cling—clang—cling—clang—cling—cling—clang—clang,* was followed by eight solemn strokes.

Mr. Gooderich made his way across Southgate Green. He found his friend Mr. Julius Fife, a man of spare frame, plain yet expensive raiment and neat personal habits. He was a gentleman of the Trade, but the house over which he had presided with considerable success had been deprived of its license on some frivolous pretext, and Mr. Fife was a gentleman at large until the brewer who paid him a hundred a year and a bonus could find him another sphere for his activity. The most salient prejudice of Mr. Fife's mind was his wolfish ferocity towards those bigoted gentlemen who had persisted in interpreting a license as a document of merely annual validity. According to Mr. Fife, a license was as eternally valid as a fiat from God—indeed, had he had the duty of bearing his license, engraved on tables of stone, from out of the thunder of Sinai, he would never have broken it. His mind, as I have intimated, was warped in its attitude towards the justices, "a party of old women" none of whom had any real living financial interest in the Trade, and who actually thought three public-houses in fifty yards of street an excessive number. Ah—h, these Radicals: for Mr. Fife the Liberal Party had no existence. Like the *Globe* newspaper, he knew only Radicals, who read "Radical Rags." This alliterative animadversion acted as a sedative on minds like Mr. Fife's. And it was an apparent and curious fact that the words Trade and Union, taken apart, thrilled Mr. Fife to the core of his being, but when coupled together these roused in his soul a ferocity even more wolfish than did the benighted magistrates. Such was the person, amiable enough in exterior, who nodded good evening to Mr. Gooderich as the latter entered the decorous precincts of the "Apple Tree" parlour.

The community of interest which had led these two
gentlemen to fraternise was racing. Mr. Gooderich's personal acquaintance with race-horses was as intimate as his
knowledge of elands and spotted lemurs, though he
watched their form with a tenacity of purpose and a
fatigue of brain sufficient to carry him successfully to
the head of the Wrangler's List at Cambridge. Mr. Fife,
on the other hand, was acquainted with Newmarket. He
had, as a matter of fact, spent two years as a bar-tender
in a public-house in that very sleepy little township, and
been very glad indeed to exchange its rural atmosphere
for the more garish delights of the Brompton Road.
Moreover, so admirably organised, so extraordinarily discreet, is every one engaged in the racing profession, from
the photographers in the High Street to the stable-urchins
in the football-field, that one may live, even as a potman,
for years in the town, and never glean a "tip" worth twopence. But Mr. Fife did not tell his companion this. He
submitted tacitly to the implication that while at Newmarket he was in the confidence of every trainer and
manager who took a brandy and soda from his hands. As
for the horses, he knew them all by sight—saw them
every day. So he did, at six in the morning, each animal
so swathed and top-coated that it might have been a zebra
for all Mr. Fife knew to the contrary.

Starting from so felicitous a theme, the pair, during
several informal rencounters at the "Apple Tree," had
pursued their way among the myriad problems which beset our modern life, and had discovered such compati-
bility of temperament that Mr. Fife had cast aside the
toga of the Trade, so to speak, and addressing Mr. Gooderich as a fellow man, bade him enter the Mystic Portals
and become a neophyte in a Lodge in which, it was understood, in a manner too involved and subtle to transmit
to paper, Mr. Fife himself occupied a not unimportant
position.

The question was, could he raise the necessary twenty
pounds.

Being actually on the top of the tide of optimism which
had been gradually overtaking him for days, and very
soon flushed with spirit, Mr. Gooderich saw no difficul-

ties. He spoke of having to draw on his reserve of late, work being scanty, but thought he could manage it "very shortly."

"Well, of course, you know your own business best, Mister, but I thought it best to mention it you—understand?" Mr. Gooderich swallowed and nodded.

"Course, if it is any particular trouble, seeing I'm the one who's puttin' you up to the idea, and, 'without prejudice' "—(here the voice of Mr. Fife flattened to a close-lipped whisper)—"draw what you like, up to fifty, at fi' p' cent."

Mr. Gooderich fixed his eyes critically on No. 3 *Mariage à la Mode,* and revolved the matter in his mind. It was a great relief, for it removed the necessity for telling lie after lie all to cover the naked fact that his bank account was seventeen and eightpence. He had no objection to being lent money. As for the interest, what improvident man ever did worry his head about interest? And then look at the ultimate advantage. How they all backed each other up, looked after the orphans and widows and all that. . . . Even the King——

Vague visions of a happier future floated before Mr. Gooderich's eyes. I have mentioned in a previous chapter his ideal of existence, in a tavern by the sea. Something of this possessed him now—if he could only possess the substance! It was not impossible—he was sitting beside a man who had been in that glorious position, who would be in it again shortly. Through the fumes of the whisky Mr. Gooderich contemplated happiness, a happiness which consisted almost entirely, dear reader, in not having to work. That improved circumstances would enable him to educate his children, buy them books and instruments, send them abroad to become acquainted with the civilisations of Europe, would place within his wife's reach a respite from her abominable and ceaseless toil, give her fine raiment and decent retirement—these trivialities did not obtrude themselves upon his outlook at all.

There had come into his usually quiet eye a look of the anxious ferrety sort, intended by him to indicate a knowing, worldly, and cynical turn of mind.

By ten o'clock his optimism brooked no opposition from

anything. The question of security was disposed of with a laugh. If he couldn't find security for twenty pounds—well! What did Mr. Fife take him for?

At ten-fifteen Mr. Fife looked at a rolled-gold hunter, compared it ostentatiously with the neat black clock on the chimney-piece, clicked the lid to, put it away and reached for his stick. He was sorry, but he had an appointment at eleven with a brother-in-law of his—a little matter of business. He would see Mr. Gooderich the following evening and talk it over further. No need to rush it. Go into things bald-headed, and you get singed! (Greater men than Julius Fife have mixed metaphors.) Take your time and you didn't regret it. Well, was Mr. Gooderich going too? In the opposite direction of course. Well, goo' night. Goo' night, Miss!

And Mr. Fife, relighting his pipe, made off in an easterly direction towards Palmer's Green.

Mr. Gooderich paused in front of the Assembly Rooms to collect himself. He was sanguine, there was no doubt of that. Equally undeniable was the potency of the spirit within him. He straightened himself up, set forward westward, but did not notice, so deep were his cogitations, that he was taking the road through the village instead of that by the church, until the brazen front and acetylene lights of the "Green Dragon" recalled him to the world of sense. He went on, reflecting that just a little ahead on the opposite was a signpost and a gate, which led to a path across the fields—one of those fortuitous and illogical trails I have mentioned—over the stream at the bottom of the valley, and so out upon the East Barnet Road. It was a fine night, a beautiful night for a sanguine man to take a walk. It was early yet. And he passed over, sighted the gate, made it safely, and resumed his walk and his musings.

"The intellectual power, through words and things, went sounding on its dim and perilous way."

For Mr. Gooderich assisted his reverie by a series of disjointed sentences, not always to the point, sometimes profoundly obscure. Like some great poets, whose most impassioned moods and loftiest flights are the most difficult to construe, so Mr. Gooderich's mentality, as it soared

into the empyrean, became less adapted to our common
speech, and the "way" would have seemed "dim and
perilous" had there been any one near to listen. Frequently enough he encountered lovers, but the respectability which he wrapped round his soul even in drink
came to his aid and he stalked by them impeccable. And
as he advanced the sheltering trees were left behind, the
path lay down across wide misty meadows, destitute of
the seclusion so dear to the lover, and Mr. Gooderich
wavered onward, a solitary man. The cool night-wind
after those potions of warm water and whisky, did not,
as many inexperienced folk imagine, allay the disorder
of the brain. It seems almost as though, when the spirit
has risen to the head, it is confirmed there by a cooler air.
Moreover, that terrible white radiance in which he moved
is no friend of sanity.

"To be—be a——I'm all right, now I'm a—what a saucy
bitch that gel is! So help me Gawd! I'll tell her—*phoo!*—
where's the matches—her mother knows she's a—what a
life!—'f I wasn't married I could get on, oh yes,—sh'll
look ol' fash'n'd when she knows she's a—a Mason!—
me I mean—wimmen bob down then—whupp! dam the
fence—like daylight this moon is. Where's me matches?
—now hold up, Jeddah! O my Gawd, Jeddah!" He
dropped the match flaming to the ground and stood staring into a vacancy of horror. That day! How the name
of the horse brought back that terrible Derby! Slowly
he struck another match, shaking his head. "Fort'n o'
war!" he muttered, moving on. "Are we down-hearted?
make anybody down-'earted, t'live wi' 'er. *R—r—r!* yer
little slattox! Than-gaw' you ain't mine, wi' yer chin
stuck out."

His dislike, or impatience or whatever it was, exacer-
bated by alcohol, flickered tremulously from wife to
daughter, from daughter to wife. And so in a zigzag
way he came to the bottom, where the path ran into shade
again, and an old tree leaned over the stream by the little
wooden bridge.

A lady and gentleman, communing after the manner
of their kind upon the mystery of elective affinities (How
strange! And I was goin' to school then. Fancy ever

comin' to this:) and possibly other astonishing aspects of their lives which they perceived reflected in the stream, were leaning on the rail, he idly cutting his initials with his knife. With some impatience they turned on the interloper, who had paused behind them to pursue his interminable pipe-lighting. With no loss of dignity, the gentleman, outraged by this infraction of the unwritten Laws of Love and Courtship, shut up his knife, took the lady's arm and moved on, leaving a neatly carved R and a halffinished S (very difficult to do an S decently) on the mossy rail. Mr. Gooderich, wasting matches, looked after them stupidly for a moment, and then leaned on the rail himself, glad of the support. The unmistakable displeasure of the pair cast a shadow over his optimism. What had he done? He was a respectable man, goin' to join a lodge, wasn't he? Well then, where were the matches? He looked at his pipe, trying to capture an idea that had flitted across his mind just now. Ah! It wanted cleaning. He ran his hand along the weather-worn rail until a split in the wood caught his fingers, now intertwined. They 'adn't *bought* the bloomin' bridge, 'ad they? Well then. He continued to pull abstractedly, not noticing that the split opened obliquely across the grain. Gaw dam't, come off! He gave a wrench which dislodged the rail at the far end, and leaning in his surprise still more heavily upon it, it gave way and plunged him headlong into the stream.

Little Hanny and Hiram, returning stained and weeddraggled from Littler's Pond, came past the church and down the steep hill, triumphant with three fish of negligible size.

Arrived at the stone bridge they began a discussion of the huge fish to be had in this stream, and sitting on the northern parapet they stared at the three-foot weir over which the water was pouring with a faint musical sound.

"That's what keeps 'em down here, I guess," said Hiram, jerking his stick towards the weir. "There ain't no fish up there, 'cause I tried it at that little wood bridge on the path. It's deep and got stones at the bottom, but there ain't no fish."

"There is over 'ere," said Hannibal, flinging his thumb over his shoulder.

"You git summoned quick if you're copped."

"Um. Not 'alf." They swung their legs in unison.

"Say, Hanny, what's that comin' down there? See it?"

"I dunno. Ain't a dog, is it?"

Out on the shining whiteness of the meadow-bordered stream beyond the trees they saw a black blob moving quickly towards them.

"Lummy!" said Hannibal, and Hiram echoed "Lummy!" and with that absurd ejaculation their feelings passed into the region of the inexpressible. Sometimes it disappeared, that curious blob on the shimmering whiteness of the water, sometimes paused and turned slowly on itself, caught by some invisible snag, then vanished into the shadow of the trees. They waited, trembling and voiceless, for the splash, and jumped when they heard it, straining their eyes to pierce the darkness. Simultaneously they saw it, saw it with a chill at their hearts and a crawling sensation of their skins, immediately beneath them, turning horribly on the footing of the bridge, and slipping under them. With a quick intake of his breath, Hiram ran across the road, climbed the parapet and looked over the wooden fence that rose above it. Hannibal, in a trance, followed, afraid, grating his knees on the stones as he tried to mount beside his companion. Hiram put his hand against Hanny's face and pushed him back.

"What's up?" Hanny whispered, looking up scared and trembling.

Hiram slipped down and pulled up his stockings.

"It's a man." He breathed. "He's dead, I guess. I'll run an' tell Ma. You stop here, Hanny." And he ran off up the road as hard as he could. The child looked after his friend as though wishful to follow. A dead man! He put his knees against the stones once again and clambered up. The full light of the moon came strongly upon the water just there and he saw it grounded on a sandy shoal, the hands swaying purposelessly in the current, a quiet and memorable picture.

With a little cry the boy slid to the ground, and there they found him, huddled against the wall in the darkness, one hand pressed on the stones, the other covering his face.

XVII

MRS. WILFLEY, when she heard of the domestic bereavement from Minnie herself, sprang at the opportunity like a lioness upon her prey. Minnie, somewhat fatigued by the emotional stress of the previous night, and rendered a little uncertain of herself by an encounter with the young man in the coal-agent's office, was borne down, swept off her feet and carried away by a torrent of gush unparalleled even in Clifford's Inn. When it subsided she found herself, limp and bewildered, on the Chesterfield by the window, sniffing a handkerchief drenched in Florida-water and listening to Mrs. Wilfley's plans for the future.

These plans were in the main altruistic. In spite of her frail health and an urgent request from a northern editor to write a series of articles on the moral tone of the town, Mrs. Wilfley was resolved to interest herself in the welfare of the Gooderich family. She had done this sort of thing before, and knew that swiftness of initiative was imperative if some one else were not to prevent her. Of course nothing could be done publicly until the funeral, but much might be accomplished privately, so that at the psychological moment, a phrase dear to her, she might burst forth in the very forefront of the movement as honorary secretary of a committee of prominent people, including one or two local people, to arrange a grand concert in aid of such a deserving case. Mrs. Wilfley placed much reliance on her influence with the local religious life: her articles, she had reason to believe, were read omnivorously in Nonconformist circles. Possibly a lecture by her on "Slum Life" or "A Flower-Girl's Tragedy" might be a further contribution.

All this, as it became clear to Minnie from Mrs. Wilfley's explanation, was profoundly distasteful. She realised that neither she nor her family had the slightest claim upon the neighbourhood. Her father had not been a member of any club or church, they had done nothing individually or collectively to identify themselves with the community, they had merely lived rather meanly and obscurely amidst a number of other mean and obscure families. Moreover, she had the nobility of soul which is libellously miscalled "proper pride"; she resented the interference of strangers in her affairs. She was not a good girl, she was not a "nice girl," she went, eventually, far from the paths of virtue; but at least she stood on her own feet; she took the wages of sin, not the spongings of the pious. But Mrs. Wilfley considered Minnie's distaste not at all. She was resolved to take an interest in the case, and she did. She told Minnie to go home and look after her mother and leave the matter entirely in her hands. Which Minnine was willing to do, only—here she sat up and faced her benefactress—was she to start on her new work?

"Ob certainly," chanted Mrs. Wilfley. "My dear girl, what can you think of me? I will send you a cheque for a month's salary at once. Have I the address? Yes; well, I will forward it at once."

Nothing could be more generous, more charming.

When Minnie was gone, Mrs. Wilfley, who had the constitution of a cart-horse when she found it convenient, sat down and did several hours' hard work. Then she went downstairs to a publisher on the ground floor, and borrowing his telephone (who can refuse a lady?) held communication with Mrs. Worrall, Mr. Anthony Gilfillan, and the secretary of a dramatic employment bureau. Mrs. Worrall referred her dear friend to Mrs. Gaynor, Mr. Gilfillan arguing company-law with a suspicious solicitor, professed himself charmed to assist Mrs. Wilfley, and begged to be placed on the committee as he lived in the neighbourhood, and the secretary of the dramatic employment bureau ran over a list of names on his desk which, he believed, would suit such a concert as Mrs. Wilfley suggested, and hoped to hear further shortly. Terms, he added, as usual, five per cent, committee to pay all travelling expenses. These matters adjusted, the lady thanked the publisher prettily, ascended to her own flat again, and wrote a tactful letter to Mrs. Gaynor. She knew, she said, from what their mutual friend Mrs. Worrall had hinted, that Mrs. Gaynor would prove a valuable ally in this projected charity, and begged Mrs. Gaynor to assist her by suggesting a suitable prominent local resident as president and chairman. Hoping for the pleasure of a meeting shortly, she begged to remain, etc.

To this Mrs. Gaynor replied briefly, saying that while quite unfitted for any active participation in the proposed affair, she had no hesitation in advising Mrs. Wilfley to approach Colonel Corinth-Squires, of Chits-hill Place, to assume the chairmanship, he being quite the proper person and well able to give solid financial support as well as social prestige. And she begged to remain, etc.

And so, almost before the coroner had packed his black bag, the preliminaries had been settled, the parties had been approached, and the musical artistes had had word of a possible engagement in North London.

Colonel Corinth-Squires, on receipt of a letter from a total stranger, remembered with a start that he had promised to speak to a friend commanding the Wessex Fusiliers concerning the lad who had so dramatically stated his intention to be a soldier.

He had made a note of it at the time, but one thing and another had caused the affair to slip from memory. Now the name Gooderich recalled the whole matter. While writing at once to Casterbridge Depôt, his daughter came in and expressed surprise that the authoress, Olga Wilfley, should be writing to her father. The Colonel was gratified. Even he had heard of the book *The Licencees of Love,* and he delighted his daughter by permitting her to answer Mrs. Wilfley favourably, adding an invitation to dinner to enable them to discuss the whole proposition.

"As a matter of fact," said the Colonel, half to himself and half to his daughter as she sat writing her note, "as a matter of fact, it's quite unnecessary to use any influence to get a lad into the Army except physical force, which will never happen in this wretched country. On the other hand, if I send him to Casterbridge, and he thinks some one is interested in his good behaviour, he will probably stick to his work and turn out well. If I don't, he may not go into the Army at all, and become a counter-jumper or a—a something useless." Miss Corinth-Squires carefully ignored her father's cogitations and bent all her attention to the writing of the note. She was not a good penwoman, and the letter, when written, resembled the horoscopes sold by Hindoo fortune-tellers in Bombay. She had, moreover, a difficulty in striking just that chord of dignity, patronage, and cordiality which she felt would be acceptable to such a distinguished woman as Mrs. Olga Wilfley. She was really grateful to dear Dad for giving her this chance to overtop the Barlows, the Revingtons, and even the Plunket-Downes with their insufferable Newnham daughter who read Ostrovsky in the original.

When Mrs. Wilfley received the note, she dismissed from her mind the notion that it was written in an Oriental language, and at once fell upon its exegesis. She knew by experience the deplorable state of education among the upper classes. Perhaps this word is not sufficiently strong. Exegesis, as Doctor John Browne kindly explains to us non-classical folks, means bringing out of a passage all there is in it. Mrs. Wilfley did this, but I think she also followed that brilliant school of commentators and art critics who read into a work vastly more than the original Father or Master ever dreamed of. Certainly Miss Carolyn Corinth-Squires would have been agreeably tickled had she known how far-reaching Mrs. Wilfley imagined the results of this encounter to extend. But Miss Corinth-Squires was not a public person. She had never reflected on the fact that all fame is built up of innumerable microscopic transmitted opinions, of myriads of inconceivably small enthusiasms which, like coral insects, live out a brief life among their fellow specks and die, leaving a tiny hollow shell of sounding reputation, and form, with the coming of the years, a reef round which the breakers roar and on which many a cock-boat, useful in itself, is dashed to atoms. I do not say that Mrs. Wilfley ran this thought to earth in exactly the same way as I have done, but she was keenly conscious of the fact and welcomed any means of extending its application to herself. Both ladies, indeed, had so much to occupy their immediate deliberations that the bereaved family almost dropped out of memory altogether. Not so the

Colonel. He had told the story at White's with approval, the story of that masterly manœuvre on Trinity Green, that Napoleonic stroke of genius of the feint, the ambush, the final furious mêlée. Give the boy a five-poun' note and pay his fare to Casterbridge, eh? By George, it had done him good when that young ruffian had stuttered out "Soldier, sir," all among his mates in the class. Good stuff there!

Bert appeared.

"Still o' the same mind, eh?"

"Yessir," replied Bert.

"That's good, that's good. Well, I'll give you a note to the Colonel at Casterbridge—here it is—and here's a trifle to help the mother. Oh, that's all right, my lad. Stick in and step smartly. Make a man of you in no time. Always trouble somewhere in the Empire, yo' know; may get your chance any day. That's right, that's right. Good-bye."

And Bert, armed with his note and a small bag of movable dunnage, made his way to Casterbridge and dropped civilian's life and clothes forever and without regret. He was glad, he admitted, that the inquest decided his old man " 'adn't done hisself in," Bert having deep-laid and quite inarticulate views on self-destruction; and he was glad to feel that he would not be round when the grand concert came off.

For the grand concert, thanks to Mrs. Wilfley's unflagging efforts, came off, in the Assembly Rooms, in style. She had dined at the Corinth-Squires' and had been begged to assume the secretaryship. That accomplished, she made many friends among the religious denominations, secured the editor of the local paper, engaged her artistes, contracted for the hall and printing, did everything, in fact, in a clever and expeditious manner. Minnie, proceeding day by day to Clifford's Inn, did most of the clerical drudgery, it was true; but could she do less, she who was to benefit so largely, she who had received a month's salary in advance? And it was during these days, when Mr. Gilfillan, as a member of the committee, called frequently to confer with the secretary, that Minnie's nature became softer and more pliant under his dominant personality.

The widow, addressing her bed-posts before turning out the light, remarked:

"Tony takes an interest in the child"; adding, as she reached out to the switch:

"And she looks very effective in black."

XVIII

MINNIE was, however, the only one of the family who did look effective in black. Mrs. Gooderich was not an effective woman at the best of times, and she supported the rôle of widow neither with dignity nor composure. She was harassed, she said, with so many things. Truly the sudden removal of the companion of so many years was a shock; but tears? She felt that her position involved many tears, so persistent is the hypocrisy of modern life. Mrs. Gaynor was of no avail against the enormous weight of tradition. Her silent yet powerful personality was baffled in its attempt to assuage the lachrymatory flood. Unwittingly, no doubt, she was of too fine a type to deal with the woman, for her patience broke down after the funeral, when the returning cortège halted at the "Northern Star" and the mourners filled the saloon-bar with crêpe. With an indignation unexpressed in words, but patent in her carriage, Mrs. Gaynor walked slowly home. This adjournment was not proposed by Mrs. Gooderich, though she thought it only the thing to do. Her husband's sister's husband, father of Amelia, Thomas, Ethel, and John, who bulked largely in the first carriage, was the author of the scheme. They were all there, the builder in a small way in Camberwell, his large languid wife, his pre-eminently respectable children, Amelia, Thomas, Ethel, and John, black-garbed, quiet and interested. Little Hannibal sat opposite little Amelia; and they two, destined in happier years to walk as sweethearts to and fro, regarded one another with the mysterious resentment of children. Mr. Brown himself was, as I said, a bulky man, with a firm mouth, conventional whiskers, and a humorous blue eye. Perhaps it was his humour that led him to call at a licensed house for the funeral baked meats. Perhaps he fathomed Mrs. Gaynor's racial antipathy to gin-palaces, and desired, after the manner of Gothic humorists, to emphasise the grotesque. Perhaps he was merely con-

ventionally anxious for a drink, for he made no remark
when she stalked away from the spot, and doubtless
forgot her while consuming pork-pie and stout.

He was unfeignedly pleased to hear that local people
were fixing up a concert in aid of his sister-in-law, for
he held no sentimental views of his duties towards the
widow and the orphan. He had four growing children to
feed and clothe, his own wife was "delicate," as witness
her partiality for invalid stout and port wine, his business
was small and profits precarious, what *could* he do? He
was surprised, he said, that Herbert had not been "in"
anything but his trade-union, who had provided the
funeral expenses, but he and him had never had much
truck with each other. Live an' let live was *his* motto.
Ah, well, we all 'ad to go some time. Any little thing he
could do, he declared, at any time, he'd only be too
glad.

Minnie, watching him with mercilessly steady eyes, and
ignorant of the high courageous humour that balanced him
on his slippery little vantage point of life, decided that it
was *very* little *he* would ever do. Which was unreasonable
of the girl, for she had no wish to be beholden to him;
but she was in an unreasonable mood all that day. The
coal-agent's clerk, not satisfied with her politely evasive
answer at the station that morning, after the tragedy, had
called and asked if the occasion might not pave the way to
a reconciliation, and Mrs. Gooderich had silently implored
her daughter to be human and generous. Almost the evil
spirit in her had prompted her to say, "If you want him,
mother, you can have him—now," but she had flinched
from that viciousness and left the room with a shake of
the head. Mrs. Gaynor's defection had disturbed her too,
for she had an enormous respect for Mrs. Gaynor, a
respect which that lady would never have drawn from
either Mrs. Gooderich or Mr. Brown, Minnie being of a
finer texture, her mind of a subtler cast. And though Mr.
Anthony Gilfillan's unmistakable interest was softening
her attitude towards life, transforming her own private
phantom-universe, it did not make her any easier to live
with, which proves the earthiness of Love.

So Uncle and Aunt Brown went home with cousin

Amelia, Thomas, Ethel, and John, and trouble neither the
Gooderich family nor us for some time.

Little Hannibal profited most, I imagine, from the
whole business. He had an entire new suit of black cloth,
new boots, his first bowler hat, a bath (which he needed),
a hair-cut, a whole new set of ideas, and a week's holiday
in which to set them in order. I pass over his joy in playing at funerals: that is an inhuman drollery common to
most children and was checked with the thoughtless
ferocity of the average adult. What seemed to me interesting was the nature of the reaction from the first Terror
that overwhelmed him, child that he was, when he saw
his father's face in the moonlit water, the Terror of the
unknowable. It is true that the new mood was retarded
by his mother's intermittent gusts of affection for the
poor little orphan, retarded still more by the embarrassing
questions of his schoolmates after the funeral. "Are you
sorry?" they would ask him as he stood in a ring of
staring interested eyes. "Are you sorry?" "I d'n know,"
he would reply, chucking a stone unconcernedly, and the
others felt they were being defrauded. They had all, of
course, been rogued of threepences and sixpences to pay
for the School Wreath, which an insane teacher had proposed in order to gain some notoriety for himself, and
they felt dimly that in return they should have been given
some details on which to gloat, some ghoulish tale from
the House of the Dead. But when these ephemera had
passed away, little Hannibal's mind took on a yet more
emphatic tinge of reflectiveness, his thoughts moved in a
closed circle round and round the huge and shadowy
enigma of human change, and death became but one more
manifestation of it. Bert had changed, had become coars-
ened and redolent of tobacco, and was about to vanish;
Minnie had changed, had grown from a flinty-eyed
Medusa who petrified his adolescent gambols to a tolerant
semi-stranger, and was in the act of evanishment. Viewed
in the light of these overwhelmingly salient facts, and
slowly and clumsily excogitated, the problem of his father's
high adventure took on a similar hue of irrational change.
The paraphernalia of interment was to him an entirely
irrelevant matter, as to most children who are spared

the shocking ordeal of inspecting the coffined dead. I suppose, if you had bullied him and driven him into a corner, you might have extracted an opinion that his father was "in there," but this by no means invalidates the contention that the whole business was a rather entertaining show, ending up with a sip of port wine at the "Northern Star" and shrimps for tea. To "become aware suddenly," in the Paterian phrase, "of the great stream of human tears falling always thro' the shadows of the world," a young soul must have a higher conductivity, a closer identity with Nature, and possibly a clearer atmosphere, than obtained with little Hannibal. Be that as it may, it certainly seemed as though the boy's spirit, immersed in that illimitable ocean of the unconditioned of which I have already spoken, had been drifted away by an invisible yet resistless current, such as exist in our terrestrial atmosphere, had been carried neither high nor low, but *beyond* the radius of his mother's arms. Had fate been propitious here we might have proceeded to record the history of a genius, an iconoclast, a seer, an artist. The materials were there, if you consider the boy's crystal-clear vision of mind, his corporeal swimming and full brown eye. But the fuel was slow-burning, the flame wandered uselessly, and while the heat was to no purpose, there was no explosion, no power. And that is the need of the man nowadays, as of old, power. The dreamer, the thoughtful ones need this most of all. Without it they are peculiar, but ineffectual, sometimes also abominably sensual. You shall see.

Here ends, therefore, this part of this book. To what good purpose were it to proceed laboriously with the disintegration of this family, having shown you the spiritual fact accomplished. That they emerge later, coagulate to a certain extent, disperse once more, and finally pass, making through Hannibal Gooderich, "a small tribute to the ascending effort" of the world, will be manifest in the conclusion, if your patience will carry you so far. But that a promise may be redeemed, we may interpolate as an episode (at this time of day!) the love-story of the girl.

END OF BOOK ONE

BOOK TWO
THE CITY

"All virtue which is impracticable is spurious."—BURKE.

PART I

I

IN A few days, after Minnie had brought a wheezy ill-strapped dress-basket and a paper bag containing her Sunday hat, and taken up her quarters on a truckle bed which was hidden during the day under a yellow cover, she declared open war. In the first place, Minnie discovered with some surprise that the companionship of Mrs. Wilfley involved housework in all its branches, from washing dishes to cleaning hair-brushes with cloudy ammonia. Certainly the dishes were only breakfast dishes, and the latter task was begged from her as a favour, but the vertical furrow in the girl's forehead deepened for all that. Then again, Mrs. Wilfley was conversational in the sense that she required some one else to be present while she talked to herself about herself. It was not reliable information because, to tell the truth, Mrs. Wilfley knew remarkably little about herself, but it was an integral part of the lady. She had dreams of a *salon* where she could gather about her all her clever friends, a *salon* that would become famous like those of Rambouillet and Lady Jeune. They of course would talk, but it would be her own golden voice that would weave them all together and make of them a shining and memorable community. In the meanwhile she practised on Minnie, a young woman whose soul, she decided, was dormant. She had practised for some time on Anthony Gilfillan, who possessed sufficient humour (toward women) to escape unharmed. But Minnie's nature could not sustain without distortion such a heavy panoply of glittering harness as Mrs. Wilfley's companionship soon became. Superimposed upon the girl's as yet unexploited ambition lay a stratum of satire, a thin layer of æstheticism and a thick mass of marble indifference streaked with vivid and tangled veins of red anger and love. Of sensuality you could find but little, that being found most often with religiousness ; and of the latter the most exhaustive assay detected no trace. It might be wondered therefore why a woman so emotionally destructive as Olga Wilfley should have "taken to" the girl as she had done, and the faint-hearted investigator might be tempted to refer the puzzle to the "attraction of opposite types," and leave it at that. Such a solution, however, is not clear enough to be strictly honest. An explanation of psychological phenomena should explain, and this the above generalisation does not do. We must employ some reagent that will precipitate the turbidity and leave the whole thing clear. That reagent consists in the statement that Olga Wilfley and Minnie Gooderich, though widely dissimilar in age, experience, and emotional activity, were on exactly the same sex-plane. Neither of them had the slightest propensity for motherhood. In neither of them did the life-force direct the imagination towards domestic fecundity and economic ease. To Mrs. Wilfley a man was a being to get something out of, even if it were only a cab-ride or the use of his telephone ; to Minnie a man was sometimes that, sometimes a person to be avoided. But to neither of them was a man a lovable and ridiculous chap who hugged them and kissed them and gave them hats and sweets and jewels because he wor-shipped the ground they trod on. To hug Mrs. Wilfley was unthinkable. You might as well have hugged Lady Hester Stanhope or Margaret Fuller, to take two notable examples. And Minnie Gooderich, dissimilar as she ap-peared to the unpractised eye, was at this time in the same case. To Mrs. Wilfley marriage was a thing to cackle about, to Minnie it was distasteful and irrelevant. To both of them Love was a powerful but far-off god.

All this, however, was subterranean and unknown to the two protagonists. Minnie, her sleeves rolled up, wash-ing from plates the grease of what Mrs. Wilfley called "the matutinal bacon," Mrs. Wilfley herself, flitting from office to office in Fleet Street, were alike ignorant of it all and preoccupied with immediate concerns. One of these was the hour of rising. Mrs. Wilfley, having an artistic temperament, could not possibly get herself out of bed before ten o'clock ; while Minnie, being physically sound and well-balanced, woke naturally enough about half-past six. To lie for three hours tossing about on a truckle bed was torture and led to a discussion.

"It seems such a waste of time," she said incisively, and she regarded Mrs. Wilfley, with her dishevelled hair and her dirty dressing-gown, with disfavour. "Can't I do something?"

Mrs. Wilfley disliked noise. Her nerves were mere rags where noise was concerned, though she could listen to the sound of her own voice for a long time. Minnie submitted unwillingly to the ten-o'clock breakfast, and, after the housemaid's work, lifted the lid from the typewriter and bent her level brows upon a batch of manuscript. This was interesting. The first and second essays were chaotic failures, of course, but Minnie found herself wondering what, after all, there was in it. It may be doubted if she would have made equally swift progress in a school, for overlooking and fussy guidance were irksome to her. She was one of those people who seem to learn with an economy of failure inexplicable to minds whose interests are more diffused. She was, to use an old-fashioned phrase, neat-handed. To use a still older word in a new yet permissible connection, she was "feat." One must attribute this to the concentration of her small and compact intellect upon whatever she was engaged. It explains, too, the curious fact that she paid no attention to the *subject* of the article she had transcribed, which was an interview with the Prioress of the Convent of the Sacred Heart. Quite without malice did she join up the maimed members of a split infinitive and substitute a comma for a semi-colon. Common people do not split infinitives any more than they split hairs, and semi-colons are to them needless refinements. The humour of the thing was that Mrs. Wilfley did not notice either modification of her own grammar.

The completion of the article brought Minnie to one o'clock, and putting on her hat she went out, locked the door, and descended into Fleet Street to get herself some lunch. To her, unused as she was to the great hubbub of the City, the meal in a vast tea-shop was novel, thrilling, stimulating. The "café-habit" came to her at once,

naturally and irresistibly. It abolished the messing with
dishes and the smell of cooking. It gave her endless oppor-
tunities, too, of studying men and women of countless
types. The interest was unalloyed, moreover, with any
literary base-metal, for it did not occur to her that she
might write. Nor did she desire very much to know all
these men and women who thronged the streets, who filled
the 'buses and cabs and cafés of the street. Had one of
them spoken to her, the amused reflectiveness in her expression would have vanished behind an icy reserve, and
the stranger would have needed the will-power and assur-
ance of Mr. Gilfillan to have dispelled it.

Towards Mr. Gilfillan she had developed an interest
that was a blend of respect and curiosity. With her usual
economy of emotion, and this is a common occurrence with
girls of small imaginative power, she had transferred to
him all that she liked in the Tiberius of the story, and left
him, so to speak, to justify his apotheosis. Mr. Gilfillan
was, as already stated, quite ignorant of his present rank,
finding the chairmanship of *"Gilfillan Filaments Limited"*
quite enormous enough without assuming the purple of
romance. During the days previous to the grand concert,
when Minnie was busily employed in putting letters into
envelopes, writing addresses, stamping and posting them,
her frequent though brief meetings with that gentleman
had strengthened in her mind the notion that she enjoyed
his company. Instantly she was on her guard. She had had
that feeling before. Certainly Mr. Gilfillan was the exact
antithesis of the coal-agent's clerk. He was keen, clever,
efficient, untrammelled by silly ideas. But all the same, she
had had that feeling before, and the thin stratum of
æstheticism in her make-up induced a horror of emotional
mess and untidiness. She had talked of her feelings on
one occasion to Mrs. Gaynor, who had struck out a good
phrase to describe such a state of affairs. "You feel all
at loose ends I suppose," said Mrs. Gaynor, and Minnie
had replied that that was just it.

"I suppose Mr. Gilfillan makes a lot of money," she had
said that morning.

For a fiftieth part of a second Mrs. Wilfley's unwashed
eyes flickered as she poured hot water into the teapot.

"Yes, he makes thousands a year," she replied.

"Eh?" said Minnie, sitting up straight. "Thousands a year? And lives in Stamford Hill?"

That was Minnie's way. Her clear brain bit right into the heart of Mrs. Wilfley's luscious statements and showed the rottenness of them. She *knew* he couldn't live at Stamford Hill if he made thousands a year. There lay a striking difference between the two brains. Mrs. Wilfley liked to think she influenced a man with thousands a year, she imagined that only people with huge incomes floated companies, and she had the emotionalist's habit of slipshod statement. Minnie, on the other hand, at once selected from her scanty knowledge of Mr. Gilfillan the entirely sufficient fact that he lived at Stamford Hill.

"Well," went on Mrs. Wilfley, "he must control huge sums of money. His company is a hundred and fifty thousand, or something like that."

"What is it?"

"Something to do with electric light, I believe. I don't know much about that sort of thing, it's not in my line, you know. He's awfully clever, isn't he?"

Minnie was silent.

"I know he's awfully interested in you, my dear."

Another silence. Mrs. Wilfley looked a little pained.

"He took the greatest interest in the concert. You really ought to thank him. Such a busy man . . ."

Minnie clacked her knife and fork together and looked straight at Mrs. Olga Wilfley.

"I think the less you say to me about that concert, Mrs. Wilfley, the better. I'm fed up with the concert."

"Some people are very difficult to help," said the lady, sipping her tea.

"Who asked for your help? And what did the help amount to anyhow?"

Several times in rapid succession Mrs. Wilfley's eyelids flickered.

"My dear child, the balance was handed over——"

"Fourteen pounds, I know. That was a fat lot to get out of seventy pounds eighteen, wasn't it? It's a paying business, I should think, getting up concerts for people."

"I don't think you quite realise who you're talking to,"

said Mrs. Wilfley, rising and going towards the bedroom door. "I can refer you to numbers of the best people——"

"I don't want you to do that. All I want is to hear the last of that concert. Mother'll give you thanks for two."

When Mrs. Wilfley emerged again from the bedroom she was dressed for walking, and going over to where Minnie was sitting over a magazine, she stood there pulling on the fingers of her long white kid gloves. Her face was composed, and she had captured for the day the lustrous yearning look which was even then becoming famous among the inmates of rescue homes and night-shelters. "Nosey Mary" they called her among themselves, which is a damning proof of their depravity and shamelessness. Just as Minnie was beginning to grow restless under the soft insistent sound of the kid gloves and the silent proximity of the lady, the latter bent down suddenly and put her arm round the girl's shoulders.

"My dear," she crooned, "you have a terrible habit of blazing out at people, you know. I'm sure you are often sorry for it afterwards. We are all so utterly weak and despicable at heart that we should not *dare* to judge others. Do you not feel that? Sometimes when I have been talking to some poor girl, trying to give her some little tiny bit of hope, I have suddenly broken down and just cried."

"You!" said Minnie, looking up and putting the book down. "Why?"

"Because when I began to speak to her I felt terribly sorry for her. It was just pity, you know. Then I would feel rather glad because I had escaped so many of the horrors of her life. And suddenly I felt how utterly impossible it was for me to really *know* about any one who was struggling alone against evil. I felt as if I was talking to her on the telephone hundreds of miles off in the wilderness and all the while she needed some one to be close to her, some one who had suffered with her. I felt so weak and helpless; and do you know, when we feel like that we are on the sure way to be really strong and helpful. Mine has not been a very happy life, you know, as the world counts happiness, but sometimes I feel that I have been overpaid when a poor miserable girl has written to me and thanked me, not for money, not for advice, not for anything material, but for *sympathy,* just that sudden feeling of weakness and ignorance which made her see I was not doing it out of pride, but out of love."

For a space there was a silence in the room with the dark oak rafters and quaint old lanterns. Minnie sat lacing her fingers, looking down at them intently. When she spoke it was in a quiet, even voice.

"It seems to be all *feeling* with you, Mrs. Wilfley," she said. "I don't take things that way at all. I suppose I'm selfish or proud or something or other, but I never bother with other people's affairs. If they let me alone, I let them alone. As for *helping* people, I can't afford it. I've got to make a living somehow and be independent as soon as I can. If I was rich, like Mr. Gilfillan," here Minnie smiled a little, "I might give a lot."

"Oh, it isn't *money* that matters, my dear child. It is sympathy a broken heart wants, not *money.*"

"Is it? Well, it seems to me that people with plenty o' money never need much sympathy. When you've got money you can buy *anything.* It's not the trouble that makes you wish you were dead and out of it, it's the nag, nag of being without enough cash. I know what it is, I can tell you. I don't mean being poor with a little money put by for a rainy day, I mean having a rainy day all the time, and all the week's money owing before you get it. It's all very well to talk," here Minnie rose and stood by the window. "It's all very well to talk about sympathy and helping others when you've got a bit, but you don't get much sympathy when you owe money. *We* never used to. Only Mrs. Gaynor. I do believe it makes no difference to her how poor you are, but Mrs. Gaynor's all right herself. She can afford it."

"You will change, I am sure of that, my dear. You find the world hard. Yes, why? Because *you* are hard. You think every one is on the make——"

"Well, aren't they?" asked Minnie without turning round.

"Of course not! That is a horrible idea to get hold of. I know hundreds of men and women who live unselfish lives, who give themselves to others to try and make the world less unhappy. There is no joy like service."

"I daresay what you say's true," answered Minnie. "What I mean is, all these good people you know: are they worryin' about the rent? It makes a lot of difference, they'd find."

Mrs. Wilfley turned from the table where she had been pouring out a lukewarm cup of tea. She put it down again now and sat down.

"Come and sit down, my dear."

Minnie came over unwillingly and leaned against the table.

"You talk about nothing but rent and money and things like that. My child, your whole view is distorted and wrong. Look at me. You think I know nothing of these things, I suppose. You wouldn't think I have been a hospital nurse, would you?"

"Were you?" put in Minnie, looking down at her.

"Of course I was. You'll read all about it if you read my book. It's over there. You see, you are very ignorant of life, Minnie, and when you blaze out at people you ought to be very sure you're quite right. Now let me tell you something. I belong to a profession in which we are always looking for fresh ideas and fresh people. It is a profession in which experience doesn't count for very much. Some people I know, men and women, have been in this profession for years and yet are not much good. And I have known a girl who had hardly any experience at all do very well because she had just the right temperament. My friend Mrs. Worrall is of great assistance to me in my work among girls because she has the right temperament to find out what they can do. Mrs. Worrall sent you to me because she believed you would be useful in my work. But what I was going to say was that in my profession we are always struggling even more than other people against material wants, and yet we have to think first about ideas and people. If I were to be always worrying about money I should never do anything else. Worry won't help me."

"That's what Mrs. Gaynor says," admitted Minnie, but in a sceptical tone.

"Of course she does. She's one of us. Mr. Gilfillan is always laughing at our ideas, but he really acts on them himself very often, though of course he is on the make, you know. So," concluded Mrs. Wilfley, standing up, "you mustn't run away with the idea that because you are a sharp, clever girl you know better than anybody else how to run the world. As a dear old friend of mine says, 'We all have our funiosities,' and you wouldn't believe how strange that sounds from him because he has so many 'funiosities' of his own that he never dreams of."

For some time after Mrs. Wilfley had sailed out of her flat and down the stairs into Fleet Street, Minnie Gooderich stood thinking seriously. She began to clear the table and talk to herself, as was her habit.

"She's a coughdrop," she commented several times. "I wonder what it's all about. I s'pose people do get fed up with me. Can't help it. Sharp clever girl, eh? Don't seem very sharp and clever to stick here washin' up for her. She *is* buttery." Minnie stopped still with some cups and saucers in her hands, her head uplifted as if listening. "No," she said, going quickly into the back room and through into a tiny scullery. "No fear! I've had all I want of that. I'm goin' through with it. I'm goin' to keep on my own somehow. Anything but that! But O Lord, I must keep doin' something or I shall go dotty!"

She began to wash up, working with quick, nervous movements, working with that precision and economy of effort which distinguished everything she did or said. One after another the dishes were wiped dry and polished and put away. Then she went back and made the beds, quickly if not perfectly, folded up some stray garments and laid them away, and then, without pausing, she entered the front room again and took up Mrs. Wilfley's book, *The Licencees of Love*.

It may be doubted if the girl understood a great deal of this book, which dealt with the lives of those women who have always been a problem in European civilisation. Mrs. Wilfley's solution of the problem may have been correct or erroneous; it matters not to us. The fact to be noted is that much of her book was enigmatic to Minnie, because the girl had no knowledge of the matter to guide

her. She knew of girls at the factory, of course, who
"did overtime" as they called it, girls who had gone for
"trial-trips" and so vanished from view. But of the great
underworld, Minnie, having been born and grown up
before popular fiction had made the subject peculiarly its
own, before really popular fiction had cast off the
trammels of respectability, knew nothing. She understood
trouble and misery to mean lack of money, for she could
not go outside her experience. The agonies of soul of
Magdalens in high places she could not feel. She was a
child of Mammon in the sense that everything translated
itself into *cost*. Moreover, she had a vague subconscious
instinct, one might almost call it, that when men and
women did evil for *money,* when they fought for their
stands in the market-place and paid their way for all the
world like other people, the evil receded. These girls Mrs.
Wilfley was so solicitous for struggled as bravely in their
way as waitresses and retouchers did in theirs; they had
rent to pay and clothes to buy. The evil of their lives did
not come through to Minnie, and Mrs. Wilfley's emotional
stress (in print) left her cold.

She put the book down at length and turned to a tiresome exercise that Mrs. Wilfley had recommended as
conducive to accuracy and speed.

*Now is the time for all Good Men to come to the Aid
of the Party*. Over and over again she banged at the
keys, each time increasing in speed, and the drone and
click of the machine was soothing to her nerves. She was
still at it when Mrs. Wilfley returned.

"How do you like it?" she asked, smiling and drawing
off her gloves quickly.

"It's a change of occupation, of course," replied Minnie
as though that implied everything. "I don't say as I should
like a lot of it, but it can't be more monotonous than
dabbing prints."

"Don't forget what you know about photography, my
dear. It may be useful to you in the future. Now I've got
something for you to do. I have an article to write. I want
you to put on your hat and go down west and just note
down the things in the shop windows."

"Everything?" said Minnie, aghast.

"Of course not. New things in the big shops. And if you see a woman with something really *chic* on you can make a note of that. You'll want a note-book and pencil."

"It's a new job for me," argued the girl.

"I know. That's why your notes will be of value. You have innocence of eye, as the artistic people say."

"But I shan't know what they call some of the things. I haven't any dress-making experience."

"Then go in and ask. I'll give you one or two of my cards. Don't be afraid."

"Oh, I'm not afraid. Don't you think that, Mrs. Wilfley! What I don't see is what the good of it is."

"Worrying again! That independent spirit of yours will get you into all sorts of trouble." Mrs. Wilfley had taken off her hat and jacket and now seated herself at her table and opened her bag. Seeing no further use in discussion, Minnie pinned on her hat, put the cards in her purse and went out. In Chancery Lane she purchased a note-book and pencil and mounted a 'bus going west, a white Kensington 'bus.

On the top of the 'bus sat Anthony Gilfillan, deep in a thick pamphlet and smoking an oval cigarette.

II

Mrs. Wilfley had shown unusual penetration (for which we give her due credit) in remarking that Anthony Gilfillan *was* on the make.

Difficult and impertinent as it is, and futile into the bargain, to sum up our brethren in one smart phrase, a jury of the average sort would have confirmed the verdict. Yet, like many other curt judgments, it meant, on scrutiny, nothing. We say of a millionaire that his god is money. Is it? Very flattering to ourselves, no doubt, our mediocre selves who know nothing of the man's soul. It is stated with some truth by the psychologists that the roots of a man's virtue are inaccessible to us. So for that matter are the roots of his vices. Often a fungoid growth, the mere result of early darkness and unusually rich soil, will hide from us the latent and unlooked-for goodwill. Later, when he became rich and powerful, when his sayings became quotations beyond the business world, when he was hated as an evil influence and hailed as a master of affairs, the tale of Anthony Gilfillan's life was dotted over with these toadstools of unworthy acts, blots on his scutcheon, and people who were neither clever enough nor brave enough to do likewise shook their heads. "If I'd done that, I'd get into jail," they would say; or, "Clever chap; d'you know how he got on? Why, some poor devil or other— I forget his name—went to him with an invention. . . . Yes, *Stole* it! . . . Made a pot o' money out of it. His Knighthood, too. How'd you s'pose he got that? Didn't you see it? Why, *Bought* it . . . !" And so on. And all the while the man himself was as hidden as it was on this autumn day when he sat on the 'bus deep in his pamphlet.

The 'bus jerked and started again as Minnie mounted, and she had sat down beside him before she recognised him. Without looking up he drew closer to the side of the 'bus to make room for her, and she felt a curious tingling

148

sensation at being so close to him. She had felt it when in his presence before at the lecture in Mrs. Wilfley's rooms, and now she wondered vaguely why she felt like that. It was quite different, she summed up, quite a different feeling from the mere self-satisfaction she derived from the attentions of the coal-agent's clerk during the first part of their courtship. She looked round and smiled, wondering what he would say when he saw her. Her pulses were beating quickly, and a flush spread over her face as her thoughts raced away into that spatial vastness which for some of us is our only playground, but which is, alas, like so many real playgrounds, vacant and dusty. She recalled Beryl Brentano and Tiberius, and wondered what she would do in like circumstances. Act haughtily, Minnie surmised, but was not sure. After all he was not so very like Tiberius: that was only a first impression. He was much more human in some things; he had a little daughter, for example. And she was not Beryl, not by several streets of houses.

Her mother, had she seen her sitting there waiting for the man to look up, would scarcely have recognised her daughter. An unwonted softness had invaded her face, the indomitably hard little face that set itself like flint against the Maple Road ideals. There was much of unsuspected childishness in her face now, much of goodness. It was like the bloom on fruit. Touch it and it was gone, mere soilure on your hands. The presence of some people brushed it away from Minnie's face at once. But as she sat there beside this absorbed magnetic man, her whole conscious self was submerged in that ocean of feeling in which we all swim, and the warm currents of it sent a thrill of inexplicable happiness through her physical frame.

And all at once, as he turned a page, he glanced up.

"Is it possible?" he said, as he withdrew his mind from the pamphlet. "Well met indeed! Are you going far? Why didn't you speak?" And he threw away his cigarette.

"You seemed so interested," she answered, shaking hands. "I didn't like to disturb you."

"Rubbish! You've been having a good look at me, I expect."

"Yes, I have," she replied.

"And you are satisfied?" he smiled.

"No," she hazarded. She was a novice in tit-for-tat conversation, but her pleasure in it and her native acuteness assisted her. "No."

"That's a cryptic answer. How shall I take it?"

"Take it as you like. I can always say I didn't mean it that way."

"Wise girl! I am going to take it to mean you are not satisfied and want to look at me still more. Is that a risky shot?"

"You think a good deal of yourself, if you think so. A cat may look at a king, they say."

He threw his head back and laughed.

"You are a most remarkable young woman," he said. "I said as much to Mrs. Wilfley when she told me how you disliked that concert business."

"I dislike it still," she answered gravely.

"Who wouldn't, who had any character at all? I thought the whole business very ill-advised when I came to study it, but one must compromise in this old world. I have lived in all sorts of places, and that is one grain of wisdom at any rate that I have treasured up. One must compromise."

"I don't see now why she did it," said Minnie.

Mr. Gilfillan handed up a penny to the conductor to pay for Minnie's ticket.

"It is a species of advertisement with her," he remarked under his arm. "You see, she makes her living in a way quite different from either you or me. You, for example, do so much work, perform so much duty, and receive in return so much money. It is a simple commercial transaction, the first step beyond simple barter or exchange. I, on the other hand, have a number of people, whom I never see, working for my benefit. I provide them with wages, pay the rent and other expenses, direct the policy and receive my emolument in the form of dividends."

"I see," said Minnie. She was interested in the matter because she was interested in him and he in her.

"Mrs. Wilfley, on the other hand, is what they call in journalistic parlance a 'free-lance.' That is, she spins out of her head the stuff she sells. There is in her business no 'good-will,' as we say in commerce, except her own name. Everything which can assist her to extend the knowledge of her name and so increase the 'goodwill' of her business, she must be ready to do. She saw a chance, I suppose, of increasing her prestige in North London by taking a leading part in a charity."

"It's a funny thing mother only got fourteen pounds out of seventy-odd taken," said Minnie, and her face clouded again.

"Twenty per cent? Don't you think that a business which gave fourteen pounds' profit out of every seventy pounds' worth of business done would be a pretty good spec? I do. I only hope my company will do as well."

"Where's the rest gone?" asked Minnie, still vague.

"Expenses: rent, lighting, wages of artistes, printing, stationery, postage, fares, telegrams, refreshments, gratuities. You see, all the various people who are employed in such an affair have no intention of working for nothing—they can't be expected to do so, can they?"

"No, I suppose not," admitted the girl. "It seems a great waste of time and money to get so little out of it though."

"My idea exactly. As I said, a most ill-advised affair. Here is Charing Cross. Where are you going?"

She told him. He raised his eyebrows.

"Do you think you can do it?" he asked.

"No," she said frankly, "I don't. I think Mrs. Wilfley's making a mistake. I think she's making a mistake in several ways. Don't you want to get off?" she said abruptly.

"I'll go through St. James's Park," he answered. "Go on. What are the several ways in which Mrs. Wilfley is making a mistake?"

Minnie laughed a little at the mimic in his tone.

"Well, in the first place, she believes, or says she believes, I'm not exactly a fool and can do this sort of thing easy. In the second place, she thinks I *am* fool enough to do this work for her for twelve shillings a week; and in the third place, she thinks I'd do anything rather than lose the job. She's wrong all the way through."

"Have you told her this?"

"No, of course not. Let her find out. Besides, you see, Mrs. Wilfley isn't known all at once. She's got all sorts of queer fits and starts. She was talking to me this morning as if I was the Woman Taken in Adultery."

Mr. Gilfillan turned silently to the Haymarket to hide a smile.

"Where did you get *that* illustration?" he demanded.

"Oh, there's a chapter in her book called that," said Minnie, turning her ticket into a little cylinder of paper. "I was reading it this morning. I didn't understand much of it, but I remembered that bit."

"Well," said Mr. Gilfillan, "I cannot say once and for all that you are right or wrong in being so certain about your lack of ability, because I have always made a rule to believe I could do anything if I only tried. For instance, I am a journalist at times, for I write articles in technical journals, and what is more, I get paid for them. When I started I had never written anything and had never been taught. I sat down with the fixed idea in my mind that I could write. And I found I could. When I was asked, two years ago, to make a speech at a dinner, I had never made a speech. But I got up believing firmly I could speak, and I did. That is my rule of life. If fate means you to lose, give him a good fight anyhow. Do you remember Henley's magnificent lines:

> '*Under the bludgeonings of chance*
> *My head is bloody but unbowed*'?

That is my gospel. What do you think of it?" And, preparing to rise, he turned and smiled down into the girl's face. She was silent, but her face was aglow.

"What are you doing this evening?" he asked.

"Nothing."

"Well, my sister and little girl are away at the seaside just now, so if you are disengaged I should like you to come and dine with me somewhere, will you?"

"I should like it."

"What time? Say seven."

"All right."

"Charing Cross Post Office, eh?"

"All right."

"Then *au revoir*." And lifting his hat he went down and dropped off the 'bus.

A moment later Minnie temporarily recovered her self-possession and found herself opposite a big shop in Regent Street. She descended hastily and joined the crowd on the pavement. But she was unable to form any clear notion of the contents of the windows. Her brain was still humming as a harpstring might hum after the hand that plucked it had gone away. *To dine, to dine, dine, to dine.* So the thought reverberated through her brain, and set all the chambers ringing. He was a man, she chanted voicelessly, he was indeed a man. *He* would never finish head-first in a brook. *He* would not nag interminably about some trivial matter. He was a man, with brain, with energy, with ideas, and he had asked her to dine, to dine. . . .

Lunch time passed and she moved up and down in front of the shops unheedingly, her note-book clipped in her fingers with her purse, untouched. Now and again her slim black figure would attract a man's eyes approvingly, but she saw nothing save men and women as trees walking, and the shining sunlight.

And then about three o'clock, she awoke.

"Oh, what shall I do?" she whispered in her heart. "What shall I do?"

The honour of the wage-earner, that honour which is so common among us that no man questions it, turned her face to the window of the shops, but the emotion of the moment still interfered with her vision. With a determined effort she braced up and walked to one of the great glass doors. Autumn shopping was at its height. The calm, serene atmosphere of the place was soothing and laid a steady hand upon that aggressiveness which always seized Minnie when she was nervous and undecided in aim. The frock-coated gentleman who approached her at once had appraised her before he had completed his bow. Shop-lifters do not dress in plain shabby dresses and sailor-hats. He was agreeably respectful therefore. What did Madame desire? Minnie gave him one of Mrs. Wilfley's cards on the corner of which was engraved the name

Sunday Words. This was the periodical for which Mrs.
Wilfley did the domestic and fashion notes, she being
neither domestic nor fashionable and so eminently fitted
to give *ex-parte* opinions. The shop-walker, to Minnie's
surprise, seemed prepared for such emergencies. She did
not know that the fashion notes of *Sunday Words* were
copied by dozens of local papers and provincial weeklies
throughout the kingdom, were sometimes pirated by American papers of the same type and then re-pirated by
English weeklies of a much higher type. Minnie, of course,
knew nothing whatever about the matter, but the shop-
walker did not know that. He merely begged her to step
this way and that way through the different departments
to a private room where a tall, severe-looking woman
dressed in a gown of plain faultless black was watching
the slowly-turning figure of another woman in front of
the largest mirror Minnie had ever seen. He spoke a few
words in the ear of the lady in black, and retired. Minnie's
nervousness intensified, for she was feeling to her very
bones the shabbiness and uncouthness of her attire. Needless agony. In this great repository of purple and fine
linen the personal appearance of a fashion-journalist was
not a matter of trivial moment, it was a matter of no
moment at all. Quite oblivious to Minnie's presence the
woman before the mirror continued to turn slowly, emitting a dropping fire of criticism, and the woman in black
muttered continually in a low refined tone. "Yes, Madame." "Oh, quite so, Madame." "Quite impossible,
Madame, I agree," never taking her eyes from the
woman's body as it turned and turned, head thrown back,
eyes downcast with an expression of imperial disdain,
hand raised slightly as though dismissing some regal
suppliant, a tragic and, when you realised the moment,
slightly ridiculous spectacle. For it was not a virgin Empress who stood there, it was not even a great artist
rehearsing her part in some decorative drama, it was
simply a rich man's daughter trying on a dress. The dress
itself was pinned and tacked from neck to floor, a thing
of shreds and patches, thread-strewn and unfinished.

"Yes, Madame, I can loop it up, right up to the armpit.
I understand perfectly, Madame. Yes, and pearls—one row

right round the shoulder : exactly. The sleeve will hang
down close. Yes, to a point, like a wing. And the red
band, you are decided on that? *Very* narrow I should
suggest, say about three-eight's of an inch, stiffened with
canvas. Yes, it is distinctly a conception. No other colour
whatever? Very good, Madame."

The woman before the mirror turned her back to the
mirror once more, threw her head yet further back, and
took a last long look at the billowing folds of the train,
met her own eyes for an instant in cold scrutiny, and then
advanced to an inner door. The woman in black sprang
swiftly to open it for her; she passed in and the door
closed.

The woman in black now turned to deal with Minnie.
She seemed quite as well apprised of Minnie's needs as
did the gentleman in the frock coat.

"We have several very *chic* things," she said affably,
for even dressmakers are affable to those who provide free
advertisements. "That was one of the best. Cream Mous-
selin-de-soie, pearl embroidery and a single narrow band
of geranium velours at the waist but higher than is worn
just at present. Here's a note of it."

She took a sheet of paper from a big table against the
wall and handed it to Minnie. The table was covered with
press-cuttings of designs, dress-cuttings, long tangled
strips of material pinned to figured slips, needles, pins,
stationery, and order-books. The modiste took up a sheaf
of papers similar to the one Minnie held and turned them
over rapidly.

"I think the most striking are here," she said. "Did
you see anything outside particularly . . . ?"

"A yellow hat," said Minnie promptly, rather to her
own astonishment. "I saw a yellow hat."

"With puce simulated wing under the brim? Quite a
creation, but of course only for race-meetings. That would
not be suitable for description in *Sunday Words,* would
it?"

"Chronic," said Minnie. "I was wondering who wore
that sort of thing."

"Kit-fox is coming in," went on the lady, ignoring
such an irrelevant remark. "You might make a note of

that. Ten guineas as an average. Oh, and there is this."
She held up a half-tone print of an impossibly tall female
encased in fur. "This is tail," she remarked, "very classical
and sure to be popular in October."

Minnie put the papers between the leaves of her note-
book and had an inspiration.

"That'll do," she said. "I've got a lot of other shows to
visit."

The customer emerged, dressed in a smart outdoor suit
of pale grey-green serge, yellow gloves, and a white felt
hat with a raked cock-feather. She was buttoning the
gloves and did not look up, for being in business as a
rich man's daughter is sometimes a very absorbing occupation.

The modiste opened the outer door, the customer passed
through, followed by Minnie.

"Thanks," the latter said over her shoulder. "Good
day."

Out in the street she paused for a moment to see the
departure of the customer. An Irish jaunting-car waited
at the curb, a sumptuous shiny and silver-plated equipage
such as Cavan or Clare had never seen, attended by a
red-haired little groom in green coat, white breeches, and
yellow-topped boots. He touched his hat, leaped into position, and held out his gloved hand for his mistress's foot.
A little crowd collected, clotted, and melted away in a
moment, one of those innumerable momentary coagula-
tions which are a feature of our streets. The lady held
herself rigidly erect, and her clean-cut yet commonplace
features conveyed a new and startling impression of
savage authority and power as she raised the whip. The
little groom ran round, scrambled up on the off side and
assumed the ridiculous attitude of his class. The raked
cock's feather on the lady's hat touched the rosette on his
glossy hat. The horse stepped high, shaking his silver
harness-bells, and they vanished among the traffic of
Regent Street. She was a rich man's daughter.

Minnie stood looking in that direction for some little
time, lost in thought. She had no clear indictment in her
mind against the rich man's daughter. Indeed, I think her
attitude was strictly neutral. "She's got it, she can do

what she likes," might express it succinctly. "When I get it, I'll do as *I* like," was the corollary, accompanied by gritted teeth. She had, moreover, the acuteness to perceive the keen pleasure a young woman can derive from driving in an uncommon turnout through West London. You drew the town, people could see your crest on panel and harness, people stopped and looked and "got to know you," as their hideous jargon has it, in course of time. There was skill in it too. You had to know your business to drive a horse like that safely through the traffic of heavy pair-horse vans, swift hansoms, cyclists, and view-obliterating 'buses. The rich man's daughter, I imagine, had Minnie's respect, and this had a certain steadying effect upon Minnie herself. These moods of preoccupation with another person's destiny inevitably react in the healthy mind, and teach it something of itself. Minnie had nothing of the late Mr. Gooderich's purposeless optimism and belief in luck. She thought the chances of wealth coming to her were fantastically remote, which is one reason why she never attained it. Mrs. Gaynor, in this connection, may be cited as a reliable authority when she said to Minnie:

"Folks often miss what they're after because they didn't wish hard enough."

Nevertheless, her brief consideration of life as it might appear to the rich man's daughter led her to sound the probable springs of the woman's happiness, and this re-acting, she found her thoughts darting and fluttering round Anthony Gilfillan like moths round one of his highly patented metallic filament lamps. She was looking into one of those long narrow panels of mirrors that were becoming popular for shop-fronts just then, and she en-countered a pair of rather frightened dark blue eyes, a face whose even pallor was tinged with one of her slow blushes. The adventure was calling her, and not in vain.

She took out her note-book and proceeded. An autumn *négligé* of white fleecy wool, with French blue silk fac-ings and sash, a hat of écru straw on which a young ostrich seemed to be sitting, a gown that Mrs. Gaynor would have called "a party dress" of blue taffeta with beads and transparent sleeves—all these were mentioned on a page of the note-book. And then observing a clock pointing to four she realised that she was very hungry and tired. She was undeniably tired, yet she had merely loitered away the day. She did not know that the wear and tear of the emotions exhausts one's body and lines one's face much faster than the work of a stoker or a navvy; she was too young. She had always felt disparagement towards those girls at the factory who had told her how "done up" they were on some days, they themselves not understanding the cause of their supineness. However, food was to be got; the three hours to seven o'clock were to be passed somehow. Mrs. Wilfley was to be seen and fought with on the usual lines, so Minnie climbed once more upon a 'bus whose ultimate destination was Peckham via the Strand.

III

THE meeting was swift, unexpected in detail, and satisfyingly spectacular. It did not, of course, compare with an Irish jaunting car in the least particular, but far surpassed Minnie's imagined encounter (he lifting his hat genteelly as he took her hand, and she smiling in a rather fatuous way). Mr. Gilfillan, it happened, did not do things that way. His agile intellect never missed the smallest opportunity of doing a thing in an original and effective manner. Minnie was standing near the kerb in front of the Post Office when a hansom came up at full speed from Whitehall, the Trafalgar Square policeman, noting the silk hat pushed back, the preoccupied stare of the eyes, the crushed appearance of the occupant, had imagined him to be, if not in the Cabinet, at least an under-secretary, and let him pass through. At first the girl did not notice him, and when the doors crashed back she stood away to make room for the stranger to alight. He leaned out, extended his hand.

"I'm five minutes late," he said with a smile as she took a deep breath and stepped in. The doors crashed together again, and half a dozen pairs of curious eyes watched the brisk little drama from the sidewalk.

"Paoli's," said Mr. Gilfillan to a massive purplish face which gazed down upon them with Olympian indifference from the little trap door. The trap fell and they were alone, aproned from the world, speeding toward a new mystery called Paoli's.

"How did you get on with the job?" he asked, lighting a fresh cigarette and examining a spot on his face in the mirror. Minnie told him.

"Ah!" he said. "I wondered how that business was done. I see. Though why the readers of *Sunday Words* want—ah, well I see that too, I think."

"They're servants mostly, poor people anyhow, so I

suppose they fancy themselves a bit when they read about nice things rich people wear."

"Yes, and they make up their own things and get ideas from the pictures, I expect."

"Yes, but what I can't make out is what good that does Bellamy's," said Minnie, Bellamy's having been the shop she had visited.

"Oh, undoubtedly it does them good. It *must* do so. It is all advertisement. Every time the name Bellamy is repeated in print or in speech, their hold on the public is tightened. In the same way, I am paying thousands a year now to journals throughout the world simply to repeat my name. In the course of a year or two, when any man says *Gilfillan,* the other man will say almost automatically *Filament.* I intend the words *Gilfillan Filament* to become a sort of obsession with mankind. You cannot take any isolated case of advertising and say, 'There, what actual profit do you get from that?' You must take the whole thing in review."

"It seems to me that there's nothing else but advertising nowadays. And when you buy it it falls to pieces," remarked Minnie. "I know mother sent ten shillings once to some firm in the country for some stuff for a dress. It only lasted till the first shower. 'Conquering-Hero' Navy Serge they called it. You ought to have seen it when the rain got it!"

"Ah, that is unavoidable. There have always been and always will be unscrupulous humbugs to catch the unwary. That is no argument against advertisement, however. You see, Miss Gooderich, you must put yourself in the place of a person who has something to sell. It may be the finest thing of its kind that ever existed; if people don't know of it, how can they buy it? Another thing. The Great British Public, on whom we all live, doesn't really know what it wants. The natural tendency of all communities is to be satisfied with what they have. The community says, 'Gas is good enough for me!' and the man with a new burner has to spend thousands convincing them that he can give them something better. The community with the new burner won't have electric light, they distrust it, it's too newfangled. When they've got used to it, I or some other man comes along with a new idea by which they can save nine-tenths of their current and get two hundred per cent more light. You'd think they'd jump at it, wouldn't you? Well, as I said just now, they compel me to form a company of people who have money and believe in me, just to spend that money like water in dinning into the public's ears that they will profit by using our Filament. They don't know what's good for them and so we have to tell them."

This thrilling and romantic explanation of certain phenomena of commercial psychology brought them to Greek Street, where Paoli's was situated. The interlude was useful to Minnie to adjust her thoughts to hansom-cab conditions, and she was grateful for it for that reason. When she jumped down to the pavement of Greek Street and waited while Mr. Gilfillan satisfied the purple-faced driver, she was ready to meet him on his own ground, aggressively feminine, an alluring touch of malice in her eyes. They entered the *ristorante*.

Paoli's was one of those diminutive eating-houses which make the metropolis endurable to a cosmopolitan of limited means. To give you a six-course dinner for eighteen pence, a flask of excellent last year's *chianti* for a florin, bread, butter, and table-napkin for nothing, and the most cheerful of *Milanese* to wait on you for whatever you are pleased to give her, were noticeable features of Paoli's establishment. It is true that the food was the refuse of the great clubs of St. James's Street and Piccadilly, you dipped your knife in the salt-cellar instead of using a spoon, and you used the same knife and fork throughout the six courses, exactly as you would in Italy, but the cosmopolitan of limited means neither knows nor cares about these things. He may be an Irishman who has studied art in Paris, a German who studies law in Gower Street, or, like Mr. Gilfillan, a transplanted Scot who has engineered in many lands. Paoli's have a welcome for him. Their snowy tablecloths and battered cruets stand waiting, the cheerful waitresses flit to and fro, and many a man of the above types, looking round while he bolts salted almonds and digs his fingers into his crusty roll, has thought to himself, "How homelike. I must bring the wife." For Mrs. Paoli sat enthroned at the desk, rouged, massive of bust, benign.

"I thought you'd like this place," said Anthony Gilfillan as they took a table about halfway down the long narrow room. "Personally, I prefer it to those big pandemoniums with brass bands and commissionaires, and all the rest of it, don't you?"

"I've never been to any of them," said Minnie. "And it's no use asking me to give an opinion. I suppose this is a foreign place, isn't it?"

Mr. Gilfillan was studying the menu which a freckled French girl had dropped between the knife and fork. Minnie caught the girl's eye for a moment and found it friendly. There lay its charm, I suppose, for Paoli's was a friendly place. Great bearded men in evening dress used to go there, neglecting the sublime gloom of White's and its multitudinous cutlery, the cheap wine recalling their strenuous days of exile and obscurity, and when they left, smoking a cigarette, would drop gold carelessly among the debris of the meal, as a sort of libation to the kindly spirit of the place. Minnie responded at once to it, and laughed sympathetically when Mr. Gilfillan addressed the girl in rapid but evilly pronounced French, and the girl replied in still more rapid *argot* and stood smiling, her underlip between her teeth and her grey eyes shifting from one customer to the other.

"What do you say?" he asked, handing over the card. "Shall we have the lot?"

"Please don't ask me," she said, a little confused. "You know, anything you say will do for me."

"Well." He took the card back and examined it judicially. "What shall we say, Juliette? Eh, *ma mie? Dîner, Juliette, et vin Toscane.*"

"*Chianti? Bien. Flacon, M'sieu?*" rippled Juliette, her hands hovering over the table. "*Poulet ou canard, M'sieu?*"

"Chicken or duck? I think chicken is safer, eh? *Bien, ma chère, Poulet, avec des pois, des asperges et du jambon, eh?*"

"*Merci, M'sieu.*" And Juliette, her red heels clicking on the hard wood floor, fled kitchenwards.

Several disconcerting happenings delayed Minnie's

longed-for serenity. There was the arrival of a party of
men at the next table, two of whom wore evening dress
and the third was dressed in an old tweed Norfolk jacket
and straw hat. Then again the *hors d'œuvres,* a bewildering array of indigestible rubbish (so Minnie thought
them), gave her food for thought if not for body. Juliette
would sail up, slap down a pepper-box and some tooth-
picks, smile brilliantly, and whirl round upon a sedate
Frenchman and his wife, who tucked their napkins under
their chins, and ascertain their views on the jam omelette.
The mirrors reflected to infinity the bizarre advertisements
of foreign table waters, stuffs called Strega, Salubra,
Cognac, and the like, daring drawings of a strange race
of women who had legs and (one regretted) did not mind
showing them. And the panels between the mirrors were
filled with drawings of men and women who knew nothing
of Maple Road, men and women whose beautiful brown
limbs took them over strange hills, whose red lips breathed
other air than ours, and whose fathomless eyes peered
through dim haunted forests, and down the vista of palaces
where white peacocks strutted, and ivory girls sat on
golden thrones. Of course, so blunt is our modern sense
of art that even cosmopolitans of limited means, even a
conventional girl like Minnie took all this as mere decorative drivel. "These bally artists!" Or if appreciative:
"That's clever, eh? Rather fussy all those snakes, don't
you think? Good motif yes, but Lord, man! you can do
anything with peacocks, and it's all repetition." And so on.
Anthony Gilfillan, who had reached a conclusion on this
as on every other subject under the sun, could have explained it very clearly. But just now he was explaining
something else clearly.

"I am not a domestic animal," he was saying over his
soup, "though that may sound strange from a man who
has a small daughter at home. I draw on all sorts and
conditions of people for my existence, and when a man
does that he cannot be called domestic."

Minnie put down her spoon and wiped her mouth.

"Is it a game?" she asked bluntly. Anthony Gilfillan
pulled up short his intellectual chariot, took out the
horses and put them to bed.

"It's the most absorbing game in the world, making love to everybody and everything in it," he said over the rim of his glass. "Here's to my next affair!" And he drank, his eyes fixed on hers and twinkling.

"*Now* I don't know quite what you mean," she answered, lifting her glass and holding it near her lips. "Do you mean you're *interested* in everything, including me?"

He nodded. "Just that," he said.

"And will it be any good to me?" she went on, still holding the glass up. For a moment their eyes met. For a moment all the nice analysis of his mind was dimmed and softened, all the calculation and antagonism of hers was effaced. Their eyes met; a spark passed.

"It will be the time of your life for you," he said gravely. "If you are the girl I think you. Now will you drink?"

And putting the glass to her lips, she drank.

It was her first glass of wine, and the beginning, in a way, of the time of her life. For from this on, she showed less of that intractable materialism which had been expressed in her intense preoccupation with money. From this on, even in her days of degeneration, when Anthony Gilfillan had passed from her life and gone on his upward triumphant way, she retained something of the joyance of that first red wine. It discovered in her a pagan carelessness, all too transitory, which Maple Road had had no power to lure into view.

The sharp tang of the wine whetted her appetite, and she ate the fish, the rissole, and the chicken with increasing freedom and zest.

"I like this sort of thing," she said, reaching for the massive pot of French mustard. "This is one of the things I've always wanted to go in for."

She began to tell him of some of the things she wanted to go in for, of Mrs. Gaynor and her sententious sayings, of Mrs. Wilfley and her curious compound of altruism, selfishness, cleverness, and purblind idiocy.

"She's always taking me in a fresh place," Minnie told him. "This evening, when I got back and asked her if I'd got enough, she said, 'Oh, damn *Sunday Words*.' I told her straight she wasn't goin' to damn me, and she got off the sofa where she'd been lying and put her hands on my shoulders. It does make me wild, that sort of thing."

"And what did she say?" asked Mr. Gilfillan.

"Ask me something easier to start with! A lot about how upset her nerves were, and she didn't always have command over herself. And then, after she'd lain down again—fetch her fur slippers and take her shoes off! What beats me," continued Minnie, "is how she gets me to do it. I didn't feel like taking her shoes off. I felt a good deal more like smacking her face."

"She certainly has a personality," agreed Anthony.

"Personality! I'll give her credit for this, that she can do the creeping Jesus turn better than anybody else I've ever seen. And we had several holy-willies up at the factory."

Mr. Gilfillan did not reply in words, but his expression showed he was interested in Minnie's view-point. She looked round hastily at the three at the next table, who were deep in their own concerns, put her elbows on the table and her chin in her hands. "I haven't said anything wrong, have I?" she asked. He shook his head.

"When I met you on the stairs, you know," she continued, "when I first asked you"—he nodded—"if Mrs. Wilfley was a bit cracked, you laughed and said no she wasn't. Didn't you?"

He nodded again, pouring out more wine.

"Well, in a way you were right, I s'pose, but for all that she's funny. Why has she taken such a fancy to me? She knows heaps o' people. They were coming in all day yesterday."

"Oh, that is a matter that can never be threshed out by talking. When you come to think it out we always want to give a false reason for our likes and dislikes except the one case of man and girl who fall in love. For instance, a man likes another man and he explains it by saying they have similar tastes. A girl likes another girl and puts it down to their common ideas in dress and books or games. A boy likes another boy and is not even allowed to explain it at all, the attraction is so objectionable. Now all this is due to misconception. Each one of us has an attraction for certain other persons irrespective of sex, age, or race. I believe that even when there is intense friendship between the members of the same family it is due to the mysterious attraction which is called love, affection, palship, affinity, and all the rest of it. You can understand?"

Minnie, sipping her wine, her third glass, smiled but shook her head.

"Well, you've got some idea of what we mean by magnetism?" She nodded. "Very good. Certain dead things, or things we call dead, have a curious attraction for other things, just as—but can you imagine what I mean by chemical affinity?" Again she nodded.

"I did chemistry when I was at school," she said.

"Better still. Don't keep on telling me you don't understand these things. You are better equipped for learning than a dozen Mrs. Wilfleys. Just as, I was saying, certain chemical bodies and compounds have a mysterious affinity for other bodies. Sometimes the attraction is slow yet sure, sometimes it is violently sudden, as an explosion. And it's just the same with people, only we don't know enough about people to say what will happen when they meet. Sometimes it is just repulsion, sometimes slow attraction, and sometimes a violent explosion. And it's often the case when they attract each other most violently that you get the most violent explosion."

"That's your idea, is it?" she said, marking the tablecloth with her finger-nail. "As it happens, I haven't any affinity, as you call it, for Mrs. Wilfley."

"Did I say you had? I dare say, as a matter of fact, that you hardly know yourself well enough yet to decide who or what you like. Mrs. Wilfley, on the other hand, has a certain amount of experience of the world which——"

"Oh, bother her," interrupted Minnie brusquely. "Let's talk about somebody else. Talk about yourself, will you? I'm not—interested in her peculiar ideas.".

"You won't be bored? It used to be a bad habit of mine, when I was a young chap, to talk about myself."

"No, I won't be bored. I like to hear about people who do things."

And he began to tell her. He took her back to his child-.

hood, a childhood spent on the road when his father, a bootmaker, tramped southward from his Fifeshire home to London, finally taking a tiny shop in Stoke Newington when Stoke Newington was surrounded by green fields. He told her of his early penury, when he tramped at dawn to an engineering works in East London, down by Thames side, to his long day's work, and tramped home again at night worn out in body and mind. He told her how he toiled by smoky lamplight, how he plodded through the dark ill-lit streets, how a dream came to him of a City of Light, where night was like day, and how he held that dream through years of bitter struggle. He told her of his first fruitless strivings to get his knowledge of electricity, when books were dear and polytechnics only just beginning; how, when he had risen to be a leading hand, he had been sent away to China to assist in putting up some machinery, and thereby saved a hundred pounds. He told her how he had come home, working his passage on an old tramp steamer, a wheezy box of corruption, a common sailor before the mast, how he walked the London streets looking for a job, so that he might save his capital for his scheme. He told her how he had met the woman he married, his landlady's daughter, how he had lost his job the day after he was married, and the ensuing bickerings of his mother-in-law. He told her how the mother-in-law had died suddenly and left him with a sick wife and baby and a houseful of lodgers to look after. How he had taken off his coat and set to work at keeping a lodging-house in grim earnest, how he had succeeded, taking the next house and working that too, finally selling the business for three hundred pounds. Then he told her of his wife's death of pleurisy and the addition of the hundred pounds of insurance money to his slowly accumulating hoard. Then came his sister into the story, a sweet-tempered girl who had never met *her* affinity and who came to live with him and mother the little girl while he went out into the world again. For he had never given up his dream of a City of Light, studying French and German that he might be apprised of all the science of Europe, even groping after the perfect stuff he believed was somewhere in the world.

He told how he had gone out to Buenos Ayres, then a sprawling, untidy city of crime, a sink where flowed all the dregs and refuse of humanity, a place where a dark street meant a knife-stab and every ditch floated a corpse. Of his lonely life out there, first a driver on the new railway, then water clerk to a Polish merchant who was coining money in various obscure ways. Then came his turn of fortune, when he met a mining engineer who wanted a manager on a new mine; of his hermit life in the mountains, master of hundreds of polyglot desperadoes. But it was good money he was earning then, and the sister in London received half of it every quarter, until she begged him to come home. But he did not come home. He had found something in the mines, something his long hours of research among dry German books of science told him was worth looking into. And look into it he did, with eyes that blazed with a furious passion for knowledge, with acid and battery and tiny forge he looked into it until he saw the thing he sought, the thing he had meant to find. Then came the time for action. He came home and began afresh, learning step by step the tortuous ways of finance, floating a small company to get the capital to purchase the options on the areas where he knew he could get the precious stuff he had found. It had been a stiff fight, the business of convincing a few Englishmen that he held the secret of mighty wealth, but he had done it, living almost from hand to mouth, borrowing here, borrowing there, sinking all his tiny savings into the venture, risking everything and luring men by his gift of speech against their cooler judgment. It was all, he reiterated, a matter of personality. If men saw you were in dead earnest, if they *felt* you believed in yourself, they would do the most extraordinary things. One man, a dour and cautious Scotsman, had sold Consols to invest with him. Another had done something even more reckless for an Englishman, he had sold *houses* and bought shares. As a rule, he said, an Englishman would not sell houses to secure an option on Paradise. And then, when he had given lectures, had written article after article, had fought single-handed against the non-metallic filament clique, he had promoted his international company, had travelled all over Europe, over Germany, France, Spain, and the Low Countries, seeking out men of capital to watch his interests in their native lands, men of brains ready to manufacture when he gave the word. Now it was all done, the company was an accomplished fact, shares were being bought even by investors, by brokers and directors of big electrical concerns, the underwriters were sanguine and financial editors were asking for particulars. He was safe now to a certain extent, and yet, he admitted, he regarded this as only the beginning of his career. She opened her eyes at this rather, but he repeated that it was, in his opinion, only the beginning.

"Why?" she asked, as she stirred her coffee. "You'll have bags of money now, I s'pose. Surely you don't want to go all through it again?"

"Money?" he said, his eyes strained with the long recital. "Money! I'm not doing this just for money. It's something quite different I'm after. No man could have done what I've done just for money."

"Of course it means a good position," she admitted a little doubtfully.

He turned to call for his bill and to hide a look of disappointment which he could not help crossing his face.

"When I first came to London from the mines," he said, turning to Minnie again, "I began a book which I shall call *Success, by a Successful Man*. Well, in that book I am not even mentioning money. I am of the opinion that the man who regards riches as success is damned. It is not even power or fame, 'position' as you call it, because when I began that book I had neither. Money and power and position are only the outward signs of what a man is. The rich fool, the titled ass, have no interest for me. It is the man with Ideas who has my love and respect. Ideas are the prime mover of this world we live in; without them we are mere masses of inert ineptitude."

"Has a woman got to have ideas to get your—respect?" she asked gravely.

He was paying his bill, and she watched him carefully counting the change left from his sovereign.

"A woman?" he repeated abstractedly, slipping a shilling under his plate. "A woman! Let us get out of here and go to a music-hall, and I'll tell you what a woman must have."

"I should like to know," she said as he opened the door.

DURING the few minutes while the hansom was whirling them towards Leicester Square, their brains humming with wine, coffee, and the motion through the glittering streets, they did not speak. He was taking her to the Empire, another haunt of the cosmopolitan of limited means. The girl was excited more than she knew by the story Anthony Gilfillan had told her. Something within her responded to the indomitable will of the man. Pride in knowing him and being his confidant, pride in his winning battle with dullness and inertness, pride engendered by the mere swift motion of the cab; these were the *motifs* of her exaltation as she jumped, almost into his arms, at the entrance.

Men and women, some in evening dress, were going up the great gilded staircases with them, solitary men of distinguished appearance, men carelessly dressed and smoking pipes, young men in groups, exquisites smoking cigars and laughing uproariously at some inane smoking-room jest. There were solitary women, vociferously attired, making their way up to the promenades, women of undeniable beauty and grace who lived the strenuous lives of West-End courtesans. These scanned Minnie with a glance that seemed never to pause, yet which saw everything, from her sailor hat to her worn low-heeled shoes. And when they pushed through the doors into the great gilded auditorium, Minnie saw yet more women of this type moving slowly to and fro, leaning on the backs of the seats, passing into the lounges, a ceaselessly moving kaleidoscope of women.

They went to seats near the front of the circle, and Minnie found herself gazing for the first time in her life at a ballet. For a while she sat silent, stupefied by the blaze of colour, the intricacy of the movements, the sensuousness of the music.

"A ballet," he replied to her vague query. "You see, there are no words, you know. Everything is expressed by gestures and movements of the body and limbs. I am sorry we missed the beginning of it."

"What's it about?" she whispered timidly.

"They call it——" he looked at the programme in his hand, *"Parthenia,* and it seems to be a sort of review of Woman throughout the ages. This is a duel, I think. Yes, you see, they draw."

The scene was the illumined court of a castle of old Italy. In and out of the many portals there danced fantastic figures, on balcony and terrace cooed lovers, in silk and velvet, singing a sweet minor love-song to the lilt of the viol and the soul-piercing scream of the flute. In the foreground two men stood confronting one another with long daggers, swaying to and fro, advancing and retreating, their faces drawn with agony, the while a bevy of fair women stood and watched. One of the men was clad in the absurd garments of a mediæval jester and poetaster, those poor devils with a knack for repartee and stinging verse who followed a ducal court as boys turn cart-wheels behind a *char-à-banc,* and his mask, just flung aside, grinned from the stones where it lay. His adversary stood stiffly angular and stark, a silhouette in grim black, his sardonic features writhen and set, his dagger flashing in the many-coloured lights. And as they met thus, a woman among those who watched, a woman superb in body and face, whose dark hair was a midnight of starry gems, on whose alabaster breast there blazed a cross of diamonds, came towards them with light step and rhythmic motion, indicating in the subtle hieroglyphs of her art woman's hot passion and fearful joy in bloodshed. In languorous measure the music swept on, the fantastic figures in their quaint garbings flitted in and out among the fairy lights, the daggers darted to and fro, as the assailants stabbed and stabbed until at length, soft thud-dings of the drums heralding a change of motive, the black phantom sprang and struck, and the merry-andrew in his gay-coloured dress staggered and fell dead. And then the music in crepitating crescendos held the audience steady on the crest of the emotional wave while the woman, the

Parthenia of the ages, flung herself in wild abandon upon the victor and received his dagger in her breast.

As the curtain fell and the music crashed and thundered and the audience clapped louder and louder, Minnie found herself withdrawing her hand in some confusion from Anthony's, whither it had fluttered in the excitement of the moment. The dull red colour slowly flooded her face and neck as she sat back in her seat and waited for him to speak and break the spell.

But for a space, he did not speak. He himself had been somewhat carried away by the magic of theatric art, inured as he was to Wagner and the intensity of Spanish-Italian opera. The dramatic anticlimax, the cruel contrast between the *ensemble* and the episode, the fidelity to the primitive passion of humanity of it, had gone home, and he was silent. He sat there in his favourite crushed attitude, his deep eyes staring moodily at the figures on the curtain, unconscious of the girl at his side. A movement of her shoulder where it touched him roused him.

"There in part," he remarked, "is what I think a woman must be." A memory of the lodging-house keeper's daughter flitted before him for a moment, but he ignored it and continued: "There too is what many women are, evil in life, yet redeeming everything in death. Parthenia! H'm! The man who wrote this thing out has brains. What d'you think?" he added suddenly, rousing still more and taking her hand again. "What do *you* think— of it all?"

And she, with softened features downcast and the slowly deepening colour flooding her body, said nothing in reply, for it was one of the few moments in her life when she thought nothing, only felt.

"You're not bored? You're glad you came?" he asked quickly.

"Rather!" she answered in a quick breathless whisper. "Don't—don't hold my hand, please."

But he held it, and the curtain rising as the lights dimmed, continued to hold it for some time. The new scene was a Fête Champêtre, such as you see in Antoine Watteau's "Prince of Court Painters." But it was Watteau in movement, Watteau interlaced with light music

and that wonderful thing which is neither movement nor
music nor colour—the play of emotion on the human
face. To show folly was the artist's intention here it
seemed, and to provide a way of gradual descent from the
high emotion of the previous adventure. For here woman
was soft and of a sugary pinkness, she sat upon the
mossy banks while satined young gentlemen bent in adora-
tion before her. Through the glades of the great green
forest the sullen red of the château roof could be seen
glowing, boys and girls in tinsel dresses pursued one
another with gilded darts, the pink arms of the ladies
twined picturesquely about the necks of the satined young
gentlemen, who were resigning themselves to a future
of endless caress, when the clear cry of a horn tore across
the gossamer tissue of the music, and the king entered
with his foresters and gentlemen. And there came the
change as this king of theirs, in his feathered hat and
laced shirt and diamond shoe-buckles came swaggering
by. Each lady, springing to her feet, made her deep obeisance to his majesty, and majesty, offering his hand to
kiss, signified by a gesture that he would accept her company. And as he passed into the forest again towards
the red-roofed château, he was surrounded by the fair
false creatures who had smiled and languished with the
satined young gentlemen so short a time ago. And the
pretty effeminate affair came to an end with soft lamenting music as the children pelted the dolorous satined
youths with their gilded darts and tinsel balls.

Instinctively his hold of her hand had loosened as they
watched this ballet of artificial and false sentiment. The
mind sometimes reacts very swiftly to external stimulus.
If he had not let her hand slip away she would have read
into the retention some of the insincerity of the scene before them. And he would have thought her a little common if she had left her hand there indefinitely, as common
as if she had snatched it from his grasp at the first. The
grossest of men and women, however dense and obdurate
in response to eye and voice, are marvellously sensitive
to touch. It is a circuit of infinitesimal resistance, yet
capable of carrying currents of prodigious volume and
pressure. Not for nothing is the hand-clasp, the shoulder-

touch, the waist-girdling arm, the kiss, held by us to be potent factors of drama. Physical touch is indeed the coarsest, yet at times the subtlest, method of communication betwixt soul and soul.

"Do you like it?" he asked. "Is it like anything that you had imagined?"

"I'd never thought *what* it would be like," she answered, smiling. "I like it though. It takes you out of yourself, doesn't it?"

"That is the intention. We come here to get away from ourselves, our ordinary office-worn selves, and see some of the light and colour of life. For myself I like this place, and I like the ballet. For you mustn't imagine you can go anywhere in London and find things like this." He indicated the stage. "Most of these ideas come from the Continent, where ideas are more common than in England. The people who live in the suburbs, now, would think all this very immoral, wouldn't they?"

"I suppose it is," said Minnie soberly.

"Indeed it is nothing of the sort. It is just what you bring to it and no more. Art by itself can only produce art. When the sun shines on a swamp and breeds disease, you don't blame the sun, do you? Well, it is just the same with this sort of thing. Because some people abuse Art, that is no reason why we should not enjoy it."

"Then you'd do this? come here, anyway? You think religious people, and people like Mrs. Wilfley, are wrong?"

"Mrs. Wilfley?" he queried. "Why do you couple her with religious people?"

"Why, would *she* come here?"

"Just as often as she can get some one to take her," he replied, with a slight smile.

"But she writes for religious papers. That book of hers is full of religious ideas."

"Yes, but . . . You don't understand, I suppose. People can't be labelled, my dear girl. Give yourself a label, now."

"Me?"

"Yes. I have here in my pocket, let us suppose, a lot of labels. You must choose one. Religious, Proud, Humble,

Moral, Immoral, Careless, Strict, and so on. Which one would you pin on yourself?"

Minnie knit her brows. The curtain was up again and a white clown, his eyes and mouth crimsoned, was busy with his patter. She felt the force of her companion's argument, but he could not go far enough to apply the argument to every one she knew. The natural indolence of the human mind, together with its natural cattishness, confirms the habit of labelling people and makes it irresistible.

"Mind, a label need not be a libel," Anthony put in, and she nodded and went on thinking.

"It's not so easy done," she decided. "I suppose it's because we know too much about ourselves."

"Partly. Also because we are too close to ourselves to sort ourselves out. But what you will find, if you keep your eyes open, is that labels are of no use. You must meet each person as something unique in the world."

"Oh, there's a lot alike," she insisted.

"To you."

"Really."

"You will find your mistake."

"Does it matter?"

"Ah!" He patted his knee softly. "You are a strange mixture. I don't wonder you hesitated to label yourself."

"What label would you give a girl like me?" she asked.

"Well, you see, you wouldn't take any joy in watching two men fight for you, would you?"

She shook her head slowly.

"Nor would you run away from me if a King or a Grand Duke took a fancy to you?" he persisted.

She looked at him narrowly for a moment, then dropped her eyes towards her hands. He laughed softly.

"What label should I give you? Who can say? You are unique, with a uniqueness that responds to my own, and there is the charm. Shall we go out, or would you rather see the rest of the show?"

"As you like. I've had enough if you have. It's rather hot here."

They rose and walked slowly past the banks of faces watching the Clown, faces set in a smile of good-natured tolerance, breaking into ripples of laughter when he made his points. They walked through the slow-moving procession of the promenade to the exit, and Minnie's eyes were busy.

"What are all those girls?" she asked as they went down the staircase. "Just walking about like that?"

They were out in the street before he answered.

"Don't you know?"

She bent her head forward in a quick way she had and peered at him.

"Oh!" she said, and made no further remark. They walked on each busy with thoughts, each trying to recapture a certain mood which the departure had banished. She had developed enormously in the last three hours, her range of emotion had doubled, and she felt as though she were standing in front of a door waiting for it to be opened. And he, who had opened many doors, sometimes with a touch, sometimes with a sledge-hammer, was pausing as if in irresolution, his hand on the latch. He glanced at her.

She was walking with her head raised slightly, her small finely moulded chin thrust out. Had she been merely precociously coy she would have had her eyes bent on the pavement. So they walked on under the stars that looked down on the multitudinous uproar of the great city, two souls among millions, waiting for that supreme moment that comes, we know not when, "like a thief in the night," when our lips are touched with the divine flame and our hearts burn within us. Terrible and sublime thought, that every moment is supreme for some man and woman, every hour the apotheosis of some passion! Who can remain unawed by this colossal pageant of human love? Who can doubt again the divinity of his kind if this vision have been vouchsafed to him?

But the moment was not yet. Through Chandos Street up through the narrow winding Strand, the Strand we strive in vain to visualise, now it is gone, they walked through the press of people streaming homeward from the theatres. The night was noisy with wheels and hoofs, whistles and laughter, and the raucous yelps of newsboys. *"Grave News from Pretoria"* was the burden of the last,

Pretoria where an old man sat at a council board, an ominous enigma. Strange to say, Anthony Gilfillan did not buy a paper; he was occupied with other things. There was a lull in the roar when they reached the Law Courts, only the lumbering 'buses and scurrying hansoms interfered with the solemnity of the night. They looked up at the great gold face of the clock, and as they looked the hour of eleven tolled. The eleventh hour! A lad hot from Fleet Street rushed past them at top speed, his poster bearing the words *"At the Eleventh Hour."*

They turned into the dark entrance to the Inn. The gates were closed, the girl noted in dismay and laid hold of his arm. But he, knowing the custom of the place, jangled the bell, and they stood, dwarfed among the giant shadows, till the night porter opened to them. An old withered man he was, bent and oblivious, a remnant of City wreckage washed into this quiet nook each night, to open to late-comers and patrol the dark quadrangle.

She turned to Anthony, but he touched her gently.

"Just to the door," he whispered, and they went on through the chapel archway and across the cobbles to her door.

"Here," she said. "No more, please."

He put his arm about her, holding her face up to his in the darkness.

"What is it—what is it?" she whispered hoarsely, not knowing what she said.

"Here—you remember?—we met," he answered, and kissed her.

V

WHEN a girl is in love, when she wakes in the morning with a thrill of unreasonable happiness, the material effects, trifling though they be compared with the emotional cataclysm itself, are apt to prove trying to third persons of normal and limited perception. If she be a maid, things of worldly import, things like beds and salt-cellars, the corners of window-panes and the wicks of lamps, slip through her memory like ashes through a sieve. If a mistress, she has a wider range of catastrophe and generally uses it to the full. In either case, she presents to the third person a spectacle of tragic incompetence and irreclaimable futility. Mrs. Wilfley, whose descriptive powers drew largely from an apparently inexhaustible stock of *clichés,* had said once that it was "very beautiful to watch Love dawning in young hearts," that one felt instinctively (she meant intuitively), "that one had not lived utterly in vain, if one had been privileged, even in a trifling way, to unobtrusively assist some shy lover to the temple of Hymen."

Perhaps because Minnie was not shy, perhaps because her previous efforts in this direction had been chiefly imaginary, Mrs. Wilfley's language did not fit the situation during breakfast. That blend of calculation and sentiment, honesty and obliquity, fluency and ignorance, which eventually lifted her to eminence in journalism did not choke the development of feminine curiosity. She had been informed with disconcerting brevity, that Minnie was going out with Mr. Gilfillan. Her desire to learn how the evening had been passed might have been satisfied in peace and quietness had she abstained from a certain patronage, which arose from her conception of herself as an intellectual. She conceived herself as unbending to take an interest in the child. To her pain and mortification, the child behaved unfilially, blew up in fact, and refused details.

"I don't see," said the child after the explosion, wandering as she spoke into a dreamland of ineffable vagueness, "I don't see—what it's got—to do—with you, with anybody."

"You are very *brusque*," said the lady, retreating into *cliché*.

"Eh? What's that?" asked the child dreamily.

"To be plain, it means rude," was the nettled reply, as Mrs. Wilfley looked into the teapot. "And quite apart from that, it's ridiculous to make a secret of it." Mrs. Wilfley shook herself as though to shake off the contagion of the girl's mood. "Ridiculous! Tony will tell me all about it. He's a dear old friend of mine. Tells me all his affairs."

Minnie brought her gaze back to the realities of life and rested it upon Mrs. Wilfley.

"Then there's no need for me to say anything about it," remarked the girl, and rose from the table. She saw Mrs. Wilfley gathering herself together for a spring, so to say, a spring which generally landed her with a splash in a pool of sentiment, and Minnie dreaded the drenching.

"What is it to-day?" she asked in a matter-of-fact tone. "Give me something to type. I get sick of that line about coming to the aid of the party."

Mrs. Wilfley, switched away from the pool, took the chance of peace with alacrity.

"Here is my interview with Lady Gophir. Do you think you could make it out? It's rather abbreviated, you know. *W* means 'who' or 'which' according to the sense." Here she showed Minnie a sheaf of pages torn from a reporter's notebook. "And I've just scribbled in my impressions. This is the beginning," showing the last sheet but one, "and this is the end." And she held up the first.

Minnie examined the pages without enthusiasm.

"You can improve it if you care to try," Mrs. Wilfley said brightly as she left the room to dress. "I was too exhausted last night to do anything with it."

"Anything else?" asked Minnie, possibly in irony. Even she could see a hard day's work deciphering the interview, to say nothing of the proposed improvement, to which no doubt Mrs. Wilfley's work was susceptible.

When Mrs. Wilfley was gone, after trembling for a

moment on the verge of heart-to-heart monologues,
Minnie sat in front of the typewriter, her chin on her
hands, thinking, and, as was her habit, talking to herself.
Her eyes were fixed on the square of blue sky visible
where the top of the window was open, a square of blue
sky invaded at the corner by the grey beautiful roof of
the Record Office. It was a bright, blustering autumn
day, a day to call one out to the wind-swept country
roads where horse-chestnuts were falling in showers and
blackberries shone like jet beneath their leaves. No day
to sit in a chair puzzling at some other person's hasty
scrawls. Who was Lady Gophir, that her unhealthy preoccupation with fallen women should be of interest to
any one?

"I wish it was tea-time," Minnie said to herself softly.
"Oh, I wish it was tea-time!" She paused, and her eyes
that were watching a white cloud crossing the blue square
glinted with laughter. "So Tony tells her all his love-
affairs, does he? What a baby in long clothes she thinks
I am! Every girl fibs like that when she wants to cut
you out. I must ask him some time on Saturday. Let's
see. This is Thursday, to-morrow's Friday; two days to
get through. Oh, well!"

She rose, seized the manuscript and dropped into Mrs.
Wilfley's Chesterfield, frowning to concentrate her mind
on the writing. But it was of no use. Her mind refused
to concentrate. A mental view of Charing Cross Post
Office at six o'clock continually interposed itself between
her eyes and the paper. And then there was a step on the
stair and a gentle knock at the door. She stepped to the
door and opened it to a young man with a fair moustache
and a high double collar. He hesitated in the manner of
one who meets a stranger unexpectedly.

"Er—Mrs. Wilfley—is she in?"

"Just gone out."

"Well, I called about a little matter—p'raps you can
deal with it." He took a long envelope out of his breast
pocket, drew forth a strip of typed paper and began.

"Come in," said Minnie, and he did so.

"It's on business, I s'pose," she added.

"That's so. You see," he put down his hat on a chair

and showed her the long strip, "It's this thing she done for us for Reaver's Stomach Mixture. It's all right except it don't go into details enough. We want more medical terms, you understand. That's what we want, more medical terms, more realism."

"Oh," said Minnie sapiently. "I see. I'll tell her."

"F'rinstance," went on the young man. "This bit 'ere," he indicated the bit with his pencil, "it wants expandin'. She might make another par out o' that, I reckon. Something about the gastric juices and the parenchyma. See?"

"Oh, yes, I see," said Minnie again. "Anything else?"

"Yes. This 'ere," he indicated another passage lower down. "Now that's a bit over people's 'eads, that is. You can't put that on the back of toilet rolls, you can't reely."

"Back of what?" said Minnie, forgetting herself.

"Well, I know it ain't the sort of thing to discuss with a lady, but, you see, Mrs. Wilfley she's doin' the job and we can't let it stand as it is. I've made a note of it 'ere, see? A bit more popular like, more snap to it."

"Anything else?"

"You want to get rid o' me, I can see that," he replied, quizzing. "Busy?"

"Yes, rather."

"Oh, I see. Well, that's all. If you'll just tell Mrs. Wilfley and ask her to let us 'ave it by Monday, will you? Nice little place she's got here. Just suit me. 'Andy for the business. You 'ere for some time, I s'pose?"

"Very likely."

"Well. P'raps we'll see more of each other. What's on to-night? Anything special? I'm on most all free lists, y' know. Care for a run roun' the Tiv'li?"

Minnie regarded him with composure. She was admirably adapted in temperament and experience to deal with him. His was a type that she knew well.

"You are rapid?" she remarked, almost as though in admiration for his unexampled celerity.

"Yes, it's a 'abit. See a chance o' doin' a bit o' business, I'm on it like a bird. Same with the ladies. Always ask, is my motter; they can't eat you. As a rule, y' know, ladies take it as it's meant—kindly."

"Mrs. Wilfley, does she——?"

"Oh, no! She's an auth'ress, yer see. Besides, she knows the guvner. I always keep off the grass—good policy."

"Oh, she knows the guvner, does she? Does she go out with him?"

He opened his eyes and blew out his cheeks.

"You bet!" he said slowly. "Why, didn't you know that? 'E's away just now, you see, on the Continen'. Any time you care to look roun' for a cup o' tea!" He took out a card and gave it to her, a card giving an address in Whitefriar's Street. She took it and put it with the strip of paper.

"All right," she said. "I'll tell her."

He looked at her, the expression on his common smart face changing from easy familiarity to guarded indecision. His speech lost its careless trip and grew official again.

"Of course, anything I may say's in confidence between friends, I 'ope?" He looked at his watch. "Well, I must be off. Got to see a man at Shep'ard's Bush at twelve." He took his hat and smiled at her doggishly. "So I'll leave the lovely lady in her lonely tower, eh?"

He made an abortive effort to shake hands, but she did not move until he had reached the door. She stood there for a moment as he went down the stairs, and saw him pause at the bend, look up, smile doggishly again, hesitate as though he might return, and finally disappear. She closed the door and went over to her work again.

It was very mysterious to her, and she decided she must ask Anthony. She had an idea that he knew a good deal more about Mrs. Wilfley than Mrs. Wilfley knew about him. She had never reflected that advertisements did not write themselves. That Mrs. Wilfley did this sort of work seemed, for all that, strange.

"Reaver's Stomach Mixture!" she repeated to herself, her lips curling a little. Mrs. Wilfley's enthusiasm for this proprietary quack medicine was extreme, to judge by her eulogy on the strip. In her opinion it was, next to Magna Charta and the English Constitution, the most precious element of national life. You felt, on reading her burning words, that if some one died in defence of Reaver's Stomach Mixture, Mrs. Wilfley would not have been surprised. Nor would she. She would have promptly interested herself in a memorial to the hero.

"Frederick the Great once said," so ran the opening passage, *"that an army was like a snake, it travelled on its stomach. This is as true of civilians as of soldiers, as true of the Battle of Life as of the Battle of Trafalgar. How true it is only those know who have dropped behind in the march and are losing heart for the struggle. Why is this? . . . See how insidious are the means by which the Foul Spectre Disease makes his way into the Fortress of the Soul. . . . Even when the enemy is in full possession, the wretched victim is unaware of his condition."*

Minnie read the advertisement through and laid it on the desk by the typewriter. The humour of the thing did not strike her. She had not troubled to think who wrote advertisements, and, now that she knew, she dismissed the matter from her mind. It was of minor importance. As far as she knew she had neither Gastric Catarrh, Gastric Colic, Incipient Cancer, nor Gravel. Reaver's Mixture was irrelevant. "Are your Nerves worn to rags?" chanted Mrs. Wilfley in fat capitals at the head of one paragraph; but Minnie felt no response, no desire to throw herself unreservedly upon Messrs. Reaver's hands and try the efficacy of a trial bottle at one shilling and three halfpence. She took up the interview with Lady Gophir again. Did Lady Gophir take Reaver's Stomach Mixture? she wondered. Was it part of the great scheme for reclaiming Magdalens to dose them with that Golden Elixir? Certainly she must ask Anthony Gilfillan some questions. And when Minnie came to that conclusion for the tenth time in the course of an hour, she smiled and forgot the interview. There was a more interesting interview to ponder over, an interview that would begin by Charing Cross Post Office at six, and she sat for an hour dreaming.

Was she mad enough to believe that Anthony Gilfillan, a man who was on the eve of making a large fortune, would marry her? Was she besotted enough with pride to figure herself as mistress of a houseful of servants, stepmother to a girl at a boarding school, the equal of other financiers' wives?

To tell the truth she was not. She was a young girl for whom marriage had no intrinsic allurement. Nor had she an exaggerated opinion of her sway over men. She was not a fool or an idiot, and she would have been one or the other if she had been bashful and amazed because Anthony had kissed her. His attitude might possibly be enigmatic, but she knew her own feelings well enough, though she lacked the ability to analyse them. His intentions were part of him, and therefore acceptable to her. His dethronement from the imperial chair of Tiberius had not degraded him to the level of a common man. He was still of the royal blood, and therefore entitled to dispose of her future.

She closed her eyes, leaning back in the seat, and gave herself up to the genuine pleasure of anticipation. To-night would be happiness certainly, with talk of many things, including Mrs. Wilfley, but Saturday would be crucial. He had mentioned that he always spent the week-end out of town. He was, he said, one of the inventors of the week-end out of town. He had told her it was delightful for him to get back on Monday to the bracing air of the Metropolis after the Sunday stagnation. She had a tingling sensation of terror and pleasure blended as she thought of Saturday. Her mind evaded again and again the question, "What will you do?" She quieted it by trying to think what he was doing at that moment, and the logical counter-problem roused her. What was *she* doing? Nothing. After all, she was supposed to do as she was told if she wanted to be paid. She took up a sheet of paper, seated herself at the desk and began to translate the interview, page one.

Lady Gophir, it appeared, lived in Mount Street, where Mrs. Wilfley had seen her, "seated in her dainty pink boudoir which was a perfect bower of flowers, from clusters of cream roses to great sprays of stephanotis, all from the magnificent conservatories in Herefordshire. Lady Gophir has them sent up specially every day. 'I could not live without flowers,' she told me with a smile as she deftly arranged a great Persian bowl of yellow asters."

In short, Lady Gophir was experienced in interviews, and told Mrs. Wilfley, whom she suspected of vulgarity, just what that lady desired. They then warmed to their subject, which was Lady Gophir's projected Home of Reclamation to be built on some unprofitable land in a desolate part of Essex, where a distant view of the North Sea would compensate the inmates for the surging tide of Piccadilly. All the best people, so Mrs. Wilfley learned, were warmly interested in it. One might wonder why? Plain good food and clothing would be given, or rather loaned, the refugees. Lady Gophir almost shuddered as she said she dreaded *pauperising* them. Surely their lives were sufficiently evil and unhappy without a stranger, even a friendly stranger, pauperising them. Here followed an almost illegible reference to *panem et circenses,* of which Minnie made a hopeless muddle. Anthony Gilfillan, whom she interrogated on the subject during the week-end, told her it meant "Bred in Piccadilly Circus," but his chuckle told her he was making a joke at Mrs. Wilfley's expense, and she let it go at that. An hour passed in this way, and Minnie looked up to find the quaint little copper clock pointing to lunch-time and the breakfast dishes still unwashed.

"Can't do both," she muttered, and fell again to work.

At two o'clock Mrs. Wilfley was still out, but the interview was fairly coherent. Rather proud of such sustained labour, Minnie put on her hat and was going out to get some lunch, when she heard some one scampering up the stairs. It was a telegraph boy, and he came right up past the ecclesiastical architect's door on the right.

"Gooderich?" he said to Minnie as she stood withdrawing the key.

"Yes," she said, and took it.

"Reply paid," said the boy.

She opened the door again and shut it, looking round the room in a scared way she had when a new experience assailed her. It was her first telegram.

> *"Meet Westminster Office three—urgent, reply*
> *Gilfillan."*

The white reply form fluttered to the floor as she stood reading the message. She picked it up and spread it out on a corner of the breakfast-table. Taking a pencil she wrote her answer to

> *"Filament London*
> *   Coming, Minnie."*

and opened the door.

"How do you get to Westminster Bridge?" she asked the boy.

"'Bus or Underground," he replied, putting the telegram in his wallet.

"How long does it take?"

"Quart' of 'n 'our," he chirped, and clattered down again, whistling.

It was ten minutes past two. Minnie followed the boy down, left the key at the porter's lodge, and went out into the roar of Fleet Street. She would have a little lunch first, she decided, as there was plenty of time, so she turned into an A.B.C. and sat down.

Eating her scone and butter and drinking her tea, she sat turning over various solutions of the new position. She took the card he had given her the previous evening from her purse.

> ## THE GILFILLAN FILAMENT
>
> ### MR. *ANTHONY GILFILLAN*
>
> "FILAMENT   82 OLD QUEEN ST.
>   LONDON"   WESTMINSTER, S. W.

He had told her that it was close to the bridge, and now she was to go there and see him. Two or three times when the cup was near her lips she set it down again, as she grasped the significance of the fact that she was going there to see him. It would be an irrevocable step forward, this meeting in the middle of the afternoon.

She was glad she had gone to work on that interview. She wouldn't have liked the telegram to have found her in a lackadaisical fit. And then as she sat in the glow of this beautiful thought, a sudden possibility swept over her like an icy wind. Suppose something had happened that it was all over, that his wife had been found to be still alive, had come home and claimed him, that he had lost all his money. . . .

For a moment she sat still looking straight before her, waiting for her native common sense to rise up and push the cold fear gently back outside. If any of these things had happened, was it likely he would wire for her to go to the office to meet him? *Was* it likely? Already she had enough of the free-wit current in the world to know that in such a case she would have gone to Charing Cross Post Office, at six, and simply—waited in vain. In old stories, when the devil took people they were wont to vanish, which demonstrates the sound psychology of the old story-teller. In modern life, especially modern commercial life, when people go to the devil, they also vanish, and we hear of them no more; we, that is, who have been in merely social contact with them. So slowly but surely, Minnie regained her previous condition of sanguine expectancy, and finished her lunch with a piece of Russian pastry, the latter indicating the genesis of a reckless mood. After viewing the telegram from all points of her compass, she found herself unable to hit upon a satisfactory motive for sending it.

She looked at the clock and rose to leave. It was twenty-five minutes to three, and she wished to be on time. A paper-man told her to get on the Victoria 'bus and get off at the bottom of Whitehall. She climbed on top, and the blustering autumn wind made her hold her hat. It made her face glow, too, as it rushed eastward, carrying stray pieces of paper high in air and making the little flag on the 'bus rattle and slap sharply just over her head.

At the bottom of Whitehall, when the conductor called up the steps "Here y'are, miss!" she began to hesitate, and half unconsciously resented it. She felt aggrieved that in so serious a crisis her mind should be clouded by an uncertainty of route and the superficial shyness natural to strange surroundings. It put her at a disadvantage, and in his presence, in his own office in the plenitude of his power, she was alarmed lest she should become what she would

have called "jumpy." Her *aplomb* in matters of ordinary
daily life was not due to brutishness, mere dead insensi-
bility to psychic influence, but to a nice balance of recep-
tivities, the same balance which makes even little girls
sometimes behave sweetly to strangers, whom they hate,
makes them sometimes pause in a sentence about the gover-
ness and say, "Isn't that pretty?" pointing to the flowers
in a wet ditch. As Minnie walked down towards the park
gates at the end of Great George Street, she felt keenly
alive to the tactical advantage Anthony would have in this
interview.

"Oh, I wish I knew what it is he wants," she whispered
to herself. But she went on, holding her head high, for the
adventure still called to her. After all, was not this a
greater thing than would have ever happened to her up at
the factory? Whom could she meet who would be able to
intimidate her? And she went on round into Old Queen
Street, gaining courage as she walked.

Number 82 was a high narrow house on the western
side. On either jamb of the white door were painted names
—names of architects, of typists, and civil engineers.
Above was a long copper plate bearing the words in red
letters:

GILFILLAN FILAMENTS LIMITED

On a white board in black letters in the entrance hall was
the statement that the registered offices of the company
were situated on the top floor, and the reader was informed
also that he or she would only be seen by appointment.
Minnie read this gravely and went on upstairs. At the top
she once more encountered a door marked with the name
of the company. The name was getting on her nerves.

"It's as bad as Little Liver Pills," she muttered, and
pressed the bell-push.

A slide in a glass panel shot back and a young girl with
a spotty, cunning face peered out.

"Mr. Gilfillan in?" said Minnie, musing.

"What name, please?"

"Gooderich." The slide slammed to again.

In a short time, too short for Minnie to experience any
change of mood, the door was opened by the young person.

"Step this way, please."

She led Minnie along a linoleumed passage through a
door, then along a carpeted passage into an office where
two men sat at big desks each absorbed in calculations, and
thence to another door whereon was inscribed in fat red
letters, *"PRIVATE,"* and at the bottom in small italics,

Mr. Anthony Gilfillan.

The young person knocked, opened the door, and Minnie, with her habitual scared look round, entered. The
door closed behind her.

The room was small and exquisitely furnished. A red
Turkey carpet covered the floor, on either side of the fire-
place was a great leather chair, and the walls were hung
with etchings in wide mounts. A rose-wood desk stood
open by the window, littered with papers and supporting a
reading-lamp, a telephone and half a dozen speaking tubes.
The window itself was noteworthy, for it was of stained
glass, the design being Diogenes hunting for an honest
man with the aid of a Gilfillan Lamp. But the most noteworthy object in the room was Anthony Gilfillan himself,
as he stood with his elbows on the red marble mantel,
looking down at the wood fire that glowed and crackled in
the grate.

Minnie stood by the door for a moment wondering.
Was this really one of the secrets of his power, this
faculty of making a surprising situation? If he only drank
a cup of tea in a café he would do it in a way that made
the girl, the manager, and the cashier remember him. Wonderful discovery of modern life—publicity! For Anthony
Gilfillan it had passed from being merely a pleasing fancy,
a business proposition, an admirable policy. It had become
the measure of his existence. All things, from the High
History of the Holy Grail to the mysteries of the Upani-
shads, were for him the Instruments of Publicity. All
emotions, trained by his iron will, were units in an army
fighting for Publicity. Just now, an emotion had mutinied
and he was deliberating. He turned and faced the girl
standing by the door, so that she could see the haggardness
of his face.

"What is it?" she said, coming to him. "You sent for me. What for?"

"To see if you'd come," he answered slowly. "To test myself. Since last night I have been uncertain of myself. This cannot go on."

"What can't go on?"

"Sit down." He pointed to one of the great chairs and she seated herself. "What? I was speaking half to myself. This state of mind cannot go on. I cannot give my mind to my work. I have done nothing to-day. So I decided to settle it once for all. I could not leave the office for some hours." He waved his hand towards the telephone. "I wired to you to come to me. And you have come."

"Yes?" she said, looking at the fire.

"Will you come to me?" he asked, looking down at her. "I need you. And what appeals more to you, I think, you need me. I can help you to what you want, Life. I can show you many things. For a time we shall be happy, I believe."

"It's wrong," she whispered.

"It is up to you," he replied, staring at the fire. "To marry would be madness, I can see that. You are of a different type, a type quite as necessary as any other, especially to men like me. But . . ."

"No," she said.

"But as a rule," he went on, "girls like you have no choice."

"Well," she said, standing up in front of him, "have I got any choice if—if I say I'll come?"

"I said it's up to you, my dear," he answered, putting his hands on her shoulders. "Isn't that a choice? Or do you think, are you afraid, I cannot make good my promises?"

"No," she said, finding her vein at last. "I want to. I'm not afraid. I want to have a good time. But——" she paused, touching the edge of his coat with her fingers. Anthony Gilfillan followed her eyes and divined the cause of her trepidation.

"No," he said. "There are no buts. Why distress yourself like this? You are trying desperately to talk to me now as though we were equals, and this strange room frightens you." He shook her gently and her eyes returned to his. "Leave the thinking to me. Leave everything to me. Can you get into that mood?"

"Just do what you tell me?" she queried.

He nodded. "Just that," he said, and there was silence. He put his hand to her hair where it escaped from her hat, her plain little old sailor hat, and touched it lightly. Her small pale face was composed and her bosom heaved regularly. The unrest was dying out of the dark blue eyes as they fell and reflected the flames on the hearth.

So came the proposition to Minnie, in a guise she could scarcely have foreseen. She moved a little to one side, holding to his coat the while, that she might watch the red heart of the fire. She had been barely four minutes in the room, yet her attitude toward Anthony had undergone a change. Though he had insisted on her inferiority, yet— she felt nearer to him. The words "I need you," are as potent as ever, and Anthony Gilfillan had made a slip in psychology when he imagined that the converse "You need me," would weigh much. "I need you" changed the atmosphere, changed their relative positions, changed everything. As she stood looking into the fire, she began to see still further the possibilities of the new situation. The material side opened out before her. Here was this shrewd business man, this tireless inventor, a man who had built up a syndicate, master of those silent men outside, telling her that he needed her. And as her mind slowly grasped this new view it was startled and stimulated by the shrill buzz of the telephone. In a moment Anthony Gilfillan had grasped the receiver on his desk and began to talk.

"Hello, Hello! Yes, this is Filament. Yes, speaking to you now, Hello!" A pause, and Minnie stood motionless and tense. "Hello! Yes? Somebody else cut in, I think. Yes, this is Mr. Gilfillan. Is that Mr. Quaritch? Good afternoon, Mr. Quaritch. I say! Did you get my note? Yes?—Oh, really? . . . That's very interesting. Is he coming to town? . . . I see. Oh yes, I must see him before he goes out East again. Our *Light of Asia* Filament is the proposition for him you know. . . . Well, I'm engaged all this week. Shall we say Monday, at—let me see?" He turned over a scribbling diary on his desk. "Monday at twelve. How would that do? . . . Yes, certainly, I'll write him. I've been planning a trip East, you know, and it would simplify matters very much if we could get a representative in Pekin first.—What?—Oh, quite so. You did quite right. Anything extra, of course, I'll see goes through. What hotel is he staying at? Royal, Glasgow? Right. I'll write him this evening. How's everything in your section?—Good. Yes, all right. Good-bye."

He put the receiver back, pressed an electric button in the wall and sat down to write an entry in his diary. There was a knock at the door, and a trim young woman entered with pencil and note-book. Minnie regarded her with piercing interest. Here was another of Anthony's satellites, a mere cog in one of his many wheels. The girl stood at his elbow without uttering a word, merely whipping open her book and waiting. In an even voice he dictated a brief letter to Yuen Shi Loo, Esq., Royal Hotel, Glasgow, begging him to favour Gilfillan Filaments Limited with a call on Monday next at noon, when their Mr. Gilfillan would have much pleasure in going into the question of an Asiatic Agency already touched on by their Mr. Quaritch. They begged to enclose particulars of their *Light of Asia* patent, in which, no doubt, Mr. Yuen Shi Loo would be interested.

"Enclose *Light of Asia* No. 17 and the General Catalogue," he remarked in conclusion.

The young woman made a few more hieroglyphics in her book and departed. Anthony turned to Minnie, whose eyes were bright with interest.

"Well," he said, taking her hands. "What is the verdict?" She looked up at him.

"I wish I could help, here," she said.

"Here? No, I have something better for you to do. I do not share Mrs. Wilfley's opinion of you, you know. She is not competent to analyse a character like yours."

"You think I'm not capable, I suppose."

"That does not explain it. You can help me better by being my friend. I have not many real friends, you know," he went on, as though thinking aloud. "A man cannot in business. *Les Affaires sont les affaires.* I never see any of these people here except in office hours. It would not do."

The young woman, after a light tap, entered again with a basket of letters to be signed. Minnie watched her as she stood there with downcast eyes, and wondered what her thoughts were. She was a smart, graceful slip of a girl. A curb chain bracelet hung on her wrist and a ruby ring glinted on her finger. Engaged, evidently, Minnie surmised.

Anthony sat down and read each letter carefully, making a trifling emendation here and there, finally signing it with a scrawl. When they were all finished the girl took up the basket and retreated without a word.

"Send Mr. Fitchett in, please," said Anthony.

He turned and looked at Minnie.

"Time's up," he said, smiling. "I wish you would sit down." She did so, leaning forward and looking at him earnestly.

"Time's up?" she said curiously.

"Yes, it's too late to draw back now."

She leaned back in the chair and closed her eyes for a moment, letting herself drift quiescent in the stream of circumstance. It was a novel and delightful feeling to her, this surrender of will to a stronger power. In this mood she tasted to the full the flavour of adventure in her life. Curiously enough she recalled the strange, beautiful figures on the painted panels of that little café of Paoli's, the girls seated on thrones amid fountains and peacocks, girls wandering with their lovers through enchanted forests. A tap at the door aroused her. A young man with thin hair, brushed straight up, entered with papers.

"Oh, Mr. Fitchett—just draw up a chair will you. I'm going away for a few days. Shall be back on Monday morning at ten sharp. The chief matter is the Tunisian Contract. If Monsieur Couvrier calls to-morrow, you will have to go through the whole matter with him. His *pourparlers* with the Marseilles firm should be fairly complete, and it rests with him to bring pressure to bear upon them to take the goods from our licencees there. He has a prejudice in favour of British-made goods, you

know. Use tact, of course. Then with regard to the
Asiatic Agency. I have just spoken to Mr. Quaritch in
Glasgow and arranged to see Mr. Yuen Shi Loo here
on Monday. If a wire should come in the meantime, relay
it to this address."

"Very good, sir. Anything else?"

"Yes. This proposition from the Bullard Company of
San Francisco is worth taking up. They know the terri-
tory and can localise the publicity to much greater advan-
tage than we. We shall need a guarantee, of course. Mr.
Godalming can deal with that. He will be back from
Manchester to-morrow morning."

"Very good, sir."

The young man with the thin hair took up his papers,
permitted his eyes to flutter in Minnie's direction for a
moment, and then retired. Anthony Gilfillan leaned back
in his chair staring abstractedly at the figure of Diogenes
on the coloured window. He had arrived at a curious
condition of mind, this financial visionary. Almost against
his profoundest convictions he had succeeded, for like
most dreamers he had an underlying touch of pessimism
in his nature. Beyond his wildest hopes he had trained
his mind to one end, publicity. And now, with regard to
this girl whose frank unimaginative nature formed so
happy a contrast to his own experienced enthusiasm, he
found himself nonplussed. Publicity was not desired
here, he was aware. Mrs. Wilfley, if she heard it, could
be trusted to give it quite sufficient publicity among their
acquaintances. Mrs. Wilfley in this respect was his superior, he knew. She could make her way into privacies
and obtain advertising commissions where even his indomitable personality had failed to gain an entrance. In
this particular he admired her immensely, but he saw in
dazzling clearness the need of keeping her ignorant of
this present adventure. He turned suddenly to the girl
and found her watching him intently.

"What am I to do?" she asked.

"Go back," he said. "Go back and wait for Saturday.
Can you do that?" He rose and leaned over the chair
where she was sitting. For some moments they looked
into each other's eyes without speaking, and then he

stood up, and spread out his hand with a gesture of help-lessness.

"Can I have forgotten?" he said dreamily. "Can I have forgotten? Or have I never learned? My dear." He took her hands and drew her up to him. "My dear, what can I say to you, you little snow-flower? Why do you watch me? Are you afraid, after all?"

"Go back?" she repeated. "I don't understand."

"Will you ever? What do we know of romance, we two? And yet we will never know each other save by romance. That's why I say go back. Here," he stopped, unlocked a drawer in his desk and took out some bank-notes. "Take these, buy whatever you like, and be ready on Saturday."

"What—what shall I buy?" she stammered, holding the thin crackling papers.

"Buy? Romance, my child. Ribbons, flowers, scents, silks, chiffons, rings for your fingers and bells for your toes."

She looked up at him with a smile breaking from her lips and eyes, a smile of comprehension.

"Is that romance?" she asked. "Was I right after all, when I said it was money did everything?"

She looked at him and laughed in his face. "Wasn't I right? What's the good of anything—without it?"

He stared at her. Even he, clear-headed as he was, had never fastened to a prime truth as this girl had done. The rosy mists of illusion had clung about his eyes so that he still talked of the utter irrelevance of money to the soul of man. He was like Mrs. Gaynor, like Mrs Wilfley, an idealist, while this smiling slip of a girl in her cheap worn dress and the crackling bank-notes in her clenched hand, was instinctively a realist. She might give him the purple buskins of imperial romance while she thought of him regardless of time and condition, but instantly, when the dream condensed to fact, when they met face to face, she could only be reached by the cash nexus, by dinners and theatres, by things that cost money. Love in a Cottage. Noble Poverty and conjugal struggles with the world, the splendid friendships which keep artists from self-destruc-tion and inspire their finest works,—all these things were

mere vague outlines to her, she curled her lip slightly at
their approach. That she loved him was indisputable, but
her love was not the supreme surrender which many
would have it, the deathless clinging many think it to be.
She was Danaë in her tower of brass, and Jove himself
could only enter in the form of a shower of gold.

"What's the good of *anything*—without it?"

And as they stood there she recovered her position. He
had been her master while she sat in the chair with her
eyes closed listening to his sharp staccato speech through
the telephone and to his subordinates, her master when
he had caressed her and called her his "child." Now she
was his mistress. She saw more clearly than he the exact
poise of their attraction, the fulcrum of their relationship,
the metallic pivot on which they were balanced, and she
smiled into his face with blithe triumph at his discomfiture. He roused himself in a moment.

"You really believe that?"

She waved the notes before his eyes.

"You see!" she said. A thought crossed her mind, and
she touched each of the notes with her forefinger, counting them. He watched her, amused at her sedate pleasure.

"You see!" she said again, and rolling them up stuffed
them in her purse.

"You haven't even said thank you," he said gravely.

"Haven't I?" She bit her lower lip, and her slow flush
mounted her cheek. A sharp peremptory ring at the telephone made them jump. Anthony looked at his watch.

"You've had twenty minutes of my time," he exclaimed, taking the receiver. "Saturday now, don't forget.
Saturday noon." He turned to the instrument and talked
swiftly for some moments.

When he looked round she was gone.

He threw himself into one of the big chairs and watched
the fire under his hand.

"Of course, I might have known that I would have no
other attraction for her. She is only a chrysalis just now.
When she has money to spend she will be another creature, with wings probably. Well, I shall have what I need,
psychic change. What is it to me if she has wings? Wings
are pretty. Money! The little vampire! And yet, no. She

has a pride. She could not be bullied, I am sure. One ought to call her grasping, callous, mercenary, yet one doesn't. Why? Pride, I suppose. What a study her temperament is!"

There was a tap at the door, the young man with thin hair entered and they proceeded to discuss the draft of a new advertisement.

"I had a very pretty fancy just now," said Mr. Gilfillan. "What do you think of a girl with gossamer wings caught in a tangle of golden filaments, eh? Light caught in a net, you see?"

"Excellent, sir!" said the young man.

"Publicity!" remarked Anthony Gilfillan.

VI

MRS. GAYNOR was sitting in her front room in her rocking-chair, reading. Outside in Maple Avenue the leaves were being blown about and defying the efforts of an old man to sweep them into little heaps. Now and again she would look up and watch him through her curtainless windows, a bent rheumatic old mortal, feebly battling with the gusts. When she looked at him she imagined she saw a Parable. He was Humanity toiling to accomplish something which the winds blew away. Then she would go on reading her book. She was glad of the wind, for her Monday washing was done and the clothes on the line in the back garden were being blown taut by it, and by evening they would all be dry. Her neighbours said she was rather "near" to do her own washing, for they were sure she could afford to pay some one else to do it. But Mrs. Gaynor went on her way serenely, doing her washing in less time than her neighbours took to steep it, and then sat down to read a book. Little Hiram was seated on his hassock doing a lesson. Sometimes he would rouse up with an "Oh, Ma, how's this?" and she would bend down to show him how. When he looked up and said quickly:

"Ma, there's Minnie Gooderich!" his mother looked up too, and saw Minnie coming up the path.

"Mercy! So it is. And isn't she tittivated out? Get up and open the door, child."

"Well now, if you haven't struck oil, Minnie! Sit down, dear, and we'll have a cup of tea."

Minnie sank into the rocking-chair and patted the boy's cheek, as he stood smiling beside her.

" 'Ullo," he said genially. "Where bin?"

"Oh, ever so many places, Hiram—where'd you think?"

"Not 'Merica, eh?"

"No, not America. Not nearly as far as that. Mrs. Gaynor," Minnie turned to where Mrs. Gaynor was busy with her spirit-lamp, "where do *you* think I've been?"

"A department store, I should think, for one place," said the quiet lady, looking at the girl's clothes.

"I should think so, but I've been to the seaside too."

"I thought you'd gone to work at Mrs. Wilfley's."

"Yes, so I have, but I'm leaving there, I think."

"Why, don't she suit?"

"She doesn't a bit. We've had a row."

"And she's paid you off?"

Minnie shrugged her shoulders.

"No, she hasn't."

"Well, I'm sure I can't imagine where you've picked up the style along with those things."

Minnie smoothed down the skirt with a smile.

"Do you like it?"

"It's just perfection. And a bracelet, too!"

"It's real. You see, Mrs. Gaynor, I'm going to have a good time. A friend of mine's given me some money."

"She's a real friend now."

"It isn't a she."

"Hiram, go right out, and take your hoop with you. You can finish that cyphering by and by."

Mrs. Gaynor went on with her spirit-lamp and tea-things and allowed Minnie to take her own time.

"I'm not going to be married," she broke out at length, and still Mrs. Gaynor kept silence.

"Mrs. Gaynor, say something," said the girl. "I s'pose you think I'm frightfully wicked?"

"What do you want me to think? What have you come back to me for?"

"Because I wanted to talk to you about it. Mother, she'd be wild about it, I s'pose."

"Mothers are poor things, aren't they, child? How can I help you? Is he a rich man?"

"Yes, he'll be very rich soon."

"Then why don't he marry you?"

"We don't want to be married. He's got a little girl. His wife died a long while ago. We want to be just friends. I told you, I told you, it's to see the world I want. I s'pose I *am* wicked, but I don't care, and—I thought you'd understand, from what you said."

The girl paused after her outburst and sat with her face

in her hands. Mrs. Gaynor came over and put her hand on her shoulder.

"Minnie," she said in her even voice. "Are you real certain you don't care?"

"No—I don't."

"Then I can't do anything. I always thought you were a queer child and needed careful looking after, and I'm sure of it now. What's worrying you, if you don't care? Other women have done the same thing. Sometimes they've bitten off more than they could chew, and then they've gone down and down. Sometimes, they've won through and it's been for the best. But it's a big job, child. *You* can't come to anybody for help, you know. This man, is he a real man, or only a whittling?"

Minnie raised her face, put up her hands, and unpinned her gay hat.

"He's a real man, as you call it, and he's got brains as well as money."

"But I can't see why you don't go to him."

The girl put the hat down on the table and lifted her face again to Mrs. Gaynor's earnest look.

"I don't go to him," she said proudly. "He comes to me. He needs me. I can't explain it at all. He is very lonely for all his big business and his brains. He wants me to help him to live. No, that doesn't explain it. But when we went away on Saturday, and we were down at Clacton, I understood it plain enough. We were so happy. He can talk and I can talk too when I'm with him. We walked on the sands in the dark, and he told me so many things, and I told him things, too. It was never like that— before, you know. He was just like a boy telling about his troubles. But this morning, when he left me at Liverpool Street and went away to his office, I felt as if I couldn't go on to Mrs. Wilfley, and I was lonely and wanted to talk to some one who'd understand. So I came out here."

Mrs. Gaynor looked into the teapot as though its dark polished interior held the solution of her difficulty. In accordance with her habit, she held her peace for a moment after Minnie had ceased speaking. The lid of the copper kettle began to flutter, a thin and beautiful jet of the steam came from the spout and hung, cumulous, in the atmosphere. Mrs. Gaynor fixed her eyes upon this as she began to speak.

"A long while back, Minnie, when I was a girl, I knew a school teacher like you. She was mighty clever, and when she went from Concord to the seminary at Boston she just swept the board with her essays and literature work. Her family were a rather united one as a rule, and couldn't make her out anyway. When she was through they naturally expected her to come back and get married same as other girls. She came into the store where I was selling underwear, and she gave me a shock same as you did just now when I saw you in those clothes. She came right on up to my corner, and when she saw me she smiled and sat down to have a talk. She was going to Europe, she said, and was laying in a stock. I said folks generally laid in stock on the other side, and she said that was so and went on talking about her friends. She asked me how the 'old folks' were, and I told her she knew as well as I did I hadn't any, for they never came back from Sacramento after—'49. That was the gold year—I s'pose you've never heard of it. Well, then I saw something was wrong with Terry—her name was Teresa—and just let her talk away. At last she said he was outside in the phaeton and she'd have to go, but I was to come and see her at the hotel. When the store shut, and it was some open in those days, I went along. A grand place, all maple and mahogany panelling, and thick carpets on the stairways and landings, and Terry was in a big suite right over the vestibule. And, do you know, Minnie Gooderich, that girl told me the very same story as you have. She was going to have a real good time and she didn't care one rap for what people 'ld think, only she wanted to tell me, just because she felt I was safe and had never been very censorious. When she'd finished she asked me what I would do, and I asked her back if he was man or a stick. He worshipped the ground she trod on, she said, and I told her that was no good to the ground. I asked her how long it would last, and she turned and got back on me by crying she didn't care about how long or how short, she was just going to drift. So I said, 'Well, Terry, by that you mean, if it isn't one man, it's another.' And she said, 'Well?' and I picked up my umbrella and went straight home. I'm afraid I was a little censorious in those days, when I was younger. I had no patience with a girl who'd deliberately spoil her career that way. Well, she came a good deal to the store and bought little things as an excuse to talk to me, until the day they sailed for Liverpool. The last time she came in she gave me an address in Paris where they were going, and I was to be sure to come and see her some time. She'd got all her smiling courage back by that, and all my black looks didn't signify. And the strange thing was that when I tried to imagine that girl's family, all crazy with the worry and disgrace, I couldn't. I was taking her point of view in spite of myself."

The kettle needed attention, and Mrs. Gaynor rose to make the tea. Minnie watched her with strained attention, her palms pressed between her knees.

"Mind, child, I'm telling you the truth and thinking the truth at the same time, and so I don't believe it will do you any harm to hear it. I didn't know as much as I do now, but I had the Light even then and held my peace. My way was plain enough, and I walked in it. I was always for the quiet side of life. When I was married and my husband came over here, he got word of Terry. He brought back a book he'd bought which she'd written herself, and do you know, Minnie, it was wonderful. It was just the story of a quiet New England girl and how she had become a nun. There was a piece written by a Frenchman in the front, and he told how the writer had come to Paris, no one knew how, and settled among them, and how she had attracted a lot of young men round her who listened when she talked and got ideas from her. The Frenchman said he couldn't explain it in the usual way, but she did them all *good*. She hadn't much time, for she was teaching folks English all day and the young men used to come in in the evenings. I guess they pretty near worshipped Terry, from what that Frenchman said. And when she took sick and died, they all went to her funeral, a whole string of them, with wreaths. And then they found this story in her room, and they got it printed and translated, and there it was."

Mrs. Gaynor paused again to pour out the tea, and Minnie waited for her to go on.

"Now I expect you're wondering what Terry's story's got to do with your case, eh? Well, it showed me that we can never be sure what a girl's vocation is in the world. If we were all cut off one stick it 'ld be an easy matter. But we aren't anything of the sort. Every single one of us is a new and wonderful creation, and it 'ld be a *miracle* if we fitted right into the place where we dropped, wouldn't it now?"

"Yes, I s'pose so. But I can't write books and all that."

"Who said? No one ever knew she could write anything worth while, though to be sure no one would have been surprised. It was her *influence* that made those young men flock round."

"You do take her part," said Minnie, accepting a cup of tea from Mrs. Gaynor's hand.

"No, child, I don't, any more'n I take yours. I'm just sitting here trying to see your view of it, and it reminded me of Terry. From what I could find out, she had a hard struggle for two or three years, but then I can't see myself what that's to do with it. She might have had more trouble if she'd stayed in New York and married. People don't ever seem to realise that doing what's right's no guarantee against misfortune. Look at me, for instance. My way's always been along a quiet road, and yet, I've had a terrible struggle at times, especially when my husband had small-pox and died when Hiram was six months old. It's the people who're comfortable who have time to worry over little trivial things. All the talking in the world wouldn't change your plans, I'm quite sure. You wouldn't have come out here unless you'd made up your mind."

Minnie gave a short laugh as she stirred her tea.

"You seem to think I'm in for it anyway," she said.

"Deep sorrow means deep joy as well, child, for those who find the Light."

"Light? What Light is it you mean?"

"I don't think you'd understand yet, Minnie. Your mother asked me the other day just the same question. She said, 'Is it conversion you mean?' I said, 'No, not quite conversion, because I've never been converted, and you can't judge by things you've never experienced.' It is thought-power, I should say, which helps you to understand yourself. And when you can do that, why"—here the quiet-voiced woman stood up, her grey-green eyes opened wide towards the light, and her serenity touched with the fire of a profound emotion—"why everything is as plain as plain can be. That's why we call it the Light. Now you are in the dark, you can't see what's going to happen. Some day, perhaps, you'll get the Light."

Minnie went on drinking her tea and looking out of the window. Mrs. Gaynor's explanation of her own mental evolution was not particularly clear to the girl, but that perhaps did not matter. Mrs. Gaynor's genius was subliminal; her influence was catalytic. She seemed to effect, by her presence, changes of soul-periods in which she herself had no part, remaining quiescent at the back of things. She was indeed the right person for Minnie to seek at this time, for she was the antithesis of Anthony Gilfillan, the dynamic giver-out of energy, the restless dreamer. She was static and receptive. Her mental pictures were etchings, quiet landscapes set against the dry unearthly Light of which she so often spoke. And as she sat a little back in the shadow near the fire-place and looked out at the driving leaves, she had one of those pictures clear-cut before her mind, a picture of herself and her husband seated on the verandah, he with his face raised from his paper as he listened to her justification of Terry. It passed quickly enough, even as Mrs. Gaynor set down her cup and looked at Minnie with a smile.

"I don't know how it is, Mrs. Gaynor, I'm sure, but it does me good to talk to you. And besides, you know, in a way you're responsible for this, because if you hadn't sent me to Mrs. Worrall and so on to Mrs. Wilfley, I shouldn't have met Anthony."

"We're all responsible that way, but it doesn't amount to a row of pins. Responsibility's like a string we can only see the middle of. Both ends are out of sight."

"Yes, that's true, but I can't help thinking of it, all the same. Have you seen mother lately?"

"Just passing."

"I think I'll look in and see her."

Mrs. Gaynor looked at her in surprise. "Like that?"

"Well, why not? It's all black."

"It's a gay black, child, with those feathers. Oh well! Go on, go right in then. I was only thinking how much English women value mourning."

"Will you come in too?"

"Surely. But wouldn't it be better to send Hiram and ask your mother to step in and have a cup of tea, here?"

"Yes, if you like."

Mrs. Gaynor went out to beckon to the hoop-trundling Hiram, who had flashed at intervals across their field of vision.

Minnie suddenly became aware of a nervous aversion to meeting her mother. That rather round-shouldered and insignificant figure presented to her a novel and disturbing front. Her mother of course was an honest woman. She was, moreover, her mother, and would scan her daughter's face with a merciless searing gaze. It appears, therefore, that a daughter who does not care, for whom the stony path of conventional virtue has no allurements, whose contempt for her mother is above the average, can nevertheless flinch from the ordeal of encounter. Why was this? Not vulgar fear: Minnie's reserve of pugnacity was enormous. Not economic dependence: she could feel against her flesh the gratifying abrasion of three of the remaining bank-notes. Not contrition: when a woman is well dressed contrition is with her a mockery and a sham. Not even physical unfitness, for Mrs. Gaynor's tea was mild and Minnie never felt better in her life. What then? I think it must have been that the contrast between herself and her mother would be so sharp that she doubted her ability to "carry it off." And then if she were to . . . but as to the upshot of offering her mother money she had not the imagination to divine.

Mrs. Gaynor returned. She knew the value of a hiatus in a heart-to-heart talk, how often it slackens a taut thread or bridges a perilous gap. Minnie felt the relief of her absence for a moment, and turning round set the feathery hat over on the head of the sofa somewhat in shadow. She remembered this act afterward; she remembered also that almost the first glance of her mother's eyes went straight at the nodding plumes. At first nothing was said while they waited for Mrs. Gooderich. Minnie wished Mrs. Gaynor would speak, but to tell the truth, Mrs. Gaynor, who was observant and had seen the postman deliver a letter at No. Eleven that morning, was slightly apprehensive of "a scene." She knew it would be better and more decorously played in her house than in theirs.

"You didn't write to your mother, I suppose?" said she at length.

Minnie shook her head. "Why?"

"I saw the postman go in this morning after he'd passed me," said the lady quietly finishing her tea and turning to the spirit-lamp.

"Oh!" said Minnie, quite unmoved.

And then Mrs. Gooderich in her weeds appeared and came up the path.

Something made Minnie, when the door opened, stand up.

"How is it you're here?" said Mrs. Gooderich, sitting down on the sofa. "I thought you'd got a place with Mrs. Wilfley."

"That's right, so I have."

"Have you? Then why does she write to me to tell me you've gone away with some man, eh?" And she drew an envelope from her pocket and held it out.

"Is that what she says?"

"Yes, it is, and I can see it's true."

"Well, don't shout, mother."

"Shout! Wouldn't it make anybody shout? To bring a child up respectable, to bear with her every whim, and take her sauce, and then have a letter like that from a stranger? And your father not cold in his grave. You know you ought to be at home with me; and I'm quite sure if you'd only been civil to people at the factory, you could have stayed on. Ethel Tanner's gone back."

"Mother, if you want to know why and how Et'iel Tanner's gone back, I can tell you, but I don't think you'd like to hear it. Leave her out of it."

Mrs. Gooderich looked at her daughter's composed, colourless face for a moment without speaking. Minnie, in spite of her apprehensions, was "carrying it off." Her

new black dress, with its high-necked collar and its skirt
clinging to the hips and trailing a little behind, gave
Minnie, as she stood there looking down on her mother, a
tall and commanding appearance. With a characteristic
lack of dramatic instinct, Mrs. Gooderich had placed herself in the most ineffective position she could have chosen.
Letters, indignation, maternal authority—all were discounted by this, that Minnie was better dressed and she
towered over her mother as she stood by the table. Mrs.
Gooderich took out a black-bordered handkerchief. She
lacked the dignity which weeds demand, somehow, and
Minnie saw this. She waited for her mother to speak.
Silently Mrs. Gaynor offered the widow a cup of tea. The
fit of anger which had been fed ever since Mrs. Wilfley's
letter had arrived was spent. Tea and tears were to follow.
She refused bread and butter weepingly.

Minnie was ill at ease again for a moment. She herself
never wept and thought it silly.

"Don't, mother!" she said at last.

But Mrs. Gooderich wept on silently, impassively, the
tears rolling down her small tired face and into the teacup.
She had been sorely tried mentally and spiritually of late.
Her appearance in deep black at the chapel the day before
had resulted in a certain change of heart. Little Hannibal,
also in black and in thick-soled boots which kicked
occasionally at the pew in front, had wondered when the
minister had patted his cheek and smiled benignantly. He
had wondered still more when his mother had sent him
to the Sunday-school after dinner while she herself had
gone to the cemetery. Mrs. Gooderich was vaguely seeking
consolation. The loneliness of widowhood has often this
effect. She had always been desirous of joining the chapel
—church was too grand—but somehow there had never
been time. But now there was plenty of time; at least
she hoped so, tremulously. She had tried to pray, for Bert
in the barracks at Casterbridge who wrote of his chance of
"going out," for Minnie away in London, for Hannibal
kicking his legs about by her side, for herself, whose
future seemed dark and desolate; and she had gained
strength, she thought. And then that letter from Mrs.
Wilfley, the kind lady who had so generously arranged

the grand concert, had upset her. She had wasted energy
by giving way to anger, talking to an imaginary Minnie,
neglecting her work and puzzling Hannibal with unexpected blows, so that when Hiram told her Minnie was at
his mother's, she had been taken by surprise. And as she
sat there weeping into her tea, she felt with a pang her
utter impotence in the face of her child's frowardness. It
was a strange paradox, this erring daughter standing unconsciously contemptuous, "over her mother." If the latter
remembered the stockbroker's wife of long ago, she
showed no sign of that lady's tact. Our conduct is indeed
of a piece with ourselves, and Mrs. Gooderich could not
have behaved as her mistress had behaved. Driven to
silence, she wept. It may seem paradox again, but even if a
recital of her own misfortune could have brought Minnie
back to her, she would have died rather than utter it. That
was past. She had done the right thing, and her fault was
buried forever. And so it did not even occur to her to
speak of it.

Mrs. Gaynor, somewhat perplexed, had gone on ad-
ministering to material needs and turning the situation
over in her mind.

"Why don't you sit down, child?" she said to Minnie;
but Minnie only shook her head and looked over her
mother at her hat. She felt instinctively the advantage
her position gave her.

"I'm goin'," she said briefly.

"Minnie!" her mother started up and seized the girl's
arm, but Minnie drew away, bending over the table.

"It's no use, mother. You don't understand and you
won't understand, so it's only wasting breath." She reached
over, took the feathered hat and set it on her head.

"Never look to me!" burst out her mother.

"That's one thing you can depend on, mother. I shan't
do that."

Mrs. Gooderich stepped back as though she had received
a blow.

"Minnie," said Mrs. Gaynor in a clear authoritative
voice, "promise me one thing."

"What?" said Minnie without turning from the glass,
her hands still fixing the hat.

"Promise me you'll always write to me and tell me where you are and how you are getting on."

"Yes," she said, "I'll do that."

"Then, Mrs. Gooderich, I'll do the same to you. And now, Minnie, kiss your mother."

"Good-bye, mother."

It was a tragic moment.

"Now don't forget," said Mrs. Gaynor.

"I won't," said the girl, and went out.

PART II

I

"THEN, Madame, what do you propose to do?"

"Stay here a little longer."

"But I have mentioned already to Madame that there is a fortnight's account due."

"He may return this morning."

"But if he does not?"

"I will let you know."

"Madame will not misunderstand me if——"

"No, no. That will do now."

Somewhat nonplussed, the landlord of the "Three Pigeons" returned to his wife. He had been glad of Madame's custom a month ago. She and Monsieur had taken rooms at a time of the year when but few visitors came. Truly, Monsieur appeared to be a commercial, yet he was free with money, and going away a fortnight since had ordered everything to be continued for Madame as before. Now they were somewhat doubtful of the issue. Monsieur was to return in a week. At the end of a fortnight, which was this morning, the landlord of the "Three Pigeons" made known his anxiety to Madame, who continued to look out over the balcony at the bustling life and noise on the Quai. He had no desire to be harsh: quite possibly Madame was in a quandary herself. A day or two . . . no harm could surely come of a day or two's delay. His wife leaned her fat elbows on the desk where she sat and hoped so. Tiding over October to April was the problem of their lives, for commercials did not as a rule come to the "Three Pigeons"; they preferred the hostelries near the station. If Monsieur returned all would be gay, if not all would be desolation. So closely are small businesses run that one bad debt will precipitate disaster. Both landlord and the fat lady on the desk looked grave.

Upstairs, leaning over her balcony, Madame watched, with apparent content, the scene below. The Seine, bearing on her broad placid bosom all manner of craft, waspish destroyers, huge snub-nosed lighters, swift petrol-launches, slim white yachts and rusty ocean-going tramps, was spread out before her. Immediately below the sun shone down on the red and white striped awnings of the cafés that line the Quai. Carts rumbled over the setts, tramcars clanged and whined over the metals as they moved off up to Bonsecours, over the bridges, down the Rue Jeanne d'Arc, out to Darnetal; and now and again a fussy Benz motor-car would thutter and hoot its way among the throng of people who waited for the trams. Up and down in front of the cafés the merchants of the City prome- naded, discussing their affairs with gestures that seemed droll from above. The whole scene was animated by the spirit of spring, and Madame, in spite of the landlord's gloomy forebodings and disquieting interview, smiled to herself. At length she turned away into the little room and took from the mantelshelf a letter. That it had been already perused was obvious, for she displayed no haste. Smiling thoughtfully, she unfolded the thin foreign sheets and laid them on her knee.

9 MAPLE ROAD, N.
Feb., 1906.

My dear Minnie,
I received your letter from Antwerp and was very glad to hear you were well. Hiram and I have had colds for some time. He's been home here a week now, and I'm glad to say he is getting on fine in his profession. He certainly likes the sea, and I have great hopes of him. As soon as I got your letter I wrote straight away to your mother. She says she doesn't like East London at all, nothing but rain and slush all the time. As she's said this for four or five years now (how time does fly!) I sup- pose it has become a habit with her. She says Hannibal is giving a lot of trouble. He seems to have lost his job at a warehouse and is running about and getting into mis- chief. I'm afraid your mother is not a very good manager. She wasn't here, I know. She is just scraping along at

*the work your Uncle George got her, and not venturing
to get anything better. I must say I respect your mother
for sending back that money you sent. Did you get it
back safely? She won't go against her views whatever
any one says.*

*Now, Minnie, what are you doing with yourself? Are
you really happy, now you've seen the world and gone
gadding round for so long? I often think of you and
wonder. You say you guess you've got all the pleasure
any one gets out of life, but I don't think you quite grasp
what I mean. And that reminds me that I saw Mrs.
Wilfley the other day when I went over and had tea
with Mrs. Worrall. She was very interested in your
career, she said, because you impressed her tremendously
with your will-power when you were with her. And although she believes you were quite wrong, which was the
reason she wrote to your mother that time, she still
thinks you have a future. She has just published another
book on the subject of Women's Rights and Moral Duties
and hopes you will read it.*

*Hiram sends his love. He goes back to his ship, the
"Cygnet," in a few days, and I've just thought I would
take the opportunity to look in and see your mother.
Certainly London is a terrible place to get about in. I
always find myself in the wrong train in that awful Circle
Railroad. And you know I still live in hopes of seeing
you and your mother reconciled. I suppose you will shake
your head, but I do believe if you came back and asked
your mother to forget the past, she would.*

Your sincere friend,
Ann Butterick Gaynor.

Minnie let the letter slip from her fingers and sat meditating upon the vicissitudes of her life. She was, as a
matter of fact, once more at a turning point. Since that
evening five years ago when she had returned to Clifford's
Inn and found Mrs. Wilfley with some friends at tea, she
had maintained a steady indifference to the obligations
of friendship. Her brief notes to Mrs. Gaynor had been
but the fulfilment of her promise, and contained little
save a record of her changing address. Mrs. Wilfley,

indeed, had been hard put to it at first to explain her
interference, though the subtle suggestion, seized when she
gathered that Minnie had not seen the letter, that there
was nothing to conceal since Minnie was now an emancipated woman, checked the girl's withering invective. The
word "emancipated" held Minnie's fancy, drew her attention back from petty details and she saw herself in perspective once more. And she found, moreover, that the
only drawback to her full enjoyment of the evening lay
in her own ignorance of literature and art. Her contempt
for Mrs. Wilfley was shorn of its edge when she heard
that lady discussing a recent and famous novel. Certainly
the criticism was of no value and might have annoyed the
author, but it sufficed to emphasise Minnie's feeling that
she was "out of it." She left the flat, promising to return,
and sought Anthony at his hotel. The experiment had
satisfied her she would not be able to remain in Clifford's
Inn. To his question she had replied that she looked to
him. He was busy at that moment composing an arresting
piece of publicity called "The Shrine of Indolence," but
he put it to one side at once and took her out to dinner.
She remembered that dinner. They did not go to Paoli's
that time but to one of the great caravansaries of the
West, where the panels of the walls were of pale pink
satin, where the waiters wore claret and gold uniforms and
the lights on the tables had rose-coloured shades. A great
orchestra in the distance made a pleasing tumult that
drowned the noise of cutlery and dishes, and Anthony had
ordered a bottle of port wine. In many ways Minnie
measured her present life from that port wine. It marked
the end of the prelude of her emancipation. Thereafter
she stepped deliberately into the milieu of the first act.

And now it should be succinctly stated in her defence,
that her life had been in many ways restrained and modest.
That she had been the mistress of more than one man
stands clear against her. She should have been faithful, I
admit, just as men should be perfect. She failed, I suspect,
for the same reason that men fail, for the same reason
that a sow's ears are unsuitable raw material for silk
purses. But of riotous living and dishonest dealing there
had been none. Her failure to realise her first vague inten-

tions as a sort of modern Aspasia did not drive her to
the quagmire of pilfering and blackmail. In this I hold
her honourable, and she herself had no qualms at all,
now, concerning her way of life. This fact I have already
remarked, that even crime, if co-ordinated and run on
business lines, loses its essentially criminal aspect; and
you may hear intelligent folk concede a half-envious admiration for the skill and courage of a bank-thief or
company-promoter—this fact, I say, has a vital bearing
upon the outlook of a woman such as Minnie Gooderich
is now as she sits looking out over the Seine from her
pavillon on the Quai. You may, if you please, sit at
home in your family and deplore the profligacy of her
life. You may, like Mrs. Wilfley, grow in goods and fame
by writing books to prove that she cannot escape destruc-
tion and death. You may, like Lady Gophir, interest yourself in refuges for her in her dreary and squalid decline.
You may do all this and fail to grasp the essential points
of her defence, that feelings control men and women, not
thoughts, that effort is non-moral, that finally you yourself, in your comfortable home, are as responsible as she.
Mr. Gilfillan's fine Flowers of Publicity are no more
inevitable products of our age than Minnie's callous independence of soul. We have cackled of the romance of
business until business is our only romance. We have slain
Poesie, and her pale phantom stalks amid our stark
realities unrecognised and undesired. We have seen Art
on the street selling herself for money, but we have lost
the right and the impulse to rebel.

Quite unconscious of this trend of existence she sat
there looking out at the busy life of the old City of Rouen.
She had altered, as we say, since the days at the factory,
altered somewhat for the better. Her face was a little
thinner, her mouth had more decision than ever, but her
dark blue eyes were less belligerent in their steady gaze.
Her simplicity in dress was noticeable too, she having
cultivated a certain severity of line which suited her spare
figure and graceful deliberateness of movement. Her weak-
nesses were perfumes and *négligés*. To spray her clothing
with aggressive essences, to sit, without corsets, watching
the up-curling spirals of cigarette-smoke, sufficed to her.

for recreation, literature, and the fine arts. She became
in a way a work of art, odorous and phantasmal. On some
men this aspect of her was the limit of fascination. And
she could smile too, exposing faultlessly even teeth, con-
veying in her glance a profound knowledge of human life.

Of her wanderings there is small need to speak at
length. She had made Western Europe her seminary, her
Didascalion, learning rapidly and intuitively the things of
which she had need. As Mrs. Gaynor had said, "If it was
not one man it was another." Let it be said, at least, that
she appealed generally to men of superior quality, and
appealed, moreover, to them as men and not as beasts.
She was no Circe, turning men into swine, but rather
attracted them by her subtle air of detachment and held
them by an implication of mystery. That men are more
generous to their casual loves than to their wives and
families cannot be laid to her door. She benefited by it as
your business profits by idiosyncrasies of the market, and
she thought no more about it.

But just now, as she sat by the window, she was somewhat weary of the play, and was meditating the possibilities of a return to a less nomadic existence. Her anxiety
as to the return of Monsieur had been genuine though
veiled before the landlord of the "Three Pigeons." The
latter's dulness had prevented him from connecting the
departure of Monsieur with that of a certain steamer a
fortnight before. Minnie was aware, however, that that
same steamer was due from Antwerp even now. But she
was wondering, nevertheless, whether it would be better to
make an effort on her own part and return to England
for a time. She would prefer that the captain of that
steamer should pay her bill at the "Three Pigeons," and
on that account alone did she prevaricate. A repetition of
that unique experience, a voyage cooped up in a berth in
a rolling tramp-steamer, did not appeal to her. She reflected
with disgust upon the nausea and fatigue, and the un-
pleasantness of the clandestine exit, to prevent gossip, at
midnight.

She rose at last, and picking up the letter opened her
trunk and took therefrom a writing case. It contained a
thick packet of letters from Mrs. Gaynor, for they had

each kept the promise made that afternoon long ago, and these letters were Minnie's only link with her early life. Strained through Mrs. Gaynor's fine sieve, her mother's attitude towards her seemed devoid of bitterness, and lacked any positive note save that she was as determined as ever to take no money from her daughter. Minnie laid the last letter on the packet and tied it afresh with a piece of ribbon. She would answer it by and by, when she had decided what to do.

When she had dressed herself for walking she went out and descended the stone stairs of the hotel. Times were certainly slack with the "Three Pigeons." The café was deserted save for the landlord, who sat on the red-plush lounge reading the *Petit Journal,* and Madame at her desk, engaged in her interminable accounts. They looked up quickly as Minnie appeared and passed out, nodding nonchalantly. They exchanged glances and shrugs, and relapsed to their former abstraction in news and figures. Minnie did not speak French fluently. She had never remained long enough anywhere to feel the need of a foreign language, and was accustomed to leave such bargainings as were necessary to her protectors. At the same time she could ask intelligibly for her meals, and even convey to the landlord that his fears for Monsieur were unfounded. She turned now up the Rue de la Grosse Horloge, and halting under the very shadow of the grey arch, entered a restaurant where she was accustomed to lunch. She liked it because it reminded her of the little places in Soho where she and Anthony Gilfillan had occasionally dined, little places more popular and more congested even than Paoli's, where you all sat at one big board like a family, and called the waiter by banging the pepper-box on the table. So much did Minnie concede to sentiment; she thought of Anthony without regret. But then she thought of everything without regret; even of their parting, effected suddenly and quietly when he went to Mexico to arrange the formation of a new subsidiary company. It had been looming for some time, he growing more and more absorbed in his great schemes, she gaining more and more interest in trivial things. She had met his daughter too, a grey-eyed convent-bred made-

moiselle, perfect in language and *savoir-faire,* and had
been stricken suddenly with a deep conviction that the
girl would later on effect her dismissal in summary
fashion. She was indeed no longer necessary to the dreaming capitalist and inventor. His advance in fame and
riches had brought him in touch with famous men and
brilliant women, women who knew more than he, who
had travelled and studied, who knew courts and kings,
who helped right and left to acquire ascendency over their
husbands and brothers, who led him into great country
houses and Mediterranean villas, whither Minnie, for all
her restrained refinement, could not go. So they had
parted, amicably enough, he to his suite on a West-bound
liner, she to her new attraction, a square-jawed, brown-
faced naval officer on leave, who found in her small flat
in Fulham a novel and delightful haven after his China
Station.

It was noon and the room was full, for others besides
Minnie appreciated the home-like cosiness of the place.
The waiter stood lashing the crumbs from the table with
his napkin and listened to Minnie's quiet, hesitating voice
as she enumerated her requirements. Removing her long
gloves and laying them beside her as she bent over the
carte, she became aware of the scrutiny of her neighbour,
a middle-aged woman clad in faultless black. Minnie looked
up at her and met a pair of wide-open brown eyes in a
face of powdered pallor, eyes shaded by a large black hat
that was set far forward in the style of the moment. The
woman's smooth white hands had rings on the short,
slightly pointed fingers, and heavy drops dragged at the
lobes of her small ears.

"Ingleesh?" said the lady with a smile as she dissected
her cutlets, and Minnie regarded her with fresh attention.

"Yes," she replied. "Do you speak it, much?"

The lady nodded, munching.

"I live zere, in Inglan'."

"Do you? Where?"

"London!"

"Do you?"

"Ver' good place, London. I have a bizness zere. You
have a bizness?"

"No. I'm here for a holiday."

"Ah!"

The soup came and Minnie took her spoon and began to eat it. Her neighbour cut a piece from the yard-long roll on the table and put it down beside Minnie's plate.

"What is your business?" asked the latter.

"Modiste an' chapeaux. A ver' small place but ver' good. I like Inglan'."

"Yes," said Minnie. "It's a good place. I was thinking of going back."

"An' ze Inglishmen, I like zem. You like Inglishmen, eh?" The brown eyes glittered.

"Sometimes. Do you know many?"

"Ah yes! I have many frien's Inglish, wiz plenty money. Inglish sweet'eart, 'e spen' plenty money."

"Yes," admitted Minnie, tipping her plate away from her. "That's true. You have an English sweetheart?"

"Certainly!" drawled the lady, eyeing Minnie as though doubtful of her comprehension. "An' you?"

"Perhaps. But not now. When do you go back to England?"

"To-morrow, by ze night-train. An' you?"

"I—I don't know quite. I am waiting for some one."

"Ah! An' if he no come?"

"Then I will come back to England with you if you like."

"Can you do the dressmaking?"

"Not much. Why?"

"I wish for assistance in my bizness in London."

Their eyes met for a moment in a challenge, and then Minnie finished her soup.

The meal went on and they became acquainted, in the manner of their class, with each other's condition. Marie Antoinette Letellier heard with approval of Minnie's reasons for awaiting the return of the steamer, but she, with her somewhat wider experience of the ways of seafarers, was not certain of Monsieur's return.

"Ze Capitains, zey come zey go," said she, and Minnie seemed to imply, by her grimace and her slightly raised shoulders, that persons who pursued such a precarious calling might be quite capable of a little uncertainty in their movements. Her companion suggested coffee at the Café Victor, near the Municipal Theatre, and she assented. They paid, rose, bowed to Madame and went out into the busy little street which had been so busy and so beautiful for so many centuries. Neither of these women noticed anything about this narrow thoroughfare, save that it was narrow and the shop-windows small. They walked down towards the river, Madame Letellier leading in the press and talking over her shoulder.

"You, you have no frien's 'ere in Rouen?"

Minnie shook her head.

"Ah, I have many. I will show you."

"At the Café Victor?"

"Ah, perhaps. But if not—but I will show."

Arrived at the Quai, Minnie scanned the shipping quickly, and then called her companion's attention to a funnel with a yellow band.

"So?" said the lady. "He is arrive, ze sheep. You will see him then, you zink?"

"I'll wait and see," said Minnie gravely, and her companion led the way along towards the Café Victor. But at the theatre she paused, turned up to the left towards the great garage in the Rue de Charettes and entered an apparently empty café. A ghostly attendant rose from a chair in the rear and they exchanged remarks unintelligible to Minnie, and then Madame Letellier ascended the stairs to the first floor. Here again the room was large and vacant, save for a little group of women lunching by a corner window which admitted a limited view of the Quai. A chorus of exclamations greeted them as they appeared; Madame explained her companion with a wave of the hand, and sitting down entered into the conversation with zest. Here Minnie became isolated, for the ceaseless inter-jangling *argot* of the women was beyond her. She gathered that one of them, a thin-faced good-natured girl, was describing an indescribable midnight ride in the tonneau of a motor-car, describing it with a wealth of gesture and detail that sent her hearers into paroxysms of laughter. How the friend of her friend who was supposed to be driving, tried to turn round and look into the tonneau, how they missed a wagon by inches and finally demolished a fence. *Quelle vie!* They all screamed, and bent over their knees in ecstasy.

Minnie, sitting where she could see the water-front if she cared to look out, and drinking her black coffee, watched them curiously. She had, as a matter of fact, rarely come into touch with the middle classes of her profession, the hardy *demi-mondaines* who occupy a place between the Minnies and the tenants of the tiny cubicles above their heads and in the Rue Victor Hugo. She did not wish to come into touch with them exactly, for women like her became accustomed to regard other women as either rivals or servants. So she sat, well content to be a mere witness of their mirth, drinking her coffee and looking out towards the sparkling river.

The women themselves eyed her with quick appraising glances as they laughed and talked, and assisted by Madame Letellier's succinct hints, placed her accurately enough. So placed she received their respect as one of the *élite*. It was their finest ideal to be the mistress of a rich man, an ideal too rarely attained in these days of competition and high rents. There was a certain reproach to their boisterous fun in her unobtrusive presence; but none knew better than they that her repose was the result of her position. Wait till she had to enter their ranks, and she would soon find the need of companionship and high jinks to keep her spirits up.

For Marie Antoinette Letellier their respect was less evident than their admiration and envy. She was a smart business woman as well as fastidious in her caprices, lucky woman that she was! The lucky woman had no pride, however, and talked in torrents of persons and places they knew and understood.

Keeping her eyes on the people passing along the Quai, Minnie saw a little man in a blue suit and black bowler hat, and carrying a brown leather case, pass and disappear. She leaned over and touched her friend.

"*Violà!*" she said. "He is come."

"*Bon,*" said her friend. "You are going?"

"Yes, I shall be at the 'Three Pigeons,'" replied Minnie, and nodding to the others, went out.

II

"I DON'T mind admitting you can make it very awkward for me, very awkward," said Captain Briscoe, as he ran his fingernail along the ship's name on his brown leather case.

They were sitting in the Museum, facing the "Death of Madame Bovary," and the good captain was obviously ill at ease. He was a small neatly-made man, with weathered features and reflective eyes which were contemplating the tragedy on the canvas. Whether he appreciated to any extent the sublime pathos of that scene did not transpire. Seafaring captains are not as a rule susceptible to the appeals of Art. He was looking at it, however, and he continued to look at it because he knew that Minnie was looking at him and he felt the delicacy of the situation.

"I don't suppose, Mabel," he went on—(Mabel was the name he knew her by)—"I don't suppose, Mabel, that you quite realise what this means to me. You think I'm too easily scared. But then you don't know Shields."

Minnie, *alias* Mabel, admitted that she had scarcely heard of such a place before he had mentioned it, that she was hazy even now as to its whereabouts.

"It doesn't matter, you haven't lost much. It so happens that the new mate I've with me this time not only lives in the same town, but in the same street. So it follows that I simply can't afford to give him the slightest chance. . . . If my people were to think that I was going about . . ."

"Thank you," said Minnie. "You needn't apologise. I only go where I'm wanted. You might have left me in Antwerp, though, since you are so particular. I was much more at home in Antwerp than I am here."

"Now don't say you regret it!" said Captain Briscoe, turning to her in consternation and putting his hand on her arm. "Don't say that, Mabel! I shall never forget it

222

myself, as long as I live. That fortnight here and that week in Antwerp I shall not forget. I thought you were different from the rest. I thought you wanted to come."

"Oh, that's all right, but what use is it my wanting if you're so afraid of your mate you daren't see me in the street?"

"Well, I am. If his wife wasn't a cousin of my sister-in-law it might not matter so much."

"I suppose the fact of the matter is you're married all the time and afraid she'll know," said Minnie, with good-tempered irony.

"Not on your life! Do you think, if I was married, that I'd . . ."

"Thanks again," replied Minnie amiably, and Captain Briscoe returned to his explanations.

"Oh well," remarked Minnie, who knew the utter folly of losing her temper with men, "I shall have to manage as well as I can, that's all. I will say this. You've come and told me, and that's more than some sailors would do, so I've heard."

"Ah," he assented, "and some shore-people too."

They were silent for a moment, contemplating the "Death of Madame Bovary."

"I'll tell you what I'll do," said the Captain at length. "I'll pay the hotel bill at the 'Three Pigeons' and cover the fare back to Antwerp. I feel this way about it. I'd hate to think you had any bad feeling for me, thinking I'd bilked you out of a single cent. I want some time perhaps, when I get to Antwerp again, and all's clear—you understand?"

She patted his cheek lightly. "All right, George," she said, smiling. "I'm sure I don't know the fare to Antwerp. Do you?"

"Fifty francs'll cover it, I'm certain," he said, opening his leather satchel.

"Mind, I don't ask you for this," she observed.

"No, I offer it. I can afford to pay my own way, my dear, and pay for my fancies too."

He looked at his watch and stood up.

"I must get back to the ship," he said. "Well!"

She sat looking up at him, almost winsomely. He

stooped, and with his hand on her shoulder, kissed her cheek. "Write to me," he said.

She promised.

. . . .

For a long time she sat in front of the picture by Albert Fourné, which is entitled "The Death of Madame Bovary."

III

WHEN Minnie re-entered the hotel of the "Three Pigeons" it was six o'clock, and no one had yet ordered any dinner. Madame sat as usual, her great account-books before her, eternally casting up. Her husband, having read all the advertisements of the *Petit Journal,* was perusing a back number of *Le Rire,* but with a woe-begone face.

When Minnie passed through alone, they looked up and exchanged shrugs. Evidently there was a misfortune in store for them. Taking the ponderous key from the board, she ascended to her room. There was a smile on her lips as she took off her walking things, and then removing her blouse, began to wash. One of her passions was cleanliness of body, another was the purity of her linen. The latter had become a cult. Perfume and feathers, laces and even jewellery she would have abandoned in indigence before linen. A woman might catch a man's attention with her finery, but it was, in her opinion, the immaculateness of the intimacies which would hold him if he were worth the holding. But of this she was not thinking as she laved her bare arms and neck, the small flat oval of transparent soap gleaming like a topaz in her fingers. She was thinking of the good captain's ethics and wondering if he were a type. For Minnie with leisure had developed an interest in types, and was often amused with the serious moral theories held by her lovers. These theories never held them back from anything they desired, she noticed. Captain Briscoe was a case in point. The trim little man, with his knowledge of the world as he conceived it, a world of agents who wanted to rob his owners, crews who wanted more than they signed for, respectable friends and relatives who demanded a flawless reputation of him in return for their favour,—this trim little man, I say, in spite of all this, had a touch of real romance in his soul. But to his misfortune he had met Minnie as a courtesan and he could not rearrange his ideas to suit the change in

his feelings. Had she been only rated as respectable when
he first encountered her, she would have been his choice,
she would have been offered his name and the privilege
of kissing numberless female relatives whenever she met
them, besides the command of a semi-detached residence
in Shields. But she had not been so rated, and the tangle
of emotional and ethical impulses seemed inextricable.
It had led him to a comical contradiction in his language,
had led him to caress and insult her in almost the same
moment.

She smiled in the glass as she remembered the parting.
What extraordinary creatures were men. There was that
young chap, a Consul's son of all people, who had expressed his unplumbable contempt for "any bounder who
would bilk a woman," and had vanished from the scene
like a morning mist, leaving her in the lurch. . . .

There was a knock at the door.

"Come in," said the lady, taking up a small soft white
towel.

"Pardon, Madame," said a voice as the door opened and
closed quickly.

"Oh, come in, Monsieur, come in! Is it anything very
important?"

"Only this, Madame." And the landlord, still holding
the knob of the door with his left hand, as if in protection
from the lady's charms, sidled into the room and extended
a card held between two fingers. Minnie paused in her
vigorous use of the towel to crane her head to read the
inscription.

"Tell her to come up, please."

"Certainly, Madame. And—er—is it impertinent to ask
what Madame's plans are?"

"Yes—I mean No. Give me the bill to-morrow morning.
I am leaving by the night boat at Dieppe."

"Excellent, Madame. I will make it out up to to-morrow
night. You will require dinner?"

"Send Madame Letellier up here," cut in Minnie.

Madame Letellier appeared, cool and composed, with
her perfect-fitting corsets and attention to details.

"I did not think you'd be so soon," said Minnie as she
shut the door.

"Peste! What a climb! What for you live zo 'igh?"

"Fresh air. I saw him."

"Ah! An' it is all right?"

"All right." Minnie took up a powder puff. Marie Letellier watched her critically for a moment, and then
espying the open trunk, began to rummage. She herself
was already dressed for the evening. Her black jacket
was open, showing a sheer voile blouse with a blone net
collar carried almost up to her ears. Minnie heard the
soft creak of her corsage as she stooped and lifted some
garments. Clapping her hands together to rid them of
powder, Minnie came over and took out the blouse she
intended to wear. Unlike Madame's it was buttoned in
front, for Minnie had never been able to afford a maid,
and details like that are important.

"Ver' nice!" commented her friend, eyeing the smooth
handkerchief-linen material of snowy whiteness. "How
much?"

"Bon marché. Twenty francs," was the reply, as
Minnie's small fingers slipped the big pearl buttons into
place and settled the waist.

"Too much. I make that for ten shillings."

"Oh well! *I* could make it, but look at the fag."

"Eh?"

"Too much trouble!" And Minnie proceeded to fix the
soft loose collar and blue sailor's knot. She fastened it
with a brooch made of three sovereigns soldered to a
back-plate, a notable example of ornament and utility
combined.

"There," she said. "Now I'm ready. Do you know I'm
supposed to be going back to Antwerp."

"Yes!" Marie Letellier drawled the word, as she stared
up at Minnie from the trunk. It was evident from that
drawl that she understood Minnie's statement in its
entirety. "He like you ver' much?"

Minnie's mind reverted to her musings on Captain
Briscoe's dilemma, and she smiled as she said that such
was the case. The Frenchwoman regarded her with fresh
attention—and respect. Minnie, then, could do that, hold
a man in invisible fetters of steel and—let him go! There
are no students of applied psychology like the women of

the half-world. It is the chief subject in the Didascalion
I have mentioned, and Marie Letellier was proficient in
it. As her bright brown eyes scanned the other woman
standing there, slim, sweet, and cool, a film of envy crept
across her eyes, for she herself was thirty years old and
she could not forget it.

Minnie broke into her musings with a bundle of used
things which she flung into the trunk and brought down
the lid with a bang.

"Where are we going?" she asked, picking up her hat.

"Folies Bergère," said Marie, pulling her blouse down
and going over to the dressing-table. "Zere is an Inglish
company zere. Ver' good!"

IV

THE Channel was as smooth as glass as the two women, heavily clad, leaned on the lee rail and talked earnestly together. They were travelling second-class, and the stuffiness of the cabin had driven them out on deck. At intervals they could see a light flashing on the English shore, and Minnie, while she listened to her friend's story, kept her eyes on the grey line now coming into view, waiting for the flash. She was trying to understand why Marie Letellier, the cool, experienced woman who had so thoroughly enjoyed her evening at the Folies Bergère, was confiding the story of her early life to one she had met so recently. It was a sad story, Minnie admitted, containing elements of drama which her own lacked, and it was told with an intensity she herself could not compass. Marie had been at school near Paris and had been allowed leave to visit friends in the City, where she had met and loved an Englishman. He had persuaded her to marry him, and she had gone back to school with their secret locked in her breast. And then each week-end she had gone to Paris, ostensibly to visit her friends as before, but really to her husband's flat. With a certain Gallic *verve* Marie conveyed to Minnie the fearful joy of that period, and Minnie's hands tightened on the gunwale as she figured it. And what had happened? Well—the voice of Marie dropped to a whisper—one night she had wakened for some reason, and needing a drink tried in vain to rouse her husband. She shook him, in vain, for he was dead. Ah, mon Dieu! And then the temporary paralysis of brain, the sudden decision, the flight back to school, the subsequent illness and removal home. Her life, Marie insisted, had been blasted, though Minnie, with her lack of imagination, could not see it.

To her the Frenchwoman's tragedy was of her own making, the product of sentiment and a love of theatricality. If not, why had she become what she was? Why had she not remained by the dead man's side and faced the thing out? Minnie could not understand. She stood there watching the great light under Beachy Head flash out nearer and nearer, stood there in the pride of health and clear intellect and perfect nerve-poise, unable to feel the throb of remorse in her companion's voice. And the Frenchwoman felt this and was awed. To each of her loves, however evanescent, however mercenary, she gave something of herself. With each passion virtue went out of her. But with this English girl it was different, apparently. To her it was the man who gave, more even than he knew. For all the difference it had made to her soul, she was as virginal as when she worked at the factory in North London. "I need you," Anthony Gilfillan had said to her, and so said they all. For her, she had no need of them, they could go or stay, which perhaps explained why they often stayed. Marie, gaining intuitively some inkling of this fundamental fact, shivered.

"You zink I was a fool?" she said.

"No, no," said Minnie, taking her arm and walking to and fro. "Most people think *I* am a fool. I can't—I can't feel that way."

The syren let out a long, wailing cry which ended in a shriek. Minnie looked up and saw the dark figures striding to and fro on the bridge. She thought of Captain Briscoe, and remembered how he came down one night, his face wet with spray, and how she had seen the hard bright glitter of command in his eyes soften when he saw her curled up on the locker. Men! They needed her.

"I think we're going in now," she said.

V

It was late in April of the same year when Minnie, seated by their window on the first floor in Lower Sloane Street, put down the morning paper and watched the postman crossing the road. For over two months she had been with Marie Letellier, and as yet that woman of perfect figure and imperfect saintliness had failed to fathom her. And indeed Minnie did not quite understand herself. Accepting the Frenchwoman's offer of tuition, she had endeavoured to make her work a success. This was hardly in the tacit contract which lay between them. The two assistants, heavily coiffured girls from Walham Green and Streatham, were nonplussed by the incongruity of her calm air of superiority and the bungling incompetence of her work. Minnie ignored them and smilingly caressed her friend, who deplored such a turn for prudery, and visited her favourite resorts alone or with less intimate friends. And yet she made no suggestion that Minnie should withdraw from the atmosphere of the genteel half-world. For she had conceived an affection for the cold English girl who took her occasional outbursts of emotional excitement without rancour, and had such a fund of quiet counsel and ironic wisdom.

Yet Minnie would have been at a loss to explain in measured phrases why she retreated from the further pursuit of the existence she had followed for four or five years. She would not have admitted that Captain Briscoe's letter, forwarded her from the "Three Pigeons," had influenced her so far. For he had written, thinking her still there, regretting his behaviour and asking if he might see her again. She had sat for a long while thinking over that letter, and wondering whether she had the courage to answer it or just let him drop out as he proposed to do. And she had answered it frankly, telling him how she had changed her plans and come to London, that she supposed they would be hardly likely to meet again, but expressing no displeasure at the possibility. And then had followed the blank silence usual when one corresponds with those who follow the sea. All her worldly knowledge, all her common sense, told her that he had vanished. She did not disguise from herself the fact that she liked him, and liked him the better for his letter. And, in spite of her worldly wisdom and her common sense, she remained absorbed in needle and thread, and wondering at intervals if she were a fool.

And now, on a morning late in April, she sat at the window watching the postman cross the road. She did not have many letters now. She had not told Mrs. Gaynor of her coming to London. With this new leaven working in her mind, she had grown a distrust of Mrs. Gaynor. When she wanted to see her mother she would go to her direct, she decided. She had no reason to suppose that she would have any letters to-day. Yet, when Marie, in her bronze-green kimono and with a cigarette between her lips, came back across the room with a letter in her hand, Minnie saw the foreign stamp without surprise. She opened it and read it calmly, while her friend, sinking into the chair behind her, waited for news. Minnie raised her eyes and met the Frenchwoman's gaze squarely.

"Yes, Marie, it is from him. What do you think of that?"

"He is comin' 'ere?" enquired Marie, and Minnie shrugged her shoulders.

"That depends. He is coming to London."

"To you?"

"He says, to marry me. What do you think of that?"

"Mon Dieu!" Minnie laughed.

"Not bad that! You don't know him. He says he has another ship, a bigger one, 'a command' he calls it, with more money and—and he says he loves me."

"But marry! For why?"

"I should like to get married," remarked Minnie, in a low voice. "Very much."

"You! For why?" The voice was shrill.

"Children, kids, brats, whatever you like to call them. Don't look at me like that, Marie; it's a fact I do. Don't you ever want . . . want . . . oh!" And Minnie opened her arms, half-rose from her chair and sank back into quietness again. Marie Letellier regarded her attentively, blowing thin spirals into the air.

" 'E say 'e love you, eh? An' you?"

"Yes," replied Minnie in her usual voice, folding up the letter. "He is a man. I don't know as I'm crazy about him, but I have been feeling lately that I ought to make a change. And that's what it all amounts to: I want a change."

And as she spoke she remembered her mother, resolving to go and see her.

"An' you will leave 'ere?"

"I suppose so."

"Leave me 'ere all 'lone?"

"Good Marie!" Minnie rose and put her hands on her friend's shoulders. "When are you ever alone? Answer me that!"

And hard upon her reply to his agent in Billiter Lane, came an impetuous telegram to be at a certain place at a certain hour. She went out, a little late, and found him fuming. He took possession of her, carried her in cabs to restaurant and theatre, ordering wines and the delicate fruits of the earth, denouncing the tyranny of female relatives in sailorly language, and damning the world in general. Evidently he had been drinking, but not deeply, and she saw with a certain satisfaction that he scanned his change correctly. She took this surprising conduct good-humouredly, appreciating to some degree the natural elation of a man raised from two to three thousand tons net register. His new ship was a daisy, and she could have ten or twelve pounds a month to keep house on. Now, would that be enough? Because if not, damn him if he wouldn't draw on his account. He wasn't going to have the dearest little, etc., etc. She cut into his baby-talk with a hint as to the lateness of the hour and he was all attention at once. There must be nothing indiscreet now. He ordered the cabman to drive toward Sloane Street, and as they passed through the solemn gloom of Eaton Square he circled her finger with a ring, and abandoned coherence for good and all. In Sloane Square she insisted gently that she must leave him and alighted, ordering the hansom to return to the "Three Nuns," where he was staying. She laughed to herself as she answered his farewell wave, and wondered why he should choose a hotel with such an incongruous title. It reminded her of the "Three Pigeons" in Rouen. That was absurd too. Everything was finely absurd to-night. She felt the elation of those who win though unaided. Her independence of soul had remained immaculate. Once more she reflected with pride that a man needed her, and she had been successful in concealing her own longings. After all, the fripperies of love, the flowers, the lights, the implied sentiment of the ring were pleasant. With a start she recalled that early affair with the coal-agent's clerk. Had she dealt unkindly by him? Involuntarily she shook her head. In the perspective of the years her cruelties, her unconventionalities, were but a part of life. He was probably happy now with a girl whom he could understand. Her mother? Well, there she admitted freely to herself as she undressed, that there was something to be done. She had the sense to know, and feel shame in the knowing, that her mother came out of this business more bravely than she. She decided that she would go and see her mother. The thought carried her on to a matter of which she profoundly disapproved, and that was her mother's dependence on Uncle George. She wondered if after these years of separation she would be able to live with her mother. Or better still, when she was married, why could not her mother come and live with her? She was thinking of this as she fell asleep, and it was not until next morning that she remembered there was Hannibal. Little Hanny would be big Hanny now, and she had no intention of taking him in as well. That was a difficulty, and she decided to go down and see them.

For Marie Letellier she had but the flimsiest of compassions. That emotional being regarded marriage much as a libertine regards children, with a mushy sentiment, unstable and only half-sincere. She had a habit of sighing when matrimony was mentioned with an "Ah, not for me!" expression on her face. It was extraordinary how much comfort this capable woman extracted from her

early tragedy without ever permitting it to hamper her
practical everyday business of extracting money from the
world and his wife. It was this trait which extorted
Minnie's admiration. There was no earthly reason why
Marie Letellier should not be as respectable a widow as
any other dressmaker in southwest London; only her
temperament forbade it. Sensuality had for her the same
fascination that sensuousness had for Mrs. Wilfley. It is
not too much to say that, had they met, they could have
fallen in love with each other. Indeed, I have often wondered whether they did not eventually collide, and I have
figured the dishevelled Marie pouring her terrible story
into the ears of a lady with a note-book on her knee, a
lady who could not hold back her tears but leaned her
head on Marie's shoulder and "sobbed like a little child,"
as she herself told a reporter. And then I see on the book-
stalls among the best sellers a slim pale volume on whose
cover is a pierced and bleeding heart, and I read the title
The Licensees of Love. A card sticks from the pages
informing me of a new and enlarged edition just out,
and as I hurry along the corridors of subterranean
London, I see posters—for Mrs. Wilfley will be a person
of importance then—posters showing her in her best soul's
awakening pose, raising a transfigured Marie Letellier
from a stern and rockbound sea. Nothing would please
either of them better than such publicity. It is quite possible that Marie was the original of Mrs. Wilfley's *Magdalens of Mayfair,* published under the auspices of Lady
Gophir in aid of her Refuge. Popular taste had come
round to Mrs. Wilfley's way of thinking, and as becomes
an astute business woman she was there with the goods.
People wished to know how these poor creatures to whom
men paid the wages of sin (sometimes as low as ten
pounds a week) lived. Mrs. Wilfley knew and sold her
knowledge, sobs included, photos extra. We may even
imagine her drawing from the willing Marie the story of
how she met an English girl abroad (sensation in the
Sunday papers!) and induced her to come to London.
Mrs. Wilfley would make a good thing out of that.

The English girl, however, did not permit these con-

siderations to alter her purpose, and when Marie weakened to tears (this was on Sunday morning, when most
women of her class weep) Minnie shook her.

"Do for goodness' sake be sensible," she remarked.
"Any one would think you had something to cry for.
Marie, how much money have you in the bank?"

"Tree—tree 'undred an' forty poun'," said Marie,
lowering her handkerchief.

"And the business? And your health? And plenty of
friends? And me only going round to Tedworth Square?"

"You will not see me when you marry!" the huddled
figure in the bed announced gloomily. "I know ze Inglish
madame. You will spoil yourself."

"Fat lot you know, old girl. Get up and dress. You're
growing lazy."

Minnie met her gallant captain an hour later at Victoria
Station, where she instructed him in the ways of Sunday
trippers to Brighton. He was, for all his million miles of
ocean travel, nearly as unsophisticated as a young man
from the country. The luxury of Pullman travel was new
to him; the plated fittings, the telephone by which he
ordered a whisky and soda for himself and a glass of
port for her, the adjustable seat backs, all excited his
pleasure. He was one of those men, so common at sea,
who have really no idea at all of enjoying themselves
except in a disreputable manner. This manner with the
years becomes distasteful to them, they sink into themselves, grow morose and taciturn, and the result is that
bleak phenomenon, a merchant skipper. Captain Briscoe
had gone to sea when he was eleven years old, and being
now forty, had spent about sixty per cent of his total
existence upon the ocean. As the train fled away through
the smiling country that Sunday morning, he realised
how little of life's ease he had had. He was inordinately
proud of the woman at his side. Ah! he knew an A 1
copper-bottomed craft when he saw one! Now he would
have a home of his own and a dear darling little wifie, etc.,
etc. The reflections of a sea-faring man are very much
like those of a bank clerk or any other man in the same
position. Suffice it that Captain Briscoe had the unusual
experience of feeling himself a thoroughly respectable

engaged man and yet a bit of a dog for all that. He had
read of trips to Brighton, and here he was, travelling
Pullman and all the rest of it. After all he could afford
it. He had grown so accustomed to investing his money
that he had almost forgotten that he could afford it.

And coming back in the evening had been the capping
of a perfect day. It might be surmised that he, having
spent so many weary years at sea, would have no supreme
emotion at the sight of it from Brighton Pier. But Captain Briscoe's sea was very different from the boat-flecked
panorama which confronted them at every turn, the gay
esplanade, the music and minstrelsy of the populous
beaches, the toy breakers that rolled lazily in the sunshine. At times he looked out at it grimly as he remembered some particularly strenuous gale off Hatteras or
the joys of getting away from Valparaiso with the
Norther hard behind him. The memory gave the present
a greater zest.

She told him in the train, as they returned to Victoria,
of her intention to visit her mother and her proposal to
take her to live in the flat in Tedworth Square.

"A very good idea!" he agreed, pleased at the opportune appearance of a relative. It seemed to cut Minnie
off from her past life, for her to produce a relative. "But
we aren't goin' to live down there for long, eh? I thought
of a place in the country, with a few fowls and a pig. I
always wanted to be a farmer."

Sublime illusion!

"Later on," she soothed him. "When you've retired."

"It's unlucky to talk about that," he reminded her.
"No seagoing man ever speaks about swallowing the
anchor."

"Why do you call it that?" she asked.

"Well, it's a pretty hard thing to do," he replied briefly,
and his blue eyes grew grave as he recalled cases to his
mind of men who had tried to do it, tried to fling from
their souls the terrible thrall of the sea.

"And the country's rather awful in the winter," she was
saying as the great yellow face of the clock-tower came
into view.

"That's right," he agreed. "London's not so bad after

all. It's a friendly place." And he really felt as though he were coming home.

"It's home to me," she assented. "And there's another thing, George. I've an idea I might make some money here."

He looked at her in alarm. What did she mean?

"It's like this," she explained. "When I was here, a long time ago, I knew a woman who wrote things."

"Wrote things?" he repeated vaguely.

"I can't explain very well," she said. "I'm not sure it would come to anything. But when I get settled I'm going to have a try. I've been thinking."

He gazed at her in admiration. What a clever little woman she was!

"There's no need for you to earn money," he declared proudly. "*I* can do that. You leave it alone, whatever it is. I want my wife to be a lady!"

"It's not unladylike," she replied, "and we might as well have as much money as we can get. I shall have a lot of time on my hands."

"You can do sewing," he suggested jocularly, and her lip curled.

"Not in my line," she returned coldly, "and there's no money in it."

She did not pursue the matter further at the time, for the idea that had taken possession of her mind was indeed too shadowy yet to put into words. But it was true that she had been thinking, and as the future proved, thinking to some purpose. Often, during the past few years, her thoughts had gone back to Mrs. Wilfley and that lady's connection with publicity. Had she missed a chance in not staying with Mrs. Wilfley? Too late to bother about that now. But it had become a habit with her to scan the papers and magazines that came her way, noting the advertising matter and wondering if Mrs. Wilfley had written it. Everywhere she would see whole pages devoted to the Gilfillan Filament, pages of glowing rhetoric framed in allegorical designs by eminent artists. And then, in a reckless mood, she had wondered whether she could not do "that sort of thing." She had ideas, she was sure. If she could only get a start. . . .

That would take too much time, she had reflected, and put the subject out of her mind. But now that she was going to be independent, the idea had come back. She had experience of life now. If another woman could do it, she could do it. But since the man at her side did not like the notion, since in his opinion it was unwomanly, she would say no more. She must be a lady, do nothing. Very well. She would wait until he was away at sea again, and then she would have a look round.

BOOK THREE
THE SEA

241

"To all whose souls are weary,
   To all whose souls are sad
With piteous days or dreary,
   To all whose hearts are glad
The great sea's soul has spoken,
   The great sea brings release,
And even hearts half-broken
   Win something of its peace."

MRS. GOODERICH sat near the carefully curtained window of her house, or rather her one-third of a house in Jubilee Street, E. The third consisted of the use of the front passage, the ground floor fronts, and a curious middle chamber, lighted by transoms, which served as a scullery and coal-shed. The ground floor back was ruled by an Irish woman from Cavan, who also washed for a very respectable Bohemian family who disseminated themselves over the rest of the house. The Bohemian family had evidently seen better days, probably before Bohemia got its bad name; they were astonishingly quick to see the respectability of Mrs. Gooderich, who had curtains, and the impossibility of the Irish woman from Cavan, who had none. They at once invested in curtains, and there they were at the upper windows, the colour being that sombre grey which is the London equivalent for white, and providing for the Bohemian females an effective screen behind which they could look down at life in Jubilee Street or peer curiously across at the occasional excitement of a scuffle, a fight, or an arrest in Assembly Passage. They tell me that all this is changed now, that Jubilee Street is so congested with respectable people that Irishwomen from Cavan and anarchists from Oran are crying out, "No room to live!"; that Assembly Passage is a Valley of Peace, and policemen no longer find it expedient to patrol it in couples. It sounds Utopian and unreal; if it is true, who shall despair of the Ultimate Reclamation of the World?

It was a bright and eager spring day and about half-past four in the afternoon that Mrs. Gooderich sat near her curtains occupied with a book. For she had of late years discovered, somewhat to her surprise, that reading "took her mind off her worries." Certainly she did not discover this while she had such worries as her husband's death, her daughter's defection from the Right, her elder boy's brief but glorious career in South Africa, and the loss of her position as a home-keeping woman. They had left her small time for reading; but now, in the lull of the past four or five years, with no greater worry than a somewhat unstable Hannibal, she had been led by Mrs. Gaynor, be it said, to follow the fortunes of heroes and heroines as described by certain masters and mistresses of Romance. As she sits there, bending her head over her book, following the words pointed out by her finger through spectacles that add twenty years to her age, and whispering inaudibly to herself, she is greatly changed from the dark-haired, blue-eyed little creature who stood before the late Mr. Royce in his nice little house in Caroline Road so long—well, twenty-four years ago. And there is a change from the slightly hysterical widow who stood facing her recalcitrant daughter that windy autumn day in Mrs. Gaynor's front room. When a woman drops in social position from two servants to one, or from one to a weekly charwoman, her spirit is unbroken; she can brazen it out and defy the neighbours to prove it isn't because she is independent and prefers to do her own work. But when she ceases to be her own servant and enters the service of another, when a thriving brother-in-law, instead of leaving her to die in her indigence, perpetuates that indigence by "putting her in the way" of a debasing employment, then there comes a change in the outward seeming. She can no longer brazen it out even to herself; a terrible apathy becomes visible upon her. As she confronts you, you see in her shoulders humility, in her hands unwilling respect; but in her eyes there slumbers an impotent anger, and her mouth has the tremulous droop of despair.

Mrs. Gooderich read on in her romance, and as we see her, she looks not unhappy. But ever and anon she looks through the window and up Assembly Passage as though expecting a familiar figure. There is no one visible in the Passage save some four or five youths who are loitering near a blacksmith's shop. As Mrs. Gooderich looks up she sees one of the boys dart from the shop pursued by a tall and powerful old man in a smith's apron. He clutches the youth by the shoulder, but quick

as lightning the lad twists his arms from the sleeves and
follows his companions in a wild stampede into Jubilee
Street. The tall old smith is left standing with the coat
in his hand.

Mrs. Gooderich put down her book and stood behind
the curtains, an expression of pain on her shrunken features as she looked out upon this scene. After a moment's hesitation, she went out and opened the front
door. The youths were leaning against the wall opposite
laughing among themselves; the coatless one regarded
with glances of admiration.

"Hanny!" called Mrs. Gooderich, and the youth turned,
the laugh dying away.

"Come here!" and he came, hands in pockets, dissatis-
faction on his face. "Where's your coat?"

"Lost it."

"I saw how you lost it. How often 'ave I told you to
keep away from that lot? You take no more notice o' me
than if I spoke to the lamp-post."

She closed the door and followed him into the room.

"You'll stay here while I go and speak to Mr. Gills,"
she ordered, and she put on her hat with trembling fingers. "You can't think how I hate to have to go to respectable people about a thing like that. It was bad enough
when you got the sack. You might behave yourself till
you get something to do!"

He sat sullenly in a chair, hands in pockets, his feet
spread out with the heels dug into the floor. He remained
in this posture while his mother crossed the road and disappeared into the blacksmith's shop. His liquid full brown
eyes were clouded with moody self-reproaching anger.
He knew it was all wrong, this tearing about the streets,
this wanton pilfering and bell-ringing. He ought to be at
work. That was the respectable thing for him, a great
lout of nearly eighteen. But he had got "fed up" with
Cortington's Repositories, the devil of "larking" had led
him too far, and on the previous Saturday the foreman
had given him his money. What would it all end in? His
mother with some asperity had told him he would go
wrong. The son of the Irishwoman from Cavan had gone
wrong already, had stolen a watch one night in the Great

Assembly Hall and had got "pinched." The Bohemian family never had any disgrace like that. With an almost uncanny facility they had got themselves into divers occupations, living malodorously behind their grey curtains, but with no breath of scandal ever hanging about their stairway. With the lack of logic often associated with villainy, Hannibal disliked the industrious swarm upstairs. Why didn't they stop in their own country, instead of taking bread out of the mouths of Englishmen? This argument was not Hannibal's, of course, he had it from a man in the Repositories, a man who had strong views about aliens.

He was sunk in one of his sullen moods when his mother returned and flung his coat over to him.

"It's gettin' past a joke!" she broke out at him, as she took off her hat. "I'll go over and see your uncle at Kennin'ton to-morrow morning, and see if *he* can't put you to somethin'. Nothin' *I* say makes any difference. It's stealin', no less, whatever your beautiful friends call it."

He made no reply, but sat looking down at the floor. She looked at him with attention for a moment.

"What's the matter with you, Hanny?" she cried. "Why don't you put your coat on?"

"I'd no'," he grunted. "Can't 'ave a bit of a lark now."

"Bit of a lark! To steal an honest man's iron so you can go sell it in the Mile End Road and buy cigarettes? It's sort of lark you'll get six months for, my boy, and so you would this time if Mr. Gills weren't a gentleman."

"Oh, all right, all right. I ain't pinchin' 'is old iron all the time, am I?"

"You tell your uncle that."

"I ain't goin' to tell 'im anything. I ain't goin' to 'ave any truck with 'im."

"Why not?" demanded his mother, setting the table. Her voice faltered, for she knew in her heart she agreed with the boy.

"Don't like him," growled Hannibal, getting slowly into the coat. It is noteworthy and curious that the mute anger which had flared into Minnie's eyes when she heard of her uncle's generous provision for her mother, had its counterpart in Hannibal's untutored and undeveloped soul. And Mrs. Gooderich, lifting her head to speak, felt the invisible power of this antipathy, felt a responsive something in her own humiliated heart, and was silent.

"Come and get your tea," she said at length. "I must be off by half-past five." Hannibal drew his chair to the table and began.

"What are you goin' to do?" she asked. "I can't keep you 'ere eating your 'ead off." Hannibal squirmed in his chair.

"Give me a chance," he mumbled, his mouth full. "I'll 'ave a look roun'." Mrs. Gooderich sighed.

It is due to her to say that she did not sigh from mere selfish grief. She had never expected fortune to be particularly kind to her; she had always been thankful that she was a respectable woman instead of a nameless derelict. She sighed because of the apparent futility of her life, because she seemed so helpless before her children. Minnie and Bert had simply ignored her, and what was the result? Minnie was a lost one, a shameless denizen of the half-world whence she herself had been rescued in the nick of time. Bert, against her wishes, had gone into the Army, had rushed gallantly to meet fate, and fate had met him more than halfway in the shape of a Schneider shell that had smashed him to a blackened pulp. There they were on the grained and varnished wall behind her now, Minnie almost faded out of recognition, a demure damsel of fifteen, Bert in a group of his chums, with their yellow uniforms coming out badly in the photo, and their dog, who had moved and so seemed to have two heads. Was she proud of her soldier-son? Who can say, since she never spoke of him? Nor can we speak with exactitude of her feelings towards that wilful daughter now that time had softened the hard outlines of her wrongdoing.

And now little Hanny was growing insurgent too, and she sighed as she cut the bread and spread it with margarine. Little Hanny, who was a head taller than his mother, ate without speaking after his appeal for a chance. He ought to have some one to look after him in the evenings, but what could she do? It was sometimes nine or half-past before she had finished in the City. She had tried to get him to "go in" for something at the People's Palace, but Hannibal was not that kind of a lad. The Bohemian family took to the People's Palace with avidity, lapping up knowledge in the classes and developing their Slavonic muscles in the gymnasium from September to May, another example of alien presumption. But not so Hannibal. Later on, as we shall see, he acquired the reading habit, with disastrous results, but for study and the social fidgets he had no facility. Behind the Bohemian curtains there was a silver shield, won by the *juvenilia* for athletics, and on the mantelpiece they showed their friends with pride an ormolu clock, the reward of the second daughter for swinging Indian clubs for an unheard-of time. Mr. Gill's little boy, even, a precocious Christian of five-and-a-half, had sung a solo at the Assembly Hall, which, so it was rumoured, had brought sinners staggering to the penitent form. Hannibal had shown no signs of eminence in any department of life. He himself was dissatisfied, though it is not in youth to admit it. The natural prankishness of adolescence had led him away from those strange dreams of his childhood, those dreams in which he saw the phantoms come and go, and Cortington's Repositories were no place to dream in. Cortington's Repositories, in fact, were a pretty good miniature of the whole world to Hannibal, being a dusty, noisy place, full of other people's property. Hannibal was "fed up" with them, which was equivalent to saying he was fed up with the world as he found it. To dart into Mr. Gills's shop, seize an old file, a hammer, a nail-head or a piece of bar-iron, vanish round the corner into Jubilee Street, stroll through Stepney Green and out into the Mile End Road, and bargain with the Russian Jew who kept the second-hand tool and metal shop—well, it might not be respectable, but oh! it was a blessed change from the eternal expression of the Repositories. He was not a bad boy. Had he been sent to Eton at thirteen and Balliol at eighteen he would have turned out an admired specimen for the governing-classes, though he had no faculty for governing. Had he gone to Merchant Taylors and passed into an old-established business, he would

have proved a fair though somewhat dreamy junior partner with a taste for bric-à-brac and Persian Prints. But he
was none of these things. He had, according to the Log-
Cabin-to-White-House school, an equal chance with others
to become Lord Chancellor or President of the Board of
Trade. I do not think he had. As I have said, he lacked
the vital spark of heavenly flame which is indispensable
if one is to become a Lord Chancellor of a kingdom,
President of a Republic or a Captain of Industry. He had
nothing of the sublime genius of a Lipton, a Roosevelt,
or an Alfred Jones. While in the Repositories he had no
hair-raising schemes for economising the expenses of
storing pianos, no heaven-born invention for simplifying
the work and so throwing half the staff out of employment. He has given the biographer, so far, very little
material for rhetoric. Lacking the genius for making
opportunity, he had had none. Evidently he has no turn
for Greatness. The Bohemian family have long since outstripped him in the race, one of them even attaining to
Cambridge and a wranglership. Something must be done
with him. Mrs. Gooderich travelling Cityward on the
Aldgate train is wondering. Hannibal himself, as he
lounges along the Mile End Road, is wondering. Possibly
the reader, if he has survived so far, is wondering too.

Let us see.

II

It was just eleven o'clock next morning that Mrs. Gooderich, pausing in her efforts to tidy up the front room, looked through the curtains and beheld Mrs. Gaynor and her son Hiram pushing open the gate and approaching the door of her home. Mrs. Gaynor's visits to her old friend had not been very frequent. The difficulties in those days of travelling from a northern suburb to Mile End Road were sufficient to deter the most hardy explorer. You may go to Japan via Siberia at the present time with less anxiety and exhaustion.

"Well now, how are you?" said Mrs. Gaynor when the door opened. "I dare say you didn't expect me, did you?"

"No, I can't say I did," said Mrs. Gooderich, leading the way into the front room. "What's brought you down here so early?"

"Hiram," said Mrs. Gaynor. "I was going down to see his ship and I thought I'd make one journey of it and see you too."

Mrs. Gooderich looked at Hiram, who smiled pleasantly and stood turning his cap over. He was dressed in the uniform of the Merchant Service Apprentice, a double-breasted coat of pilot cloth with big brass buttons, and his cap was adorned with gold cord and a badge. His cheerful face was as brown as a berry, as were his hands, which were big and muscular, the happy result of much strenuous toil.

"He does look well," sighed Mrs. Gooderich, and Hiram's mother regarded him with approval.

"Why don't you send Hannibal to sea?" she asked, when they were seated. "It'ld do him a world of good."

"What can I do?" complained Mrs. Gooderich. "I thought he was doin' well at the Repositories, and now they've discharged him without a reference. He's so

250

rowdy too, and he won't listen. If I was to suggest anything he'd go against it for certain."

"That's so," assented Mrs. Gaynor. "That is so. I shouldn't suggest it. Just pack him off."

"How! I don't know anybody. I'm sure I'd be very glad, though I've no great fancy for a child of mine to be a sailor and get drowned."

"We don't all get drowned, Mrs. Gooderich," said Hiram, laughing. "I've been to sea two years and here I am safe as houses."

"Yes, but you might. There's always a danger."

"So there is in the Cambridge Heath Road," said Mrs. Gaynor. "I was nearly run over this morning."

Mrs. Gooderich smiled.

"One gets used to it—all this traffic—after a time."

"If you'd like to get Hannibal away on a ship, Mrs. Gooderich, I'll speak to the Skipper. He might know of a chance," said Hiram. "It's hard work though, and hard grub too. P'raps he wouldn't like it?"

"I 'ardly know what to do," she replied wearily. "Where is your ship?"

"Surrey Commercial Docks."

"And there's Hannibal, isn't it?" exclaimed Mrs. Gaynor pointing with her umbrella. Hannibal was visible leaning against the wall across the road, a cigarette in his mouth, conversing with another youth. Mrs. Gooderich bit her lip in her anger as she went to the door and opened it. He saw her beckoning, and slouched across holding the cigarette so that it was hidden in his sleeve.

"Throw it away," she said quietly. "Here's Mrs. Gaynor and Hiram. They want to see you." Hannibal, flinging away the sodden mess, took off his cap and followed his mother into the room.

"Why, Hanny, you're as big as Hiram!" cried Mrs. Gaynor, who forgot for a moment the intense dislike young people have of all references to their growth. Hannibal stood uneasily shifting from one foot to the other.

"Goin' away?" he managed to remark to the trim young sailor, who nodded cheerfully.

"We were just saying, Hanny, that you might do well at sea, too," suggested Mrs. Gaynor.

"Me!" said Hannibal, eyeing the pilot-cloth and the gold buttons.

"Sure, you. Why not?"

Hannibal was silent. This was a new idea, and neither he nor his mother were adepts in dealing with new ideas.

"Blow'd if I know," he replied at length. " 'Ow d'you get a job to start?"

"You ought to be apprenticed," said Hiram.

"P'raps his uncle would help him," suggested Mrs. Gaynor.

There was another silence which Mrs. Gooderich relieved.

"I'll see him," she said, but she spoke reluctantly.

"Wouldn't you like to come down and see the ship with us?" asked Mrs. Gaynor.

"If you like," replied Hannibal, looking at his mother. "I'd better 'ave a wash."

While Hannibal was having a far from unnecessary scrub in the scullery, Mrs. Gaynor took a letter from her bag and handed it to her friend.

"From Minnie," she said briefly, and sat silently while Mrs. Gooderich got her glasses and read it.

"She's comin' 'ome," she said, handing it back.

"To London," replied Mrs. Gaynor. "Will you see her?"

"If she comes to see me I can't turn her out. But do you think for a moment she'd come 'ere? She isn't like you, Mrs. Gaynor. She's a fine lady, lives on the best, I dare say. She won't come down 'ere, I'm quite sure."

"You see?" said Mrs. Gaynor, looking over the letter. "She speaks of going into some business with this friend of hers. It may be—a change."

"It would be—if it was honest. No, she'll come to me when she's sick and got no money, not before."

"Mrs. Gooderich, I don't believe she would," said the American woman earnestly. "I think she's too much pride."

"You mean she'd be ashamed of seein' her mother livin' down here? I dare say. Gels like her 'ave plenty of that sort o' pride."

"Well, we'll see, and I'll let you know when she writes to me. We must be charitable."

"Oh, I'm very charitable," assented Mrs. Gooderich with unwonted waspishness. "I can afford to be, in my position."

And then Hannibal returned, and Mrs. Gaynor switched the conversation away to literature. Mrs. Gaynor, while admitting the genius of Augusta Wilson, thought Mrs. Southworth her superior in novel-writing, and it was that lady's *Ishmael* which Mrs. Gooderich had been reading.

"How do you like it? Isn't it a great story?" asked Mrs. Gaynor.

"Beautiful," agreed Mrs. Gooderich. "He does marry that Countess, I s'pose?"

"Sure, and the poor thing he'd married in secret dies. Haven't you got to it yet?"

"No. I read so slow," admitted the widow. "I was wonderin' if the Countess 'ld get him, and then I couldn't think how he'd manage with the wife he had."

"She dies," repeated Mrs. Gaynor solemnly.

"That's the best of stories," remarked Mrs. Gooderich. "You can always let them die if they're in the way. It's different in real life."

It is.

Hannibal had washed his hands and brushed his hair and boots, and now appeared ready for the expedition.

"Will you be back to dinner?" asked his mother.

"I'll see to that," said Mrs. Gaynor. "Hanny'll have to escort me back to the City. The ship don't sail till to-night, but I'll have to be getting back this afternoon."

"I'll be out a bit, so if he's not to be back at dinner-time I needn't hurry."

"Not a bit o' need. You go right along and do the errands. Hiram, where's that—oh, here, it's in my bag." And Mrs. Gaynor placed a pot of her home-made jam on the table. "Victoria Plum. I hope you'll like it. Now we must be getting along."

They got along, and Mrs. Gooderich, looking through the curtains at them as they walked towards Stepney

Green, noted with a certain satisfaction that Hannibal was bigger than Hiram, and would no doubt look as well if he had the same uniform. This brought her back to the half-formed decision which had led her to hint she might be out for a while. Should she go to see her brother-in-law, Mr. Brown, and ask him to assist her in sending Hannibal to sea? There was much against it. She did not like either the idea of the sea or the idea of asking her brother-in-law's help. But was it not her duty? That was the worst of Mrs. Gooderich. She never knew whether any course of action was her duty or not. As a rule, when she did an unpleasant thing, it was not because she was convinced it was her duty, but because she was afraid it might be. It was in this mood that she made her way, after an early dinner, towards Kennington. She would ask her brother-in-law's help, he would very likely decline; she hoped he would; she would have done her duty and would then proceed to do something which was not her duty, namely, leave Hannibal to get some casual employment.

The curious thing is that Mr. Brown and his family were quite unconscious of any reason why Mrs. Gooderich should not accept assistance at their hands. Mr. Brown was still the man with the humorous blue eye who had stayed the funeral cortège at the "Northern Star" and regaled himself with pork-pie and stout. He was more successful, that was all. He had got on. From a slippery little ledge on the lower slopes of the mountain, after a period of peril so terrible that only a single rope held him dangling over the Bankruptcy crevasse, he had reached a narrow path which led each year higher and higher. That dangle on the rope had greyed his hair, but it had not destroyed his sense of humour. He had no pride at all in the sense that Mrs. Gooderich understood pride. He would have puzzled in vain to know why his sister-in-law was reluctant to be under any further obligation to him. He had gone out of his way to get her recommended for the work of cleaning those offices in the City, he had got her that quite desirable third of a house at a ridiculously trivial rent. What could he do?

But as a matter of fact, Mr. Brown was too busy getting on to do any puzzling at all. He understood his business, and now that he had ceased to dangle and had good solid rocks under his feet, he took a great pleasure in increasing his business and so gave his sister-in-law very little thought. It may be that this was one of the reasons why she was loath to ask more of him. The widow and the fatherless are very quick to discern whether your sympathy be perfunctory or really from the heart. They have no business to be so fastidious, seeing who they are, but the fact remains that a poor foolish widow like Mrs. Gooderich, and a poor ineffective orphan like Hannibal, will have more pride than a prosperous builder like Mr. Brown, who really could afford to be stuck-up.

It could hardly be expected that Mrs. Brown, who was so helpless an invalid in the old days that she had to drink port and oatmeal stout, would be any better now that her husband had got on. She was not. She had grown steadily worse until nothing but Bournemouth and Heidsieck could keep the breath in her body. It was a great relief to Mrs. Gooderich to know that she was not called on to meet Mrs. Brown. There is bound to be patronage and stubborn resentment in such encounters between sisters-in-law until humanity is scrapped and made over afresh. The daughters were much more bearable, Mrs. Gooderich thought, they being quite unaffectedly pleased with their prosperity and glad to see their aunt.

The neat bow-windowed house, with its little office built out at the side, was in one of the many turnings off the Kennington Road. As Mrs. Gooderich came up to the gate, Mr. Brown was standing in the way leading to his yard at the back, talking to his foreman. He did not hasten out to bid her welcome, though he was glad to see her. He just waved his hand and waited for her to come up to him. Another piece of presumption and foolish pride; the widow resented it.

"Well, Mary, how's things? Come over to see us?"

"Yes, George, I thought I'd just run over and have a word with you. How are you all?"

"Oh, fairish. The missis is just as usual. She goes out in a bath chair a bit, y'know, but she don't seem to get any stronger. Beef-tea an' Bengers, an' a glass o' champagne. Nothin' else yet, doctor ses."

"An' the children?" Mrs. Gooderich began to be sorry she had come. It seemed more difficult than ever to ask a favour.

"A-h," replied Mr. Brown. "That reminds me of something. But what's the trouble? You said you'd come over to 'ave a word with me."

All this time he stood there in the yard entrance, his broad body planted firmly on his great stout legs encased in black leather leggings, his thumbs in his waistcoat pockets, and his humorous blue eyes glancing over his little sister-in-law. She had walked nearly a mile from the train and she looked round vaguely as though in search of a seat.

"Well, I was thinkin',—but if you're busy——"

"Not for a few minutes. Let's go indoors, and see Amelia, she's somewhere roun'."

He led the way through the little office and into the drawing-room.

The house, like most of those owned by people who have some money but no pride, was rather over-furnished. It was scarcely safe to stand still in the drawing-room, so congested was the space with goat-leg chairs, curio-cabinets, Chesterfields and small tables. Everything was covered with photographs and vases, the walls were re-inforced with oil-paintings of sheep in fields, enlargements of the family-portraits in colours, and plush-framed mementoes of Margate, Bournemouth, and Ilfracombe. Mr. Brown pointed to a straight-backed chair and settled himself in the Chesterfield.

"Amy!" he called, adding to Mrs. Gooderich, "She'll be down in a minute."

She was down in less than a minute, and so was Ethel. They had seen their aunt from a bedroom window and had lost no time in changing their blouses and repinning their hair. They entered together, two buxom well-looking young women, and offered their cheeks to be kissed.

"How are you, Aunt?" said Amelia.

"How are you, Auntie?" said Ethel. Then they patted

their hair, glanced at their reflections in the overmantel, and sat down carefully.

"Now to business," said their father. "What was it you wanted to see me about?" It occurred to him as he sat there that it was delightful to do any one a good turn, especially a poor relative.

"It's about Hannibal. I've thought of sendin' 'im to sea."

"Sendin' 'im to sea!" repeated Mr. Brown in consternation, and his daughters repeated the words—

"Sendin' 'im to sea!"

Mr. Brown was British to the backbone, and he had the Britisher's horror of the sea, but his astonishment was not merely at the idea. To think that his sister-in-law had hit on such an extraordinary scheme! And he said the words again, quite unable to frame any other comment for the moment.

"Sendin' 'im to sea!"

"Yes," replied Mrs. Gooderich in a low, nervous voice. "You see, I was talkin' to Mrs. Gaynor the other day, an' her boy's doin' well on a ship, an'—an'—so——"

"Did *she* give you the idea?"

"We thought it might be a good thing," faltered the widow.

"And leave his job?"

"He left it last Saturday."

"Sacked?"

"Some little thing. . . . He's been there eighteen months," flared the mother, defending her son, her heart sinking.

"Fancy!" breathed the two sisters, watching their aunt with the unwinking gaze of young women destitute of pride.

"Any reference?"

"The foreman was that short I had no chance—they won't listen to a woman," she muttered.

"Well—and so, what is it you wanted—my advice?"

"I—Mrs. Gaynor thought you might be able to—to get him on a ship."

Now this was, in all justice to Mr. Brown, a most un-

reasonable request. Mr. Brown knew as much about ships
as he knew about the Differential Calculus. He was as
far from the shipping world as he was from Mahomet's
Paradise, and he felt aggrieved that his sister-in-law
should show such ignorance of life as to expect anything
else.

"Get 'im on a ship? Why, Lord bless me, Mary, you
'aven't took leave of your five senses, 'ave you?"

"I didn't think it 'ld be much use," she said. "I told
Mrs. Gaynor it wouldn't be any use."

Ethel looked at Amelia and Amelia framed the word
"Fib." And Ethel nodded.

"I should think not. Why—why—if Mrs. Gaynor's so
fond o' the sea, why don't *she* do somethin' for 'im?"

"They've only got one ship, she said, and they don't
take many boys. An' there's a premium too."

"That's it, is it? Me to pay the premium? For a boy
as gets the sack an' no reference. Mary, I'm surprised."

He was. He hadn't a particle of pride, but he was surprised that a widow woman who was glad to take a
sovereign a week for cleaning offices, should have dreamed
of an apprenticeship for her boy. Young John was in the
engineering and costing a pretty penny in books and keep,
Ethel had served an intermittent novitiate at the gentle
art of winding wire round flower stems and making up
buttonholes and wreaths. But Amelia had faced life un-
flinchingly behind a tobacconist's counter, and Tom, his
beloved Tom-tom, the right-hand man of his business, he
had never had no apprenticeship. True, Mr. Brown had
been dangling by a rope at that time, with but few
thoughts to bestow on any of them, and Tom had proved
one of those adaptable mortals who can see money in
anything and can extract it without fuss. But what has
all this to do with the case of the widow who sits on
that straight-backed chair? By what law, human or divine, can she lay claim to such a start for her boy?

As Mr. Brown himself said *sotto voce* when a liner
was wrecked and all the survivors were saloon passengers: "What's the use of goin' first-class, if the steerage
stand as good a chance as you do?"

He was not proud, but he could not see it.

Mrs. Gooderich rose.

"It don't signify—I thought very likely you wouldn't fall in with the idea."

"Well, hold on a bit—sit down—we've got something to say first," said Mr. Brown. "It's really Amelia's business and she can tell you." Mr. Brown peered through the thick screen of plants, gold fish, and curtains which obscured the window. "I see Tom's out there with a man I want to speak to."

He went out, and the two girls sat looking at their aunt for a few moments. And then Amelia began to explain.

"The fact is," she remarked, with numerous little feminine movements, "I've had a little legacy left me. You didn't know our Uncle Bartholomew, did you, Auntie? He wasn't really uncle, only a cousin o' dad's. Well, anyway, he took a fancy to me when I was little, and what does he do but leave me something in his will."

"I've 'eard of 'im, Amy. He 'ad 'ouses, I think."

"No, property," corrected Amelia gravely. "But he didn't leave that to me." She tittered and looked at her aunt as if to say, "I shouldn't be wasting my time talking to *you* if I'd been left real property." "No," she went on, "this little legacy is the unexpired lease of a shop in Billiter Lane. Goodness knows how he got 'old of such a thing, but I expect it was a bad debt—it generally is. It's a hosier's business now; the old gentleman used to pay a man to run it. Now he's gone and left it to me. I'm not goin' to pay a man thirty shillin' a week to make a pound profit. You see? So we had a sale and cleared it out."

"What are you goin' to do? Let it?"

"The lease has only four years to run and any tenant 'd want alterations no end. So I'm goin' to get dad to fix it up as a tobacconist's, which is a business I know something about, and look after it myself. Dad's great on shop-fittin'. He says there's a fortune in it. But I told him he wouldn't make any fortunes out of me 'cause he was to do it cost price."

"I see," said Mrs. Gooderich because she didn't see.

"So that brings me," continued Amelia, "to the reason

I'm tellin' you all this. You know where Billiter Lane is?"

Mrs. Gooderich shook her head vaguely, and both sisters sat with pursed lips. They were very patient and good-tempered about it, but Aunt Mary was slow.

"Well, it's off a turning this end o' Fenchurch Street."

"Near Aldgate?" said her aunt, now thoroughly cowed. The two girls nodded.

"Well then, it's not so far from your place, and I was thinkin' that as I couldn't be tied hand and foot I'd have to have an assistant. An' so, to keep it in the family, it struck me Cousin Hanny 'ld find it a good opening. Not much to start, of course, but in time he'd get on, and it's much more gentlemanly work than a furniture warehouse. Don't you think so?"

"Oh, yes, Amy, yes, my dear. It's very good of you. You'd teach him the business, you mean?"

"I'd teach him the business," assented Amelia, seizing a fresh point of view with the quickness of a lightning flash. "Free of charge, and he can open the place in the morning and close it up at night."

"Oh, you won't be livin' there?"

Amelia closed her eyes in mute despair, and then looked appealingly towards her sister, signalling to her, *"Do you think it's any wonder she's poor?"*

"Aunt Mary," she said, "do you know the rents in Billiter Lane?"

Aunt Mary shook her head sadly.

"Well, for a room no bigger'n this one you're sittin' in, they get five pounds a week!"

"Good gracious!"

"I should think so! My place is only half as big as this, and I could get three pounds a week for it if the lease had any time to run; but as soon as people know it's up in four years they're off."

"I see," remarked Mrs. Gooderich. "Hanny could walk, I should think."

"If he's got legs," agreed Amelia amiably. "I suppose he has the usual number."

"Here's father comin' in again," remarked Ethel.

She was two years younger than Amelia and always undertook the irrelevant remarks. "Isn't it a lovely day?"

she enquired of her aunt. It was a lovely day to the two girls, no doubt, but I don't think that, so far, it had impressed Mrs. Gooderich as being very lovely. So she only smiled weakly and looked up at her brother-in-law.

"Well, how is it now?" he asked, taking the Chesterfield again. "What do you think of Amy's idea?"

"I think it'll do very nicely," replied Mrs. Gooderich. "It's very good of Amy to give 'im a chance."

"To learn the business," added Amelia, with a look at her father which was at once accepted, answered, and filed for reference.

"Bit better'n goin' to sea, I reckon," he suggested, with a smile. "I suppose," he added, "I suppose he'll take it on, won't 'e?"

"Oh, yes. I'll speak to him about it as soon as I get 'ome."

"That's the style," he replied, looking meditatively at the small bent figure and thinking about an investment he had had on his mind for some time. A successful man, or even a man achieving success, has many things to think of. "That's the style. It'll make a man of him. Let's see, 'ow old is 'e now?"

"Eighteen nex' birthday," said the mother. The two girls looked at each other for a moment. They had not realised that even poor people grow up. It is very presumptuous of them, but they will do it. Not even "stunted," according to slumming rules, for Mrs. Gooderich added, "An' big for 'is age."

"It must be two years since he was 'ere," mused Mr. Brown. " 'E was only a lad then."

" 'E's been runnin' up," she explained apologetically.

"You ought to bring 'im over sometimes," he told her, and she made no reply to this except to rise once more.

"That's not the time?" she asked, looking at the gilded clock which had stopped at half-past five three weeks before. Mr. Brown looked at his gold watch.

"Three," he said, clicking the lid and polishing it with his thumb. "Just three."

"I must be goin'," said Mrs. Gooderich, holding out her hand. He took it heartily.

"Well, bye-bye. Let Amy know as soon as you can."

"Yes. Good-bye, Amy. Good-bye, Ethel."

As their aunt was passing through the hall, Ethel looked at Amelia and Amelia shook her head.

"Take care o' yourself," was Mr. Brown's remark as he closed the door.

"Eighteen!" exclaimed Ethel, when the little servant had brought the girls their tea up to their snuggery. Amelia stirred hers meditatively.

"He may be a handful," she remarked. "It's plain he's too much for her to manage."

"She never said a word about Minnie."

"It's not likely, is it?"

Ethel's eyes were round with interest as she stared at her sister. She was growing up and approaching the time when Amy would confide fully. She knew in a vague way that Aunt Mary had a past, and she knew in a way somewhat less vague that Cousin Minnie had, so to speak, a present which would ultimately develop into a lurid subject for non-primitive young ladies to discuss. But as she stared at her sister, Amelia took up her novelette and resumed her perusal of the adventures of a poor heroine who had been wronged. So Ethel resigned herself patiently to a little more waiting, and continued her initiation into womanhood by taking up her own novelette, which treated of the adventures of a fascinating widow who visited country houses, broke guardsmen's hearts and stole diamonds.

III

As Mrs. Gooderich hurried home she had a great fear
gripping her heart, a fear that transcended all her feelings of sadness and jealousy which had been aroused by
the visit to her successful brother-in-law. It was the fear
that by foolishly letting Hannibal go to see Hiram's ship,
she had spoiled the chance of getting him to fall in with
the new scheme. For Mrs. Gooderich, in spite of her
reluctance to accept favours from Kennington, was heart
and soul in sympathy with the commercial career as compared with the nautical life approved by Mrs. Gaynor.
What if Mrs. Gaynor had induced Hannibal to ship himself away immediately? What if he were already tossing
about on the ocean? Mrs. Gooderich's ideas of maritime
procedure were vague. And it must be remembered that
the sea was connected inseparably in her mind with running away. The Mercantile Marine, she imagined, was
entirely manned by disreputable young fellows who had
done something and run away to sea. The Navy, of
course, was different. If you were in the Navy, you wore
low-necked jumpers, very baggy trousers, and appeared
in your native village at long intervals on leave with a
bundle done up in a blue handkerchief.

But Amelia's plan, apart from its Kennington origin,
promised to be an admirable start in life. Mrs. Gooderich
had never heard of Napoleon's famous taunt. She would
have seen nothing libellous in it. She would have only
wished we *were* a nation of shopkeepers and she herself
one of them. But while in a general way you needed
capital, in this case that terrible difficulty was overcome.
It was a fine idea, but all the way home she had recurring fits of panic as she thought of Hannibal preparing
to run away to sea.

But Hannibal was there when she returned, still in
his clean collar and his hair not yet tousled. An unusually
quiet and self-contained Hannibal, who made no re-

marks of any importance while his mother hastily prepared their tea.

"Did you see the ship?" she enquired; and he nodded.

"Is it a big one?" And he nodded again.

"I've seen your uncle," she told him nervously. "He says he can get you a job."

"On a ship?" he asked, turning round from the window.

"No. He says 'e don't know anythin' about 'em. It's a tobacconist's, in the City."

"Oh," said Hannibal, and resumed his contemplation of a game of tip-cat in Assembly Passage.

"Your Cousin Amy's 'ad it left 'er, and she wants a lad to look after it, open it and lock up at night, you see," she went on hurriedly. "It's a good openin' to learn the business, as she's been in that sort o' thing, so I thought —you'd better take it. What's the matter? Why don't you answer?"

He turned on her again.

"Why do other people 'ave all the fat?" he asked hoarsely. "Why didn't father git on same as Uncle George? Nobody leaves *us* tobacconist's shops, as could do with 'em."

"'Ere's a chance to get on," she replied quietly.

"So they say; 'ow much a week?"

"I didn't ask. It wouldn't be much at first, till you'd learned the business." He made no answer and she went on again. "It'll be more'n you get at sea." He laughed grimly.

"It couldn't be less, old lady," he assured her, thinking of Hiram's statement that he was in receipt of five shillings a week until he was out of his time.

"There you are," she argued. "This idea of Amy's is the chance of a lifetime, and you'd better take it. She may not ask twice."

"I ain't ast her once yet," he replied in a low voice.

"What's the matter with you, Hanny?"

"I'd'no. Some'ow I get fed up with it, seeing everybody else 'avin' a good time. Look at Hiram now——"

"What does 'e get a week?" she asked.

"Get? He gets nothin'! Mrs. Gaynor 'ad to plank down twenty quid to put 'im there, and they give 'im five bob a week out of it. That's what I mean; 'e don't 'ave to earn anythin'. And 'ere's Amy 'avin' shops left 'er. I git fed up with it, that's all."

He sat sideways on his chair, staring moodily through the grey curtains into the street, and struggling with a vague, formless desire, a desire that became in time a reincarnation of those purposeless imaginings of his childhood. Like many inarticulate souls, he was compelled to falsify his emotions by his expression of them. He did not really envy others for their good fortune. What he felt was that at bottom he was unfitted for the life in harness which seemed his only destiny. Whichever way he looked he saw the collar of servitude and toil waiting for his neck. And as he stood on the deck of the great beautiful ship, the white yards and endless complexity of her cordage soaring above him, as he had stood there looking across at the great steamers and caught, as it were, a hint of the vast heaving world through which they had ploughed, a passionate hatred of his dullness and impotence took possession of him. If he could only get away out of it.

Hiram, showing him the berth he shared with another brawny, brown-faced youth, had supplied in some sort an answer to Hannibal's hazy questionings. Hiram said that he *might* get a job on a steamer as an ordinary, but the pay was poor and the work was filthy. Or he might go— here Hiram looked at his chum who was twenty and smoked a pipe—he might go as a steward.

"Me!" scorned Hannibal. "I don't know nothin' o' steward's work."

"Mess room," said the pipe-smoker. "You soon get into it. It isn't sailoring, I know, but it runs to a pretty good job later on. Six or seven pound a month besides what the Old Man gives you."

Hannibal looked at the speaker respectfully as he stood there against the bunk, his muscular arms crossed, his brown face clouded with the smoke of his briar.

"I'll think it over," he said. "How d'you get a job; just go on board an' ask?" And they nodded courteously. And then Mrs. Gaynor, who had been talking to the captain's wife, came along and said they must be off.

Hannibal often thought of that excursion down to another world, a world of which Londoners least of all seem to have any consciousness. And he remembered the journey up into the City with Mrs. Gaynor. He was not very clear as to her meaning sometimes, but he felt she was to be trusted. Mrs. Gaynor never failed to give that feeling, even though you were antagonistic to her. You could not for the life of you suspect her of advising some course for her own aggrandisement. And so, when she said to Hannibal in the 'bus, "Now, Hanny, you're the only one left over to your mother now, so you must be a man and take hold," he interpreted, "taking hold" as doing something for his living at once.

"D'you reckon I could get on a ship—like Hiram?" he asked hesitatingly.

"Why, I spoke to Captain Baines about it, and he said he didn't know what he could do until the other apprentice is finished, and that'll be next voyage. But do you think you'd like it? You see, your mother'll be lonely all by herself."

"Same's you," he suggested.

"I'm never lonely," replied Mrs. Gaynor, her grey-green eyes illumined by a curious light. "Your mother isn't like me, she needs company. She's not like me, and you."

"Me? Why me? I ain't particularly fond o' bein' by meself."

As he uttered the words he realised that they distorted the truth, that at bottom he despised his friends and their chivying, and would have withdrawn to quieter haunts if the common cravings of human life had been more rationally and adequately sated.

Mrs. Gaynor had not answered him at first. She had sat there in the 'bus leaning forward and grasping her umbrella and bag firmly, thinking that though Hannibal was about the same age as Minnie when they had gone for a little jaunt together, yet she could not make Hannibal understand like Minnie.

"You used to be," she had said at length.

"Ah," he replied, looking out at the crowded street. "I used to be a lot o' things I ain't now."

"You're running up," said Mrs. Gaynor, looking at him earnestly, "and you'll soon be a man. And yet you have no friends."

"I know a lot of chaps," he persisted, in spite of himself.

"I said friends, as Hiram and Harry Grantley are on the *Cygnet*. I feel as safe as safe about Hiram since he's been to sea, because he wrote and told me about his chum. Now, Hanny, you ought not to grow up without a real chum."

"I'll do whatever you tell me," he declared. "Shall I go and try for a job on a steamer, or stick 'ere in London?"

"You must do what your mother thinks best. I don't believe she'd stand in your light, but all the same, Hanny, don't forget she's had a great deal to put up with, and try to make it easier for her."

Hannibal was wondering why, if this green-eyed lady was as rich as his mother surmised, she didn't dress better and offer to pay his premium to indenture him to the sea? But that was not Mrs. Gaynor's way at all. She did a great and rare service to the world by living in it; her influence made a great deal of difference to those who experienced it, and she felt that this subtle psychic beneficence would have been vitiated by any traffic in money. Hannibal, of course, did not know this; he merely wondered, and came to the conclusion that Mrs. Gaynor was not so very rich after all. Which was as near the truth as any one ever attained.

Perhaps it was the result of that influence that he returned home from his visit to the good ship *Cygnet* in a somewhat chastened mood, which was only marred by the chafing effects of the Brown family's success. When he made his statement to his mother that he was "fed up," she put down the bread-knife and came over to him.

"Fed up? And don't you think I'm fed up with it too, long ago? Do you think I want to go and take their leavin'? But we can't starve. We've got to take what's offered. Beautiful countesses don't come round with bags of money nowadays," she continued bitterly, thinking of the novel she had been reading. "And even if you've got relations as are well off, it's as bitter as death to take it from 'em. What right 'ave we to pick and choose?"

"There y'are," he replied in a low tone. "That's just where I bring up every time, and I'm gettin' sick of it."

Mrs. Gooderich was standing "over him," staring through her curtains. She roused with a start.

"But you'll take it, Hanny?" She almost whined. "Don't let them say we threw it back at 'em."

"Yes, I'll do as you like, old lady," he assured her, getting up and going to the table. As he rose and towered over her, rumpling his hair with one hand while the other stretched out horizontally, Mrs. Gooderich was struck by a new thought. She was nearly strangled by the suddenness and the lunacy of it, but she could not dismiss it.

"Hanny," she said, "when did you last see your Cousin Amy?"

Hannibal yawned again, and reaching out took a piece of bread and margarine by the edge and dropped it flat on his plate. He began his tea.

"I d'no," he said, his mouth full. "Which is the oldest, Amy or Ethel?"

"Amy," said his mother, looking hard at him and still turning over her new lunatic idea in her brain.

"Ain't been there since I was at the Repositories," he said. "Why?"

"Nothing," said his mother, and changed the subject.

IV

THE meeting was under the eye of Mr. Brown and therefore formal; Hannibal was somewhat tongue-tied and conscious of his clean collar. But in spite of these disabilities he made a favourable impression upon Amelia, and Ethel, had she been yet further advanced in knowledge of life, would have detected an unwonted softness in her sister's face.

"Well, young man," said the humorous uncle, "you've been takin' the law into your own 'ands lately. Chuckin' your job, an' threatenin' to run away to sea! Tut tut!"

Young John, who was in the engineering and who therefore was presentable to strangers at week-ends only, looked up at this, and the story had to be retold for his benefit. He did not seem so shocked as his father had been, seemed in fact more interested in Hannibal than before.

Thomas, his father's Tom-tom and right-hand man, followed his sisters, trying to make the young man feel as though he were one of the family. They plied him with all the provender of a high tea, for the Browns, having no pride, were still far from that stage of success which is accompanied by late dinner. The servant did not wait as yet, merely bringing in the food and returning later to clear away. And Amelia, by whose side he sat, was gracious and encouraging.

"Anybody'd think I was a terror!" he laughed, when the panic occasioned by so many dishes had passed from him. He did not look like a terror as he sat there, his hair brushed up from his forehead with a wet brush, the blinding light of three incandescent mantles descending upon him. The Browns were still under the impression that their success should be demonstrated to themselves by excess of light. They had worked up from one mantle to three on the gasolier, with two (never used) on either side of the fire-place. This greenish radiance disturbed

strangers and made the girls look plain, but they had not
yet attained to subtlety in such things.

Mr. Brown ate steadily with the appetite of a healthy
and unembarrassed man, leaving his daughters to make
the conversation. This they proceeded to do after their
own fashion. The business of making Hannibal one of
the family went on apace.

"Have a little more tongue, Hanny?" said Amelia, who
was hostess.

"Tom, pass the mustard," said Ethel, pushing the salt
towards her cousin, who was holding his plate for more
tongue.

"Have you been to any theatres?" asked Ethel, who
was fond of them.

"Not much. I've been to the Paragon now and then."

"We saw the *Sign of the Cross* the other night."

"What's it like? I've 'eard of it."

"It's splendid! So real, you know."

"Did you see it?" Hannibal asked Amelia, and she
nodded seriously.

"It's a lovely piece. You ought to go and see it. It's
always on somewhere."

"What's it about?"

"Oh, the Christians in Rome, you know. It's very religious."

"Is that so? Fancy! At a theatre too!"

"Clergymen go to see it," observed Ethel, looking into
Hannibal's cup. "More tea?"

"Thanks. I seen a piece called the *Fightin' Parson* once,
but I didn't see any clergymen there," remarked Hannibal.

"That's only a sketch!" said Amelia, with a contempt
difficult to imagine now. "The *Sign of the Cross* is quite
different."

"I must see it," said the young man, wondering where
he would find the money to go to theatres.

"Aunt Mary doesn't like theatres, does she?" enquired
Ethel, and Hannibal looked grave.

"No," he said, "she don't." He tried to imagine his
mother at a theatre and failed.

When tea was over young John offered Hannibal a

cigarette. Somewhat embarrassed he took it, knocking
the end on his thumbnail in a way that damned him as
one experienced in cigarettes. His cousin Amelia watched
him lean over towards John's match, and hoped it wasn't
a vice with him. She had not been prepared for a cousin
quite so grown up as he had proved to be; in fact her
intended attitude of patronage would have been impossible
if Hannibal had been more sophisticated. She was half
angry with herself for liking him, yet like him she did.
He had the full swimming eye that draws women, and
though the cigarette habit might breed trouble in a tobacconist's, it made him seem more manly and—subtle
point—independent of his mother.

I have reiterated, perhaps to weariness, the lack of
pride in the Brown family, and it is a fresh demonstra-
tion of it that, so far, they had not conceived any notions
of consolidating their position by means of advantageous
marriages. The lady who might have engineered any such
campaign was on her back in a Bournemouth hydro, entirely preoccupied with her own interior and the stimu-
lants which alone retarded dissolution. Amelia and Ethel
had no "fancy" idea which prevented them from enjoying
the society of "boys" of whose financial status they were
quite ignorant beyond their ability to pay for chocolates
and seats in the upper circle. Ethel was still in the engagement period, her clandestine attachments varying in dura-
tion from two days to a fortnight, with intervals of a
week. It may lower her in the reader's estimation, but it
will certainly convince him that she was not proud, when
it is stated that for the whole of the preceding September
she had been engaged simultaneously to a junior clerk at
Bournemouth (*ætat* nineteen) and a pattern-maker, a
chum of John's, at Camberwell. The temperament which
survives, nay flourishes, on such quick-change passion is
the temperament most often found in families who are
getting on, who are healthy in body, active in mind, and
who find in the *Sign of the Cross* a sublime moral lesson
for their souls. Nothing can stop these people in their
onward career; they fill up every ditch as they go. They
take no chances, are prepared for every emergency. Does
one part of the business fail? They recoup one another.

Is their house burnt? They are insured. Does a great disaster overwhelm their investments? Sons and daughters have each a calling and are at once earning wages. This temperament needs no pride to bolster it, it shines upon them and upon all their works as the incandescents glare down upon their sumptuous high-teas.

Amelia, of course, as became a girl who had a legacy, no longer entangled her emotions so promiscuously as Ethel; and it was characteristic of the Browns that she had no word of reproof for her sister. But Amelia had no particle of the snobbishness which would have led her to regard her poor cousin as so much East End dirt. The keen though unconscious pleasure which she took in cowing her aunt had its origin in quite another quarter. It had in fact two origins. One was Mrs. Gooderich's stiffness—her pride in fact—when the Browns were in the depths, and the other was Amelia's knowledge, through her mother, of the circumstances that led up to Mary Higgs marrying Amelia's Uncle Herbert. But the girl who refrained from babbling of those circumstances to her sister was not likely to let them affect her attitude towards the honestly-born blood-relative Hannibal. Behold here another point in the Brown breed. The good Berkshire blood which had gone to water in Mrs. Brown was red enough in her children, and carried with it a sane ethic which set a limit to the ostracism of bastardy. For them a man honest in business was the noblest work of God, but an honest woman was a frequent and gratifying spectacle and nothing to make a song about. Ethel's indiscretions ran not beyond sitting on a park seat with her lips glued to those of the hour; but her father had no fear whatever that she would overstep the somewhat elastic bounds of suburban propriety. And for the very reason that they felt passion in a healthily subordinated manner, they affected books and plays wherein passion is a wild and murderous emotional debauch, and regarded the Aunt Marys of life with piquant interest and wide-eyed wonder at their foolishness.

Hannibal, therefore, as he and Amelia, followed by Ethel and John, walked down the Kennington Road, lay under no ban in his cousin's eyes. She found herself again and again speaking without patronage. He, on the other hand, was discovering the charm of untrammelled speech with a young and attentive woman. It is encumbent upon us to acknowledge the genius of the Brown family, for they had succeeded, for a time at least, in banishing the look of suspicion and fear that had always sprung into the boy's eyes at his mother's mention of them. It had an intricate origin, that look, for it was born of an instinct that told him in quiet hours that their way led far from his, but it had become merged into the more superficial "pride" which was the bane of his mother's life. This dispersion could not have been entirely effected by artifice or even genuine lack of pride; the secret lay in the fact, hardly manifest to Amelia herself, yet, that she was interested in him.

"I shouldn't like any one belongin' to me to follow the sea," she told him, after they had discussed his visit to the *Cygnet* and he had tried to convey to her the strange charm of looking up at those vast spars and dizzy topmasts, the unique personality of a ship, and her mute message from the great Beyond. "An' the figger-'ead, it's an angel, 'oldin' one 'and to 'er breast and pointin' upwards like with the other. An' all gilt. Hiram Gaynor says she dips right in sometimes when it's a storm." He had tried, but without much success. Ships and the sea had to come across the theatre footlights to make any impression on Amelia. Her mind was like the old-fashioned cameras; the image appeared on the ground-glass screen upside down, and it needed the condensing lens of dramatic art to make any permanent impression at all. He had grasped his coat and pointed "upwards-like" with the other to show her what he meant, and she had smiled and drawn down the corners of her mouth in a way he came to know well, and looked round to see if any one had noticed his theatrical pose. Had he been on the stage she would have thrilled at the gesture and called it splendid. In the Kennington Road it was "silly."

"Don't!" she had muttered, and a flash of the old suspicion had darted across his face, only to vanish when she smiled. "Why," he said, following her glance round. "Where's Ethel an' John?"

"Somewhere along," she answered, as though the matter were of trivial interest. "We'll see them at the theatre; John's got the tickets."

When they reached the theatre and were working into the crowd that moved about in front of the main entrance, Hannibal found himself pressed up against his cousin, and it was the most natural thing for him to put his arm across her back and steer her along in front of him. She looked up at him once or twice, her lower lip between her teeth, and they exchanged glances and trivial remarks.

"It's always a crush on Saturday nights."

"Yes, s'pose so. Don't worry; I'll look after you."

"We'll have to wait here for John. This is the upper circle staircase."

"Right; where is 'e?"

"There he is."

John appeared forging through the crowd, alone.

"Where's Ethel?"

"We met Arthur, so I gave 'em the tickets an' came on," said the young mechanic. "They're gassin' about some'ink. Here y'are."

"John, you know father's pretty easy, but he draws the line at Arthur," said Amelia as they went up. "And I must say I agree with him too. If he had any idea——"

"Oh, rats, my, it's all off in five minutes."

"I know that. I'm not afraid of her doing anything so silly as that. What I mean is, I know and you know that Arthur's nothing more nor less than a bookie. That's what I'm so afraid o' father hearin'."

"Only now and again."

"No, it isn't now and again. I see him myself in the Kennington Road loitering round the gates, day after day. I wouldn't give much for his neck if father catches him with Ethel. You know how down he is on that sort of thing."

John did know, and winced. Hannibal listened to this little passage of arms with a deep interest. It is significant of the amorphous morality of our times that he should have grown up tolerant of betting and distrustful of theatres while the Brown family took theatres as a babe takes milk and held betting to be one of the seven deadly sins. For this latter sentiment is a natural outcome of their theory of life. They hold their positions by virtue of their capacity for industry and commerce, and by some instinct implanted in them in bygone ages they know the gambler and all his works to be their foe. There is no religious feeling in the matter, it is a plain strong morality fashioned to suit their temperament and condition. Ethel and John were young and had not yet arrived at full conviction. They played with fire, but played knowing as well as Amelia or Mr. Brown that it *was* fire; they never tried to palliate the offence.

To Hannibal the question took a different form. His street life, in conjunction with his employment in the Repositories, following a childhood in which early editions and talk of horses and their form passed without criticism, had familiarised him with the idea of betting, and the bookie was a mere detail of daily experience. Beyond the mild dissipation of a Derby-sweep his conscience was clear, for his interest in sport was small. But Amelia's strong sentiments on the subject, her obvious opinion that such practices were bad and not respectable, led him to fear that he himself might have some difficulty in appearing stainless before her. The prevailing sentiment in Assembly Passage, and even in Stepney Green, was that a bookie, unless he were a welsher, was a hard-working citizen with rights like everybody else. If he made a bit now and then, as no doubt he did, what of it? This view seemed to have no stability at all in the presence of Amelia's low-spoken denunciation of the wicked young Arthur. And with a sudden pang of wholesome shame Hannibal recalled the affair in Assembly Passage when he had evaded the blacksmith's attempts at capture. He coloured deeply as they passed into the theatre, and Amelia, catching sight of his face in a mirror, mistook the cause of it and fell to pondering upon the future.

V

"A BIT of all right," agreed Hannibal, stepping back to the kerb of Billiter Lane and surveying the ensemble.

You would scarcely have known him in his grey spring suit, his oiled hair, his coloured shirt with the cuffs turned back, his preoccupied business-like air. Something of the past lingered in the creased tie, the ill-fitting collar, and particularly in the boots. Boots are extraordinary things. When a man has raised himself in the world his boots are always the last to follow him up. He is never sure he will not slip back until his boots assume a permanent improvement. For one thing they are so expensive. Perhaps the use of trees has a good deal to do with it, and no one who has not gone through it can realise the tremendous difficulties of acquiring the tree-habit. With women, success—in boots—sometimes lingers until the daughters are grown up, and dancing is an obligation. Small wonder then that Hannibal's best, nine months old and eight-and-eleven in the Cambridge Heath Road, should contrast poorly with the spring trousers and the oiled hair.

He stood on the kerb oblivious of his boots, however, admiring the ensemble of Amelia's venture, which was to open next morning. Mr. Brown's incursion into shop-fitting had been recent but thorough, and he had taken a genuine pleasure in putting good work into his daughter's premises. The premises themselves, if plurals are not to be denied to a floor area of eleven feet by nine, had been provided with a sufficiency of shelves and electric lights (Gilfillan Filaments being specified by Amelia), a patent till and a rubber mat. Outside over the shop, Mr. Brown's sign specialist had had the pleasure of seeing a fancy of his own affixed: ground glass with red letters which were illumined at night.

Amelia, who was a hotbed of ideas, finally decided on a fancy name, "The Little Brown Box." Everything was mahogany in the shop, it was no larger than an ordinary shipping case, and her name was Brown. Again, it was customary, Amelia knew, for tobacco wholesalers to provide stock and fittings, charging the returns until the balance was paid off. This she described rather tersely as robbery, explaining to the scared Hannibal (in whose heart Assembly Passage still rankled) that by that method you could easily pay fifty pounds for ten pounds' worth of stuff. So the capable young woman, who had not been in a shop in the Strand and another in Holborn for nothing, ordered her stock for cash, and thereby was enabled to provide her customers with what they wanted and not with what some wholesale firm wanted to get rid of.

And now it was all ready, window dressed, lights in order, scales polished, everything; and he stood on the kerb approving. Amelia came out and looked up at the sign. Then she looked at Hannibal, biting her lip roguishly. It was growing dusk, and she tripped inside again and pressed the switch that illumined the sign. Vanity! She joined Hannibal on the kerb, and together they stared entranced at the words, the red glowing sans-serif letters of the sign:

THE LITTLE BROWN BOX

"Think it'll take?" she said.

"Rather!" he breathed.

"Worst of it is, it uses so much current," she mused, and then, Vanity having had her turn, Amelia ran inside and switched it off.

"If we were on a street, now, I'd leave it on to-night as an advertisement, but nobody ever comes down here at night except——" She pulled herself up and entered the shop again. Hannibal thought it very delicate of her not to say "cleaners."

Mrs. Gooderich would have stood any insults now, however, for Hannibal seemed to have turned the corner and to be on the upward path of commerce, industry, and respectability. She gathered, moreover, from her son's remarks that he and Amelia were on no mere commercial footing, that he admired his cousin for her business acumen, her strong sense and activity.

"She is a manager," he told his mother.

"Oh, Hanny, suppose you got to like each other?" she had said, and he had replied,

"So we do, old lady, but look at us. She's older'n me and she's the boss."

"That wouldn't make any difference," she said, trembling.

Hannibal thought it would. He stood in a curious position toward Amelia, a position which her cleverness had managed to disguise. She had soon found that any hint of patronage on her part roused the latent fear in his eyes, and she had adopted a blend of sisterly authority and business brusqueness that enabled him to find his way among his own feelings and sort them out, so to speak, while the coarser adjustments of human intercourse were being made. This was cleverness, for Hannibal's nature was really very delicately balanced. By virtue of that gift of his for seeing things in three dimensions instead of flat outlines and absurd silhouettes, it was necessary to be most circumspect in dealing with him. If Amelia had not felt her own weakness towards him, her downright criticism and tuition would have scared him away. This was not desirable, since an alien assistant would have been expensive.

Moreover, she liked him.

Hannibal did not discover this all at once. He might not have discovered it at all if she had not helped him. As, for instance:

They had been busy opening the cases of tobacco and cigars, Hannibal solemnly assisting with a brand new claw-hammer, while Amelia ticked off the items on a long advice-note which had come by post. It was all depressingly methodical and business-like, and Hannibal, festooned with straw, was reminded of the Repositories and felt the tentacles of Commercialism closing around him. He looked through the window; even Billiter Lane was flooded with spring sunshine. Across the way a steamship company exhibited a picture of a great liner at

anchor in some tropical port of the Far East, the white
hull surrounded by boats full of naked brown men, the
blue sea rimmed by mountains of a deeper blue and
crowned by a violet sky. To see "strange lands from under
the arched white sails of ships!" . . . He woke suddenly.
Amelia was calling out "What next?" Soberly he held
up a canister.

"Shag seven pounds," she ticked. "That goes into the
jars. We'll sell more of that than anything else. I don't
know how it is. You never see men smokin' shag, but
that's the stuff that goes quickest."

Briskly the work went on, Hannibal stealing a glance
now and then at the picture of the ship and wondering.
Hiram would be out that way now; he had been bound for
Singapore. Singapore! The name haunted him. Was that
it in the distance on that picture, that blur of gilt and
white far down the harbour? Billiter Lane! Singapore!

"That's the lot!" came Amelia's voice into his dreaming. "Well, Hanny, if we sell all that in a week, we'll be
rich, won't we?"

"We?" he said vaguely. "We? It's yours, ain't it? I'm
only the shopman."

He turned that full swimming brown eye upon her and
she quivered and laughed nervously.

"Don't be silly."

"It's a fact. Ten shillin' a week," he persisted.

"And a commission," she corrected.

"But it ain't 'we,' for all that."

"It may be. It might be better to be partners, p'raps,"
she whispered, making little dents on the advice-note with
her pencil.

So far had they attained when he had stepped to the
kerb to see the effect of the ensemble. So far that he
neglected to glance again at the picture of the steamer.
The Little Brown Box was now all swept and garnished;
all the debris had been put into the largest case and stored
under the counter. They gave it one last look round before
Amelia shut the door, drew the lattice gate across and
double locked it, giving Hannibal one of the keys.

"You'll want a ring," she said, and then stood, thunderstruck at her own madness. "For the keys, I mean," she added, smiling.

"Not for you?" he countered, shaking the steel gate.

"Oh, go on!"

It was plain sailing after that. The fact that he had only a few shillings of his own worried him at first, but the sisterly manner that Amelia cultivated prevented him feeling hurt when she paid for their tea. After all, he had been working nearly a fortnight and so far had had no wages. His reluctance to "take hold," as Mrs. Gaynor phrased it, to be really businesslike and alert, was in her favour. "You are a manager!" he said to her as to his mother. And I think that very defect of his was one of the reasons that Amelia liked him. His frank admiration of the speed and skill with which she stocked her show-cases and glass window-shelves was sweet as civet to her hardy spirit.

"I'll be down at nine sharp in the morning," she told him as they stood near Aldgate Pump. "I don't suppose there'll be any customers for the first few minutes. I've a good mind to send circulars round, after all father said," she mused. "A neat little folder, p'raps. Lamport and Gooling had a very nice one, I remember. It was like a smoker's cabinet and opened, you see, and inside were the prices and all particulars. I wonder if I could have something like that?"

Love is a subordinated passion in the Browns, remember! Amelia's hand was in her cousin's as she made these reflections, and it was no use expecting Hannibal to get these ideas. She would have to do it. And moreover she liked it. She had imagination and saw her little Brown Box thriving and throwing off other Brown Boxes until London was studded with them. Another idea seized her as she stood there saying good-bye, the idea of using flowers to decorate the Brown Box. Would the scent of tobacco kill them? Hannibal didn't know. Then she must ask Ethel. Ethel, who had been at a florist's in Knightsbridge, would know.

"It's a job to keep up with you," he laughed. "All these ideas!"

"You see," she explained pleasantly, "what you want

to be always on the watch for is something that'll make
people come in again, something to remember you by. I
forgot to tell you never to say 'Don't keep it.' It don't
matter what it is, if we haven't got it, we must get it
before they come in again. That's what a man likes. Perhaps he won't come in for a fortnight; doesn't matter. I
remember a gentleman comin' into Lamport and Gooling's
in the Strand, and asking for Capstan Full Strength.
Nobody ever used to smoke it then. He didn't come in
again for a month, and then he asked for cigarettes. When
I told him I had his Full Strength, he *was* pleased! And
he came in often after that."

"I see," said Hannibal.

"Now people like flowers and they're very cheap, with
all these girls about the city. So I'll see what Ethel says."

She left him with a cheery wave of the hand, her underlip in her teeth, and Hannibal took his way eastward
meditating on his good fortune. It speaks loudly for the
unreasonableness of his character that he should be un-
convinced and sombre on this evening previous to the
great event. She had signified unmistakably that she was
not indifferent to him. Was he grateful? Surely he should
be, when she had taken him up like this, made him smart
and useful and self-respecting. Surely this was better
than Assembly Passage, eh? his conscience almost
screamed at him. Eh, what? Going to sea? Yes, better
than going to sea, too. Hiram? H'm! Hiram didn't tell
the whole story. What about fevers and insects and salt
pork? What about scurvy and frost and blinding snow?
Eh? Hiram indeed!

So his conscience, pecking here and there from his
memory of maternal and avuncular oratory, answered and
overwhelmed him.

"I see I'm in for it," he remarked to himself. "And
I s'pose it might be worse."

I do not think his mind carried him as far forward as
marriage. Indeed, his mind never carried him in that
direction at all; all his excursions were made unhampered
by time and locality. The most trivial little thing was
sufficient to set him off, as that shipping poster had
carried him to Singapore and the unchanging East. What

ineffable happiness! To wander among strange peoples and palm trees! Palm trees, and white minaretted shrines, surf-torn beaches and blue mountains!

As he strode eastward toward Jubilee Street he thought again of these things. He figured Hiram on his ship with her great bellying sails driving through the deep dark blue waters of the ocean, Hiram lying in his narrow bunk in that tiny cabin by the mast, "rocked in the cradle of the deep." He figured him away ashore in one of those wonderful dream-cities, buying strange shells and boxes, seeing astonishing sights, living every moment to the full. And then he tried feebly to look forward along his own track, the humdrum beaten track Amelia was pointing out to him.

Some one bumped into him and he awoke with a sigh. The roar of the great London artery was all around him, the noise and the glare of the shops, the clatter of hoofs, and the ringing of bells. Hoarse voices cried their wares from barrow and stand, boys darted to and fro in play, sweethearts loitered arm-in-arm before the windows, mothers with their children trailed in and out. The life of the millions seethed and bubbled around him, leaving him solitary and sad. Once or twice during the last fortnight it had come to him in a fugitive way that he lacked character. Why did he feel so helpless before Amelia's resistless energy and capable knowledge of the world? She was only twenty or so, yet he was as a child in her hands. Why was he always wandering from the point, dreaming of far-away, seeing himself in extraordinary and fantastic regions? Was he an idiot? Was he predestined to fail in this great roaring world into which fate had pitched him? He wondered.

He was silent at supper that night, his mother failing to elicit more than monosyllables. Anxiously, after the fashion of mothers, she supplied his wants, for your dreamy unpractical youth is as ravenous as any one, in spite of the food of dreams on which he feeds in secret.

"Everything all right, Hanny?" she asked him.

"Yes, I s'pose so, old lady," he mumbled.

Later she bent over him as he slept, after the foolish fashion of her kind, trembling, yet with an unwonted gladness in her eyes. To launch one frail craft safely, to see him on his way secure and ballasted with gold. . . . What happiness! After long grief and pain, after tragic failure and the bitter bread of indigence and neglect, to sink back and sigh "nunc dimittis." Could it be?

She knelt down and prayed incoherently to God that it might be so.

VI

IT WAS a custom in the Brown family to have occasional reunions in their house off the Kennington Road. For Mrs. Brown, of course, it had of late become out of the question, but the young people kept it up. Tom-tom, of course, was engaged, and to a very nice girl too, who was in an office, in the City, and helped him in his book-keeping. John's steady flame burned before a pale young lady, "very refined," in black, whose people had had losses. Ethel, not to be outdone at these gatherings, would hastily select from among her loves a presentable specimen (not necessarily engaged, but eligible), and bring him to her father as "Friend o' mine, dad."

And Amelia brought in Hannibal.

Mr. Brown brought in a battalion of old friends on his own account, and all these people, shovelled together and wedged in the neat villa, were very bewildering to Hannibal. But the Browns enjoyed it. They had, to its fullest range, that glorious gift of enjoying vulgar pleasures. The apple of their content was not cankered by the worm of culture and fastidiousness. They ate their high tea, passing each other salt and bread and great trenchers of provender; they stood up and made silly, laughable speeches while they cut a pie and pulled a cork; they joked in a quite impossible way about affairs of the heart; they sang comic songs that were not comic, and love-songs that reached to the depths of banality. They had a gramophone and used it, sometimes during the meal. They had mandolins, and Tom-tom went regularly every Monday and Thursday to learn the banjo. Ethel, that youthful Messalina of Kennington, played after a fashion on the piano, by which I mean she vamped, and having a good ear and a non-critical audience, she did better than many. Later on in their career they took up piano-players and the gramophone was put in the breakfast-room. For the

Browns are the real supporters of progress in the Arts. They are always the first to take up the new idea. Who had incandescent mantles first? Neither you nor I; but the Browns had them while we walked in darkness. Who first discarded the old musical-box and bought the gramophone? Who seized the safety bicycle and made it their own? Who listens to the voice of the inventor crying in the wilderness? Not the cultured and leisured ones of the land, not the literary and scientific, but the Browns, the Cerebos of the earth. They are the people who read the advertisements.

The subject of the hour when Hannibal first attended one of these functions was dancing. John was taking lessons and was very serious about it, by which I mean he was "taking hold" and studying the subject. Ethel seemed always able to hop about, and quite surprised them all by stating her intention of "taking it up."

"Why, I thought you knew all about it," said her father, carving cold beef. Ethel smiled in a superior way.

"Oh, I've only picked it up, dad. Lessons are different."

She took it up, dropped it, took it up again, and then, in consequence of a disappointment (the young man going to Honolulu without warning), abandoned dancing for professional rinking, which rolled her, almost before she was aware of it, into the arms of a husband.

Hannibal sat amid the clatter of knives and forks and the babel of the reunion ill at ease. Here was another of his defects being painfully shown up. When Amelia asked him if he could dance, he shook his head mournfully.

"Then you must learn," she informed him. What a girl she was for ideas! He hadn't thought of that. The same with cards. After tea he sat beside her, cards in hand, trying to keep his attention on the game. If you can't do a thing, take hold and learn. How efficient they all were! Even Mr. Brown was winning a whole heap of wax vestas at whist. Later they began singing. Tom-tom led off with "Sing me to sleep," accompanied by John's sweetheart, all joining in the chorus. By this time Mr. Brown and his senior friends were sitting over cigars and whisky in the dining-room, leaving the youngsters to themselves and

their love-making in the drawing-room. For the Browns
had no pride and no false shame in making love under
three incandescent mantles. They kissed each other, and
sat on each other's knees in a most refreshingly frank
fashion, and when John trod on Amelia's skirt and brought
it down, there was a roar of merriment and every one
helped to fix it up again. And then when Ethel was forced
on to the piano stool and they began whirling round to
the measure of a waltz, Hannibal found himself seized.

"Come on, I'll show you," said a laughing voice in his
ear; and before he was aware of it he was holding
Amelia's waist and watching John's agile feet in an
endeavour to glide. He was terribly self-conscious and
awkward, but to the Browns self-consciousness while
learning to do anything was a forgotten myth. All they
demanded of you was that you should try, and be good-
tempered. "Keep on your toes," commanded Amelia, doing
her best to avoid shipwreck against the corner of the
piano. If she had added, "And keep off mine," the advice
would not have been out of place.

At length the "dreamy" waltz tune was shut off in the
middle of the bar in the irritating way amateur musicians
have, and the sliding molecules of humanity stopped and
broke away with laughter and gasps for breath.

"Do you like it?" asked Amelia, readjusting a hairpin.
Her cheeks were flushed, and when she showed her even
teeth she looked almost pretty. Hannibal felt to see if his
tie was up at the back, and then laughed.

"Don't know if I'll ever be much good at it," he replied.
"I never went in for that sort o' thing much."

"But you will?"

"Why—I s'pose so."

A shadow crossed Amelia's face as she looked at him.
She liked him; he seemed all right in the Little Brown
Box, and he looked a very desirable young man as he
stood there, his face flushed and his attractive brown eyes
smiling at her. But she did not like this streak of ineffec-
tiveness, this lack of "go." To her it was silly for a man
to be reluctant when you showed him the way. She looked
over to where John was explaining to Ethel and Tom-
tom the intricacies of his last lesson. Wild horses, Red

Indians, all Hell would not stop John in his pursuit of the art of dancing now he had taken it up. But Hannibal did not seem interested.

It was quite true that he was doing pretty well at the Little Brown Box. Each morning he opened the collapsible gate and pulled up the brown blinds, each evening he lowered those same blinds and locked the gate. He was slowly acquiring familiarity with the stock, and had even made one or two ventures in the direction of "patter," that light conversation which many customers ignore when it is offered, yet miss when it is denied them. To Amelia it came as naturally as breathing. Comments on the weather came pattering from her lips as pearls fell from the lips of the lady in the fairy story. As for Hannibal, if his remarks had been frogs they could not have been more difficult to bring up. People seemed to answer Amelia, giving her an opening, so to speak. She would say, "Looks as if it was clearing, doesn't it?" and the customer would laugh grimly and say he hoped so, but was not going to put his money on London weather. If it were gloriously fine, she would suggest it was a good day to change a sovereign, and the customer would cackle with amusement and ask her what she did with herself during the long evenings. But if Hannibal, after severe thought, alluded to the fineness of the day, the customer would either ignore him altogether or point out with biting politeness a shortage in the change which Hannibal was tendering.

He began to hate the weather.

Eventually, however, Amelia contented herself with a daily visit to let him go and get his dinner. They got on very well when they were by themselves. It was in the company of the Browns and their kindred that she found something lacking in his spirit. When they were alone, I think she rather preferred his quietness and the little affectionate way he had of touching her cheek with his finger, of settling her collarette under her jacket, and other habits that he practised but did not speak of. It is possible, though it seems madness to suggest it, that the Browns' scheme of existence had left one of the human instincts unprovided for, that the jolly, efficient, sociable

Brown religion was at times a little trying even to its communicants, and that Amelia was unconsciously drawn to her cousin by reason of his deficiencies. Those flowers in the Little Brown Box led me to think there might be something in this view, those flowers and the canaries who sang high up among the cigar stock. Perhaps there was a streak of poetry in Amelia, a thin vein of gold in that quartz of her nature. The worst of the Browns is, that when they become aware of the vein of gold they turn it into money. The Little Brown Box was getting a name for its flowers and canaries. They brought custom and business was good.

To Mrs. Gooderich there came one benefit of all this: she escaped from Amelia's bullying. It sounds harsh when written down, but no other word is to be found to express so justly the attitude of well-fed young women towards a dispirited widow who is cursed with pride. Attaining to a certain vague sympathy with Hannibal's nature she found her feelings altered towards his mother. She paid visits, unknown to him, to Jubilee Street. She met Mrs. Gaynor there once, and experienced that lady's soothing influence. It was at this time that she was made aware of her Cousin Minnie's presence in London. The details were meagre enough; she was in partnership with a French-woman in Ebury Street, in a dressmaking business. Enquiry from Ethel elicited the fact that Ebury Street was "all right, down Chelsea way, penny 'bus from the top of Sloane Street." But Amelia was in no mood now to make up any scandal about her relatives. There was nothing to be got from Mrs. Gaynor anyway. She had the strangest way of hoping and believing Minnie was behaving respectably, and if she was, Mrs. Gaynor said, what were you going to do about it? Being a Brown, this was a little bewildering to Amelia, but she rested content with the facts.

And Hannibal behind the counter—what of him? We have seen him at the reunion, a rather unadaptable youth bewildered with novel ideas of amusement, abashed equally before the giddy Ethel and John's refined young lady. He was not "at his best" at the reunion. But behind the counter, beneath the canaries and within sight of that picture of the steamer across the way, how did he fare, this inarticulate lad with his long thoughts?

The fact is, he had formed another habit of which Amelia was not aware. Even chartering-clerks and water-clerks, to say nothing of shipowners hurrying to and from the Baltic, are not in continual need of tobacco and cigars, and Hannibal had periods of inaction when the shop was deserted. He could not smoke continually (Amelia discouraged smoking behind the counter, anyway), and he fell into the newspaper habit. It gave him subjects for conversation, if a customer were not in a hurry. But the newspaper, admittedly a great and glorious institution, has its limitations. *The Literary Year Book* tells me it is primarily for the dissemination of news, and I am willing to believe it, though I find a good many advertisements. Hannibal's paper, for example, which cost him a half-penny, devoted the front page to a New Corset. The back page was occupied by a "heart to heart talk" by the write-up expert attached to Gilfillan Filaments Limited. It was called "Darkest London and the Way Out," and the new form of filament now offered was modestly described as The Light of the World. Opening the journal, you found inside still more appeals to your better nature by the retailers of Cocoa and Whisky firms. You found elixirs which reduced your fat, secrets which increased your fat, "home treatments" which, if you were a lady, would develop your bust until you resembled a pouter pigeon. Illustrations were provided to show you the gradual inflation. It may add to your opinion of Mrs. Gooderich to know that Hannibal did not care to look at those illustrations; they seemed to him unpleasant. If you were a man and suffered excruciating agony in your spine, as per illustration of a pain-racked *laocoön,* you were informed that you had only yourself to blame, since Elixerine was just two-and-ninepence a bottle and every chemist kept it. Furnishing firms pleaded with you to avoid wrecking your happiness and Hers by senseless delay. Home! Was it not the sweetest word in our noble English tongue? Had you no duty to the Motherland, to Love, to your unborn children? Were they to come into the world and find you—married, no doubt—but without that exquisite drawing-room suite at six shillings down and the balance at threepence a week? Hannibal became quite disturbed when he read some of these, but they were *pastiche* compared with the shrieks arising from the columns where the unguents "distilled from rare herbs indigenous to the Upper Himalayas" were described. "I was a mass of scabs," reported a lady in high society; and did not seem a bit ashamed of it either, for there was her portrait, with jewels and scabs complete. Hannibal's notions of high society were confused enough, but he thought "it was a case for a 'orspital" when one's face got as bad as that.

Eventually his wandering mind was caught by an item of news hidden away in the middle of the paper, far from the madding crowd's ignoble strife, a brief report of a fire in China, where a couple of hundred thousand had been driven from their homes by the flames. His imagination was caught by the news; he tried to figure to himself all those terrified yellow men and women battling with the fire, the roar as the wind blew it onward, the cries of the dying, the desolation of the smoking ruins. He wished there was more about it, but somehow the newspaper had no room for any more. There was a most eloquent article just below—over half a column—giving the circulation figures of the paper for the previous month. There he saw another paragraph stating that a sailing ship had been lost with all hands off Cape Horn, and Hannibal's thoughts went back to Hiram on the *Cygnet*. He would close his paper and put it away under the counter with a sigh. The agony of those yellow men, that last fight with all-encompassing death in the storm, these things seemed trivial indeed to the newspaper. Evidently people did not want to be told what was happening in the great world. They wanted to be told what to buy.

He had an idea one day, though this has nothing to do with the habit. Amelia came in with her usual briskness, and after smiling a greeting she stood looking round critically at the counter-dressing, considering improvements.

"Goodness me! What's that?" she exclaimed, as a faint squeal reached her ears. Hannibal grinned and beckoned her to come round. She came round quickly and stopped short at the sight. A small grey kitten was trying valiantly to climb up his leg, a tiny atom of a thing, with a pointed tail and scared eyes.

Amelia did not like cats, and she was about to say so sharply when something in his attitude as he stooped and took the little thing in his arms made her pause. His face was apologetic, yet——

"Thought it 'ld be company," he muttered. "They was goin' to drown it, so I fetched it up."

"Nasty little things," she muttered. "I can't bear 'em."

The kitten clambered up on his shoulder, and erecting the pointed tail seemed well pleased.

"Mind you don't leave the canaries down on the floor then when you clean the cage," she warned him.

"That's all right, Amy. You don't mind me 'avin' it?"

"If you really want it, only we don't want a menagerie in the shop, do we?"

"No. Only time 'angs a bit in the mornin's, you see."

"You ought to follow the news. Keep up with the times."

"So I do, but there's nothin' in the paper 'cept advertisements."

"Well, why not get a book out of the libr'y? It passes the time."

"That's a good idea!" he remarked, stroking the kitten. "There's an ol' book-shop in Aldgit I pass every mornin'. There's all sorts in the tuppeny box. I'll 'ave a look at 'em."

"You don't want to *buy* books!" she nearly screamed. There are some things the Browns of this world cannot and will not stand, and spending money on books is one of them. Buying a book is with them a sign of a mind unhinged.

"Now an' again," he suggested, cowed. "They're only tuppence."

And that was how he contracted the habit which led to acquaintance with Mr. Brober.

VII

It was he who spoke first as Hannibal shyly took up book after book in the twopenny box and scanned the pages for something that might interest him. The twopenny box did not seem to contain much of that sort. In fact, whatever the authors of those books had aimed to accomplish, it was not to thrill the reader.

"Student?" enquired Mr. Brober, a black briar in his mouth. He was an elderly unclean man, in an old frock coat and a golf cap of uncertain shape, and his shoulders were bent as he accosted Hannibal.

The young man put the book down nervously and laughed.

"Me? No, Mister."

He might have been, thought Mr. Grober, looking him over. He often had poor students at his shop, dressed in shabby suits and amorphous boots. For Hannibal's new spring suit, following the eternal law of spring suits selling ready-made at twenty-seven shillings (*vide* advertisement twice a week in Hannibal's halfpenny paper), was now, after six months' wear, decrepit, without form and void of symmetry.

"I was going to say," continued Mr. Grober, "that if you were, I have a stock of text-books inside at extremely low prices. Come in."

"I was only lookin' fer something to read," explained Hannibal apologetically, as though such a motive were unheard of by a bookseller. And he followed the old man into the gloom of his shop.

"Here they are," said Mr. Grober, indicating several shelves of thin books with gilt letters on the backs, Classics, Mathematics, and Science.

Hannibal shook his head.

"No use to me," he assured the old gentleman. "I've got no 'ead for that stuff."

"Then what?" asked Mr. Grober, sitting down in his chair again. "What is the sort of work you require?"

"Work?" echoed Hannibal blankly.

"I mean book," Mr. Grober corrected. "What sort of book do you require?"

Hannibal gazed round helplessly at the dusty shelves. "Something to read," he replied.

"Novels?"

"No, not novels." Hannibal's notion of novels was confined to the formidably long romances his mother had been accustomed to read. "Not novels."

"What then? Books of travel or——"

"Ah! Something about the sea. I s'pose you 'aven't anything like that—cheap?" He waved his hands.

This was the beginning of Hannibal's induction to literature. For nearly an hour he sat in the dusty shop while Mr. Grober descanted upon the decline of taste in good literature. Many of his remarks fell upon empty air. It was evident that Mr. Grober only required an audience, he took replies for granted. Eventually, however, he came round to the subject of immediate interest to Hannibal. He directed attention to a box of paper-covered books and explained his system. When you had read it, you brought it back to Mr. Grober in good condition, and he gave you twopence for it. By this scheme you paid a penny only for a volume published at sixpence or a shilling. To Hannibal the scheme seemed admirably adapted to his needs, and begged Mr. Grober to select something for him. Relighting his black briar, Mr. Grober complied, laying out volume after volume. Many of them seemed to the lad to belong to that class of literature known to illiterate folk as "blue." There was *Manon Lescaut, Mon Uncle Barbassou, Moll Flanders, Madame Bovary,* and those beautiful short stories with which Emile Zola lightened the sombre burden of his days. Then Hannibal's eye lighted upon *An Iceland Fisherman,* and he took it up.

"It's about the sea," he said, and Mr. Grober nodded.

"One of the most exquisite idylls of the sea," he remarked. "I doubt if you will quite appreciate to the full the genius of Loti."

"I think I'll take this for a start," said Hannibal, producing threepence. "I was thinkin' o' goin' to sea once," he confided.

Mr. Grober was not interested in this. He was one of those men who can be reached by no other channel save that of literature. He would have passed every fisherman from Dundee to Southwold without noticing they were fishermen, but *An Iceland Fisherman* was literature, *ergo* he knew all about it.

How shall we describe the boy's delight in the new world that now opened out before him? Ravenously he followed the fortunes of those French sailors in the stormy north seas, in the treacherous Channel and out in the burning East. Sometimes he would draw a long breath and look out long and earnestly at that steamer in the blue harbour, while the grey kitten climbed over him, purring in his ear, and the canaries sang above him. And then, when the door opened and a customer came in, he would return to reality with a jump and pursue his business of selling tobacco.

"It's all right, that," he told Mr. Grober when he brought it back. There was a slight crack in the cover which he feared had not improved the volume, but Mr. Grober did not notice it and motioned to him to pick out another.

It was late, for he had been for a walk with Amelia, and near closing time, and Mr. Grober seemed taciturn and uneasy. As Hannibal turned round he saw the door at the back partly open and a sharp-featured woman peering out. The door closed abruptly as he turned. Mr. Grober followed him outside to bring in the boxes preparatory to shutting up. Hannibal, sensing Mr. Grober's desire to explain something, flung his thumb over his shoulder.

"Old lady?" he asked in a low tone. Mr. Grober bowed his head over the threepenny box.

"The same," he said.

"I see," said Hannibal, though he saw nothing.

"The fact is," said Mr. Grober, straightening himself with the box on his hands. "The fact is, my young friend, that though many of our master minds have described Hell, and many of our great painters have endeavoured to represent it on canvas, not one of them has succeeded in portraying anything so ghastly as a square peg in a round hole!"

And Mr. Grober marched slowly into the shop and deposited the box on a chair. Hannibal stood waiting for further revelations, hoping they might be clearer than this one. When the old man emerged and bore down upon the twopenny box, he said:

"'Ow d' you mean, Mister?"

"I mean," said Mr. Grober, "I mean that the torments of a Lost Soul are radiant bliss compared with the life of an Idealist in a world of Stark Reality!" And in he went, his old golf cap askew on his grey head, his untidy head on his breast, a forlorn and weary figure.

"What's up, Mister?" enquired the youth when he reappeared to pull down the shutters. Mr. Grober grasped the pole and held it out at arm's length, looking sternly up the street. The few people who were passing took no notice of them.

"Under your arm," remarked Mr. Grober, "you have the story of a man who never married. Eventually he drowned himself. He chose the better part."

And pulling down his shutter with a jar and a bang, Mr. Grober re-entered his premises.

Hannibal, *Toilers of the Sea* safe in his pocket, went home in deep thought. To a certain extent he understood Mr. Grober's cryptic utterances to refer to domestic affairs. Things, he concluded, had gone wrong between 'em. Old chap was fed up, perhaps. She didn't look over good-tempered. He told his mother about it over his supper.

"P'raps he drinks?" said Mrs. Gooderich. "What 'ave you got this time?" She looked through Victor Hugo's pages. "What is it, a novel?" she asked.

"I reckon it's a story from the look of it," he returned "but not like that one you're readin'." And he pointed with his knife to where Mrs. Southworth's works lay among the things on a side-table. Mrs. Gooderich would not argue this point with a young man. One of the remnants which made up her ethical bundle was a disbelief in too much reading for children. Certainly her children had never indulged themselves in this vice. She regarded the book with suspicion. About a man who never married, eh? And Mr. Grober said he chose the better part. What a difference between such books and *Ishmael,* which was about a man who had two wives at once! Of course, it was all a terrible mistake, and didn't he pay bitterly for it? But that was so true. We do pay for our mistakes, Mrs. Gooderich thought.

"He's a funny old chap," Hannibal went on. "He talks like a book."

"I only 'ope," said Mrs. Gooderich, "that 'e won't go puttin' ideas into your 'ead, that's all."

It would be a grave offence, she thought, to put ideas into people's heads.

VIII

WHEN Amelia came briskly along Billiter Lane one evening in May, she crossed over to the other side to obtain
a good view of the Little Brown Box. Everything was in
apple-pie order in the window, she noted, the sign had
been cleaned, the door-handles were bright, and her face
expressed calm approval. What a pity Hanny was such a
stick to go out with! He didn't seem to have any idea
what to say to a girl. That reading habit of his seemed
to be spoiling him. She stood a few moments watching,
but there was no sign of him coming out to meet her.
H'm! Reading, very likely, or playing with the kitten.
She stepped across, opened the door, and found the place
empty.

For a moment she looked round helplessly, her brain
stunned by the enormity of the thing. A canary trilled
and twittered at her, but she took no notice. The kitten,
asleep on the counter, stretched and curled up again.
Amelia drew a quick breath, stepped behind the counter
and took off her things. She hardly knew what to think.
Had there been an accident? Had he . . . ? She darted
to the till, unlocked it and counted feverishly. No, it
seemed about as usual. What then? Suddenly a figure
passed the window, the door opened and Hannibal came
in. Her face hardened.

"This the way you look after your work?" she asked.

"Just went out for some change, Amy," he replied, his
eyes faltering as he glanced from the open till to her
face. He came round and put some silver into the drawer.
She looked at him coldly.

"Why didn't you lock the door?" she asked. "The whole
place might have been cleared out. How long have you
been away?"

"Only a minute."

"I've been here five," she said, and a curious look came

over her face. "We'd better have it out now or we'll get into a bad way," she went on.

"I can see who comes in from—from the other place," he said sullenly.

"What other place?"

"The pub down—on the other side," he said.

"Oh, you get change at the pub, do you? What's the matter with the bank? I thought we'd arranged all that. You've got all the change you need there, as far as I can see."

"Oh, all right, all right," he muttered.

"It isn't all right, all right," she retorted. "This shop's mine, and I can't afford to have it left alone, that's all."

"Anybody'd think I was out all the time," he complained.

"As you will be if nobody says anything." She turned away with a gesture of vexation. "I was comin' up to ask you to come over to supper this evenin', and—and this spoils it all." She finished with a break in her voice. Hannibal was silent, shifting uncomfortably from foot to foot.

"It won't 'appen agen," he said at length.

"How do I know?" she flung at him passionately. "I thought we were goin' to get on so well, too."

He turned and put out his hand as though to touch her, but she moved away and his hand dropped irresolutely. A customer came in and broke the spell, and Hannibal busied himself with the stock while Amelia served. When the man had gone out, she began again.

"Promise me," she said, steadily. "Promise me you won't go into a pub again."

"All right," he answered in a low voice.

"Can't you see," she queried, "how important it is not to leave the shop for a minute? It's all for your own good, isn't it? If people come in . . . why the business'll drop right down if people come in and find nobody here!" She looked at him wide-eyed. All the tradition of the Brown family was outraged by this terrible and unheard-of defection. Hannibal twisted uneasily under her gaze.

"Yes, I know," he muttered.

"I only hope," she said, "you're tellin' me the truth, and

you didn't go to the pub for anything else. I don't like those places. They never did anybody any good yet."

He was silent.

"You haven't promised me, Hanny," she added gently.

"All right," he said. "You know best, I s'pose."

"I do, that's a fact. Now, are you comin' down to Kennington?"

"Yes, I'll come. I was goin' down to get a book though."

"Well, it isn't far, is it? I'll come down with you."

At seven o'clock they shut up the Little Brown Box and walked down Fenchurch Street towards Aldgate, joining the dense throng of homeward-bound toilers who were tempted by the summer feeling in the air to avoid the 'buses and wear out their shoe-leather instead. It is marvellous how difficult it is in London to get any pleasure without paying for it. Amelia looked at the girls who passed with interest. She knew them all well, knew what they worked at, how much they earned and how they lived. She was not above them just because she had a shop. No thought of superiority ever entered her head. If she had had "property," of course it would be different.

"These Sheenies!" she said laughingly to Hannibal as a tall, stylishly-dressed Jewess passed them in her panoply of velvet and lace. "What a rig to work in!"

Hannibal started guiltily. He had been far away from Aldgate just then.

"Ah," he said.

"I shall have to keep an eye on you," said his cousin archly, "or perhaps you'll be keepin' company down here."

"Not me," he asserted with vivid sincerity. "One's enough for me."

"D'you mean it?" she asked, not quite certain of his drift.

He paused in front of Mr. Grober's faded shop.

"This is it," he said. "I shan't be a minute." And he went in hastily. Amelia regarded the place with some disdain. A second-hand bookshop was not much in her line. Hannibal had explained how he got his books for a penny each, and she had expressed a hope that there was no danger in them. "You never know where they've been," she remarked.

Mr. Grober was glad to have a visitor. He offered Hannibal a battered and ill-printed copy of *The Flying Dutchman* and begged him to take a seat.

"I can't. I got a little friend waitin' outside," he explained.

Mr. Grober was visibly depressed. He had hoped, he said, that Hannibal would have a chat and possibly some refreshment.

"Not now," said the young man hastily, looking through the shelves at Amelia. Mr. Grober looked also.

"Ah," he remarked. "A counter-attraction, I see."

"Some other time," said Hannibal, moving off. "Goo' night, Mr. Grober."

"Good night, and heaven help you," said the old gentleman, watching Amelia from behind the books. He came to the door, and when she looked in his direction bowed in an old-fashioned way. But Amelia did not include Mr. Grober among her charities. He was dirty and untidy, and he looked incompetent, her critical glance told her. She moved off quickly with her cousin.

"You aren't taking up with that sort of people, are you?" she asked coldly.

"Me? Oh, I have a chat now and then," said Hannibal, trying to be unconcerned.

"Well, I shouldn't if I was you. At least it's this way: We can't afford to be friends with such people. They always want something, generally money."

"He don't want anything," remonstrated Hannibal.

"I'm only tellin' you. He looks as if he could do with some, anyhow. I hate these untidy people. Let's take a 'bus."

When they were on the 'bus, she began again. She took possession of his mind, stowing away axiom after axiom, fact after fact, until he was bewildered and sullen. She felt that she must lose no time in formally educating him up to the Brown standard.

"If people aren't gettin' on, they're slippin' back," she told him. "They can't stand still. And if they're slippin' back it's best to keep away—you can't do anything."

"Why not give 'em a 'and same as you did me?" he asked.

She folded her hands on her purse and looked steadily ahead towards the Surrey side.

"Relations are different," she observed, and thereby handed him another piece of family philosophy. "That old fellow has never done himself any good and he's not likely to do you any. Keep yourself to yourself, except among those you know."

" 'E's 'ad a very good education," ventured Hannibal.

"So I should say by the dirt behind his ears," said Amelia. "I've seen his sort in the Strand, or something very like it. They want tick, these people with wonderful educations and long hair. Mind you don't encourage him."

"All right, Amy. What's on to-night?"

"I was goin' to tell you, only so many things put it out o' my head. Mother's comin' home from Bournemouth to-night and we're goin' to meet her. It's at eight-thirty at Victoria."

"Is she?" said Hannibal dubiously.

"Well, you don't seem very enthusiastic," complained the young lady. "Mother's very delicate, but she manages at home now the weather's warm. I suppose you haven't seen her for a long while?"

"Not since the funeral," he replied briefly. To Hannibal and his mother there was but one funeral, and they had used the phrase to cover a number of things. "Since the funeral" meant since Minnie had left them, since Maple Avenue had become a memory, since Bert had gone.

"Well," said Amelia, "you'll see her now." To the Browns their mother's illness was not a thing to joke about. If they had been poor they would have gone without the necessaries of life to get her wine and beef extract. They were a brilliant example of the family who owe nothing to their parent save their being, yet who worship her and revere her weakness as though she had sacrificed everything for them.

"What's the matter with Aunt Eliza?" asked Hannibal, in the same tone as he would ask "What's the matter with the chimney?" if it smoked.

"Kidneys," said Amelia in an awed voice. Neurasthenia had not been discovered then, and nervous disorders were located in the body by an unimaginative faculty. "She had breakdowns too. Doctor says that she mustn't exert herself at all. It's a great strain on her, this railway journey. Dad went down this morning to bring her up."

"I expect she's forgotten all about me," Hannibal surmised.

"I told her, you know, when I wrote about the shop and all that."

The conversation dwindled, and Hannibal found himself faced by the problem which had been growing and growing in his mind for some time. It was a curious problem for a young man of reflective mood to find before him, like a black cloud which he could not elude, being none other than this: "What am I doing?" To such clarity of vision had he arrived by this time, aided undoubtedly by the books he had been absorbing day by day. For, unlettered as he was, unskilled in the fine analysis of motive and feeling, he saw plainly enough that the difference between himself and these men in the books was simply they were doing something, while he was dreaming his life away amid cousins, canaries, and cigarettes. The thought grew and grew within him, and his eyes became less and less observant of the material world. It was an intensely interesting question for a young man, for he was aware in a dim fashion that, if he liked, he could batter down the walls of the prison, he could struggle out into the fresh air and join those heroic souls who do things in the world.

He was unfortunate perhaps in this, that Amelia had none of the fine, careless admiration for courage which had been so fashionable among young women a few years ago, when the war-spirit was upon the nation. It died away, if you remember, afterwards, a wave of religious and social uplifting swept across the land, knights in shining armour were seen no more, khaki-clad bank-clerks went again into the black livery of their calling, and the army lost its prestige among women. Amelia was a very accurate reflection of her class. Had she been touched with that lust for romance which was, we are told, inseparable from mediæval womanhood, she might have given Hannibal the necessary impetus to perform

some deed of daring. This, however, was not to be. Amelia
was a child of her time, a time of peace and music-halls,
of social reform and municipal enterprise. To her, as to
all the other girls of that period, courage and high endeavour, romance and beauty, were not to be found in life
but on the stage and cinema-film. Hannibal felt this, and
gave no sign of the difficulty that confronted him. She
would have looked at him blankly at first, and then the
corners of her mouth would have come down in contempt.
To her a craving for a fuller life would have meant simply
an excuse to get out of working. Her world was littered
with people who dodged or tried to dodge their natural
destiny—labour. She classed Mr. Grober with these. For,
strange to say, running a tobacconist's was work, but a
second-hand bookshop was "mooching about."

Their entry into the Brown homestead caused a diver-
sion of their thought from matters purely personal to
those of the family. Ethel it was who, in a white blouse
with short sleeves and a narrow band of velvet round the
throat, answered the door and gave them a wide-welcom-
ing smile.

"Good old Amy, here at last!" she said. "Come along,
Hanny, we're waiting for you. Father'll have a fit if we're
late."

They were all round the supper-table; John and his
young lady, Tom and his, Ethel with a brand-new and
extremely eligible looking young man in a tail-coat, who
was in fact the laundry-manager who afterwards levanted
to Honolulu. It was obvious that to them this home-coming
of an invalid mother was an event of importance. Hannibal felt that if he could feel no interest in Mrs. Brown
he could not possibly be one of the family. In some de-
jection he admitted to himself that his interest was *nil*.
He regarded Ethel's new young man with envy. With all
imaginable ease the laundry-manager slid into the stream
of conversation, picking up the threads of past topics with
dexterous precision, and receiving confidences in a way
that showed unmistakably the Browns were forgetting
how recently he had joined their ranks. Hannibal demanded of himself with some bitterness why he could not
do that, but without eliciting any clear reply.

"I see you're one of the thoughtful sort," said Miss Sanderson, John's refined young lady, who sat next to Hannibal. She smiled indulgently at the bread her long fingers were crumbling, and looked at him kindly. He gave a sigh of relief and returned her gaze frankly.

"It's only because I 'aven't anything to say," he told her in confidence. "Somehow I never do 'ave in company," and he sighed again.

"Perhaps you think all the more," she insisted, with another smile.

"I'd'no," he said. "I reckon if a chap thinks, he can spit it out, don't you? If he thinks real, I mean."

"How do you mean by real?"

"Why, when a chap thinks o' something and then does it. 'E's got something to talk about then."

"Why not do something then?" Miss Sanderson's eyes were smiling. She was enjoying herself with the young man.

"How can I, selling fags?" he asked simply.

"What do you want to do?" she queried.

"That's just it," he told her, a far-away look in his eyes. "That's just it. I'm blowed if I know."

"But aren't you trying to get some idea?"

"Oh, I got millions of ideas, but what's the use if you 'aven't got the dough?"

"John's got ideas by the thousand for patents," she laughed. "But I'm afraid he'll never get the dough, as you call it."

"It's different with 'im," Hannibal mused in confidence to her. "He's got 'is dad. I daresay 'e'll put up the tin some day if John wants it. I feel a bit out of all this," he added, as they rose from the table, "though I don't know why I should be tellin' you."

"I'm interested," she said, with a glance at once arch and sympathetic. "You must tell me about some of those millions of ideas."

"What are you two flirting about?" called Ethel, who was pinning on her hat in front of a mirror and could therefore see behind her.

"You be quiet, Eth. Hanny and me are having a little chat all by ourselves."

"John, you'll have to be careful," said Tom, brushing his hat. "These young tobacco merchants, they know how to pick peaches without treadin' on the grass."

The laugh that followed Tom's sally was shared by Miss Sanderson, but it did not prevent her joining Hannibal on the pavement when her own black straw was adjusted. She was, as I have hinted on a previous page, "very refined," and she was treated by the Browns as the daughters of Royal Dukes are treated by Society—with respect. She was permitted to do things another girl could not very well do; for example, appropriate Amelia's young man. If you feel astonishment at this in view of her family having had losses, I can only point out, in commiseration for your ignorance, the fact that, with the Browns, indigence after competence was a very different thing from indigence *per se*. The Browns argued logically enough that to have had losses it is first necessary to have had something to lose. In this case Miss Sanderson's people had had property and had lost it in a perfectly respectable way. Miss Sanderson, then, was a bright angel fallen from the heaven towards which the Browns were endeavouring to climb. About her there still hung a trace of the brightness of that sphere, a faint perfume of gentility. You saw it in her walk, in the way she held her handkerchief to her nose, or the distinguished manner in which she sat back in her chair at table and crumbled her bread. She was, though you might not know it, an acquisition to the Browns. She had "style." Even Ethel knew that. Even Ethel knew her own pert mannerisms would not have deceived the manager of a fifth-rate musical-comedy troupe—they were pure Kennington, with an edging of Knightsbridge and Brompton. As I say, you might not know all this, but the Browns knew it, knew it so thoroughly that the paltry embroidery of words was unneeded. They felt it in their bones. Miss Sanderson was superior. When she elected to walk with Hannibal they had nothing to say. Ladies like Miss Sanderson don't need watching like some people.

That Hannibal felt the full weight of his good fortune may be doubted. He did not at that time feel the full weight of anything—until the weight had been removed.

But he did feel with great keenness the immense difference between talking without effort to Miss Sanderson and
trying to talk to Amelia about the things in his mind.
Miss Sanderson was interested; she said so, and she made
him feel she was.

"Of course, when I say millions, you know what I
mean," he began, as they hurried towards the 'bus.

"You want something better than the tobacconist business?" she asked. He looked round to calculate Amelia's
distance.

"Well, you see, I 'ardly like to say it to meself, but
some'ow I do get full up with it. Got no business to be,
I s'pose. My old lady ses I ought to be very thankful to
'ave such a comfortable job. I dessay she's right, though
it don't make me feel any different about it. An' yet I
don't like to say anything, see?"

"You mean seeing it's for Amy you don't like . . . ?"

"That's it to a T," he replied.

"Ask her," argued Miss Sanderson.

"No," he whispered. "She wouldn't understand."

Miss Sanderson laughed gently.

"What is it you would like? Go for a soldier? Farming
in the Colonies? (My brother's in New Zealand.) What
is it?"

"I don't reckon I'd care what it was if I could only see
something. I been readin' a good bit lately, and I feel all
out of it. This shop-work's all right, if you don't want
to see things. But it's Jubilee Street in the mornin', Billiter
Lane all day, and Jubilee Street at night. It's chronic."

"I suppose you think you'd like a life of adventure."

"You mean Buffalo Bill an' Sherlock 'Olmes? Not
particularly."

"Or a life on the ocean wave?"

"Ah!" Hannibal started a little as Miss Sanderson
touched on this matter of the ocean wave. Out of his
reading and much fugitive thought he had evolved a
strange sea-world of his own, a world of tropic sunshine
and white cities, blue water, and anchored ships.

"With a wife in every port?" went on Miss Sanderson,
who had a reputation for prettiness in wit. Hannibal
looked at her in alarm. She was dangerous, this long-

necked young lady who had plighted her troth to the mechanical John. For it was true; he had dreamed of fairer women than he had ever seen, the quick heat of his adolescent mind had fashioned them dark and fair, pale and bronzed. But so shadowy were they, so lightly did they play their amorous part in those dream ports of his mind that he recoiled from Miss Sanderson's smiling jest. He coloured and was silent.

"I say, Lil," said John, catching them up. "Did you go and see——" His voice died to a whisper, and Hannibal heard no more. The others came up and effected a re-distribution of partners. Ethel, voluptuous with her thin revealing blouse and well-shaped hips, put her arm through Hannibal's and steered him toward the waiting 'bus. She was humming. It was characteristic of Ethel to hum. Presently, when they had mounted, she began:

"I wonder if the girl I'm thinking of—is think-ing—of—me!"

"Oh, dear, what a life! I say, Lily," she screwed round and called to Miss Sanderson, "which button do you press to make this figure talk?"

"Why, won't he?"

"Not to me." She examined Hannibal with humorous criticism. "Perhaps he's in love with me and don't like to show it. Or don't you like fair girls, Hanny? That must be it, Lily. He admires brunettes."

"Chuck it!" pleaded Hannibal.

"What's the matter, Ducky? Doesn't this old 'bus roll about! It's like bein' on a ship," and she began to hum.

"On the ro-o-o-o-l-ling deep!" ending up with an absurdly high squeak that made him laugh as the 'bus threw her against him.

"Mr. Simpkins 'll be gettin' on to me, sittin' 'ere," said Hannibal, feeling the warmth of her body. Mr. Simpkins, the laundry-manager, was deep in conversation with Amelia.

"Is that your way of sayin' you like my room better'n my company?" asked Ethel, looking at Hannibal in a way that made him uncomfortable. Her moist red lips and full blue eyes were close to his face, her thigh was pressed against his own, and he could not help seeing her bosom as his eyes dropped. He put his arm over the edge of the rail to give himself a little more room.

"I don't mean that," he stammered. "I only thought 'e might feel out in the cold."

"He knows you're one of the family," she returned. "How's the Little Brown Box? Is Amy behaving herself?"

"Oh, yes," he laughed. "We manage somehow."

"No lovers' tiffs?"

He shook his head.

"How's Auntie?"

"Pretty fair."

She gave it up at last. Her quick ears caught the drift of John's conversation with Miss Sanderson on the seat behind, and turning half-round she joined in. Hannibal looked at her blouse which was, like most young women's blouses, partly open at the back. He took the edges and slipped the buttons into place with one of his gentle caressing motions that all unconsciously reached feminine hearts. She turned to him.

"Hanny," she said, "you're a stick, and I'm goin' to make you talk. You told a fib when you said you and Amy hadn't tiffed. She told me all about it."

"About what?"

"You know. She feels it, Hanny. When a girl gets engaged she likes to be cuddled and made a fuss of. You treat her as if she was in a glass case."

"Fancy 'er tellin' you that!"

"She didn't! I didn't say she did. How dare you twist my words? She only told me how you said, 'Yes, Amy,' and 'No, Amy,' and," here Ethel laughed, "shook hands when you said good-bye."

"It is funny, when you come to think of it," he remarked coldly.

"Well I never!" Ethel regarded her cousin with some curiosity. "It isn't off, is it?" she whispered, feverish to get the first news.

"It will be if people can't mind their own business," he replied. Ethel's hand strayed to his knee. It was a hand too plump to be pretty, with well-kept nails and looped with silver bangles. A white openwork mitten reached to her elbow.

"Hanny," she said, "don't show it before mother, will you? She can't bear any excitement."

"I ain't excited, Eth; you needn't worry about me. I wish you wouldn't do that," he added, as she pressed closer to him.

"Why, what am I doing?"

"Squeezin'?"

"You are a funny boy, Hanny."

"I know I am, everybody laughs as I go down the street. I'm a walkin' *Comic Cuts,* I am," he agreed acidly. "It's the way I'm made, I s'pose! Family weakness."

If Miss Sanderson, with her delicate psychic apparatus, had alarmed Hannibal, it was he himself who was now causing some perturbation in Ethel's plump bosom. This was a new Cousin Hannibal indeed. She felt a little afraid of him, a little suspicion that there might be something in him neither in accord with the Brown philosophy nor actually bad, something different. Evidently he had a temper, quite cutting. Poor Amy! They had to get off the 'bus as Ethel arrived at this conclusion, and Hannibal was not surprised to see her push through to her sister who was descending the steps. Bumping against Tom, who was holding his young lady in a firm grip, Hannibal was glad to exchange humorous comments concerning the facility in what Tom called "chin-chewing." Tom and his young lady did not indulge in the gay amorousness of the younger members of the family. They courted strictly according to regulation, they kissed each other on the cheek at greeting and parting, but Miss Bax felt that her position as senior assistant in the actuarial department of Messrs. Krehbiel Ganz & Co., London Wall, precluded any frivolity in her attitude towards love. She realised that in a little time she would, as Tom's wife, assume the virtual headship of the Brown community. It would not do to place herself exactly on the same level as Ethel, Amelia, or even Miss Sanderson. Miss Sanderson and she had measured swords already; it required all the prestige of

Krehbiel Ganz & Co. (capital seventeen million dollars) to balance Miss Sanderson's position and refinement as the only daughter of a gentleman who had had losses. They were too conscious of the good opinion of the Browns to show any hostility, but one could imagine them later, each in her holy-of-holies, dissecting each other before sympathetic allies, and lamenting the shortcomings of human nature. Tom's deference to the opinion of Miss Bax showed him to have the makings of an admirable husband, fitted to carry the business forward to heights undreamed of by Mr. Brown in his dangling days. Indeed, the secret of their continued prosperity lay in Tom and Miss Bax, who were at this moment descending the steps of the 'bus. Hannibal looked down upon them as curiously as though they were beings of a different species. Joke as Tom might, and he was not a gloomy young man, he made you feel the responsibility that lay upon him. His dark, simply-cut clothes, his leather watch-guard, his plain tie and slightly old-fashioned collar, his square-toed boots with elastic sides, the bowler hat which covered his head winter and summer—all these little points were points of difference which set him subtly apart from the men of straw. Joke as he might, Tom evidently regarded this pilgrimage to Waterloo to meet his mother as a sort of ritual. Mrs. Brown was the Queen Bee of the hive. She had done nothing but give them birth, which was sufficient. You felt as you watched him and Miss Bax arm-in-arm, he on the outer side, that this was for them a solemn moment. The authors of their being—for Miss Bax already considered them her parents—were even now enduring that almost interminable purgatory, the wait at Vauxhall; they had yielded up their tickets, were removing the luggage from the racks, collecting magazines and rugs, looking out upon the illimitable roofland of South London. Hannibal, following the Browns up the incline that leads to the platform, was conscious of their feeling in the matter. Unknowingly he was up against the very foundation of our national life. It was the lack of this solidarity, this community of interest, which had caused the Gooderich family to fall apart like dry sand. It was Hannibal's privilege now to behold an apotheosis of the Brown religion as the train came slowly to rest, and Mr. Brown's head, covered by a soft grey felt hat, protruded from the window of a second-class carriage. Simultaneously the party moved towards the compartment, pushing past strangers and porters, splitting round a barrow and re-uniting in an intense little group. An incoherent murmur of welcome rose from them. Hannibal saw Tom, bare-headed, tugging at the door, handing out luggage and passing it on to the others. Hannibal found himself holding a portmanteau. Then Mr. Brown, broad breasted and summery in thin grey serge, bent his head and descended amid handshakes and kissing. So far the Queen Bee had not been visible. Mr. Brown, looking round, spoke to Tom in grave tones and re-entered the compartment. Shawls emerged one by one, John was detached to call a four-wheeler to the kerb, porters, like vultures when the traveller staggers, began to hover on the outskirts, and then Hannibal caught sight of a large woman slowly emerging from the dimly-lit train. With much assistance she came to rest on the platform, and after a pause for welcomes and filial kissing, moved across to the cab. All were in strict order of precedence. Mr. Brown and Tom guided the lady's slow footsteps, Amelia and Ethel carried intimate things like shawls, rugs, and chatelaine, John of course stood holding the door of the cab, Mr. Simpkins and Miss Bax came next with pillows and dressing-case. Miss Sanderson, who seemed to have adroitly avoided becoming a beast of burden, held her own skirt and looked interested, while Hannibal peeped over her shoulder.

It was very impressive. I have seen a foreign monarch arrive at a London railway station with less impressiveness than did Mrs. Brown. Even the driver of the four-wheeler twisted round on his box and looked on with respectful interest. There was a pause as Mr. Brown took his seat beside his wife; the group on tip-toe stood as if expectant of a miracle. Mrs. Brown raised her hand and waved it gently. Tom, still bare-headed, closed the door with reverence. Suddenly Mr. Brown gave a hasty glance round, looked at Tom with the look of rigid horror assumed by Englishmen when they have lost personal property, and breathed the word "portmanteau." The news was spread like fire in stubble through the group. Where was the portmanteau? Hannibal was surrounded, relieved of the burden, patted on the back as though he had done a noble deed, and the bag was hoisted to the roof. Mr. Brown was heard to remark in reply to Tom's earnest enquiry, that the boxes were coming on to-morrow in advance. The word "advance" is used by railways in England much as "express" is used by parcels companies in America—facetiously. At length the cab moved off and the Brown group gazed at the back of it until it was lost to sight. The next thing to do was to get home as quickly as possible. Much discussion between Tom and his sister produced a definite policy. It would not do to be late, therefore Amelia must take a cab. She could not travel without an escort even in a cab, so Tom was elected to go with her. But Tom could not desert Miss Bax. What then was to be done? Ethel turned round and sought Hannibal.

"Let Hanny go with you, Amy," she said. Tom had no objection. He could travel in a cab whenever he liked, but the pleasure of abstaining from luxuries, while knowing he could have them if he wished, far outweighed the childish joy of spending money. He was quite willing to let the young fellow go. Almost before he knew it, Hannibal was inside a second four-wheeler which had drawn up at the kerb. Amelia was seated next him. Ethel's generosity in this matter is explained by the fact that Mr. Simpkins, the laundry-manager, had already pledged himself secretly to a hansom. John's plans were not known. John's plans could not reasonably expect a great deal of attention since he was only an apprentice as yet. In fact, had John not been one of them, the Browns would have been mildly curious to know how he had come to fall in love with Miss Sanderson. Even after marriage, when John got a gaffer's job, the exact relations of the pair were not ascertained by the family. On one occasion, when his lady had signified with tigerish emphasis the importance of recognising her as boss in her own house, John had surprised the family by endorsing her claim. But when the squall blew over and the blue sky of connexional harmony smiled upon them they found themselves as vague as ever as to John's standing with her his wife. And so, in the excitement of four-wheelers and hansoms, pervaded as it was with Tom's growl and Ethel's high-pitched chatter, John and Miss Sanderson faded away, to appear at supper (taken on the knee in the drawing-room) mysteriously happy.

"She looks wonderfully improved," said Amy, as the cab wrenched round the corner into the street. "Bournemouth always did suit her." She did not seek for any answer to this. She was wrapt in a dream, an ecstasy of pleasure at seeing her beloved parent again. You might have imagined that Amelia, being the elder daughter, would have felt reluctant to take the second place again in the house. But she knew that her mother would be an invalid still. It had become a habit almost impossible to break for Mrs. Brown to have things done for her. She would sit among cushions with a rug over her knees and receive her lady-friends in state, and those lady-friends would be under Amelia's thumb. They would have to accept tea and pastry from her table. They would have to admit her to their confidence or they would not come again. Miss Bax might be Tom's sweetheart, but until she was Tom's wife, Amelia was in charge. She sat there in the cab in a fit of glad abstraction planning out the summer. Hannibal looked at her furtively in the darkness and saw that he was forgotten. A sudden perception came to him, that in all probability he would be forgotten in the future. He could not for the life of him enter into that unity of thought which distinguished the Browns and their satellites, and it followed that sooner or later he would be forgotten. In his mind this momentary lapse of Amelia's thoughts became typical of her world. Very likely Ethel was right. They thought him dull and uninteresting. Very likely, too, Miss Sanderson would have got tired of him after a while. Now that he came to think of it, he had used his opportunity to talk to Miss Sanderson very poorly. It was always the way. He was dazzled by close contact with women and did not know what to say.

He felt depressed and disheartened.

"What did you tell Ethel about us for?" he asked, looking solemnly out of the window. One of the priceless advantages of possessing a small mind is the power to train it upon any problem in a flash. So with Amelia.

"She's my sister, I suppose?" she enquired.

"Givin' me a fine name."

"What name?"

"Stick."

"Well!" Amelia laughed suddenly. "She wasn't so far off, was she? You know, Hanny, your mind isn't on your job. You'll never get on if you go round fly-catchin'."

"Think not?"

"Positive. That's all Eth meant by 'stick.' I wouldn't let her call you names as a general thing, and she wouldn't want to. But she can't help noticin'."

"You ought to 'ave left me in the Repositories," he remarked. "I feel all out of it 'ere, ridin' in cabs."

"And give up the shop?" she cried.

"You can get somebody else for that job."

"Oh, don't be so silly! I s'pose you're grousing because I didn't like you leavin' the shop. I might have said a good deal more'n I did this morning."

"I noticed that. Why didn't you?"

Amelia turned and looked at him, astounded at his perspicacity.

"I thought we had an understanding," she faltered.

"I 'ad an idea that way too," he admitted.

"Then why do you ask me why didn't I fly out at you when I noticed it? Do you think I wanted to have a row? If I'd known you knew, I would have." And she flung herself away from him.

"'Ere's the 'ouse," said Hannibal as the cab drew up. He got out, put his hand in his pocket and found a florin. He gave it to the driver and turned to his cousin.

"I'll see Aunt Lizzie another time," he said briefly. "I've 'ad just about all I can stand for to-night."

And turning away, he went off down the street without giving her an opportunity to reply.

IX

ON WATERLOO BRIDGE he paused, and leaning over one of the embrasures studied the amazing scene spread before his eyes. On either hand the embankment was picked out in a curve of lights, the great hotels loomed up on the right bank, and away westward the clock of Westminster glowed like a yellow moon. Below, the dark water reflected the illumination of the shores; here and there a deep red or green light marked a moving craft. From the Strand came a dull roar of traffic; police whistles called shrilly for cabs; behind him the omnibuses rumbled and carts rattled. Far away on Westminster Bridge lights of swift hansoms sped across continually. The night was clear and warm. There was no despair in his heart; rather was there the exultation of revolt. He had by some strange effort, some reaction quite alien to his ordinary apathetic attitude towards life, broken from the Brown influence. That influence would claim him again in the morning. He had no confidence in himself if Amelia appeared next day in a melting mood. How did he get the courage to state the facts so bluntly? He did not know. It seemed almost as if he had heard some one else saying it. To tell the Browns that he had all he could stand of them—my word! Amelia would think him off his chump. She had said he went round catching flies, had she? Well, he had given her something to think over now. He was not going to be absorbed into the Brown system so easily after all, he was not quite devoid of individuality. Miss Sanderson had realised there was something in him. And Ethel, too, had had a shock. As he looked out across the dark water, the young man's eyes hardened a little. He would not give in. Again there came to him the consciousness of his power to break away. What did he want to do? He did not know nor care. He would find his way to the world he had dreamed of, never fear. Under the

stress of his thoughts he moved a little, and became aware
of a shadow. He looked up quickly to see the huge bulk
of a policeman standing over him. He started back with
an exclamation, instinctively avoiding the law.

"You'd better get along," suggested the law. "I thought
at first you were goin' to do yourself in."

Hannibal laughed and stood back a little further from
the parapet. "Not me!" he answered, taking out a pipe
to show his easiness under scrutiny. "I was only 'avin'
a look roun'. I don't come this way often. What's that
street up there?" He pointed towards Covent Garden.

"Strand," said the law. "Where do you want to go?"

"'Ome, Mile End Road."

The policeman, who was only waiting for ten o'clock
to go eastward himself, nodded.

"Up there, and round the right. Tuppence on the 'bus."

"Thank you. Good night."

The brief conversation restored the young man's balance and solidified his belief in himself. The recoil from
the Browns' influence led him to contemplate confiding
in his mother. Now this casual contact with the world
left him standing on his feet again. He strode on towards
the Strand, and seeing an East-end omnibus waiting across
the road, ran over and sprang upon it. The noise, the
lights, the movement of the great teeming street exhil-
arated him. He felt outrageously glad that he had af-
fronted Amelia so brazenly. He cast about him for something that would embody his revolt. If he went home that
would be a tame ending—he would have gone home anyway. Ah, he had it! He would have a drink, for a start.
He felt in his pocket and found a shilling and some
smaller coins, about one-and-ninepence. He regretted that
florin now.

He descended at Aldgate and entered a bar. To push in
and out of a pub is part of East-end education. Even
people who are strict abstainers in that part of the world
have a certain familiarity with licensed premises. These
gin-palaces, as Mrs. Gaynor was accustomed to describe
them, are the clubs of the poor. It is necessary to remember this when reflecting upon Hannibal's behaviour. To
him and to the majority of East Londoners, entering a

public-house signified nothing. Even to Amelia it signified nothing in itself. In the old days when Mr. Brown was in a comically small way of business, when Hannibal's father was buried, for instance, it was a right and proper thing to go into bars. Now they had reached a higher plane where they were limited to hostelries like the "Bull and Bush" and the "King's Head" at Roehampton. And it might as well be explained here while Hannibal was entering that bar, that Amelia would have had some trouble to explain in stark language why she cherished such an objection to the faint odour of liquor which lingered round her cousin when he returned to the shop. It could not be any prejudice against drink. The Browns were all too much alive, too interested, too intelligent to have any craven fear of it. Possibly it was because, taking Hannibal at his own valuation, she did not consider him one of the family, and so came unconsciously to the conclusion that drink was a possible vice with him. Perhaps the rumours current when her uncle died, that he had had a drop too much, weighed with her. Perhaps it was merely a feminine desire to find fault with a young man who offered a too easy mark. Whatever her ultimate motive, it would have been formidably strengthened had she seen him now breasting the mahogany bar asking for a bitter and selecting a match from the sheaf that stood near his elbow.

The bar was a saloon, semicircular, with seats in the corners of the room. As he turned to glance round after a sip, Hannibal was surprised to see his friend Mr. Grober in a chair by a small table, enjoying his black briar and a tankard of ale. The young man nodded, and Mr. Grober, regarding him with attention, withdrew from his reverie far enough to respond. Hannibal felt a singular excitement on beholding the old man thus occupied. He took up his glass and went over to him.

"Good evenin'," he said. "I'd no idea you were in 'ere."

"The surprise is mutual," responded Mr. Grober. "I thought you were engaged for the evening."

"Oh, we went to see 'er parents come back from the seaside," explained Hannibal. "I got sick of it and cleared out."

Mr. Grober looked at his young friend with some curiosity.

"You are fortunate," he said simply.

"'Ow d'you mean?" asked Hannibal, drinking.

"To be able to clear out, as you express it, whenever the mood takes you. It will not be always so, believe me."

"Oh, I'm not goin' to be bossed," said Hannibal.

Mr. Grober's face expressed pity.

"And how do you propose to avoid it?" he asked. "When the greatest men are ruled by women, while they have it in their power to make our lives either a hades or an elysium, how, I ask, do you propose to escape the universal fate?"

"Oh, it ain't as bad as that, Mister," Hannibal protested.

"You are young and time will show," said Mr. Grober. "You imagine that your young lady is merely a female. A woman is only a manifestation of her sex. Except in rare cases she has no essential nature of her own. Men speak of having been under the influence of various women. Never was there such a puerile misconception. They are all one woman. He escapes from one only to succumb to the enchantments of another. He may fly from England to China, from China to Peru, but it is all in vain. Ultimately she gets him, and deals out to him the destiny ordained from the beginning. Happy the man who can snatch some happiness in the intervals of the pursuit, and steel his heart with philosophy against the unforeseen tragedies of his life. You will read," continued Mr. Grober, "you will read in that book in your pocket the story of a fruitless attempt to evade the eternal question of sex. That is what I mean by all women being one and the same. Woman has been told so often that she is an angel, that she has grown to believe it. The most cursory examination of a few examples of women is sufficient to disprove this monstrous fallacy."

"I s'pose you're a woman-'ater, Mr. Grober," said Hannibal, looking judicially into his pipe.

"By no means. I am merely giving you, a young and inexperienced man, the benefit of close observation. I am what the world calls a failure, which means I have the

right to criticise the world. Disraeli said of critics that
they were those who had failed in literature and art. I
may transpose Disraeli's dictum and say that failures are
those who exchange success in art or in life for the right
to criticise. A little thought will show that only the failure
can pass unbiased judgment upon the world. The majority of people imagine that because a man has failed in
this particular world, he's failed absolutely. By no means.
Many a man who sinks down and dies and is forgotten
might, by one infinitesimal turn of fortune's wheel, have
landed beside Cæsar and Napoleon. Still more men who
struggle furiously with poverty might, by a chance movement of the hand, a furtive roll of the eye, light upon
some hidden spring which, when touched, would transfer
them to an Aladdin's Palace. Chance, chance, chance!
Take myself; at any moment I may turn over an old folio
and discover some document which will draw upon me
the attention of every learned society in Europe. So far
a ten thousand to one chance had been against me."

"You aren't countin' on it, I suppose?" asked Hannibal,
whose mind was puzzled yet attracted by the old gentleman's fluent monologue.

"I count on nothing. I am a fatalist, by which I mean
that I disbelieve in the future. It does not exist. To an
age debauched by erroneous systems of logic it may
sound strange, but the future does not exist."

"I am afraid that's a bit too deep for me," said the
young man. "Take me. Can't make up my mind what I'm
going to do to-morrow."

The question recalled Mr. Grober to the immediate
present.

"Well," he said, finishing his beer, "I should imagine
that you can answer that question better than I."

The young man lifted his glass, glanced with a roving
eye round the glittering bar, drank off the liquor and set
down the empty glass.

"That's right," he said. "I can. I 'ave," he added.

Mr. Grober looked at the clock over his head and rose.
"I must go," he said hurriedly. "I had no idea of the
time. Come over to the shop."

They went out together through the swing doors.

"You speak as if you had made up your mind to do something extremely important," Mr. Grober began when they had crossed the road. "Now I am ready to admit that there is one incalculable element in human life, and that is Youth. It is unique. If it were not for Youth there would be neither joy nor sorrow in the world. If it were not for Youth—come in, come in,—if it were not——"

Mr. Grober's stream of eloquence was cut off short as he entered the shop and beheld his wife standing by the inner door. Hannibal felt acutely uneasy as he noted the light of battle in the lady's eye. He withdrew to the book-encumbered entry. Mr. Grober's entire personality seemed to shrivel beneath his wife's viperish regard. His hands faltered and made deprecating motions in the air, he slithered sideways to his chair and sank into it as though beaten down by the torrent of her vituperation. There was neither skill nor meaning in her words, but a mere unimaginative repetition of foul phrases. Hannibal was appalled, and drew further out towards the street, pretending to examine the volumes on the shelves. Not one word of retort did the old man offer to stem the rushing flow of profane upbraiding. He sat wilted and diminished, his arm dangling over the back of the chair, the black briar between his fingers. Only once, when she hurled the opprobrium "Lousy old soaker" at him, did he move as though to reply. She was not an old woman; had she been lapped in luxury she might have been pretty, and at most she was forty. But the evil rage in her heart, the gnawing penury of body and spirit had distorted and maligned her features so that now as she stood swaying in her passion, she might have been one of the Furies pursuing her husband with implacable hatred.

"What d'you want?" she turned hoarsely to Hannibal. "Standin' there listenin'? You're like all the rest o' them, lookin' and lookin' and puttin' 'em back, an' never buyin'." She paused, exhausted, put her right hand to her throat and coughed weakly, making motions with her left for him to be gone. Hannibal stepped out into the street and paused irresolutely. Then he walked back into the shop.

"Why, what 'ave I done, missis?" he asked boldly.

She waved him away without turning to him.

"Sling yer 'ook," she croaked, for her voice was gone. "Sling it."

"Shan't," said Hannibal, and the old man looked up at him, mumbling, "Youth! Youth!" to himself. "Mr. Grober 'ere ain't said anythin' about chasin' me out, 'as 'e?"

The storm was over; Mrs. Grober repassed the inner door and vanished. Slowly the drooping head of the old bookseller revived.

"I regret, my young friend," he said, "that you should have witnessed such a scene. For the young it is undoubtedly an unfortunate spectacle. Mrs. Grober is subject to occasional fits of depression. Possibly the profits accruing from the sale of second-hand literature might be larger. I may be mistaken, but I have never heard of any one making a million out of it. And that is a curious feature of the profession. We have it on the word of Monsieur Heineffethermatt that there are over a thousand million printed volumes." Mr. Grober was off again, his hands waving, his dull blue eye fixed on Hannibal's face. "Let us take a conservative estimate, ten per cent for second-hand matter. That gives us one hundred millions. One per cent of that, say, for England, which leaves at the disposal of a hypothetical dealer one million volumes. Surely, by means of business acumen and judicious handling of capital it would be possible to control the sale of those million books. You need, say, a text-book."

"I don't," grinned Hannibal.

"We will make the supposition," replied Mr. Grober gravely. "You come to me. Having in my control the whole of the second-hand books in the country, I maintain price. You offer a shilling. I keep the price at two shillings, even three. You are financially at my mercy."

"People 'ld buy new ones then," surmised Hannibal.

"Ah! You have put your finger on an important point. The scheme would involve negotiations with the publishers, and that is a fatal defect. I have discovered, young man," Mr. Grober remarked with energy, "that anything which involves negotiations with a publisher is apt to prove unfortunate for the other party."

"Were you the other party?" asked Hannibal curiously.

"For my sins, I was," said Mr. Grober. "If you will assist me to shut up, I will tell you about it."

"All right, mister."

Hannibal set to work at once. He put down his pipe, strode out to the front and began tumbling the books into the boxes. Mr. Grober turned out the gas in the front and carried in the various cards which announced to a careless world the sacrifice of certain special lots at prices hardly compatible with Mr. Grober's imaginary trust. When the boxes were inside and the shutter down, he motioned Hannibal towards the back room. To the young man's look of scared enquiry he indicated the ceiling with his forefinger, pursing his lips to imply that while Mrs. Grober had retired to an upper floor, quietness would ensure her remaining there. With some apprehension, therefore, Hannibal passed the glass door and found himself in a small, dirty room furnished with sofa and chairs of dark green velvet, an oval table with a black oil-cloth cover, and a stunted sideboard. A naked gas-burner over the table gave a scanty illumination. Mr. Grober followed, rubbing his hands. Into his seamed and bloodless features had come a certain exultation. Stooping before the sideboard he took from it a square bottle and two thick glasses. Setting them on the table, he regarded them for a moment in deep thought, as though he were struggling to realise the solemnity of the moment. Hannibal, his cap in his hand, sat on the edge of the sofa, watching him shyly. At length Mr. Grober, still keeping his cap on his head, removed the cork and poured out some whisky. Then he looked round as though he had lost something. Feeling in his pocket for matches, he struck one and searched in a cupboard near the window. He brought back a jug containing water.

"The lower classes of the metropolis occasionally use milk," he remarked, filling up Hannibal's glass and adding a tiny trickle to his own. "I believe it is considered vulgar, though it would puzzle a philosopher to explain why. I mentioned something about publishers, did I not? Well, many years ago,—but drink, my friend, drink," and he pushed the glass to the abashed Hannibal. A sud-

den vision of his mother waiting up for him at home
flashed across his mind. Was he, after all, effecting anything particularly heroic by associating with this old man?
And then the great desire to press forward into experience, to pass somehow beyond the narrow bounds which
had been hemming him in, came over him, and he lifted
the glass.

He heard Mr. Grober clinking the square bottle against
his tumbler as he poured out another measure of the
spirit. What was it Mr. Grober was saying? Hannibal
felt astonishingly buoyant and optimistic. He tried to keep
his attention on Mr. Grober. "I believed in those days
in the future. For me it existed as a bright and roseate
dream of ineffable power and joy," so ran Mr. Grober's
thin voice, quavering now with excitement as the spirit
pervaded his brain. "I dreamed in my folly, that since
ambition had marked me for her own, I would find recognition, fame, wealth, ultimate illimitable happiness. I
deemed that, having Youth, I had every requisite to invest the manifestation of my life with the form of Art. I
—what was I saying? Invest—aye, a fatal word! The
damnable materialism of the age has covered the very
language of art with its offensive slime. Had I but lived
in the glorious days of the Renaissance, when Cellini,
Michael Angelo, and Aretino lived out their fierce and
tragic lives!"

The young man sat on the edge of the sofa listening
to the old man's wandering and incoherent speech in some
perplexity. The spirit was potent within him; his mind
soared to a sense of supreme accomplishment. Mr.
Grober, after all, was not so important as he seemed to
think he was. That old chap over there was gassing away
—poor old blighter! Now he, Hannibal Gooderich, had
something in him. He was going to do something. What
was it he was going to do? Never mind. He shook his
head portentously in front of Mr. Grober, who was pointing at him with the stem of his pipe.

"Have you," asked Mr. Grober, "ever reflected that a
man's destiny may be determined by a trivial matter?"

Hannibal shook his head. "Don't understand," he said.

"I speak of men, not failures, not even those so-called successful beings who plod along year after year and never muster courage to turn and grapple with their fate. I speak of men, not of the great majority like ourselves. We never give hostages to fortune, we never dare to burn our ships behind us. We creep along in the mud until the grave opens and takes us in. I speak of *men!*" The old man's voice rang out on the word with an energy and resonance that startled himself. He shrank into himself again, listening fearfully for any sound above.

"I don't see why I shouldn't do somethin' on my own," whispered Hannibal. "I'm goin' to try, any'ow."

"Beard Destiny in his den? Brave youth! Think of the millions round you. If they fail, can you succeed?"

"Who's goin' to stop me?" asked the young man.

"Yourself. Your own craven spirit!" cried Mr. Grober, striking the table with a soundless blow. "Do you think I have not tried it? Aye, tried, and at the first roar of the monster I ran screaming back to my accustomed haunts. Not for me the great world of action, not for me the glorious struggle with unknown perils. I realised all too soon the fundamental difference between men and men. Fear, grim Fear sent me to my kennel, chained me there, and here you behold me. The Philosophy of Fear! When will the genius rise to proclaim it? Foolish dream! Grim paradox, my young friend! For if a man be held by Fear, he will never rise to proclaim it."

."I see what you mean," said Hannibal in a new voice. "I reckon I've got into that 'abit myself, thinkin' as I can't go off on my own. Various things, me bein' engaged and all that—they do make you feel kind of 'elpless."

"Bound to the Caucasus," assented Mr. Grober, pouring himself out more whisky.

"But I've been thinkin' jus' lately that I'd like to get out and see things. F'r instance, a friend o' mine, 'e's a sailor, and——"

"You propose to follow his example? Excellent! Tell me."

Hannibal told him. He told it disjointedly, going over the ground with interminable repetition, growing more fluent as he proceeded, encouraged by the nodding of the

old man's head. He told it ungrammatically and egotisti-
cally, told it to an elderly failure with years of systematic
alcoholic stimulus, and whose brain cells were sagging
with reaction, whose dull blue eyes peered at him through
the curling smoke of a malodorous tobacco. He told it in
a way that debars it from transcription, and yet in spite of,
perhaps because of this disability, he communicated for
the first time his own view of the world; he did that thing
which so many of us fail utterly to do, he put forth his
hand and touched the garment's hem of Romance, he
thrilled as he felt his soul pushing slowly, blunderingly,
yet surely through the veils of custom and law. He saw
once more those strange shapes that had haunted his
childhood, realising suddenly how sheath after sheath of
his immediate life had closed round him and shut him off
from that vast rhythmic dream-world beyond. . . .

He paused, and found himself sitting strained and stiff
on the edge of the sofa, his glass in his hand, staring at
the rigid features of the old man.

"An' so," he concluded lamely, setting down the glass
and looking round in a dazed way—"an' so I thought as
I might find it agen, if I got out o' the net, see? I ain't
'ad much education, an' I can't put it very well. That
sailor-chap in the Iceland book—when 'e was away out
there, fightin', 'e found it, such a long way from 'ome. I
don't reckon you can ever see these things while you're
at 'ome, eh?"

He looked into the bowl of his pipe as though he could
read the tremendous riddle in the ashes. Mr. Grober was
silent for a space, the frayed fabric of his deteriorated
mind catching at odds and ends of the narrative. An
expression of bewilderment and grief struggled through
the mask as the memory of his own youth was recalled
by the young man's words. A sudden vision of himself
as he might have been, had he held to his own, came
with appalling clearness before him. The rickety scaffolding of hypocrisy, plastered with the gaudy lying show-
cards of quack philosophy, which concealed his failure
from his own eyes, fell away.

He closed his eyes for a moment, close-locked in his
own mute agony, and then reached for the bottle. The

young man had not asked him for advice, had not craved his judgment upon the world, and he felt the unconscious slight. He was nothing, a mere vacuum in the surrounding density, a vacuum which had sucked from the lad his story. He bowed his head as though to the decree of an invisible fate.

"I—I am scarcely in a position to say," he remarked in a dull, spiritless voice. "My own experience of the great arena of action has not been exactly exhilarating."

Hannibal sat unheeding, absorbed in his own gnarled and tangled thoughts. The clink of the bottle against the glass roused him. He looked round to see the time.

"I must get along," he said, standing up. "The old woman'll be wonderin' where I've got to."

"Have another drink," said Mr. Grober, filling his glass. "Success to your new resolutions. I wish—I wish—but never mind, my wishes generally escape the notice of providence. I shall merely wish you joy of your adventure."

Once more Hannibal swallowed the strange liquor that felt like hot velvet in his throat and sent a shiver through him, and then he took his cap.

"Goo' night, mister," he said. "I'll look in agen."

"Like a ship passing in the night," said the old man, his dull blue eyes straying over Hannibal as they passed into the shop. There was a sound of footsteps overhead, a creak of the stairs, and Mr. Grober's expression changed. Tiptoeing across the floor, Hannibal let himself out.

"Good night!" whispered the old man, peering forward with strained, ghastly features. "I give you a crumb of wisdom—not mine, alas! Be master of yourself. The world is not an oyster to be opened, but a quicksand to be passed. If you have wings you can fly over it, if not you may—yes, yes, I am coming now, my dear!—you may quite possibly be sucked in."

The door closed abruptly and Hannibal found himself under the huge dome of the starlit sky. For a moment he looked up and down the broad thoroughfare with its endless rows of street lamps, its late tram clanking up from Mile End, its occasional swirl of yellow radiance from tavern or ham-and-beef shop, its hurrying pedestrians and leisurely policemen. Oblivious of the ferment in his brain, the world was settling down to a few hours of rest. Hannibal set forward, crossing the road in front of the tram. The lateness of the hour—for the East End is unlike the West in this—came to him with fresh force, and he hurried on. Assembly Passage seemed unusually long in the darkness. Its one lamp, bracketed high up and flaring through a broken pane, flung a darting and ghostly light athwart shutters and windows. Emerging into Jubilee Street, he saw a light in the front room. The old lady was waiting up for him. A shadow rose and crossed the blind as the gate whined at his touch.

"Why, Hanny, wherever have you been? I was gettin' anxious."

He told her briefly, flinging his cap on a chair and sitting on the sofa to unlace his boots. Mrs. Gooderich followed him in and stood watching him.

"I've had a visit," she said, sitting by the table and leaning her chin on her hand. "I've had a visit from Minnie."

Hannibal, flushed with stooping, raised his eyes to his mother's face.

"Eh?" he said blankly. Mrs. Gooderich repeated the remark.

"After all this time?" he queried.

"After all this time."

"What'd she say?"

"She was very quiet," said Mrs. Gooderich. "Very quiet." And then she added as an afterthought: "She always was."

"She ain't—comin'—'ere?"

"No," said Mrs. Gooderich. "She isn't."

"What'd she come for?"

"To tell me she was goin' to be married."

"Ah!"

"She's a fine lady now, by her clo'es. Do you know what that means, Hanny?"

Mrs. Gooderich's face was pale with resolution. She too had been going through a crisis. The sudden apparition of her daughter had flung her thoughts around her son. It was time Hanny was told certain things. Hannibal set his boots down in a corner and shook his head.

"I'm tired," he said, rubbing his eyes.

"What's the matter?" said his mother sharply.

"Bit worried," he answered. "'Ad some words with Amy. She's always gettin' at me."

"Oh, Hanny!" Mrs. Gooderich sprang up. "You aren't goin' to spoil everything now! Think what it means to me." And she made a gesture of despair.

"It ain't my fault," he argued. "I can't 'elp it. I don't reckon we'd get on very well. We ain't Uncle George's sort, any'ow. You know, mother," he went on, his hands in his pockets, "I feel sometimes in that shop as if I'd go off me head. I seem to be jus' rottin' there. And I been thinkin' as 'ow it's got to come some day, so it might as well come now. I'm goin' to try and do somethin' on me own."

"What?" she asked dully, sitting down again. "You goin' that way, too?"

"It's like bein' in prison," he said, "since I left off goin' about with the chaps. Prison, excep' 'avin' somethin' to read. I been thinkin' a lot lately an' I want to clear out."

"I see you readin' *Flotsam* the other day," said Mrs. Gooderich. "You'll be flotsam if you don't take care. I was afraid you'd be gettin' ideas."

"I don't care," he growled. "Better be flotsam than moochin' in a tobacconist's all me life. Little Brown Box, Little Brown Box. Eh? Stop there till I'm ready for another little brown box? Ugh!"

"What can you do?" she asked, distressed.

"I'll find somethin'. Mr. Grober, 'e ses 'be your own master.' So I will. I don't want no Uncle Georges nor Aunt Elizas neither. All very well for them with their seaside an' cabs an' nice 'ouses. Let 'em 'ave it. I'm goin' me own road, damn 'em."

"Hanny, you mustn't say such things!"

"I tell you I am! What'd you want to go to 'im for, anyway? I could 'a' got another job without 'im. They're only makin' a convenience o' me, any'ow."

Mrs. Gooderich was silent. Minnie, sitting there cool and composed that afternoon, had said the same thing in other words, had offered her mother money, which had been refused with scorn.

"Ain't she comin' any more, then?" he asked suddenly, recalling his mother's news.

"I don't know. She said something about lookin' in again to-morrow."

"An' she's goin' to be married? Who to?"

A shadow crossed his mother's face.

"She says he's in a very good position, and they've been waitin'. She says 'e put up the money for that business o' theirs in Sloane Street, and those 'olidays she 'ad on the Continent. I don't understand it myself. People don't give you money, if they don't want somethin' in return, especially men."

"Well," said Hannibal, yawning, "she's done all right for herself, I should reckon. Any supper, mother?"

Mrs. Gooderich rose to get him something to eat.

"It's past twelve," she remarked reprovingly. "I don't think you ought to stay out so late."

"I wasn't out," he retorted testily. "I was sittin' in the room behind the shop, talkin'. That's where it is," he continued, "all the time, you an' Amy. You don't think this, you don't think that! Why can't you lea' me alone? I ain't Jack the Ripper, am I? Nag, nag, nag!"

He plumped himself down and began to eat in sullen silence.

"I'm your mother, I think." Mrs. Gooderich intended to convey cutting sarcasm. "By the way you fly out at me, I might be dirt. Minnie's the same, she always was. I did think you were goin' to be different, Hanny. I did think Amy was going to make a man of you."

"Amy can get somebody else to make a man of," he replied. "I'm no use to 'er. She as good as told me I went round catchin' flies, my mind ain't on me work, and all the rest of it. She's got the idea she can bat me round jus' as she likes."

"Then you must have been doin' something or other," said his mother.

"I went to get a drink an' some change, an' I was away from the shop about a minute, that's what I was doin'. *That* was only an excuse! I ain't their sort down at Kennington. She come down to ol' Grober's shop this evenin' wi' me, and turns up her nose at the place. Don't approve of 'im, I s'pose. Every bally thing I do is wrong. The kitten was all wrong too—an' jus' because she's got the tin. She can 'ave it."

"Oh, I am sorry you can't get on there, Hanny. You know, she's right in a way. You do need someone to look after you."

"No use arguin'," he answered. "Let's go to bed. My 'ead aches."

"You smoke too much," began his mother.

"Oh, drop it, do," he cried desperately. "Do say somethin' without findin' fault. What am I made of? Tell me that! What am I made of? Wouldn't it drive anybody balmy?"

And without waiting for his mother's reply, he went out and shut the door behind him.

X

WHEN Hannibal had washed his hands in his little basin behind the counter after sweeping out the shop, polishing the brasswork, dusting the rows of canisters, replenishing the canaries' seed-pots and the match-jars that stood by the cigar-cutter, he took up a booklet that had been lying on the floor by the gate when he had arrived. It was an attractive little pamphlet, with a sap-green cover on which was represented a young man with sharp, clean-shaven jaws holding his crooked fingers over the floating form of a young lady lightly clad. In eye-piercing lettering the title ran *Raising the Dead*. Desirous of knowing something about this subject, Hannibal silenced the inner voice that told him it was only an advertisement for a Pill, and sat down to investigate.

Outside was a May morning. Even Billiter Lane was of cheerful aspect. Clerks, hastening to their offices or to the Baltic Exchange, vendors of violets, bananas and dates, maps of London and copies of shipping newspapers, made the little dark canyon between the great blocks of buildings seem gay and debonair. The kitten, with her blue ribbon askew on her neck, sat by the door and carried out an exhaustive personal examination. From Fenchurch Street came the drone of a great traffic, punctuated at intervals by the call of a newsman or hoot of a motor horn, hoarse, poignant, and unmusical.

Hannibal read the pamphlet in some perplexity. It implored him to pause and realise the terrific power which lay latent within him. This power was described as Hypnotic Suggestion. Up to the present this power had been used merely for such trivial purposes as medical science had indicated. That was now to be changed. He, the reader of that booklet, had power to raise the dead. Was this an exaggeration? By no means. People without ambition were dead, practically speaking. We referred to such as "dead to the world." That was to end right away.

That dead ambition was to be resuscitated. Why did people remain in this coma of inaction? Why did people find it so difficult to succeed? Because they did not know their work. INEFFICIENCY! the booklet replied in double leaded capitals. Why did they not know their work? Because they did not utilise the amazing facilities of the Pallas Athene School of Tuition by Correspondence. Never mind others. Hypnotise yourself. Raise yourself from the dead wreck of inefficients. Nowadays the incompetent man was kicked out. He was scrapped. His ultimate destination was the casual ward. He lay under sentence of death before the Bar of the Modern Business World.

Hannibal, with some misgivings, stared at the illustrations. There was Pallas Athene leaping full-armed from the head of Jupiter, for your really smart advertiser has no time to discriminate between the mythologies; there was a trembling inefficient standing before a court of stern captains of industry, who were sentencing him to death; there was a broad-shouldered efficient sitting at an immense roll-top desk, with a background of scores of other inferior efficients toiling at typewriters; there were little pictures of young Arabs, Russians, Japanese, and Hindoos, poring over the sheets issued by the Pallas Athene School. Occasionally wetting his thumb to turn the thick, highly-glazed pages, Hannibal went through the pamphlet over and over again. He wondered if Mr. Grober had received one. Most probably. And what would Mr. Grober think of it? Here was Mr. Grober's teaching in a modern and biting form. At the end was a page of "Axiomatic Aphorisms, the Double-distilled Quintessence of Philosophic Thought, boiled down and left in a cool place to set." As thus:—

"Jupiter reached Danaë in the shape of a shower of gold. It was the only way he could reach her."

"A man can do the same—go through towers of brass —if he has the gold."

"We show him how to get the gold."

He laid it aside at length, and went to the door to think. He stood there in his shirt-sleeves, smoking a cigarette and trying to arrange things in his mind. Was there any truth after all in that little green book? Was it a certain thing that he, having a desire not to amass gold, nor acquire a position among captains of industry, but to see this great wonderful world in which he had been born, and enjoy the beauty of it—was it certain he was doomed to sink down into the mire and die? He felt greatly perturbed. He had a sort of panicky feeling whenever he compared himself with those same captains of industry, those rigid-featured geniuses who think in millions. Once he had read in a weekly paper an account of the marvellous career of one Sir Anthony Gilfillan, the inventor of those same Gilfillan Filaments which illuminated the Little Brown Box. He had read Sir Anthony's maxims for success. The faked photograph of the man, with deep-sunken eyes and bulging brow, had given him that panicky feeling. And he had wondered why his mother, seeing the picture, had taken the paper away from him. To tell the truth, when Hannibal read of these great men, that they had once been poor boys like himself, he did not believe it. They may have been in moderate circumstances, but they had had some sort of luck. And as he grew up, there had grown up along with him a dim conviction that the cause of their success was their intense desire for it. So that in the end, Hannibal and Mrs. Gaynor and the Pallas Athene School had all arrived at the same simple psychological fact, so ably expressed by Mrs. Gaynor herself when she said that many people fail to get what they wish because they don't wish hard enough.

Hannibal decided, as he stood there beside the kitten, looking out into the street, that very likely these efficient folk were right. But there came his difficulty. He could not see why, if a fellow like himself wanted to look on at the show, he couldn't do it without being considered a criminal. Everything he himself took an interest in seemed to have no money value. There was Tiny Tim the kitten, Bob and Bill the canaries. He loved them, loved to watch them and feel that they knew him. It was a great deal to him that the canaries would jump on his finger if he put it between the bars, that Tiny Tim would climb upon his shoulder and go to sleep as he sat behind the counter reading. And although a certain diffidence of soul led him to say nothing to Amelia about it, he loved the flowers too. They did not shout at him that he was not succeeding in life, that he was guilty of inefficiency, that he must get on or get out; and yet, for all that, they told him many things. So too with books and pictures. I have mentioned some of the books with which Mr. Grober supplied him, but I have not mentioned the ever-present influence of the book-stall and picture shop. There were certain windows before which the young man always paused, windows in which were pictures. There was one which had given him a great deal of pleasure, a painting of a wide stretch of green, rolling Atlantic, and it was called "Across the Western Ocean." He was sorry when that picture was taken away. But all this was of no profit to him, according to the Pallas Athene School. Of what use, they asked, were fine ideas and delicate thoughts if you made no money out of them? And he sighed as his attention was drawn to two men who emerged from the office of the steamship company across the way and came over towards him. One of them was a short, thick-set little man with a beard, who carried a brown leather satchel like a young lady's music-case. Hannibal retreated behind the counter. They entered, and when the little man had ordered some fine-cut pipe tobacco, continued talking.

"And there's nothing else, I suppose, Captain?" said the tall young man, whom Hannibal had served occasionally.

The gentleman addressed as Captain, busy lighting a cigar, shook his head. He had laid his satchel on the counter and Hannibal could read the name on it in sloping gilt letters:

s.s. *Caryatid*.

Hannibal placed the required canister on the counter and looked respectfully at the Captain.

"The chief said he wanted a lad," said the latter, putting down some silver. "I don't think he can get anybody here; he doesn't know London much. I said I'd mention it while I was up in the City."

"Why doesn't he go to the Sailors' Home?" said the young man, lighting a cigarette.

"He can't get away. And besides, he says he doesn't want a lad who's been to sea before. They know too much. Always trouble with 'em." He looked up and saw Hannibal's strained, attentive face.

"D'you know anybody?" he asked abruptly.

"What—what sort o' job, sir?" stammered Hannibal.

"Mess-room Steward. Good job for a handy lad."

"On a ship, sir?"

"Sure."

"Yes, sir, I know somebody."

"Goin' right away?"

"Think so, sir." Hannibal put down the change.

The Captain took it up and pointed to the name of the ship on the satchel.

"Victoria Dock. Sailin' to-morrow. He'd better go down and see the Chief to-day. Say Captain Briscoe sent him down."

"Yes, sir."

They went out and other customers came in, the usual ten-to-eleven stream, and Hannibal served them like one in a trance. What a strange world it was! Here was a job on a ship; and this determined little man, in his dark blue suit and bowler hat, his slow authoritative manner and freckled hairy hands, seemed to have a different view of life to those appallingly efficient people who had printed that pamphlet about Raising the Dead. Hannibal wondered if he had after all dreamt it. Here was a job where the holders of it could easily know too much. Was it not too good to be true? Surely this was an oversight on the part of the Pallas Athene School of Efficiency.

He turned it over in his mind as he served the customers. He hardly dared think of the thing to which he was committed. To desert the shop and Amelia, to trample on the Brown Ideals! The s.s. *Caryatid*. He looked out across the street at the picture. Was that the *Caryatid* in some far-distant port? The kitten jumped on the counter and rubbed herself against him unnoticed. One thing cheered Hannibal immensely, and that was the promptness with

which he had seized the opportunity. After all, it was
strange that skippers of steamers had not patronised the
shop before. Another characteristic of the affair gave him
a certain comfort. It almost seemed as if the control of
things had passed out of his hands. It was fate. He was
destined to go away.

And then he came down to earth again as he thought of
Amelia. He had left her with frightful abruptness the
night before; would he be able to carry on that attitude
when she came in to-day? He felt sadly that he would
not. He figured her trim figure suddenly appearing at the
door, her bright nod of the head, her rapid glance round
the shop to see if all was right, her brisk inspection of
the cash-register. How she did take hold, to be sure! What
was he to do? He tried to avoid thinking of what he was
to do, tried to fix his mind on the ship. A feeling of delicious terror ran through him as he thought of the
strangeness of the life to which he had committed himself
by his headlong plunge into Captain Briscoe's conversation. He recalled that visit to the Docks with Mrs. Gaynor and Hiram, the great spars of the *Cygnet* overhead,
with the sails dropped partly down to dry, the immaculate
cleanliness (so different, by the way, from steamer cleanliness, or even workhouse cleanliness), the air of invisible
authority that informed every movement, the mystery of
curtained port-holes and impregnable teak doors. And now
if he did as he had promised, he was to see that life complete, he would step aboard of this steamer, the *Caryatid,*
and she would bear him outward on the tide, beyond the
mud of the estuary, out into the sharp cool air and cloud-
rimmed circle of the heaving sea. He caught his breath
quickly as he tried to frame for himself out of his
ignorance some credible presentment of a streetless and
mobile existence. There would be no Little Brown Box.
His imagination staggered and halted before that for a
while, for he had grown up among little brown boxes of
various kinds, he had lived in spirit for many years in a
little brown box. He remembered his father in a brown
box in the front room. And when they had left Maple
Road their belongings went into a brown box. He could
hardly conceive of an existence apart from that emblem of

discreet security. And yet, had he not read with vague
gropings towards ultimate liberty, of folk who dwelt far
out beyond the Narrow Seas, who lived casual lives, sor-
rowful sometimes indeed, but free?

Leaning on the counter, his head on his hands, he fell
into a waking dream of the future. The kitten crouched by
the door in the shaft of warm sunlight that struck slant-
wise into the street, and the canaries twittered and trilled
riotously above him. So his cousin found him when she
came, and remembered it afterward, that pose of quiet dis-
traction and the vacancy of the eye which he turned upon
her when he spoke. A shadow crossed her smiling face
when she saw it. She had been inclined to forgiveness as
she came through the sunlit streets, though his behaviour
had been very reprehensible. Rancour had but small place
in the Brown character, and she had deflected the enquiries of her relatives with jocular evasions. But here he
was again, up in the clouds!

"I was getting anxious," she said. "Last night you were
so short I thought you must be ill. What was the matter?"

He stood up, and the kitten having sprung in friendly
agility on the counter, he brushed her away. The crisis
was come, and he had no glib phrase to hide under.

"I'd know," he said. "We all get the 'ump at times."

"The hump," she flared. "A nice way to describe it. Tell
me to my face you have had as much as you can stand of
us and call it the hump." And she took a handkerchief
from her pocket and held it to her nose, keeping her eyes
fixed upon him. This was, I think, because she could not
trust her mouth as she could her eyes, frequently the case
with young women of the Brown type. A slow colour
flooded Hannibal's cheeks and the eyelids over the brown
eyes flickered ominously.

Amelia failed to read her cousin's face accurately. She
imagined him humiliated. She had done very well at
school, but there were some things she could not understand. She could not understand anyone in their senses
saying such a thing as Hannibal had said. She lived in an
England which of all the Englands known to man is immune from criticism, the England of the Middle Classes.

This England is told, day in and day out, that they do the
work, fight the battles, pay the taxes, uphold the Flag,
and maintain the kingdom of God at a time when lords
and wage-earners are fallen away. They do not strike and
throw the nation into the periodical paroxysms that
are "so bad for trade." They do not congest the Divorce
Courts with the muck and garbage of their undisciplined
concupiscence. They are respectable. In their orderly millions they fill their microscopic destinies and their tombs.
Those who would smile, let them look well into this matter !

Amelia Brown was aware instinctively of the titanic
weight of class-consciousness behind her. She and her kind
valued their conception of the conduct of life as the goal
towards which others aimed but never reached. The idea
that there might be a side of the question which she could
not see did not occur to her as she stood watching him.
And she saw him, as she thought, humbled and without a
word to say for himself.

"It's gettin' to be a habit with you," she went on as he
did not speak. "It isn't as if you were that smart you
could afford to be saucy. You were half asleep just now."

"No," he said, lifting his hand in gentle deprecation.
"Not 'alf asleep. Only thinkin'."

"Not thinkin' of anything to put money in your pocket."

To her surprise he lifted his head and looked at her with
a quiet eye.

"No," he agreed, "it wasn't. You're quite right there."

She put up her hands and took off her hat with an
irritable movement.

"I can see what it is. I'll have to do it all," she muttered, as though in conclusion to some previous train of
embittered thought. "I don't see why you couldn't bring
your dinner with you," she went on, reverting to the
moment. "Aunt Mary could have something hot for you at
night. That's what John does."

Hannibal seemed impressed with John's habits.

"Ah," he said, "I might do that certainly."

She looked at him curiously.

"You're sensible enough now," she told him. "Go and
get your dinner. I want to get back to mother."

Obediently he took his cap and stepped to the door. He paused for a moment as though he were going to speak. He even turned towards her, looked up at the ceiling, and then, laughing gently, went out.

And never went back.

XI

THE *Caryatid,* in ballast, was steaming down the river at half-speed, and Hannibal, after the most strenuous twenty-four hours of his life, was leaning over the bulwarks and watching the coast-line slide ever away from him. He was at sea. He could feel the beat of the engines down below him, the rattle of the rudder-chains in the wheel-house, the occasional deep clang of the telegraph as the pilot altered her speed to slow or fast, after the manner of pilots. Far below him the turbid waters of the Thames received the outpouring discharge water from the pumps, great curved cataracts of yellowish foam. It was evening, and the City lay behind them wrapped in crimson and purple gauze as the sunset strove to pierce the great pall that hangs for ever over London.

Hannibal took a long breath as he looked out over the Essex flats and tried to fix those grey distances, those mist-blurred forms of chimney and tower, in his memory. And a breeze with a tang of salt in it came up the river and ruffled his damp hair deliciously. He turned away with a feeling of triumph in his heart. He had done it at last, done something on his own, something, moreover, that was unheard of among the Browns, something disreputable. He had run away to sea. Certainly there had been a great deal of red tape about that signing on in the Shipping Office, but for all that the essential vagabondage was there. He had no doubt that Amy was finished with him for ever. What a base trick he had played upon her. To go away without a word, to leave her to look after her own shop. Was there ever a more diabolically ingenious scheme to wring the Brown withers? He tried to imagine her there in the shop the previous afternoon waiting, waiting. . . .

They were all busy on deck coiling up ropes and putting on tarpaulins, and Hannibal went along the alley way to his room on the port side which he shared with another

lad who was "on deck." He wanted to think out how it
had all come about. And indeed he had a great deal to think
of. For when he had reached home the night before, his
mother had confronted him with a pale drawn face, and
over his mother's shoulder he had seen another face, a
face framed in a large hat, with steady dark blue eyes
and slightly smiling mouth, the face of his sister. And
when his mother had said, "Hanny, this is Minnie," he
had said, "Ullo," as though they had parted the day before.

"You've grown," she told him, and then had taken but
little notice of him. Evidently he had come in upon a
scene. He could not gather a great deal of it, but it referred to a plan Minnie had suggested. His mother would
have none of it at first. Minnie was going to marry someone she had met abroad. They were to be married—he remembered Minnie laid great stress on that—and then he
was going abroad again, and she was going to live in a
flat off the King's Road, Chelsea. Hannibal gathered that
the difficulty lay in his mother's doubt of this story. For
Minnie suggested that her mother should come and live
with her, and Mrs. Gooderich, with an unusual imagination, pictured herself being lured into countenancing a
ménage which was not respectable.

It is easy to make fun of Mrs. Gooderich and her ball-
fringe morality; but to her it was not funny, it was not
trivial. To her it was the very plinth of her life. She might
be poor and stupid and shiftless. She might be only a sort
of glorified charwoman, but she would fight like a tigress
for that thing she had so nearly forfeited years ago. She
had never forgotten during the long dragging years of
wifehood, that her husband had lifted her from the nameless women. But she waited in vain for any note of grati-
tude in her daughter's voice. Minnie seemed to feel she
was conferring a favour upon this man whom she had met
abroad. Mrs. Gooderich could not understand that. She
could not understand why there should be so much going
away in her daughter's life. There was a certain quality
in Mrs. Gooderich's mind which an electrician would call
resistance. She possessed sufficient conductivity to carry
the ordinary current of her life, but these critical moments

of high tension were full of difficulty. I think it was this
resistance which roused Minnie to irony, and gave Hannibal an uneasy feeling that there was what he called "A
row on." He was disconcerted, for he wanted to explode
his own bomb. He wanted to tell his mother he had run
away from the Little Brown Box. But since he had come
in about his usual time his mother had not given him a
chance.

He had made his chance, however, and he had had the
satisfaction of making them both look at him very intently indeed. He was quite unaware of the fact that this
ability to make people look hard at you is one of the most
highly-prized faculties in the world.

"Old lady," he had interrupted, "why don't you? You'll
be all alone 'ere, 'cause I'm goin' away now."

"You!"

"Ah, I 'eard of a job and went down to see the ship and
I got it. Three pound a month and all found. You'd better
go to Minnie."

"A ship, Hanny?" Minnie had asked.

"Ah, a steamer—the *Caryatid.*"

"The *Cary*—!" Mother and son were looking at each
other, and did not see Minnie put her knuckles to her lips
and draw back as if to avoid a blow.

"What are you going as?" Minnie now asked, arranging
her draperies as she sat on the chair by the window. And
he had told her and watched her face assume its usual expression of cool composure.

Mrs. Gooderich had sat looking at her son, too dazed
to straighten out her tangled ideas. It was staggering
enough to have Minnie come back. But to have, on top of
that, Hannibal going away, was too much for her frayed
intellect. She sat there struggling in vain to comprehend it.

"And we're sailin' to-morrow," he had informed her.

"What did Amy say?" she managed to ask him, and her
horror when he confessed that he had not told Amy about
his intention was manifest and acute. Brother and sister
looked at each other. Evidently what Amy would say was
of importance to their mother. Unconsciously they behaved
as Ethel and Amelia had behaved towards the elder woman

who sat with her chin in her hand. What was she to do?
All her fair plans for her boy's future were to be shoved
aside. He was going on his own. In spite of herself she felt
a weight of responsibility lifted from her shoulders. Then
there remained Minnie. How familiar it seemed, to have to
consider Minnie's existence! But now it was Minnie who
was in the wrong. Surely, surely Minnie was in the wrong.
And yet, as she groped freely among the facts, she began
to wonder why it was Minnie did not behave as a prodigal
daughter should. She did nothing of the kind. She sat
there with her nice clothes, her carefully manicured nails,
her pale delicate face, and exhaling a perfume that filled
the room and added to her mother's dismay. There was
nothing in her attitude to indicate contrition or even maid-
enly alarm at her approaching nuptials. And here she was
calmly suggesting that her mother would translate herself from her lowly casual condition and come and live
with her. As in a dream she heard the clear voice expound-
ing a philosophy from which she shrank. "What good has
Uncle George done you, anyhow, mother? An honest living! And he our uncle! He ought to be ashamed of himself. He sends his own wife to Bournemouth and gives you
an office-cleaning job. . . . I don't care. You tell me
I've cut myself off from you. That's all rubbish. I simply
went my own way to make a living without asking help
from Uncle George or anybody else. I've done it, too, and
how much worse am I than many a married woman who
hasn't any excuse? A lot I care for what they think. A
woman like Marie Letellier is worth fifty of them. So am
I for that matter. I must say you're very hard to satisfy,
mother. I sent you money, and you sent it back. That's
your own affair. Now I come and offer you a home independent of Uncle George and his crew, and you tell me
I'm not respectable. H'm! You're as bad as the man I'm
going to marry. *His* relations have had him under their
thumb all his life."

And then Mrs. Gooderich had tried to tell her daughter of that early time, that terrible time when she had
gone home in shame and silence to bear a nameless child,
but she had failed, had wandered away into other matters,
so that Minnie had lost patience and said: "Mother, listen.

I've got my own reason for not telling you who it is I'm going to marry. The reason is I've learned to make quite sure of things before I count on them. For some time back I've been with Marie Letellier, and I've been earning my living sewing. I'm not much use at that, never was, and I can only just manage it. I've done that because—well, because he asked me to. I don't quite know how to explain why I like him, but I do. He's genuine, as far as his relations let him. He—he gave his own name and address, and I didn't. But when I'm married he's going to give me half-pay to keep house with, and that's twelve pounds a month. And as he'll be away a good deal, I want you to live with me. I can tell you this: he's in a good profession, and he wouldn't touch a builder with his umbrella."

"It's not——?" Mrs. Gooderich had begun.

"No, it's not," Minnie had replied. "He went a long time ago. He's Sir Anthony now. Don't talk about him. We went our own ways."

And then Hannibal had come in with his bomb and exploded it among them. He was going to sea and was sailing to-morrow.

"The *Caryatid* you said?" Minnie had asked. "How funny."

And then he had gone on to tell her how he had seen the chief and got the job, how his room-mate, a sailor boy, had shown him round and offered to help him get some dunnage. And he was going to meet him at seven o'clock at Aldgate, and would have to hurry with his tea. The word tea had roused his mother. That was a side of his character to which she could always respond. And how curiously commonplace had been his parting with his sister. He had seized his cap and turned to her irresolutely, and she had nodded over her teacup and said, "Be a good boy on the *Caryatid*, Hanny." And he had gone out and hurried to Aldgate to meet his new chum, who took him to a shop where he had ordered a blanket and a bolster and a sailor's bag. He had been so full of his own affairs he had almost forgotten Minnie by the time he had got back to Jubilee Street once again. His mother, her face grey in the lamplight, had confronted him. Amelia had been, Amelia with thin lips and a bright spot in each cheek,

Amelia refusing to sit down, so that her cousin Minnie had been able to sit with her back to the light and look her over at her leisure. Mrs. Gooderich's insulation had almost broken down altogether, so tense had been the encounter. She had wrung her hands and blamed herself, to which Amelia would not agree. But——! She had gone again, coldly, had promised to write, but it was all over. Mrs. Gooderich was sure she need never look to Kennington again.

And Minnie's cool, clear enunciation had cut into her bewailing like a sword through flesh. "Can't you see, mother, they only want to make a convenience of you? I suppose Hanny's been working for her for half the wages of a stranger. Engaged? Rubbish! What if they have been walking out? Mother, you're a hopeless fossil. Girls get engaged three times a month nowadays. It gives them a thrill, silly fools. Engagement's nothing."

"But she feels it!" Mrs. Gooderich had protested.

"I daresay. Gave her a nasty jolt, finding out all of a sudden he'd slipped." And then seeing the spasm in her mother's face she had relented: "Well, anyway, I believe Hanny'll do better if he starts out on his own like this than sticking to the Browns. Good Lord, mother, he isn't going to commit murder!"

"It's a wild life," his mother had whimpered.

"Oh, it is, is it? I could tell you something about it if I liked. Mother, I'm going to marry a sea-captain. There! Now are you satisfied? That's why he's to be away so much."

The mother's universe had been tottering for some time, and then it nearly capsized. She had thanked God with many tears that a working man had deigned to marry her and give her a name, and yet here was Minnie triumphantly closing her career of shame by wedding a professional man.

"And you want me to live with you?" she had queried, after Amelia had faded away.

"After we are married, and you shall have the certificate if you like," said Minnie emphatically. "I don't know whether you will understand me, but if there's one thing I hate more than being suspected of something I haven't done, it's being forgiven for something I *have* done. So don't let's have any fuss. The ship is going to Swansea, and if we can't get married to-morrow, he'll come back next week from Swansea. That's why I'm not anxious to blab. He may be drowned, he may be killed in a railway accident, he may drop dead, he may change his mind and I'll never see him again. You can't tell you've got a man until the papers are signed. I've seen too much of woman's sweet trusting nature and man's noble habits to have any illusions about them!"

"You'd never listen to anythin' I was to say," Mrs. Gooderich had remarked forlornly, and the exquisitely dressed creature had risen and come over to her. "There's no need to worry over that, mother. I've learned a good deal in the last three or four years, and if I can't take care of myself, I'm sure you won't be able to help me. I suppose"—here Minnie had laughed—"I suppose you think because I'm well dressed and use scent I'm a helpless sort of woman. Think, mother, think. I may be a rogue, I may be a fool; I can't be both. I'm not a fool for making you this offer, am I? I do it because you are my mother, how-ever much we differ, because you ought to rest now, and, most of all, because I hate the Browns and want you to be quit of them. Mother, do! Do the same as Hanny has done. Don't go to these offices any more. Just don't go. Let Uncle George explain it as he likes and be damned to him!" In her excitement, all the more terrible because it was so rare, she had clutched her mother's shoulder, and her mother had flinched from the pain of it. And then recovering herself, powdering her face in a little mirror drawn from her bag, she had smiled again and kissed her mother.

"I'll let you know as soon as I can," she had said, and so had gone into the night, firing the respectable curiosity of the Bohemian family behind their curtains.

It had certainly cleared the air, for when Hannibal returned his mother had made up her mind to do some-thing. It was as though the chambers of her mind had been swept by a mighty rushing wind which had cleared out the accumulated detritus of the years, and left her wan and reluctantly sane. It was not in her nature to do what Minnie had urged: to drop her brother-in-law and his employment. She would have to retire by easy stages. But to have inured her mind to two such revolutionary ideas in one evening, to desert Mr. Brown and permit Hanny to go to sea—no wonder her face was grey and drawn when Hanny returned to supper.

He had had a momentary panic, he remembered, when he had learned that Amelia had put in an appearance. But his mother's news that Minnie was going to marry a sea-captain drove out all thought of the Brown family. That was very curious indeed. Fancy Minnie doing that. But even Minnie, dominant as she was, did not hold him long. He was hungry, he had made a new chum, he was to be on board the ship at five o'clock the next morning. A youth of eighteen recks little of his sister's affairs in such circumstances.

"Five o'clock!" Mrs. Gooderich had echoed blankly. "I'll never get you up before six." But she had forgotten that the tense excitement of the adventure would keep him floating on the very edge of slumber all night, and indeed he was on his feet soon after three that morning, padding round in his bare feet and knocking dishes over in his nervous anxiety to save her trouble. She asked him when he was coming back, having years of separation in her mind; and when he said he didn't know, as the ship had no orders yet, she looked grave and piteously lonely in the twilight of the passage. So he remembered her now as he sat in his berth listening to the thud of the engines and the boots clouting on the deck over his head, a grey-faced old woman in a yellow flannel wrapper with her hands on his breast. He remembered with a feeling of almost uneasy shame how he had towered over her, his bundle of clothes in his hand, how, when he had gone out and closed the gate, he had looked back and seen her peering from behind the door, a bewildered pathetic figure.

And then it had been a strenuous day indeed. He had reached the dock all right and got aboard, and Tommy, his new chum, had shown him where to get the things he needed. The cook had to be placated, an irascible man of brutally frank utterance and having an aversion to "new-

starters" generally. But eventually Hannibal had made
coffee and toast and carried it down into the engine-room
safely. That had been an experience! The interminable
iron ladders which had to be negotiated with one hand
on the polished oily rail, the hot oppressive atmosphere,
the smell of oil and steam, the sound of water dropping
somewhere far below, the occasional hiss and spit of a
blowing steam-pipe, the shimmer of brass, the half-
revealed glory of shining steel, the purr of the little
dynamo, the lazy flutter of the forced-draught-fan—all
these things smote his senses and filled him with a sort
of solemn delight. This was indeed what he desired. This
was worth while. And down there, too, he had encountered the man whom he understood to be his boss, the
Second Engineer, a spare, wiry young man whose hair
was greying at the temples, and whose eyes had crowsfeet
in the corners. He came abruptly round from behind the
engines, his singlet stained and splotched with black oil,
which can no more be washed out than printers' ink, his
greasy peaked cap stuck on one corner of his determined-
looking head, and a cigarette in his mouth. "Ain't it 'ot
'ere?" Hannibal had remarked, looking in awe at the great
silent engines. And the Second Engineer, after glancing
at the thermometer, an instrument of softly glowing copper, had looked at Hannibal over the edge of the mug
without speaking. He was not a man of many words, having to deal with so many crises where words are of no
avail, and he could not express his opinion of a youth who,
at five-thirty in the morning, thought a temperature of a
hundred degrees anything extraordinary. After a sup and
a bite at the toast he had set them down and disappeared
again, and Hannibal heard a clean hard burst of steam, a
choking splutter and a sudden jar as of something brought
up standing, and then, as though that something had experienced a prodigious relief, a sigh, followed by a regular
throb. How interesting it was! He turned and watched the
shining little engine that drove the dynamo, and saw the
blue fire that snapped now and again from the brushes.
This was indeed the heart of things. And then the Second
Engineer reappeared, summoned by the whir of the tele-
phone-bell, and he spoke in a low voice to someone above:

"She's just on the sixty-mark now, sir. . . . All right, sir. . . . It's eased back quarter turn, sir. . . . All right, sir. Just begun circulation. . . . Quite cold, sir. . . . L.P.'s warmin', though. . . . Yes. . . . All right, sir." And he had hung up the receiver, and seeing Hannibal staring at the engines, had pointed with his thumb to the ladder, a gesture of enormous expressiveness, and Hannibal had taken the hint.

And then had come trials and difficulties, the inevitable trials and difficulties of those unaccustomed to the ways of ships. He felt now that he would never have got through if it had not been for Tommy, who told him how things were done. But Tommy was out on deck pulling ropes, working the winch (he called it "vorkin' the vinch"), running hither and thither at the bidding of a tall strong man, the Bosun, doing an amount of work out of all proportion to his size. Tommy could not spare the time to go everywhere with him, and so Hannibal had made numerous mistakes, such, for example, as asking the Chief where the sugar was kept, and enquiring of the cook the whereabouts of the tablecloth. He even committed the unpardonable crime of opening the Third Mate's door (quite by mistake, they were so alike, those doors), and inadvertently arousing a young man who had been ejected from Frascati's at twelve-thirty A.M. But in spite of these troubles, Hannibal felt that he was learning, and having taken off his coat and "started in" in earnest in the messroom, turning out all the "gear," he found little difficulty in getting the breakfast. And then, when that was over, the dishes washed, the cloth shaken and folded up, the tapestry cover spread over the table, he had found time to pause and draw breath. After all, he had not done so badly. The four engineers had filed in and seated themselves without comment. Hannibal had looked at them curiously, from the taciturn Chief who ate nothing, down to the grimy-faced Fourth who ate everything he could reach. Only the Second carried on a low monologue which was intended for the Chief, who replied by nods. The Third, who seemed to suspect the Fourth of a tendency to hilarity, fixed a glassy eye upon the new mess-room steward and made him extremely uncomfortable. Hanni-

bal hardly knew whether to out-stare him or turn away.
The Chief had a fashion of pointing silently for anything
he wanted, which was rather disconcerting, but it was a
glorious change from "nagging." Another thing that
reconciled him was the prodigious quantity of food left
over. A great dish of rump steak and onions swimming
in gravy, a plate of liver and bacon, potatoes, jam, marmalade, and coffee. Evidently he would not starve. And
then, when he had washed up, it occurred to him to go
through the cupboard from which such an astonishing
stench arose. He pulled out numerous tin boxes containing
fragments of bygone loaves of bread, a piece of cheese
rivalling the Stone Age in antiquity, a pot of jam turning
rapidly into cockroaches, some oval cabin biscuits, a pot
of marmalade turning into sugar, and various vessels
which had at one time held chutney, pickled onions, sar-
dines, ketchup, and mustard. The whole of this collection
was alive with an army of insects varying in size from
the huge brown cockroach to the diminutive black objects
with many legs and enormous antennæ, with which they
appeared to be signalling in semaphore fashion to unseen
battalions in the interstices of the fabric. Hannibal was
not quite unacquainted with these uncertificated members
of the ship's company, but he was somewhat amazed by
the number of them. There seemed to be an illimitable
supply, for no slaughter ever sufficed. So he carefully
emptied the tins, swept the cheese, the crusts, the dirt,
and the empties into his dust-pan, and threw them on the
ash-heap on the bridge-deck. He had found a dirty white
jacket with silver buttons such as the cabin stewards
wore, buttons with the curious zigzag figure which appeared on the funnel, on the house-flag at the masthead,
on some of the crockery, and on the badges which the
mates and engineers wore on their caps. It was the Greek
letter K and it was what Hannibal, in his ignorance, called
the "Trade mark of the Firm."

But now it was evening, the toil and excitement was
over for a time, and he could think about it all in peace.
He looked round his berth and felt that he would do very
well there. In the next room were two apprentices, young
men about his own age, who were now on deck with the

others carrying out the orders of the gigantic Bosun and the Chief Mate, who was always whistling for someone to run up and down and do something that had been forgotten. Once Hannibal had caught sight of Captain Briscoe walking to and fro on the bridge, had seen him pull the lanyard that ran to the great bronze whistle on the funnel and blow an ear-splitting blast. This was to warn the ferry-boat at Woolwich. Hannibal had leaned over the side of the boat and watched the tiny people waving on the ferry, and the sight made him realise what he had done. He was a seafaring man now, one of a class apart. Those people on the ferry were Browns, tiny respectable home-staying Browns, builders and shopkeepers. How distant they all seemed, as he watched the ferry slide sideways to the pier!

He busied himself putting his gear straight, though he had not brought a great deal. Tommy, the omniscient Tommy, had advised him to buy all he wanted in Swansea, whither they were going to load. The previous mess-room steward had been what Tommy called "a dirty feller," but his "donkey's breakfast," the straw mattress in a case of sacking, seemed all right, and Hannibal spread his blue blanket over it and settled the pink flannel bolster in place. Then he stowed all his clothes away in the drawer. Tommy slept in the top bunk, and Hannibal noted how "tidy" he kept everything belonging to him. That was Tommy's mania, "tidiness." Hannibal was looking at the little photos on the bulkhead when he came in with his kid of hash and a tin of tea.

"Ullo, how's things?" he asked cheerily, and slipped off his sea-boots, which were all wet with washing down the bridge-deck.

"Pretty fair," smiled Hannibal. "You finished?"

"No. I go to the veel at eight bells," replied Tommy, taking a knife and fork from a drawer, and seeing a puzzled look on his new chum's face, he went on: "You don't know de bells, I s'pose? It's one bell in de dog vatch now. Quarter to eight's one bell too. Eight o'clock's eight bells, so's twelve and four. I'll show you. Hain't you bin to sea before?"

Hannibal shook his head.

"I bin to sea two—nearly three years now."

"You? 'Ow old are you, then?"

"Fifteen and a 'alf."

Hannibal looked at the round rosy face and clear sea-blue eyes in astonishment.

"You been all round then?" And Tommy, his mouth full of hash, nodded.

"You ain't English, are you?" And Tommy shook his head.

"Amsterdammer," he said. "Don't you like Dutchmen?"

"I never seen one before," Hannibal confessed. "I've been in London all me life," and he tried to imagine how life looked to this little seafarer who toiled so cheerfully in foreign ships and spoke a foreign tongue so well. "D'you speak Dutch?" he asked in wonder. Tommy nodded.

"And German and Flemish too. I vorked as mess-room on a German ship three months," he said. "Dat was no good. Germans gib bad grub an' bad pay."

"What do you get here then?"

"Three pounds, like you."

As time went on, and especially after they had gone out of Swansea, Hannibal learned something of the life of his new chum, Drevis Noordhof, of his childhood in Amsterdam, of how he ran away to sea when he was thirteen, of his sufferings on the German steamer, so that he ran away from her in Petersburg and, getting lost in the city, was found by an Englishman, who put him on a British ship and sent him home again. He learned of Tommy's "oppu," his mother's mother, who had brought him up, for his mother was dead and he had never known who his father had been. But the next day after they left London, when the *Caryatid* was below St. Catherine's Point, she began to roll, and Hannibal's interest in life vanished like the morning mist.

It was in the mess-room, as he felt round among his gear for the tea-things, that the cataclysm overtook him, and he stumbled out on deck and over to the side in an agony of hope that vomiting might relieve him. The cook saw him hanging, limp and heaving, to the rail, and threw a rotten spud at him for luck, but Hannibal was past being offended. The bitterness of death, it seemed, was at hand, and each choking retch was like to prove his last gasp. Those who can experience seasickness in the comfort of the saloon know nothing of its terrors. To be compelled to do one's daily work at the same time is a different matter. It is no jest, until it is all over. Weak and listless, Hannibal tried to make the tea and take it round. In the room occupied by the Third and Fourth he saw the latter in his pyjamas on the settee, a pipe in his mouth, a couple of pillows behind him, reading *Sapho*. The rolling had no effect on him. Was it possible, thought Hannibal, that he would ever be like that, be able to loll on a settee and smoke while the ship lay over in this disgusting manner? The roll flung him against the alley-way stanchion and he looked down at the grey-blue waters of the Channel with an unutterable loathing.

As the day advanced he grew worse, and at tea-time he thought he was really going to die. Only the callous gibes of the others reassured him. Of course, everybody had an infallible panacea for the complaint. The cook said he ought to drink a pint of salt water every half-hour, and Hannibal wondered if the man were mad as well as heartless. The Chief said nothing except to order him to put the racks on the table and leave nothing loose. The Second suggested putting a finger down his throat to make himself sick and get it over; but Hannibal, with tears in his eyes, answered that he had no difficulty in being sick, and proved his words by rushing to the side and casting his dinner into the sea. Then the Carpenter, a tall, hardfeatured man in enormous sea-boots that reached to his thighs, asked him how a little fat pork would suit him, and the young man's face turned ashen-grey with nausea. It was all very tragic and ridiculous, and when he came reeling into the mess-room with the potatoes falling out of the dishes, and the stew under his arm, the juniors cackled with delight and the Chief made grumbling remarks about the "ballast run."

It was dreadful to watch four men voraciously devouring a big meal of stew, potatoes, pork, jam, and tea, and lighting pipes of full-strength tobacco afterwards. It seemed inhuman, to him, struggling with a bucket of hot water and breaking dishes at every turn. The fragments slithered about the floor, and when he got down on his knees to look for them, the sickness came on and he had to rush out on deck.

The sea was not really very rough, though the *Caryatid* rolled rather heavily round Land's End, but a tall ship in ballast is at the mercy of the slightest swell, and Hannibal thought it very tempestuous indeed. It was good for him that he was compelled to go about regularly. If he had lain down as he wished he would have been relieved, like a passenger, but he would have been all the longer finding his sea-legs. The Second knew this and kept him mercilessly to his work. Hannibal used to watch the Chief out on the after-deck walking to and fro, sloping his body as the ship rolled, his pipe sticking out from between the upturned flaps of his pilot-coat. The Second would come up from below and stand near the engine-room door talking to the Chief as he walked, his cap hanging to one corner of his head, his knotted arms all smeared with grease, and he would look over the side now and again to see if the bilge-pumps were working right.

They were in the Bristol Channel, coming up past Lundy, when Hannibal felt able to sit down and light a cigarette again. He still had a queer subdued feeling of disquietude, but the sickness was gone, and he had lost the horrible sensation of his stomach being loose inside him. The natural optimism of youth, aided by Tommy's cheerful conversation, took Hannibal's thoughts away from himself and he began to observe once more. He revelled in the immensity of sea and sky, the huge piles of tinted clouds driving before the south-westerly wind, billow on billow of cumulous vapour, through which the straight slanting rays of an invisible sun poured like the celestial glory in Italian paintings. He liked the ceaseless onslaught of the waves against the bows, and he would watch breathlessly as the ship rose and fell, to see her plunge just as a swell advanced, and see the sheet of spray flash across the water. And the perpetually-recurring attacks of the defeated waves as they licked the sides of the ship away below, rushing along the plates, running up

strake after strake and vanishing with a vindictive slap—
this was a source of continual delight to him.

Tommy came down from his two-hour trick at the
"veel" and told him they would be in Mumble's Roads
before dawn, and then of course he had to explain what
he meant by Roads, which was an anchorage. Hannibal
asked him what sort of a place Swansea was, and Tommy
proclaimed it "all right, all right."

"I got a girl there!" he informed Hannibal, who
laughed.

"You!"

"Ah. You want a girl? Dere's mine, see?" and he
showed Hannibal a picture-postcard with a photo of a
dark young lady with one hand on a carved table and
a panorama of tropical jungle and river scenery behind
her. "She's got a sister. You come wid me, I'll show
you."

"You got one in every port?" asked Hannibal facetiously.

Tommy smiled as he stripped off to have a scrub.

"Girl's all right, I reckon," he opined, stretching, and
rumpling his tow-coloured hair. "This one here I like
good an' plenty." And he plunged his arms into the basin
and began to wash. His round little face came out dripping
suds and he reached blindly for his towel.

"Some of them are no dam good," he remarked, towel-
ling vigorously. "One I had in Liverpool, over at Bootle,
when the ship was laid up, she said she'd write to me. She
didn't at all, and when I came back she'd got anoder feller.
I 'ad one in Glasgow too, and she did de same. See? Dat
de worst o' bein' a sailor-boy. Ven you're away, she gets
anoder feller."

"D'you go out with 'em?" asked Hannibal, lying back
luxuriously on the settee.

"Sure! Vat else? See? You get dis oder girl, de sister,
and we'll go out to de Empire, eh?"

"I'd' now," he replied. "I've 'ad enough of 'em."

"What you been doin' ashore?" Tommy asked, dragging
a comb through his hair.

"In a shop, a tobacconist's," replied Hannibal, blowing
rings.

"Gee-whiz! Dat 'ud be all right! Why the 'ell d'you come to sea, den."

"I wanted to 'ave a look around."

"It's no good, dis sort o' life, I reckon," said Tommy, slipping his head through a singlet and straightening up. "People ashore get plenty more money'n us."

"Not all found," argued Hannibal, who was beginning to see things.

"Better grub, though."

"This 'ere grub's all right. More'n I can eat."

"You vait till we get to sea. Dis 'ere's coastin'. Vait till de salt meat start and de tinned stuff. One trip we went from Shimonoseki to Honolulu. No peas, no spuds, noding but tinned stuff. You vait!"

And Tommy climbed into his bunk to have his eight-to-twelve sleep. Hannibal went out on deck to have a think. He could not quite understand how Tommy should take things so gaily. And yet, when he got ashore in that strange place whose lights would soon be twinkling ahead, would he not feel more free himself? Would not the romance of youth surge in him and tempt him to see the light in women's eyes? He was away now. He was in the eyes of the Brown family, a scapegrace, a defaulter, a youthful prodigal. He would have to live up to the character. His eyes danced as he thought of the possibilities before him. Even now, the voyage scarcely begun, he had nearly half a month's pay in hand,—twenty-seven shillings. Of course, he would have to lay in a sea-stock in Swansea, as Tommy had told him; but even then he would have some money to "blow." He stood with the wind ruffling his hair, watching the light on Lundy Island dying away behind them. The tide was on the turn now, and the quick thud-thud of the engines came up to him more faintly now that they were in slack water. Up on the bridge dark forms flitted to and fro, and every now and then the Mate's whistle shrilled through the night air and a sailor would hurry aft with a lantern to look at the patent log.

It was four-thirty in the morning when the cook dug him in the ribs and he rolled out on the floor, rubbing his eyes. The electric bulb glowed in the ceiling, a towel

wrapped round it to screen the light from penetrating
Tommy's curtains, where he lay in the profound slumber
of those who keep the middle-watch. Hannibal scrambled
into his clothes and hurried out on the deck. They were
going in. Just ahead he could see the deep red light that
marked the entrance to the lock-channel. Rubbing his
eyes, he took his coffee-pot to the galley. The junior apprentice, a freckled young man with a jaw that receded
into his thick woollen comforter, was standing in the
galley, talking to the cook.

"Is that a fact?" asked the cook, as Hannibal lifted
the dipper from the hook.

"The Third Mate swears blind it is," said the apprentice. "I heard him tellin' Mr. Brail. Saw the Old Man
comin' out of Frascati's with her last night before we
come away. So he followed and ran against him accident'ly
for the purpose. You know Mr. Cadoxton."

"He's certainly got the gall," assented the cook, search-
ing among his utensils.

"Well, he apologised and all that, and the Old Man,
who scarcely knows Cadoxton yet by sight, seeing he only
joined himself last week, ups and introduces him. I reckon
the Old Man was a bit on, you know."

"Frascati's!" said the cook, throwing up his eyes to
heaven as though he had been a sad dog there in the past.

"Well, the Old Man ups and introduces him—'Mister
—er,' and Cadoxton prompts him a bit—'Mister Cadoxton, my future wife.' And the Third Mate says chin-chin,
and shakes hands with her. A peach, the Third Mate
says."

"And she's comin' the trip?" asked the cook, passing
out a great schooner of coffee to a fireman.

"So the Third Mate says. He says the Old Man told
'em at the Cabin Table he was goin' up to London on
business, and the Mate said something about the Old
Man tellin' him he wouldn't be back for several days. I
shouldn't wonder."

"I don't like women on the ship," growled the cook.
"It's all sorts of extry work for the Steward, and that
means more for me too."

"Well," remarked the junior apprentice, "there it is.

The Mate knows more than he lets on. We shall see to-day, very likely."

Hannibal went out and made the coffee. The Chief was passing up and down in his thick pilot-coat, and said to him as he passed:

"Make coffee for all, boy. They're down below."

He went back and toasted four big slices of bread as he had been told by the Second. This time he saw the senior apprentice standing by the galley door, talking furtively to those within.

"I was talkin' to Mr. Cadoxton just now when I left the wheel," he said, "and he told me he could swear blind he's seen her or her picture somewhere. He's tryin' to think. He's goin' to turn over his letters. Anyhow, he's sure it's some time since she left the infant school."

"He's no chicken, the Old Man," remarked the junior apprentice.

"He's all right. Don't come interferin' with the work on deck. Yes, sir!" he howled, and darted away to where the Second Mate, a rotund little man in uniform, was standing by some ropes.

"Tod always thinks he gets exclusive information out of the Third Mate," said the junior apprentice in some indignation.

"He's next 'im," said the cook significantly.

"Not in this case. I heard the Mate say myself, 'Mr. Cadoxton, you're making a mistake. Better not let on you've seen her before if the Old Man brings her down.'"

"Oh, 'e said that, did 'e," said the cook, chopping onions. "'E knows somethin' then."

"His brother-in-law's Second Mate o' the *Torso*, this Old Man's last command, and I'll bet my rubber boots he knows something. His brother-in-law lives near the Old Man's people."

Hannibal ran out with his toast, buttered it, and took it down the engine-room ladders to the starting-platform. The telegraph clanged deep and resonant as he reached the plates, and he saw the Second throw the engines into gear with a lightning twist of his hand. The Fourth was standing by the handle of the great enamelled dial where the peremptory finger was pointing to "Slow Ahead." The

Third strolled to and fro on the middle grating, feeling here and there, a cigarette hanging to his lower lip, and a spanner in his hand. Suddenly, just as Hannibal set down the steaming cups on the vice-bench, the gong went again, this time with a shrill poignant clangour that drove the blood back to one's heart. The pointer had swung round to "Full Astern." With a turn of his hand the Second sent the reversing engine flying round, the huge links of the main valve-gear slid over the position, the cranks paused, trembled, and then sprang to their work as though whipped into activity by some invisible titanic hand. With infinite *aplomb* the Third leaned over the shining hand-rails feeling the plunging masses of metal as they flew up and down; the Second eyed the gauges and beckoned to the Fourth. Hannibal stepped up to him as he began to speak.

"Coffee, sir?" said he above the rush and thud of the engines.

"All right. What was that about the Old Man? Goin' to get married?" said the Second, addressing the Fourth and spitting into the high-pressure crank-pit.

"The Third Mate's got a yarn about meetin' him in Frascati's the other night," said the Fourth, opening a drain-cock to ease the water hammer in the low-pressure cylinder. "Tony lot, they mates! As a matter of fact, I was in the cabin this afternoon askin' the Old Man about my half-pay note, and he was writin' the address on a letter."

"An' you saw it?"

"Ay! Miss Gooderich. He writes plain enough, you ken. I didn' have time to spot the address. S. W. anyway. That's London, is it not?" he addressed Hannibal, who was standing with a curious look of amazement on his face.

"Ah," he assented with a nod. "Sou'-west that is."

"And he put sealin' wax on the back," added the Fourth, reaching up and handing the Third an oil-feeder. "Shall a book it?" he asked, breaking off, and when the Second nodded he wrote on the log board. "And then he pushed his ring on it and stamped it. It was her all right, all right."

"An' Cadoxton don't know you know it?"

"Na. He knows it all, does Cadoxton, him and his Frascati's! What's a sailor-man doin' to Frascati's, any-way? Gatti's was always good enough for me when I was in t' Castle Line."

"His ma has means," sniffed the Second, eyeing the telegraph. "Surely we're backing into Port Talbot?"

"'Tis to swing her," said the Fourth. "She's like a brewer's lorry to swing. Full ahead, she is!" he shouted as the deep mellow ahead gong gave out its warning note, and answered.

"He'll be takin' her the trip," vociferated the Second, as a fireman entered and signalled expressively for the fan to go faster. The Second nodded.

"Maybe. Easy! Slow ahead," chanted the Fourth, writ-ing on the log board. "She'll be waitin' of us in the Prince o' Wales Dock."

"Mess!" called the Second to Hannibal, who was still standing trying to get the hang of this tremendous affair. "Do you go up and ask the Chief to speak down, will you? Savvy?"

Hannibal roused and nodded.

"Yes, sir," and he climbed up toward the dawn.

When he had told the Chief, who ran to his telephone and spoke to the Second, the *Caryatid* was safely through the dock gates and she was being swung round to move up to her berth under the coal-tips, huge latticed structures with pale lights on their upper cabins, their shoots drawn up and pointing to the delicate blue sky, stark emblems of utility deriding the azure. All around were sleeping steamers, their galley lights winking in the twilight, the huddled figures of night-watchmen leaning over their bul-warks, observing the new-comer with the insatiable curi-osity of the sea. A small boat, loaded with a hawser and propelled by a stern-oar, waggled to the dock wall and made fast. The *Caryatid's* forecastle-head vibrated with the working of the windlass. With ceaseless industry the sailors ran to and fro on the decks. At intervals the hum was torn by a short blast from the whistle or the far-off chaffering of megaphones. Slowly, slowly the tall hull drew in to her appointed berth beneath the silent tip. The telegraph orders grew less frequent. With a thuttering roar the safety valves lifted and a billow of white steam flew from the 'opper waste-pipe on the funnel. Now and again Hannibal saw the Old Man waving to the Second Mate on the poop, saw the Third Mate at the Old Man's elbow discussing something. Men appeared on the quay, men in blue uniforms, men in black coal-grimed apparel, men in new serge suits. The red disc of the sun rose up above the hills and flooded the port with the light of a May morning. Birds sang under the eaves of the weighing-houses and flew across the railway sidings, and sea-gulls, gossiping on the buoys or perched in solitary grandeur on the trucks of the sailing ships, viewed with easy familiarity the advent of the *Caryatid*. At length the stern ropes were made fast, the blue-uniformed man on the quay cocked his eye to the bridge, calculating the chances of *coomshaw* from the skipper, the gangway, urged by twenty willing hands, slid over the bulwarks and down to the black earth, the drum of alien heels sounded on her decks, and the bridge, so authoritative, so omnipotently urgent a moment since, was silent. She was no longer a sentient thing in the sea, she was become but a line in the shipping news, a factor on the Exchange. There she had not even a name, she was simply a semi-hypothetical capacity, "8000 tons, Las Palmas, 8s. 3d.," a bucket in the endless distribution chain that creeps across the world.

Hannibal, busily laying the table for breakfast, wondered after all why he should feel so excited over the news that had come to his ears. He had already enough of the sea-habit to be pretty sure that any amount of relationship made but small mark on the hard and shining discipline of the sea. And he was not unmindful, moreover, of Mr. Grober's valediction, to be master of himself. Poor old Mr. Grober! Hannibal was sorry now he had not looked in and taken that book back. He thought of him now, feebly setting out his boxes of rubbishy books, standing by his door looking out with rheumy eyes upon a world which, he said, was not an oyster to be opened but a quick-sand to be passed. Surely enough he had no wings, or they had been pulled out long ago. He would sit in his dusty shop, his pipe in his mouth, his spectacles on his nose, slowly reading a dead book, slowly sinking into the sand. . . .

That was not to be his way, Hannibal thought fiercely, clattering the cups and saucers. No fear! He was not going to be "sucked in," as Mr. Grober had phrased it. As for this astonishing information which had come to him so fortuitously, he was going to be his own boss and earn his living independent of anybody. He knew now, though, why Minnie had said "Be a good boy on the *Caryatid*." She knew this! But what did it matter? The Old Man was the Old Man certainly, but he had no truck with the engineers' department. Hannibal, going over the matter in the cool light of morning, decided that his freedom of soul was unimpaired. If it had been the Browns, now——! But that was grotesque in its impossibility. As he carried the porridge in from the galley he laughed in sheer light-hearted conviction that he had nothing more to fear from the Browns. He would do his day's work and go ashore, oblivious of Minnies and Skippers and Amelias, go with Master Drevis Noordhoff and investigate, in impartial spirit, the world, the flesh, and the devil. He would have no more shilly-shally, this piddling game of hanging like a puppy to its mother's dugs. He would go out and see for himself. Was he not a man, a seaman in the British Mercantile Marine, with a number and registered rating? Had he not come into direct conflict with organised government, looking a supercilious shipping-clerk in the eye and taking a neatly-stamped advance-note from the hand of the gilded creature who wrote them out on that polished mahogany counter? Had he not gone down into the depths and prayed for dissolution in the agony of sea-sickness? What were the petty details of domestic life to him, lord of himself and a twelve by fourteen mess-room? He was almost hilarious when he hastened round to call the engineers to breakfast.

"What's the matter? Somebody died an' left you a farm?" asked the Second, mildly surprised at Hannibal's genial face.

"Wife got twins?" enquired the Fourth, looking between his legs as he washed in a bucket in the alley-way.

Hannibal laughed.

"There's nobody dead!" he laughed; and the Third, fixing him with a glassy stare, a stare that concealed a violently romantic soul, remarked, "He must be in love."

"He wouldn't grin if he was in love," said the Second, hunting for a clean shirt. "I was in love once, and it was rotten. Ever been in love, Tich?"

"I'm goin' to get a grip of her waist to-night," said the Third. "Spink!" he addressed the stooping Fourth. "It's your night aboard, me bonny laddie, d'ye ken that?"

"Don't you be so free wi' your nights aboard," growled the Fourth. "I'm goin' to ask the Chief for an exemption, it bein' a home port."

"You in love, too?" enquired the Second, locking the door. "Boys will be boys! Don't keep the Chief waiting for his grub."

At breakfast the main theme of conversation, the theme which was vibrating in every department of the ship, from the Chief Mate's berth to the lazarette where the cook was cutting up joints, overrode the minor topics of the casual loves of the sea. Even the dour Chief, nibbling his toast and sipping his tea, for he was a victim of dyspepsia brought on by early carousing, made sundry disjointed references to the rumours afloat. Mr. Spink, devastating a trencher of steak and onions, contributed his own precious tid-bit to the news, a tid-bit undeniably confirming the general impression. Hannibal listened, but forbore to speak. The knowledge that he might give their curiosity a perfectly unendurable fillip amused him, but he felt quite unable to cope with the ensuing situation, and so refrained.

"Mate's got an idea's somethin' fishy in it," the Chief murmured, looking into his tea with profound distrust.

"Cabin talk, a reckon," said the Second with his mouth full. "Cadoxton had his foot on the rail in London and he wants us to know it. D'you reckon she'll be comin' the trip then, sir?"

The Chief looked round as though lost in an uncongenial maze of psychological problems. And in truth he was in no wise competent to grapple with either drama or romance.

"I could'na say," he murmured softly, pointing to the

butter, and Hannibal moved it towards him hastily. "Better let the Fourth put a new rubber in the deck reducin' valve, eh? I heard it pop this morning."

The Second cast a sidelong look of surprise at the Chief, who was always surprising him by unexpected knowledge.

"Aye," he said, digging at the butter. "I'll let him all right, all right."

"An' the Third can help him," droned the Chief discontentedly. "I'd like you to go through the bunkers this mornin'."

The Third fixed his eye on the cruet and tried to ignore the exquisite agony of the kicks of the joyful Spink.

"Is Mrs. Hopkins comin' down this time?" enquired the Second, waiving the bunkers as an unsuitable subject for the table. The Chief nodded and passed his cup to Hannibal.

"So a believe," he returned.

"I should 'a' thought you'd 'a' fetched her to London."

"Too far. Didn't care to ask the Old Man. Bachelor skippers don't carry women round the coast."

"The Mate says his brother-in-law's Mate o' the *Torso,* where this Old Man was," began the Fourth, who had been talking to the senior apprentice before breakfast.

"Ay, so I heard," commented the Chief coldly, and so shut him up.

"That's a fact, sir," urged the Second, unabashed by the Fourth's discomfiture. "They both belong to Shields, you see, and from the yarn, this Old Man has no particular objections to women on the ship. Anyway, he's goin' to do himself in now."

The Chief stirred his second cup of tea sombrely.

"Forget it!" he muttered. "You'll get caught some day."

And Mr. Spink, spreading marmalade with a liberality that would have given the owners cold shivers, giggled.

XII

FREE of the numbing paralysis of Billiter Lane and
Jubilee Street, free of the day's work on the ship, Hannibal selected a clean collar, brushed his clothes, lighted a
cigarette, and accompanied Master Drevis Noordhoff,
ordinary seaman and cheerful optimist, ashore. They
wound their way along the dock side, debouched upon the
Port Tennant Road, crossed the North Dock, and passing
under the railway arch ascended Wind Street, Tommy
lightening the way with chatter of his many experiences
in distant lands. Hannibal listened abstractedly, his eyes
wandering up and down, taking in the novel details of
foreign aspect. At the top in Castle Square a crowd were
gathered about a young lady who was singing a hymn.

"Sally's Army!" remarked Hannibal, sniffing.

"No good to me," said Tommy, brushing past.

"Where will you go when you die?" asked Hannibal,
shocked that one so young should be irreligious.

"In a box," replied the boy promptly, and Hannibal's
smile died away. He thought of the Little Brown Box
from which he had escaped, and shuddered.

"That ain't the end," he protested uneasily.

"You can search me then!" said Tommy joyously, and
led the way along Castle Street, which was narrow and
populous in those days, a congested artery leading to the
freer air of High Street and beyond. Suddenly the boy
turned into a sweet-shop and rolled sailorwise up to the
counter. A fluffy, dark-haired vision rose up and simpered.

It was an edifying spectacle. All the worthy gentlemen,
from Cobbett and Ruskin onwards, who have prescribed
early matrimony, would have purred with delight had they
seen that encounter among the candy. Hannibal watched
them from the entrance. He was meditating flight. But
Tommy, with a grin of delight, turned and beckoned
vigorously, and Hannibal came unwillingly to the front.

"Dis is my gel," he whispered. "Friend o' mine," he told

the fluffy young lady, who laid her head on one side and held out her hand. She must have been at least fourteen.

"Where's de sister, Girtie? My friend 'e wants a gel, too."

Hannibal tried to protest, but he was too weak. Girtie smiled gloriously into his eyes and laid her head on the other side.

"She's goin' to the station to see a friend of hers. She's coming from Cardiff about a job."

"What time train?" asked the pertinacious Amsterdammer.

Girtie looked down at the oxidised watch that hung on her blouse.

"Seven-forty."

"We'll go and see her, eh? Then I come back for you. You finish nine o'clock? You get my post card?"

Girtie nodded. She had a drawer full of post cards from every conceivable port of the world. Wherever the Merchant Service had penetrated, throughout the Seven Seas, from the ports of the Danube and the fever-ravaged reaches of the Amazon, came picture post cards to Girtie. But she did not tell Tommy this. Girtie's success as a sailor's sweetheart rested in part upon her ability to make each guileless youth imagine himself the one chosen Jason of the Argosies. It is not an easily classified virtue, this innocent beguilement of the idle hours of wandering souls, but it implies a certain talent in the charmer. Very few can do it successfully year after year. Miss Bevan, that amazing genius of Barry Dock, raised it to a fine art. When she withdrew into the comparative retirement of matrimony, the gaiety of the nations was eclipsed, she became a legend, and it is whispered that her post cards, in five hundred albums, are to be presented to Lloyds. Girtie in the confectioner's shop in the old Castle Street was but an humble follower of the greater light. She dealt, after the manner of her age, chiefly with apprentices, junior officers, and Tommy. He, at least, had that distinction. His artless audacity had led him to ask her how she would like him in the family. She had replied at first that "she couldn't be dead," the Welsh girl's potent phrase. But Tommy was a good spender. The silver for which he toiled so hard on the *Caryatid* passed through his fingers like water when he was with Girtie. And Girtie smiled. Even Third Mates didn't run to eighteenpenny stalls at the Empire, and beribboned boxes of chocolates. Those who did, didn't bother to take her out, anyway. Life to Girtie was a string on which boys were strung like beads. Some of them were blue, some red, some white. As yet there were none of Gold. Tommy came sliding through her hands at the bidding of the freight market which had wafted the *Caryatid* to Swansea, and being a maid of modest imagination she was content. And moreover, this solicitude to provide her sister with a boy was kind. Girtie felt deeply that it was not easy to attach Lilian to any one. Lilian was not a peach, she was not a genius, and she had bad teeth. Obviously it was Girtie's duty to do her best for Lilian. And when Tommy produced a well-grown young man with the full liquid brown eye so dear to women, she smiled.

"Yes, of course," she replied. "I suppose you've had a gay time in London whatever. You off the ships?" she asked Hannibal, who nodded and cleared his throat.

"It's nearly half-past seven now," he said to Tommy, who was stealing chocolates.

"Come on then. Chin-chin, Girtie," he called. "Back in a jiffy."

"She's all right, eh?" he asked Hannibal, chewing.

"Is her sister older?" Hannibal wanted to know. He did not care for very young creatures. He was afraid of their eyes.

"Yes, a good bit. She's all right though," he added, for after all, if a girl *was* eighteen she couldn't help it. The tone in which Tommy uttered his encomium, however, did not express any desire to deprive Hannibal of Lilian's charms. There are few things in nature more terrible to the middle-aged than the contempt which films the gaze of boys and girls when they notice some stiffness of ligature, some flaw in perception, some lack of interest in life. Tommy, in the clear healthiness of body and soul which was his sole heritage, was condescendingly cruel towards Lilian, whose complexion, compared with his, was as a used blotter to plate-finished Japanese paper.

"She don't work in a shop, she lives at 'ome," he remarked. "Looks after de 'ouse. And Girtie say, she goes to de mission too. Tryin' to get a feller, I s'pect."

Even Hannibal was not entranced by this information.

"She's respectable, then?" he surmised.

"Sure thing. Here's de station, right ahead."

They crossed the road and entered the subdued melancholy that seems to be inseparable from a small terminus. A train appeared as they gained the platform, a creaking deliberate interminable local affair; from whose opening doors leaped some dozens of impatient passengers. Far up the platform the two youths saw a young woman in a large straw hat scanning the compartments.

"Der she is," said Tommy, pointing and beginning to hurry, but Hannibal was staring into the window nearest to him. A plump young woman was trying to open the door. He stepped forward and twisted the handle, and she desisted, smiling joyously.

"Much obliged," she said, jumping out. "I never can manage the bally things." She shook herself and looked round shrewdly. "I'm expecting a friend o' mine," she confided, "but, as usual, she's not here. Oh, there she is!"

"We come up to meet 'er," said Hannibal, gazing at the young woman admiringly. "Is 'er name Lilian?"

"Just fancy! What a coincidence! I haven't had the pleasure, have I? I meet so many gentlemen in my business."

"No," said Hannibal, warming to his work. "Matter of fact, I don't know your friend either. My friend there, 'e's goin' to interduce me. 'Er sister Girtie said she was up 'ere."

"Oh, I see! My name's Ffitt, Eleanora Ffitt, and I don't care who knows it. Welsh, and I don't care who knows that either. What a life! How are you, Lilian, darling?" They kissed vehemently, and Hannibal lost all desire to win the affections of Lilian. He regarded Miss Ffitt with the frank pleasure so difficult to recapture in later years.

"I was tryin' to get the door open when your friend—I didn't catch your name—oh, yes, Gooderich, when Mr. Gooderich did the honours. How funny! Like a novel, isn't it? Well, Lilian, and how's the flat-iron? You look as if you hadn't been out for a month. Isn't it just a peach of an evening?" She turned beaming to Hannibal, "I wish I was young again and able to enjoy it. The older we get the harder we have to work. Ah, well, p'raps it keeps us out of mischief. You two off the ships? I thought so. How do I know? Ah, that's telling. Get behind a bar and you can give a lady fortune-teller all the points and beat her. Your friend's on deck, isn't he? There you are again. How do I know it, indeed!"

So she ran on, this incomparable young woman, this queen of all whom Hannibal had ever met. He was entranced. This was seeing life indeed, to listen to Miss Ffitt's ceaseless stream of kaleidoscopic prattle. If it be true that each one of us has in him or her some faint trace of the artist temperament, with but an infinitesimal gift of expressing it, then I may say that Miss Ffitt expressed herself in prattle. She was an artist in prattle. Her mastery of the lights and shades of conversation was astounding. She could stipple away at some imaginary portrait of herself until it was a mere mass of dots without *i's,* and yet you understood what she meant perfectly. She could work with the etching needle or in dry-point, and if another customer called her away she would finish the sketch hastily in mezzotint and leave you marvelling afresh at her versatility. Even after marriage, which in-- evitably slackens the speed of such vivacious persons as Miss Ffitt, she still maintained an astonishing power of prattling. Hannibal as he listened thought he would never tire of it, and as a matter of fact, he never did.

It was not very far from the station to Castle Street, but it was sufficient for Miss Ffitt to detail her life-history down to the present moment, and the account included a succinct relation of the cause of her coming to Swansea, not, she intimated, for her health, for she found Swansea relaxing, and Cardiff, though you might call it dirty, doubtful, and even disgusting in certain phases, was at any rate alive, which was more than you could say for dear old Abertawe in the rain. Her comfortably pink face glowed with satisfaction as she explained that a certain licensed victualler needed a barmaid and was prepared to make her a most advantageous offer. This person, Snickery

by name, was opening a temperance-house next door to
his present hostelry, and being unable to hold the license
and the new establishment as well, wished to strike a bargain with Miss Ffitt concerning the joint management.

"He thinks," she observed, pausing to scan the latest
family groups in a photographer's window, "that I'm going to run his jam-roll shop for him, I do believe. He
thinks I'm going to wash the floors and let him deduct a
halfpenny for every saucer we break. And I'm going to
tell him," she turned to Hannibal like a burst of sunshine,
"I'm going to tell him I can't be dead, and no more at
present from yours truly. Just look at that girl's hat,
Lilian. It's like the sky-sign of a chamber of horrors."

Lilian, fearful of further criticism nearer home, for
Miss Ffitt was as frank as she was good-natured, en-
quired what house she referred to as kept by Mr.
Snickery.

"The 'Stormy Petrel,' Ryder Street, down here and turn
to the left," Miss Ffitt replied promptly. "I must hurry,
for I must get the nine-fifteen or my character is gone for
ever. Aren't you coming? Well, good-bye, Mr. —— I
didn't catch your name—that's it, Noordhoff—Irish, isn't
it?—Give my love to Girtie."

"I'll go with you, if you don't mind," said Hannibal, getting pleasantly red in the cheeks.

"Not at all; a pleasure, I assure you. Good-bye, Lilian;
take care of the little boy." She smiled ravishingly. "I'll
look in before I go back, of course."

Lilian, looking over her shoulder with a serious look on
her disdainfully plain face, nodded, and Tommy, who was
familiar with that elusive psychological phenomenon which
we call "fancy," waved his hand encouragingly to Hannibal.

"Isn't he a cherub?" asked Miss Ffitt delightedly. "He
ought to be in a crèche instead of walking out with that
brazen Girtie."

" 'F's been all over the world and 'e speaks four
languages," replied Hannibal, pushing Miss Ffitt deferentially out of the way of a cyclist as they crossed over.
"Nice little chap, if 'e is a forriner."

"And so are you," she informed him. "Here. Don't you

know you're a foreigner in Wales? Englishmen take the Hot Cross Bun!"

"Easy," protested Hannibal. "We're all under the same flag, ain't we?"

"Of course, I was only joking. Anyhow, you're from London, aren't you? I thought so. We often have them in Cardiff, only they call it Cawdiff."

"Ever been there?" he asked, reluctant to see her wit spraying over his native place.

"Not once. I was in Liverpool two years ago. That was enough. Wild Wales for me all the time."

"I like to go about and see places," he returned.

"And quite right too. That's man's work. Do a lot of these boys good to be chased out to see the Empire. But men must work and women must sweep, while the private bar is moaning. Here we are. The 'Stormy Petrel.' Doesn't it look the part? Go in and have a drink for the good of the house while I talk to Mister Snickery. I shan't be more than a minute."

Her neatly-shod feet tripped up the three steps of a private doorway beside a quiet-looking tavern in a quiet bye street, and Hannibal, with mingled feelings of pleasure and astonishment, pushed open a glazed door marked Private Bar. Several young men in large caps and refulgent neck-wear leaned over the bar to catch the fairy accents of a young lady in pink who raised her eyes and looked at Hannibal as though he had insulted her. Meekly asking for a glass of Scotch, he took a match and lit a cigarette. Slowly the habitués examined him, and he felt uncomfortably warm under their gaze. A touch of Minnie's aggressiveness under fire came to him.

"Lost anything?" he enquired, projecting his jaw towards his silent critics. After all, he reflected, they couldn't do much to him. London wasn't going to be done in by a lot of Welsh nuts. Somewhat taken aback, they turned once more to their little glasses of beer and left him in peace. Perhaps the whisky inspired their respect even more than his belligerent attitude. Neither their heads nor their means were yet up to the spirit mark. Hannibal diluted it to a genteel half and half and drank it down as quickly as he could. He did not want to keep

Miss Ffitt waiting a single moment. Avoiding the bar-maid's resentful gaze he went out again, his chin in the air, and walked up and down building blissful castles in the air, of which Miss Ffitt was the plump presiding goddess. He was quite unable to explain to himself why she should seem so alluring to him, and fortunately for himself he felt under no necessity to seek for such an explanation. Perhaps his sea-sickness had caused him to throw over-board the callow reluctances of early immaturity. His opening of that railway carriage-door was not youthful impudence, but genuine gallantry, perhaps the first con-scious act of its kind in his life. I am inclined to think, however, with my foolish partiality for the lady, that Miss Ffitt, being a law to herself, revolving in a hilarious orbit amenable to no definition, swept him off his feet by the sheer buoyancy of her personality. She kept his fresh resilient mind on the bounce, whereas Amelia was con-tinually allowing him to come to rest and then expecting him to leap of his own volition. As he walked up and down he laughed continually to himself. Wasn't she just a wonder? He did hope she was coming to Swansea right off. With a pang he remembered a rumour in the mess-room that the *Caryatid* would not be more than ten days in port, if that. Surely this most opportune meeting would lead to something more than a hasty farewell at the nine-fifteen? As though to chase away this sinister contingency, Miss Ffitt came down the steps with a run and a jump and beamed upon him.

"Sorry to keep you waiting," she chirped, shaking her shoulders in a way she had, very much like a canary as he prepares to sing. "Here we are again. That's over, thank goodness! Yes, it's all right. I'm starting the day after to-morrow, and next week we'll see what we shall see. Nice old man, Snickery. What do you think? He says he's changed his mind, a thing a man has never done before. Changed it for the better too. He's going to run his temperance place himself—see it with the whitewash on the windows?—And I'm going to take charge of the 'Stormy Petrel.' What sort of angel has he got in that bar?"

" 'Aughty blighter," said Hannibal, resentfully. "Looked as if she wanted to bite me."

"Poor little lamb! Did ums! Now, aren't some girls idiots? She'll wonder why she gets the office. There's a girl in my place in Cardiff, just the same. I know them. Any one 'ud think a man came into a licensed house just to get a drink with a scowl at the back of it. And a smile is just as cheap."

"She 'ad some fellers in there," Hannibal began loftily.

"Worth about three half-bitters a night each. I know them too. And she thinks she's got the good of the house at heart when she lets them play the goat all the evening."

"You goin' round to the other place now?"

"Just to see Girtie dear and her mother. You see, this is my native. I was born at Crwmbrla, and if you can pronounce it I'll give you a threepenny-bit to put on the plate on Sunday! Girtie was a little thing when I was at school. I'd love to go for a ride round to the Mumbles this evening. You ought to go out there."

"With you," he ventured.

"It 'ud be a pleasure," she answered winningly. "I suppose you'll be sailing away on the briny ocean though. Crossing the bar, so to speak."

"Not before Sunday," he assured her.

"Lovely. And is that dear little boy with the rosy cheeks on your ship?"

"We share a room," said Hannibal, laughing.

"Well, I do hope you tuck him up at night. Only suppose he caught cold."

" 'E can look after 'imself all right, all right," said Hannibal. "Didn't I tell you he speaks four languages and 'e's been at sea nearly three years? 'E's 'andy too. Showed me my job when I started."

"I don't know what the world's coming to. It's cradle-robbing. All the same, I'd rather see boys go out like that than have them messing about at home. A boy's best friend is his mother when she boots him out to look after himself."

"That's right," agreed Hannibal. "To see the world."

"And the Empire," added Miss Ffitt, who had a weakness for the Empire, and spoke of it as if it were the next station beyond the World.

"Ah!" said Hannibal, and they turned into the sweet-shop in Castle Street.

"Hullo, Girtie! Mother in? How's business? Now don't you tell this little boy any of your saucy stories, you young thing. I'll just run in and say chin-chin." And Miss Ffitt ran round and disappeared behind the counter.

Tommy appeared to be getting on famously, his cheeks full of sweets and gaiety in his eye. Lilian had disappeared. It was probably only a variation of Lilian's usual bad luck, to lose a swain. Girtie put the slightest touch of distance into her reception of Hannibal when he came up to the counter.

"Where been?" asked Tommy.

"Having a drink and waiting for Miss Ffitt," replied Hannibal.

"You goin' wid her," whispered Tommy, and Hannibal nodded, looking at his boots.

"We're goin' to de Empire."

"All right. I'll see you to-morrow."

Hannibal had an inspiration.

"Give me quarter of a pound of chocolates," he said to Girtie, who smiled upon him again and executed the order, putting a redundant chocolate into her own small red mouth.

"'Ave another," suggested Hannibal, putting down sixpence. "'Ave one, Tommy?"

Every bone in Tommy's head was working already, but he made room for a lump of chocolate ginger the size of a walnut.

"No," said Hannibal, in answer to Tommy's gesture, "I don't care for 'em. I'm smokin'," and he pocketed the sweet until Miss Ffitt reappeared. This she did in a very short time. The door opened and out she came followed by Girtie's mother, an amiable dark-eyed woman of fifty, with something of the Amelia glance with which she swept the shop and her customers. She smiled as Girtie slammed home the drawer of the patent till and gave Hannibal a halfpenny.

"Well, I must be off, Mrs. Rees. See you again in a day or two. Good-bye, Girtie darling. Good-bye little boy. How these children eat! Yes, this gentleman's going to see me safe into the train. High Street's so dangerous at night. Toodle-loo."

And they were outside walking merrily up towards the High Street.

"'Ave a sweet?" he asked, tendering the box of chocolates. Miss Ffitt gave vent to a miniature and strictly private scream of delight.

"Goodness! You're a mind-reader, Mr. Gooderich. Thanks. Won't you? Well, it's a silly habit for men." She munched for an instant.

"Don't go well with whisky," he remarked loftily.

"No, I suppose not. I'm glad you're not teetotal. That's what's ruining this country, this gassy stuff men are going in for. That lager too!" Miss Ffitt selected another chocolate and skipped ahead to avoid a stranger.

"So long as you don't go on the booze," agreed Hannibal.

"Oh, yes! I've no patience with soakers. A man who can't take it or leave it alone isn't a man, that's all I can say. You said you lived in London, didn't you? Any family?"

"I ain't married," grinned Hannibal.

"Of course, I know that! I mean any brothers and sisters."

Hannibal told her.

"Goodness! And she's been away for years. And only just goin' to be married?"

"I don't know much about it. You see, she's a lot older'n me. Since the dad died I ain't seen much of 'er. I don't 'ave much use for relations," he remarked, throwing away his cigarette.

"Well, I always say we don't pick our relations and we do our friends. I'm that way, too."

"I 'ope you'll call me one of your frien's," he said.

"Only too pleased. You must come up to the 'Stormy Petrel' and see me."

"And Sunday?" he asked.

"Sunday? Oh, the Mumbles! Yes, rather. It'll be like

going back to childhood's days," Miss Ffitt said, with a flicker of sentiment.

"I wonder if you won't 'ave too many old friends to bother about me," Hannibal remarked as they entered the station.

"Of course I shall, heaps of them," she told him. "And I must keep them all up, and try and get more business. Business is business, isn't it? But if you like to be a very extra-friend, well—we do get on together, don't we?"

"Business be blowed!" Hannibal growled, opening the door of a third-class carriage. Strange to say, Miss Ffitt smiled at this heresy.

"On Sundays, yes," she replied, and her quick bright glance fell over him so that he thrilled from head to foot. "But you'll do me a favour, won't you?"

"Bet your life I will."

"Only tell the other men on your ship about the 'Stormy Petrel.' You see, it all depends on making a good start. If Old Snickery sees business going up quick as soon as I get in, he won't bother me afterwards." Hannibal nodded vigorously.

"And if they come, I'll make them come again. And another thing, don't be silly and get jealous, will you?" He looked up into her eager eyes and nodded again. The carriage lights had not yet been turned up, and her face came out of the gloom clear and piquant. Obeying some obscure impulse, he sprang into the compartment and sat down by her.

"Now, don't be silly—well I never. There! There! Let me give you one, little boy."

There was a silence, short, sweet, mysteriously significant. A porter halted at the end of the carriage and moved a lever, and the lights went up. Hannibal jumped out of the carriage and closed the door. His face was transfigured. The vague seriousness with which he was wont to look out upon the world was supplanted by an expression of idiotic self-satisfaction. The porter, accustomed as porters are to such expressions, passed them without comment. Strange to say, Miss Ffitt's prattle did not run on as before. She sat with her purse in her hands and her eyes fixed on the floor in front of her. She had

lost confidence in herself for a moment. Hannibal reached
through the window and touched her cheek gently. Slowly
her gaze rose from the floor and met his, searchingly, piti-
fully, clear white and blue, and childlike too, now that her
cheery worldliness had dropped for an instant from her.
The young man smiled and took her plump gloved hand in
his.

"Good-bye," he said.

"Good-bye, little boy. Be good."

"To you, sure!" he laughed. "Send me a picture post
card."

"I don't know your address."

"S.S. *Caryatid*, Prince o' Wales Dock. An' tell me
when you're comin back. I'll meet the train."

The guard blew his whistle and Hannibal stepped back.
The train moved with a jerk. He stepped to the window
again.

"Sunday?" he said, and she nodded, and the train
moved out carrying her into the darkness.

"I'm on it!" he said to himself, as he strode down the
street.

XIII

ENGROSSED in his work of laying the breakfast-table the next morning, Hannibal did not hear the door leading to the Chief's room open; the roar of the coal pouring from the up-ended truck into the empty hold, the tramp of feet overhead, the soft slither of ropes and hissing of steam, overpowered all minor sounds. He turned and found a sharp-eyed lady looking him over.

"Good mornin'," she said. "Are you the new boy?"

"Yes'm."

She smiled. "From the village?" she asked, and he grinned comprehendingly.

"That's right," he said easily, setting the cruet straight. And then he added, "Mrs. 'Opkins?"

"That's me," she nodded, and looked at the table.

"You'll be havin' breakfast, I s'pose," he said, opening the drawer hastily and setting another knife and fork. "I'd 'now where the Fourth 'll sit," he mused, scratching his head.

"On a stool," she informed him genially. "You've not been to sea before, my 'usband tells me?"

In a few minutes she had his story. Deep called unto deep. Hannibal perceived that her eyes, though sharp, were friendly. Her Cockney accent smote his ear gratefully. His knowledge of Whitechapel won her heart. The Steward's bell jangled above them, the sound coming down through the ventilator. Mr. Hopkins, rather grimy about the hands and face, appeared and pointed upwards.

"Shut it," he said laconically, and Hannibal ran out and up the ladder to put the cowl over the opening.

Evidently Mrs. Hopkins ruled her lord and his satellites while she was at the table, though even she could not shake the melancholy from her husband's soul. The Fourth brought in a canvas stool and sat on the outer side of the table, well within the reach of the marmalade.

"How's Cardiff lookin', Mrs. Hopkins?" asked the Second.

"I was sorry to leave it," she answered simply, passing him his steak and onions.

"Hear that, Chief?" he chuckled. "The Militia must be up."

"I had to put off one very pressing invitation," Mrs. Hopkins continued, nudging her husband, who was looking into his tea. "Such a nice young man, off a liner."

"A liner in Cardiff?" queried the Third, demolishing a saucer of pickles which he ate, American fashion, with hot meat. "That must be the Black Funnel Line."

"He wanted me to elope and fly with him," the lady added, spreading butter on her toast. "He told me he'd seen my husband in Singapore with a Japanese girl on each knee."

The Fourth giggled and choked over his tea.

"I wondered why he was ashore so long that night," said the Second, and the Chief regarded him reflectively.

"These married men!" moaned the Third, looking round for the mustard. "Fancy! One on each knee."

"*I* never had such luck," observed the Second moodily.

"Why didn't you fly with him?" enquired the Chief in hollow accents, pointing to the bread.

"Because the half-pay might stop, old dear," his wife informed him, patting his shoulder, and the Fourth, to whom half-pay notes were as yet in the dim and terrible distance, cackled heartlessly. "What are you laughin' at, Mr. Spink?"

"Cap'n Briscoe's goin' to leave half-pay at home now," said the Second.

"So I hear. What sort of man is he?" Mrs. Hopkins asked. "Mr. Hopkins says he's one of these here new-fangled skippers, but that don't tell me anything."

"Chief means he's very interested in revolutions," replied the Third Engineer, looking at the Chief, whose face was concealed behind his teacup as he drained the contents. "I've heard that he's one of those hermaphrodite curiosities who have passed as Mate in Steam. In case we should all suddenly jump over the side with our pockets full of half-inch bolts, Captain Briscoe is certified by the

Board of Trade to go down below and take charge o' the main engines."

"Oh, dry up!" remarked the Chief, and passed his cup to Hannibal, who was listening open-mouthed.

"Sort of all-round man?" surmised Mrs. Hopkins, who was not interested in technical details. "Doesn't any one know anything about him or her?"

"I daresay we'll have all we want of her if he brings her down," the Second surmised, rescuing the marmalade from the Fourth.

"That's a nice thing to say!" exclaimed Mrs. Hopkins indignantly. "You don't mean to tell me you're one of those miserable wretches who don't approve of ladies on the ship?"

"Depends on the lady," said the Second diplomatically, as he divided a slice of bread with extreme care.

"They take a man off his work," surmised the Third.

"Ah, I don't suppose it needs much to take you off *your* work," retorted the lady, and the Third, amid some laughter, replied that such was the fact.

"Second means he don't mind old women like you," said the Chief, looking up. "It's the young ones that play the devil."

Mrs. Hopkins was speechless.

"Twenty-two ain't old, Chief," sniggered the Second.

"Twenty-two? Fifty-two, more like it," said the Chief, a pale smile breaking over his grimed face.

"Ted! You know I'm only forty-two——" Mrs. Hopkins pinched her husband.

"Ah, but you look fifty-two, Jane. That fast life you led before we were married——" Another pinch silenced Mr. Hopkins, and he resumed his contemplation of his tea.

Hannibal found as the days passed that this was the usual tenor of the conversation when Mrs. Hopkins took her meals in the mess-room. Her complete and contemptuous confidence in her husband, her genuine interest in everybody, her total lack of ladylike stand-offishness, her genial scepticism, her unmistakable London origin, all these things attracted the young man in the mess-room, and he became her willing slave. In due time, in a manner that is a secret among women and will die with them, she led him to talk of his present life, and the grotesque desire to make money. He, the refugee from the Brown Box, desired money! It was Mrs. Hopkins who took him up and showed him the promised land. She multiplied his three pounds by twelve, and the result, a year's pay all found, took his breath away. "A young man would have to toil all his life in a Little Brown Box to save thirty-six pounds."

"Of course he would," Mrs. Hopkins said; "and when you get on, you'll have more than that. But," she lifted a warning finger, "mind the foreign ports, my boy."

Hannibal nodded. He supposed so, though he couldn't be expected to know. He did know the money went quick enough in Swansea. It was irresistible, but very expensive, that nightly visit to Miss Ffitt at the "Stormy Petrel."

Of course Mrs. Hopkins was interested in Miss Ffitt, for Mrs. Hopkins had herself been a barmaid at Plaistow at a time when Mr. Hopkins had been paid off with two years' wages. He had been rendered abjectly miserable by the possession of so much money, and had requested her to take charge of them both. She believed that this was really a woman's proper destiny, to look after a man's money for him and see that he didn't buy rubbish with it. So she lived cheerfully in a little house (freehold) in Penarth, among scores of other sailors' wives, thoroughly satisfied with her condition, receptive of all the stories she heard about husbands and sons in far-distant lands, and scornful of them all. Having no children, she felt a brusque and kindly affection for those children of the sea over whom her husband was supposed to reign. For Hannibal her London origin predisposed her in the favour. The Londoner, though destitute of the savage clannishness of the Scott Tyke, or Welsh, yet has a certain community of feeling. He likes to call London "the village," he accepts meekly the alien's extensive and peculiar knowledge of the metropolis, and he will never make you understand exactly why he loves London, for he will never make the attempt. Certainly Hannibal never did.

Mrs. Hopkins, I was saying, was interested in Miss Ffitt, for she was an ex-barmaid. I am inclined to think that she had been a successful barmaid, though not in the way Miss Ffitt or Miss Bevan of Barry were successful. Mrs. Hopkins probably had to do with men of middle-age, men who would have regarded ebullient conversation with pained surprise, men who talked over affairs at little tables, and went out with their wives on Saturdays.

She had no cash-register in her bar in those days, no gramophone, no sandwiches or lager beer. Mr. Hopkins, for example, was not the man to be lured by fluffed hair and effervescent chatter. No doubt there was in the Penarth home a tasteful little presentation clock or card-salver from her middle-aged customers, as a token of their esteem. Mrs. Hopkins was the sort of woman who grows a little more frivolous as she grows older. Some twenty or thirty grey hairs were apparent to the relentless observer on the top of her head, and the quantity that came out occasionally made her stop and think, comb in hand; but her heart was very green, and the nice lad with the brown eyes and his Miss Ffitt interested her. She would stand at the door of her husband's room, when he was out on deck or down below, and talk while Hannibal did his work.

"Why don't you do something with more money?" she asked one morning.

"What else can I do?"

"You could go in the engine-room, couldn't you?"

"Me?" incredulously.

"Why not? This isn't man's work."

"Not this?"

"No; it's girl's work, washin' dishes. You're strong enough. You ought to go in for something more—more— I don't know how to say it exactly. You aren't afraid o' bein' dirty, are you?"

"I don't know, Ma'am. I never thought of it."

"Some men are. Others seem to enjoy it. Mr. Hopkins doesn't think he's doin' any work if he isn't smothered."

"I don't see 'ow I can change now," Hannibal said doubtfully. "The chief wouldn't let me."

"I'll make him!" she said promptly.

Hannibal advanced another step on his upward road to manhood. He paused in his work of polishing the big lamp in the mess-room and put his hand on his hip, looking frankly into Mrs. Hopkins' sharp eyes.

"Why d'you bother?" he demanded, an involuntary gruffness in his voice.

Mrs. Hopkins was taken a little aback. Then she smiled.

"Ask Miss Ffitt," she answered lightly, and retreated into her husband's room.

He did not do that. Youth-like he was not sufficiently self-conscious to bear such instruction in mind until Sunday, when they merged into the holiday throng that spotted the cliff walks on the Mumbles or fretted the evening sky-line on the pier. And even had he asked her, it is doubtful whether he would have received any truthful reply. Had she told him, it is probable that she would have lost him. And Eleonora Ffitt, though she had never heard of Bernard Shaw and would not have understood him if she had, had no intention of losing Hannibal. He was netted more safely than he knew. With woman's cunning she held back from him in the glaring lights of the bar of the "Stormy Petrel," and in the noise and rumour of the town, and waited until they sat above the gentle wash of the rock-bound shallows. With infinite artistry she allowed herself to become identified in his dreams with the harsh cry of the gulls, the presence and murmur of the sea. He remembered that evening always when away; the silver hoop of the moon, serene across the shimmering channel, the subdued whispers of lovers, the drone of the music, the clash of the tiny waves round the solemn wide-sweeping lantern on the reef, the long crescent of lighted roadway that curved with inimitable beauty into the mysterious darkness of the port, the lamp-spattered loveliness of the encircling hills. Of all this, in his memory, she was a part. Her warm womanhood became inextricably mingled with that Nature toward which he strained with inarticulate desire. So he recalled her out on the tropic seas, and with that evening still vivid within him, he worked out his probation and returned to fulfil his destiny, a casual of the sea.

XIV

LOADED to her summer marks, the *Caryatid*, in the endless hours of the middle watch, lay waiting for the tide. It was that hour when time seems to stop and the stars, dragging slowly across the sky, fade imperceptibly into that first faint premonition of the dawn. On the coal-littered decks, cumbered with wide-straddling booms and the gleaming sheets of thin iron over which the coal slides to its place, the silence hung heavily. Now and again a restless sailor came out of the dim-lighted galley and hung, listening, over the outer side, the smoke of his pipe passing like a spirit above his head. Out on the shiny water loomed the tall hulls of the old steamers at the buoys. They lay there patiently month by month, awaiting their turn to be broken up. They had run their race, poor casuals of the sea; with cold hearts and sightless portholes they strained gently at their moorings, and their pale figureheads stared in blind agony to the westward, as though they prayed that the end might be soon.

The hours dragged on, and with infinite deliberation the eastern sky became informed with that awesome pallor that precedes the sunrise. An iron door clanged sharply on the *Caryatid*, a rat, creeping craftily along the plating to the pump, fled in wild terror beneath a winch, there was a blaze of brightness at the engine-room door, and once again, silence and darkness. The Second, his pipe blowing great clouds, seated himself on a plugged ventilator near the galley, and folding his arms, looked out upon the familiar scene. So still he was you would have thought him graven in stone, save for the dense rolling upward of the smoke. In a few moments another ghost appeared from the port alleyway, a dark, huddled figure in a heavy coat of pilot cloth, with the cap pulled low over the eyes, the collar turned up, and the hands in the pockets. Quietly he moved across the deck, now grey against the white galley, now silhouetted against the glowing fire.

"All right?" he whispered to the Second, who did not turn his head.

"All right, Chief," he answered.

"Wing fires away?"

"All away," replied the Second.

"What's she carryin'?"

"Sixty-five," said the Second, meaning a hundred and sixty-five.

"Dampers shut?"

"Aye."

There was a pause. As they stood there, a thick-set man in a big woollen muffler came down from the bridge deck and spoke. It was the Old Man.

"All ready, Chief?"

"All ready, sir," said the Chief.

"Windlass?" the Captain's eyes glittered.

"All on, sir," muttered the Second.

"How's things, Cap'n?" whispered the Chief, looking on the ground. "All well at home?"

The Captain threw back his head and laughed.

"Champion!" he said. "Time of my life. I'll tell you another time. But——" As he paused the Second twisted round on the ventilator and looked at him. Captain Briscoe took out a cigar and bit the end.

"Eh?" asked the Chief.

"Think of it!" The Master threw out his hands. "Think, man. I never thought of it before. You're a married man, Chief? You know. Leavin' the warm bed——"

Neither answered him. The Second resumed his contemplation of the grey waters. All the east was aflame with rose and silver. The dock lights shrank to pale points of flickering radiance. Heavy boots drummed on the bridge deck, voices growled in the distance, the noise of a chain block flung down crashed against their ears, an avalanche of sound. Another man suddenly appeared above them and blew a shrill call on his whistle. The world of men was awake. The Old Man lit his cigar and pulled himself up the ladder with his brown hairy hands. A gold signet ring flashed on the third finger.

"H'm!" The Second shifted his feet and waited for his companion to make a remark.

"It's a hell of a life," whispered the Chief, and moved slowly across the deck. The Second wondered if it was. It seemed as though he were not alone in feeling the inexpressible sadness of the dawn. What a banal remark! A hell of a life! As if he didn't know that. Even he had some knowledge of the tragedy of the warm bed. . . . He stretched, twisted round so that he could see the galley clock, and relit his pipe. He slipped from the ventilator and disappeared into the steering house. Putting his lips to a tube he blew, and a faint querulous whistle sounded below in the engine-room. He looked down solemnly on the scene of his continual toil, critical, not ill-pleased. She was a good old girl! The Third swung up the ladders, his long oily arms playing with a prehensile grace upon the shining rails.

"What's to do?" he asked, wiping his face with his sweatrag.

"Coffee," said the Second. "What's the steam?"

"Seventy," said the Third, meaning a hundred and seventy.

"Then she'll blow off, sure as hell," said the Second gloomily. And he plunged with the speed of long use down the ladders. He passed along the plates, dived into a tunnel between the boilers and emerged into the stokehold. Two Greeks and a German were sitting under the ventilator.

"Look at it!" he snarled, dragging the fire doors open and then flinching from the white glare. "Why don't you put green coal on—— Look at it! Gimme the shovel."

"She's all right, Mister Seccon," clicked a Greek.

"Is she hell?" He seized a bucket of water and drenched some fine coal, turning it with the shovel.

"Put it on," he ordered, dropping the tool and peering at the gauges.

Sullenly they obeyed him, and the German disappeared into the bunkers. The Second returned to the engine-room, looked at the water, moved the throttle of the dynamo engine a fraction of an inch, and wiping his face, seated himself on the vice-bench, and filled his pipe. It was a habit with him to meditate upon the hellishness of his life. He felt resentful that a man like this skipper, who had just got married, should realize it so soon. After all,

why didn't the man bring her to sea with him, if he wished
to? What did skippers know of the reality of loneliness?
They were free to go as they pleased, to sleep, to gorge, to
find fault. There was the Chief too, mewing like a kitten
because his wife was gone home to Cardiff. What about
him, Hilary John Jesmond of Jarrow-on-Tyne, First-class
Certificate and Engineer-Lieutenant R. N. R.? Well, perhaps he ought to get married. He was engaged to two or
three girls, certainly, but marriage was a step! He had
arrived afresh at this conclusion, that marriage was a step,
when the Third descended, followed by the Fourth, who
was rubbing his eyes, and Hannibal, who looked as if he
would like to rub his, but was too occupied with the coffee.

"What's to do?" asked the Third, sipping the coffee.
"The pilot is in no hurry."

"He says," remarked the Fourth, "the gate's opening
but he'll not shift her for another half-hour. What's the
time? Just gone four. Seems to me I've only been turned
in five minutes."

"You'll die in your bunk," commented the Second.

"I'm sure I hope so, mister. I don't want to die down
here."

"I've lived down here," said the Second pensively, taking a large bite of his toast, "for sixteen years. What a
life! Once I had ideas. All gone now. My dungarees are
dirty and God hates me."

"I don't reckon he takes that much trouble over sailormen," muttered the Third, drinking deeply. "Why jouse
yourself, mister?" His drawn, slag-grey face creased into
smiles, he moved his feet in a rhythmic rattle on the
polished plates and began to sing:

> Oh I met a maid on Hornsey Rise,
>   And kissed her on the lips,
> I looked into her limpid eyes
>   And told her all the dear old lies,
>
> But she started off in wild surprise
>   And her hands went on her hips,—
> Said she, I'm the wife of a sailor-man
>   Gone down to the sea in ships!

"Stow it!" growled the Second. "Isn't the Johnny Walker out of you yet? Hie, boy! what's the matter? You look as if they were all dead."

Hannibal, leaning against the hand-rail of the ladder, laughed. His face was still soft and puffed under the eyes with sleep, and dark rings encircled them. His mouth was dry and distasteful from tobacco and drink, and his mind muggy.

"I was only thinkin'," he said, and shifted his feet.

"You shouldn't do that," warned the Fourth, measuring his toast with his eye. "It drives men crazy sometimes at sea."

The Third pinched the young man's ear.

"It's a hell of a life, eh?" he whispered, and the Second stirred in irritation.

"What do you know about it?" he asked in annoyance. The speaking tube whistle whined, and he leaned over and drew it out. "'Ullo, sir!—Ah! Seventy or thereabouts. Half an hour? All right, sir. Yes," he resumed, putting the whistle into the tube again, "you think you have a rotten time, don't you? There's another up there. Now what has *he* to worry about? I'm here. Why can't he stay in his room and leave me alone? There's the skipper too, tellin' me it's a hell of a life, just because he's got to leave a nice young wife at home."

"You'd grouse, too, if you'd just got married," said the Third boring him with his eye. "Especially if she's young. And all the time you're at sea, thinkin' and thinkin' of the men round her, and you far away on the ocean. Wouldn't you?"

"Easy to talk," snapped the Second. "The younger you are the more you yap. Here's the Mess. I daresay he's thinkin' how hard it is to go away, eh?"

"Yes," said Hannibal simply. "I'm engaged, mister."

"You! There you are!" said the Second in moody triumph. "I told you so. Silly young blighter. Who is it?"

"That's—that's my business, mister," replied Hannibal. "I was only answering your question. An' I'd like to know if the Chief said anythin' to you about me—coming down 'ere?"

"What's that?" said the Fourth, as the Second shook his head.

"I don't approve of it," remarked the Second, finishing his coffee. "We'll see later. I expect some o' these noble fire-boys'll slope in Las Palmas. What d'you want to change for?" he demanded.

"More money, sir," said Hannibal. "I can do man's work now."

"You think so. Chasin' a coal-barrow in the tween-decks is very different from washin' dishes."

"I know it is. There's no reason why I shouldn't 'ave a go at it."

"What you goin' to do, buy a farm?"

"No. Git married."

They stared at him, these young men, in awe, as he collected the empty mugs. Somehow the simple statement had set him away beyond them. He was going to get married! The Second slipped from his seat, and went over to the gauges, patting the curved syphon pipes with his hand. He returned as Hannibal put his foot on the ladder.

"Forget it!" he called, in a strange voice.

"Not me," said Hannibal, going up.

"He's not plumb," said the Third, watching him. "The excitement has turned his brain. Spink, why don't you get married? You look all right when your face is washed."

"I've tried, often," said that young man, pulling a wad of waste from a bundle in the store. "But it's no use, they won't look at you if they think you haven't got a ticket."

They moved, as by some subconscious thought common to them all, over to the telegraph.

"Is the whistle on, Spink?" asked the Second.

"Aye, on stabbard main," replied the Fourth, and leaned against the wheel of the reversing-engine.

"You know what's the matter with us?" queried the Third, blinking. "We're all scared."

"Scared?"

"Ah, scared. We come to sea and get into the sea-habit, and then when we go ashore, we're like damned kids. I think it must be the condensed milk gets into our blood and we funk comin' to the point. See that young feller? He's only been at sea three days and *he* goes up town and gets engaged. Says he's goin' to get married. You daren't say that, Jack. Nor you, Spink?"

"I wish I was a rich lady's pet-dog," remarked the Fourth. The whistle whined, choked, and then burst into a terrifying roar above them.

"So do I, but what's the use? Pet-dogs aren't bred on condensed milk." The Second looked up and saw the Chief gazing mournfully down from the steering house.

"Throw her over," he said. "Spink, open up and forget it. You'll be out on the West'ard to-morrow. All right, sir! Stand by! Where's that greaser? Here, Snyder, put the syphons in. Right, Spink? Swab the tails, Snyder."

With a great sigh the cranks moved, woke up, jerked backward, and came to rest.

"Condensed milk!" said the Second to himself indignantly, as he peered round the engines. "What does he know about it."

.   .   .   .

High up on the flying bridge Captain Briscoe walked to and fro, a proud man. Preoccupied with his own private pleasure and pain, he yet watched with relentless attention the manœuvres of the ship ahead. She was the *Vechstrom,* a slim, long-nosed three-thousand-ton freighter from Rotterdam. Captain Briscoe found time to envy her commander. With admiring eyes he watched her swing round as her twin-screws revolved, one against the other, churning the dock-water into cream-coloured foam. And then, as her sharp thin nose pointed toward the open gates, both engines went full ahead, beating the foam into tumultuous waves, her whistle blared, and she was away. Seventeen knots she went, that little clipper! with her rows of steel derricks, her self-trimming holds, her patent rudder, her collapsible lifeboats, and all the rest of her. Captain Briscoe gazed sourly at the tricolour flag flaunting on her flush poop. Damn these Dutchmen! Why didn't British owners have modern ships? To-morrow night she would be safe in Rotterdam. And he resumed his scrutiny of the checkropes, glancing first at the Chief Mate on the forecastle and then at the Second away aft. As the latter swivelled his signal disc from red to white, the Old Man raised his hand. Mr. Cadoxton, natty and fresh-shaven, thrust the telegraph slow ahead. As the Old Man passed him he spoke with the seriousness of youth.

"Funny thing, sir! I was looking at the articles last night, checking the discharge-books, and I noticed something."

"Eh?"

"The mess-room Steward, sir. His name is a rather unusual one. I don't know whether you noticed it."

"Eh?"

"Gooderich, sir."

"Give her a kick astern, slow," said the Old Man, watching the pilot's hands. "Port! You at the wheel there." In the wheel-house behind the glass windows and teak framings the round face of Drevis Noordhoff could be seen at the wheel. "What's that you said, Mr. Cadoxton?"

"Not a usual name, sir," said Mr. Cadoxton, deferentially. He was a rather exasperating young man, with his courtly manner and boyish face. He had grown up in the new tradition into which the Old Man desired to be an adept, and he had a way of impressing his superiority upon people.

"No," snapped Captain Briscoe, relapsing into the older tradition. "What of it?"

"Well—shall we ease her, sir?"

"Stop her! Mess-room, did you say?"

"Yes, sir. Joined in London. Belongs there, I believe. He hasn't a discharge, of course."

Captain Briscoe walked up and down, making signs to Tommy at the wheel and waving to the men on the pier heads. He remembered now. It was the lad in the tobacconist's shop, of course. Certainly it was, as the Third Mate said, curious. He turned suddenly and walked back.

"Half," he said. "Port there—that'll do. Slow, Mr. Cadoxton."

"Quarter-cheek's away, sir," said Cadoxton.

"Half, then. What made you mention it?"

"Well, as a matter of fact, sir, the Third Engineer was telling Mr. Brail of a friend of his of that name, and Mr.

Brail, he said his brother-in-law on the *Torso* knew a lady of the same name, you see, and so——"

"What was he on the *Torso?*"

"Mate, sir, I believe."

The Old Man turned away again. He leaned over the end of the bridge and watched the piers receding. Once more he was going out to sea. But this time he was conscious of a difference. He had left something behind. As the distance widened he felt as though an invisible thread were drawn taut. She was already far away in her little flat. A sudden pain shot through his heart. Had he been a fool? He was terribly proud, this master mariner, proud of his career, of his yeoman ancestry, of his ship, of his wife. But had he been a fool over the wife? Had his impulse led him wrong? Somehow this news of the lad in the mess-room disturbed him, he scarcely knew why. Surely he had gone into the whole business with his eyes open. Minnie had not deceived him. No, dammit, she had graciously accepted him. The pilot touched him on the shoulder.

"Pleasant voyage, Cap'en."

They shook hands and the pilot went down to wait for the tug. Captain Briscoe resumed his thoughts. Was this to be his portion for months now? He had read of jealousy. Was he to dream of that little flat? to pace the bridge at night thinking of her as he knew her in Antwerp, of other men ringing the bell, and of coming in? Oh, that would be a hell of a life! The perspiration stood on his face though the morning wind was cool. He went down and drank a glass of whisky. What was his nerve coming to? He understood now why married men stood motionless by the rail, looking out across the sea. As he went into the chart-room to set the course, he bethought himself of prayer. Could he pray? God! What a life!

Mr. Hopkins stood on the lee-side of his house and inspected the discharge water as it foamed below him. Like most men with a ruined digestion he rarely looked happy. The Second Mate had stopped on his way to the bridge to inform him that the Old Man had written a ten-page letter to his wife the night before, and he had received the news with calmness, merely spitting into the sea. What fools men were! He listened to the beat of the engine, suspicious of trouble. He was always anxious until the Second came up and stood by the rail smoking, silent and disdainful, as though wondering what land was for anyhow. He would look thus at the eternal hills round the Piræus, at the glittering domes of Venice, a sarcastic sphinx. As he came up now, the Mumbles Head received his disparagement. The Chief looked at him furtively. What was he thinking about, this wiry and tireless lieutenant? He wasn't married. Was he disappointed because he never attained promotion? What a fool! He was better where he was. He could eat his meals anyhow—blessed privilege!

"All right?" he asked, looking towards the shore.

"Intermediate Rod's blowin' a bit. It'll take up," said the young man.

"Aye, it'll take up," echoed the Chief. "Swab it good."

An expression of contempt crept into the Second's face, but he did not answer. When the Chief looked round to speak to him again he was gone, and the Third went past him with a long slouching stride. He was going to the forecastle, Mr. Hopkins knew. Some damned scum was sleeping off the drink instead of taking his watch on the fires. The Chief let his mind wander gently to the days when he was young and indignant, and when he fought with the soddened and desperate seamen who fill the stokeholds of our merchant navy. His hand wandered to his thigh whence he had once pulled a Dago's knife. Fierce work on those Manzanillo boats in the old days, eh? He saw the Third returning along the foredeck pushing and punching a reeling brown-bearded man. Up the ladder to the bridge deck he came somehow, pummelled from behind, falling prone by the cabin door. The Third heaved him up and along again until they reached Mr. Hopkins. Mr. Hopkins regarded the brown-bearded man with disfavour. His big blue eyes were bleared with drink, his mouth worked convulsively and his clothes were dropping from him. He leaned his shoulders hard against the house, and his head sank.

"Goin' to turn to?" asked the Third, shaking him.

"What's his name?" asked the Chief.

"I dunno. He's a Dutchman."

"What's your name?" repeated the Chief.

The man's eyes opened, blinked, and closed again, as he hiccoughed. Four bells rang clear and distinct on the morning air, and a sailor ran up the bridge-ladder to relieve at the wheel. Tommy came clattering down to get his coffee, running along the alley-way. As he passed the little group, the fireman's eyes opened and roved round glassily. They settled on the boy's face as he stood there trying to pass.

"What's your name?"

"Jesus! My name!" The man struggled to his feet and stood grasping the rail. A shudder of nausea ran over him and he raised his brown-bearded face to the blue sky. . . .

"Better get down below," said Mr. Hopkins to the Third. "Leave him to me."

Slowly the man turned his eyes aft, where the boy was talking to the Bo'sun.

"My name," he whispered huskily. "Mister, I'm bad. Lemme go and turn in, for God's sake." Again he looked. "Better this afternoon, sir."

"Git out of it," said Mr. Hopkins, turning away.

Hannibal was fixing up a photograph in his berth when Tommy came in.

"You got a gel all right, all right," he remarked approvingly. "We'll write post cards each place, eh?"

"Sure," assented Hannibal. "Letters too."

"I don't know what to say in a letter, in English," said Tommy, feeling elbow-deep in his canvas bag. "I only write to 'im in a letter," and he nodded to a sketch of a clean-shaven man with a loose tie that was pinned over the lad's bunk. Tommy fled out again and left Hannibal to examine the picture at leisure. Tommy was not loquacious about his friend. He called him "the man dat looks after me." He had a bundle of long letters from him, addressed to "Mein Fliegende Hollander," which Tommy had explained to Hannibal's puzzled ears. It appeared that this man "made pictures" and had "bags of money," that he had been a passenger on a ship, the old *Eumenides,* where Tommy had been cook's boy, and he had taken an

interest in him. And being something of a power, through
relatives in Billiter Lane, he had got the Amsterdammer
on the *Caryatid* as a sailor. That was why, Tommy said,
in answer to Hannibal's query, he was in a room amid-
ships instead of in the forecastle. Some day, when he had
finished his time, the picture-man was going to get him
a mate's job, and then he was made! "You see," Tommy
had said simply, "he ain't got no liddle boys, and he want
me to be smart an' get on, and den, he'll help me. When
I done four years, I'll get my ticket an' go third mate.
I call him my fader, 'cause I never had one, see." Hannibal thought of this now as he put up the photo of Miss
Ffitt on the bulkhead over the settee, and his mouth hardened. There was no "picture-man" to take an interest in
him, that was plain, nor did he want one. He was going
to make his own way. He had something to work for now,
something to think about. Unlike Captain Briscoe, no
doubt assailed the young man's mind. Nellie wasn't that
sort. Of course, she had to be easy and good-natured to
the customers, but what of that? It was business. His
luck almost took his breath away. She had told him that
old Snickery would have to vest the licence in some one
else, as he could not hold the new premises as well. And
he wanted to hold the new premises very badly, for they
were going to pull it down later on, when it would be
valuable. Anything might happen, they decided as they
talked it over. Hannibal wanted to rise to this new development. With Nellie he felt it possible to accomplish won-
ders. He would hold the Chief to that promise Mrs. Hopkins had extracted from him and try and save money.
By money Hannibal did not mean thousands. He really
had no conception of a hundred pounds. He was like those
Bushmen who cannot count beyond a certain figure. Fifty
was a golden dream, but he determined to get as near as
he could to it. By the time he went in to tidy up the Second's room he felt confident about fifty. And then, coming back again, rolling home across the sea! He tried to
realise his position. Outward bound, and all the world to
see!

XV

WHEN he turned out one morning at half-past four and looking through the port saw no land, he felt that the irrevocable had happened. For the first time he was out of sight of England. Tommy, taking his hour on deck, looked out of sleepy eyes at the round cloudless sky-line and said that that was nothing. Hannibal supposed it was. He grew accustomed to being told that the things he felt were nothing. This nihilism of the seafarer is a sort of half-way house, where he dwells awhile before he goes on to the final acceptance and despair. But Hannibal did not think it was nothing. He thought it was wonderful, these familiars of the sea. Day by day, he would watch the great panorama, the sudden rifting of the clouds, the downward dart of the straight strong beams like the pillars of a golden tower reaching up to God. He saw the black massing of the rain-clouds, the swift movements of their shadows across the sea, the gulls wheeling in endless circles above his head, black against the sunlight, white as snow against the clouds. He saw huge liners loom upon the horizon, burst into clear view, with all their panoply of boats and ventilators and glittering windows, flash past with proud funnels belching smoke, and drop out of sight. He saw oil-tanks towing slowly and painfully eastward, the stunted little steamers with their ugly high-perched bridges, the unwieldy lighters with their tall steel masts and solitary deck-houses. Humbly indeed they swam on the ocean, bereft even of a name, and expressing in their dangerousness and preciousness the ignoble ideals of those who send them forth. He saw tiny fishing boats bobbing buoyantly as they toiled to reap a scanty harvest on the broad fields of the Bay. He saw white winged sailing ships come up out of the dawn, flying clouds above grey hulls that lay over to the wind. And when the weather changed and the *Caryatid* bored her way through the sloping green, when the sky was thick with great clouds racing easterly and the wind-swept decks wet with the leaping spray, he saw the sea in a fresh phase. For hours, when his work was done, he watched the mountainous waves rolling up and crashing against the stubborn bows, listened to the boom and rattle of the plating, the sough of the wind in the ventilators and the scuffle of the propeller when the stern lifted in the swell. And when the weather roughened, he would stand by the galley and watch the green seas leap over the bulwarks and thunder upon the deck in furious splendour. Sometimes they missed and he would wait breathlessly for the next. Like most ships which have had their load-lines raised, the *Caryatid* was a wet ship. Sea after sea came over the weather side, and Hannibal would note the sailors with their heads bowed, drenched to the skin, hanging to the life-lines that ran along on either side. This was summer weather in a steamer! To them it was nothing. They did not call it going to sea, these leathery beings who had been round the Horn in sail before Hannibal was born. This was summer time. Day by day they chipped and scraped and washed the paintwork, moving about with a sort of lumbering ease adapted to their arduous and humdrum labour. Only in the forecastle, where Hannibal did not see them, did they drop their mask and try, pathetically enough, to be human. He saw the black squad too, now and again, dark forms hunched against the funnel-casing awaiting the eight-bell chime: or he would come upon a trimmer, emerging from the hatch, filthy and breathless, his sweat-rag in his teeth and a smoking slush-lamp in his hand. The Second would often appear abruptly from the sliding coal, and discuss professional problems with the Chief, who awaited him. Day by day and night by night each one of these men had his appointed hour and toil. He saw the Old Man in his double-breasted coat with the brass buttons and his long sea-boots, pacing the bridge like a caged animal, silent and supreme. It was inconceivable that he should be Minnie's husband, grotesque, absurd. Once or twice, he had paused in his walk and eyed Hannibal as he hurried to and from the Steward's pantry. What was he thinking about? Was he angry because his wife's brother was a mess-room stew-

ard? Did he know? Hannibal gave it up. He knew so little about his sister. Only when in thought he placed her
side by side with Nellie did he feel certain of his ground.
Nellie was different from Minnie. He felt that. There was
something strange about Minnie, superior as she was.
With the sublime omniscience of youth he brought all
morality to the measure of his embryo mind. And in his
embryo mind the thing that was strange was antagonistic.
That was why he loved the eternal heave and rhythm of
the ocean. But in his love for Nellie he instinctively shrank
from anything so strange as Minnie. Why did his mother
never speak of her? She must be more than strange, more
than antagonistic; there must be something evil in her
life. To him evil was not a devil with horns and tail, not
even a fiery furnace. It was rather a vague uneasiness, a
dark cloud at the back of his mind. To Tommy it was
something sharp and very real, hunger and the bodily
pain of cruel whipping. But Hannibal had never been very
hungry nor had he been drilled in the religion of an aveng-
ing deity. He did not know what it was, save that when
he thought of Nellie and Minnie, he was afraid. And yet,
there was the Old Man. He gave it up and went on living
his own life, dreaming of the future, and watching with
insatiable interest the common flow and return of sea
and sky.

And as they drove southward towards the Canaries, a
new wonder came to him. The clouds rolled away across
the world and the air grew warmer. Down in the engine-
room Hannibal thought it unbearable. In that maze of
flying rods and gleaming metal, men toiled, stripped to the
under-vests. The oil-laden atmosphere stifled him, but the
Third sneered amiably at the bare suggestion that it was
anything unusual. With the sweat running from his grey
face in streams, he would tell the young man that it was
"just a nice workin' heat." And he would lift the chatty
from its hook in the ventilator and drink long and thirstily.
"You're not born yet," he would tell Hannibal. "You'll
be marked before you see old England again. This is
nothing. The stuff'll be up at the top o' the thermometer
and tappin' to be let out, yet."

"Is it 'ot in the bunkers?" Hannibal asked timorously,

lifting his mouth fish-like to the cool of the ventilator.

"Hot in the bunkers? Just a wee. Still set on it? Ah! You'll get a bellyful before you're paid off then. Fine healthy exercise for a young chap, trimmin' is."

The Chief saluted the lower parallels by changing into a weird costume of stained khaki, and ordering Hannibal to remove a blanket from the bed. That bed-making was a trial to him at first. The engineers one and all broke out into open insurrection over his entirely new and original method of folding the bed clothes so that no mortal could insinuate himself into them. So he went humbly to Tommy, who knew everything, and asked to be shown how. Tommy's blue eyes opened in wonder upon a young man of eighteen not knowing how to do a simple little thing like that.

"You thick!" he said, grinning. "'Ere, I'll show you." He dropped the clothes off his bunk and began. "First," he said, "take all dese off, see, and put them on the settee. Now tuck in de bottom blanket. Engineers 'ave sheets, see? Den put de piller straight an' tidy. Den you vatch me. Take de blanket and de sheet an' lay 'em along de edge o' de bunk like so, see?"

Swiftly Tommy laid the bedding across the bunk-board and folded the tops neatly back.

"Who taught you, Tommy?" asked Hannibal, trying to imitate him.

"Me? De steward o' that German boat, 'Amburg-Amerika Line, 'e show me. It was 'im gimme de belt, an' den I run away, see."

"That feller's a good friend to you," said Hannibal, remembering what Tommy had told him, and nodding at the photograph.

"Sure thing! He gimme my sextant, and plenty clo'es. He's a *Man!*" stammered Tommy, a far-away look in his eyes. "A Man, by *God!*"

"Why don't he get you a job ashore?" asked Hannibal.

"I dunno. Not so easy. I'm a sea-boy, I am. I reckon it's got to be. And it ain't so bad, if you're smart and try to get on, eh? Everybody got to work! He works, making pictures same as Rembrandt. When we come back I'm going to see him in London. He's away now."

Bit by bit Hannibal, friendly-eyed and unobtrusive, learned the obscure histories of his shipmates. Bit by bit he picked them up, piece here, piece there, a vivid patch next week, and tried in his unskilled way to put them together. What a wonderful patch-work it was! He would talk at times to the apprentices, who had imagination, and they helped him to join up stray fragments of gossip. They told him of Mr. Cadoxton's lordly connexions, of the Second Mate's bigamy case a year before, and they fed him full with amazing stories of the Old Man's wife. He was interested in this last, as may be imagined. The senior apprentice certainly told his tale well, though Mr. Cadoxton's artistry was visible in the sketches. But Hannibal's was a detached interest tinctured with a furtive pride in his exclusive knowledge of the lady. They told him, too, of the Old Man, how he tramped the bridge hour after hour staring across the sea, how he let meal after meal pass without uttering a word, thinking, thinking. "It's on his mind," said the senior apprentice darkly. "He was going to bring her the voyage, but Mr. Cadoxton says she's quite impossible. He tried it on the *Torso,* you see, and he had to leave. She kidded him she's got bags of money, you see, and now he's stung, he can't forget it. I shouldn't be surprised if he jumped over the side one of these days. My brother was with a skipper who cut his throat." And so on. Hannibal listened to it all, the inane conjectures of the sea. He could not help seeing that, though very human, these men were a race apart. They believed all this cackle that passed from lip to lip, yet it altered their attitudes toward one another not at all. . . . They accepted man as desperately wicked, they knew him to be inconceivably foolish, and these special examples were only faint outlines of what they might be. Under them all the screw kicked them ever onward, over their heads the sun rode with undeviating rectitude. What recked it, if men were purblind and given over to a lie? It was but a tale to be told in the dog-watches. The iron grip of the articles held them for a time, and then, when they jostled into the shipping office once more, they would fall apart, disintegrate, and their gossip would become a lurid fable, succulent but incredible. But to the Old Man, it was no fable for idle hours. As they slid through the summer sea the possible became a nightmare certainty, and he writhed with no soul to ease him. He remembered with shame his indiscreet outburst before the Second and Chief, when the bitterness of the dawn was upon him. Mechanically he took his bearings, checked the reckonings, and wrote his night-orders. Over and over in his room he fumbled with the scanty notes that she had written him. She had no gift for correspondence, she had said lightly, as she held the match for his cigar. He groaned inwardly as he recalled that every one of her charms was the charm of the odalisque, save that immaculate calm, that maddening indifference; and was not that after all a supreme effort of the genius of the odalisque? She had led him on by thrusting him back. . . . Yes, by God! She had sent him away. And he—the infatuate fool—but stay, he loved her!

He would drop his cigar into the tray as he sat in his room, and stare with strained eyes into vacancy, holding the edge of the table. Sometimes he would draw out his writing-materials and begin a letter. *My own dear darling little wife,* and so sit an hour on end, in an agony of doubt. Sometimes he would start up, resolved to break the spell, light a fresh cigar, drink a stiff peg of whisky, and go along to the Chief's room. But the Chief did not understand, and resented interruptions when he was reading Scott. He had no interest in Scott, and he hated Scotsmen as only a Welshman can hate, but he had got into the habit. He fell asleep over *The Talisman* in the afternoon, and after ten he would take down *Quentin Durward* and start half-way through. Was he curious to peep furtively into that mysterious world of mushy heroics in which he had no part? Did he believe after all in anything beyond his propeller? Who can say? He would lay the book aside and clear the litter from his settee, and wait for the Old Man to speak.

"Pretty fair run," the Old Man would say, and Mr. Hopkins, reaching for his pipe, would nod.

"Wednesday morning, I should say, eh, at two hundred and fifty a day?"

Another nod. "How's things going? All right?"

Another nod, and silence. And then the Old Man's eyes would move around the room, as though he had never seen it before. He would look at the bookshelf stuffed with dime-novels and Scott, built solid with magazines and a copy of *Breakdowns at Sea*. A photograph of Mrs. Hopkins, taken some years back, in a widespreading skirt and with her sharp eyes cast down on the pages of a book, was fastened in brass clips over the bunk. Other photographs there were, groups of embarrassed men in uniform, with backgrounds of ventilators and life-buoys, faded portraits of old ladies and gentlemen. Colour-prints there were too, gaudy trashy things with sentimental rhymes tagged to them, picture post-cards of quite indescribable bathos. Mr. Hopkins would sit, his head on his hand, listening to the steady drum of the engines. He had no opinion of his wall decorations; they did as well as anything. Once he had gone over the side, his watch in his pocket and his certificate in a tin case in his teeth, and from the lifeboat, lifting to the early morning swell, had peered through a thin fog at the steamer that settled slowly by the head and finally vanished. He thought nothing of it. It was, he would have told you, nothing. The idea of using such an incident to make conversation was grotesque. Captain Briscoe, desirous of being communicative, would have felt no interest in such a commonplace triviality. He himself had spent three days of his life on a raft, equipped with a most inadequate supply of provisions, so inadequate in fact that two out of his three companions, somewhat run down by the fine weather and the tropical sun, went to sleep and never woke up. The minds of such men are like locked chambers of horrors of which the keys have been lost. Mr. Hopkins gave one the idea at times that he was looking for the key, that he was trying to think where he had seen it last. Perhaps that was the reason that he read Scott. As the Old Man's eye moved restlessly round, he would fill his pipe and reach out with incredible deliberation for the matches.

"She's a comfortable ship, this," the Old Man would say.

"Ah, I've seen worse," Mr. Hopkins would mutter between the puffs, and he would hold the match interminably over the ash tray, and letting it drop at last as though it was his life, and he was weary of it.

"You've been here a good while now?"

Mr. Hopkins nodded.

"How'd you get on with old Middleton?"

"Not so bad."

"Used to carry his wife, didn't he?"

A nod.

"All the time?"

"Mostly."

"I wish I'd brought Mrs. Briscoe now. She'll be lonely all this time."

Only five days out! There was a shade of expression in Mr. Hopkins' face, an expression of contempt.

"Oh, I mean, you know, the voyage? Oil's way up now, you know, Chief. It's all on the cards we take case-oil out of New York to Japan, eh? They told me so in Billiter Lane."

"A year perhaps, that's nothing."

"It's some waiting when you're a married man, I think. I wish I'd brought her with me."

"Why didn't you?"

"She didn't like the idea—said she'd had enough . . ." The Old Man stopped, pulled himself up short; you could almost hear the brakes screaming. "She's a bad sailor. Even crossing the Channel's too much for her, she says. She travelled a good deal," he ended lamely, looking at the end of his cigar. Mr. Hopkins, on this occasion, made no remark. His poise was admirable.

"I suppose a man gets used to it," the Old Man added. "In time, eh?"

Appealed to directly, the Chief allowed his eyes to travel to Captain Briscoe's knees. Perhaps the question struck a chord within him. Perhaps his imagination was fired by the counter-idea of a man actually not getting used to it. He was stirred. He became, comparatively speaking, dramatic. He shrugged his shoulders and reached for another match.

"Got to," he whispered.

XVI

It was a pleasant life, trading the wide world round, and the scenes came so rapidly before him that Hannibal felt the need of a readjustment in his mental process. No longer was it possible (and the change from mess-room to forecastle made the process imperative) to brood over the rich phantasmagoria of sea-life as he had brooded over the easy monotony of youth. When you are going to and fro across the Seven Seas, carrying coal to the Islands, loading oil in the West, taking sugar from Java to Germany, and salt from Germany to New York, your attitude towards the eternal verities becomes strained. You begin to understand the men about you, why they say continually that these things are nothing, and revolve on your own pivot. The ship takes on an importance you could not conceive before: her very vilenesses are dear to you. You become a part of her. You hear, in the night watches, her voice as she labours onward, the little intimate complaints of her fabric. And then, when in the forecastle you hear the incredible clangours of the chain-locker as the anchor plunges headlong to the mud of the harbour, it is to you more than the fall of empires, and the first look through the port is like the discovery of a new world.

So he changed, this young man from London, and into his eyes came the look of those who have seen the great distances. He grew lean and wiry and tanned, and a small black moustache, like a charcoal smear, came into being on his upper lip. The refinements of urban life, such as he had, fell from him, and his speech became supple with the *lingua franca* of the sea. He took his meals seated on a soap box, with the platters on his knee, and he learned the wisdom of eating from the middle of the kid, where a man's thumb cannot reach. He became, as is necessary in the forecastle, primeval, contracting his visible personality to a canvas bag and the boards on which he slept. Day and night disappeared from his view and he judged men and

404

things by the middle-watch. Each night and noon he took his way along the fore-deck, under the stars or beneath a furnace sky, and descended into his appointed place. Here again were conditions astonishingly inimical to the conventions of the "Little Brown Box." He never forgot his first day, leaving sunny Las Palmas, in the bunkers. The Second had taken him down through the stokehold, where men stabbed furiously at burned-down fires, and great heaps of glowing clinker spattered and stank as water was flung over them, through a small door and up, up into blackness and pungent odours to where small yellow flames burned smokily in the fog of a coal slide. He saw yawning openings in the decks into which he was to tumble barrow after barrow, openings into which he nearly tumbled himself once or twice. And he had been left there, with instructions to get a move on and keep it running. He had set to work in feverish fashion, shedding first the blue dungaree coat, then the shirt, and finally stripped to the skin, shovelling, shovelling, eyes and nose and mouth full of the acrid impalpable dust and the sweat making rivulets of white skin on his chest. He had gone at it bald-headed at first, after the manner of the tyro, and at two o'clock lay panting on the coal, too exhausted to climb up or down. The Second, crawling cat-like over the hummocks, found him and diagnosed the disease. "You won't last a week if you slog at it like that, man," he had said, his eyes gleaming in his soot-darkened face. "Take it steady, pitch-and-pitch. Like this," and taking the great square-mouthed shovel he drove it deep into the coal, swung it back and out with a long measured lunge and shot the mass, clean and solid, into the hole ten feet beyond. Hannibal watched him attentively, saw the sense of slow-moving persistence, and tried again. He got into the way of it in a day or two, and kept her running easily enough. And when the agonising stiffness of biceps and thighs had worn away he even enjoyed it. It was fierce, but it was nearer being a man than anything he had ever experienced before. At first he had regretted the flesh-pots, and sighed on Thursday for the ham-and-eggs of the mess-room, but he soon discovered that the most important part of a meal was the pipe that followed. He had discarded his short stumpy briar, and divided his affections between a thick clay and a thin-stemmed corncob. He learned to cut up the sweet Boreen, paring it into his hand, rolling it with a slow circular motion, and packing it away skilfully into the bowl, wasting none of it. He would take his corncob up on the forecastle head after tea, which was his favourite time, and with his back against the windlass drum look out from under the low awning at the opal and turquoise of sea and sky. It was quiet up there, and he discovered the sense of separation that this gives, far away from the immediate tumult of the engine-room. Even in the bunkers he heard them but faintly, muffled throbs mingling with the scroop and rattle of the shovel, the croon of the dry barrow wheel, or the thunder of heavy lumps against the bulkheads. Up there he would sit and sometimes watch for Tommy. Half-way up the foremast was the crow's-nest, and after tea, if it was his watch, Tommy would climb up to the ladder and ensconce himself there for an hour, peering out across the level floors. Sometimes he would look down and grin at the sedate Hannibal puffing luxuriously under the awning. It was in this way that Hannibal learned the beginning of a story that had its ending the day before they reached Japan. The brown-bearded man with the bloodshot blue eyes who trimmed on the four-to-eight watch, and who slept in the bunk over Hannibal's used to join him at eight bells, and sweeping the kid clean with a crust, discourse upon life as he had found it. He was bitter concerning life, apparently, blaming it for many things, and bitterer concerning women. It was difficult to discover exactly what his grievance against them was, for from his own telling they had been kind to him in a casual way, helping him in divers trouble, giving him money, and asking naught but love in return. He was very proud of his power over women. They would do anything for him, he said. It was possible, for women are foolish, and he had the mobile mouth and unabashed eye that lures them to folly. And yet he spoke of them with bitterness. They were all no good, except one, and she was dead. Perhaps this was his grievance. She had died while he was away, and her mother, the old hag! had demanded money to keep the child. That was years ago, when he was young, and might have settled down. He had had every intention of settling down if she had only lived. Of course, he only told his own side of the story. He said nothing of his desertion of the woman. How was he to know she would have a child? And he never had any money, it seemed to go somehow. But he had been thinking, and he was going to make a change; he was going to save this trip's money, not get drunk at all, go back to Amsterdam and get a boatman's job. He would put ten pounds in the bank at least, and buy a boat and some clothes with the rest. Sailormen were fools, he argued.

Hannibal would listen and nod, letting the brown-bearded man go on, and in this way they grew friendly, exchanging tobacco and matches, pooling things like butter and tea, and doing little kindnesses to one another. They shared the bucket that the Second had given Hannibal, and took turns in washing clothes on the fore-hatch. Little as there is to steal in a forecastle, men will steal it, and these two would guard each other's tiny belongings in the watch below, taking one another's part in the wrangle over the tinned milk, and so cultivating a certain humanity that makes for the soul's good. It was Jan who took Hannibal ashore in New York, when they were loading there, and led him across the Brooklyn Bridge into the unimaginable uproar of Manhattan. Hannibal's breath stopped as he stood there, that Saturday afternoon, among the tangle of iron rods and flying trolley cars, and looked out at New York. It was to his unaccustomed eyes the City of a Dream. He walked through the deep streets, a pigmy among pigmies, dazed and frightened. The roar of it, and the immensity of it, appalled him. But when they walked down to the Battery and saw the great ferries sliding back and forth like shuttles on the bright water, saw the blue sea shimmering beyond, he felt reassured. Jan laughed and said it was nothing. He had worked there once for a time, got four dollars a day until he went on the booze and lost his job. It had not been his fault. Some one had put knock-out drops in his liquor and cleaned him up while he was unconscious. All his money gone, he had shipped away again on a German ship, and tried to start afresh. But Hannibal's gaze returned again and again to the tremendous buildings with their innumerable windows, tier on tier to the sky, their giant towers and stark outlines. It seemed to him that there was a personal antagonism in this monstrous conglomeration of alien energy, and he felt afraid. What would they think of it at home? How would Mr. Grober regard it? It did not occur to him that he might find Mr. Grobers in New York as in London. It seemed impossible. This was a place for men who had leaped the quicksands of life, who were not to be sucked in like Mr. Grober. And yet as his eyes took in the more immediate details, he saw old men and slatternly women on the seats around them dozing in the heat, very like people on seats at home. It was when they boarded a surface-car and went away uptown that he saw a difference. There was a brisk, unrelenting hardness in the faces, a ceaseless striving after smartness in the clothing, a disquieting lack of humanity in the way the conductor pushed an old man off the step, that seemed in keeping with those prodigious structures among which they crept. Hannibal's uneasiness deepened. The atmosphere was charged with unrest. The brown-bearded man and his young companion in their rough and crinkled clothes seemed out of place. They got off and walked along aimlessly, suddenly tired. Hannibal felt that he was not equal to it. He wanted to get back to the ship. He remembered that he ought to write a letter.

So he saw the world in fugitive peeps, and began to comprehend why seamen in the fulness of their knowledge called it nothing. He felt that too; all those millions of people hurrying to and fro were nothing to him. He was but an alien, a haphazard atom of humanity dropped among them for an idle hour. A day or two, and he was on the sea again. He preferred it that way. As the weeks grew into months he became aware of a fuller and more passionate love of it. The cool wind at evening, when he sat by the windlass and thought of Nellie; the endlessly changing panorama of clouds, the sublime galaxies of the tropic sky, the friendly moon flooding the wide ocean with silver light, the lonely tramp passing a mile away—all these things touched him and filled his heart with peace.

He had had no letter yet from her, he remembered, as

they drove southward toward the Cape. Of course, it was a difficult job to time a letter properly to catch a ship that was wandering hither and thither. Plenty of other men on the ship had missed letters they were sure had been mailed. Perhaps he would get one in Durban. He tried to feel worried but he did not succeed. He longed for the time when he would return, and yet he was very happy as he was. He liked it, this life of strenuous toil. He liked the monotony of it. It gave him time to think about things. He acquired a sort of spiritual stoicism often cultivated at sea. It is the ultimate good to be derived from the sea by those who dwell in the hot, unhealthy huddle of towns. In there among those roadways, in the clashing din of the market and the bawl of the money-changers, you cannot see mankind for the people, you cannot feel for your nerves. At sea, you behold the ignoble rabble in perspective, the black many-headed swarm lie on the fair earth like a blight, you perceive the contemptible insignificance of their passions in comparison with the terrible passion of the sea, and if you have been living "according to your lights," you will have time and space to see the lights of eternity, to listen to the west wind, and to harken to the voice of the storm.

He had too much to reflect upon to become morbidly interested in himself. No man can be an egoist in the fore-castle. The lack of privacy and the communal discipline of toil precludes it. When the *Caryatid* pushed her blunt nose across the thirtieth parallel, and the cool rushing trade-wind poured down the ventilators and flapped the shirts bent to the forecastle rails, Hannibal would sit amongst his mates and listen to their vague maundering speech. They were scarcely to be called men, if you selected, say, Sir Anthony Gilfillan as a typical man. Rather were they dumb-driven cattle, capable neverthe-less of turning, the red light of battle in the dull eye, and rushing upon their owners. They did this once—and it may happen again.

For the most they slept or read penny stories of true love and virtue triumphant. There were twelve of them there in that dark triangular cupboard. Three small ports admitted a dim twilight upon them as they sat about on boxes or lolled in their bunks. At night a single bulb of light behind a ground-glass screen burned like a relentless eye watching them. When they moved, vast shadows swept across bulkhead and ceiling with idiotic speed. Men hung pants and towels over their rails to obscure the light, while others read. Fritz, the German greaser, had fashioned a hinged tin box to cover it in the night-watches, and this box had a habit of working loose from its hook and, coming down with a bang in the middle of a desultory conversation, plunge them in darkness. The floor was littered with matches and soiled with black boot-tracks. Here and there some one had laid down a piece of sacking in an attempt to keep the place tidy. One or two bunks were neat and clean. Often you might see a half-naked figure rubbing with sweat-rag and soap at some unpremeditated soilure on his bunk-board, the petty motions of his arm repeated in gigantic grotesque across the wall. But these were exceptions. The great Greek, whose feet hung over the bunk-board near the door and tended to obtrude upon the incoming stranger, terrifying him with their very vastness, blackness, and sprawling articulation, was not a clean man. Hannibal would sit on his box and look up at this recumbent enigma, wondering what he thought about. It was his duty twice a day, at four o'clock, to arouse the man. Once—the day they left New York, to be precise— he had been unable to arouse him. Pinching, punching, shouting into the sooty orifice of his ear, was of no avail. Hannibal called the Second Engineer, and received some instruction in the art of turning out the watch. The Second placed his oil-smooth hands on the Greek's enormous abdomen and rolled him slowly from side to side. If you have a nervous temperament this will cause you to sit up, knocking your head against the bulb-iron of the ceiling, and shrieking with simple terror. But the Greek was fathoms deep in an aftermath of carouse, and he only sighed, flinging one great arm over his head. He lay there in magnificent pose for a sculptor, the eccentricities of the lighting throwing his profile into sharp relief. The Second was not a sculptor, and he merely scratched his hand and cast his eyes down at the bottom bunk. A tow-haired Norwegian lay there, wide-eyed, watching him.

The Second crooked his finger. "Get out," he said shortly.
The man came obediently, feet first, hitching his grey
flannel underclothes as he stood up. The Second got into
the bunk, lay down and put his feet against the loose
boards of the top bunk. What followed was almost too
rapid for Hannibal to take in. The body of the Greek rose
as though in some terrible physical convulsion, swayed,
and fell over the board, belly first, clothes, mattress and
all, in one tumultuous cascade upon the floor. Hannibal
and the Norwegian stepped back to avoid the crash. For a
moment the malodorous heap lay still. A man putting on
his boots on the other side of the room muttered "Jesus
Christ!" rose up and slouched away on deck. Slowly the
Greek raised himself to his knees, coughed and spat, the
saliva dribbling in discoloured threads from his lips. He
looked round as an ox looks round in the pen, suspicious,
bewildered, the whites of his eyes rolling.

"Goin' to turn to?" asked the Second.

Once again the man spat, and struggled to his feet
blindly.

"Serve you right," said the Second, looking down at
the disarray of the bedding. "Too much whisky, Angelatos. Get busy now! There you are!"

High up in the crow's-nest the bell tanged sharply, eight
strokes.

And Hannibal went down to wash himself in the stokehold.

It was somewhere in that interminable crawl across the
Indian Ocean from Durban to Sabang that he got his first
taste of the fever that seizes the Northerner by way of
carelessness. Day after day they followed the long slant
north-easterly, crossing the burning line at an angle of
twenty degrees. Day after day the sun blazed down upon
them, and night followed night in breathless succession.
And then one evening there came a change. The light air
that Hannibal sought so eagerly after tea on the forecastle-
head, dropped entirely, the black smoke of the Natal coal
rose in a spectral column from the funnel-top. Up on the
bridge the white figures of the Captain and Mate showed
against the teak wheel-house where they talked. Out of
the ship's side a great tin wind-scoop could be seen stick-

ing from the Steward's room, twisting round and round as he endeavoured vainly to catch the slightest draught. Late into the first watch Hannibal lay up there winking at the stars, turning in hot discomfort on his pallet, and watching a black line thicken and spread over the horizon. As the hours crept past it grew, a dense blackness like a smudge of charcoal on dark blue paper. When he was called at One Bell the blue dome was blotted out, and he had to feel his way to the ladder. It was about half-past one, as he stood under the ventilator in the stokehold dripping with sweat after cleaning the ashpits, that he heard the thin clear call of the Chief's whistle. As he climbed the ladders a heavy blob of warm greasy rain smote his cheek, another fell on his hand. The Chief, ghostly in his white sleeping-suit, was standing by the fiddle-top.

"Yessir?" asked Hannibal.

"It's goin' to be some shower," muttered the Chief, taking hold of his arm and pointing to the skylights. "Better get up and shut 'em. Turn the ventilators aft. Quick!"

Hannibal climbed quickly, but the rain was quicker. As he thrust the first skylight lift hard down, it came. Each great drop, as it struck his vest and pants, seemed to pin them to his body. He bowed his head to shield his eyes, and the rain poured down his neck in streams. The sound of it battering on the awnings and canvas covers of the life-boats was deafening. He had to feel for each lift as he struggled round. He could see the Third, far down in the glittering radiance of the engine-room, looking up, wondering at the noise. In less than half a minute Hannibal was as wet as though he had been dipped in the sea. His boots were full, his pants clung to his limbs, and the rain ran from his hair into his eyes. He jumped down to the deck, felt for the rope ladder that was lashed in the bunker hatch, and disappeared, swaying, into the deeper darkness of the coal. Anywhere to get out of the rain!

"Gor lummy!" he muttered to himself, crouching on the coal, and wondering how long it would last. And as he sat there he began to shiver. He tore off his singlet and tried to wipe his body with his sweat-rag. He stripped and went on wiping, his teeth chattering. He hardly knew what to do. All his dry things were in the forecastle. He went to the ladder and looked up. The breeze was cooler now, a tear in the black canopy showed a strip of velvet blue sky studded with stars. He decided to chance it before it came on again, and climbing up, he ran swiftly forward, his white body gleaming in the darkness. He found a dry cotton vest and clean dungarees and put them on. Certainly it had been "some shower."

The next morning, when they called him for his breakfast, he lay on, shivering with cold and streaming with sweat. His stomach seemed tied into knots. The Second came along and looked at him, scratching his head. When he asked what was the matter, Hannibal turned over in utter weariness and said he was sick. There was something wrong with his inside. The Second went away and the Steward came, bringing the simple therapeutics of the sea. He put a slim glass tube in Hannibal's mouth and told him to keep it there for a minute. When the Steward took the thermometer out again and looked at the temperature he said "Sufferin' Moses!" and ran away to speak to the Old Man. They returned together, white figures overwhelmingly incongruous in the dim kennel. Captain Briscoe looked down at the youth lying motionless under the blanket. You would not have thought, to look at the Captain's immaculate drill suit with the gold shoulder-straps, the white-covered cap with its ornate badge and cord, his neatly-trimmed beard, his pipe-clayed shoes, that he had lived many years in the forecastles of sailing-ships. He stood looking down, his hands clasped behind him, while the Steward tried the temperature again.

"Hundred and one—hundred and two, now, sir! Better give him the fever-mixture, I should think."

"And a dose of salts," added the Captain. "What's his name?" he asked generally.

Nobody knew his name. Jan, lying in his bunk, leaned over and looked down at the young man.

"Hanny, what's your name?" he called. "Captain wants to know your name."

"Gooderich, sir," he whispered, and the Captain gave a scarcely perceptible start.

"What's he been doing?"

"In the rain, I expect, last night," said the Steward. "I felt it on me face. Had to shut the port, sir."

The Captain went out into the daylight and walked up and down the bridge for an hour, pulling at his beard. Mr. Cadoxton, in exceedingly fine raiment which he had got, at great expense, from a Liverpool tailor, surveyed the ocean with a satisfied smile. He was a nice-looking lad, with a complexion tending to ruddiness and freckles beneath the eyes. His teeth were white and regular and he used a manicure set. Captain Briscoe had not made up his mind about Mr. Cadoxton. Finding him playing cards one evening in the dog-watch, he had remarked that he would be better employed studying for his Master's ticket. This was excellent in its way, only Mr. Cadoxton, who was a little older than his clean-shaven and fresh-looking features betokened, already possessed an extra-master's certificate, and Captain Briscoe should have found it out before. He knew, and he knew that Mr. Cadoxton knew, that *he* himself would never get an extra-master's certificate if he lived to be a thousand years old. Mr. Cadoxton looked down even on "Conway boys." As he stepped jauntily to and fro, keeping his eyes with exasperating vigilance upon the empty horizon, Captain Briscoe, walking fore and aft alongside the wheel-house, reflected with some bitterness upon the puzzling tangle of existence. He would have given fifty pounds for some one to talk to. He dared not open his mouth to the Mate, the man's every movement implied his unappeasable hunger for promotion. The Second Mate was fat and secretive, and his record was clouded by that grotesque bigamy charge. With the curious contrariness of human proclivities, Captain Briscoe desired greatly the confidence of Mr. Cadoxton. He felt that the young man had the indefinable requisites of gentility; his voice betrayed him when he spoke of "my people." Captain Briscoe, with an effort, remembered to lay his knife and fork together before the Steward removed the plate. Mr. Cadoxton did it without remembering just as he took his soup from the further edge. Captain Briscoe had every reason to hate the young man, and did hate him at times, and yet he felt that if only they could gain one another's confidence in some trivial accidental way, he might derive comfort from the circumstance. They approached each other automatically in their walk, and Mr. Cadoxton withdrew his eyes from the ocean.

"The Steward tells me there's a trimmer sick, sir," he remarked in his small refined voice.

"A touch of fever," assented Captain Briscoe. "It's a very curious coincidence," he went on, "that young feller's name is the same as my wife's."

"Is that so, sir? It is curious, certainly. We all have poor relations somewhere."

Captain Briscoe thought this an excellent notion, and democratic.

"A matter we can't be held responsible for," he suggested.

"Of course. It may be only a coincidence though: I have heard the name before. That's the chap who was in the mess-room, I think."

"That's him."

"Very decent young chap, sir. I spoke to him about the boat-drill last Saturday and he was very civil. Most unusual in the firemen class."

"I can't say," said the Old Man—"I can't say as I'd like to have anybody belonging to me in the forecastle, nowadays. Still, I don't know anything against it, if the man's respectable."

"Not at all. A man isn't responsible for the others. But why don't you ask him, sir? Has Mrs. Briscoe mentioned any of her relations who follow the sea?"

"No," said the Captain, taking out a cigar. "She didn't."

"Perhaps he's one of the independent sort, quarrelled with his people, perhaps."

"Maybe. What is it, Chief?"

The Chief, in his suit of blotched khaki with the brass buttons enamelled with verdigris, stood looking up at them. He pointed to the forecastle.

"Oh, he'll be all right to-morrow, Chief. Put' em on six-hour watches," and the Chief walked slowly back to the afterdeck.

"You think he's quarrelled, eh?"

"I had a cousin who went to Canada," remarked Mr. Cadoxton, reaching for the binoculars in the box by the telegraph. "And I believe he did something of the sort. Left the Army and went out for good."

"Fireman?" asked the Captain hopefully.

"Oh, much worse, sir. I believe he's a billiard-marker in a club."

Captain Briscoe resumed his walk. The long voyage was telling on his nerves. Fifty days out, and still they crawled in an unbroken circle of cobalt blue. They were making, according to orders, for Sabang, a new coaling station somewhere in the north of Sumatra. This was the second time they had crossed the line. Twice more they would have to pass that mystic circle ere they started northward up the China Sea. He reflected with impatience upon the absurd regulations of the Canal which made case-oil prohibitive if carried on that route. In Sabang he would get coal and fresh meat, and what was more important, letters. He had had a letter in Durban, a brief scribble without any of the luxuriant language of newly-wedded love and therefore unsatisfying. She said she was busy with her flat, had joined a women's club, would write more next time. He could not help being proud of the stylish handwriting, the embossed lettering of the address, the thick square envelope. She knew how to do things all right. But he longed for a little gush. Was it anyway possible she disliked being called his own dear darling little wife? A warm flush of vexation came over his face, and he went down to get a peg of whisky.

Two or three days of breathless inaction and semi-starvation, racked by diarrhœa and headache, and Hannibal crawled out into the daylight again. The Second told him to take it easy, and gave him a stiff dose of whisky. It did him good, though he found the shovel strangely heavy, and often he would grow dizzy and have to lie on the hatch with his face on his arm, exhausted. Swansea seemed a long way off. Was she thinking of him? He hoped so. He found now, in his weakness, that tears came easily. He was sorry for himself. And one night as he sat in the cool breeze that blew from the Nicobars, he heard the mates and engineers in the Second Mate's room singing "Rolling Home":—

Rollin' home, rollin' home,
Rollin' home, rollin' home,
Rollin' home—across—the sea,
Rollin' home to dear old England,
Rollin' home—dear heart—to thee!

He felt a terrible pain in his chest, and the tears came unbidden to his eyes. He heard a growl from some one of them, overwrought.

"For the Lord's sake sing something else! I can't stand it!" And Hannibal understood perfectly.

Twenty-eight days after they had quitted Durban, the *Caryatid,* rounding Acheen Head, passed slowly into the land-locked harbour of Sabang and made fast to the white timbers of the jetty. Angelatos went to the door of the forecastle as the Mate shouted, "Make fast!" and looked round, licking his lips. He had been this way before, had Angelatos, and he knew that gin was a shilling a bottle.

XVII

IT WAS the end of the day, and the *Caryatid* lay off in the middle of the land-locked harbour. From where Captain Briscoe sat in his deck-chair no break could be distinguished in the high, densely-wooded hills that enclosed the sheet of waveless water in which he laid moored. It was as though some mad millionaire had brought a great ship over the mountains and launched her on his ornamental lake. Here and there in the velvety gloom a light hung, a drop of liquid yellow. The riding light shed a pale glare on the forward awnings. For the rest, it was darkness save for the dim light of the stars. The oil-lamps in the chart-house failed to penetrate the curtains. Captain Briscoe, in his pyjamas, his pipe gone out, lay in his deck-chair and stared out moodily towards the bows. He was distraught in more ways than one. The owners had cabled, counselling speed, and he had cabled back diplomatically, regretting a non-existent delay. That was bad, on his first voyage in a bigger ship. What was worse, he had received another brief letter from Minnie. She was busy and could not think of a great deal to tell him. Throwing down the letter petulantly he had torn open the newspaper, one of those bulky weekly journals that appeal more particularly to the love of the dramatic and spectacular in human beings. On the front sheet was an article with big headlines relating the successful and burglarious entry of some suffragettes into the House of Commons. Captain Briscoe regarded the suffragettes very much as he regarded Dagos, with loathing and contempt. He felt they ought to be crushed with an iron hand. If, he argued, a woman was a woman, she would never do the things these hemaphrodite beings did so persistently and publicly. Mr. Cadoxton had agreed with him in this. He read on, trying to interest himself in the paper, when he came to the list of the prisoners who had been hand-cuffed after a stiff struggle with the police. With something like paralysis numbing his brain, he had seen Minnie Briscoe on the printed page, and had let the paper drop.

At tea-time he had sat there at the head of the cabin-table, seeing nothing, eating nothing. With a certain sense of relief he saw that Mr. Cadoxton was absent, taking watch on deck. What was he to do? He wanted to run away and hide himself. He felt that if he could only go out and kill something it would ease the agony of mind. They would all see it. Every one would have a look at the papers. He had a wild notion of going round and stealing them from the different rooms. He turned again and again, when he reached his room, to the vile rag that had recorded this hateful thing. There it was, "Minnie Briscoe, 303 Tedworth Square, S. W." She, his wife, was in prison!

So far, he reflected as he sat in his chair, sucking at a cold pipe, so far, thank God, he had seen no hint of any suspicion in the faces of the others. But to-morrow, and the days to come! His hands clutched as he thought of it. And on top of this, the trouble with the men. Gin was a shilling a bottle in this place, and somehow, in spite of his care, they had got it. The Chief had told him laconically that steam was impossible until the men came round. They lay in an abysmal stupor; nothing could be done. Only one, that young chap out of the mess-room, was doing his best with the Third and Fourth to clean one or two fires during the night. Captain Briscoe thought bitterly that he need have no cause to look down on the young man now —he was at least respectable. He rose from his chair and went down the ladder, leaving the Third Mate leaning over the rail. Hannibal stood by the fiddle-grating, cooling himself after a turn with the shovel. He felt rather up-lifted by the fact that he was the only fireman sober. It had been a wild time in the forecastle that afternoon. Men had drunk themselves mad. Angelatos had grown furious with a big red-haired Liverpool Irishman, had lunged for-ward with a bottle in his hand and gone down with a crash against the bulkhead. Jan was drunk too, and it took a lot of gin to make him drunk. Hannibal saw the Old Man pass into the cabin, and went over to the hatch to sit down. The Fourth would call him if he wanted him.

He had had a letter from Nellie, a real letter, full of cheery gossip from his own love-a-duck. Another from his mother did not contain much news. Mrs. Gooderich had not felt able to explain what had happened to Minnie. When you come to think of it, it was rather a difficult thing to explain to a boy, as Mrs. Gooderich still thought him to be. As he sat there thinking of all that had happened since he had left the Little Brown Box, he became aware of two crouching figures moving across the dim whiteness of the cabin bulkhead. They paused at the entry, gesticulating in the darkness. Perhaps they wanted the Steward. He didn't know. Why should he bother? He had plenty to do. And as he was asking himself why he should bother, he heard a thud, and a growl.

He rose up and went on tiptoe to the cabin door. At the far end of the white panelled alley-way was a swaying curtain. He heard a struggling sound, and a smothered "Ouch" and an imprecation. He went in feeling his way along the wall, leaving black finger-marks on the glossy enamel, and drew the curtain.

It was the Captain's room. The oil-lamp was turned down low by the broad bunk. Across the room, just in front of a mahogany locker, were three men locked together. Captain Briscoe's sleeping suit showed up against the dark forms of the other two, who were on their knees in a curiously bowed attitude. His arms were about their necks, and he was striving to crush them down. One of them had worked his arm loose, and wrapped it around the Captain's neck. So they strove there, almost in silence, rocking to and fro.

The sound of the Third Mate's footsteps in the ladder roused Hannibal to action. He turned and beckoned, and then ran in and seized the fireman's arms. Mr. Cadoxton followed him precipitately. He had been dozing and dreaming of the pleasant Leicestershire country, when he heard the first thump below him.

"What's up, sir?" he called, and threw himself upon the man's neck. Freed from the embrace the Old Man sprang to his feet and dealt the man blow after blow in the neck and face. For an instant he was mad, and struck blindly, but the Third Mate's voice recalled him. He paused.

"Get the handcuffs," he ordered briefly. "And call the Mate." The men rose to their feet, cowed and noiseless. Hannibal saw with amazement that one of them was Jan.

The Mate came hurrying in with the shining steel things in his hands. Captain Briscoe turned up the lamp. He seemed relieved by the exertion. His face was calm as he turned to the men.

"Mr. Hutchins," he said to the Mate, "handcuff these men and put them in the lazaret. In the morning I log them for breaking into the spirit-locker. Mr. Cadoxton, you're a witness of this. You!" he said to Hannibal. "You saw this, eh?"

"Yes, sir, I heard a noise as I was sitting on the hatch."

"Take them out of it," ordered the Captain. "And call the Steward to put the place straight."

To Hannibal, standing in that unaccustomed privacy, there was something horrible in the submissively extended wrists of the two men who had been bludgeoned into a craven acceptance of manacled seclusion. And one of them was Jan, the man he had been ashore with, his chum in a way, and not a bad fellow at all. As the Mate led the men away and Mr. Cadoxton followed, he remained standing on the soft red carpet. The Captain turned and saw him. Checking a gesture of dismissal he looked the young man over.

"See what it does for a man!" he remarked, feeling for a bruise near his eye. "Keep away from it."

"I do, sir. Never take much. Makes me 'ead ache."

"Good for you. What's your name?"

"Gooderich."

"Oh." The Captain went over to a little mahogany table and took a fountain pen and paper. "You belong to London?"

"Yes, sir."

"Any relations there?"

"Yes, mother and sister."

"Sister, eh?"

"Yes, sir."

There was a pause. Hannibal's eyes came away from the table and met the Captain's squarely. The Captain went over and took the door off the hook. The Steward came in with a run as the Captain was closing it.

"Never mind, Steward," he said. "Clean it up in the morning. I've changed my mind." And he shut the door.

"Now," he said. "You did me a good turn coming in here just now."

"It was the Third Mate, sir."

"Yes, you did, and I'm going to do you a bad turn in payment for it. Don't you know anything about your sister at all?"

"Just a bit, sir. We never 'ad much truck with each other since I was a kid."

"You know, then?"

"Something, sir."

"You know what she used to be—when I first knew her?"

Hannibal looked down, his hands behind him, vaguely disturbed.

"I didn't," he muttered at length. "But I can make a pretty good guess."

"And do you know where she is now?"

"Married, sir."

"She's my wife!"

"That's right, sir."

"And do you know what she's done since we left home?"

"I—I haven't 'eard, sir. My mother don't say much about 'er. She's almost a stranger to me," he pleaded in a low voice.

"Look here!" And Captain Briscoe held up the newspaper. "She's in jail. My wife and your sister in jail. That's a nice thing to have coming after fifty-six days at sea." Holding the paper to the light Hannibal read the particulars of the raid and the ensuing arraignments.

"A nice thing!" muttered the Captain, feeling the bruise swelling beneath his eye.

"And then this on top of it. My God!"

He turned, and putting up his hands on either side of the port, looked out. A black mark ran across his shoulders where the man's arm had laid hold of him.

Hannibal put the paper down and looked round in a

scared way. The moment was beyond him. He couldn't ex-·
press what he felt save that he was sorry for the Old Man.
This man had been kind to him, had given him a job. He
was, moreover, his brother-in-law. That was what staggered him. All these months they had been within a hundred feet of one another and no words spoken. What a
strange world it was! And his sister, the quiet-eyed girl
who used to take him with her to the Botany Class in
Trinity Road, in jail!

"What is to be done, sir?" he asked in a low voice.

"I don't know. Upon my soul, I don't know. Only this.
Keep your mouth shut, do you hear?"

"I ain't likely to blab," Hannibal said, surprised.

"See you when we get home, understand?"

"Yes, sir."

"You see what this means to me?" He ceased abruptly,
a look of fear coming into his eyes as though he himself
were only just then seeing what it meant to him. His trim
beard was twisted around his set mouth, his pyjamas had
lost a button or two, and revealed the hairy chest, faintly
tattooed with red and green markings, a heart, hands
clasped, a Union Jack.

"I won't say anything to anybody," said Hannibal. "It's
a mixed-up business, I can see that, for you."

"I'll have to cable," the Old Man muttered, staring at
Hannibal. "What shall I cable? I must think. But it's all
over now. They'll get six months. We'll be home by then.
God!"

There came a knock at the door. It must have been low
enough, but it sounded like the crack of doom to the two
standing within. The Captain went over and opened the
door. The Chief, looking as though he were deliberating
upon some stupendous problem, stood on the mat. He
raised his eyes.

"Trouble?" he asked, feeling in his pocket for matches.

"Oh, Chief, come in. I've been taking this man's
evidence. He came in after those two toughs and assisted
me. All right, you," he said briskly. "You'll sign the log
in the morning."

Hannibal stepped out into the alley-way and the door
closed.

"Trouble?" the Old Man whispered, taking the Chief's arm. "Don't it take the biscuit? Here we've come twenty-eight days without a break, saving coal, as they told us, and they want to know where we've been. And then this on top of it. This means twelve hours lost."

"Gin's too cheap," said the Chief, putting the match carefully in the ash-tray. "I've been along. Fo'c'sle's like a pigsty. Stinks. Hell let loose. I'd jail them if I was you."

At the word jail the Old Man looked hard at the Chief, who was staring at the wall. "Jail," he whispered, and said no more.

"You've got a bat in the eye?" asked the Chief, looking at him for a moment.

"Isn't it a hell of a life?" snarled the other, suddenly raging. "Isn't it a beautiful life? Here am I, lying on my bed worried enough with one thing and another, God knows, and those scum crawl across the room to the whisky." He tore the pyjama jacket from his body and flung it in a corner.

"Jump on 'em?" enquired Mr. Hopkins.

"I landed right on top of them, and by God, I'd have killed one of them if nobody'd come in. And been sorry for it!" he added, stepping, nude and shaking with anger, to a chest of drawers.

"All they're fit for," growled the Chief, going towards the door.

"Hold on, wait till I get some clothes. Have a peg? It's on the locker."

"Get any letters?" asked the Chief, pouring some whisky into a glass. The Captain came up to him and poured another.

"Yes," he said, drinking.

"All right at home?"

The Captain reached up for a cigar-box and selected a cheroot. He turned the light down till it was a blue shadow in the shell of the burner.

"So damned hot," he said huskily. "Sit down, Chief. I've got to tell you something, about my wife. You may hear from some lying hobo who'll put all sorts of frills on it. I can trust you to keep mum, can't I?"

Mr. Hopkins, drawing steadily at his pipe, grunted and inclined his ear.

"The fact is," went on the Captain, "my wife's got some peculiar ideas. She's taken up with the Suffragette business and there's been some trouble. She got run in with a lot of others, and there you are. You can understand of course, it's only a case of her being led on."

"I saw it," said the Chief, staring at the carpet.

"You saw it!" repeated the Old Man drawing back. "Then why in thunder didn't you say so?"

"No business o' mine."

Captain Briscoe sucked at his cigar.

"They've all seen it, then?"

"No. What of it?"

"Suppose it was your wife. Think of it—handcuffed!"

"Say nothing."

"It's all I can say. I only told you in confidence. I've got to speak to somebody. I'd go mad if I didn't, Chief."

"It'll pass. This business will make 'em forget it. You're making too much of it."

A silence fell upon them, and they sat there in the darkness, each thinking, in his own way, of the tremendous problems that beset them whenever they touched the land. All real trouble came to them from ashore. Mr. Hopkins turning over in his mind a certain mortgage, almost regretted the necessity for receiving letters at all. Captain Briscoe sought relief from his present disorder in reflecting upon the easy way in which sailormen were fooled. Everybody fooled them—owners, ship-chandlers, house-agents, charterers, women, everybody! Fooled them and forgot them. He found himself back at the old point again. Minnie had forgotten him, else why had she not written to him in her trouble? He stirred uneasily on the red-plush cushion as this new grievance flooded his mind. As though he understood, as perhaps he did, for he understood more than he could express, Mr. Hopkins put his hand on the Old Man's arm.

"Wait, wait," he muttered. "You're all worked up. Turn in and sleep. You can't do anything."

He stood up, and the room filled suddenly with dazzling radiance.

"He's got some steam," remarked Mr. Hopkins. "We'll get away at daylight. Good night."

He went away quietly, and Captain Briscoe, turning out all the electric lights save one by the bed, sat for a long time at his table, his chin on his hands. Gradually the tide turned, and a semblance of peace came into his eyes.

"No," he said to himself gently, as though in answer to a voiceless query. "No, she's mine. I took her, knowing what she was. Some day I'll stay ashore and look after her. A little house in the country, with honeysuckle and bees. God! The years I've worked! I don't ask much, eh? Just a few years, and a few things some men have all the time. Surely she'll understand. She's cleverer than me, she'll understand."

It was midnight when he rose, and the habit of years sent him up on the bridge to have a last look round. The Third and Second Mates stood in the shadow of the awning, talking earnestly together. They fell apart as he came up.

"All right, Mr. Brail?" he asked.

"All quiet, sir."

"Call me at four o'clock," he ordered. "I'm going to turn in."

"Very good, sir."

He went in again, and lying down on his bed he extinguished the light and fell into a tumbled sleep.

XVIII

THEY had been out two days from Sabang, when Hannibal, hanging over the side of the starboard bunker-hatch, discovered it. He had come up for his two o'clock spell and a faint breeze blew off the mountains of Sumatra and fanned his face. His body was naked to the waist, a black sweat-rag hung like a rope's-end around his neck, and he spat inkily into the blue water that lapped the rusty and peeling plates. Without knowing exactly why, he found himself waiting for the occasional wavelet that reached the starboard strake and ran aft with a flicker and a scarcely perceptible hiss. He bent his head lower and watched carefully. The next time the slight heel of the ship aided the ripple, the immersion was deeper, the hiss unmistakable. He got down on his knees and felt the ship's side. Hot, yes, but not so hot as all that. There it went again. He waited until the ship rolled to starboard again and watched. This time he saw it for certain. It was steam.

He stood up again and tried to think what to do. He was a man now and he wanted to make sure. Where could he get another view of that bunker? He went down the ladder and saw with disappointment that he could not get to the inboard side of it. It was too near the funnel. But the bottom of it, he reflected, would be the ceiling of the engine-room down below, over the forced-draught fan. He descended and passed under the boilers into the engine-room. The Third was standing under the windsail, whistling: *"That's how I need you."*

"Hello," he said, "what's to do?"

Hannibal's eyes wandered about the ceiling over the fan and dynamo, and the Third looked at him in some surprise.

"Say, mister," remarked the young man, raising a black arm, "what's up above that there?"

"Coal, my child. Stabbord engine-room pocket. Wan'

some?" But Hannibal had run three steps, and stopped, looking up at the smudge on the white paint.

"Can you get up there?" he asked. This time the Third saw the smudge and understood. In three springs he was on the fan, another, and he was hanging to a stringer within the reach of the smudge. He touched it, and withdrew his hand quickly. He dropped down beside Hannibal and took up the telephone.

"It's the Third, sir. Come down for a minute."

"Is it?" asked Hannibal.

"Stinkin'," replied the Third. "Now be a man, and say nothing to anybody. This is a business for the Chief. What made you come in here?"

"Saw the sea spitting on the side, sir."

"Bully for you! Here comes the Chief."

He came, incredibly agile for so phlegmatic a man, four steps at a leap, swinging by the hand-rails like a monkey.

"What's to do?" he asked, and the Third pointed.

"Put the Sanitary pump on deck. You go and take the hatches off quick," he added to Hannibal.

As Hannibal knocked the wedges from the cleats and let the battens clatter on the deck, the Captain paused in his walk on the bridge and looked along at him. When the tarpaulins were folded back and the hatch lifted, and he saw Hannibal fall away from the opening, Captain Briscoe came down quickly.

"Eh?" he said, bending over and touching the coal. "What's the matter?"

"Chief told me to take it off, sir."

A thin lazy thread of smoke crept out from among the lumps of fuel and blew away. The Chief came along from the engine-room. He had relapsed into his wonted taciturnity. He looked at the thread of smoke and searched for matches.

"Going good," he commented.

With a great slither the fire-hose was flung across the saddle-back hatch abaft the funnel, and began to straighten out with the urging of the water. The Chief put it into the coal.

Soon they were all there. Bosun and mates, carpenter, engineers, all craning their necks to look at the hatch. The two apprentices, painting the ice box aft, looked on from afar with an agony of curiosity. Everybody knew it inside of five minutes.

"Who discovered it?" asked the Captain.

"The Third told me," said Mr. Hopkins, resenting the crowd about him.

"The trimmer noticed the ship's side was hot."

Immediately the rail was adorned with downward-looking heads. Hannibal felt self-conscious and rather glad. It is nice to feel you are some use after all. Captain Briscoe spoke low to the Chief.

"All right," the latter nodded. "The best way is to wet it and try to smother it. Go down," he said to the Fourth. "Go down and ease the pump. And tell the Third to watch his starboard bilges."

Later in the day it became known that the fire was inextinguishable. Down there in the coal somewhere the combustible stuff had fretted into flame, and was burning with a dull solid glow, spreading, as they could tell by the hiss of the strake further forward and the discolouration of the ceiling in the engine-room. Rumours passed to and fro that they would have to stop. Mr. Cadoxton spoke of Singapore, and the Third Engineer gave a touch of science to the deliberation by mentioning spontaneous combustion. At the end of the day Singapore had become a certainty. They could not afford to pass a British port like this; stories of oil ships on fire were at a premium after tea.

It was something to talk about, at any rate.

Hannibal came into the engine-room soon after midnight to fill his slush-lamp, and the Third told him they'd be in Singapore by dinner-time. The name seemed familiar to him. Of course! That was where Hiram's ship, the *Cygnet,* had been bound. It all came back to him. The picture of the ship in the office in Billiter Lane. The drone of the traffic out in Fenchurch Street, the twittering of the canaries, the *cling-clash* of the cash register. How infinitely far off that life seemed now! He could not help smiling as he recalled his dream of distant lands. Well, it was not so bad. It was different, certainly, from what he had imagined it, yet he was not disappointed. He was a man now, among men. Not so dusty either, when he came to think of it. He had savvy, they said, at the mess-room table, and the Third treated him with cautious familiarity. Hannibal laughed when Singapore was mentioned, " 'cause I'd a friend of mine on a sailin' ship what went there," he explained to the Third.

"Those are the passenger boats, the *Samos, Lesbos, Chios,* and *Delos*. White hull with buff funnel. I know them. I was Fifth of the *Samos,*" said the Third. "What d'you quit a job like that to come to sea for?"

"Have you ever had a job like that, mister?"

"No such luck!"

"Well, it ain't so nice as it looks. I know *I* found it pretty slow. I don't mind work, so long I can get about and see things. I wanted to see Singapore, somehow."

"You're a funny chap," said the Third. "What about gettin' married? I thought you were all for the beach when we left Swansea."

"So I am in a way. I don't know as I can explain how I feel about it," Hannibal replied, screwing the top of his lamp tight and wiping his hands with a piece of waste, "I always 'ad a hankerin' to get away, only I didn't know 'ow to go about it."

"It's a wasted life, I reckon," said the Third, looking up the windsail.

Hannibal shook his head decidedly. "No it ain't, mister," he said. "Not for us. It's the married men as gets the worst of it at sea, not us. I can see that."

"And yet you're going to get married!"

"So I hope," he returned simply. "I expect I'll have had enough of this by then. But even suppose——" And Hannibal put his finger on the Third's singlet. "Even suppose I did. I ain't going to say it's a wasted life." He wiped his forehead with the waste and put it down thoughtfully.

The Third watched him stoop, lamp in hand, and open the iron door under the boilers. "He's a funny cuss," he mused, and looked up at the ceiling. "I wonder if he's right." And he went round behind the engines to watch the evaporator.

They anchored far out in the harbour at sundown, just as the last rays caught the gilded roofs and set them on fire. Hannibal lay on his pallet on the forecastle and watched it. Jan smoked beside him. All round the red ensigns were dropping from the poops and across the water came flying skiffs with many-coloured sails.

"Look, Jan!" he said, flinging out his hand. "See that sky?" Jan looked with moody eyes upon the purple and crimson glory of the western heavens, but his soul was dull within him. He had awakened in the lazaret, and found the handcuffs on his hands. "What was the use?" he asked himself. He could not keep away from the drink. Every time he swore to reform, and every time the evil thing mastered him. Up on the bridge-deck Tommy was waving flags to the next steamer, sending a message. Up and down and across the flags moved, making the simple words by which the seaman calls to his brother-wanderer round the world. Jan saw him, and a strange look of longing came into the blue eyes. He turned to Hannibal.

"Reckon the Old Man'll send us ashore here?" he asked in a whisper.

"I—I can't say," faltered Hannibal. He had heard a rumour that it might happen.

"I won't go," muttered Jan. "I'll sink first, so help me God! I've been in here."

"Don't say that," said Hannibal.

"Here," said Jan, "you're next him, you are, I don't know why, but you are. One o' the sailors told me something. You speak the skipper. Tell him"—here he bowed his head and shook with a wheezing cough—"tell him I'm done for. I'll be finished anyway soon. Tell him no let me die in the calaboosh. Eh, will you?"

Hannibal looked at him carefully. His brown beard was long and dishevelled, his eyes dry and bright, and his mouth worked under the moustache. Hannibal remembered that since Sabang he had eaten nothing, turning with loathing from the contents of the kid. Suppose he could do this thing for another man? He might. It would be another step in the ascending effort to full manhood. He nodded and put down his pipe.

"I'll 'ave a shot at it," he said, and went aft to the cabin door.

Captain Briscoe was sitting at his little table, writing.

"Come in," he said, when he heard the faint tap on the panel. "Oh, it's you! What's the matter?"

Hannibal told him, and the Old Man stared at him in astonishment.

"What's he to you?" he asked.

"Just a chum sir. 'E can't keep off the booze. 'E's been in quod 'ere before, 'e says, and 'e thinks it'll kill 'im. 'E's sick, sir, sometimes. If it don't make any difference to you, sir?"

"What do I care about the scum? You ought to keep clear of that lot. A respectable man has to be careful."

"They ain't so bad, sir," he answered, lifting his hand in protest. "Only the booze sends them silly. They're men, any'ow."

"Are they?" returned the Old Man bitterly. "A lot you know about it. Jail's the place for them, I tell you. Let them off, and they go and do the same thing again."

"I don't reckon jail makes 'em any better, sir. If they got any friends, they'll feel bad about it, same as us."

The Old Man remained silent, drumming on the table with his knuckles.

"Is that why you came here to ask?" he enquired at length, and Hannibal nodded.

"I'll see," said Captain Briscoe, and the young man went away with a curious feeling of gladness in his heart. It was nice to do a thing like that, if you had a chance.

Jan's sickness was not a fake, as the Second, inured to fakes, grimly pronounced it. He took his watch all the five days they lay at anchor in Singapore, took it feebly for the first fortnight of the long pull up the China Seas. Hannibal helped him by working hard all his own watch, so that Jan had very little to do. But as they left the islands of Loo Choo melting into the blue Pacific, he lay in his bunk helpless, and breathing through dry, cracked lips. The Captain went along with the Steward and saw at once that the man was sick. He ordered them to carry him out and lay him on the hatch. A tarpaulin was put over the boom and hung over the edges, making a sort of tent with open ends. For two days Jan lay there, drinking a little barley water, his eyes closed, his breath coming in irregular spasms, the face above the brown beard like death. Hannibal would creep in after tea and sit beside him, with his knees drawn up, smoking a companionable pipe.

" 'Ow's things?" he would ask cheerily, and Jan would open his eyes and look straight up at the boom. Then he would close them again, while Hannibal told him the gossip of the day. On the third day his eyes were open, and looking for Hannibal. By his side was a milk pudding and a tumbler. One wasted arm lay across his chest, in the other was a key.

"Eh?" said Hannibal. "What is it?"

"Book in my bag. Little book. Savvy?"

He took the key obediently and, finding the bag, unlocked the brass ring that secured the neck, and felt in it for the book. Then he relocked the bag and returned to the hatch.

"This it?" he asked.

Jan nodded, and whispered "Open it."

Hannibal turned over the leaves. It was in some strange language, full of harsh cries, croonings, and abrupt dissonances. He shook his head doubtfully. The fly-leaf fell away, and he saw a photograph of a young woman. The print had been stuck in to the book by some unpractised hand, askew, and with a thumb-mark on the edge. Above was written in thin graceful characters, *"Greta Noord-hoff, Amsterdam,* 1895."

Hannibal looked up and saw the man's bright feverish eyes watching him. He put down his head.

"You look at that picture?"

He looked at it again. The full oval of the face was framed in severely arranged hair, which deceived his inexperienced eye at first. But the eyes were unmistakable. He noticed the name again. "Tommy?" he thought.

"Yes," he thought to himself, in some excitement, almost forgetting the man who was watching his face. Yes, there were the same long-fringed eyelashes, the same shadows under the eyes, the same soft mouth and rounded cheek.

"Who is it?" he asked.

"Girl I told you was good to me. I went away, and she

had a baby. When her mother got on to me for money I
say I got none, see? I think it somebody else's. She died,
same as I told you. Now you see that! Savvy?"

"Yes," said Hannibal, "I savvy. I'll fetch him."

He had not seen Tommy much of late, and now as he
walked aft it occurred to him that he was bound upon an
errand beyond his powers. Here were man and boy, aliens,
the man dying in a desperate plight of irreparable neglect,
the boy very much alive and ignorant of the man's history.
And he, Hannibal Gooderich, only lately seller of tobacco
in Billiter Lane, he was to go along to the boy and say to
him, "That man on the hatch is your father. He's dying,
and wants to speak to you." It was preposterous, a crazy
dream. Tommy would tell him he was not plumb. And yet,
there was the name, the date, the photograph.

He went along the alley-way to his old room. The door
was open, and the boy was sitting with a big red book on
his knee, scribbling figures on a sheet of paper. He looked
up with a smile.

"Hello," he said. "What's de matter wid you?"

Hannibal stepped inside, closed the door, and sat down
beside him.

"You know that chap who trims on the four-to-eight
watch?" he began. "'E's a Dutchman."

"He!"

"Yes, and 'e's dying. 'E's got a touch o' the fever 'e
got out 'ere years ago, and the booze has crumpled him
all up. 'E's an Amsterdammer."

"Hey!" Tommy put down his book.

"Yes, and he's got a book there with a photo in it of
a girl, and the name's same as yours. It's—it's your
mother, I reckon." The boy's face relaxed. For him the
situation, perhaps, was not quite so complex as it seemed.
Say what you will, blood-ties are like blood-stains. They
can be obliterated. The hardy convention of the ages still
persists that the dark blotch on the floor remains so forever, that some deep ineradicable instinct drags forth the
shuddering cry of "Father!" But to this alien child, who
had been sent begging around the ships as soon as he
could walk, who had grown as a sparrow grows, who had
been beaten and starved and frightened by the blackguards

of the sea, who loved where he was loved, and answered as a dog answers, to him the "call of the blood" was less than nothing. To him had come no accumulated tradition of parentage, no childhood enervated by the delicately insidious business of family affection. It had been a slogging fight between a courageous young spirit and a cowardly old world. It was only natural that the love of his heart should go to the man who had stepped in and helped him in his struggle, who had seen with an artistic vision the eager young soul as he might be if he were put upon the road. What had he to do with a father? And so his face relaxed. He reached for his coat.

"I'll come," he said, and together they went forward to the hatch. The man lay as before, one hand across his chest, the other by his side, the top of the dishevelled head towards them. The milk-pudding and the tumbler had not been removed, and they introduced a note of irreconcilable bathos, for he was dead. They saw that, and paused beneath the boom. It was as though the grim Spectre, seated in there beside his last victim, undaunted by the milk-pudding, had raised his hand.

And so, having sailed the seas for many years, having debauched the gifts of God, and the love of women, having avoided with incredible dexterity the esteem of man and the joy of accomplishment, Jan Ostade went out into the void.

XIX

NINETY days after the *Caryatid* had crept out of the shadow of Staten Island, her stockless anchors broke into the glassy surface of the Gulf of Osaka, and she was at rest. Only those who have been through the ordeal can have the dimmest comprehension of the sigh of relief that passed the lips of every one of the ship's company. The *Caryatid* herself seemed aware that for a little while at least she could brood upon her destiny unharassed by the insistent urge of her propeller; and the hoarse roar of the safety-valves, the white feather of steam that floated on the off-shore wind, intimated to her distant colleagues the fact of her achievement.

The Third Engineer came up from the scarcely-endurable heat of the boiler-tops, where he had been shutting the mains, and looked out contemptuously upon the kingdoms of the immemorial East. His colourless face was lined and stippled with black grease, and the bridge of his undistinguished nose was made diabolically incongruous by a patch of soot, scraped from some unnoticed projection. He stood there, in easy pose, neglectful of the chatter in the galley, incurious as to the ensign at half-mast which Mr. Cadoxton was hastening to pull down, and moving only when he heard a step behind him. Mr. Spink, his hair standing many ways, his torso glistening with friction, a bath towel around his shoulders, and a briar pipe hanging from his teeth, joined the Third in his contemplation of the Orient.

"Spink, son," said the Third softly, "call me at one bell, will you, as usual?"

"What on earth for?" asked the young man.

"Not for anything on earth, Spink, but for the heavenly glory of goin' to sleep again. Think of it, O my Spink! Ninety days have I kept the graveyard watch, and now, once more, I'm going to have an all night in. Oh! it's too good to be true."

"You'd better go and get yourself washed then, instead of wasting valuable time," remarked the prosaic Spink. "I'm getting into the hay right now. We'll have to get busy on them pump-links in the morning. They've been bangin' something 'orrible."

"Don't talk about it, Spink. Let the morning bring its own troubles. Let the giddy young Jesmond go round spyin' out unnecessary jobs. Use your time, while you've got it, free from responsibility. Behold the land of the Japanee!"

"I got the log-slate to write up," sighed the Fourth. "The Chief always grouses if I leave it till the morning, even if he don't enter it until next week. Ah!" he put his elbows on the bulwarks and looked attentively at the shore-lights. "Say, Tich, this is some scenery, eh, lad?"

The Third nodded. In a vast semicircle lay the blue mountains crowding upon the twilight sea. From Hyogo, away westward, to the multitudinous brilliance that was Osaka, the lights ran round in interminable chains and galaxies. From the harbour at Kobé flared at intervals a crimson storm-signal, and electric tramcars, like golden beads on an invisible thread, slid back and forth, bursting ever and anon into blue fire as the trolley jumped the wires. High up, the lights of a monastery burned faintly, showing where sad-eyed monks looked out across the darkling sea. Over the water came the cries of the fishermen, the shrill call of a locomotive, the plaintive clang of a mysterious bell.

"Yes," said the Third with a yawn, "very pretty if it wasn't so far from Charing Cross. I suppose that's the launch going around the breakwater now." And he extended a finger towards Kobé. "I suppose he'll bring back the letters."

"He will that," said Spink, and they went into the alley-way.

"I was beginning to think," remarked the Third, as he drew the red ball-fringed curtain across the door of their room, "that I should never be respectable again. I'm not sure now whether I've got a clean collar to go ashore in. How fortunate, Spink, that we both take fifteens!"

Mr. Hopkins, removing a three-days' growth from his

chin, was more concerned about his boilers, I think, than anything else. The Second, leaning against the door-jamb, his head and body in shadow, his face in the light, like a dreadful mask, outlined in a monotonous undertone his campaign of toil. Mr. Cadoxton patrolled the deck overhead, and unfolded to the Second Mate his theory that the Old Man was a victim of premature senile decay.

"Take my word for it, Charlie," he said, as they walked to and fro, "if he doesn't get good news he will be a dithering idiot before we get home."

"Yes, it's nervous tension," said the fat Second Mate, who had a habit of startling people by asking if they had read Herbert Spencer. "That's what it is—nervous tension." Mr. Cadoxton laughed lightly.

"Under the circumstances," he replied, "I think we may call it that."

It was nearly half-past nine when, stopping for the hundredth time to scan the dark waters of the bay with his night-glasses, Mr. Cadoxton detected the approach of a sampan under sail, and moved to the head of the accommodation-ladder. The craft came around in a circle towards the steamer, the tiny lantern on the rail sending out an eerie radiance. As she seemed about to strike the ship end-on, for the off-shore breeze was blowing freshly, the bamboo gaff slipped down and the sail fell in soft folds about the dim, naked form of the boatman. A few skilful manipulations of the big stern oar brought the boat to the foot of the ladder, and Captain Briscoe came slowly up the steps. Mr. Cadoxton, peering over the rail, watched him with intelligent interest. The Captain's head came in line with a lighted port, and appeared a moment as a vivid intaglio. As he stepped upon the deck, and you could tell he was the Captain by the way he did that seemingly simple thing, he handed the Third Mate a bundle of letters and newspapers. Mr. Cadoxton, offering his arms for the load, looked his commander in the eyes.

"Everything all right, sir," he observed.

"Where's the Mate?" said the Captain in a strong vibrating voice. He stood solidly on his feet, his broad figure black against the gangway lantern, the cigar in his fingers glowing. The Chief Mate came down from the chart-room.

"I want to speak to you," said the Captain in the same domineering tone. "Get the men out——"

They walked off together, and Mr. Cadoxton, putting the mail down on a hatch, blew his whistle for aid in drawing up the accommodation-ladder. The Second Mate came over the deck from his room on the port side.

"Letters," he crooned, turning them over. One by one the crew came up, holding eager hands.

"Here you are. *Bosun, Borgan, Skettles, Rathorne*—who's *Rathorne?*—*Nystrom, Noordhoff, Hutchins*—that's the Mate—*MacCuskery, Angelatos, Stolypin*, here you are. . . ."

Some, leaning towards the lantern, held but one thin letter, others had three or four; some, lonely shell-backs, took away a bundle of newspapers but no letters. The pride of these men, their simple chuckling pleasure in receiving their quota, their good-humoured triumph over some eager shipmate who waited patiently until the distribution was over and found nothing for him, was a curious sight. And very soon the bridge-deck was deserted. In top bunks, in lower bunks, in the galley, in rooms with curtained doors, men sat and poured over intimate communications, public trials, news of fire and flood in that far-off country across the world. Mr. Cadoxton, seated on the Second Mate's chest of drawers, lit a cigarette.

"Did you hear him, Charlie? Well, he was terse. There is no other word for it. Never even answered me. It's my opinion, Charlie, that the nervous tension you spoke of is relaxed. He's got his grip again. He'll be nosing around in his pyjamas at five o'clock to-morrow morning." And he sent the smoke in fine jets through his nostrils. The fat Second Mate folded a letter and sighed. "Let him nose," he remarked. "I've forgotten more about my work than he can tell me."

Captain Briscoe, having astonished his chief officer by a number of unnecessary orders concerning the breaking of bulk early on the following day, unlocked his room and entered, shutting the door after him. As he proceeded to divest himself of his shore clothes, he whistled a tune. He even paused, half-naked, to pour out a glass of whisky. As his head emerged from the singlet, he smiled into the mirror. He took a photograph from over his bunk and kissed it. When his sleeping suit was adjusted, he lit a fresh cigar, took a packet of letters and newspapers from his leather case and extended himself on the settee. Once again he went delightfully through the letter he had already perused a dozen times.

It could not be called a long letter, the small neat handwriting only covered three sides of the thick square paper. Minnie, in her imperturbable way, discounted the incident which had given her husband so much misery. It was true she had been down to Westminster, with a petition.

An old friend of hers, a Mrs. Wilfley, had taken her down there. And in the uproar that followed they had been arrested along with many other innocent women. One of the witnesses was Sir Anthony Gilfillan, M. P., who knew Mrs. Wilfley very well, and he had bailed them out, had given evidence that they were innocent. It was very foolish of her husband to take such a thing seriously. She belonged to a Woman's Club, but she had no sympathy with window-breakers. She and Mrs. Wilfley were suffragists, but not suffragettes. She was going on very well at her flat. Her mother lived with her, and she would be glad when he came home. She missed him.

It was flawless in its restraint, its quiet undercurrent of humour, its complete comprehension of his state of mind. The last paragraph was redolent of her personality.

"You know, George, I never had the gift of the 'gab' very strong, and writing letters tires me. But I should like you to know that I think too much of your opinion to do anything that would hurt you, even if you never heard of it. I do really. And if I could explain, which would do no good, you would understand what that means sometimes. Good-bye, dear, write to me as soon as you arrive. I was at Mrs. Wilfley's flat the other day to tea, and a gentleman was telling us about Japan. I almost wish I was with you. It must be a beautiful place. I do miss you sometimes."

That was one letter. The gem of the collection, he

thought, as he laid it down reverently. The next one was shorter, posted a week later. It referred to her brother. She didn't quite know what it was he was doing, but he had thrown up his job and gone to sea. She knew now he was on the *Caryatid*. Her mother thought he might be in danger as he had written saying he might be put on the fires. What in the world was that?

Captain Briscoe laughed happily to himself. His mind leaped the months before he would be home again. This was September. By Christmas? It was possible. To the mariner, getting paid off for Christmas is a foretaste of Heaven. It is a lovely mirage held ever before his eyes by a sardonic Fate. Captain Briscoe had not had a Christmas at home for eighteen years. He had sailed out of Leith in a snowstorm on Christmas Eve, he had run ashore in the Savannah River, in a fog, on Christmas morning, and remained there for two days. He had every reason to be suspicious of that festival. Nevertheless he lay on his settee making hasty mental calculations. Certainly they ought to do it if they got despatch in Java. Even if they went to a Continental port he would get over for Christmas.

His mind reverted to the letter concerning the young fellow. Minnie could not be expected to understand the enormous gulf between her husband and her brother on the *Caryatid*. He smoked hard as he tried to think of some way in which he could act upon her hint. He shook his head. It was not possible. And after all, the young fellow was all right. He seemed quiet, civil, sober, contented. He expected nothing. When they were paid off, then he might do something. But here it would be subversive of all discipline if the Captain interfered with the Black Squad. He decided it could not be done.

He had gone ashore that afternoon with the dead body of Jan Ostade, neatly wrapped in canvas, and had superintended the formalities which that troublesome individual had imposed upon him by dying within sight of land. It is to be surmised that Captain Briscoe did not feel much of this minor tragedy of the sea. When you have lived in the forecastle, where men die at the most inopportune moments, and are shot over the bulwarks without benefit

of clergy, you cannot set aside your own personal troubles
to weep over a foreign trimmer. Sympathy stretched to
cover so wide an area grows thin. To Captain Briscoe, in-
asmuch as his charge of the incubus ceased as he received
his letters, it was as though the man had been a source of
bad luck to the ship. With an entry in his log and a
declaration before the Consul his responsibility ended.

But to Hannibal, seated in his customary place against
the windlass, the matter was not to be so dismissed. He
felt it more even than did Tommy, who was at an age
when tragedy is an irksome conundrum. Hannibal tried to
comprehend the workings of Fate, tried to fathom the
sublime mystery of death. In the dim recesses of his
mind, he fumbled for the key to the enigma. He remembered that away back in childhood, in the days when he
had played about Maple Avenue with little Hiram, he
had been able to look with unfrightened eyes into the
phantom world where mysterious shapes moved to and
fro. Why could he not see them now? It puzzled him,
as it has puzzled many of us thoughtful folk, this paradox, that the more we learn the less we seem to know.
He had a sudden and tear-blinded vision of the innumerable failures, the incredibly foolish failures, with which
the progress of the world was strewn. He remembered,
as he sat there smoking in the darkness, that pamphlet of
the Pallas Athene School, *Raising the Dead*. Was it possible that those sharp efficient people were right? Was
it entirely the fault of Jan and Mr. Grober, and his own
father, that they had gone down the Dolorous Way that
leads to ultimate failure and oblivion? He wondered.

And then another vague idea grew up in his mind, an
idea that perhaps a man's life was not a complete thing
in itself, that perhaps it was but a bead on a string, a
link on a chain, the visible part of an invisible continuity.
In the light of that thought, death seemed a small and
theatrical affair. Was that, then, a solution? It did somehow link up the confusing accidents of existence. It did
make the pain seem less sharp. The essential product of
one's life was indestructible, and lived on. Jan was dead.
Tommy was very much alive.

It had not taken him long to read Nellie's letter, Miss

Ffitt's fluency of speech communicated itself to her correspondence. To tell the truth, she was one of those who endeavour to conceal a tendency to ramble by means of dashes. Old Snickery was a drunken old beast. She sometimes wished herself back in Cardiff—fancy that! She was talking of a certain Mr. Gooderich to a friend of hers the other night—did his ears burn? She saw Girtie the other night—how was that ittle cherub of a sailorboy with the foreign name?—She was out at the Mumbles with her sister-in-law last Sunday—only day she could get off—it made her very anxious, now she held the licence—if anything happened—and anything might happen when those mates and engineers got going—such a time the other night! The barmaids were frivolous things —needed a tight hand.

It is rather refreshing to find artlessness in correspondence in our time. Miss Ffitt wrote very much as if she would have written five thousand years before—in jerky pictures which were quite unintentionally arresting, and sometimes funny, as when she described a German captain with "a carroty beard, a beetroot nose, and onion eyes—but very well bred." Or the mate of a Scotch sailingship, who spent the whole evening over one glass of whisky—"it was a very close night." She made no endeavours after tenderness at all, though I think her simple conclusion, praying that the Lord stand between them while they were absent one from another, indicates with a certain naïve charm and dignity the plane of her permanent emotion.

XX

SHE came into view slowly, for she was deep laden and the tug was contemptibly small. Across the burnished floor that led the eye into the intolerable brilliance of the Inland Sea, she came reluctantly, her yards thick with blobs that were men, her sides cluttered with sampans. She seemed to hang back, as indeed she did in that current, like some beautiful sensitive creature ashamed of the noisy vulgarity of the tug, whose stubby funnel belched a rolling fuliginous vapour and whose whistle sent forth a raucous and disquieting bray. As she drew nearer and, simultaneously with the fall of the anchor the sun dropped behind the shoulder of the Hill of Hyogo, the still water changed from shining bronze to a clear silver, and hull and spars showed up sharply like a dry point etching against an amber sky. With a valedictory shriek the insufferable tug swept round and made off in the direction of the breakwater, and the ship, coming up by indistinguishable gradations upon her clanking cable, took on an aspect of repose, which received its final confirmation from the dispersal of the sampans, and the slow ascent of a riding light in the rigging. She lay a mile to the westward, and Mr. Cadoxton, viewing her through his binoculars, informed the curious that she was the *Cygnet* of London, an unusually fine ship.

Hannibal, hanging underwear to dry on the fiddle-grating, heard the information with pleasure blent with a species of diffidence. His appreciation of the infinitely subtle sense of caste that runs up through the ranks of the Merchant Service was too just to permit any dallying with the notion of the well-bred sailing ship apprentice receiving a steamship trimmer with unfeigned joy. He knew as well as Captain Briscoe now, that you cannot do as you like in such matters. It would have been nice to go ashore with an old friend, he admitted, and sighed. It would be nice to go ashore anyway. This was Friday.

He reflected. To-morrow he would receive ten shillings. He did not want to go ashore urgently, and yet he felt restless. Since they were arrived at the end of the voyage he had tried to take up reading again, having got a bundle of shilling novels from the Third Engineer. Perhaps the Third Engineer was not quite the man to lend a young fellow books, for his taste in literature was sophisticated. Hannibal had a feeling of uneasiness as he read some of those novels, as though he were being forced to peer through the keyhole of a bedroom door. It was not that what he read was so very shocking. It was going on all the time anyhow, he agreed to himself. It was the way they put it, "they" being in the most cases ladies. Further analysis eluded his untutored mind. The stimulating effect upon his imagination was the root cause of his restlessness.

They were going to make a party in the forecastle, to economise in the matter of sampans, it being clearly understood that on setting foot ashore each one should be free to go as he pleased. Angelatos asked Hannibal if he was going with anybody, and he answered quietly that he was on his own.

"I'll go with you," announced the Greek. "Tees fellows all bums." Hannibal reflected that if he really desired to see life and put in what the Third called "a pretty tough evening," Angelatos was the man.

But he did not so desire. The rough work in the furnaces and combustion-chambers, the stifling and blinding toil of tube-sweeping was not to be compensated by an insensate carouse. He had seen Angelatos in his cups, and the sight was not a beautiful one. And yet it was obvious that, in his own poor way, the man was desirous of going ashore with a respectable shipmate who might perchance keep him away from evil. "Tees fellars all bums" was a plain though tactless condemnation of the others.

Allowing for the difficulty of keeping a suit of clothes in a canvas bag, Hannibal presented a fairly decent appearance as he stood waiting for the sampan. Captain Briscoe, patrolling his bridge, observed with satisfaction the young man's respectability. Collars were a rarity in the fireman's forecastle, and Hannibal, unlike the Third, had made certain of his, and it chafed his brown neck with unaccustomed severity. Angelatos, in a suit of violent stripes and a purple silk scarf knotted at the throat, leaned negligently against the rail, a cigarette between his lips. Captain Briscoe came down the ladder.

"Get forward if you want to smoke," he ordered sternly, and the big Greek, flinging the offending thing into the sea, moved away with a muttered imprecation. Hannibal met the Old Man's eye tranquilly.

"Better keep clear of that lot," said the Captain. "They'll get you into trouble."

"I'll watch that, sir," he answered.

The sampan arrived soon after and they all descended, somewhat abashed before the supercilious gaze of Mr. Cadoxton, falling over each other as they stepped upon the bobbing gunwale. The naked boatman heaved his sail, and as they cleared the ship's side the breeze bore them across toward the *Cygnet*, under whose stem they would pass. Hannibal looked out eagerly as they neared her. She seemed much smaller than when in the London Dock. Only when beneath her did he appreciate again the enormous span of her main yard and the perilous height of the masts. And then he saw Hiram and waved his hand excitedly. The young man was leaning over the side and answered involuntarily, as one will. With some surprise Hannibal found the sampan rounding the stern and steering for the *Cygnet's* ladder. The boatman lowered his sail, seized a rope flung out to him, and made fast. Hannibal came to a decision. He grasped the rope-handrail and stepped out. The boatman took a basket from under the seat and handed it to him, pointing upward.

"Hi!" called Angelatos. "Where goin'?"

"See a friend o' mine," replied Hannibal, holding the basket firmly. "See you later." And he climbed the ladder. Several brown faces appeared over the bulwarks and examined him curiously as he ascended. A man with a full black beard under a peaked cap held out his hand for the basket.

"I'm off the *Caryatid*," Hannibal explained. Already the sampan was standing away towards the breakwater. "The boatman gi' me this. There's a friend o' mine—oh, there he is!"

Hiram came up, a brown hand extended.

"Friend of mine, sir," he explained to the Mate, who nodded and went aft. "Well!" Hiram went on. "Where on earth have you sprung from? I thought you were working in London."

"Don't you remember?" asked Hannibal, smiling. "I asked you—that day I come down to the docks—about gettin' a job on a ship?"

"I never gave it a thought," said Hiram. "Come into our room." He led the way along to the forecastle. "I can't wait now. We're just going to wash decks. Will you wait here till we're through? We shan't be long."

Hannibal nodded and sat down. He felt somewhat shy in the midst of all the spotless cleanliness of the sailing ship after the unavoidable dirt of a steamer. He found himself looking up at a photograph of Mrs. Gaynor, and the sight of it brought back with a vivid clearness the life in Maple Avenue. Her calm amiable features, with the slight touch of ironic resignation in the corners of the mouth, reminded him, by contrast, of his mother. He had always been the least little bit afraid of Mrs. Gaynor. She savoured of the efficient class somewhat. He remembered dimly conversations, mainly monologues, in which she had advised his mother of "the best way" to do things. She had even commented upon the folly of putting collars on children, and he recalled little Hiram's blue woollen jerseys. Obviously his mother attached too much importance to appearances. He turned his neck irritably in his collar as it scratched him.

It was not long before he heard the swishing of water on the deck, the brief orders of the bosun, the pattering of bare feet and the scrubbing of brooms. Out on the water the *Caryatid* lay, strangely insignificant. He fell to wondering if he had done wisely in succumbing to that great desire to go out and see the world. He was seeing it sure enough; but was he happy? He decided that, taking it all in all, he was. And then he thought with anticipating pleasure of going ashore with Hiram. Hiram had changed vitally to Hannibal's eyes since boyhood. This was natural. Three years at a grammar school are potent factors in any personal equation. He had a "tone" which Hannibal was sensitive to appreciate but too untutored to ape. When he came in, his trousers rolled to his knees, his legs wet with salt water, his grey eyes smiling, Hannibal felt that he had not made a mistake in acting upon that impulse and coming aboard. But he set out to make quite sure.

"I say," he said, "I came aboard 'ere accidental, you know, I didn't think the sampan was comin' alongside."

"Well, I'm very glad you did, Hanny. Here's my chum. Harry, you remember this chap in London?"

"I saw him come aboard," said the brawny youth, shaking hands. "How d'you like the briny ocean?"

"It's none so bad," said Hannibal. "What I was goin' to say," he went on to Hiram, "is that I'm in the fo'c'sle on the *Caryatid*. I'm—a trimmer."

"What a job!" exclaimed Hiram. "Pretty thick, isn't it?"

"Ah, at times. But I soon got sick o' washin' dishes. I'm tellin' you 'cause I know what the deck thinks . . ." His eye wandered to their faces. Harry Grantly, working socks on to his damp feet, grunted.

"I've been scraping the bilges in the fore-peak all the morning," he said. "I don't know what trimming's like, but if it's anyway worse than bilges you have my sympathy."

"Or guano," said Hiram, holding his nose.

"You understand?" said Hannibal. "Or p'raps you don't. What I mean is, deck keep to themselves on a steamer, and don't 'ave any truck with the firemen. I don't blame 'em either," he added. "They're a pretty tough lot."

"Were you going ashore?" asked Hiram.

"Yes. Are you?"

"What is it, Harry? Beach to-night?"

"Might as well. We'll take a walk up to the Quarter, eh?"

"Where's that?" Hannibal asked, and they laughed.

"Don't you know?" said Hiram, and they laughed again.

"I've heard," remarked Hannibal, and flushed. "I've never been to any o' those places, though."

"Oh," said Harry, peeling. "We just go and have a look round, you know."

"I see."

They laughed again.

They began to talk of their voyages, and Hannibal told them of the *Caryatid's* long pull across the world, the fire in the bunkers, the dust-up in Sabang, and all the little incidents that make up the simple annals of the sea. And they in their turn told him of their manifold wanderings, of wonderful places like Rangoon and Hong-Kong, places with names that reverberated in the mind like the solemn boom of a temple bell. He found it very pleasant to talk to these hard-bitten, clean-limbed youths with the brown faces and clear, steady eyes. They had acquired a certain quiet dignity, engendered of their long lonely cruising, that sat quaintly enough upon their young shoulders. Had you compared them in your mind with a couple of clerks, you would have seen the enormous gulf that lay between. There was a precision of speech and gesture, a sureness of touch, an expression of energy in repose in the boyish features that is the inalienable heritage of the sea.

It was when they were ashore that Hannibal found it more difficult to absorb the full spirit of their emancipated outlook. "I'm engaged," he protested, when they plagued him with the sailor's catechism, and the dull red flush mounted to his cheeks. He followed them in a sort of panic. The heat, the dust, the multitudinous sounds and colours, the jolting of the *rick-shaw* over the uneven roadways, the astounding vistas of temple-gardens and the vivid blue of the mountains beyond—these things disturbed his wonted balance. And he realised with a certain subconscious shame that in the panic was pleasure. He felt as though he stood before a great gaudy curtain hung across the pathway of life, and he trembled all over as he thought of what lay behind. By obscure yet infallible channels he understood that these two young men had already explored this exquisite secret.

As in a dream he found himself with them in a strange room up a dark stairway. It was dark now, and the semi-transparent wall glowed with the light of a lamp in the room beyond. They sat there on chairs, their faces showing dimly to one another in the strange twilight. At times a form would suddenly grow enormous on the paper-screen, fade away, and vanish with the inconsequence of a nightmare. A small figure appeared abruptly, a sharp silhouette that reached out a hand. The panel slid silently.

"Here they come," said Harry.

They came, three dark heads bowed low in a line, three quaint little creatures in kimonos of violet, orange, and pink, with vivid splashes of crimson, with fans fluttering in their tiny hands, with hair coiled so firmly it seemed carved in jet. They came in little runs, smiling out of inscrutable almond eyes. The young men watched, as though the East held them in its mysterious grasp. Hannibal heard the low musical murmur of a gong. The whole thing was preposterously unreal. He remembered his dreams of what seemed centuries ago. Dreams of fair creatures who were his slaves, phantoms of the night. They were cold logic compared with this tiny being who floated to him, whose porcelain skin caressed his face, and whose baby arms crept about his neck. He felt suddenly the enormous humour of the thing. He was a Gulliver among these Lilliputian women. He burst out laughing. Here was richness of experience. Here indeed went up in flames the last of the Little Brown Box. None again could say he had not lived. . . .

The murmur of the gong rose and fell on the air. There was a nervous quality in the sound that made him laugh. He felt that otherwise he would be unable to look across and meet his companions' eyes.

"You love me?" cooed the strange little creature, pinching his ear. He looked round before answering and found a paper wall obstructing his view.

"You love me, eh?" persisted the girl.

"You," he said, patting her cheek. "Why, you look as if you'd come off a Christmas tree, you funny little baggage."

"You no love Jappy gel?" she said, with her eternal smile. "All same. Chop?"

XXI

THEY were sixteen days out from Shimonoseki, going eleven knots. Captain Briscoe and Mr. Cadoxton exchanged trite irrelevances to relieve the tedium of the watch.

"What's the matter with him anyway, sir?"

"Blest if I know. I thought—'pon my word, at one time it was cholera. But it would show itself before now if it was."

"He was jolly sick. I heard him chattering away in that spare berth one night. Absolute rot, of course."

Captain Briscoe took a turn up and down the bridge. Mr. Cadoxton, smiling in the darkness, examined the horizon with care through his night glasses.

"See it?" said the Captain.

"Nothing so far, sir."

"Ought to raise it soon. We'll be at anchor by breakfast-time. What was he talking about?"

"Well, I hardly care to say, sir. A man says anything in delirium, you know."

"What was it? Anything about me?"

"As a matter of fact, it was, sir. That was why I didn't care to repeat it. He was quite 'all abroad.'"

"Shows how murder will out, eh?"

"I haven't repeated it, sir," replied Mr. Cadoxton, and he resumed his scrutiny of the darkness. Captain Briscoe went into the chart room and studied the Madura Strait. He had never been through here before, but he was under no anxiety. It was absurdly simple for a ship in ballast. The soundings near the point were somewhat vague, certainly, but the light on the shoal to the eastward was clear. It would be a feather in his cap if they caught the charter, and here they were fifty miles from port, with two days in hand. He had promised each one of the black squad a pound if they made Sourabaja in seventeen days. It was good going for the old *Caryatid,* with her bottom cur-

tained and festooned with weed and shell. He relit his
cigar and went out again into the night.

"There they are, sir," murmured Mr. Cadoxton, and
pointed. There they were indeed, dead ahead.

"Not so bad," remarked Captain Briscoe.

"Very good, sir," assented the young man. "The currents are beastly hereabouts. I was ashore a week on Laut
Island, three years ago."

"Laut's a day behind. I am going to keep as near the
shoal as I can. I don't like that end of Madura at all."

"No, sir."

The Old Man struck a match and relit his cigar. The
Third Mate observed a look of pride in his face.

"I told you that story was all a fake, in the papers about
my wife?" Captain Briscoe began.

"Oh, yes, sir."

"You see, it don't do to take these things too much at
heart, does it? I knew my wife wouldn't do a thing like
that. She's not that sort."

"No, sir."

"Now the young feller has been telling things about me
in his delirium, I suppose you think you've got a pull on
me, eh?"

"I shouldn't put it that way, sir. As I said, I have not
repeated it, and have no intention of doing so. Hadn't we
better shift her half a point to the west'ard, sir?"

"No, keep her as she is. Go and look at the patent log,"
said the Captain in a sudden pet. Mr. Cadoxton took an
electric torch from his pocket and fled away aft. Captain
Briscoe went to the wheel-house and altered the course a
point.

"Forty-eight, sir. That's a hundred since noon," said
Mr. Cadoxton.

"You see, Mr. Cadoxton, I'm navigating this ship, I
think."

"Precisely, sir," said the young man stiffly, and moved
away. The Captain came over and stood by him.

"Forget it," he said. "I get worked up, sometimes. You
understand, Cadoxton? Worked up. That young feller's illness has worried me."

"Oh, don't mention it." Mr. Cadoxton still spoke stiffly.

"But I must. It isn't enough to know you won't say anything about what he said of me. What did he say? Out with it."

"Merely that you were a relative of his by marriage, sir. I can't see——"

"Nothing else?"

Mr. Cadoxton was silent. He felt quite unable to say what else he had heard the sick man saying. One had to draw a line somewhere.

"My God, Cadoxton! Do you tell me——" The Old Man broke off.

"I didn't speak, Captain."

"Then why don't you?"

"Very unpleasant thing to discuss. Best to let it drop," said Mr. Cadoxton shortly.

"But suppose you can't let it drop, Cadoxton? Suppose you had it with you day and night for months?"

"Well, sir?"

"Well, Cadoxton, that's me. You heard things, did you? Well, *I* heard things, to my face too. I went in to see him one morning, and he says 'I can't make it out.' 'Can't make out what?' I asked him, and he says, clear as a bell, 'Sister!' I took his arm to put the thermometer under it, and he looked at me like a scared kitten, and says, 'Why, I ought to have told 'em about you. You're the man,' he says. I tried to keep steady and shoved his arm down in the bunk. 'Keep quiet,' I said; 'it won't hurt you.' 'Oh, no,' he said, laughing to himself. 'A little thing like that won't hurt me. My father's dead, my brother's dead, and here's me dead too. Sister's all right,' he said. 'Catch *her* being dead. Wonder why mother ain't dead too, though? that's funny. I must ask the Old Man about that.' And so he went on. I couldn't stand it, and came out and got him a sleeping draught. You see what I'm going through? And it isn't as though it was just for the voyage either. It's for every voyage; it's for all time, Cadoxton."

"I'm sorry, sir," said the young man, but he never took his eyes from the two lights ahead.

"Some men," said Captain Briscoe, "would go over the side." He pulled himself together and laid his hand on the telegraph. "I knew a chief once who was in something

of the same position. Came back to Swansea and found
the girl he'd been leaving half-pay to—you've heard the
story, eh? Ten years! My God! It got on his mind, you
see. But I'm going to beat this, Cadoxton! I'm going to
win this hand. You're young. You've got your tickets in
your pocket, and all your life in front. You're pitying me,
the poor fool of a shell-back that's done for himself by
marrying out of his course. Well, you may be down and
out yet, but you'll find I'm still living and sticking in at
it. I've got one thing the women can't touch. I'm master,
and I've never had an accident yet. Coal-fever I've had,
but that's nothing. The Chief's to blame there. Up here
my record's clean. That's all I live for now. Eh? what's
that?"

The look-out on the forecastle had shouted something.
The fifteen-second light on the shoal threw a whitish green
glare over the ship.

"He says he can see the beach this side of the lighthouse, sir," said Mr. Cadoxton.

"Port," barked the Old Man, but it was too late. The
bows of the *Caryatid* rose up as though she were rearing
back from some unseen terror of the sea, and she rolled
over to starboard and lay trembling. The Third Mate had
dragged the handle of the telegraph to full astern, and the
perspiring Spink, who had picked himself up from under
the forced-draught fan, had the time of his life, throwing
the reversing-gear over all alone. It was glorious, he
thought. They were ashore, and him on watch. No doubt
about that. Look at the chatty hanging all askew in the
ventilator. The Chief came pouring down the ladder,
looked at the telegraph, found his pipe and hunted on the
vice-bench for matches.

"Let her rip," he muttered, puffing. "They've piled her
up on a coral reef. Open the fan a bit." And he went up to
look around.

The *Caryatid's* stern was in deep water, her bows were
up on a beach of gleaming coral within two hundred yards
of a steel-verandahed lighthouse. The heavy bucking of
the propeller going astern at seventy revolutions palpitated
throughout the empty ship. Mr. Hopkins peered over the
side as the light swung around. Far away below him he

could see the white bunches of coral in the shallowing water. Humph! He became aware of the Old Man standing beside him.

"Nice little business, eh?" said the Captain, as though he were admiring a greengrocer's shop in a market town. "That's working by chart, you see."

"Miss the charter?"

"Looks damn like it. Here, Chief, just keep that, will you? Give it me back when we get home."

Mr. Hopkins found something heavy drop into his pocket. For some moments after the Captain had gone forward again, he remained motionless, looking over at the water pouring in torrents from the discharges. And then he withdrew for a moment to his room.

. . . .

Hannibal, sleeping in the spare berth, woke to find his face pressed hard against the bulkhead. He turned his head and listened. Yes, the engines were going—how the ship trembled. Going—going astern. He sat up feebly. A faint glare flashed across the room, and vanished—came again—and vanished. He felt the curtains of the bunk tickling his ears. He leaned over and turned up the lamp—it was leaning away from him drunkenly. His trousers on a hook on the wall displayed the same crazy propensity. His thin frowsty face, with the brown eyes ringed with blue, leaned out over the bunkboard. Suddenly he realised that he might be in danger, and he lay back on the pillow. He heard footsteps pass his door hurriedly. He was forgotten. Languidly he put a white, bony leg over the board, then the other, and sat up pressing his hands over his eyes. He felt very weak and ill. Tommy had looked in that evening, and told him he'd been crazy for a week. Crazy! What did Tommy mean by that? Why, Tommy meant he had been talking queer and not knowing what he said. He could not remember. It made his head tired to think.

Kobé? Yes, he could remember that. And a day or two in the bunkers. And then? No good. And he wanted a drink of water. Where was the bottle? Of course, empty. He put his head out to the chest of drawers, and explored with his left foot for the settee. Where was it, dammit? At last!

Still the ship shivered, as the engines raced astern. He crept to the hooked door and looked through the crevice. A man, somebody, one of the crew, went past, and Hannibal called in a husky whisper, "Hi! What's up, eh?" But he did not hear. Every few seconds the light came in his face and made him flinch. He fumbled with the hook and the door slammed in his face. He sat down on the settee and fingered the sweat on his forehead. What should he do? He heard footsteps overhead, the hoarse growl of the bosun, the crack of a block striking the boat-deck. Boats! They were getting the boats out. He made another effort to rise, succeeded, and laid his thin hand on the door knob. It was stiff, and when it turned he had to lean against it to get it open. He stepped out into the starlight, shivering. Upon the bridge he saw figures moving about, other figures standing rigid, their elbows stuck out stiffly as they looked through glasses at the lighthouse. Two ruby red lights hung from the foremast rigging, one below the other. Then with a crack and a groan of protest the boat above his head swung out-board, and the bosun shouted, "Make fast." Hannibal saw some one squatting down against the funnel-casing. He crept along the bulkhead, shaking and with his teeth chattering, and spoke to the man. The light swerved around upon them, and he saw the flattened smiling features of the Japanese fireman—Jan's successor.

"What's matter, Jappy?" he whispered and the Oriental smiled, showing all his teeth. He clashed his hands together, with a gesture of collision, and pointed overside. Hannibal stumbled to the rail and looked down. The tide was going out and the *Caryatid's* port bow was high and dry. She was tilted and listed horribly. And the engines had stopped.

The sailors came down from the house and drifted aft to get out a tow rope. Tommy was one of them, and he ran up to Hannibal, his eyes bright with excitement.

"She's ashore, all right, all right," he spluttered. "See de bottom? Dere! Nearly hit de lighthouse. In de morning we goin' to de lighthouse. I'm going. Dey speak Dutch."

He ran away after the others and left Hannibal on the

bunker hatch. He wondered what he should do. It seemed wrong somehow to go back to his bunk while all the rest were busy. He struggled to his feet and went slowly along the alley-way abaft the engine-room. The Chief was standing there talking to the Second, who was in his pyjamas.

"What are you doin' out here?" they asked him. The harshness of their voices appalled him. He leaned against the house.

"Can't—can't I do anythin', sir?" he quivered, and they laughed brutally.

"Get away and turn in," said the Second, taking his arm. Hannibal resented this weakly.

"Are they going to leave me 'ere?" he asked, hanging back.

"Aw, go on wi' ye! What's the matter, man? We don't quit a ship because she's ashore. Come on! Here you are. Now get in and go to sleep. We'll be off in the morning."

But it was not so. When the dawn rushed over the Java Sea, the *Caryatid* lay there, sullenly indifferent to charters, engines, everything. The Mate had lowered a kedge anchor into a boat, and rowing off had dropped it in deep water. And then with the winch he had hauled it in again, a few rags of weed and crumbs of coral hanging to the flukes. Three times he did it, and then desisted. A small Dutch gun-boat, grey-white in the dawn, all awning and brass hand-rails, hove to and offered to tow. She towed and towed, her screw kicking the blue water into useless effervescence, and the *Caryatid* lay on, disdainful of gun-boats, her nose sticking up rudely to the opaline sky. And to-morrow her charter expired.

At six o'clock Mr. Cadoxton, his usually ruddy face grey from lack of sleep, took a crew of four, including the linguistic Tommy, and rowed over the shallows to the spidery lighthouse. It was like a many-verandahed bandstand, and they could see the occupants swinging in hammocks. Far off on the silent water, black proas with vast multicoloured three-cornered sails hovered like enormous butterflies. Up on the bridge, Captain Briscoe walked swiftly to and fro, his hair and beard criss-crossed, his hands clenched in his pockets in impotent rage, counting the never-ending minutes as the Third Mate gesticulated with the lighthouse-keeper. At last they descended the invisible iron ladder, cast off and began to row back. He went down, and waited by the ladder, as Mr. Cadoxton came up hand over hand.

"Well?" he asked, his voice harsh with anxiety.

"He says, according to Noordhoff, sir, that the highest tide of the year is to-morrow morning. She may come off."

"How many fathom?"

"Three and a quarter metres, sir—that's well over ten feet."

Captain Briscoe turned away.

"All hands there!" shouted the Third Mate. "Now!"

And the boat came up, the blocks screaming over Hannibal's head.

At breakfast, Mr. Hopkins sat in his accustomed place, eating the dry toast of the bilious. The low hanging brass cuddy lamp, that formed the only ornament of the room, was swung forward into his face. He ignored it in his impassive way. Spink, still flushed with the excitement of being "down below at the time," found it necessary to prop his plate up with a piece of bread to keep the porridge in. It was an irksome business sitting at such an angle. Suppose she rolled over! The Third's glassy eye fixed on the boy as he put the fish on the table, a phlegmatic irresponsive boy, impervious to hints, and cherishing a permanent grievance because he had been transferred from the Steward's pantry to the mess-room. He returned the Third's stare without emotion.

"Suppose she rolls over!" said the Third. "You remember that Italian ship at Spezia, Chief? Brand new, launched without ballast, went over on her side. 'Straordinary thing that: took half an hour to do it too. They got a cinematograph down and made a film of it. There she is now."

Mr. Hopkins looked into his tea, merely raising his eyebrows.

"Ah, but Tich, that was different, man," said the Second. "We're in deep water aft. She isn't making any water. Did the Old Man say anything about lightening her, Chief?"

"Two hundred ton," gloomed the Chief, handing his cup to the boy, "after breakfast."

More excitement!

They were breaking open the hatch between the funnel and the bridge when the real fun with signals began. All the morning coasting craft and fishing proas had hung about them, hungry for pickings. Some even landed on the coral by the lighthouse and obtained information. The gunboat had gone away up to Sourabaja for coal, incidentally taking word to the agents. The word flashed across the wires to Singapore, to Suez, to Malta, Marseilles, Hamburg, London. The price of sugar in England quivered a decimal point. A notice was up at Lloyds, giving her price at eleven guineas per cent for reinsurance. At noon she was still there, and the price was eighteen guineas. At tea time, just as the Fourth proposed a game of bridge and the Third Mate agreed to take a hand, silk-hatted men, running between the Baltic and Billiter Lane, spoke of twenty guineas per cent.

But the real fun was not in the Baltic; it was on the *Caryatid,* and the cause of it was the incoming string of steamers. One after another they hove into view—Dutch liners, German liners, British liners; they caught sight of the *Caryatid,* rushed up to her and burst into cascades of flags. As Mr. Cadoxton told the Second Mate, "You could see them licking their lips." Salvage!

Their enquiries were urgent and sincere. Do you want assistance? Shall I stand by? Send a boat! Do you need a tow? And so on. To all of which the *Caryatid: "Am all right. Require no assistance."* They swung there, reluctant to leave her, their rails lined with passengers, their innumerable portholes sprouting white wind-scoops, their decks awninged from stem to stern. They would get tired at last, go astern and swing round, heading in disgust for Sourabaja.

Meanwhile the coal came up in baskets and splashed into the sea on either side. All day long Hannibal heard the rumble and bump of the barrows in the 'tween-decks below him, the splutter of the winch and the dry hiss and plop as the coal hit the water. All day long he lay there in his bunk turning things over in his mind. Sometimes his head got light and time passed unconsciously. Sometimes he dreamed and woke with sweat on his face. All the time the bolster was wet under his neck, turn it as he might. He drank all the water in the bottle, and found himself weeping because he could not call for more. At noon the Steward brought him some broth and a milk pudding. "Water!" whispered Hannibal, showing a hot tongue.

"My Gawd!" said the Steward. "Drunk it all? I only filled it at breakfast time." And he went to get more.

Hannibal took a little of the soup and lay down again. He did not want milk pudding. He remembered with awful clearness the milk pudding beside the dead Jan, on the hatch. At four o'clock Tommy, with his face as black as a nigger-minstrel, popped in to give him the news.

"I been trimmin'," he chirruped, "down in de 'tween-deck. It's pretty hard work, eh? Second Mate 'e says we come off soon. How you feel? Bad?"

Hannibal nodded with closed eyes. Tommy looked at him gravely for a moment and went away to wash himself.

"I reckon," he said to the junior apprentice as they scrubbed industriously at their buckets, "I reckon dat chap'll be a stiff soon, eh?"

"Oh, he'll be all right, when we're homeward bound," said the other. "It's only fever."

To Hannibal everything seemed an immense distance away. The noises on deck sounded dim, mere ghosts of sounds, the light of the ten-inch port was a far-off moon. He was not conscious of having a body at all. He seemed to float idiotically in the bunk. Only his head ached, and the warm sticky perspiration trickling behind his ears worried him.

Nevertheless he was better. He knew that, in a vague impersonal way. His wasted body had been purged clean, and his mind, or his soul if you like, that was purged too. It seemed to him he had been an awfully wicked young man in Japan. He had given way to his desires, regardless of everything. He tried to think what the Browns would say if they only knew. Or his mother. Fancy him, of all people, rioting, drinking beer, making himself sick on that beastly sâki, sleeping in tea-houses. It was true he was not the only one. Even Hiram! He wondered what

Mrs. Gaynor thought. Did she know? She seemed to know a good deal more than she ever let on. What a time it was!

But it was all over and done with. The sickness had cleared all the dross from his nature. He was going home. Oh! how glad he would be to get back to Swansea, to lean his head on Nellie's shoulder and pray her to look after him. The tears gathered under his eyelids and ran down his cheeks to his ears as he thought of it. The sea had been too much for him. He loved it, for all that. The great beautiful round blue sea! It had lured him, tempted him, crushed him, purged him. He did not want to die. He was young, yet how old he felt! Sometimes it seemed as though he had lived through a lifetime in the last six months. And Billiter Lane, where even now silk-hatted men discussed the re-insurance of the *Caryatid,* seemed a hundred million miles away.

It was tide-time at seven o'clock that evening, but the bridge party on the after-deck, gathered on stools round a wicker table the Third had bought in Las Palmas, cut and played as though they were in port. Mr. Hopkins, grown tired of *Ivanhoe,* leaned over the bulwarks and eyed the little island of coal alongside. It made his heart bleed, for it was good Moji stuff, and he knew the vile Bengal rubbish awaiting him in Sourabaja. Suddenly he threw up his head. He put his fingers in his mouth and sent forth a piercing whistle. The bridge players looked up. "Movin'!" he called hoarsely. "She's shiftin'. Get the stops open, Spink."

Over went the stools, tables, cards, everything. The bridge-party had vanished. The Old Man on the bridge tugged at the telegraph, for he too had been leaning over the rail and noticed the slight movement. Down below the Second was breaking every recommendation of the Board of Trade, getting steam into the engines. The excited Spink splashed oil round on the cups, in the crankpit, on the Second's head, everywhere. The Third stood to the stokehold, and told Angelatos that his mother was no better than she should have been, and watched the steam gauge needle crawl round. The engines responded to the Second's efforts with much hammering of water traps, much groaning of journals. Then, with a rush and a storm of escaping steam she started. Away aft the water surged under the shuddering counter, and the Second Mate strained his eyes to detect any movement of the ship. Mr. Hopkins, wondering if the Second had bust anything, kept his eye on the lighthouse. Some one shouted, "She's goin'!" And some one else, less sanguine, drawled, "No, is she?"

But she was. This time the sanguine one had it. Down below, as they raced round thumbing the bearings, shifting the checks, and doing all the little things overlooked in the first mad turmoil, Spink created a sensation by pointing to the chatty hanging in the ventilator. It was straight! It quivered, swinging slightly from side to side, as though it said, "There! what do you think of that? I'm straight again!"

"She's away sure enough," admitted the Second. "Floatin'," and he watched the telegraph.

"Home for Christmas, Spink!" bellowed the Third, as he twirled the swab-bush in the pot. "Stories round the fire—mistletoe—stockin's—brandy round the duff, Spink!"

"No wonder I sold a farm to go to sea," grinned Spink.

XXII

THEY made up a bed for him on the poop, just by the ice-box, and from there he caught sight of Perim, as they began the race neck-and-neck with the deserts up the Red Sea. It had been a long hot day across the Indian Ocean via Colombo, and the Red Sea was fifteen hundred miles long. Six days they ploughed onward, and Hannibal wondered why it was called Red. It certainly was red-hot. The winds from the desert struck his face like a furnace blast, and little birds dropped dead on the deck with the heat. He used to watch them flying, screaming with agony as the death-hawks pursued them. Poor little things, to come so far to find death! One night he looked up at the ice-box and saw two of them asleep side by side, their beaks laid together for comfort. He raised himself gently and drew near to them, but they slept on. "Poor little dicks," he muttered, feeling a lump in his throat. It moved him profoundly, the sight of those tiny casuals of the sea, and he never forgot it. Somehow they seemed akin to him, and the yellow death-hawks with their spotted plumage and horrible faces—they were efficients. Their wings were strong, their sight was keen, their beaks were sharp, like those clever people who made money and looked down on him at home.

One morning, as the Gulf of Suez loomed ahead and the cool breeze flapped the awning, he asked for his clothes. He wanted to get up and work. The Chief lounged along and inspected him. There was not much of him except skin and bone, and Mr. Hopkins shook his head. The Second joined him.

"If you want to turn to," said the latter, "come into the engine-room. I'll put Snyder in the bunker, Chief. There's worlds of scouring to do. I daren't go into Liverpool with an engine-room like a ship-chandler's store. You go on day-work, six to six, see? What you want is plenty of soup and greens. You'll soon pick up."

So into the engine-room he went, and picked up to a certain extent. It was amazingly good to be about again, to feel one was useful, and the Third made him laugh so much that his weak body ached. They were all very joyful because, barring accidents, they would be home for Christmas. All day long they toiled, painting, scrubbing, polishing. Hannibal went all over the hand-rails, and even Mr. Hopkins made humorous signs that the brilliance was painful to his eyes.

They passed through the Canal at night, and Hannibal, with his overcoat buttoned up, for it was piercingly cold, watched the great beam of the searchlight cutting into the darkness. What a treat it was to be cool again! And then Malta. He thought Malta very beautiful that morning, as they came in among the warships and liners. He bought himself a blanket and some clothing, for all the old ones were nearly done for. And just as a little luxury after his long privations, he bought a box of cigars. It reminded him of the Little Brown Box.

He had letters at Malta too, from Nellie and his mother. Mrs. Gooderich did not excel in correspondence. She said they were getting on very well. Minnie was out a good deal—had grand friends that Mrs. Wilfley introduced her to, and they had a little servant. Altogether they were not doing so badly. She never heard from Kennington now. They had their own friends. Mrs. Gaynor had written saying she had heard from Hiram, how they had met in Japan. That was very nice. Mrs. Gaynor said Hiram wrote fine long letters, telling her what he saw and all the wonderful places he visited—why didn't Hanny do that too?

Nellie's letter didn't contain much, but it was enough. When was he coming home? She had no idea this silly old world was so big. Old Snickery was breaking up. The old fool would drink himself crazy soon. The "Stormy Petrel" was doing big business—she had no time at all. With "love from his chatter-box" and a quaint "God bless you, dearie," at the end.

And almost before they could realise it, there was Gibraltar "grand and grey," like a lump of England dropped down in the Mediterranean, on the starboard bow. Well! He had seen it; seen Singapore, seen the "far-flung battle line" of old England. He was a man now, he thought, as he scoured and polished the brass-work, a man with money coming to him, and a girl wait-ing for him. This at least the sea had done, and he was not dissatisfied.

They ran into the Bay and found it in a bad mood. The sky shut down on them, and the great grey-white waves came out of the west and crashed aboard. The ship looked very bare with all the awnings stowed away. He could hardly realise it was winter time. Only a week or two back they had been in the Red Sea. The water was freez-ing cold, the forecastle-ports leaked, and the bogey wouldn't burn. He would squat in the store in the engine-room for warmth, and watch the engineers swaying to and fro as they did their work. And then one morning, just as he was coming down the ladder, the engines pulled up with a bang. He never forgot the Second's face at that moment. He took his pipe from his mouth, and in one glance looked at the gauges, the levers, the throttle, the fan. He did not run wild. He just used about three sec-onds to think, and then he went quietly to the fan and stopped it. The Chief came down the ladder at once in his pyjamas, and gave the same keen glance at the vital parts.

"Eh," he muttered, putting the telegraph to "Stop."

"Stopped dead," said the Second blankly. "Slide's bruk?"

"Get 'em all out," said Mr. Hopkins. "I'll go and tell the Old Man."

The Third and Fourth came tumbling down as soon as Hannibal told them, and they began. There was no fuss, no excitement, no profanity. The *Caryatid* rolled in the trough of the great Atlantic waves, and it was difficult to work quickly, but they stuck to it, silently and with infinite care and patience. He could not help feeling proud, ridiculously proud. They were foolish, silly men in fine weather, grumbling at everything, cursing their fate, and judging many things wrong. But here, in a pinch, by God, they were men! It took them three blistering hours to get the broken throttle valve out and repair it. As the last nut was screwed up, the Third began to sing, *"I fear no foe in shining armour!"* and the volatile Spink made a spring for the fan.

"Go easy now," said the Chief, wiping his face with a piece of waste. And he looked round vaguely for a box of matches.

Up on the bridge the Mate and the Old Man steadied their bodies to the roll and looked sombrely at the two black-balls swaying in the wind. They felt very helpless, as sailors do when the coffee-mill goes wrong. Mr. Hopkins had been far from clear in his accounts of the trouble. How long? H'm! They could search him! and he had gone down again. Their oilskins flapped about their legs as the wind rushed in wild gusts about the charthouse. It was weary waiting.

Captain Briscoe waived breakfast and kept his place, waiting, waiting for the telegraph. Half-past eight passed and no sound. Overside the seas boiled and fell up against the bulwarks in dull thuds. How slow time moved! What was the matter down there? Eight months those engines had run without a murmur, and here, almost in sight of England, something had gone bang. Were they hiding something? Was that Chief afraid to tell him? Fancy being towed in after being aground, and his first voyage! But he knew in his heart that the silent little man in charge was not likely to be afraid to tell him. Still, why didn't they hurry? He wanted to get in and get finished. He had something to do when he got the ship in. He would be up against another problem. But to be towed in! He felt he would rather . . .

And then the pointer of the telegraph whirled round as Spink worked the handle, round and back, round and back, and then on to *"Full ahead."* He answered at once, and turned to find Mr. Cadoxton at his elbow.

"I went down below to have a look, sir," he said. "It's all right. Mr. Hopkins says it'll take us into Liverpool."

"Cadoxton," said the Captain, "I've been twenty-eight months in a wind-bag, and felt it less than this run."

"Yes, sir, it has been a bit of a strain. But we'll be in Liverpool inside of a week."

The young man looked up at the sharp, drawn face under the sou'-wester, the fierce eyes straining into the grey weather, the bleak crinkled nose wet with moisture. Not a bad little chap, even if he was a bit of an outsider, don't you know. And he began to think of Christmas in the pleasant Leicestershire country; snow perhaps, and skating. His brother the barrister would be down, and his young brother at Oxford, with his chum; awfully jolly it would be. Such a treat to get into one's dress clothes again. The weather? Oh, blow the weather! This was nothing, so long as they could keep punching into it.

And Hannibal down below, he too was disdainful of the weather. As he cleaned up the place after the battle with the broken valve, he felt unreasonably glad that he had been there, if only as a helper. There was something in that little tussle with the forces of nature that appealed to him. You didn't meet men like them in warehouses and retail shops, did you? He had watched their faces as they had toiled, faces set hard under the grease and sweat. He heard the Second talking quietly. "Now, Spink, don't get excited, son." Spink, the youthful hilarious Spink, with his teeth gritted together, one sinewy hand hanging to the grating, while his body writhed to reach a reluctant and exceedingly hot nut. And the Third too, surpassing the others in his skill in making slings and knots, producing little steel wedges unexpectedly from his pockets at just the right moment like a conjurer, his face an impenetrable mask of contempt.

"It's moving," said Spink. "Aye, like a little dog's tail," said the Third. "It's coming," squeaked Spink. "Aye, but Christmas is near." And down on the plates the Chief stood with upturned face watching them, watching the gauges, watching everything, with never a word. They knew their work, didn't they? Well then, and sometimes, but quite casually, he glanced at the clock.

The young man felt he had seen something worth while that morning, something he could remember with keen pleasure. It was not that these men feared death or that they loved the owners, that they had done this thing so valiantly. No, there was something deeper than that. That grey old master, the sea, called them, and they answered. They would be paid off in port, and be scattered abroad over the earth, never to meet again—no matter.

The sea called, and they answered. To each other they said it was nothing. They had heard of real breakdowns, crank-shafts snapped, air-pumps gone to glory, cylinder-heads blown out. Dreadful were the stories with which they passed the dog-watch that night. The Third lied brazenly about "the last ship I was in," until the Chief muttered, "Forget it! I heard that yarn twenty years ago, and it was old then." What a life!

What did it matter? They would be home for Christmas.

And so they were. The gale hauled off, or else they did punch through it, everybody forgot which; and on a fine, clear winter night, they picked up a pilot off Angle-sea. Almost with a feeling of sadness, Hannibal took his bag down to give it a scrub. He felt all right now, though a little shaky on his pins, as he told the Chief. Even the cloddish occupants of the forecastle were bestirring themselves. Men got out stubby pencils and figured on old magazines the possible total of pay, forgetting to allow for all little advances—the ten pesetas in Las Palmas, the two dollars in New York, the twenty yen in Kobé, the five guilders in Sourabaja. But Mr. Cadoxton, sitting in the cabin surrounded by documents, did not forget them, and it was wonderful, when they were added up, how much there was to come off the total.

Fog held them in the river, a dripping low-lying bank so thick you could not see your hand before your face. All around them sirens screamed and whistles bellowed, and sometimes a ghostly ship came perilously close, the thump of her propeller sounding with startling distinctness for a moment. Hannibal sat on the warm fiddle-grating, and looked out. Fog? He laughed at the idea. He had been brought up to call this white cotton-woolly stuff *mist*. Fog, to his metropolitan consciousness, was different. How homelike it was, though, after the burning crystalline East, after the interminable days of shining blue water. It seemed like a beautiful, dreadful, unforgettable dream, a dream from which he was returning, through a sleepy phantasmal fog, to real life again. Beyond that vaporous mystery lay Nellie and warm fires, home, love, long mornings in bed. After all, he was tired.

And once or twice he coughed huskily.

At length, after much waiting and manœuvring, after long hooting and ringing of bells, they came into the dock. It was morning, and the mists had rolled away.

Beyond the river wall lay a huge liner at anchor, her great funnels reared up against the sky-line. For a moment Hannibal forgot the imminence of his departure, forgot the insistent calls to come ashore and have a drink. He leaned over the bulwarks and stared at the broad stream and the steamer. How he loved them, those splendid runners of the sea! Men lived there, toiled and rejoiced, cursed and did their work. And the old out-classed steamers laid up alongside—he loved them too, unkempt, rusty, and bluff-bosomed though they were. They were casuals of the sea, going blindly as the markets bade them up and down, across and across, so they fetched and carried to feed the roaring looms and busy mills of all the lands. And when no hand was lifted, no charter signed, they lay there silently, patiently, in one side, paying no heed as tides ebbed and flowed, claiming humbly but space in which to rest, their masts flaunting no joyous ensign to affright the spirit of decay that crept up the river on the dripping fog.

"Hi, man! Get yourself ready. They pay off at ten o'clock," called a voice from the forecastle door.

"I'm coming," he replied, turning. The voyage was over at last.

XXIII

A SHIPPING office is a region given over to the commonplace. Inside of the heavily-latched doors you are out of the hearing of the great happenings of the sea. On those distempered walls of ashen grey are pinned curt notices of trumpery court-cases, fines for over-loading, imprisonments for falsifying discharges, nagging circulars or recommendations, illegible lists of bygone salvage crews, pathetic appeals for seamen's homes. Behind the broad mahogany sit disdainful young men in immaculate raiment, industrious, distant, and incredibly skilful with the pen. There is something of the workhouse office about it all, with its bleak cleanliness, its chilling silences, its penetrating odour of documents, its dry disregard of the souls of men.

At eleven o'clock Captain Briscoe walked into the discharging room quickly, a brown leather bag hanging heavily from his hand, and lifting the hinged leaf in the end of the counter, went round behind. A clerk looked up from his writing and nodded good morning, which the Captain returned, setting his hat and umbrella in a corner. Seating himself at the corner he opened his bag with a curious air of preoccupation. He took out the ship's papers, set them to one side, and spread before him a crumpled telegram.

In twos and threes the crew sidled shyly into the space before him, their boots ringing on the clean bare floor. Gradually they separated into little groups, sailor seeking sailor, fireman fireman; the engineers standing aloof at the far end, their bowler hats held decorously against their chins. Mr. Hopkins, forbidden by the law to smoke, stood with his left hand in his overcoat pocket as though feeling for matches, his untidy moustache drooping, profoundly depressed. The Third stood with his back to the others, reading without emotion a notice which mentioned that

if he, Eustace Richard Titheradge, applied to the offices
of the Board of Trade, or any shipping office in the United
Kingdom, he would be put in possession of a bronze medal
due to him as one of the crew of the steamer *Pharos,* who
had rescued the crew of the Norwegian barque *Ingeborg*
in the Bay of Biscay, six years before. Having read it,
he turned and surveyed the crew of the *Caryatid* with a
blank stare. Tommy, his round cherubic face appearing
above the grey muffler, leaned on the radiator and studied
a slip of paper—his account of wages. Hannibal stood
beside him nibbling the edge of his tweed cap, and watching the Old Man.

The door opened again and admitted Mr. Cadoxton.
Mr. Cadoxton did not remove his hat like the rest of the
crew. He betrayed no sign of being overawed by the
atmosphere of the place. He walked quickly to the leaf,
ducked under it, and appeared beside Captain Briscoe.
From his pocket he drew a gloved hand containing a
bank envelope. The Captain closed his hand on the telegram, crushed it up and put it in his pocket. Every now
and again the door would open and a strange face would
peer round the room, only to withdraw hastily.

Captain Briscoe laid a thick wad of bank-notes on the
counter, and poured the bag of silver and gold upon them.
Hannibal looked at the money curiously. It was the first
time he had ever seen hundreds of pounds. He tried to
imagine how it had come there. By what magic was the
skipper, coming up out of the fog of the river, out of the
great sea spaces, able to persuade these shore-people that
he was the rightful steward of all that money? It was very
marvellous. Only a few hours ago, you might say, they
were down there in the Irish Sea, and here, with the
speed of a fairy tale, gold appeared, the gold for which
they had toiled so long. He looked at the wages list. He
was to receive as a final balance thirty-two pounds. He
felt suddenly timid as he tried to realise the immensity
of the sum. He would have to put it in a safe place—
he might be robbed. He wanted to be rid of it before he
had received it. He had heard stories in the forecastle of
men who had met friends outside the shipping office. As
he nibbled his cap he heard his name called by Mr.

Cadoxton, and stepped forward. All around him men stood with heads bent over curved palms making hasty calculations. The clerk swung the articles around and pointed to the place where he was to sign. Mr. Cadoxton peeled off six banknotes, selected some loose gold and silver from the heap, and pushed them towards him. There was a whispered conversation between the clerk and the Captain.

"Wait," said the latter. "Wait for your discharge-book. Go and get measured. Over there."

Hannibal turned uncertainly, and the beaming Tommy pointed to a blue-uniformed officer who was beckoning him to the wall. Hannibal went over and stood with his back against a graduated pillar, and the official slid the gauge down until it touched his head. Five feet eight. He smiled sheepishly as he caught the eye of Spink. He saw them pass up one by one and sign the paper. By that delicate reversion of precedence affected by ships' articles, Mr. Hopkins appeared last. Hannibal, looking at him, had a sudden conviction that the whole business was a dream. That drooping, untidy little man with his sagging overcoat, his green neck-tie up over his collar, his ill-kept nails, his expression of hopeless melancholy—was he the man who had been his boss for so long? Hannibal stared at him, as he grasped the pen to sign against ninety-four pounds seven and a penny, and saw his left hand come out of his pocket holding a paper parcel.

"Here," said Mr. Hopkins to the Captain, "want it now?"

For a moment the Old Man looked blank. And then he remembered. He put out his hand.

"Thank you, Chief," he said clearly. "Much obliged."

Mr. Cadoxton's eyes strove to appear unconcerned. When the shiny blue discharge-book had been made out and handed to him, and Hannibal turned to go, he found the place empty, save for the official who had measured him. He opened the door to go out into the chill wind that blew around the corner. He felt lonely, and strange. And there was the money.

"Why don't you put it in the bank?" asked the man in the blue uniform, as though reading his thoughts.

" 'Ere?" asked Hannibal, and the man nodded. "Come this way," he said, and led the young man into another room with brass railings over the counter. In a few minutes he had made out a form which would entitle him to draw his money in Swansea.

"Keep the two pounds odd," suggested the official; "you'll have to pay your fare."

"Of course," laughed Hannibal. "I forgot that." He put the warrant in his pocket and went out again.

"Dirty weather," he remarked. "How do you get to the station from 'ere?"

"Car at the top of the street. Take a Lime Street car," said the man.

"Thanks. Oh! 'ere's the Old Man!"

Captain Briscoe, accompanied by Mr. Cadoxton, came out, putting up their coat-collars.

"Tell the Mate I'll be back for dinner," said he to the Third Mate. "Here, Gooderich, come with me."

Somewhat amazed, Hannibal found himself hurrying up the road beside Captain Briscoe.

"Understand," said the Captain, "you can't come back in the ship."

"I'm going to Swansea, sir," he replied quickly.

"There's no need to sir me now. You are off the articles, and your sister is my wife."

"I can't imagine it," said Hannibal, coughing. "But then I don't know her very well."

"Do you know where we are going?" demanded the Captain.

"No idea," said Hannibal. The Captain took the crumpled telegram from his pocket and handed it to him. His unaccustomed eyes wandered over the carboned scrawl.

"Staying Mason's Hotel. Saw *Caryatid* due this morning. Minnie."

"Why," he exclaimed, "she's here, then!"

"We are going there now," said the Captain.

"Me!"

"Yes, you. We've got to get acquainted. On the ship—impossible—discipline against it—Understand?"

They swung up on a tramcar going up Church Street.

Hannibal felt troubled about this business. He resented being dragged into other people's affairs.

"I want to get a train to Swansea," he mentioned.

"What for? Get another ship?"

"No, sir—I mean—I got a girl there."

"That so? Thought you'd be going home for Christmas."

"It's going to be home for me," he returned.

"Well, I'll show you—get a time-table at the hotel. You see, I must see the wife first thing."

"But why me?" quavered Hannibal fretfully. "I don't know 'er as well as you do. She's always been on 'er own. It's nothing to do with me, anyway. My relations never done me any good. I'm going my own road." And he looked sombrely out of the streaming windows of the car.

"I was wondering whether you had quarrelled. The wife never mentioning you, you see," said Captain Briscoe.

"We ain't quarrelled," he insisted. "We've just gone our own roads, that's all."

He could not explain the lack of sympathy between himself and the rest of his family. It was one of those subtle things that are always overstated in words. And indeed, how could he, the untutored young man, give expression to the distinction between Minnie's fastidiously unconventional mind and his own simple appreciation of life and love? How could he be expected to see any resemblance, any common origin, of Minnie's absence from home and his own sudden desire to get to sea? He felt oppressed by the weight of the problems confronting him. It was like the fog in the river. He wanted to get away to Nellie.

A sudden exhilaration came to him as he thought of her. She would look after him. With her he would be safe.

Captain Briscoe sat watching the streets as they went on. Mason's Hotel was temperance, and he knew where it was. Had she come on alone? That would be foolish. Hotels did not like solitary women. He had had no idea, when he forecast a probable date of arrival, that she would come to him so quickly. Was she in trouble? His lips worked under his beard as he tried to take a view of the whole question. It was a little big for him. Out on the ocean, he had seen it as a frightful morass in which he was staggering, lifting a foot only to plunge it afresh in the downward-sucking ooze, while above his soul a dark sky hung, thick with red stars. But here in the City the problem was more difficult, though less terrifying. As he pondered he became dimly aware that the solution lay in his wife's future integrity and his own courage. He had undertaken a colossal task when he married her. He saw that now. He saw that the walls of convention are low within, but terribly steep and high without. Perhaps that was why it was so easy for the folk within to look down on you.

He stood up quickly and beckoned to Hannibal. They alighted and hurried through the rain, up a side street.

"Here you are," he said, stopping before a yellow stuccoed front with *Mason's Temperance Hotel* in thick gilt letters across the first floor wall.

"I'll go up first," he said as they entered the narrow hallway. "You understand? It will be better if I go up first," and he went forward to meet the thin woman in black who was coming down the stairs.

"Mrs. Briscoe? Come this way, sir, if you please." Hannibal watched them round the curve of the stairs. A faint smell of meat cooking came to him, the clink of cutlery and the murmur of voices. On the wall was a faded oil-painting of a sailing-ship in a dingy gold frame. Some one had poked an umbrella through the spanker. How dreary it was, after the splendour of the East! The shiny varnished paper, the woven carpet, the monotonous ticking of the clock in the sitting-room behind him brought home to him the fact that the life of England was closing round him once more. Well! he shifted his feet cautiously, and coughed. When he got to Swansea he would be all right. Nellie was waiting for him. Perhaps he ought to have sent a telegram. He would do that as soon as he could. What was going on up there? Why did they not send for him?

He felt curiously ill at ease at the prospect of meeting Minnie again. He had grown since leaving London, his knowledge of the world had spread over the surface of his mind, until it had reached his sister. And she was the

Old Man's wife. She was to be spoken of as Mrs. Briscoe. And she was upstairs. He heard footsteps.

"Hanny!"

He went forward blindly to meet his mother, took her in his arms and kissed her cheek.

"Well, old lady! I didn't know—you come with Minnie!"

"Good gracious!"

She pushed him back a little to look at him.

"You're a man!" she said solemnly, and touched the black hair on his lip—his own gesture. He laughed.

"Sure thing, old lady. Here I am, you see."

"You'll come up now?"

"Is she up there?" He raised his eyebrows to indicate upstairs.

"Yes, of course. And George—Captain Briscoe too."

Mary Gooderich had changed once again since we saw her last in that house in Jubilee Street. She would have said perhaps that she scarcely knew herself, for this time the change was in another direction. The cringe was gone from her gait, and in her gestures was a certain freedom, a certain air of vague authority. And she called the Old Man George. To Hannibal it was a revelation of his mother. It is certainly wonderful how adaptable a human being, especially a woman, is to environment. When you have left Jubilee Street for a flat in Tedworth Square, with a servant, even if she be only a little one, when your daughter is married to a sea-captain and travels to Liverpool to meet him, staying at hotels, your attitude towards the world becomes less strained. Your regard for the Browns may even become humorously indifferent.

Like many people of limited intellect, Mrs. Gooderich had been borne down by facts. Apparently every fact she encountered was on Minnie's side, the fact of the monthly note cashed in Billiter Lane, the fact of the flat with its furniture, its linen, its gracious labour-saving contrivances, its capable servant. There was the undeniable fact too, of Minnie's acquaintances. Surely, if her daughter were a bad girl, good kind ladies like Mrs. Wilfley would not associate with her, distinguished men like Sir Anthony

Gilfillan, M.P., would not exert themselves on her behalf, when she joined that foolish petition business down at Westminster? And behind all these was the signed bald statement that George Briscoe, master mariner and bachelor, was married to Wilhelmina Gooderich, spinster, at the Town Hall, King's Road, Chelsea. The sight of that plain sheet of paper had recalled the past with a painful vividness. She remembered her sudden choice of the name Wilhelmina, when she read of the queen-baby across the Channel—a foolish piece of sentiment that her husband had capped by naming their youngest after a horse. Mr. Gooderich had won four pounds on "Hannibal" that week and the money had been welcome. She could look back at that time now without a shudder. Somehow, in a manner so complex she could not follow it, she had emerged; her dream of an old age unspoiled by care was come partly true. She avoided the dark thoughts of her life and held firmly to the facts. It was a great comfort to have really good clothes to wear.

Hannibal followed her upstairs. Perhaps it was as well he had come. After all, he had no quarrel with any one. He blushed as he thought how he had hugged his mother. He had gone not for to do it. He had never done it before. Fancy!

Mrs. Gooderich led the way along the dark corridor to a room with a ground glass door at the end.

Captain Briscoe was standing by the fire looking down at his wife. He turned as mother and son came into the room.

"Here he is," said Mrs. Gooderich. "Take your coat off, Hanny. It's all wet."

He hung his cap on a peg by the door, and shouldered himself out of his coat. As he fumbled for the loop he heard a voice say as though amused:

"Why, is that Hanny? Good heavens!"

He turned with a certain aggression in his manner, which was defeated by a short fit of coughing. And then he saw his sister sitting by the fire, a rug thrown over her and tucked under her arms. Her face was pale, as always, and her hands lay with fingers loosely interlaced on the dark fabric of the rug. She smiled as her brother came up to her. How disconcerting she was! Captain Briscoe looked at Hannibal's doubtful face with a certain sympathy. He too had been taken back by the smiling figure in the chair. He, like Hannibal, had braced himself for a definite situation, and she had scored again in her inimitable way. You cannot be aggressive with a woman huddled in a rug. Try it.

She held up her hand, still smiling.

"Well, Hanny," she said kindly, "did they put you on the fires? You look as though you had been put somewhere. Look at him, mother. He's thin as an umbrella."

He stood by her chair, looking down at her, smiling awkwardly. Young men dislike public references to their personal appearance. Mrs. Gooderich looked at him solicitously.

"He *is* thin. I suppose it was that illness."

"He had a touch of fever," said Captain Briscoe. "I looked after him."

"And how do you like it?" said Minnie.

Hannibal, as he answered, was conscious of a feeling of amazement at her kindly peremptory tone. She spoke like a lady of position. He was sure she would patronise Mrs. Hopkins. There might be sparks flying, wigs on the green, no doubt; but that would be her attitude.

"I like it all right," he said quietly. "But I'm for the beach for a while now."

"For what? Talk English, Hanny."

"I mean," he said, "I'm going to stay ashore a bit."

"I see. I suppose you'll be coming to town to stay with us?" There was a faint sarcasm in the tone and he caught it.

"No, I ain't," he returned. "I'm going to Swansea to get married."

For a moment she studied his thin features as the firelight played upon them, his solemn brown eyes gazing into the glowing coals. It was a facer for her, for all of them. How could he have been so secretive? Mrs. Gooderich could hardly believe her ears. After throwing over Amelia, here he was after all—but Swansea! For a moment no one spoke, and he stood motionless, unconscious of the mild sensation he had caused. Minnie pursed her lips slightly.

"You!" she said at length.

"That's right," he replied evenly. "What of it?"

"Who is it, Hanny?" asked his mother anxiously.

"Girl in Swansea," he said. "We got engaged when I was there."

He was master of himself now, realising the tremendous advantage he had over his sister. She couldn't get past that, married as she was. He caught her eye for a fleeting moment and saw it flicker involuntarily.

"And you won't be coming to London?" said his mother.

"Perhaps, later on," he replied. "I—I want a time-table," he added, looking at one that hung on the wall.

"Well," said Captain Briscoe, handing it to him, "you don't seem very anxious to tell us much about it."

"There ain't much to tell," he returned simply. "There's no need to worry about me," he coughed. "I'm all right."

"You've got a cold," said his mother.

"Fog," he croaked, turning the leaves of the time-table. "I'll be all right soon." He looked round for a chair to sit down. "Here's one to Cardiff," he said without looking up. "Two-twenty. That'll do me." And he shut the book and laid it on the table. For a moment he stared at the fire.

"I thought," said his mother, a little uncertainly, "you'd be coming to London for Christmas." And she looked at her daughter, who gave no sign that she had heard.

"She'll be waiting," he replied, and stood up. Suddenly he looked at his sister. "What's the matter?" he demanded.

Minnie looked down at her hands. Mrs. Gooderich fidgeted. Captain Briscoe smiled. Hannibal glanced from face to face, and his own cleared.

"Oh," he said. "Well, I'll 'ave to get down to the ship for my dunnage. I'll 'ave to say Toodle-oo."

Minnie held out her hand, but made no offer to kiss him.

"Good-bye, Hanny," she said. "Come and see us some time, when you are a married man."

"I dare say," he answered. "Good-bye, sir." He checked

himself and laughed. "I'd never get out of the 'abit," he said.

"It's a good fault," said Captain Briscoe. "Minnie, my dear, I've just this to say for this young chap. He's done his work, and kept his place, and I've had no fault to find whatever. I wish him luck. Pity there isn't more like him." And he shook hands. "Good-bye, young man," he said.

Mrs. Gooderich went to the door to go downstairs with her son, helping him into his coat. He turned at the door, cap in hand.

"I'm glad," he said in a low voice, "glad it's turned out better than you thought. Good-bye." And he left them.

"Hanny," said his mother, when they reached the dreary passage again. "What's her name, dear? I'm so glad!"

"Nellie, mother, Nellie Ffitt. I'd like"—he paused and looked round—"I'd like you to see 'er some day, when we get spliced."

"And are you going on the ship again?"

"I couldn't say. I may. I'll write to you, old lady."

"Do, dear. Isn't it rainin'?"

"Ah, rotten weather," he coughed again. "I'm breaking up," he joked. "Good-bye." He kissed her again with his arm around her. "You all right—with Minnie?"

"Oh yes, we're very comfortable. Now mind you write."

"Sure."

And he was gone.

Mrs. Gooderich went slowly upstairs, a finger pressed into her cheek. She felt a pang, no doubt, at the young man's curt dismissal of them and their interests. She could not help sharing her daughter's temporary dismay when he dumbfounded them by the announcement of his departure for Swansea, for she had gone over to Minnie, she feared, irrevocably. There were the facts. Here was Captain Briscoe himself, an irrefragable if baffling fact, talking about living in the country. She re-entered the room.

"I was saying," said he, setting a chair and hanging up the time-table, "that it was always a hope with me to live in the country."

"And I was saying, mother," cut in Minnie placidly, "that George doesn't seem to realise that it's us who have to live in the country, not him. You'll be away all the time," she said to him. "You won't have the trouble with leaky roofs and broken windows. And do you think the girl will live in the country? Not likely. You ask her!"

"Well, Minnie, you can get a girl who belongs, can't you?" Captain Briscoe was not impressive away from his ship.

"There's another thing," Minnie went on, spreading her hands on the rug and examining the nails. "I want to take up my work again when this business is over." She indicated her condition with a faint gesture. "It's awfully fascinating," she added, looking up at him.

"Writing advertisements?" he muttered, and she nodded. He was quite surprised at this extraordinary development of his wife's character. Think of it! It had never entered his head that advertisements were written, and here was his own wife calling it fascinating, giving him perfectly incredible particulars of the money to be earned by it. Mrs. Wilfley made her twenty pounds a week out of it. And it was refined, lady-like work too, a branch of literature, you might say.

"Writing advertisements?" he muttered, and she nodded.

"Couldn't you do that in the country?" he asked. She shook her head with a smile.

"One has to be in the heart of things to get the human touch," she replied, and I defy any one to have told whether Minnie was quoting unconsciously, quoting sincerely, or quoting ironically. Her placid face told nothing.

"George," said Mrs. Gooderich—here was another phenomenal thing, this diminutive, neatly-dressed mother-in-law addressing him as George—"you're exciting her. She's tired by the long railway journey."

Minnie said "Rubbish!" but Captain Briscoe sprang to his feet and looked at his watch.

"I must go down to the ship," he said. "I want to see the Mate and Chief about dry-docking. I'll be back soon. I'm sorry you won't be able to come down and see the ship this time. She's in fine trim."

"Is she?" she answered indifferently. "Is that anything

extraordinary? You might bring me the *Morning Post* as you come back. It wasn't in when mother went for it this morning."

"Yes, all right. I'll bring it. I shan't be long."

He put on his coat and hurried out. He was particularly anxious to see the Mate at once. Mr. Hutchins was keen on promotion. Some one might come down to the ship.

"I wonder," said Minnie as her mother took up a piece of linen which she was sewing, "I wonder if he will remember to get it."

"You forgot to ask him about the name," said Mrs. Gooderich.

"Did I? No, I don't think I forgot, mother. When he came in I got an idea it would be better to leave it."

"It would be nice if you called him Hanny," began Mrs. Gooderich, smiling and biting her thread.

"I would call him anything in the world but Hanny!" said Minnie, with a touch of viciousness in her voice. "How can one tell if it will be a boy? I hope so, of course. I don't want a girl. If it is a boy—well, I've another idea."

"You have so many, Minnie—I can't keep up with you."

"I shall ask Anthony Gilfillan to be his godfather," said Minnie.

"That gentleman! Do you know him well enough?"

"I think so," replied her daughter. "I saw a lot of him at one time, when he wasn't so well known. And Anthony's a good enough name, mother."

"But George might——" began Mrs. Gooderich.

"George has enough to bother about without that," interrupted Minnie. "You didn't hear, though—you were downstairs. He's in some trouble or other about his ship now. 'Put her aground,' he calls it, and there's to be an enquiry. He talks of losing his command." For a few moments she gazed into the fire, a contemptuous expression on her face, her hands moving under the rug. "I should have thought," she broke out, "that the sea was big enough. And he's been at it long enough. It'll be a nice thing if he can't get another job and I have to earn money for two—three—four. Eh?"

Her mother looked at her in astonishment. Minnie's

face was no longer merely contemptuous, it was triumphant. To the elder woman's consternation she withdrew her hand from the rug and showed a gleaming blue-black revolver.

"Oh!" said Mrs. Gooderich, and recoiled.

"He gave me this," said Minnie, regarding it with some amusement, "to keep. He dare not trust himself until he has heard what they are going to do. Fancy!"

For some time there was a silence. Slowly the girl hid the thing under the rug again, staring into the fire.

"Mother!" she rapped at length, and her mother started.

"Yes, Minnie?"

"Mother, I was just thinking. What fools men are! What utter fools! But, oh mother, dear mother, what fools *we* are, not to find it out—sooner!"

XXIV

It was to him a physically fatiguing journey, for he was but little accustomed to trains. To the seafarer, the monotonous confinement, the crepitating vibration of the wheels at unknown and unfriendly junctions, the noxious yet draughty atmosphere and the never-ending readjustments of the body to a fresh cramp, make up a familiar and dreaded memory. To him, moreover, with his body shaken by weakness, it followed upon a sleepless night and a morning of variegated mental excitement. As he changed for the last time, and after a weary wait, into the local train at Cardiff, he wondered if it wouldn't have been easier, and almost quicker, to have gone round by sea. Tommy had told him how he had travelled from Glasgow to Liverpool and from Leith to London in coasters. Very cheap, Tommy pronounced it, and cheapness with Tommy was a cardinal virtue. Funny little chap, Hannibal thought dreamily, as the locomotive bunted into the train with a crash. He was clever too. Look how he signalled in German to that ship in the Mediterranean, just after leaving Malta! No doubt about him getting on. And, why, if it hadn't been for him, there would have been no Nellie! Just think!

He thought affectionately of every one on the ship. Strange, surely, they should be all flung apart now. He wondered if he would ever see any of them again. There was Spink, the hilarious Spink, gone to Shields to get his ticket. Not a bad young chap. Hannibal remembered little gifts of soap and matches, old magazines and plugs of tobacco—the Spartan luxuries of the sea. The Third too! He was a cough drop, he was! No soap and matches from him; he never had any of his own. For the Second, Hannibal had a species of awe. He had the wit to see how completely the smooth running of all the complex mechanism of "below" depended upon that taciturn, tire-

484

less man's labour and care. True, behind him was another
yet more taciturn, but it was not likely that Hannibal
should see how essential to the Second's peace of mind
was the silent, invisible integrity of the Chief. A good
fellow, Mr. Hopkins. He would like to have seen Mrs.
Hopkins again. She understood him. Well, perhaps he
would; Penarth was close here, somewhere.

And that led him back to Nellie. Would she be at the
station? He had accomplished the unprecedented feat of
sending a telegram to tell her he would arrive at five
minutes to eight. The mere thought of her gave him a
warm glow. Somehow he felt no alarm now at the prospect
of settling down. He was tired of roaming. To his youthful imagination, so long turned inward, so recently stimulated, it seemed to him he had lived through a whole
lifetime of vivid experience since Captain Briscoe had
entered the shop that day to buy some tobacco. That day!
The day of his emancipation. As he leaned back in the
corner with closed eyes he searched his mind in vain for
any regret at leaving Amelia. And then a thrill of pleasure
followed. His mother was clear of those Browns too. He
had been on the defensive with Minnie, but he was glad indeed that his mother was shut o' those Browns. Of course,
she was under Minnie's thumb, as was Captain Briscoe.
Fancy! The Old Man under Minnie's thumb! He found
himself pitying him. But then, and he looked at the matter
from a personal point of view, perhaps the Old Man
liked to be under her thumb, if he loved her, same as he,
Hannibal, turned instinctively to Nellie for strength. That
might be it. Anyway, it was no business of his. And he
thought with a lazy, delightful satisfaction of the thirty
pounds waiting for him in Swansea. . . . Quite a
fortune!

He was nearly asleep as the train picked its slow way
round from Landore into the town that lies behind those
huge bulwarks of coal-streaked rock, yet open to the
western rain-laden winds, open to her friend the sea. The
lights of the approach, the clatter of the wheels over
switches, roused him. As he buttoned his coat up closely
he looked out of the window. The train glided into the
station and he was conscious of a pause within himself,

a momentary doubt. It occurred to him that, so astounding had been his life recently, it would not be surprising if the whole thing turned out to be a dream. He often had this obsession, this slack grasp on reality. As he stood up in the darkness of the dimly-lit carriage it came upon him. What was it all, this curiously-coloured, inconsequent thing called life? How did you account for all these contorted shining images in his brain—the East—ship—fog—Minnie—thirty pounds—Little Brown Box—railway train—bump! The door flew open at the touch of a porter's hand, and he stepped carefully upon the platform, feeling dizzy and stiff. And then, in the midst of strange, half-seen figures he singled her out coming towards him, waving hastily, gladly.

He saw her expression change as though she were half afraid of his welcome, her full, pink, pretty face set in a frame of dark fur. They met, really, almost in absence of mind. He was thinking, "I saw her here first of all!" and she was thinking, "He's got a moustache!"

"I'm back," he said, laughing sheepishly, as he took her hand. "Nellie!"

For a moment she was silent, merely nodding and smiling as she looked him over. His big brown eyes roved over the station, came back to hers, and he laughed again. She came to herself.

"Goodness! you do look ill! I got your telegram, just as I was having a cup of tea. My sister-in-law's living with me now, and we always have tea at three. So you have come back! Where's your things—in the van? No, this end always, with Cardiff trains."

They turned as his canvas bag, corpulent with bedding, shot upon the platform.

"There it is," he said. "I'll go and get it." She caught his sleeve.

"Let the porter fetch it. I'll tell him." She told him, and they went out to the street. There she paused in her prattle, looking searchingly into his face. He coughed.

"You mustn't get cold," she announced, and walked towards a cab. Like a man still in a dream, he got in, heard her say, "Stormy Petrel," felt her sitting beside him, inhaled the scent of her clothes.

"Blow the expense!" he laughed. She turned on him, her face glowing.

"Didn't you get my letters in Malta?" she demanded.

"One," he said.

"I sent another three days after. Old Snickery fell down the cellar and broke his neck!"

"Lummy!"

"So you see, but perhaps you don't——" she began.

"See what, Nellie?"

"Why, I had the license, that's all." And she took her lower lip in her teeth and smiled into his eyes. She saw he did not understand.

"The 'Stormy Petrel' is mine now," she added.

"Yours!" he croaked. "For good?"

"Just that and nothing else. They went to law about it, old Snickery's nephews and nieces, but they lost."

"And you're—the landlady?"

She nodded.

"And you come to meet me, and take a cab?" he faltered.

She nodded again, smiling.

"Why not, Hanny? I'm no different, am I, from before?"

"The landlady!" he reflected, as though afraid. "Why," he broke out, "you've got property, then."

"That's what I'm telling you," she answered with gentle impatience. "It isn't a crime to have property, is it? You aren't one of those socialists?"

"Me? No, I ain't anything, only a chap who's been to sea. D'you mean to say," he went on, "we're still engaged? You with property an' me with—with——" And he stopped as the cab halted at the kerb.

"Come on," she said. "May's waiting to see you. Come on!"

He glanced up at the house before entering it. The door of the bar was swinging even as he looked. Electric lights inside showed a glittering array of bottles, polished wood casks, nickel-plated ware, glasses in rows, all festooned with holly and red berries. He followed her into the hall-way upstairs and into a room over the bar, a room with a big fire and a table spread for supper.

"Here he is, May," he heard Miss Ffitt say, and saw a lady turn from a glass where she had been touching her hair.

"Mrs. Lloyd—Mr. Gooderich," said Miss Ffitt, introducing them. "I just got to the station in time, dear. He didn't get my letter about—you know. I've just been telling him."

Mrs. Lloyd was a lady with a certain gentility that did not preclude good nature. She smiled and shook hands heartily, and seemed disposed to leave the talking to Miss Ffitt.

"I've heard of you," she said graciously, and busied herself with the table.

"I don't understand now," said Hannibal, sitting down after removing his coat. "It's like a fairy tale."

"That's all it would have been if I hadn't stuck to my rights. Now I'll just run down and see how things are going on. I won't be a minute." And going out she gave him a pat on his shoulder.

"Fancy!" he muttered, looking at the fire. He heard Mrs. Lloyd ask him if he had had a good voyage, heard himself answer politely, but he was far away in dreamland all the time. Surely, he thought, it would all vanish, and he would find himself on the soap-box in the forecastle, looking up at Angelatos' big feet or listening to Jan's commentary upon life. He strove to figure himself as a man of property. He remembered the awe in which Amelia spoke of such people. He wondered what they would think. Lummy! He would be able to talk to them now! He would be able to snap his fingers at Uncle George and all the rest of 'em. Buy up the Little Brown Box, eh? Not that he wanted it. Swansea was good enough for him!

But was it true? A troubled look crept over his face. Had he the nerve to ask her to marry him now she was in such a different position? Why, there must be scores after her, men of property, perhaps. Why should she take to him so? And he remembered that, in a way, women did take to him. Amelia had done so, as had Mrs. Hopkins. Was it possible that there was something about him he didn't know what?

Miss Ffitt came back. In her plain black dress that fitted her figure and made her seem slim, she was the image of a capable landlady—not too old. Indeed, the black dress, contrasting her pink face and light brown hair, made her look younger and less blowzy than her favourite pink would have done.

"Now we'll have supper," she announced, smiling. "And you'll tell us all about your travels."

"No fear," he said. "You've got to tell me all about this business of the house. I can't believe it. 'Course I believe you," he added, as he drew up his chair. "But what I mean is, it's so unexpected like."

"Of course it is, dear, but we can get used to anything if we try, even a bit of good luck. The great thing is to see it when it comes and take your chance. I wasn't thinking of anything like this happening when I first took over the license. It was simply a matter of business, me taking out the license and acting as Mr. Snickery's manager. Why, do you know, even when he was dead I went to a lawyer, Mr. Leese, who said I had what he called a technical right to the place. 'What's that?' I said. And he said it might need a lawsuit to substantiate the claim, and he would take it up for me if I liked. I hadn't anything to lose, you see, so I told him to do it. Did it very well, too, and only charged a hundred pounds altogether. Wasn't I glad I hadn't given it up as they asked me to the day after the old chap was buried?"

"What I said was," said Mrs. Lloyd, "that Nellie having really made the business what it is, she had a moral right to it, anyway. Don't you think so?"

"And then," broke in Miss Ffitt, "what do you think? Those nephews of his tried to take my character away. Began to tell people I'd been their uncle's kept woman, and I'd wheedled it out of him. Mr. Leese wanted me to let him take that up. He said he'd get five hundred out of them for defamation of character. But I didn't want to do that. I let him write to them and threaten proceedings if they didn't apologise, as he had six witnesses. They did too, so that's over. Kept woman indeed! I'd be hard up for a new dress, I can tell you, before I had anything to do with a poor rickety old boozer like Snickery!"

"What a lot's been happening while I' been away," said Hannibal.

"I should think so! Let's see, it's eight months nearly, though I thought, after you wrote from Japan, you'd been lost, it was such a long time before another letter came."

"I was bad," he returned, passing his plate for more ham. "And we were ashore on a coral reef. I woke up and found the ship all on one side."

"Fancy! Do tell us all about it."

He told them, growing descriptive as he warmed to his subject. Perhaps he drew his own figure a little large in the picture, perhaps the unaccustomed stimulus of an attentive and easily astonished feminine audience led him to paint the dangers of sea life somewhat luridly. It is a very easy sin to commit, for though most women are too shrewd and too practical to believe the preposterous for long, yet they do actually believe anything at the time of the telling, and make you feel they believe it too, which is very charming and delightful, when you are young and just off a ship.

"And what are you going to do now?" enquired Mrs. Lloyd, as they pushed their chairs back from the table.

"Me? I'm going to ask a young lady I know if she's thinking o' getting married," he replied, a fine courage in his brown eye. "You see," he added as he put his arm round Nellie's waist, "I'm like Nellie with the lawyer. I didn't reckon what I was in for. But the great thing is to see good luck when it comes, eh? And you don't get much—if you don't ask."

XXV

Not for many months did he arrive at any sort of ordered comprehension of the things that had befallen him. Indeed, I fancy that just as he had passed his childhood in fantastic dreaming, as he had roamed with East-End gamins without much contamination of soul, as he had gone among the brisk and successful Browns without understanding their clear and immediate view of things, as he had voyaged across the world and seen life touched at the edge with the prismatic colours of romance, so now he did, with that slow-fusing imagination of his, transmute the daily happenings of his present existence into a delightful and—alas!—incommunicable dream. Even at the end, which was near, he found yet another matter for supreme wonder, another confirmation of a previous discovery that the essential spirit of life is indestructible and divine.

One minor cause for astonishment awaited him, as soon as the excitement of marriage was done with and he could give coherent utterance to irrelevant and profane thoughts, and that was the way in which money made money. Especially, he explained, in his own case. He could hardly understand how any one could be induced to go out and work, when money made itself so easy. Why, he observed, it was as easy to be a publican as to be a sinner, and the unexpected pithiness of the remark, its acceptance by one or two who heard it as genuine humour, induced him to say it often. "At least," he would add, "that's what I tell the wife, but she won't have it at all."

It was not to be expected. Doubtless a consciousness of his dependence on her capacity came to him in time, for it was plain to the meanest mind that hers was the directing genius of the establishment. She it was who made a snap-offer for the goodwill of the restaurant next door, who shut it up, gutted the "Stormy Petrel's" jug department, cut a way through from the private bar, abolished a dark back room and transformed it all into a tasteful grill-room. She it was, too, who went through the lists, wrote complaints to distillers and kept the mineral water dealers in terror of their lives. It was her business, it came natural to her to tend the details of a tavern. And moreover he was satisfied that it should be so. From time to time he asked questions, sat watching the smooth running of the mechanism of the house. He was happy in his way, he told her, and she in hers. He wasn't going to be such a fool as to interfere with anybody who knew their business.

It was a source of some chagrin to him, however, to think that he had so far no expert knowledge of any trade, and this impelled him to try to master this one, if only to the extent of supervision. So he tried and found himself grateful to the training of the Little Brown Box, which had made him familiar with the exigencies of the currency. But for the most part he let the mechanism run on, keeping upstairs out of the way, adjusting his ideas of the world in various ways. One of these was clothes. He had drawn his thirty pounds from the shipping office and put it under the tea-cosy one afternoon. When Nellie found it she counted it carefully and copied the numbers of the notes upon a piece of paper. When the notes themselves were in the safe in the bedroom, she said:

"Why don't you buy some clothes, Hanny?"

"What's the matter with this?" he asked, touching the neat blue serge in which he was married.

"Nothing, but you'll want more than one suit. I've been over your things, and you need a lot."

"Well, you buy them," he said, opening the *Cambrian Daily Leader*. "I'm no 'and at that sort of thing."

"I can't buy your suits," she protested. "Underwear and socks, yes, but not suits. You want to be measured."

"All right, old lady," he said with great good nature, "I'll go to-morrow morning."

And when fairly into the matter of it, after having got out of the one-suit habit, so to speak, he found it pleasant enough to multiply his personality in tweed and serge, to note the idiosyncrasies of the young men who came into the saloon bar and walked with lordly airs in Oxford

Street. He grew accustomed to have clothes, in time, affecting neutral tints and inconspicuous design, and eventually ceased to give the matter much thought, as other fancies took possession of his mind.

One thing he found that it was essential to have, and that was something to do. For some days after coming back from Crwmbrla, where they were married ("that mouthful," he called it), he had gone about lackadaisically. That had palled terribly. Nellie insisted he should keep out of draughts and button his coat up when he went out, for he had a habit of lounging along with his hands in his pockets and his waistcoat showing. He talked with Mrs. Lloyd until she returned to Neath to warm the hearth for her husband, who was steward of one of Elder Dempster's West African ships. And the weather being bad and (of course) rainy, at the time, he bethought himself of reading, recalling Mr. Grober and his threepenny books, or a penny if you took them back. He told Nellie about him and his smoky shop, his whisky and his "bitter half," as Hannibal called the soured woman his wife.

"Poor things," said Nellie. "Easy to laugh, Han, but what a life! It is awful how some people live."

"Perhaps he ain't to blame," surmised Hannibal, "bein' a square peg in a round 'ole."

So he betook himself to a shop where books were piled in an endless and glittering variety, a shop reminding him in no detail whatever of Mr. Grober's dingy hole, a shop full of disconcerting ambuscades of literature tended by discreet young women, who puzzled him by their amazing knowledge of books. They seemed to have read them all.

"Stories about the sea? Yes." And they brought down a heap. "What would you like? Pirates or history?"

He wouldn't say, ashamed to let them see how greatly he, a married man, desired to read about pirates. He took up *Treasure Island*.

"This any good?" he asked, flirting the leaves over.

"Yes, it has been out some time—quite a classic," said the young woman, and he nearly put it down again. But the word "pirate" caught his eye on one page and he took it, together with *Westward Ho!* and the *Frozen Pirate*.

The curious thing was that he did not notice that these stories were in any wise improbable. That they did not happen to him was no fault of the world, but himself. It was just accident, that was all. They might happen even now. And as he took up *Treasure Island* for the second time, and read the tale of the doings at the "Admiral Benbow" inn, it came upon him suddenly. "Why," he muttered, "I'm keepin' a pub, or an inn, as he calls it!" It was a great discovery. Here he was, keeping a tavern in a seaport town, with seafaring men coming in for goes of rum (sometimes), and who could tell when a pirate with a wooden leg would not come stumping in? Here he was living in romance, and never thought to look at it that way. There was the name, too, "Stormy Petrel"! It became the preoccupation of his waking moments and the stuff of many dreams, this idea of his proximity to the adventurous life of bygone days. He would look down into the narrow street and watch the townspeople hurrying to and fro, imagining desperate motives and lawless schemes to be behind their haste. He longed for a man with a wooden leg, and once as he walked down to the shore he saw with a queer feeling of delicious horror a blind man, tapping along the asphalt path. Surely it was Pew. Alas! the poor wretch had a tin cup on his breast, proving he was no pirate save upon charitable purses. So it couldn't be Pew. He told Nellie of his fancy, alluding to the name of the house. She laughed.

"I had thought of changing it," she said, to get a better class of trade. The 'Glamorgan Arms,' or something like that."

"Oh, you mustn't do that, old lady," he protested. "That would spoil it. Think! It's like a bit out of a book. The 'Stormy Petrel.'"

She consented to let it stand, if it amused him, and busied herself with the more practical side of the house. He insisted she should read the book that had so seized upon his imagination, and to please him she did so, lamenting the dearth of love interest.

"They're an awful lot of ruffians," she complained. "What on earth d'you want to read about people who are always killing somebody, Hanny? They'd all be locked up if they behaved like that now." But she caught a little of his enthusiasm after all, even to the extent of reporting the momentous fact that a man with a wooden leg had drunk a glass of beer in the public bar one afternoon.

"And me not in!" he exclaimed, laughing at himself.

He bought a parrot, too, a grey, suspicious-looking bird from Las Palmas, who loved warmth and squalled at everybody who came near. No amount of soothing reiteration of "Poor Polly, Good Polly," would soften the baleful gleam in that sombre bird's eye. "They don't talk when they're young," he would explain to Nellie, as they stood before the cage.

"He's awful bad tempered," Nellie would remark.

"Perhaps 'e's grieving over bein' took away from 'is 'ome," Hannibal would suggest, and then the parrot would vent his appalling screech, and there was nothing for it but the cloth. . . .

"I wish 'e'd learn to say 'pieces of eight,' " he would say, coughing. It became a custom with him to go down in the evening to the saloon bar and talk with the patrons who came obviously from ships. Mates and engineers learned to know the young boss, and decorative versions of his life-history passed from ship to ship, ran through enlarged editions in foreign ports, and came back unrecognisably romantic. It brought business, as Nellie expressed it, and so had its uses, though Hannibal thought little of that. It was very pleasant to lean over the bar and watch the drink passing, and add his quota to the stories of far-away; pleasant to be able to say, "When I was in Singapore," or "Yes, I saw her in New York." It gave him a certain prestige. It did not disturb these patrons that they had heard he had been only a fireman. They only wished they could get fixed as he had done. He was good-natured too, and was ready to stand occasionally himself, if he knew his company. Always he asked at some point in the conversation, "Do you know the *Caryatid?* yellow funnel, black top?"

"Out of London?" a second mate would enquire.

"Ah, Billiter Lane."

"Carry passengers, don't they?"

"Some. Not the *Caryatid*. Old sugar basket she was."

And he would laugh and tell them of something that happened "while I was in her."

Always, too, he would look round to see if any one he had known was present. It would be delightful to see Spink enter, for instance, to see his look of sudden puzzled recognition, to shake hands and ask him what he would drink. Ask him upstairs? Rather! Or Mr. Hopkins, though Mr. Hopkins did not frequent taverns. And, strangely enough, one evening as he came through from the grill-room he saw a familiar back. The barmaid was opening a bottle of soda water and splashing it into a whisky. Hannibal came along behind the bar, his eager young face alight with pleasure. He nodded.

"Good evening, Mr. Titheradge."

"Good evening," said the other, reaching for a match and scarcely looking up.

"Don't remember me, I suppose?" said Hannibal, smiling.

The late Third of the *Caryatid* regarded his host with attention and uttered a subdued and profane ejaculation.

"Why—what's to do?" he exclaimed. "Swallowed the anchor?"

Hannibal nodded, enjoying his bewilderment and the polite interest of the other customers.

Mr. Titheradge swallowed his whisky and desired information, and Hannibal insisted he should walk upstairs and see the wife.

"Wife," muttered Titheradge, with his glassy stare. "So you did it, then?"

"Bet your life," grinned Hannibal, leading the way.

It was a great experience for both of them. The Third was frankly generous in his approval of Nellie, and drank half a bottle of whisky while he detailed his own career. He had left the *Caryatid* in Liverpool and gone home for Christmas. Got a Second's job on a Hartlepool boat—not much of a gamble—poor grub and a Chief who behaved as if his feet hurt him—just in to bunker—away to-morrow to Fiume, and up the Black Sea for grain. Spink? Oh, Spink got his ticket and was away in one of Kitty Furness's ships—forget which one—B.A. and Rio run. He believed the *Caryatid* was in Calcutta on time-charter.

Awful life. He'd had some—damn glad he'd left. Yes, the Second and Chief were still in her. And Mr. Titheradge took another peg.

"You're pretty well fixed here," he remarked, looking round. "Parrot, too. Quite nautical! Some people do have luck."

"Why don't you get married too?" asked Nellie, smiling.

"Got any sisters?" asked Mr. Titheradge. And Hannibal slapped his leg and burst out laughing and coughing.

"She's married," Nellie answered, tittering.

"There you are! Just my luck!" sighed Mr. Titheradge.

"Yes, but there's heaps of nice girls everywhere. You know the song?" And she hummed the music-hall ditty:

There's nice girls everywhere,
Nice girls everywhere.

Mr. Titheradge, eyeing a photogravure entitled "The Garden of Eden," which Nellie had bought as a present for Hannibal, pursed his lips and looked sceptical.

"That's what the furnishing pirates say," he remarked. "You get married, we do the rest."

"It's worth trying," urged Hannibal.

"On twelve pounds a month?" said the other sarcastically.

"Plenty do it on less," said Nellie.

"Well, if you hear of anything, let me know," Mr. Titheradge remarked. "Anything like this, I mean," and he waved his hand round the room. "I'll be round pretty sharp, I can tell you."

"If you love each other, it doesn't matter——" began Nellie, but the visitor put up his hand.

"Don't, Mrs. Gooderich, don't—I can't bear it—I can't indeed. If I gave that sort of talk its right name, you'd be shocked."

They stood side by side, looking at him, as he rose and reached for his coat. They were sorry he felt that way. "Come down and have a look at the *Bloomingdale*," he said to Hannibal, accepting a cigar. "I used to think the

Caryatid was a wreck, but I hadn't seen this packet then. She's a peach. We're in the Prince of Wales dock, but he's not there just now."

"I will," said Hannibal.

So he did, picking his way next morning among the railway ties and discovering Mr. Titheradge in a very warm, dark engine-room, for the coal was thundering on the skylights, wrestling with an old and recalcitrant reversing-engine.

"Quite like old times," he remarked, looking round for a piece of waste.

Hannibal talked about the meeting for days, after he had stood on the pier head and waved to the old *Bloomingdale* as she crawled out into the Bay one misty February morning. Nellie listened to him as he vent over all the incidents of his sea life.

"Do you want to go to sea again?" she demanded suddenly, as she sat by a great heap of newspapers in their sitting-room.

He looked at her, startled. The drone of the electric cars in Oxford Street came faintly to their ears.

"No," he said vaguely, as he looked out into the little street. "No, I don't know as I do, Nellie. Seein' the chaps and talkin's all right, but I reckon it's the beach for me for a bit yet."

"A year, anyway," she suggested, hunting among the papers, so that her face was hidden from him if he should turn.

"Ah," he asserted.

"Oh," she said, "this is what I was looking for. This," and she showed him an advertisement. "Why not try it?"

It was a good advertisement in a way, an English way. A French or Italian specialist in publicity would have lifted his shoulders in despair of the consummate banality of it. An American of the same profession would have said it lacked punch. They would all be right; but for the English, it was a good advertisement. It proved that Minnie, who had composed it, who had, through Mrs. Wilfley, received twenty pounds for it (Mrs. Wilfley merely raking off a trifling fiver), had learned the essentials of the art, and had, moreover, a certain propensity for it. It was plain that she had studied under that cultivated lady the science of "Commercial Psychology," the chair of which Sir Anthony Gilfillan had endowed at London University. The fruitfulness of her study was apparent in the fact that she caught Nellie, and Nellie was sharp enough in her own line. She knew beer was a deleterious mess in most cases, containing saline stuff to aggravate thirst instead of allaying it; that whisky was faked with potato spirit, and port was doctored with log-wood; but she did not think that there was aught of guile in that advertisement. It was headed in exquisite Kelmscott type, *Are you anxious about some one you love?*

She was. Well, was she lying awake thinking of some precious soul who was all in all to her? Did she note, with the piercing eye of affection, symptoms that none but she could see? Was she afraid to exaggerate some possible trifle by speaking of it?

Did she realise this risk?

What would she say to herself, when it was too late?

Would she ever forgive herself if she failed to try every remedy?

Perhaps the doctor had said nothing. Oh, yes, but with all respect for the whole medical profession, was it not human to err? Was it not madness to believe in the infallibility of a poor mortal being like a doctor? Why, it was gross irreligion savouring almost of papistry.

Humanum est errare.

So far the clever spacing and arresting type had carried Nellie along, but now the advertisement got down to business and the type got down to two-line pica. And when a modern advertisement, composed by a student of Commercial Psychology, gets down to business, the reader begins to shake in his or her shoes. Nellie shrank as from a whip when she first read it. It was gross irreligion, folly, to place a blind confidence in an erring human practitioner, was it not? But what was it, then, to neglect the aid held out to you by those who had devoted their lives to your welfare? It was not merely irreligion, it was not merely folly, it was criminal neglect! In all solemnity, and with a full consciousness of the gravity of their words, the proprietors of FOCHABER'S COUGH ELIMINATOR had no hesitation in describing it as criminal neglect. No money need be sent, no responsibility was incurred, by writing to-day for a sample bottle. The poorest had no excuse, while the spread of education enabled the most humble of their brothers and sisters to learn the glad tidings of great joy which had been brought to many by this incomparable preparation.

It was a very good advetisement.

"What do you think?" Nellie asked, anxiously watching Hannibal's face as his eyes travelled down the page and rested finally upon the picture, a woman with streaming hair, kneeling by a bedside, entitled, "Too Late." Hannibal put the paper down, obviously perturbed.

"Me, my cough, you mean? Oh, it's nothing."

The same thought flashed through their minds at the same instant. That was just what the advertisement said, and then—"too late."

"It won't do any harm just to try it," she ventured, and he nodded. "All right, old lady. Go ahead."

The afternoon was fine, the first of a series of fine spring days when the white clouds raced across the blue sky and disappeared behind the green hills over the town, when the sea sparkled and curled under the whip of the westerly wind. Nellie went to a druggist's shop and purchased a bottle of Fochaber's Eliminator. It was in a tasteful pasteboard box, wrapped with testimonials, and directions in thirty-nine languages, and had a Government seal on one end. Minnie had done the work for her employers most thoroughly and well. Mrs. Wilfley had told no untruth when she said to guests at her new flat in the Temple, an eyrie overlooking the Thames, that some of Mrs. Briscoe's writings, like her own, though not to be named, had been translated into as many languages as the Scriptures. And while Mrs. Wilfley smiled and Minnie looked out upon the delicate Thames nocturne that evening, Nellie and Hannibal, in their own sitting-room over the bar of the "Stormy Petrel," carefully removed the polyglottic wrappings of the bottle of Fochaber's Eliminator, and gazed with a simple speechless awe upon the mystic bottle within, as though it had contained a god.

For it was no use trying to treat the matter lightly. There was no badinage or frivolous jesting about Fochaber's. The innermost wrapper was devoted to symptoms and medical terms. Pleurisy, Nellie read, was either diaphragmathic or interlobular. In either case prevention was better than cure. Beware of the cough, that dry cough. They looked at each other. Was Hannibal's cough dry? "Sometimes I spit stuff," he remarked.

"But it's generally dry," she argued, and he nodded.

And the next day he was better. He had been for a good swinging walk round to Oystermouth and back, and eaten a hearty tea. He felt better. They exchanged smiles and congratulations over the breakfast table.

"Wasn't it a good job I thought of it?" she said.

"Rather. I'll go on with it," he returned. And he did. Three bottles at half a crown each were purchased and used, and each time after a dose he felt better. He went out for walks, visited neighbours, looked up chance acquaintances on the ships, and amused himself devising adventurous happenings on the way. In time he would be all right. And Nellie registered a vow that she would write to Fochaber's and tell them what she owed them. It would be only right.

So time passed on, and with the coming of summer Hannibal did to all seeming improve, though Nellie thought it best for him to take his medicine regularly, in case of relapse. They paid a visit to Neath and saw Mrs. Lloyd and her husband, the steward, and Hannibal learned something of the ins and outs of that department of life. And then an event of great importance to Nellie happened.

Mrs. Gooderich Senior came down on a visit.

Hannibal met her at the station in a lordly way, and quite overwhelmed her with his fine new clothes, his watch-chain, his moustache, his cab, his cuff-links, and his cigar, which last made him cough. Was this Hanny? Was it possible that this was the dirty little rapscallion who used to go fishing in Littler's Pond?

There was a suspicion of smugness about his mother's face nowadays. The Facts, having bowled over her moral sense, had gone on to smooth out the wrinkles of existence to such an extent that Mrs. Gooderich Senior was in danger of becoming supercilious. She grew sceptical even of the genuineness of those people who couldn't make ends meet. She told Hannibal that the working-classes were a lot better off than the middle-classes, which smelled to Hannibal like a piece of Minnie's philosophy. She approved of Nellie, who was a little uncertain of herself just then, and laughed without any apparent reason, and she gave an unmistakable verdict in favour of Fochaber's —why, it was advertised all over London. She heard Mrs. Wilfley say Fochaber's had paid fifty thousand in London alone to the space-brokers. Think of that!

. She stayed two months, winning Nellie's confidence and enjoying the sea air. Sitting on the pier at Mumbles one serene evening, Mrs. Gooderich suddenly realised how extremely fortunate her life had been since she had relinquished her uncompromising sense of honesty. And yet, what was wrong with her life? Nothing. She lived with her daughter, who had married well; she had been staying with her son, who had married still more well. What could be more respectable than her existence in Tedworth Square? True, she did not dare to interfere or even show herself too much when Minnie's fine friends came. She contented herself with tending the endless needs of Anthony Briscoe, whose dark eyes gazed up at her occasionally from the cradle. Even there hers was a back seat, for the trained nurse resented suggestions. After all, she had only to be quiet, and life flowed on smoothly month after month, unassailed by money troubles. She read Mrs. Wilfley's articles in *Sunday Words* or in the daily papers, and felt uplifted. She read novels, "old favourites" like *Left With a Trust,* and all the Pansy stories. And she and Nellie found a point of joyous contact in a common appreciation of Allen Raine. Nellie, for all her shrewd practical business sense, revelled in the stories of Allen Raine. So did Mrs. Gooderich Senior when she became acquainted with them. Together they smiled on Hanny's fancies for pirates and dead men's chests, and they gave the parrot the benefit of much elegant conversation concerning "she" and "he" and what "they" did in the historical present of romance. They attended chapel together, and enjoyed in a mild way the spiritual ecstasy of comfortable prayer.

No. As she sat there on the pier that evening, Mary Gooderich felt that her lines had fallen upon pleasant places, and that she had earned a little rest.

And so, I think, she had.

It was in September that a sudden idea came to Nellie as she sat at a table covered with papers. She was enclosing a cheque for the fire insurance of the premises, when a little list of life premiums fell on her lap from the sheaf of papers in her hand. She looked up.

"Hanny?"

Hannibal came out of the depths of *Roderick Random* with a grunt of enquiry.

"You ought to insure your life!"

"Me?"

"Yes. You see, the sooner you start the better. Look here. It says——" He bent his head down to hers. "——it says, 'Age next birthday twenty, premium for two hundred pounds, two pounds five a year. Redeemable when you're fifty at three hundred pounds.' Hanny! Just think what a nice little nest-egg that'll be for—for you know!"

Hannibal, his hands on his knees, looked down at his feet.

"All right, old lady," he said soberly. "I don't reckon that'll break us."

"It says any doctor, you see?" She pointed. "You've got to see a doctor, of course."

He nodded, sunk once more in his chair and *Roderick Random*.

An intense conviction had taken hold of his mind as he steadily made his way through tale after tale of adventure and mystery; a conviction that, when he might least expect it, the True Romance would sweep into his existence. He would let the book slide, and stare away into vacancy, seeking for he knew not what. Life was a wonderful thing! Who could tell what might not happen to him, if he only had the wit to seize the chance?

"It'll come," he would say to himself, "it'll come, if I wait."

So it did, embodied unostentatiously in a very young

man, whose overcoat buttons fell away from the holes
and disclosed a uniform of stark newness. That was a
raw October night, a week before Nellie suddenly decided to go and see the doctor, for various reasons.

"You'd think I only needed a big brass helmet to be the
hero of the piece," said the young man in facetious allu-
sion to his uniform. "And when I tell you," he added,
leaning confidentially across the bar, "that I'm only the
Third Mate of her, you'll wonder what the Old Man must
be like when he's got his war-paint on, eh?"

"Passenger boat?" asked Hannibal.

"Not on your life!" The young man was evidently confronted by a situation beyond his scope. He drank a little
more whisky. "Have you ever seen a wind-bag with a
propeller?"

"Not me."

"Well, come down and look at the *Beile Glâs*—she's in
the North Dock. She's worth a squint. I joined her at
Clydebank, and she was called the mystery ship up there.
'What's her cargo?' says I to the rigger. 'Wine for the
owner,' says he. 'That's why she carries electric windlass
and winches, steam would spoil the bouquet of the ninety-
three.' All piff, o' course, but there you are. A thousand
tons, four masts, Yankee rig, a six-foot propeller, electric
lights, wireless, and the finest accommodation *I've* ever
seen. She's a floating Pullman!"

And it was all true. Hannibal went down the rain-swept
Wind Street the next day and saw her.

She was of grey steel, with four tall masts carrying
enormous booms. Her deck-houses were of teak and glittering with varnish, German silver, and electric light re-
flectors. One blade of an undeniable propeller stuck above
the water. To add to the mystery, a board marked "No
Admittance" hung forbiddingly by the gangway. There
was no reservation in favour of those "on business," no
suggestion that a man might quite legitimately stroll up
and ask for a friend, say the Third Mate. It was as plain
as one of the Ten Commandments, as terse as an act of
God. "No Admittance."

He returned to the "Stormy Petrel" thinking of
treasure-seekers, forgotten lands, rich owners, and

mouldering maps. It grew in his mind, this conviction that he had found a romance. "Pieces of eight! Pieces of eight!" Each evening that talkative young man in the shining uniform leaned over the bar, and smiled, and added fresh fuel to the fire of his imagination, mysterious hints—sealed orders—stores for two years on board— all British crew—a machine gun—tons of ammunition —marked tinned meat on the manifest of course, ha-ha!— and so on. And as the days passed, a crazy scheme took shape in Hannibal's mind, and the two heads leaned closer together, the round, dark, bullet head of the Londoner and the long, high-crowned cranium of the youth, who came, obviously enough, from Londonderry.

"Sure, man, it can be done," the latter was saying. "We're going off to the buoy about twelve. The Captain, who hasn't come back from Plymouth yet, is to join us about that time. If you come down about seven, say, and walk aboard as if you'd business with us, you understand? Seven, say. I must run now. The Stores have come for the Captain to-day—consigned from Plymouth."

"I'll be down," said Hannibal.

It was a simple scheme of his, simple, plausible, and stark mad. He would dress himself in his old clothes, slip down to the *Beile Glâs,* and get the Third Mate to show him round, and then—trust to luck to stow himself away. He must seize this chance to swing on to the car of True Romance as it passed him. He must find out the tale of this strange visitant. The *Beile Glâs!* Stores from Plymouth! Sealed orders! Lummy!

He went round whistling softly to himself, watching the clock.

"Going out to-night, dear?" said Nellie casually, and he jumped.

"Oh, I may," he remarked.

"I saw Dr. Rhys Evans to-day," she chatted. "He's coming round to-morrow morning."

"I see," said Hannibal. "Where's my old overcoat?" he asked.

"Whatever for?"

"I'm going down to 'ave a look at a ship, see? Makes the clo's so dirty."

"I gave it away months ago," she told him. "What do you want to go messing about ships for?" she queried fretfully.

"Well, I can if I like, can't I?" he answered, a little cross.

"Oh, go if you want to——" she said, and he waited for the word "dear," but it did not come. He felt aggrieved. She took no interest. He took his usual coat and cap and went out. It was already seven o'clock. He must hurry. He ran down Wind Street and full into a keen autumnal gale sweeping along the Port Tennant Road. And when he reached the dock-side he was in a bath of perspiration.

At first he could see nothing. The stretch of water where the grey ship had been was clear, sparkling, and empty. Then he understood. That dull patch in the shadow of the warehouses, a patch with a single light hanging near the bow, was the *Beile Glâs,* at the buoy. He was too late.

He stood for a moment, benumbed of brain, slowly rousing from the curious aberration that had possessed him. He sat down on one of the bitts and tried to think. What was to be done? He could not go back just now. He wanted to see the *Beile Glâs* go out. It all crystallised down to that in time. He must see the *Beile Glâs* go out. It seemed to him, as he looked across at the silent ship, that she held more than a general mystery. She held part of himself, a part he was about to relinquish, a certain delicate sense of illusion, and she was taking it out to sea, to lose it on the trackless waters where he had found it. It was in obedience to this feeling that he waited on; and when, about nine o'clock, he heard some commotion near her and a tug came out of the gloom, he turned and ran along the road again, far out on the pier where the red light burns, so that he might see her pass. It was cold and very dark there, mysteriously cold and dark, the wind blowing through the timber piles and the black water moving unseen with an ooze and a slap below him. Several times he shivered and coughed, but he took no heed. He was looking at the town lights round the bay, at the dark hills touched with the crimson glare of the steel works over by Landore. What a pity, he murmured, what a pity he had missed her! Here was a treasure ship going out on the tide, a treasure ship, and he had missed her. He would be out of all the fun after all, out of the fights with savages and buccaneers. He had hoped to see them swing at the end of those tremendous booms. Of course he would be under hatches during the fight, but when all the ammunition had been sent up and it came to the final rush, he would grab a cutlass and . . .

He became aware of her, a trembling blackness in the shadows, a faint pulsation, communicating itself to the timbers on which he stood. She drew nearer, looming large above him, her tall masts blood-red in the light of the lantern, the smoke of the tug drifting through her rigging like the smoke of battle. He saw dark forms on her decks going back and forth, he heard the clang of a bell, a gruff voice, and the soft purr of a dynamo. A shrill whistle sounded as she cleared, and he strained his eyes to see the last of her as she receded. She was gone, gone with her secret and his, and a sigh escaped him. It was gone forever, that foolish idea of his, that iridescent rainbow edging of things, and he must try and remember. She was gone and part of him with her, out into the night.

He bought a paper as he passed through Castle Square, and saw among the brief paragraphs that filled the front page the announcement that "The Special Survey ship *Beile Glâs* was due to sail that evening for Punta Arenas, under sealed orders."

Several times he had to pause, with bowed head, while a paroxysm of coughing swept him, and he felt conscious of a "pain somewhere inside."

Nellie met him on the landing.

"Where have you been?" she asked, amazed. "It's past eleven o'clock."

"What I said," he replied huskily. "Went down to see a ship off. Everything all right."

"I was getting frightened," she reproached him. "You've got a cold again. You better take some of that stuff." And she went slowly across the bedroom to the medicine chest to get the bottle of Fochaber's Eliminator. She always kept it in the house now.

"I'll be all right in the morning." he croaked.

But in the morning he was anything but all right. He lay in bed very ill indeed, while Nellie, after giving him some more Fochaber's, decided that Doctor Rhys Evans might as well see him too. He could prescribe for the cold and examine him for the insurance company at the same time.

The doctor, who was young enough to enjoy his own sense of humour, came in casually about eleven o'clock. To Nellie's surprise Hannibal had not risen at all. He did not know what ailed him. All he could tell her was that, if he lay on his left side, he could hardly breathe; if he lay on his right side it was not much better; if he lay on his back he could not cough, and was nearly strangled; and when he got into position for coughing, he thought he was going to die.

Doctor Rhys Evans came in jauntily com his runabout car, quite at ease with himself and the world. Nellie's description of her husband's cough, together with the talk of insurance policies, had not led him to expect anything serious. "Sweethearts still, and worrying about everything, as they do at such a time." So it shaped itself in the brain under his silk hat. But when he reached the door of Hannibal's room his expression changed. He stood stock still for a moment and sniffed, and Nellie behind him was puzzled. Then he drew off his motoring gloves, shot his cuffs, felt in his waistcoat pocket for his thermometer, and sat down at the bedside. He supported Hannibal's shoulders with pillows, so that he could breathe more easily; he took a stethoscope from his hat and listened for a long time to the stertorous chest. He leaned over to catch the odour of his breath.

"What are you giving him?" he asked sharply, swinging round upon Nellie, who jumped.

"This," she said, a sudden fear gripping her heart, as she held up the bottle of Fochaber's. The doctor took it, read the label, and without any apology flung it with emphasis and precision into the grate, where it shattered.

"Get a fire lighted here," he ordered. "Got any more of that stuff in the house?"

She paused in her trembling flight and turned to shake her head.

"That rubbish is poison!" he said, when she returned. "You must get me towels and a tub of hot water."

She brought up the servant and one of the girls to help her, and together they got the things needed.

"Hot-water bottles, everything hot in the house," he commanded. When the tub came, he stood the shivering Hannibal in it, scalding his thin legs with the liquid until they were fiery red. Hot towels were draped over the young man as he sat there on the edge of the bed, his head drooped on his chest.

"Now in with you!" said the doctor. And into the hot bed Hannibal was shoved, and banked high with blankets.

"It's Lobar Pneumonia," said the doctor to Nellie, afterwards, "and I may be able to get him over. He has no constitution, you see. If it gets a firm hold on him he'll go down like a pack of cards."

"I thought Fochaber's was good for——" she began.

"It's a lying swindle," he returned. "I'd like to see every bottle of it pitched over the Mumbles Head."

"But the advertisement——" she protested.

"Pooh!" said the doctor. "Advertisement! They'll say anything. You should have more sense."

She looked at him with wide, scared eyes and an expression on her face as though she was saying, "Yes, yes, all my fault. Hit me hard. It was my fault." He looked at her.

"Get some one, sister or some one, to stay with you," he suggested. "You understand?"

And Mrs. Lloyd arrived in the afternoon.

The crisis came quickly. His system, never very vigorous, had been silently but definitely undermined by his sickness in the East, his lungs were full of coal dust, and his stomach deranged by the opium and mercury and formaldehyde of that beneficent proprietary, Fochaber's Eliminator.

"Good heavens!" said the doctor to Mrs. Lloyd. "And they wanted to insure his life!"

"Get some one else down," he told her another time. "You must keep her quiet. You understand?"

And so Mrs. Gooderich Senior left Tedworth Square and journeyed down to Swansea again. When Nellie saw her mother-in-law safely into the house, she retired from the sick room. "Don't you worry now," said the doctor. "He'll be round sooner than you are. He'll soon pick up when we have something to tell him."

But to Mrs. Lloyd and Mrs. Gooderich Senior he reiterated his doubts. "Like a pack of cards," he repeated. "He has no ballast to carry him through a thing like this."

And early in the following week, on a day when Winter rushed through the streets shaking at the casements and sending pieces of paper high over the roofs, that was just how he did go down, like a pack of cards. He lay there motionless, his eyes closed, the leaping flames of the fire illuminating his face with a sudden fugitive and disturbing radiance. He lay there thinking in an absolute mental calm, looking out upon the little ocean of his life, its currents and storms forgotten, merely pondering upon its ultimate utility. What was the good of this life? he asked, without rancour or impertinence, of the silent Fates. He was not complaining. He had had a good time, and the world was an astonishing place, well worth a visit. But surely there was something else. Life wasn't just a museum, through which one wandered, delighted with the strange things all around one, going out finally into the night, nothing done. One left something behind. Where was he? He had seen that dim ship pass out, bearing in her heart his Lost Illusion. One odd fancy took him, and his mother, watching his face, saw a slight creasing of the cheeks as he smiled, a fancy that had been the beginning of the end. He was going piece by piece. Here he was lying quite peacefully on his back, and Nellie was—ah! that was hard lines. Would he not see her again? They had got on so well for their short time. She loved him, looked after him, understood that idea of his that already floated away. After all, he was not cut out for practical business, not cut out . . .

He became aware of a subdued murmur near him, near the door. Some one was bending over him, touching his hands. He heard his mother speaking in his ear, and then quite suddenly, and almost unreasonably, he found himself smiling and feeling glad. Good! A boy! Lummy! The murmur subsided and quiet reigned, broken only by the distant noise of the trams and the crackling of the fire. Was this the reason, then? Another piece broken away. Soon he would be ready to go out on his own quiet adventure. That was how he had grown to look at it. Here in this life, you were up against hard practical efficient people and things, with occasional exasperating glimpses into another world. No use grumbling; while you were here you had to fall in line. His mistake had been that he had tried to live in both worlds at once. No good. But now, out there alone? He would see.

Sometimes, during that evening, he grieved quietly for the absence of Nellie, who had been so benign a pillow when he was in danger of suffering from the ceaseless indurations of business. And from that he slipped into a renewed consciousness of this obscure joy, this scarce-won fatherhood, seeing it as a great light afar off, swinging dizzily in space, a light on the coast he was leaving behind. Little by little the light grew dim, his hold on reality slackened, and he babbled of nameless things—things that had lain in the depths of his mind for long years, words that were like empty shells of long-dead ideas. Forgotten baby talk, like strings of feathery weed, fluttered from his lips, and troubled the scarcely-comprehending solicitude of his mother. And sometimes he wept, feeling lost in the dark. "Sealed orders," he would murmur. "Going out with sealed orders." And then "Pieces of eight!" She wished she could help him, but he had always been such a tranquil child, thoughtful too, and secretive. She sat at his bedside, an anxious woman verging upon old age. And he was dying, her son was dying. I doubt very much if she realised it.

She had never seen any one die. When her husband had been carried home, the melodramatic trappings of his transition had covered like a gorgeous pall the central sordid fact. So, too, with Bert, who had died with éclat, six thousand miles away, leaving behind for her memory to feed on not even a body or a funeral, only a blue War Office form and a misspelt name in a newspaper. She knew these things as she knew of events in a book. Here was a son dying before her eyes. Already he had gone off to the buoys, and in a little while he would go over the bar. She did not realise it.

I don't suppose Mrs. Gooderich Senior changed much after this experience. She was now "set," as she said. Her blue eyes were no longer the dark blue of the days when the brisk young baker's man touched her rustic heart. Her blue eyes were nearer green now, flecked with grey, and regarding you equably from a region of peace, a sort of neutral ground common to great sinners, great saints, and great sufferers. It is really, only we are loath to give it its right name, a species of *ennui*. A human soul is limited. It grows unresponsive after a certain number of excitations, and we call it peace, whereas it is really fatigue, a kind of hysteresis. Mrs. Gooderich had suffered, and her mind could respond no more. She could not transmute her sorrow into exquisite art, nor could she share the finer ecstasies of the Church. She felt that, after all, comfort and freedom from money trouble were the cardinal things of life, and even the spectacle of her son dying did not disturb this conviction. He belonged, moreover, to another woman. She had not understood that wild breakaway when he went to sea. Why should he want to go to sea? His Uncle George had disapproved. Was Amelia married now, she wondered. She had heard that she was walking out with a water clerk, whom she had met in Billiter Lane. . . .

She was lost in a maze of conjectures, this woman verging on old age, when she noticed the thin hand on the coverlet making a gesture of throwing something away.

"What is it, dear?" she whispered.

"Cast off, cast off," he muttered. "Sealed orders." And while she was wondering if she had not better call some one, he smiled and went out into the night.

.   .   .   .

It is spring again in Abertawe, and the white clouds flit merrily across the blue sky over the white-lipped waters of the Bay. There is a joyous bluster in the wind that races around past Oystermouth, and rustles in the trees up Sketty way, whispering "Youth! Youth!" All the world is green and glorious upon the hillsides, and in the lanes lovers are walking to and fro. And in the "Stormy Petrel," as I see it in my mind's eye, there is that incomparable woman in rich black, and all the prettier in the neat widow's cap, superintending with unremitting care the red fragment of humanity in the cradle and the business he will some day inherit. I sit and see it, in my mind's eye, and think. It is an excellent business.

Mrs. Gooderich Senior is gone back long ago to the comfort of Tedworth Square. I think it was Fochaber's upon which they differed chiefly, for Mrs. Gooderich Senior, having heard of it at first hand, would believe no ill of Fochaber's. Be that as it may, she is gone back to London, to the discreet household in Tedworth Square. There she is, it is true, somewhat a cypher, save when Captain Briscoe comes home for a week-end. She and he are united in admiration of the astonishing money to be earned by writing advertisements. Sometimes Mrs. Wilfley, occupied upon a new book entitled *The Souteneur,* will call, ineffably affable, and talking heart to heart will tell Mrs. Gooderich some of her spiritual divagations. And Anthony Gilfillan is a fine boy. It will not be long before Tedworth Square forgets the "Stormy Petrel" and the pretty widow who visits a grave out at Port Tennant Cemetery every Sunday.

But for me, I have not forgotten, and I think that when the spring is yet a little more advanced, I shall run down to Abertawe. I should like to make sure that Nellie, in spite of what she says, has really given up all idea of marrying again.

THE END

Modern Library of the World's Best Books

COMPLETE LIST OF TITLES IN

THE MODERN LIBRARY

For convenience in ordering use number at right of title

MODERN LIBRARY GIANTS

*A series of full-sized library editions of books that formerly
were available only in cumbersome and expensive sets.*

THE MODERN LIBRARY GIANTS REPRESENT A SELECTION OF THE WORLD'S GREATEST BOOKS

Many are illustrated and some of them are over 1200 pages long.

G1. TOLSTOY, LEO. War and Peace.

G2. BOSWELL, JAMES. Life of Samuel Johnson.

G3. HUGO, VICTOR. Les Miserables.

G4. THE COMPLETE POEMS OF KEATS AND SHELLEY.

G5. PLUTARCH'S LIVES (The Dryden Translation).

G6.
G7. GIBBON, EDWARD. The Decline and Fall of the Roman Empire (Complete in three volumes)
G8.

G9. YOUNG, G. F. The Medici (Illustrated).

G10. TWELVE FAMOUS RESTORATION PLAYS (1660-1820) (Congreve, Wycherley, Gay, Goldsmith, Sheridan, etc.)

G11. THE ESSAYS OF MONTAIGNE (The E. J. Trechmann Translation).

G12. THE MOST POPULAR NOVELS OF SIR WALTER SCOTT (Quentin Durward, Ivanhoe and Kenilworth).

G13. CARLYLE, THOMAS. The French Revolution (Illustrated).

G14. BULFINCH'S MYTHOLOGY (Illustrated).

G15. CERVANTES. Don Quixote (Illustrated).

G16. WOLFE, THOMAS. Look Homeward, Angel.

G17. THE POEMS AND PLAYS OF ROBERT BROWNING.

G18. ELEVEN PLAYS OF HENRIK IBSEN.

G19. THE COMPLETE WORKS OF HOMER.

G20. THE LIFE AND WRITINGS OF ABRAHAM LINCOLN.

G21. SIXTEEN FAMOUS AMERICAN PLAYS.

G22. CLAUSEWITZ, KARL VON. On War.

G23. TOLSTOY, LEO. Anna Karenina.

G24. LAMB, CHARLES. The Complete Works and Letters of Charles Lamb.

G25. THE COMPLETE PLAYS OF GILBERT AND SULLIVAN.

G26. MARX, KARL. Capital.

G27. DARWIN, CHARLES. The Origin of Species and The Descent of Man.

G28. THE COMPLETE WORKS OF LEWIS CARROLL.

G29. PRESCOTT, WILLIAM H. The Conquest of Mexico and The Conquest of Peru.

G30. MYERS, GUSTAVUS. History of the Great American Fortunes.